D0424564

Nelson DeMille was born in New York City in 1943. He grew up on Long Island and graduated from Hofstra University with a degree in Political Science and History. After serving as an infantry officer in Vietnam, where he was decorated three times, DeMille worked as a journalist and short-story writer. He wrote his first major novel, *By the Rivers of Babylon*, in 1978 and has gone on to write 10 international bestsellers, with sales of over 55 million copies in 24 languages. He lives on Long Island.

For more information on Nelson DeMille contact:
www.nelsondemille.co.uk
www.nelsondemille.net

Also by Nelson DeMille

By the Rivers of Babylon
Cathedral
The Talbot Odyssey
The Charm School
Gold Coast
The General's Daughter
Spencerville
Plum Island
The Lion's Game
Up Country

Mayday (With Thomas Block)

NELSON DEMILLE

WORD OF HONOUR

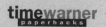
timewarner
paperbacks

A *Time Warner* Paperback

First published in Great Britain in 1985 by Granada Publishing
Published in 1987 by Grafton Books
Published in 1984 by HarperCollins
This edition published in 2000 by Warner Books
Reprinted 2001
Reprinted by Time Warner Paperbacks in 2002
Reprinted 2003

Copyright © Nelson DeMille 1985
A Bernard Geis Associates Book

The moral right of the author has been asserted.

*All characters in this publication are fictitious and any resemblance
to real persons, living or dead, is purely coincidental.*

All rights reserved.
No part of this publication may be reproduced,
stored in a retrieval system, or transmitted,
in any form or by any means, without the
prior permission in writing of the publisher, nor be
otherwise circulated in any form of binding or cover
other than that in which it is published and without
a similar condition including this condition being
imposed on the subsequent purchaser.

A CIP catalogue record for this book
is available from the British Library.

ISBN 0 7515 3119 7

Printed and bound in Great Britain by
Clays Ltd, St Ives plc

Time Warner Paperbacks
An imprint of
Time Warner Books UK
Brettenham House
Lancaster Place
London WC2E 7EN

www.TimeWarnerBooks.co.uk

To Ginny, with love

ACKNOWLEDGEMENTS

I would like to thank Tony Gleason for insights into military law, Reid Boates and Nick Ellison for their editorial suggestions, Sgt First Class Susan Rueger for her assistance at Fort Hamilton, and Kathy Haley, night typist.

NEW
YORK
CONNE
NEW
JERSEY
LONG
THE
BRONX
MANHATTAN
THE GOLD COAST
SUFFOLK
Garden City
QUEENS
NASSAU
COUNTY
BROOKLYN
STATEN
ISLAND
Fort Hamilton
ATLANTIC
OCEAN

Plum Island

ORIENT PT.

SHELTER IS.

GARDINERS ISLAND

C T I C U T

SOUND

NORTH FORK

ISLAND

Sag Harbor

COUNTY

THE HAMPTONS

LONG ISLAND
NEW YORK

AUTHOR'S FOREWORD

Many people have asked me if *Word of Honour* is autobiographical. Considering that the protagonist, Ben Tyson, is accused of instigating a massacre of civilians while serving in Vietnam, the correct answer is 'No'.

There are, however, some similarities between Ben Tyson and the author, mostly in regard to the short military careers of the fictional Tyson and me. Tyson and I were both infantry lieutenants with the famed First Air Cavalry Division, our tours of duty in Vietnam both encompassed the Tet Offensive in that memorable year of 1968, and we both shared many of the same experiences, thoughts, and beliefs. But unlike Lt. Tyson, I was not wounded in action, and my men did not participate in any atrocities.

On the home front, Tyson and I both live in a pleasant suburban village on Long Island, but beyond that, our domestic and professional lives have no similarities.

Ben Tyson is, in a way, the universal American citizen-soldier; he reached military age at a time when his country was at war, at a time when young men were still drafted into the Armed Forces, and he found himself taken from his comfortable American life and thrust into an unspeakable horror for which he was totally unprepared. This is, then, a story that millions of men and women can relate to.

Word of Honour was first published in 1985 in the United States by Warner Books, and though the Vietnam War had ended some ten years before, the aftermath of that war and those times was still colouring how we thought and how we acted as a nation. Vietnam was a war that grew larger in the national psyche even as it receded further into time.

Word of Honour was published to wide critical acclaim; was a Main Selection of the Book-of-the-Month Club; was sold to Hollywood, where it passed through a series of producers and screenwriters who couldn't seem to get it right; was translated into two dozen foreign languages in Europe and Asia; was put into audiobook form; and has been in continuous print since its debut. This last fact is what most pleases an author: the knowledge that new generations are reading and hopefully appreciating and learning something from his novel. Interestingly, *Word of Honour*, though fiction, is assigned reading in some college courses about the Vietnam War. I recall that in a college class I took in the 1960s dealing with the Second World War, I was required to read two novels: Norman Mailer's *The Naked and the Dead* and James Jones's *The Young Lions*. I still have more vivid memories of these two fictional accounts of the Second World War than I have of the textbook readings or the military memoirs that I struggled through. The same, I think, can be said for other classic war novels, such as *The Red Badge of Courage, All Quiet on the Western Front*, or *War and Peace*. This might suggest that fiction can sometimes be more educational than fact. Certainly this is true of all good war novels because war novels by their nature are parables, and parables are instructive and, hopefully, memorable.

In any case, *Word of Honour* is not precisely a war novel, but it is a novel about war's aftermath. It is a story of love, survival, loyalty, betrayal, and, ultimately, redemption. It is not literal truth in the sense that these things happened to specific people in just the way I described, but it is still the truth in the sense that the characters in the novel represent a generation of men and women who all had experiences such as those described in the book. The Vietnam War that I describe is real, and my description of the major events at the Battle of Hue is real. What I hope is most real are my characters, who act and react from the highest and most noble principles on some occasions and at other points display all their human weaknesses, fears, and prejudices.

The Vietnam War still has the ability to divide us as a people, and I was aware of that when I set out to write this novel. I purposely took no sides, made no judgements about the war (I hope), and tried to put the politics into perspective. I had the advantage of hindsight in this regard, the luxury of a cooling-off period, so to speak.

Partly for this reason, the book was well received by reviewers and readers across the political spectrum. Friends and acquaintances from both the political left and right thought it validated their opinions and beliefs. Finally, readers' letters confirmed that I had struck the right balance. An author would like people to read his novel and think about the issues raised; books that are thrown down in disgust are obviously not read and do not instruct, illuminate, or invite debate.

An honest and fair appraisal of Vietnam was almost impossible in 1968 and in 1985 when my novel was published, and it may well be almost impossible today. With that in mind I concentrated on the human tragedy of that war and focused on the moral and legal questions of a specific act – a massacre – and in doing so left open the larger questions of Vietnam. One could say this same story could have been written about nearly any war in which this country was involved or will be involved.

But to be completely honest, as a soldier who saw combat in that specific war, I was well aware then, and am more aware now, that all wars are not created equal. As Thomas Mann wrote in *The Magic Mountain*: 'A man lives not only his personal life as an individual, but also, consciously or unconsciously, the life of his epoch and his contemporaries.' For me to be totally uninvolved or majestically above prejudice or judgement is not only unrealistic but would also be somewhat dishonest. So to avoid dishonesty, whenever I consciously let my own judgements or prejudices creep into the narrative or dialogue, I was careful to create dialogue or narrative that gave the other side of the same issues. Since this is a book without villains, the good guys and the good women often surprise themselves by seeing and speaking both sides of the debate. In fact, this is not so surprising or difficult for anyone who has ever taken a formal debating course and been asked to defend the indefensible.

I'm often asked if writing this book was a catharsis for me. It certainly was *not* while I was writing it. In fact, not unsurprisingly, it brought back too many bad memories. I had left Vietnam in November of 1968 – although the war was brought back to me every day on television until the North Vietnamese entered Saigon in April 1975. It wasn't until the early 1980s that I began to put the experience behind me. By that time I was married, had two children, and had achieved some success as a writer. I had thought about writing the Great Vietnam War Novel, but I knew that most publishers weren't interested in Vietnam novels in those days. Even though the natural impulse of a man who has been to war is to talk about it, at least among friends and ex-vets, or to write about it, privately or publicly, this was one war that no one wanted to hear about.

Ironically, it was Hollywood that opened up the issue with some striking and successful war movies, such as *Coming Home*, *The Deer Hunter*, *Platoon*, and *Full Metal Jacket*. The publishing industry, while not exactly soliciting manuscripts on Vietnam, was at least willing to talk about war novels after these movies.

But had I written a Vietnam novel in the 1970s – and a few were written by others and published – it would have suffered a fate worse than the characters in the novel. Not only was the country not ready for an important and balanced look at this national tragedy, but neither was I. My notes taken during the war and afterwards seemed to point towards two kinds of stories: One was a traditional blood-and-guts, action-oriented novel; the other was a too political, bitter, and alienated book. Quite possibly I would have experienced some catharsis and some spleen-venting by writing either of those books, but the public does not pay to read an author's attempts at self-psychotherapy.

By 1985 the country and the author had calmed down a bit.

My ex-hippie, war-protesting friends were making money in the Reagan boom; my conservative, pro-war friends were doing a little coke and saying things like 'No son of mine will ever go to war.'

The men and women of my generation didn't completely give up their beliefs, but they certainly modified them to match new realities. More important, as we aged physically and grew, I hope, intellectually, we realized that the younger generation was somewhat clueless concerning who we were, what we had believed in, what we had fought for or against, and what had happened to us as a generation and as a nation.

By 1984 I knew without a doubt that the time had come for me to write about Vietnam. The decade of relative silence was coming to an end; the anger, the shame, the divisiveness and the hatreds were fading. This was good and this was bad. To sublimate a national trauma is one thing – to have national amnesia is another.

In any case, I, like many other authors – veterans and non-veterans alike – was ready to deal with the issues in fictional form. In other words, the long-delayed war novels were starting to be written.

But as I sat down to write, I realized to my complete surprise that I didn't want to write a war novel. It simply wasn't working. It took me a few months to comprehend that what I wanted to write was a novel *of* the war, not *about* the war; a novel that sprang out of the post-war American experience, a story that everyone – soldiers, civilians, and the generations then unborn – could understand and relate to.

And so I created Ben Tyson, combat veteran, suburbanite, husband, son, father, employee, neighbour, friend and citizen. His war, like my war, was nearly two decades behind him. When we meet him, he has gotten on with his life and is relatively happy and prosperous. His wife, Marcy, is a former college radical and war protester, and their marriage typifies the uneasy truce between the two halves of a once polarized nation. His teenage son, David, is blissfully ignorant of the fiery cauldron that formed his parents' lives. The lives of Ben, Marcy, and David, as well as of their contemporaries, are a picture of the calm after the storm.

But there are skeletons in Ben Tyson's closet. The closet is figurative, but the skeletons are real; they lay in the ruins of a hospital in Vietnam – over one hundred men, women, children, and babies, massacred by troops under the command of Lt. Benjamin Tyson. But there are only a handful of people still alive who know of this.

And this is part of the universal appeal of *Word of Honour* – the skeletons in the closet that we can all relate to: the things we've done that we got away with at the time but that haunt us and threaten to reveal themselves at the worst possible moment.

Which is exactly what happens in this story. An author named Andrew Picard publishes a book called *Hue: Death of a City*, about the Battle of Hue during the 1968 Tet Offensive. In that book is a description of Lt. Benjamin Tyson whose platoon massacred the above-mentioned hospital full of men, women, children and babies – nuns, wounded enemy soldiers, civilians, and foreign medical personnel.

What Tyson thought was the calm after the storm turns out to be the eye of a hurricane.

But what exactly *did* happen at that hospital? We think we know from the testimony of witnesses and from Andrew Picard's book. However, what looks like an open-and-shut case starts looking different as other witnesses give conflicting accounts. In other words, like the Japanese play *Roshomon*, the same crime is described from different points of view, and we begin to wonder if any crime at all was committed. Are witnesses lying, or are they blocking out the trauma, or does position determine perspective? Or all three?

As the story progresses, Tyson's ghosts come back to haunt him, but we know that this is just what he needs. We understand that catharsis sits at the end of a bumpy road. But for some people, catharsis is not enough, or not the goal after all.

Ben Tyson needs redemption in both the secular and spiritual sense of the word. And redemption is harder to come by than catharsis or forgiveness or a not-guilty verdict.

So, was the writing of this book a catharsis for me? Yes and no. *Yes* in the sense that it was good to get a lot of this pent-up war stuff off my chest; and *no* in the sense that by concentrating on the writing of this story for a full year, a lot of the forgotten memories came back. I didn't experience anything that could be described as post-traumatic stress syndrome, but certainly there were many days when I was out of sorts after a particularly intense writing episode. Also, I had the occasional war dream, which I hadn't had in years prior to beginning this book.

But after the book was completed, I think it did me more good than harm, and I hope I can say the same for my readers.

In January of 1997, I returned to Vietnam for three weeks with two friends who had also served there during the Tet Offensive.

In early February we arrived in the city of Hue on the eve of the lunar New Year – the Tet Holiday. It had been exactly twenty-nine years since the start of the Tet Offensive that had so changed our lives and changed the course of the war.

We checked into a three-star hotel, making the appropriate jokes about how the accommodations in Vietnam had gotten better since our last visit.

Later, we went out into the city and joined the celebration of the New Year. We ate, we drank, we watched the fireworks and the dragon dances, we spoke to the people and patted kids on the head. We told some fellow Americans about the Tet Offensive in 1968. We went to bed very late, very tired, and a little drunk. I had no war dreams that night, and I woke up in a fine mood, except for a little hangover. My travelling companions reported no nightmares either.

After I came home, I realised that the return trip to Vietnam had been emotional and a little sad to be sure, but it had not been traumatic and had not produced any nightmares while there or afterwards. So, in the words of William Manchester, 'Goodbye Darkness'.

In one passage of my novel, Tyson's attorney, Vincent Corva, says to Tyson, 'Let me tell *you* something – let me reveal to you the one great truth about war, Mr Tyson, and it is this: Ultimately all war stories are bullshit. From a general's memoirs to an ex-Pfc's boasting in a saloon, it is all *bullshit*. I have never heard a true war story, and I never told one, and neither have you.'

And so, with that fair warning, I invite you to read this war story that isn't true and isn't even a war story.

Nelson DeMille, 1998
Long Island, New York

Part 1

It is easier to find false Witnesses against the civilian than anyone willing to speak the truth against the interest and honour of the soldier.

Juvenal

1

Ben Tyson folded his *Wall Street Journal* and stared out the window of the speeding commuter train. The dreary borough of Queens rolled by, looking deceptively habitable in the bright May morning sunshine.

Tyson glanced at the man in the facing seat, John McCormick, a neighbour and social acquaintance. McCormick was reading a hardcover book, and Tyson focused on the title: *Hue: Death of a City*.

McCormick flipped back a page and reread something, then glanced over the book and made unexpected eye contact with Tyson. He dropped his eyes quickly back to the book.

Tyson felt a sudden sense of foreboding. He focused again on the book jacket. The cover showed a red-tinged photograph of the ancient imperial city of Hue, a low-angle aerial perspective. The city spread out on both sides of the red-running Perfume River, the bridges broken and collapsed into the water. Great black and scarlet billows of smoke hung over the blazing city, and the sun, a crimson half ball, rose over the distant South China Sea, silhouetting the dominant features of the town: the Imperial Palace, the high walls and towers of the Citadel, and the soaring spires of the Catholic cathedral. A remarkable picture, Tyson thought. He nodded to himself. *Hue*. Tyson said, 'Good book?'

McCormick looked up with feigned nonchalance. 'Oh, not bad.'

'Did I get an honourable mention?'

McCormick hesitated a moment, then without a word, he handed Tyson the opened book.

Ben Tyson read:

On the sixteenth day of the battle of Hue, 15 February, an American rifle platoon found itself pinned down by enemy fire in the western suburbs of the city. The platoon was an element of Alpha Company, Fifth Battalion of the Seventh Cavalry Regiment, of the First Air Cavalry Division. As a point of historical interest, the Seventh Cavalry was the ill-fated regiment commanded by General Custer at the Little Big Horn.

The rifle platoon under fire was led by a twenty-five-year-old Auburn ROTC graduate, Lieutenant Benjamin J. Tyson, a New Yorker.

Tyson continued to stare at the open book without reading. He glanced at McCormick, who seemed, Tyson thought, embarrassed. Tyson continued reading:

The following account of what happened that day is drawn from interviews with two members of Tyson's platoon whom I will identify only as Pfc X and Specialist Four Y. The story, heretofore untold, was originally brought to my attention by a nun of mixed French and Vietnamese ancestry named Sister Teresa. Further details regarding the provenance of this story may be found at the conclusion of this chapter.

Tyson closed his eyes. Through the blackness an image took shape: a Eurasian girl, dressed in white, with a silver cross hanging between her breasts. Her body was fuller than that of a Vietnamese, and there was a slight wave in her long black hair. She had high cheekbones and almond eyes, but her eyes were soft brown, and there was just the suggestion of freckles on her nose. As he held the image in his mind's eye, the mouth turned up in a smile that seemed to transform her whole face, making the features more strongly Gallic. The Cupid's-bow mouth pursed, and she spoke softly, '*Tu es un homme intéressant.*'

'Et toi Thérèse, tu es une femme intéressante.'

The enemy fire directed at Tyson's men was coming from the vicinity of a small French hospital named *Hôpital Miséricorde*. The hospital, operated by a Catholic relief agency, was flying two flags: a Red Cross flag and a Viet Cong flag.

The firefight had erupted shortly before noon as the American platoon approached. The platoon quickly took cover, and there were no initial casualties. After about five minutes of intense firing, the enemy broke contact and withdrew towards the city.

Someone in the hospital then draped a white bed sheet from a second-storey window, indicating surrender or 'all clear.' Seeing the white sheet, Lieutenant Tyson began moving his platoon up to take possession of the hospital and surrounding structures. The enemy, however, had left behind at least one sniper, positioned on the hospital's roof. As the Americans approached, shots rang out, killing one American. Pfc Larry Cane, and wounding two others, Sgt Robert Moody and Pfc Arthur Peterson. There was a possible second sniper positioned at one of the windows.

Tyson paused again, and his mind returned to that day in 1968. It had been one of the worst days of the massive enemy offensive that had begun on the lunar New Year holiday called Tet, ushering in the Year of the Monkey.

He vividly recalled the sky, so blackened with smoke that he wouldn't have known it was an overcast day except for the cold rain falling through the ash.

He heard, in the steady rumbling of the train, the persistent pounding of impacting mortars and the ceaseless staccato chatter of automatic weapons.

The train whistle blew at a crossing, and Tyson recalled very clearly the blood-freezing shriek of incoming rockets, exploding with an earthshaking thunder so intense that it took a few seconds to realize you were still alive.

And the dead, Tyson remembered, the dead lay everywhere. Trails and fields surprised you with sprawled, slaughtered corpses; hamlets were littered with the unburied dead. The Graves Registration people wore gas masks and rubber gloves, recovering only the American dead, burning the rest in pyres stoked with diesel oil and ignited with flamethrowers. Bonfires, bone fires, crackling fat, and grinning skulls. He could still smell the burnt human hair.

Tyson recalled what his company commander, Captain Browder, had said: 'The living are in the minority here.' And Browder himself joined the majority not long after.

Death, he remembered, was so pervasive in that bleak dying city, in that bleak and rainy winter, that the living – civilian and soldier alike – had almost ceased to struggle against it. People would, out of instinct, duck or take cover, but you could see in their eyes that they had no prospects for the future. *Hue: Death of a City. Hue: City of Death.* No wonder, he thought, we all went mad there.

Tyson drew himself back to the book. He skipped a page and read at random:

A French nurse, Marie Broi, attempted to stop the Americans from killing the wounded enemy soldiers, but she was struck with a rifle. An Australian physician named Evan Dougal began swearing abusively at the Americans. Clearly, everyone was overwrought; nearly hysterical might be a better term.

Suddenly, with no forewarning, an American soldier fired a burst from his automatic rifle, and Dr Dougal was hurled by the force of the rounds across the room. Spec/4 Y describes it as follows: 'He [Dougal] was thrashing around on the tile floor holding his stomach. His white smock was getting redder and his face was getting whiter.'

The ward that had been in pandemonium a few seconds before was now very still except for the dying sounds made

12

by Dr Dougal. Pfc X remembers hearing whimpering and crying from the adjoining paediatric and maternity ward.

What happened next is somewhat unclear, but apparently, having murdered the first Caucasian, several members of Tyson's platoon decided it would be best to leave no witnesses. The doctors, nurses, and nuns were ordered into a small whitewashed operating room and—

'Jamaica Station!' cried the conductor. 'Change here for trains to New York! Stay on for Brooklyn!'

Tyson closed the book and stood.

McCormick remained seated and said hesitantly, 'Do you want to borrow—?'

'No.'

Tyson crossed the platform to make his connection, wondering why this had happened on such a sunny day.

2

Tyson looked down from his office window and focused on Park Avenue, twenty-eight storeys below. One version of the American dream, he reflected, was an office aerie like this one – a commanding height from which the captains of industry and commerce directed the nine-to-five weekday battle against government, consumers, environmentalists, and one another. Having arrived here, Tyson discovered that he had no particular enthusiasm for the fight. But he had wisely not dwelt too long on this discovery. And besides, the world had changed for him somewhere between Hollis and Jamaica Station.

Miss Beale, his secretary, spoke. 'Do you want to finish this letter?'

Tyson turned from the window and glanced at the seated

13

woman. 'You finish the letter.'

Miss Beale stood, her steno pad held to her ample chest. 'Are you feeling all right?'

Tyson looked Miss Beale in the eye. Miss Beale, like many secretaries, was alert to signs of weakness in her employer. A little weakness could be exploited. Too much weakness, however, foreshadowed visions of the unemployment line for both of them. Tyson replied, 'Of course I'm not all right. Do I look all right?'

She was momentarily discomposed and muttered, 'No ... you ... I mean ...'

He said, 'Cancel my lunch date and my afternoon appointments.'

'Are you leaving for the day?'

'Most probably.'

Miss Beale turned and left.

Tyson gazed around his office. He wondered what colour offices were before the discovery of beige.

He opened his coat-closet door and looked at himself in the full-length mirror. He was just over six feet tall and he thought he carried it well. Tyson brushed his grey pinstripe suit, straightened his tie and waistcoat, and finger-combed his sandy hair. There were few corporate images he did not fit, few armies in the world where he would not be described as every inch an officer and a gentleman.

Tall people were more successful, so said the studies done on the subject of success in business. Yet the president of his corporation was five feet, two inches. In fact, most of the principal executives in the company and the parent company were under five feet six. And with good reason, he thought: They were all Japanese.

Tyson closed the closet and walked to his desk. He sat and sipped absently on a cup of cold coffee, and his eyes drifted to a piece of company stationery: Peregrine-Osaka. When Peregrine Electronic Aviation had been acquired by Osaka, Tyson had not been happy, and his spirits had not improved in the two years since the takeover.

He was no racist, he told himself, and yet looking down on Mr Kimura when they conversed was awkward, and being addressed as Ty-sun was somehow grating.

The Japanese were subtle, and their presence was delicate and gentle. Yet in some indefinable way they ruled with an iron hand. Tyson, unasked, had removed his war mementos from his walls: his Army commission, citations, and photographs – *objets de guerre* that had had some cachet with Defense Department customers, that had been looked on favourably by Peregrine's former owner and founder, Charlie Stutzman, but which now did not fit the new regime's psychological decor. Also making its way home in his briefcase was a photograph of his father in his Navy flier's uniform. His father's Grumman Tomcat could be seen in the background on the deck of the carrier *Lexington*, three rising suns painted on the fuselage. Three dead Japs.

Mr Kimura had studied the photo intently one day but had no comment. Tyson waited one face-saving week before removing it.

Tyson stood, picked up his slim attaché case, and left his office. He passed Miss Beale's desk, aware of her keen gaze.

3

Ben Tyson walked east on 42nd Street and turned into a small bookshop near Grand Central Station. On a table marked RECENT ARRIVALS sat a tall stack of them, red, black, and white spines facing him. The top of the stack was crowned with a standing display copy. Tyson took the copy and leafed through it.

Interspersed with the text were photograph sections, and every few chapters there were classical military map drawings

15

of Hue and environs. The book fell open to the title page, and Tyson saw that it was autographed by Andrew Picard.

'The author was in here yesterday.'

Tyson looked up into the eyes of a young woman dressed in jeans and a T-shirt that said 'New York is Book Country.'

She continued, 'We just got those in last week. He bought a copy for me and signed it. I read part of it last night. I try to at least scan the major books that come in.'

Tyson nodded.

She went on, 'It's in the style of the big battle through the eyes of little people.' She appraised Tyson closely. 'Were you there? Nam, I mean.'

Tyson replied, 'Quite possibly.'

She smiled, 'Well, I'd recommend it as a good read – if you were there. Not really my taste.'

Tyson said, 'There's supposed to be a part in here about a massacre of a French hospital.'

She grimaced. 'Right. Really gross.' She thought a moment, then said, 'How could we do something like that?'

Tyson marvelled at how the young used the first-person pronoun to include and indict themselves for the depredations of the government and the military. He said, 'It was a long time ago. I'll take the book.'

Tyson went to the corner of 42nd and Second and entered Ryan McFadden's, a sort of upscale Irish pub. His eyes adjusted to the dim light, and he moved to the long bar, taking an empty stool. The establishment's clientele was eclectic: foreigners from the nearby U.N., local media people from the WPIX-Daily News building across the avenue, and a smattering of literati whose presence seemed a mystery to the owners, who did not encourage that sort of trade. It was not the type of place frequented by businessmen, and he did not expect to run into any of his associates. One of the owners, Dan Ryan, greeted him warmly, 'Ben, how's life been treating you?'

Tyson pondered several answers, then replied, 'Not too bad.'

Ryan ordered him a Dewar's and soda, with the traditional Irish publican's 'Good luck.'

Tyson raised his glass. '*Slainté*.'

Ryan moved off to greet a group of newcomers. For the first time since he'd opened Picard's book that morning, Tyson's thoughts turned exclusively to his wife: Marcy was not the type of wife one saw on the news, standing staunchly beside a prominent husband accused of political corruption, embezzlement, or sexual wrongdoing. She was very much her own woman and gave her loyalty selectively, as it should be given. She was not, for instance, a good corporate wife, and in fact had a career of her own as well as a mind of her own. She had been and still was violently antiwar, antimilitary, and anti-anything that didn't fit neatly into her own left-of-centre view of the world. Her reaction to the book would be revealing, Tyson thought.

Tyson opened his attaché case and took out the book. He set it on the bar and scanned the pertinent chapter quickly, unwilling to actually read or comprehend any more of it, like someone who has got a Dear John letter or a telegram about a death. His name jumped out at him in various forms: Tyson's platoon; Lieutenant Tyson; Tyson's medic; Tyson's radio operator ...

He shut the book, finished his drink, and ordered another. After some time he opened the book to a page he had dog-eared, and read a passage:

As the platoon approached, they were presented with three conflicting signals: the Viet Cong flag, the Red Cross flag, and the white sheet. The latter may have lulled them into a false sense of security as they crossed the exposed courtyard in front of the building. Suddenly shots rang out, and Larry Cane was killed instantly. Moody and

Peterson were hit. The platoon took cover and returned the fire.

Of the two wounded, Moody's injury was slight, but Peterson's wound was critical. The morale of the platoon, not good to begin with, became worse. There was a feeling of helpless rage and impotence among the men, a feeling that they'd been duped and deceived.

Tyson nodded to himself. Yes, that was an accurate description. Rage and impotence. They'd been played for suckers. Not only by the enemy, but by their commanders in the field, their commanders at headquarters, their commanders in Washington. They were looking for something or someone to strike back at. In retrospect, Tyson realized those people in the hospital never had a chance.

Tyson skipped a page.

On entering the hospital, Tyson demanded immediate medical attention for his two wounded.

The hospital's chief of staff, a Frenchman named Dr Jean Monteau, explained rather peremptorily to Tyson in passable English that the hospital was on the triage system: i.e., there were so many patients and so few staff and supplies that those who were clearly dying – like Peterson – could not be helped and those who were lightly wounded – like Moody – would have to wait. Whereupon, Dr Monteau turned his back on Tyson and began attending a Viet Cong soldier whose arm was shredded by shrapnel and who apparently fell into the proper category to receive care.

Dr Monteau's medical judgement may have been sound, but his judgement of the situation could not have been worse.

Tyson looked up from the book. 'You got that right, Picard.' He tried to picture the face of Dr Jean Monteau but

18

he was able only to conjure up a sneering caricature of an arrogant little Frenchman. Surely, he thought, this was a defence mechanism of his mind, a justification for what happened. The real Dr Monteau had addressed him with some dignity and politeness. What may have seemed at the time like peremptoriness was fatigue. He thought again, then concluded, *No, Monteau certainly was an arrogant little son of a bitch.* But he didn't deserve to die for it. Tyson stirred his drink, then read again at random:

Tyson's platoon, as I've mentioned, had been operating independently of its company for over a week. They had already suffered high casualties in the preceding sixteen days of the offensive. Out of an original platoon of forty men, nineteen remained. Also, they had gone without rest or resupply for the seven days prior to this incident.

These facts are not meant to suggest extenuating circumstances for what happened. They are provided only as background. Certainly soldiers have been more sorely tried, more lacking comforts, more exposed to hostile action and the general horrors of war than this unfortunate platoon, without reverting to—

Tyson slammed the book shut. He lit a cigarette and watched the smoke rise, then abruptly turned the book over and looked closely at the picture of Andrew Picard. The photo seemed oddly blurred, but he saw the profile of a bearded man of about his own age, dressed in a light shirt with military-style shoulder tabs. There were lines running across the photograph, and Tyson saw that they were actually names. He suddenly realized that the photograph was of Picard's image reflected in a dark, glossy surface, and he comprehended that the surface was the black granite wall of the Vietnam memorial in Washington.

Tyson stared at the extraordinary photograph for some time, reading the etched names of the dead that ran across the black wall, across Picard's mirrored image, out to the edges of the dust jacket – that ran, he thought, across time and space; the army of the dead.

Tyson opened the book to the inside flap and read the short biography: *Andrew Picard is a graduate of Yale University. He served with the Marines as a Public Information Officer in Vietnam at Hue during the Tet offensive. He lives and works in Sag Harbor, Long Island.*

Tyson nodded. *Yale.* Probably went to Platoon Commander School the summer after graduation but had got himself a cushy public relations job and managed to avoid actually having to lead a combat infantry platoon.

Sag Harbor. A little town just north of the Hamptons. Tyson had rented a summer house out there some years before. He could vaguely recall a roadside mailbox that he passed often with the names Picard/Wells on it, but couldn't remember exactly where. It appeared that the lines of his life and Mr Picard's had converged without touching: once in 1968 at Hue, then in the summer of '76, and most recently in a bookshop on 42nd Street. It appeared too that they were somehow fated to meet.

Over his third scotch, Tyson recollected an incident nearly two years before; he had received a telephone call at his home from a man who said he was researching a book on Vietnam. Tyson recalled being as unhelpful as possible without being obviously evasive. Some weeks later the man had called again. Tyson had been abrupt and hung up. *Andrew Picard.* Tyson nodded in recognition.

Tyson thumbed through the book and regarded the photograph pages. There was the usual lineup of military commanders: Americans and their South Vietnamese allies on one side, Viet Cong and North Vietnamese on the other. Like a football programme, he thought.

Then there were the shockers: the uncollected dead, the trucks and armoured vehicles hauling the collected dead, the civilians on their knees weeping and wailing over inert bodies, the grotesquely wounded, and finally the mass graves. And it was all in black and white which he thought was wrong. World War II was in black and white. This war was in colour.

Tyson stopped turning pages and looked down at a half-page photograph. Grouped around the ruined hull of an enemy armoured amphibious vehicle were the men of the First Platoon, Alpha Company, Fifth Battalion, Seventh Cavalry. There were nearly forty of them, a team shot, taken before the Tet season began, before injuries cut the roster by more than half.

They were, he thought, a cocky-looking crew, arrogant and unfrightened. A good deal of that was posturing, of course. But he remembered that the picture had been taken in December 1967, around Christmas – before that first fateful day of Tet, January 30, 1968, when Alpha Company had lost a third of its people one morning in a village called Phu Lai.

December, though, had been a good month. The rain was light, the winds warm, and the sun not so cruel. Casualties were zero that month, and they'd tallied some kills on their side of the scoreboard. Christmas, if not a Currier and Ives one, had at least been bloodless. Ergo the smug faces of the men of the First Platoon of Alpha Company.

Tyson saw himself poised in the turret of the enemy vehicle, the warlord atop the scarred castle turret of the vanquished enemy, his victorious soldiers gathered about.

He scanned the faces more closely and was able to pick out the ones who were fated to die and those about to be wounded.

He studied the faces with the intensity of a man studying a high school yearbook before an upcoming reunion.

Tyson closed the book and slipped it into his attaché case. He picked up his drink and noticed the slightest tremor in his hand. He replaced the glass on the bar and drew a deep breath.

He headed for the door, stepped out into the bright sunlight, and began walking. By the time he reached Fifth

Avenue, his mind had settled back into the present. He considered the consequences of this public exposure. He reflected for a while on his courses of action, his family, friends, and career.

The danger seemed unreal and remote at the moment, but that was the worst kind of danger: the kind you cannot or will not meet head-on. The kind that is amorphous at first, incorporeal, but which takes shape while you're busy denying it exists and hardens into a physical entity.

It was very much, he thought, like when the jungle suddenly became quiet at night. *Nothing out there*. Then the bamboo would click in the wind, but there was no wind. Moon shadows would move across the outer perimeter, but there was no moon and no clouds to make shadows.

Then suddenly, between the beats of a speeding heart, the silent and shapeless shadows would appear, black-clad in the black night, dropping all pretence of not existing, moving towards your pathetic little perimeter of invented safety.

Tyson stopped walking and wiped a line of perspiration from his forehead. He looked around as though to assure himself he was on the sidewalks of New York. Then his mind went back once again to that rainy morning in Hue. It seemed that it had happened on another planet, in another life, and to another person. That Ben Tyson, he thought, was twenty-five years old, unmarried, had never held an infant in his arms or seen a corpse outside a funeral home. That Ben Tyson had only a vague conception of love, tragedy, compassion, or even morality. Nothing in his sheltered American life had prepared him for Hue, 15 February 1968.

The question at hand, however, was this: *Had anything since then prepared him to face the consequences of that day?*

4

Ben Tyson boarded the 1:40 out of Penn Station and took a seat in the smoking car.

The train moved out through the dark tunnels of Manhattan, passed under the East River, then broke free into the sunlight of Queens.

At Jamaica Station there were the usual garbled PA announcements and the search for the right track before he boarded the correct train.

Twenty-two minutes out of Jamaica, the train came to a halt at Garden City station, and Tyson stepped out into the sunny platform near the quaint station house.

He could smell the flowers, great coloured protrusions of them, growing wild along the track beds. Out of instinct he turned right toward his house, then reversed his direction and walked along the raised platform toward the centre of the village. He descended the short flight of steps and crossed Hilton Avenue.

Tyson realized that he hadn't been home on a weekday afternoon in some years. There were children walking and bicycling from school, housewives with prams, service vans, mail carriers, and all the other signs of activity that made up the life of these commuter towns by day. He felt almost estranged from these familiar streets where he'd spent his childhood.

Tyson stood before a picturesque brick building with arched windows. The hundred-year-old structure had served as the village stable, public school, and warehouse. Now it was a gentrified warren of law offices where Dickensian scriveners spent the day bent over plea forms and wills. Tyson entered a ground floor office and stood in the empty waiting room.

He shifted the attaché case to his left hand and was aware of the book, like a tumour, he thought, nascent at the moment, newly discovered, awaiting diagnosis.

A woman appeared from the far door. 'May I help you?'

'My name is Ben Tyson. I'm here to see Mr Sloan.'

She smiled in recognition, not of his face, but of his name. Like most of Tyson's relationships, the one with Phillip Sloan's secretary was primarily telephonic. 'I'm Ann. Please have a seat.'

She disappeared and a minute later returned with Phillip Sloan, a man in his fifties. Sloan was dressed in an unfortunate checkered suit, tassled shoes, and his club tie, whose colours never seemed to match anything. Sloan greeted Tyson effusively, then said, 'Ben, did we have an appointment?' Sloan made a silly show of leafing through his secretary's appointment book.

Tyson moved toward the entrance to the inner offices. 'This won't take long, Phil.'

Sloan shot his secretary a quizzical look, then followed. He directed Tyson into the library. 'I have a client in my office.'

Tyson took a seat at a long reading table and regarded the book-lined walls. *Corpus Juris Secundum.* The law of the land, codified and indexed, spelling out in excruciating detail and obtuse prose the rights and obligations of a uniquely lawless society.

Tyson placed an open book on the mahogany table and slid it toward Sloan. Sloan glanced quickly at the front of the book, then began to read.

Tyson lit a cigarette and stared at the far wall.

After some time, Sloan looked up from the book, a neutral expression on his face.

Tyson saw that Sloan was not going to speak, so he said, 'John McCormick showed that to me on the train this morning.'

24

Sloan gave a professional nod that conveyed nothing.

Tyson did not particularly like the man. But Sloan's father had been the Tyson family attorney for years, and it seemed natural that Phillip Sloan should continue to handle the Tysons' affairs. And Sloan was good, if not likable. Tyson stood. 'I just wanted to alert you to this before you heard it on the links or wherever it is you disappear to on sunny days. If anything comes of it, I'll let you know.'

Sloan hesitated, then made a motion with his hand. 'Sit down, Ben. I can spare a few more minutes.'

You're damned right you can, thought Tyson. *This is one of those walk-ins you dream about.* Tyson remained standing.

Sloan began speaking with a tone of concern. 'Well, this is distressing.' He thought a moment, then said, 'I suppose you've given some thought to bringing suit.'

But Tyson was only half listening. He said abruptly, 'Could this thing bring about a criminal action?'

Sloan stayed silent for some time, staring at Tyson, then said, 'That depends.'

'On *what?*'

'Obviously on whether or not there is any substance to what is written in that book.' He paused, then said, 'Will you sit down, Ben? Let me see that book again.'

Tyson sat and took the book from his attaché case.

Sloan examined it, reading the flap copy, scanning the index, then the front matter. He looked up at Tyson. 'Major publisher. The author seems to have credentials. The book is annotated and has a bibliography. Seems like a respectable job.'

Tyson shrugged.

Sloan said, 'You understand, Ben, that whatever we say here is privileged conversation.' Sloan drew a deep breath. 'Well?'

Tyson hesitated, then said, 'Look, what I want to know from you is whether or not I ... or the men who served with me ... can be called to account.'

Sloan's voice had an edge of sharpness. 'For what? You haven't answered my question.'

'For murder!'

Sloan leaned back in his chair and thought a moment, then replied, 'There is no statute of limitations on murder.'

Tyson's face was impassive.

Sloan continued, 'However, the Army would have to establish jurisdiction in this case.'

'Meaning?'

'They'd have to get you back in.'

Tyson nodded. 'Can they do that?'

'That's the question.' Sloan added, 'If they can't, then no civilian court can try you. You see, you fall between the cracks. It would have to be an American military court-martial or no trial at all. There are precedents for this.'

'I'm sure there are.' Tyson thought a moment. 'Okay, worst scenario. They get me back in. Then what?'

'The key here is witnesses. Is there anyone in your former unit who would testify against you?'

'Apparently there is.'

Sloan shook his head. 'Talking to a writer is not the same as testifying in front of an Army grand jury.'

Tyson stayed silent.

Sloan played with his pencil awhile, then said, 'Look, what we have here is an alleged crime brought to light by a writer some seventeen – eighteen years ... My God, is it that long ago? Anyway, many years after the alleged facts. The writer mentions three sources for his account: two unnamed GIs who he claims were in your platoon and whose anonymity he is protecting and one Eurasian nun, identified only as Sister Teresa, who he says is the sole survivor of the massacre—' Sloan looked at Tyson. 'Do you know this Sister Teresa?'

Tyson hesitated before replying, 'I knew the nun in question.'

Sloan did not pursue this but said, 'Anyway, here is an

alleged crime, committed in a foreign country with which we have no present relations—'

'I know all that.'

'—during a military operation, during a time of war, and you are not specifically mentioned as one of the people who actively engaged in this ... massacre.'

Tyson stared at the book lying between them. 'All right, now what's the bad news?'

Sloan leaned forward. 'You know. As the commander—'

'Responsible for the actions of my men, I bear full responsibility, and so on. Yes, I know.'

'Did you shoot anyone?'

'No.'

'Were you at the scene of the alleged murders?'

Tyson began to reply, then said, 'Picard says I was.'

'Picard wasn't there. I'm asking you.'

'No, I wasn't even there. Case closed.'

'I'm afraid it isn't, Lieutenant.' Sloan tapped his pencil on the table, then said, 'Okay, let me play devil's advocate again. Or Army prosecutor, if you like. Based on what I read here, I, as a prosecutor, want to know if you actually *ordered* those murders or if you did anything to *prevent* them. I want to know if you *knew* of them and did not *report* them, or even if you *should* have known of them or should have *anticipated* them. Because if any of that is true, then the Army will charge you with the actual murders as though you committed them with your own hands.'

After a period of silence, Tyson let out a breath and remarked, 'Rank has its privileges.'

Sloan stood and went to the far wall of the library. He pulled a large volume from a high shelf and literally dusted it off, then laid it on the table. He said, 'Any case that the Army builds against you will probably be based in part on the precedents and principles established at the Nuremberg trials of Nazi war criminals and the Tokyo trials of Japanese war criminals.'

'I'm in good company.'

Sloan leafed through the book as he spoke. 'The object of these trials was to get nooses around the necks of our enemies, of course. But some of those precedents have come back to haunt the American military.' He stopped turning pages. 'To wit: The landmark case of General Yamashita, commander of Japanese forces in the Philippines. Yamashita was accused by the Americans of having "unlawfully disregarded and failed to discharge his duty as a commander," by permitting men under his command to "commit brutal atrocities and other high crimes."' Sloan glanced at Tyson . 'Nowhere was it alleged that Yamashita personally *committed* any of the atrocities or even that he *ordered* their commission or even that he had any *knowledge* of them. The charges merely stated that during the period of his command he failed to *anticipate* what his troops might do, *should* have known what they might do, and failed to provide effective control of his troops as was required by circumstances.' Sloan closed the book. 'General Yamashita was found guilty and hanged.'

'Thanks for the pep talk, Phil.'

Sloan looked at his watch. 'I have to get back.' He stood. 'Look, the point about "should have known" and all that is somewhat esoteric. The Army is not going to charge you with anything after all these years unless you were actually at the scene of the incident. Were you?'

'Quite possibly.' Tyson stood.

'Did you actively participate in any way? I'm still not clear about what your role was in this alleged incident.'

Tyson picked up his attaché case. 'Well, it was a long time ago, Phil, and I'll have to think about what my role was.'

Sloan seemed miffed at the evasive answer. He walked toward the door and turned back. 'The best defence is an aggressive offence. That's true in football, combat, and law. You ought to give serious consideration to suing this guy Picard. If you don't sue, then this will be noted by the

28

government and the Army, and may well influence their decision on it and how to proceed.' Sloan waited for a reply, then added, 'Also, you ought to consider how your friends, community, family, and employers will look on this if you don't sue for libel.'

Tyson had already considered all of that. He knew, too, that Sloan was baiting him, asking in an oblique manner, *Of the charge of murder, guilty or not guilty, Tyson?*

'Of course I'll consider a lawsuit,' Tyson said.

Sloan nodded slowly. 'All right, Ben, keep me informed if anything further develops. Meanwhile, leave me the book to read. Get another copy and do the same.' He walked through the door, and Tyson followed. They parted in the corridor. Sloan said, 'Don't make any statements, public or private.'

Tyson looked over his shoulder. 'I wasn't planning to.'

'Best to Marcy.'

Tyson left the office and walked up the tree-shaded avenue. The danger, he thought, was more clear now and more palpable, which in a way made him feel better. But the thing had grown another head, and the teeth were far bigger than he'd thought from a distance.

Ben Tyson recrossed Hilton Avenue and entered the village library. He went directly upstairs to the reference law library. After some searching he sat at a small desk with four thick books. He pulled a yellow legal pad from his briefcase and headed the first page: *The Peers Commission Report on the My Lai Massacre*. On the second page he wrote: *Byrne's Military Law*. Page three and four he headed, respectively: *The Uniform Code of Military Justice* and *The Manual for Courts-Martial*.

Tyson opened the Peers Commission report and began reading, making notes as he went along. After half an hour, he pushed it aside and opened *The Uniform Code of Military Justice*. He was familiar with this book and was fairly certain it hadn't changed in the eighteen years since he'd last opened a copy of it. Military law transformed itself at roughly the same

29

rate as the evolution of a new species.

As an officer he'd sat on court-martial boards and had even acted as defence and trial counsel at Special Courts-Martial. Military law as written had seemed fair, logical, and even compassionate. There was a certain element of common sense to it that he knew instinctively was not present in civilian law. Yet some of the courts-martial he'd observed, especially those overseas, had a surreal quality to them; grim, dreary, little Kafkaesque affairs whose sole function was to process the accused into the convicted as quickly and quietly as possible.

Tyson skimmed the pertinent parts of the *UCMJ*, made some notes, then picked up the *Manual for Courts-Martial*. The book was actually a three-ring binder that held loose-leaf pages. He perused the book quickly, more out of curiosity and a perverse sense of nostalgia than for legal strategy. The manual was little more than a primer, a blueprint, and a script for a trial. Everyone's part was neatly spelled out in black and white. As an officer he had gone to this book only when all signs and omens pointed to court-martial. Tyson closed the book, rubbed his eyes, and stood. The light was dying from the west-facing window, and the library seemed unnaturally still, even for a library. Tyson looked at his watch. Nearly 6 P.M. He collected his notes, slipped them into his attaché case, and descended the stairs. He left the building and walked to a bench in the small war memorial park, a stretch of lawn between the library and railroad station. A late commuter train pulled in, and wives or husbands in cars and station wagons were there to meet it. Across the street the large hotel sat serenely in its own treed park.

Several things that he'd read, especially in *Byrne's* and the *Peers Commission Report*, preyed on his mind. He had thought briefly that perhaps he was beyond the reach of the law; that time, distance, and the course of his own life had forever separated him from that fetid little white stucco hospital. But now he was not so sure.

Tyson stood, turned, and began walking. He pictured himself in his pressed officer greens, sitting again in a court-martial room, not on the government side but in the accused's chair. He held on to that image as he walked, trying to make it so vivid that he felt impelled to take any steps necessary to avoid it becoming reality.

He headed toward Franklin Avenue where there was a bookshop. And then, without further delay, he knew he must head home to his family.

5

Ben Tyson walked up the flagstone path to his home, a prewar Dutch Colonial on a pleasant street lined with stately elms.

There was a good feeling to the house with its white cedar shingles, shutters, hipped roof, and Dutch dormers covered with reddish slates. Two carriage lanterns flanked the black-panelled door, and through the fanlight above the door he saw the foyer chandelier.

He opened the mailbox and extracted a thick sheaf of mail, mostly third-class junk; which reminded him that he lived in a prestigious zip code and was on every mail-order hit list in the nation. It also tipped him off that Marcy was not yet home.

He tried the door and found it was unlocked, meaning David was home. He entered and called out, 'Dave!'

A stereophonic sound emanating from the second floor reverberated through the walls and floor, about a 4 on the Richter scale. Tyson threw the mail on the foyer table and went through the living room into the rear den, or as Marcy called it, 'our office.' The first time his father heard her say that he looked as if he was about to have another coronary.

Tyson threw his jacket over the desk chair and sat in an

Eames recliner. He surveyed the room whose original masculine flavour had been altered, neutered by Marcy into a sort of eclectic potpourri of things that struck her fancy. Things that did not strike her fancy were conspicuously absent from the room, most notably his Army memorabilia which couldn't seem to find a home.

The remainder of the traditional home had undergone the same transformation. Only David's room, which contained Tyson's boyhood maple colonial furniture, circa 1953, had escaped Marcy's imprint. David had shown a strong sense of territoriality that Marcy could not crack, though Tyson was fairly certain that the boy didn't care either way about the bedroom furniture.

Marcy was, he reflected, a coercive utopian. Their house was run as though it were a commune. Decisions were shared, housework was shared, things and thoughts were shared. Yet, Tyson felt that he was somehow not getting *his* share. If nothing else, he thought, he made twice her salary and worked longer hours. Although Marcy would not use Marx's words, her philosophical rebuttal was: *From each according to his ability, to each according to his needs.* Apparently his needs were less, though any suggestion that his ability was greater met with an icy silence. He often wanted to point out to her that he'd fought a war to keep a country from being run the way his house was run. But that was a lost cause, too.

Tyson put his head back and listened to the stereo. *Primitive. Jungle music.* He couldn't identify the song, if in fact it was a song. But he could not deny its appeal on some primal level.

Tyson drew from his attaché case the two books that he'd purchased earlier, a paperback novel by Picard called *The Quest*, and *Hue: Death of a City*, which had set him back another $18.95, plus tax. At this rate, he thought, he'd drive the book onto the *Times* bestseller list and make Picard rich.

He set the novel aside and opened the Hue book, scanning some of the pages that did not relate to the incident at Hôpital

Miséricorde. Picard, he judged, was not a terribly bad writer. The book was in the style and format favoured by pop historians, stressing personal tragedy, anecdotes, and interviews with survivors – from peasants and privates to generals and provincial governors. And it was impressionistic – the big picture painted or suggested by a series of tiny points like a Seurat.

He read from an early chapter:

Hue. The city had an almost ephemeral nature to it. It was one of those small city-jewels of the world that transcended the meaning of city. It was the soul of Vietnam, North and South. It was a centre of learning, culture, and religion; an historical and evocative place, the seat of the old Annamese Empire for twenty-one centuries. And like all great cities, it was a blend of the exotic and the sophisticated, the urbane and the bucolic. It was more Vietnamese than French, but the old cafés on the south side of the Perfume River still had a colonial air about them, and the great Phu Cam Cathedral was a tribute to the city's ecumenicalism.

Hue was a mélange of sights, smells, sounds, and sensations. It was vitality and otherworldliness all in one. It was the heart and embodiment of the nation, and as long as it existed, the Vietnamese people, from the simple villager to the corrupt Saigon politician, had reason to hope ...

'Hi, Dad.'

Tyson closed the book and looked up at his son. 'Hello, David.'

'Whatcha readin'?'

'Try that again.'

'What are you reading?'

'A book. You didn't take the mail in.'

'I took the garbage *out*.'

'You left the door unlocked.'

'I took the milk and paper in. Where's Mom?'

'That was my question.'

David smiled.

Tyson regarded his son. The boy dressed well, but then sartorial splendour was in vogue at the moment. His hair was of a length that would offend only a master sergeant, and the boy was good-looking, though in Tyson's opinion too lean, like his mother. But also like his mother, his colouring was dark and rich, and he had her striking green eyes.

David drew closer and glanced at the book in Tyson's lap. 'Hew?'

'Pronounced "way." The French gave the Vietnamese the Latin alphabet, then misspelled every word for them.'

'Oh. It's about Vietnam.'

'Right. Jeet?'

David laughed. 'No. What's for dinner? You cook tonight. I have K.P. Mom serves.'

'Is that so?'

'Check the chart.' He said it with barely concealed disdain. David picked up *The Quest*. 'What's this?'

'Another book. I'll bet you've seen them in museums or on television. They make movies out of them.'

David ignored the sarcasm and studied the cover art, then read the flap copy. 'The Holy Grail. I read something about that. King Arthur. Is that a true story?'

'It is a legend, and a legend is like the truth, but a legend is also like a myth, and a myth is like a lie. Follow?'

'No.' His eyes drifted back to the Hue book. 'Is that a true story?'

Tyson did not reply.

David put the novel down on the end table, then said, 'What's wrong, Dad?'

Tyson thought a moment, then replied, 'I'd rather not discuss it at the moment.'

'Are you and Mom getting divorced?'

'Not to my knowledge.'

David smiled. 'Okay. We can hold a family council later.'

Tyson again detected a note of mockery in David's voice. 'There are some things, David, that do not lend themselves to solutions by family councils. There are things in this world that children should not be privy to nor burdened with.'

'Tell that to Mom.'

'I will. But I will speak to you privately about what's troubling me without giving you all the details.'

'Okay.' The boy hesitated, then said, 'You want me to call out for dinner?'

'Yes. Please. Make it a surprise. No pizza.'

David nodded and moved toward the door. Tyson could see he wanted to say something more, but Tyson did not encourage him. David left, and Tyson stood, moving to the bar in the shelf unit. He poured himself a small Drambuie.

Tyson sometimes wondered if they should have had more children. He was one of four children, the other three, girls. Conversely, Marcy had three brothers, and he suspected that she had been somehow traumatized by the experience. He, on the other hand, had been treated affectionately by his sisters. David would know neither sibling affection nor rivalry. The decision not to have more children had been made eight years ago when Jenny was born, lived, suffered, and died, all within a week. Marcy said it was a result of the LSD she took in college. Tyson offered that it could have been Agent Orange. His minister, Reverend Symes, said it was God's will. The doctors had no opinion.

Yet, David was healthy in every way, and Tyson sometimes thought it was worth another try. But neither of them had the temperament to cope with a deformed child who lived.

Tyson put this out of his mind and picked up the Hue book. He looked at the index to see if his name appeared anywhere other than the pages dealing with the Hôpital Miséricorde incident. There was a page reference near the front of the book and one near the end. He turned to the earlier page and read while standing:

The soothsayers had foretold that the Year of the Monkey would bring bad luck, and never had the prophets of doom been proved so right so soon. The year was not three hours old when the enemy offensive began.

But notwithstanding this dire prediction, a festive mood filled Hue that day. It was a time of traditional family reunions, feasting, and street festivals. It was like Christmas, New Year's Eve, and Mardi Gras rolled into one. Ancestors were honoured at family altars, and religious ceremonies were held at the city's many pagodas and temples. Paper dragons snake-danced through the streets, and, forebodingly, fireworks and sky rockets reverberated throughout the city.

There was a declared truce, but the military was uneasy. American troops were on normal alert, and the South Vietnamese had cancelled holiday leaves for some, but not all of their troops. Nearly half the Vietnamese armed forces and a high percentage of key commanders were not on duty. And of those who were, it can be assumed that many were engaged in some sort of celebration.

On the evening of 30 January, seven thousand soldiers of North Vietnam's 4th, 5th, and 6th regiments marched boldly, in parade formation, across the bridges that spanned the canals in Hue's southern suburbs. And no one stopped them.

Within the city, thousands more Viet Cong had infiltrated and mingled with the holiday revellers. Other enemy formations were poised around the city, waiting to strike. Hue's time had come.

But the battle of Hue actually began earlier in the day, though at the time no one realized the significance of those opening shots. Alpha Company, Fifth Battalion of the Seventh Cavalry, First Air Cavalry Division, was patrolling an area six kilometres west of the city in the late afternoon. The company, nearly two hundred strong, was commanded by Captain Roy Browder of Anniston, Alabama. Alpha Company began a standard sweep through the supposedly deserted village of Phu Lai when it encountered a unit of well-armed enemy troops, later identified as the Ninth North Vietnamese Regiment, whose strength was estimated at over a thousand men. The enemy regiment was hiding in the village in preparation for their midnight assault on Hue.

The first platoon of Alpha Company was led by Lieutenant Benjamin Tyson, of whom we will learn more later. Tyson's lead platoon was actually inside the village when, according to a survivor, whom I will call Pfc X for reasons that will become clear later, 'All of a sudden the place started to move. I mean haystacks opened up, and gooks came out of the wells and holes in the ground. Gooks were standing in the windows and doors of the hootches around the village square, and we were in the middle. It was like a nightmare. I couldn't believe my eyes. No one fired for a really long time. But maybe it was a few seconds. Then it exploded.'

Tyson found he was sitting in his chair again. He nodded to himself. It was curious to discover after all these years that his company was one of the first to make contact with the enemy before the Tet offensive actually began. But then the grunt in the field rarely saw the bigger picture. And though he never knew that he'd tangled with a thousand enemy troops, he could believe it. It was for people like Picard to supply the regiment designations and other details that seemed unimportant then, but which allowed others, veterans such as himself, to interpret what had happened. If they cared to.

He put his head back and yawned, feeling very drowsy. The book slipped from his hand onto the floor.

'What the hell are we going to do? *What? What?* What

37

are we going to *do?*'

Tyson lay in the village square between the dead radio operator and the dead squad leader. He turned to the rifleman lying wounded beside him and replied, 'We're going to die.'

Machine-gun fire raked the square, and rocket-propelled grenades burst among the living and the dead. Tyson had never heard or seen such sustained and heavy enemy fire and had never been in so exposed a position to fully appreciate how quickly a cohesive military unit could wither and die. He knew of no tactics that would extricate them from this massacre in the muddy square. One just had to wait one's turn to die, or stand up and get it over with.

A rocket-propelled grenade landed in front of his face and splashed filthy water into his eyes. Tyson stared at it, half submerged in the brown puddle, realizing it was the last thing he'd ever see. But it did not explode, and he would learn later from other men who had stared that khaki egg-shaped death in the eye that many of those Russian-made grenades were faulty. Some unmotivated, vodka-soaked munition worker in Volgograd had done something wrong, and Ben Tyson was alive for the time being.

A bullet nicked his right ear, and he yelled out, more in surprise than in pain. He saw men stand and run, only to be cut down, and he wondered where they were running to because the fire was coming from all sides of the square. They were cut off from the rest of the company, and they hadn't the men or resources to break out. He prayed earnestly for a quick death and drew his .45 automatic as insurance against being taken alive.

Then, as if God answered someone else's prayer, a bullet struck a smoke-signal canister hooked to the web belt of a dead man, ten metres to Tyson's front. Tyson watched as the red smoke billowed up slowly from the dead body as though the man were bleeding into a zero-gravity environment.

Tyson tore a smoke canister from his own belt, pulled the pin, and rolled it a few feet away. The canister popped, disgorging a stream of green smoke into the heavy, fetid air. Smoke canisters began popping all over the square as the survivors of his platoon comprehended that there might be a way out. Vivid plumes of red, blue, yellow, orange, and green smoke rose from the killing zone.

The enemy was temporarily blinded, and their fire lifted higher, as was natural in obscured conditions; they began cross-firing into each other's positions across the market square.

Tyson reached out and pulled the radiophone from the stiffening fingers of the dead radioman. He steadied his voice and called Captain Browder. 'Mustang Six, this is Mustang One-Six. We're backing out the same way we came in. Can you meet us halfway?'

The radio crackled, and Browder's voice came on with that practised cool of a man who was used to talking and ducking bullets at the same time. 'Roger. We're heavily engaged at the moment – still at the edge of the village. But we'll try a linkup. That's your smoke, I guess.'

'Roger. Guide on that. We've got to leave the dead.'

'Understand.'

'How about air and artillery?'

'On the way. But don't wait for it. Get your asses moving. Papa's coming. Good luck, partner.'

'Roger, over.'

'Roger, out.'

Tyson rose to one knee and called out through the smoke and noise, 'Pull back! Take the wounded and leave the dead and know the difference!'

The first platoon of Alpha Company began their withdrawal across the mud-slick square. They crawled, ran, and stumbled back through the smoke-shrouded marketplace to the first line of huts that bordered the open area. They set the huts ablaze with incendiary grenades, threw the last of their smoke canisters, and tossed tear-gas grenades in their wake. They blasted away with M-16s, machine guns, shotguns, grenade launchers, and pistols, expending ammunition at a rate that testified to their desperateness. They fought for each metre through the cluster of bamboo huts, leaving a burning swath through Phu Lai in their efforts to break out of the trap that had severed them from their main body.

The linkup with their company came on a small village lane that ran between a duck pond and a pigsty. The wounded were handed over to the less fatigued troops of the second and third platoons and passed down the line to a concrete pagoda where the four company medics had gathered. The enemy was still firing, but the battle lines had become so obscured that Alpha Company was not drawing effective fire at the moment.

Browder approached, a stocky figure covered with grime, moving nonchalantly along the path. He spoke to Tyson gruffly. 'Well, you're out of the neck-deep shit, sonny, but you got me wading in the knee-deep stuff.'

'Thanks for coming.'

'Yeah. Well, we can either form a perimeter here, dig in and fight it out until they break it off. Or we can make a break now and beat feet across that rice paddy dike we came in on. Any thoughts?'

Tyson rubbed his bleeding ear. 'I don't like the smell of this. Too many gooks with too much ammunition, acting too ballsy. I think we hit something bigger than we are. Time to go.'

Captain Browder said, 'But we've got nonambulatory wounded to drag out, and I've got some KIAs.'

Tyson shook his head. 'I don't think Charlie's going to break contact and disappear this time. I think if we stay, they mean to finish us off.'

Browder considered a moment, then nodded. 'Let's pull out before they get a fix on us again. Let the artillery and gunships pound the shit out of this asshole of a village.'

Browder spoke into his radio and gave the orders for a withdrawal. The Cobra gunships arrived and were surprised to meet heavy-calibre antiaircraft fire. One ship crashed in flames into the village. The artillery began landing in Phu Lai, round after round of-incendiary white phosphorus as Browder had called for, and the village began to burn as Alpha Company reached the rice paddy dike that marked the western edge of the village.

They staggered across the sodden paddies, carrying the wounded and a few of the dead, leaving a trail of abandoned equipment. Tyson saw a boot stuck in the mud. The enemy fired after them, but Alpha Company paid little attention. Their sole objective was to distance themselves from the village of Phu Lai.

The gunships and artillery covered their withdrawal, which was in reality a rout. The enemy did not follow them across the exposed paddies but took to their underground bunkers and tunnels to wait out the rain of fire and steel.

Alpha Company regrouped on a high and dry piece of ground dotted with burial mounds: the village cemetery. They picked off the rice paddy leeches and began digging in. Bones were turned up, and they littered the reddish earth as the men dug deeper. Skulls were set on the edges of foxholes, facing outward, a circle of grinning death-heads stark white against the upturned earth. Someone dug into a fresh grave, and the stench caused the man to vomit. The grave was quickly closed again.

Casualty lists were prepared by the platoon sergeants. The officers read and tallied them: five known dead, present and accounted for. Thirty-eight wounded, ten critically. Fifteen were missing, and Browder reported by radio to battalion headquarters that the presumption of death was strong, but this did not save him from a fierce dressing-down for leaving Americans behind.

Under normal circumstances, Tyson thought, both he and Browder would have been relieved of their commands for the Phu Lai fiasco. It was, after all, a defeat, and a defeat equalled a blunder of some sort. But on that particular night of January 30, in the words of Roy Browder, the faeces hit the rotary blades, and they were spared the humiliation of being fired. In the general confusion and panic that gripped the battered nation over the following weeks, trivialities such as the Phu Lai fuckup were forgiven and forgotten. After all, said Browder with a wink, everyone from the chiefs of staff to the chief of Army intelligence was a fuckup for not having noticed what was coming. Browder, when he' had a free moment some days later, put himself in for a Silver Star and told Tyson to do the same, though Tyson did not.

Alpha Company spent a restless night among the bones and pungent earth. A breeze from the South China Sea carried the sounds of explosions from the east, and they could see parachute flares and signal rockets in the vicinity of Hue. A sergeant on his second tour of duty commented, 'That's just Hue celebrating. It's called Tet. The gook New Year. Happy New Year.'

But it wasn't Hue celebrating. It was Hue dying.

At dawn the remainder of Alpha Company moved east toward the now besieged city, a journey of six kilometres that would take them nearly two weeks and, for many of them, a lifetime to complete.

'Ben!'

Tyson opened his eyes and focused on Marcy sitting in the club chair across from him, a drink in her hand. He cleared his throat. 'Hello.'

'Tough day?'

Tyson sat up. 'I've had worse.'

Marcy considered him for a moment. Then she said,

'David ordered Chinese food.'

'I smell it.'

'Do you want to eat, or do you want to talk?'

'I want to drink.' He held out his glass.

She hesitated, then stood and took it.

'Drambuie. Neat.' He picked up the Hue book and slid it across the coffee table between them. She handed him his drink.

He said, 'Have a seat, my love. I have good news and bad news. The good news is that your husband is famous. The bad news is the reason why. Page two-seventeen.'

She took up the book and began reading. She dressed well, and for all her feminism, she favoured frilly white blouses and cameo chokers. Her skirt was hot pink and fitted tightly, with a slit up the side. She wore her dark brown hair in a short shag that framed a light olive complexion. She looked vaguely Semitic or Mediterranean, though her genetic pool lay in the north of Europe. Her eyes were what people noticed first; those large watery green eyes that were able to flash anger, sensuality, and iciness with equal intensity. Ben Tyson studied his wife as she read. Finally, she sensed his gaze and raised the book.

Tyson shifted his attention to the window. Bluebirds were feeding on the back lawn, and the sun was nearly gone, leaving long purple shadows over the terrace. The room was dark except for the circle of lamplight around Marcy.

'Is this true?'

He turned back toward her. She'd rested the open book in her lap and was staring at him, intently, expectantly.

Everything that came to mind sounded evasive. 'As far as it goes, and in substance, yes, it is accurate.'

She said nothing for a long time, then asked, 'What more is there?'

'Much, much more.'

'In your words, Ben. How is this book inaccurate?'

'It's a matter of perspective. It depends on where you were standing.'

'Where were you standing?'

He ignored the question and said, 'Also, after a long time it's hard to distinguish reality from fantasy from nightmare.'

'It says here' – she tapped the open book – 'it says you and your men massacred sick and wounded people. You shot men, women, children, and babies. Burned people alive. Did *that* happen?'

Tyson let a few seconds go by, then replied evenly, 'It happened. It did happen. But not quite the way Picard says.'

'Then tell me what you remember. What you know.'

Tyson considered a moment, then answered, 'No.'

'Why not?'

'I made a promise never to speak of this.'

'Whom did you promise?'

Tyson looked off at some indeterminate point and said distractedly, 'We all promised. We swore to each other.'

She showed a flash of anger. 'That's absurd. I'm your wife.'

Tyson stood and poured himself another liqueur. He turned and looked at her.

Marcy stood and tossed the book on the coffee table. 'I think I have a right to know, and I don't really care about some vow you made ... and obviously *someone* broke that vow. X and Y squealled, didn't they?'

'You weren't *there*! You were *here*! Don't ask me to explain to you what happened in that shithole eighteen years ago. Who the hell knows what happened? Who cares—?' Tyson got himself under control and sat back in his chair. 'I don't remember what happened.'

Marcy drew a deep breath and looked at him closely. 'That's not true.' She added, 'I can remember what happened to me eighteen years ago—'

'You should. It was reported in a national magazine.'

'Cheap shot, Ben.' She moved to the door as if to leave, then walked to where Tyson was sitting and put her hand on his shoulder.

He took her hand and said, 'Just give me some time to sort

44

it out. I'll tell you. But I want to tell you the truth. And that's not possible now.'

She didn't reply.

Tyson added, 'Look, if this book triggers some sort of ... investigation, then there will be different versions of the truth ... and it's best if you wait—'

'What do you mean "an investigation"? Can they ... bring charges ... ?'

'According to Phil Sloan they can.'

She shook her head, then said, 'You went to him? Before you spoke to me?'

'He has a law degree. You don't. He was available. You weren't. The subject was murder, not marital difficulties.'

Marcy disengaged her hand from his. 'Just tell me this: Did you ... kill anyone? I mean, it doesn't say you killed anyone yourself ...'

He replied, 'An officer is responsible for the actions of his men.'

'Nonsense! That's so typically macho. Such egotistical military bullshit ... Every sane person is responsible for his or her own actions.'

He interrupted, 'I'll tell you something else: Not only am I responsible for the actions of the men I commanded, but I'm liable for crimes they may have committed. That's the law.'

'Idiotic.'

'Be that as it may, you have to take into account *military* law, institutions, custom, and logic. Not your own personal philosophy.'

'All right. I understand that, Ben. Just don't decide to be noble or stupid. If you didn't kill anyone, you're innocent of murder. And you'd better say that, if anything comes of this.'

Tyson didn't reply but walked to the window and threw open the sash. A scented breeze came into the room, and the big sycamore tree rustled in the light wind. Children were playing in the next yard. It was an incredibly beautiful twilight, he thought. One of those evenings whose smells

45

come back to you years later. 'What is that? Honeysuckle?'

'I suppose.'

'Why can't it always be May?'

'You said you liked the changing seasons.'

'Right. But sometimes I like it to be always May.'

Marcy stared at his back for some time, then spoke softly, 'I'm frightened for you, Ben.'

'I'm okay.'

'No, you're not. That's the point. I know what's going through your mind: duty, honour, country, God. Or something like that. You've got a martyr streak in you—'

'Have I?'

'You may have survived combat, but you won't survive this. Not unless you—'

Tyson turned and faced her. 'That's enough.'

'All right. But I'll tell you this: As far as I'm concerned, everything that had to do with that war was criminal. But that's no reason to offer yourself up as the chief criminal, out of some misguided sense of responsibility, guilt or—'

'Enough! I don't need a lecture.'

'What *do* you need from me?'

Tyson leaned back against the windowsill. He thought she would probably be more understanding if he'd come home and announced that he was an embezzler or a dope addict. Or better yet, that he'd machine-gunned a roomful of Republican fund-raisers. But this particular crime touched a raw nerve in her. He said, 'I just wanted you to know.'

'Thanks. I could have learned more at the supermarket.'

He forced a smile, then spoke musingly. 'Maybe I'm overreacting ... maybe this will fade away. Probably I shouldn't have even gone to Phil's office.'

She replied, 'I hope you're right,' then added, 'But you know, Ben, even if it doesn't lead to anything in a legal sense ... in other ways, here in this house, in this town, and on your job ...'

'Yes, I know. Thank you.'

She seemed to be lost in thought, and instinctively he knew her mind had returned to those pages of gory detail.

She looked up at him. 'How did they kill the children? I mean *how* ...?'

There was a knock on the door, and it opened a crack. David peeked in. 'The Chinese delicacies are congealing.'

Tyson said, 'Give it a shot of microwave. We'll be right there.'

David closed the door.

Marcy and Ben Tyson looked at each other for some seconds, both wondering how much David had heard. They turned and walked silently toward the door.

She said, 'Do you want wine?'

He held the door open for her. 'Beer goes better with Chinese delicacies. How was your day?'

'Hectic. And I have a trip this week.'

'Where?'

'Chicago. One night.'

He didn't respond.

6

Tyson awakened. He threw the bedclothes back and turned his head toward Marcy. She slept in the nude, in all seasons, as he did. He regarded her naked body, dark against the plain, white cotton sheets. He watched her full, firm breasts rising and falling as she breathed, then his eyes travelled down to her pubic hair. The miracle of their marriage, he thought, was that after sixteen years the sexual attraction was as strong as the sexual drive.

Tyson knew that nearly everyone found them a classically mismatched couple. Tyson considered himself a traditional man, a result of growing up in a home that stressed

47

traditional values and in a community that was locally famous as a conservative bastion. Unlike Marcy, he was never personally caught up in the turbulence of the sixties, partly because he went to college in the Deep South, partly because of his years in the Army, 1966 to 1969. He'd commented on occasion, 'I missed the Age of Aquarius, but I saw it on TV.'

Marcy Clure Tyson and Benjamin James Tyson had nearly opposite tastes in music, clothing, literature, and art. Politically, he was indifferent, and she was committed. Yet they married and stayed married while a good number of their friends were divorced, about to be divorced, or wished they were divorced. Tyson had often wished he'd never met her but rarely wished to see her gone.

Marcy rolled over on her side and faced him. She mumbled something, then let out a snore.

Tyson swung his legs out of the bed and stood. He walked across the carpet to the dormer windows as he did every morning to personally greet the day. The eastern sky was brightening, and he could see it was going to be another fine morning. Below in the dark street he saw two very early commuters, briefcases swinging in wide arcs, as they stepped out purposefully to catch the next train. Tyson heard the matin bells of a nearby church. *Each matin bell, the Baron saith, knells us back to a world of death.*

Tyson stepped onto the running trampoline and began to jog in place, his eyes still fixed on the east-facing window. There were lights in bedrooms across the road, and at the larger cross-street at the south end of the block, he saw cars making their way toward the parkways, expressways, and railroad stations. Suburbia was on the move, flowing westward to infuse the great city with its clean, oxygenated blood, to wow Wall Street and Madison Avenue with its tennis tans and tales of weekend bogies and eagles.

Tyson jumped off the trampoline and somersaulted to the middle of the grey carpet. He did a few minutes of calisthenics, then walked briskly into the master bathroom.

The bathroom had been modernized and sported a large Jacuzzi. Tyson turned it on. He shaved and brushed his teeth, then lowered himself into the hot, swirling eucalyptus-scented water. Through the rising steam he saw himself in a mirrored wall. He was, by any standards, powerfully built and somewhat on the hairy side. Some women liked that, others didn't. Marcy revelled in the forest on his chest. The Oriental girls, he recalled, found it beastly or amusing, but never sexy. However, they always commented favourably on his size; and it wasn't flaky, prostitute flattery. Westerners *were* bigger as he'd found out when he'd purchased a non-PX condom at a local *pharmacie*. He thought he should tell that amusing story to Mr Kimura over lunch one day.

He put his head and shoulders on the marble rim of the tub and floated in the turbulent waters. The dream had come again last night: He is back in the Army. There is a war on. It is a nameless war, with few of the elements of Vietnam. The landscape is the cold wintry woods of Fort Benning, Georgia, where he'd taken his infantry officer training. The combat fatigues he wears remind him of the foreign-looking uniforms worn by the aggressor army in the war games they played at Benning. In the dream these uniforms are filthy and torn. The weapons and equipment he carries are somewhat primitive. He does not interpret this to mean it is an earlier war, but rather a future war of long duration: an interminable, civilization-destroying conflict. Armies sweep back and forth across the scarred earth and the dying cities. That part at least is Vietnam.

In the dream he is no longer an officer, but an ordinary rifleman, and someone always says to him, 'Tyson, you have five more years to serve,' to which he always replies, 'That's not fair. I was already in. This time I'll die.'

Tyson pushed off the edge of the large tub, and let the waters swirl around his floating body. He had gone briefly to a psychiatrist who specialized in the war neuroses of upper-

49

middle-class and wealthy veterans, preferably ex-officers. That was about as specialized as you could get, Tyson thought, and only on Park Avenue would you find such a shrink. Tyson had rather liked the man, Dr Stahl, and found his insights revealing and his knowledge of postwar-related stress nothing short of startling.

Stahl and he had talked about the dream, they talked about the guilt of having survived when others didn't and spoke of the special guilt of having killed. They discussed at length the unique problems of having commanded men in battle, of having given orders that led to the deaths of subordinates and the deaths of civilians. It was in this area that Stahl earned his two hundred dollars an hour, and they were both aware of that. Popular literature and conventional wisdom were confined to the depressingly ordinary problems of the grunt. Stahl recognized that analysing the problems of the ex-officer was more interesting, more complex, and usually more remunerative.

Tyson had been on the verge of telling the man about Hôpital Miséricorde but knew intuitively that confession becomes a bad habit. After Stahl he would tell Marcy, and after Marcy the Reverend Symes. And thus having squared things away in privileged conversations with his shrink, his wife, and a representative of his God, he would eventually go to the Army Judge Advocate General. Therefore, he did not tell Stahl, and since further psychotherapy was of little value unless Stahl knew the Big Secret, Tyson had terminated the relationship, much to Dr Stahl's surprise and regret. Stahl found Tyson interesting. Tyson found Stahl too perceptive.

The last thing Stahl had said to him, in a letter actually, written in Stahl's somewhat stilted middle-European style, was this: *There is something else on your mind which is a great and terrible secret, Mr Tyson. I cannot see it, but I can see its shadow and feel its presence in everything you say.*

It would be idle to speculate on what it is, but please feel assured that in war everything is the norm. I have spoken to brave men who have had hysterics on the battlefield, who have run from the enemy, who have left their friends to die, and who have soiled their pants in the heat of battle. I have had revealed to me things of which you cannot even begin to dream. I tell you, my friend, war is hell, but take heart: When a soldier goes to war everything is pre-forgiven.

Tyson had never forgotten that cryptic last line: *Everything is pre-forgiven.* But by whom? How? When was it pre-forgiven? That line was meant to pique his curiosity; to entice him back onto the couch of Dr Stahl. And it almost had. But in the end he did not answer the letter, because it was unanswerable.

Some time after that, Dr Stahl, like a statistically significant percentage of his colleagues, had killed himself. The *Times* reported that the overdose of Quaaludes may have been accidental, but Tyson did not think so. Tyson thought that Vietnam killed by contact, association, and proxy.

Tyson floated to the edge of the tub and spread his arms out over the rim to steady himself. He stared up at the infrared lamp overhead and felt its waves warming his face. He recalled that he was not particularly surprised at Dr Stahl's suicide. For all Stahl's assurances about not being judgemental, not being shocked, the man was after all human. He had listened to an army of sick men fill his ears with grief until it had filled his heart and soul, and like a slow-acting virus, had overcome his immunities. And one day he discovered he was dead and made it official.

Tyson had been unexpectedly saddened while reading the obituary. But on a practical level, he was concerned about what had happened to Stahl's case files, though he had never made any inquiries.

Stahl had ended most of his sessions with the words 'You cannot run from the demons, so you must make friends with them.' He had advised Tyson to recall the dream in detail, talk with the characters who peopled the dark landscapes of his mind, until one day they would become familiar, friendly,

51

then perhaps banal and insipid. So, lying there in the Jacuzzi, Tyson went through it again. But this time – and there was no mistaking it – the characters in the dream had become more malevolent. The dream had taken on a special and prescient significance. In fact, the nightmare was becoming reality. *All is pre-forgiven, Dr Stahl.*

Marcy walked naked into the bathroom and lowered herself into the tub. She drew a long breath, inhaling the eucalyptus, smiled, and closed her eyes.

Tyson watched her breasts bob in the water, then turned his attention to her face. Rivulets of sweat ran from her brow down her cheeks. He thought she looked fine without makeup. She extended her legs and floated atop the misty water. Tyson reached out and massaged her toes. She murmured, 'Oh, that feels good.'

Marcy spread her floating legs, and Tyson knelt, leaning forward, cupping her buttocks in his palms. As he moved his head between her legs, she said, 'You'll drown if you try that.'

'What a way to go.'

'Ben!'

He buried his face deep in her groin, and she brought her thighs together, slipping down further into the water, taking him down with her. He struggled for a moment, broke free, and surfaced, spluttering. 'Bitch.'

She laughed.

Tyson retreated moodily to his end of the bath.

Marcy lifted herself out of the sunken tub and stood on the tiled edge, her legs parted as she stretched and yawned.

Tyson watched her and was instantly reminded of the photograph. It had originally appeared in *Life* magazine and had been reproduced a number of times in books dealing with the 1960s. It was a black-and-white photograph showing a group of students in Los Angeles' Griffith Park during the winter recess of 1968. It must have been a mild day because they were all cavorting in the nude at Mulholland Fountain.

The occasion was a rock concert according to the *Life* caption, though when the picture had been used on a network TV documentary about the 1960s the occasion had been described as a love-in. A photographic essay book described the event as an antiwar rally. Tyson had also seen the picture captioned as a happening and a be-in. Although the event may not have been clear, the picture of Marcy was. She was the most prominent of all the students, standing on the rim of the fountain much as she was now standing on the rim of the Jacuzzi, a full-frontal nude, one arm around the shoulders of a slender, shaggy-haired young man. The other arm was upraised, fist clenched, and her legs were parted. The expression on her face was a mixture of defiance and uninhibited joy. To the side could be seen two policemen approaching the fountain full of naked young men and women.

Tyson saw the picture again in his mind: Marcy's luxuriant pubic hair like a black bull's-eye, her breasts standing proud and erect. But for all the nakedness in that fountain, there was little that was erotic. The gathering was meant as a political statement, and it was.

Like other famous tableaux – the flag-raising over Iwo Jima or the girl weeping over the body at Kent State – the photograph transcended the particular event and captured the essence of an age. None of the subjects had been identified in print, their names as unimportant as the name of the photographer or the journal where the photograph first appeared. The picture had entered the public domain, the history books, and the public consciousness. No royalties were paid nor permissions asked nor rights protected. Yet for those who knew the subjects by name or who were the subjects, the famous photograph still remained personal and evoked a sense of grief, joy, or violated privacy.

Tyson looked up at his wife, still engaged in her stretching exercises. Her body and indeed her face had not changed that much in nearly two decades. In the picture, though, her hair

53

hung in long, wet strands down to her breasts. When Tyson had first met her at a party in a friend's Manhattan apartment, her hair was still shoulder-length, and his mental image of her remained that of a young girl with long hair, barefoot, with little makeup, and wearing a peasant dress. He said, 'I love you still.'

She paused in her stretching exercises and smiled at him. 'We are still in love. Remember that in coming weeks and months.'

'No matter how nasty we are to one another.'

'Right.'

Tyson shut the water off and lifted himself onto the tatami mat beside the tub. He rested his head on a cylindrical bamboo pillow and brought his knees up. He ran his fingers over the scar on his kneecap. It had turned reddish purple from the hot water. Most shrapnel wounds were jagged and ugly as they were supposed to be. This one was ludicrous: It looked like a large question mark.

Tyson said to his wife, 'There was a picture of me and my platoon in the book.'

'I didn't see it.' Marcy reached into the large, tiled shower stall and turned on the six pulsating jets. She said, 'Where did you leave the book, by the way? I don't want David to see it.'

Tyson stood and stepped into the shower with her. He thought he'd remind her that the *Life* magazine of March 8, 1968, was stuck up on the bookshelf in plain view. He said, however, 'I put it in my attaché case. But he'll have to read it eventually.'

She let the water pound against her body and ran her soapy hands over her breasts and face. 'Right. But you have to speak to him first.'

'The book speaks for itself. I'll just ask him to read it from the beginning. So my ... role will be seen in context.'

She looked over her shoulder. 'In or out of context it's gruesome, Ben, and it's going to upset him. Speak to him first.' She added, 'Perspective. Give him some perspective.

Show him where to stand when he's reading it.'

Tyson left the shower.

She called out, 'Sorry.'

Tyson tore a towel off the rack and quickly dried himself.

Marcy shut off the water and opened the stall door. 'Tell me something. How did you live with this for all these years? Wait. Don't be angry. I don't mean that in a judgemental sense. I mean it in a practical sense. How did you keep it to yourself and not tell *anyone? Did* you tell anyone?'

'No.'

She nodded and said, 'You never even hinted at it ...' She thought a moment, then added, 'You were blocking. You totally blocked it.'

'Psychobabble.' Tyson tossed the towel in the hamper. 'I never *blocked* it. I just chose not to discuss it. Unlike many people, I don't have to pour my guts out and reveal my personal history to casual acquaintances or even to friends. Or even to you.' He turned and walked into the adjoining dressing room, closing the door behind him.

He opened his closet and scanned his suits without really noticing them. It occurred to him that Marcy was going to be his toughest critic, but also his most honest one. He should listen to what she was saying so he could know what others were thinking. 'Day two,' he said aloud. 'Each day brings forth something new.'

7

Ben Tyson pulled his yellow Volvo into the drive leading to the Garden City Hotel and joined a line of slow-moving cars waiting to be parked. He moved the car up a few feet. Directly in front of him was a Cadillac limousine. In his rearview mirror he saw the grillwork of a Rolls. He said, 'Let's buy a new car. Something decidedly decadent.'

She shook her head. 'In your present situation, a new *tie* would look flagrant. Low profile, Ben. That's the word of the week.' She added, 'Also, your job may be a little shaky.'

Tyson nodded. Nevertheless, he thought, the old battered Volvo needed replacing. But now, nearly two weeks after that Tuesday morning, even the most mundane and personal decisions had to be scrutinized with one eye on appearances.

Tyson moved the car up another few feet and looked out toward the hotel. The nine-storey building sat in the centre of the suburban village, surrounded by ten acres of landscaped park. It was a new building, vaguely Georgian in style and topped by a reproduction of the cupola that had crowned the old Garden City Hotel. The setting sun blazed in red reflection from the windows, and Tyson squinted. He imagined the red brick Georgian structure that had stood there when he was growing up. The May evening recalled to him his senior prom in the Regency Room. He remembered the annual cotillion, the weddings and celebrations, including his parents' twenty-fifth anniversary party in the Hunt Room. It was, he reflected, a privileged childhood and adolescence, a very good time. A time of hope, a time before the war and the turbulence had changed him; had changed everyone. Such had been the years of his growing up in the fifties and early sixties. He said almost to himself, 'Enjoy it while you can.'

'What?'

'Life. Dance and be merry.'

She glanced at him and said thoughtfully, 'Philosophical musings don't become you.'

'Perhaps. I was just trying to put my petty problems in perspective. *That* is still the word of this week, by the way.'

'Glad to hear it.'

'Also, the last refuge of a troubled spirit is religion. I'm going to pay a call on Reverend Symes.'

She thought a moment, then said, 'Why not? That's better

56

than talking to your wife. And he can't testify against you either. Which reminds me, you never told me what Phil Sloan said.'

'Why should I? I know by something you let slip that you spoke to him yourself. Privileged conversations, indeed. I'll give old Symes a shot at being discreet.'

Marcy didn't reply.

Tyson expanded on his earlier subject. 'But life is good. At least for us. There's no war, depression, famine, hunger, or civil strife.'

'Not in Garden City, also known as the Garden of Eden. This place is zoned against reality.'

Tyson exhaled a long breath. Subconsciously, he thought, he must have precipitated this conversation about Garden City – Marcy's favourite subject – in order to take his mind off other things. Marcy was a product of Manhattan's Upper West Side, whose population leaned as far to port as Garden City's citizens leaned starboard. And Marcy, he knew, wanted to move back to her old stomping grounds. As if she'd read his thoughts, she said, 'You can't live here anymore, you know.'

'I can live wherever the hell I please.'

'But you can't.' Marcy retreated into a moody silence. Just when Tyson thought he was on the verge of a marital dispute, she laughed unexpectedly. He glanced at her. She said, 'Do you realize we always pick a fight when we don't want to go someplace?'

'Yes, I realize that. This car has made more U-turns than a boomerang.' He stopped the car under the hotel marquee. 'But this time we've arrived at our planned destination.'

A green-liveried footman with top hat opened Marcy's door. An attendant held open Tyson's door, and Tyson exchanged the Volvo for a parking chit. A doorman saluted as they passed inside to the pink marbled lobby. A hand-painted sign announced:

The arrow pointed left.

Marcy said, 'Let me buy you a drink first.'

The tables in the dimly lit Hunt Room were full, but Tyson found an empty barstool and Marcy sat. Tyson stood beside her. He ordered a scotch, and she ordered a glass of white wine. They both glanced around the room as their eyes adjusted to the low light and nodded to a few people.

The drinks came, and Tyson stirred his scotch. He said, 'Am I crazy to come here? Or just brazen?'

· Marcy picked up her wine. 'At some point you'll know the answer to that. Up to now, no one knows how to deal with you.'

Tyson leaned his back against the bar and again surveyed the room. English hunting prints on the panelled walls were a feeble reminder that the original Hunt Room had actually been a place where ladies and gentlemen of the Meadow Brook Hunt Club gathered after riding to hounds. Tyson mused, 'I liked the old place better.'

Marcy's eyes rolled. 'Oh, Jesus, if I hear that one more time *from one of you original settlers* I'll puke.'

'Well, it was a hell of a place.' He added maliciously, 'The Nassau County Republican Club had its headquarters in the old hotel. I used to do volunteer work for them. We had a Goldwater fund-raiser here in sixty-four.'

'I'm getting sick.'

He smiled, then sipped his scotch and drew on his cigarette. 'History,' he said aloud. 'Teddy Roosevelt stayed here often. Charles Lindbergh spent the week before his solo flight at the old hotel. Once, when I was on leave, I took the Lindbergh suite. Did I ever tell you that? I slept in the bed Lindbergh slept in.'

Marcy contrived a yawn and replied, 'Based on what I've

heard from people who don't romanticize the old fleabag, you probably slept in the same sheets, too.'

Tyson stared into the dark recesses of the lounge. The clientele in the pre-World War I era included Astors, Morgans, Vanderbilts, Hewitts, Jays, Belmonts, Harrimans, even Lillian Russell. But history was a continuum. Someday, someone sitting where he was now sitting would say that Benjamin Tyson had frequented the new Hunt Room.

Benjamin who?

The guy who was court-martialed for murder. Remember? It was in all the papers. The hospital massacre in Vietnam.

Oh, right. He used to drink here? No kidding?

But that was future history. In the old Hunt Room, where he was drunk, he'd conjure up images of the past especially the aviation greats who had drunk there between the world wars: Glenn Curtiss, Jimmy Doolittle, Billy Mitchell, Lawrence Sperry, Amelia Earhart, Leroy Grumman 99 Tyson recalled his boyhood dream to be a fighter pilot, as his father had been; he thought of his plastic model of the Grumman Tomcat and wondered what had become of it. The world spun too fast now, and Tyson knew he would never fly a Grumman Tomcat, but what was worse, the desire to do so was dead.

Marcy broke into his thoughts. 'Another?'

He turned his head toward her. 'One more.'

She ordered, and Tyson said to the young bartender whom he knew slightly, 'Ed, you ever heard of the battle of Hue?'

'Midway? Yeah, it was on TV.'

'Heard of the Tet Offensive?'

The bartender turned and ran Tyson's tab through the register. 'Tet? Sure. Vietnam. The VC attacked Tet and the Americans got beat.' He put the tab back on the bar in front of Tyson.

'Tet was a time, not a place.'

'No kidding?'

'No kidding.'

Ed shrugged and went off to serve someone else. Tyson said, 'Smart kid.' He sipped on his drink, then observed, 'See ... ultimately all battlefield deaths are in vain. No one really remembers any of it. So what's the big deal?'

'You tell me.'

But Tyson could not. He sensed the alcohol working its magic and felt better.

Marcy said, 'Time to dance.'

Tyson smiled and took her hand. They retraced their steps through the lobby, arm in arm, nodding to a few people as they made their way to the Grand Ballroom. As they entered the mauve-coloured ballroom, Tyson scanned the pale-blue-clothed tables set around the large dance floor. The band wasn't playing, and there seemed to be a lull in the full room. Tyson said, 'Let's split up and regroup at the bar.'

'Okay ... oh, Christ ...'

Mrs Livander, the president of the Nassau Hospital Auxiliary, had spotted them and was sweeping across the room, arms prematurely spread for an embrace. Tyson stepped forward as though he were sacrificing himself so that Marcy might live. Mrs Livander veered slightly and enveloped him in her plump arms. 'Ben Tyson. Oh, you charming man. You're so devilishly handsome, if I were ten years younger I'd be after you.'

Tyson thought twenty years was closer to the mark, but he hugged Lydia Livander and gave her a peck on the cheek.

Mrs Livander turned to Marcy and effused, 'You look *lovely*. What a stunning *dress*! How *do* you keep your figure?' She took Marcy by the shoulders as if to fix her in place and poured a steady stream of lavish praise on her. Tyson's eyes darted around until he spotted the bar.

Without warning, Lydia Livander took their arms in a firm grip and propelled them toward a photographer from the *Garden City News*. 'Sam,' she bubbled, 'Sam, you *must* get a picture of this beautiful couple this *instant*.'

Tyson and Marcy smiled, the flash went off, and before

Tyson could see clearly, Mrs Livander had him on the move again. Tyson glanced at Marcy and shrugged. If he'd intended to slip in unobtrusively, he was making a bad start of it. As Mrs Livander moved them around to meet people they already knew or didn't want to know, he had the distinct impression that heads were turning toward him.

Pleading an urgent call of nature, Tyson broke free of Mrs Livander's ministrations and made directly for the bar. He ordered a scotch and soda and carried it to a neutral corner. Shortly, Marcy came up to him and said, 'You see, nothing has changed. Lydia did that for each of the two hundred couples who arrived tonight.'

Tyson swallowed half his drink. 'I felt like the only Negro at a Liberal Party dance. There wasn't enough of me to go around.'

Marcy smiled. 'Hang in there, Benjamin Balls.'

'Right. Nevertheless, it's going to be a long evening.'

'But a memorable one. And your last public appearance, I daresay.'

'Perhaps.' However, he suspected that his last public appearance would not be a black-tie affair but a dress-green appearance in a place less convivial than this one.

Ben Tyson sat at a round table and surveyed the full ashtrays, empty bar glasses, and discarded programmes: the detritus of another tax-deductible bash. If the hospital got 10 per cent of the take, they were doing well, he thought. The tables hadn't been assigned, and he'd found himself with different groupings of people throughout the evening. Now, finally, he found himself alone.

Tyson glanced at his watch. On balance, he thought, he was glad he'd come. If there was any truth to the old saying that public opinion was in advance of the law, then he felt somewhat relieved. No one had snubbed him, and no one had hustled him into the men's room to face a committee of peers with tar and feathers.

There had been some awkwardness and strained smiles, but this was not an age of absolutes, and there was no consensus on the correct behaviour toward a suspected war criminal. Socially, he was still acceptable. Legally, he was innocent until proven guilty. Time to go home.

Tyson looked around the room. Half the crowd was gone, but he couldn't see Marcy. In fact, he hadn't seen much of her most of the evening, though he felt confident she'd danced with a good number of the men, annoyed an equal number of wives, received at least one serious proposition, and accepted one or two dates for lunch in the city.

Tyson began walking toward the door and saw he was on a collision course with Phillip Sloan. Sloan intercepted him near the exit. 'Ben. Did you have a good time?'

'Hello, Phil.'

'Where's your wife?'

'Where's yours?'

Sloan smiled tightly. 'Do you have a moment?'

Tyson replied, 'I'd rather not be seen speaking to my lawyer.'

Sloan seemed miffed at being put into the same category as a bookie or loan shark. 'Let's step out here.' They went into the large anteroom, and Sloan indicated the men's room. Tyson said, 'Branch office?' Sloan went inside and Tyson followed. Sloan said curtly, 'Is this all right?'

'If you like pink marble.'

'Listen, Ben, you haven't been the most cooperative client—'

'And you have not been the most discreet attorney, Phil.'

Sloan began to respond, but said instead, 'You know, our families have done business for years. I consider you more than a client, you're—'

Tyson turned and used the urinal.

'You're a friend. Our wives are friends.'

'We're all friends.'

'Right. So don't give me this shit that you don't want us to

62

be seen together in public.'

Tyson turned from the urinal. 'What did you want to see me about?'

Sloan glanced around to assure himself they were alone. An Hispanic attendant sat on a stool, reading the *New York Post*. Sloan said, 'I've contacted an attorney in the city who specializes in publishing law.'

Tyson washed his hands.

'He advised us to bring suit.' Sloan waited, then went on. 'His reasoning is that these alleged incidents are so old that a criminal action is extremely unlikely. That will leave Picard's allegations as basically hearsay. In lay language, Picard has his ass hanging out. Are you following me?'

The attendant gave Tyson a hand towel. 'Sort of.'

'Also, no one but you is mentioned in a pejorative way. Whenever he writes about someone shooting civilians, he doesn't give a name.'

'I noticed that omission.'

'But you are mentioned by name as a witness to the massacre. The point is made again that you did nothing to stop the killing.' Sloan added, 'There's even a line in there that suggests you masterminded the cover-up. There's also an ambiguous sentence about you ordering the enemy soldiers to be killed.'

'That certainly was an ambiguous sentence. I did not order wounded and captured enemy soldiers murdered. I ordered my men to find and destroy any armed enemy soldiers still in the hospital who continued to resist.'

Sloan seemed uninterested in the clarification. He said, 'The point is, whoever spoke to Picard was out to get *you*. I think Picard believed a lot of crap and printed it as truth. This attorney and I agree that we have a very stong case for libel.'

Tyson straightened his bow tie.

Sloan continued, 'Ben, I'd like you to meet this attorney. His name is Beekman. He's a real crackerjack—'

'What does that make me? The prize? Are you a Milk Dud?'

'You're drunk.' Sloan made a move to leave, then came back and took a deep breath. 'Beekman has handled some famous literary libel cases. You may know the name.'

Tyson looked at Sloan's reflection in the mirror. He said, 'You and I have both heard of civil trials that took on the coloration of criminal cases. All sorts of muck is dragged up, the press reports it as though it were a murder trial instead of a lawsuit, and in the end, even if the plaintiff wins, he loses.' Tyson took a bottle of Aramis and splashed some on his palm. 'Let the damned thing *die*.' He slapped the cologne on his face.

'It won't die unless you *kill* it. If you don't sue and win, these allegations will hang over you for the rest of your life. Reviewers will quote from Picard's book, other authors will pick up bits and pieces, and this damned hospital incident will enter history as *truth*.'

Tyson didn't respond.

'Actually, it may be better to sit tight for a few weeks and see what kind of media exposure this gets.'

Tyson tipped the attendant and looked at Sloan. 'What does that have to do with it?'

'Well, according to Beekman, considering the book is recently published, the damages to you are small as of now. The book could be recalled by the publisher, further limiting damages. However, we could wait and ... pretend we had no knowledge of the book. Then, in time, as a result of, let's say, author interviews and book reviews, plus the book's circulation, advertising, promotion, and so forth, your good name and reputation will be further damaged.'

Tyson didn't reply.

'Let's say,' continued Sloan carefully, 'that you lose your job. That your son is harassed at school. That Marcy is ... well, whatever. Then, wham! We sue. We go after not only Picard but the publisher, the distributor, maybe even the unnamed sources that Picard mentions. Assuming a jury finds for you, the award will be *huge*. You will be vindicated and rich.'

Tyson observed, 'The flip side of every problem is an opportunity.'

'Exactly.'

Tyson was intrigued by Sloan's offhand manner in engineering a conspiracy. He'd probably be more ethical in a criminal case where the money was paid up front, and the only thing he could lose was his client's liberty.

Sloan said, 'Libel suits are very rare things. It's not often that a person gets libelled in print. Cases like this probably make up less than one per cent of all civil suits. And the press covers them. So I understand you wanting to avoid further public exposure. But you're a fighter, Ben, and you won't let this blotch remain on your honour.'

'Cut the crap, Phil.'

Sloan pulled at his lip as though he were wrestling with a tough decision. He looked at Tyson and said, 'You probably think no one is going to zero in on your small chapter in that big book. Well ...' He reached into his pocket and pulled out a folded piece of paper. 'Beekman got this for me. There's a trade magazine called *Publishers Weekly*, and they get galley copies of books months before publication. This is a book review in that magazine published seven weeks ago.' He handed Tyson the photocopied page.

Tyson looked at it. There were six short book reviews on the page. His eyes went to the one captioned *Hue: Death of a City. Andrew Picard*. There was some publishing information, followed by a short review of about 150 words. He scanned it quickly and saw that the review was generally favourable. Halfway through he read:

There is an account of a massacre by American troops at a French hospital filled with patients and European staff. Picard's writing vividly re-creates the massacre and leaves the reader wondering why no official inquiry ever grew out of this incident that ranks with My Lai in the annals of Vietnam atrocities.

Tyson refolded the page and handed it back to Sloan.

Sloan tapped the paper against his palm. 'You see? Even in this little précis, you see what sticks out?'

'I see.'

'Imagine longer reviews in newspapers and magazines.'

Two men came into the rest room. Tyson walked out, and Sloan followed him into the anteroom. People were wandering out of the ballroom and standing around talking, or heading for the lobby. Tyson noticed a few people glancing their way. He said, 'You know, Phil, when I got that Community Fund Service Award, no one seemed to hear about it. But as soon as I get myself mentioned in some obscure book as a war criminal, everyone has heard the good news in two weeks.'

'That is life, my friend.'

'So I've heard.'

Sloan took Tyson's arm. 'I have to tell you, Ben, a lot of people kept asking me tonight, "Are you suing?" I don't know what to say anymore.'

Tyson knew Sloan was manoeuvring him toward a lawsuit the way a surgeon manoeuvres a patient toward the operating room. He knew he needed a second opinion and not Beekman's. He said to Sloan, 'If we sue and it went to trial, how many Army lawyers would be in the spectator seats? How many Justice Department lawyers?'

Sloan didn't reply.

Tyson continued, 'You see, win or lose, in a civil suit, the government will hear enough to make them curious. Did that occur to you, counsellor?'

Sloan shrugged. 'That's a possibility, of course. But still, Ben, I'm assuming that in a strict legal sense you are not guilty of murder. That's what the government will conclude if they monitor a civil trial.'

Tyson leaned closer to Sloan. 'They will conclude no such thing, my friend.' Tyson fluffed Sloan's red pocket handkerchief. 'Good night.' Tyson turned and walked toward the lobby where he found Marcy seated in an armchair. She stood as he approached, and without a word, he took her arm and they left the lobby of the hotel through the main doors. The night had turned cool and misty, with a soft wind blowing from the south. Tyson breathed deeply to clear his head. 'I think I smell the ocean.'

'You always say that after you eat canapés made with anchovy paste. You said that once in Switzerland.'

Tyson gave the doorman his parking chit. About a dozen people waited under the marquee for their cars. Tyson looked at Marcy. 'Did you have a good evening?'

Marcy considered a moment, then said, 'No. For the first time, I felt I wasn't Marcy Clure Tyson but Ben Tyson's wife.'

'Weak ego, Marcy.'

Marcy did not reply.

Tyson lit a cigarette and leaned against a pillar. He looked out across the hotel grounds toward the road. To the left was the village's main street, a long block of little shops and banks. Everytown USA; as Everytown had looked before the malls and commercial strips. To his left front was the library, and to the right of that, the small war memorial park. Directly opposite the hotel was the commuter station. In the distance, rising above the trees, he could see the tall Gothic spire of the Episcopal Cathedral of the Incarnation against the moonlit skyline, topped by an illuminated cross. This was familiar territory. Safe ground.

'Are you all right?'

He looked at his wife. 'Yes.'

'You were somewhere else.'

'Sometimes I do that.'

Marcy said, 'Your mother called today. I forgot to tell you.'

'What did she want?'

67

'She wants you to take care of yourself. Eat well. Relax. I think Florida made her Jewish.'

Tyson smiled. He'd heard from a few old friends and some out-of-town family over the past two weeks. He was a little surprised at how fast news travelled. It reminded him of the Army, the rumour mill par excellence.

Marcy, as though she knew what he was thinking, said, 'Anybody who didn't know about it when they got here, knows now. Maybe you ought to issue an official statement in the village papers and the club newsletter.'

Tyson smiled again. 'Phil said no statements, public or private.' But he himself had called a few people, close friends and relatives. And he'd been surprised by the variety of reactions: some people seemed insensitive; some were noncommittal; a good number seemed unimpressed by the seriousness of what had been written about him. A few people, as he'd noted tonight, sensed a developing celebrity status, albeit of a questionable nature, and he had the impression that these people were trying to get close to him to somehow share the limelight. Tyson said to Marcy, 'The Grenvilles, who are important personages in the old guard, have asked us to cocktails. Next Friday, if you're interested.'

Marcy replied, 'I suppose they want you to autograph Picard's book. I'll bring the *Life* magazine to pass around.'

Tyson smiled. Marcy, if nothing else, he thought, was well equipped to handle friends, neighbours, and family.

As Tyson saw his car coming down the drive, a voice behind him called out, 'Ben. Marcy.'

Tyson and Marcy turned. John McCormick and his wife, Phyllis, had come through the doors.

McCormick said, 'I didn't get a chance to speak to you guys tonight.' Greetings, handshakes, and perfunctory kisses were exchanged. McCormick said bluntly, 'I have some more bad news for you, Ben. I hope you don't hold anything against the bearers of bad news.'

Tyson rather liked McCormick, but two pieces of bad news

from the same person in two weeks might, he supposed, prejudice him against the man. Tyson saw the thick newspaper under McCormick's arm and made a guess at what the news might be.

McCormick said, 'Sunday *Times*. Just came in. The book got a major review. Your name is mentioned.'

Tyson nodded. 'Okay.' He noticed that Phyllis McCormick looked at her husband in a way that suggested this was not her idea. Tyson saw McCormick hesitate, much as he had hesitated on the train before handing him the book. Tyson had a sense of *déjà vu*, coupled with a sinking stomach, as McCormick offered him the separated Book Review section. Tyson smiled gamely. 'Do you want me to autograph it?'

McCormick's smile seemed more forced. 'You can keep it.'

The Volvo stopped at the kerb, and the doorman held the passenger door open. The Tysons wished the McCormicks good night, and they parted. Tyson slipped behind the wheel of the Volvo and put it into gear as the attendant shut his door. He pulled up the curved drive toward the road. Marcy sat quietly with the Book Review section on her lap.

Tyson said, 'Well.'

'Well what?'

'Well, with a national circulation of about two million, things are going to begin happening.'

Marcy nodded. 'I'll arrange for an unlisted phone number Monday.'

'Good idea.'

'The school year is nearly over.'

'Right.'

'Should I list the house with the brokers?'

'Don't overreact.'

She thought a moment, then inquired, 'How are your employers going to take this?'

Tyson swung the car onto Stewart Avenue. 'Who knows?' He headed west toward Eaton Road. 'I can't get a handle on that bunch. They really are inscrutable.'

'I'll let the racist remark pass, Ben, because I know you're under some strain.'

Tyson didn't reply.

She asked, 'Did Phil find you?'

'Yes.' He turned left on Eaton Road. 'Spoke to me in the men's room. Do you realize how much business is conducted in men's rooms?'

'What did he say?'

'Sue the bastards.'

'He must be under the impression you're innocent.'

'No, he's under the impression that the government is not clever enough or motivated enough to seek an indictment. Therefore, Picard is vulnerable to a civil suit. Poor Andrew Picard. He may find out that the truth doesn't pay as much as it costs.'

She looked at him in the dim light. 'Would you sue a man who told the truth?'

Tyson pulled into his long driveway and shut off the engine. He listened to the insects for a while.

'*Would* you?' she asked again.

8

Lieutenant General William Van Arken, the Army's Judge Advocate General, flipped through the personnel file in front of him. 'I see he has two Purple Hearts. Score one point for Mr Tyson.'

Fraser Duncan, from the Secretary of the Army's office, looked at Tyson's medical file and commented, 'Both wounds were superficial. Score only half a point.'

Herbert Swenson, an aide to the Secretary of Defense, observed, 'He has the Vietnamese Cross of Gallantry, awarded by the Vietnamese government for actions at Hue.

That could get sticky.'

Thomas Berg, a presidential aide, looked down the long, polished mahogany table. He said, 'We were discussing the question of possible court-martial. Let's talk about relevant facts.'

General Van Arken, sitting at the opposite end of the table, replied, 'Mr Berg, if you have ever witnessed a court-martial, you will know that is what we are doing.'

Berg shrugged. He turned to Peter Truscott, a young attorney from the Justice Department. 'I gather from what you've said that the Attorney General is not interested in pursuing this case.'

Truscott stayed silent for longer than was considered polite, then replied carefully, 'I didn't actually say that. I said it is a shaky case from a legal standpoint, Mr Berg. Also, the Attorney General feels the matter is military in nature.'

Berg looked up and down the table at the four men present in the windowless room, located in the interior of the building. Green-shaded lamps illuminated the places where the men sat, leaving dark gaps at the long table.

The outer fringes of the large room were in darkness, and the only sound that penetrated the room was the susurrant rush of the air-conditioning ducts. *Dark things*, thought Berg, *belong in dark places*.

There was no stenographer present, and Berg had seen to it that there were no tape recorders in the room. No one was allowed to take notes. This was an unofficial, ad hoc group whose agenda memos and daybooks showed they were meeting to discuss better methods of interdepartmental communication, which in fact they had discussed for about two minutes. And except for Van Arken, they were representatives of their respective government offices – special aides to their bosses. The feeling in the White House had been to keep it low key. The subject of Benjamin Tyson, if anyone ever asked, had never come up.

Fraser Duncan spoke directly to Berg. 'Could you give us

71

some insight into the White House's thinking on this?'

Berg rubbed his lip thoughtfully, then replied, 'The President knows nothing of this. His military aides asked me to prepare a background briefing in the event it becomes necessary to bring this to the President's attention. The President's only interest in this would derive from his position as Commander in Chief.' Berg thought he ought to temper the lie and added, 'His political aides are obviously concerned with the political ramifications of the case. No one has forgotten Nixon's part in the Calley case.' He added quickly, 'But politics are not the issue. The President's legal aides want to ensure that the President acts in a legally correct manner each step of the way.'

Berg looked at Van Arken, who as a young captain had been on the prosecution staff in the My Lai case. Berg said to him, 'We are here because so little precedent exists for this type of thing in this country – and thank God for that. In fact, with the exception of yourself, General, no one here has had any experience with war crimes, and no one is quite as sure of himself as you are.' Berg saw a few smiles around the table.

Van Arken replied with forced civility, 'I'm fairly certain that eventually this will land in my lap, and the Army will be obliged to proceed with a court-martial. If so, then I, too, want to be certain that we don't have a recurrence of the Calley-Medina fiasco.'

Berg nodded. 'So does the White House, General.' Berg had taken the time to read Van Arken's file and to ask questions of people who knew the man. Van Arken was fifty-five, young for his position. He was military in his bearing, language, and attitude, an oddity in the Judge Advocate General's Corps, where the opposite qualities were held in some esteem.

Berg saw that no one was going to speak, another oddity in a government meeting, so Berg said, 'Gentlemen, what we've established so far is that legally an officer can be tried for a murder, or murders, committed by his troops, depending on the circumstances. We've also noted that there is no statute of limitations on murder. Beyond these two elementary facts, we have not discovered anything. We can't even be certain a capital crime has been committed.'

The General's voice carried loud and clear across the room. 'Based on what we've all read in this Hue book, we have every reason to believe that some sort of capital crime has been committed.'

Swenson said irritably, 'Certainly you don't believe everything you read.'

Van Arken replied with less assurance, 'No, sir ... but you can't come away from reading that without getting some sense of ... of a criminal act.' Van Arken sipped on a glass of water. 'As in civilian law, where there is information or suspicion that a violation of law has occurred, then an official investigation must follow.'

Berg had realized early in the meeting that Van Arken was disposed toward a full criminal investigation, rather than an unofficial fact-finding committee as the White House had hoped. Clearly, the man was out to make a reputation for himself; or to live down his previous reputation regarding the Calley-Medina trials. However, the Tyson case, more than the Calley case, had trouble written all over it. Not only domestic political trouble, but international problems as well. Berg said to the group, 'As I understand it, there is a question of jurisdiction involved here. It is the opinion of the Justice Department that no state or federal court has jurisdiction in this case.'

Truscott nodded. 'That's correct. The alleged crime happened in a foreign country. The alleged perpetrator was at the time a member of the armed forces. However, he is not now a member of the armed forces. And that's where the problem lies.'

Berg turned to Van Arken. 'General?'

Van Arken stayed uncharacteristically silent for a few seconds, then said, 'As Mr Truscott indicated, the alleged crime was committed while the suspects – and I include Tyson's troops, of course – were subject to the provisions of the Uniform Code of Military Justice. There's no doubt about that. My opinion is that whether or not they are so subject at present is irrelevant—'

Truscott interrupted, 'It is *not* irrelevant, General. It is crucial. Tyson, we know, is not in the Army now. The others may or may not be. We will find out. But the Army is not going to try civilians. Not ever.'

Van Arken replied calmly, 'Do you mean to tell me, Mr Truscott, that if some of those men are still on active duty, only they will be unfortunate enough to be tried for murder? Will the civilians go free for the same crime?'

Truscott began to reply, but said instead, 'The question is probably moot. Let's find out first if any of these men are still on active duty.'

Van Arken continued, 'All right, assume none of them are. Tyson we *know* is a civilian. So how must we change the jurisdictional status of these men?'

Truscott didn't reply, but Berg said, 'You're suggesting, of course, that we call these men back to active duty.'

Van Arken nodded. 'Mr Truscott is correct. The Army cannot and will not try civilians. Therefore, we cannot even begin an investigation of Mr Tyson, but we can investigate Lieutenant Tyson.'

There was silence in the room, then Berg said, 'I've been advised that this question of a serviceman becoming a civilian before a crime has been discovered has never been fully resolved to anyone's satisfaction. It's apparently a glaring gap in our system of justice. Therefore, we must legally resolve this point before we proceed.'

Van Arken added, 'Every decade or so something like this comes up, and we are unprepared for a question of jurisdiction. Most of these past cases involved crimes of little importance. Here we have a crime of immense proportions, with implications beyond our borders.'

Berg said, 'Thank you, General. I think we realize that.'

'The point,' continued Van Arken, unperturbed, 'is that, while the Uniform Code of Military Justice does not list war crimes as an offence, it does list first-degree murder, and that is the charge that must be investigated. Because – and this is the point, Mr Berg – if it is not, I hold out to you the embarrassing possibility that, theoretically, the present government of Vietnam, or the governments whose nationals were alleged to have been murdered in that hospital, could file charges with the tribunal in The Hague. The charge would be crimes against humanity – war crimes.'

No one commented and Van Arken continued, 'Under U.S. law, we know neither Tyson nor his men would ever have to actually face such a tribunal. However, it is crucial that the charge of murder be promptly investigated to preempt anything of this sort.'

Berg was unimpressed by Van Arken's foray into international law and diplomacy, but he knew Van Arken had a point. He said, however, 'American citizens are not charged with murder to satisfy world opinion *or* domestic opinion.'

Van Arken replied, 'I wish that were so. But there have been cases where just that has happened to servicemen overseas. And, to some extent, that will happen with this case if you delay. This is a case where the law has to be in advance of public opinion so as not to give the appearance later that we were bending to any outside pressures. In other words, gentlemen, before a storm of media attention hits us, we ought to publicly announce an investigation.'

Berg had the gut feeling that Van Arken, whatever his motives, was correct. But the President and his advisors hoped this mess would go away if left alone. Berg knew intellectually that it would not, but emotionally he hoped also. He felt he had enough bad news to carry back to the White House for the moment. He looked at Herbert Swenson.

Swenson understood the unasked question and replied, 'From what I've heard, I don't believe this matter should be personally attended to by the Secretary of Defense. The Department of the Army ought to deal with it directly.'

Fraser Duncan smiled thinly. 'I'll recommend that the Secretary of the Army closely monitor the case, but I'm passing the buck down to the Judge Advocate General's Corps.'

Peter Truscott spoke. 'The resources of the Attorney General's office are, as always, available to the government in the interests of justice. But only in matters pertaining to questions of law. On questions of strategy, that's up to the Army, the JAG, and the Commander in Chief.'

Berg nodded. There was, he thought, little legal precedent to fall back on. There appeared to be a violation of the Uniform Code of Military Justice; there appeared to be some machinery in existence to deal with this violation. But because of the unique and unusual nature of this case, there were many subjective decisions to be made along the way to the courtroom. Berg gathered his files and said, 'I suggest we adjourn and do some homework and some ... soul-searching.' He stood. 'We'll meet again to discuss inter-departmental communications. In the meantime, keep in mind that we are not dealing solely in abstract law problems or public relations problems, but with human beings. Specifically, with a man named Benjamin Tyson who may end up in front of a court-martial board, on trial for murder, for which the maximum penalty, if convicted, is death by firing squad. Good day.'

9

David Tyson came into the kitchen where his father was sitting, drinking coffee and reading at the long breakfast counter. David said, 'I'm going to bed.'

Tyson looked up at the kitchen clock and saw it was nearly 11 P.M. Marcy would be back soon from her nocturnal grocery shopping. The night was warm, and Tyson was barefoot and shirtless, wearing only a pair of cutoff jeans.

David asked, 'What are you reading?'

Tyson replied, 'These are photostats of magazine pieces that I got from the library. Personal accounts of the battle of Hue.'

'We're up to that now. I mean Vietnam. In school. In history.'

Tyson smiled. 'When I was a soph, we only had to get up to Eisenhower sending the Marines to Lebanon.'

David pulled up a stool and sat opposite his father.

Tyson pushed the photostats aside. 'How are you making out in school?'

'Okay.'

'That's not what I hear.'

'What do you mean?'

'You're catching some flak at school.'

David looked at his father and replied, 'I can handle it.'

'Can you?'

'You always told me to handle my own problems. You bawled me out once when I was a kid and came home crying about something that somebody did to me. So I don't come home crying anymore.'

Tyson regarded David for a few seconds. 'But this is different. This is my fault. You can complain to me.'

'I'm not complaining. Anyway it's not all bad. Some guys ... and girls ... are sort of friendlier than they used to be.'

Tyson nodded. 'I'm having the same experience. But watch out for that too.'

'I know.'

Tyson realized he was looking at his son in a new light. David was one of those boys who thought their own father was a better person than their favourite rock star or professional athlete. This was perhaps a rarity these days, but perhaps it was not so rare, just unspoken and never put to the test. Regardless, it was what it was and it must run in his family because Tyson had always hero-worshipped his own father. 'Do you want a beer?'

David hesitated, then nodded. He went to the refrigerator and brought back two bottles. He opened them and slid one toward his father, then sat again.

Tyson and David drank. Tyson thought of Gene Conroy who had come up to him in the Men's Club, a man Tyson barely knew, and apologized to Tyson for his son Derek's behaviour toward David. That was the first Tyson had heard of any such problem. Yet he knew some of that must be going on and that there was great potential for cruelty among children. The children of Alpha Company had shown him the limits of cruelty. And Tyson wondered, without dwelling on it too long, if David could ever be a member of Alpha Company. In a way, he hoped his son had some of that cruelness in him, because if he did not he would not survive in the world in which he lived. 'Adults have deceived nearly every generation of youth into dying for them and their causes. Do you understand that?'

'I think so.'

'I don't want you fighting for me. I'm talking about Derek Conroy, as one instance.'

David studied the label on the beer bottle. 'I don't have to take any crap from anybody.'

'Okay, as long as you're defending yourself, responding to

personal insults, or whatever. But don't defend *my* honour.'

'Why not?'

'I just told you. Adults con the young into fighting their battles.'

'You haven't conned me.'

'Haven't I?' Part of the process of growing up, Tyson thought, of losing whatever innocence that was still part of childhood, was receiving a cruel blow from someone you cared about. It was time, Tyson decided, for David to be disabused of the notion that his father was innocent. In that way, David could grow, could fight for the real Ben Tyson if he chose to; not the idealized one. He said, 'I'm going to tell you what no one outside of my platoon knows. I'm going to tell you, as best I can, what happened at Miséricorde Hospital. Okay?'

David nodded hesitantly. 'Okay.'

Tyson said, 'First thing you should know is what Picard said in his book is mostly true. My platoon massacred over one hundred men, women, children and infants. The youngest man in my platoon was not much older than you. His name was Simcox, and I saw him shoot a nurse about the same age as himself. Do you want me to go on or not?'

David bit at his lower lip. Finally he said, 'No.' He stood. 'It doesn't matter. I knew it was all true. I don't care. I'm going upstairs.'

'And pull the covers over your head?'

'I don't want to hear it, Dad.'

Tyson nodded. 'Okay. As long as you understand that what people are saying and writing about me is at least partly true. Understand too that this has nothing to do with you. You have nothing to be ashamed of. You are David Tyson, and you are your own person.'

David walked toward the kitchen door, then turned back. 'How about what people are saying about Mom?'

Tyson did not know quite how to deal with this. Somehow he was more willing to discuss mass murder with his son than

79

the subject of Marcy's past. Tyson said, 'A man or woman's past personal life is no one's business but their own. Your mother never hurt a soul, and no one has any right to hurt her or try to hurt me or you through her. Don't respond to any of that.'

David replied, 'I have to be honest with you, Dad. It wasn't you that asshole Conroy was talking about. It was Mom.'

Tyson drew a deep breath. 'Idiotic.'

'I get these filthy notes shoved in my locker. Dad, if you want to talk to me about something, talk to me about all that crap about Mom.'

'There's nothing to say. Most of it is lies.'

'Is it?'

'Yes. Go to bed, then. It's late. We'll talk again.'

David nodded. 'Night.' He left.

Tyson sipped on his beer. *My God*, he thought, *that kid's world fell apart. Yet, he showed no outward signs.* Tyson finished his beer. David, he decided, was tougher than he'd suspected. But it would be a race between the end of the school term and the end of David's ability to cope. *Poor David. Poor Marcy. Poor Ben.*

Marcy Tyson placed the grocery bag on the breakfast counter. Ben Tyson was still sitting on the stool reading, a cup of coffee in his hand. He said. 'Hello. Back already?' He didn't look up.

'No, I'm still at the supermarket.'

'Good.' He turned a page and yawned.

Marcy said, 'It was weird. Bizarre. I mean at the checkout. There I was on the *cover* of the *American Investigator*. Can you believe it? A housewife's dream come true.'

Tyson looked up from the paper.

Marcy continued as she began unpacking the bag, 'They covered my crotch with a black strip. But my tits are right there. Jesus. Who needs it? Right?'

Tyson watched her closely as she went about emptying the

brown bag. She did not seem upset, but he suspected she was. She looked very young tonight, he thought, dressed in a cotton khaki skirt, sandals, and a navy blue knit shirt open at the collar.

He looked at the kitchen clock. It was nearly midnight, not the Tysons' normal hour to go marketing. He looked at the groceries piled on the counter. 'Did you buy that rag – what's it called?'

'The *American Investigator*.' She hesitated, then added, 'It's in the car.'

He nodded. Life in the Tyson household had become somewhat surreal, not to mention furtive and xenophobic. He had taken to varying his methods and times of commuting to New York, though Marcy continued to take her regular train. They generally avoided social contact, and he had dropped out of the tennis tournament at the club. They no longer dined at local restaurants, though he still went to the Men's Club, which was a world unto itself.

Tyson played with the sugar cubes, building a tower on the countertop. He spoke without looking up. 'As a public relations person, can you explain to me the dynamics of this thing? I mean, how did we become hot news?'

Marcy put away some canned goods. 'Lots of reasons. Andrew Picard is hot, for one thing. He's good on talk shows. Not bad-looking either. Maybe this is a slow news month. But remember, Ben, the central belief of the public relations business: "There's no such thing as bad publicity."'

'Well, this shit looks mighty like it.' He added another course of cubes to his tower. *Picard*. After the *Times* book review, Picard had appeared on radio and television, hawking his wares. And Picard knew what interested his audience. And it wasn't the battle of Hue. That was an abstract subject, too boring for the electronic media. Picard spent his airtime wisely, focusing on the Miséricorde Hospital massacre, as it was now known.

Tyson had actually heard Picard on the car radio one

morning, and if he hadn't read the book, Tyson would have believed that the entire thirty-nine chapters were devoted to Benjamin Tyson and his gang of psychotics shooting up a hospital with the rest of the massive month-long battle only a sideshow for that main event.

Marcy broke into his thoughts. 'This is the sort of thing a publicist prays for. Moving from the fluff and entertainment pages to the news pages. Authors have wet dreams about being mentioned in somebody's column.'

Tyson nodded as he concentrated on the tottering tower. *Hue: Death of a City.* The book had been given a piece in *Newsweek.* Could *Time* be far behind? The book had appeared on the Sunday *Times* bestseller list two weeks ago and was climbing. Picard must be pleased. Tyson added a flying buttress to steady the tower.

'These things achieve a critical mass of their own,' explained Marcy. 'You understand? It becomes news because it has become news. That's not to say it isn't a good story. I mean, let's be objective here. And it doesn't hurt to be twenty-five miles from the news centre of the world. We'd get off easier if we lived in Omaha. That's a fact.'

Tyson blew gently on the hexagon-shaped tower and watched it sway.

'What the hell are you doing?'

'This is the gleaming white marble tower that stands on the desolate brown plains of Formica. It is the last bastion of civilization in a dying world. The last learned men and women have gathered here—' He blew again and a cube toppled to the brown countertop. 'But savages have surrounded the tower, and—'

'Are you well? I mean, should I call a white van, or what?'

He looked up. 'Just playing. Men never grow up. I think you said that once or twice.'

'Anyway ...' She turned and put some packages in the freezer. 'Anyway, I spoke to the local fuzz this morning, and they were sympathetic. However, it seems that laws about harassment, blocking traffic, causing a public nuisance, and so on apply only to mortals and not to newspeople unless you get a court order or something ... If those shits set up their cameras outside again—' She slammed the freezer door.

Tyson recalled the local TV station that had thrown together a half-hour news show on the unfolding drama. There was an interview with Picard, alternating with stock footage of the battle of Hue. The war had returned to the American living room. And it was good footage, aerial stuff of the burning city, then close-ups of the Marines trying to cross the Perfume River over the one remaining railroad bridge, the university crammed with miserable refugees. And not your typical peasants, but upper-middle-class Vietnamese, students, doctors, priests, monks, and administrators. The cream of society, filthy and forlorn, weeping for the cameras. Very good footage.

The show had ended with a reporter standing outside a house, and it had taken Tyson a moment to realize it was his house. The reporter had done his wrap-up as the camera panned the block of substantial houses, taking in a few curious neighbours. Then the camera had zoomed in on Tyson's front door. The reporter had closed with, 'Behind this handsome door is the one man who can answer Andrew Picard's questions. But that man is not talking. And it remains to be seen whether or not he will ever talk about what happened at that hospital eighteen years ago.'

Tyson tapped the countertop sharply and watched the tower bounce, then settle back without collapsing. 'Earthquake. Severe damage, but the tower built by the world's last master builders stands.' Tyson yawned again, then turned back to his wife. 'You know, Marcy, for all the interest people have shown in me and my difficulties, I suspect that a good number of them haven't actually read the relevant chapter in Picard's book. Yet they think they all know what it's about.'

Marcy yawned also. 'They're waiting for it to be made into a TV movie, Ben.' Marcy put away the last of the groceries.

'Thanks for helping.'

'Sorry ... I was thinking.' He lowered his head, eye level to the sugar cube tower. 'I see the major damage—'

Marcy flicked her finger and the tower collapsed in a heap.

'Bitch.' He swept the cubes to the side and blew away the sugar granules. 'Do you want me to re-create the battle of Hue with sugar cubes?'

'Maybe in the morning.'

'After reading Picard's book I know what happened.' He quickly laid out a line of cubes. 'This is the south wall of the Citadel. Okay? Each wall was two miles long. All right, the south wall abutted the north bank of the Perfume River—' He looked around, spotted the milk pitcher, and poured a stream of milk over the countertop. 'That's the Perfume River. Pretend. Okay, this is the canal—' He trailed his finger through the milk and formed a small tributary. 'Okay, help me with the other three walls. Do you have any more sugar cubes? We have to build the Imperial Palace here, and construct the walled enclave in the northeast corner of the Citadel, where Picard had got himself trapped with the South Vietnamese soldiers. That's over here. Three full battalions of the First Cav were approaching from the north. Their mission was to relieve the pressure on the Marines and ARVN – that's the South Viets – and to block escape routes to the north and interdict enemy supply and reinforcement attempts. Got it? This sugar tong and these two spoons represent the three cavalry battalions. Follow? Okay, the tong is my battalion, the Fifth Battalion of the famed Seventh Cavalry. But my company was detached and we were more to the west. Here. My platoon was further detached and I was operating alone. Here. I was advancing along the north bank of the river. Hue was burning to my front. Now this little fucking sugar cube is Hôpital Miséricorde. Okay?' He looked at her. 'Why aren't you building those walls?'

Marcy Tyson turned and went to the cabinet over the trash compactor. She retrieved a bottle of Grand Marnier and filled half a water tumbler. 'Want one?'

'No thanks.'

She noticed he had completed the four walls of the Citadel without her help. 'Ben, cut it out. Seriously.'

He looked up and his eyes found hers. He smiled and swept away the sugar cubes.

She let out a shallow breath. 'Ready for bed?'

'Not yet. I was thinking ... it must have been the neighbours. I mean the *Life* magazine picture. The media didn't stumble on that by accident. You weren't even identified by name in the original caption.'

Marcy swirled the orange liqueur around the glass. 'Actually, Ben, I tipped them off. I was tired of you getting all the press.'

Tyson smiled. 'I thought a good PR person is supposed to stay out of the spotlight.'

Marcy raised the glass to her lips. 'Well, I have an ego, too.' She drank.

'It had to be someone in town. But why would anyone do that? I mean, what is gained by dragging you into this mess?'

Marcy leaned back against the sink. 'People are petty, envious, and nuts. I thought everyone knew that.'

'I thought you believed in the basic goodness of people. Brothers and sisters and all.'

'I do believe in that. Sincerely and passionately. Nevertheless, an awful lot of people are flaming assholes.' She finished her drink.

Tyson stared out the kitchen window. There was a light on in the sunroom of the Thompson house, and he could see their daughter Kerry, seventeen, parading around in her bra and panties. He saw a figure approach the sunroom. The French doors opened, and the figure entered. The lights went out.

Marcy glanced out of the window. 'Kerry?'

'Right.'

'Did you rendezvous like that when you were a horny little guy?'

'Damn right. I knew every backyard and fence in this town.'

Marcy laughed. 'God, it was different in the city. We used to neck a little in the parks, and sometimes if it got serious we'd go to the roof of our building. The boiler room, in the winter.'

'Peasant.' Tyson walked to the refrigerator and opened it. 'This is all pussy food. Yogurt, lettuce, strawberries.' He closed the door.

Marcy spoke. 'Two incidents. Hue and Griffith Park, occurring about the same time. What did the *New York Post* say? Something about the irony of Marcy making love while Ben made war. Christ, give me a break.' She smiled. 'You know you've arrived when the papers start calling you by your first name. And as a journalism major and a public relations lady, I can tell you, Mr Tyson, you ain't seen nothin' yet.' She finished her second Grand Marnier, and Tyson noticed her eyes had taken on a glazed duck à l'orange look.

Tyson sat on his stool at the breakfast counter. 'Funny, I haven't had that nightmare since this began.'

'Why should you? You're living it. "Life is a dream in the night, a fear among fears, a naked runner lost in a storm of spears." Arthur Symons.' She filled his half-empty coffee cup with Grand Marnier.

'Thanks,' Tyson said to his wife. 'We have got to get David out of here as soon as the school term is finished. The kid must be going through hell, but he hasn't said a word.'

Marcy nodded.

Tyson sipped on his coffee, laced with orange liqueur. David, he knew, had been aware of the infamous photograph long before this. In fact, about a year before, Tyson had found David sitting on the floor of the den with the original *Life* magazine spread out on his lap, staring at the picture of his mother.

Tyson had chosen not to let the incident pass without comment. Some days later, he'd sat David down and given him a brief sociological lecture on the Age of Aquarius. It was odd, he'd thought, that a middle-aged man had to defend his generation's looser morality to a teenager. But morality, like war and peace, was cyclical. Victorians did not approve of the morality, clothing, or literature of the Georgian age that preceded theirs. David's generation, while certainly not prigs, were nevertheless not quite as loose as their parents once were.

David had listened, nodded understanding, but something told Tyson that the boy did not approve, not only of the nude picture but of his parents' life-style.

Tyson realized that he himself affected a certain sophistication regarding the photograph, Marcy's past in general, and the marital relationship. Marcy had once observed to friends, 'Ben has become more liberal and less inhibited, and I've become more conservative in my middle age. That's the story of the 1980s.'

Tyson understood, too, that he was titillated by Marcy's past, as well as by her present job, which brought her into close contact with successful men. There were the business trips, the breakfasts, lunches, late dinners, late office nights, and the publicity events. There were ample grounds for jealousy, and in fact there had been some rather intense discussions on occasions when Marcy had staggered home in the small hours of the morning. The one thing this marriage did not suffer from was boredom. He said to her, 'You're handling this well. And you're right. You don't need this.'

She poured a third drink. Her voice was slightly slurred. 'For better or for worse. That's what the hell it's all about.' She thought a moment, then added, 'You're handling it quite well, too. I ... I always respected you ... but there were times ... you know, when I felt you were wishy-washy. I guess I promoted that ... I never wanted to emasculate you ... never ... And I'm glad to see you show real balls ... I mean, adversity builds character, right? We all need a little stress to feel alive ... it can strengthen us and our marriage ... but too much stress and strain ...' She tipped the glass back, drank, and suppressed a belch. 'I don't know.'

Tyson nodded. Marcy, he knew, was a self-assured woman. And she was alive, and where there was life there were problems.

He looked at her. 'I just remembered that time I brought Kimura, Saito, and their wives here for dinner. And you served them take-out Chinese food from the containers.'

Marcy said innocently, 'Did I fuck up?'

Tyson smiled.

'You never said a word about it.' She grinned. 'I served the shit with chopsticks, for Christ's sake.' She added in an injured tone, 'And I made up that neat drink out of saki and bourbon. The Hiroshima Bomber. Everybody liked it.'

Tyson laughed.

'Don't laugh at me, you pompous, uptight twit.'

Tyson stopped laughing and took a step towards her. 'Who's uptight?'

'You, you stuffy, anal-compulsive—'

He seized her by the shoulders, lifted her in the air, and laid her out on the breakfast bar, amid the coffee cups, sugar cubes, and newspaper.

'What the hell are you doing, Tyson?'

'I'm going to fuck you, lady.'

'*Here*?'

'Here.' He unzipped her skirt and pulled it with her panties down around her ankles, over her sandals, and threw the bunched clothing on the floor. 'Spread your legs.'

She spread her legs, knocking cups and ashtrays off the counter. Tyson slipped his shorts off and lifted himself onto the counter between her thighs. Without any preliminaries, he mounted her, finding her wet and receptive.

Marcy extended her arms and clutched the edges of the counter.

Tyson's thrusts were short and rapid, but he found his knees had no traction on the smooth countertop. He rocked

88

back on his haunches. 'Turn over.'

Marcy flipped herself onto her stomach, then rose to her hands and knees. Tyson clutched her shoulders and entered her from behind, ramming hard a dozen times in quick succession. Marcy slid forward, and her head rested against the splashboard. The counter shook, and the sugar bowl vibrated over the edge and crashed to the floor, followed by the milk pitcher.

Marcy spread her knees further apart and lowered her head, looking back between her hanging breasts at Tyson's sliding penis and dangling testicles.

Tyson came suddenly, withdrew, and hopped back off the counter. He slapped her buttocks and strode out of the kitchen, calling back, 'Clean up that mess.'

Marcy remained motionless for a full minute, feeling the wetness running over her thighs, dripping onto the breakfast counter. Slowly, she lowered herself to the floor and surveyed the debris. Still naked from the waist down, she swept the milk and sugar together with the smashed ceramic, then knelt and pushed the mess into a dustpan with a sponge. She stood and began wiping the breakfast bar, wet with milk and splattered sperm.

Marcy stopped suddenly and stared down at the glistening streaks along the brown plastic counter. She felt humiliated and used. But tonight that was how she was supposed to feel. That was part of their sexual repertoire; Marcy taunts Ben, Ben treats Marcy like chattel. The acting out of a common sexual fantasy. And she enjoyed that submissive role about once a month. But this time there was something different ... something was wrong ... Tears came to her eyes, and her hands shook as she continued wiping the counter.

10

Thomas Berg said, 'Change of venue, gentlemen. I trust this suits you.' Berg motioned around the small, tastefully decorated room in the Victorian-style Old Executive Office Building. Berg added, 'We are getting closer to the White House, physically as well as metaphysically.' He nodded toward the window at the Executive Mansion a few hundred yards to the east.

Berg lowered himself into a wingback chair. General Van Arken sat in a suede upholstered chair near the window. Peter Truscott, from the Attorney General's office, sat by himself on a leather couch. Absent were the representatives of the Departments of Defense and of the Army. Berg explained, 'We're limiting our options, so we're limiting our membership in this group to us three.'

The air-conditioning in the hundred-year-old building was balky, and the east-facing room was warmed by the late morning sun. Truscott and Berg had slipped off their jackets and loosened their ties. Van Arken kept his green tunic on, and as per regulations, it was fully buttoned. Berg felt warm just looking at the man. He thought that the military had developed discomfort as a separate art form. A tray of carbonated mineral waters sat on the coffee table along with a bucket of ice and glasses.

Berg cleared his throat. 'All right, at our first meeting, we discovered we had a potential problem. By our second meeting last week, General Van Arken's prophecy of media attention seemed to be coming true. General, any other prophecies?'

Van Arken sat forward. 'I have no crystal ball, Mr Berg. But I am in closer contact with the real world than the people over there are.' He jerked his thumb over his shoulder at the White House.

Berg nodded. 'Perhaps.' He thought a moment, then said, 'The President has a press conference scheduled in three weeks. This subject will come up unless it is ruled out beforehand. But the press doesn't like that. The President can, of course, take cover behind the fact that it would be improper to comment on a possible legal matter. But we'd like him to be able to say something more substantial than that.' Berg looked at the two men. 'We'll think about that.'

The room fell silent, and Truscott helped himself to a glass of sparkling water. Outside on the White House South Lawn, a helicopter was landing, and the muted sound of the rotor blades penetrated the stillness of the small sunlit room.

Berg addressed Van Arken. 'Another of your prophecies has come true, General. To wit: The State Department has, this week, received inquiries from the ambassadors of France, Holland, Belgium, Germany, and Australia, asking what is being done to investigate the alleged murders of their nationals by American forces in Vietnam, and so forth.' Berg paused, then continued, 'I am happy to report, however, that the Swiss ambassador, who as you know unofficially handles the affairs of Hanoi here, has not received any such note from the People's Republic intended for us. But that may be on the way. Also, no one in the U.N. has raised the issue as yet.'

Van Arken interjected, 'It would be hypocritical in the extreme for Hanoi to attempt any propaganda from this, considering what their own troops did at Hue.'

Berg shrugged. 'My theory is that Hanoi will let the countries involved and the Catholic Relief Agency make problems for us.' Berg looked at Truscott. 'Anyway, between our first and second meetings, General Van Arken contacted the Army Records Center at Fort Leonard Wood, and we believe now that no one who was in Tyson's platoon at the time of the alleged massacre is still in the military. So, based on that, we agree that it would be best to offer the former

91

enlisted men in that platoon immunity from prosecution in exchange for sworn testimony.'

Peter Truscott responded, 'As in the Calley trial, you have to let the small fish go, in order to land the big one.' Truscott added, 'Anyway, it's nearly impossible to recall enlisted men to duty. Tyson, as an ex-officer, is an easier catch. Correct?'

Van Arken said nothing, but Berg could see he was unhappy.

Truscott said, 'Incidentally, I made some discreet inquiries at the Nassau County Clerk's office – that's the county where Tyson lives. It appears that Tyson has not initiated a libel suit against Picard or the book publisher.'

Berg said, 'What can we construe from that?'

Truscott shrugged. 'Any one of a dozen things.' He thought a moment, then said, 'Sometimes I try to put myself in Tyson's place ... I wonder what I would do.'

Berg smiled. 'I'd think about it in Brazil.'

Truscott smiled, too, then said seriously, 'I believe that Tyson, like us, is playing a waiting-hoping game. And, like us, he doesn't know what he's waiting for or hoping for. And, like us, he's frightened.'

Berg nodded slowly. After some time he said, 'Well, that brings us to our next order of business – Mr Tyson himself. How far can we delve into this case before it becomes necessary to recall Mr Tyson to duty? Mr Truscott?'

Truscott replied, 'The Attorney General's office feels that you can proceed as you are now with informal meetings and research, until you feel there is substance to these allegations.'

Berg looked toward Van Arken. The General shook his head and offered, 'We are right now in a tenuous legal position.'

Neither Truscott nor Berg replied.

Van Arken expanded on his opinion. 'You must understand that a recall to duty would place Mr Tyson not only under the *jurisdiction* of the Uniform Code of Military Justice but under its *protection* as well. As you noted in our first meeting, Mr Truscott, the Army cannot court-martial a civilian. So, by extension, the Army cannot investigate a civilian. Such an investigation by my office or the Army Criminal Investigation Division would certainly be a violation of the man's civil rights.'

Berg nodded to himself. Clearly, Van Arken had thought this out. Clearly, too, Van Arken was making a power play. Berg turned to Truscott.

Peter Truscott was rubbing his chin. 'Well, this is difficult ... Perhaps the White House could order my office or the FBI to begin an investigation, then we could pass the findings on to the JAG—'

Van Arken interrupted, 'I cannot accept the fruits of a civilian investigation in a case like this. Gentlemen, if you want this case killed or weakened because of procedural errors, then you are doing a fine job of it.'

Berg glared at Van Arken for a few seconds but said nothing. Obviously, they'd reached an impasse.

Van Arken said suddenly, 'I suspect that the White House doesn't want Mr Tyson in uniform.'

Berg stood and poured himself some mineral water. 'Well, they see that as a point of no return.'

'We've already reached and passed that point. Read the newspapers.'

Berg ignored this and continued, 'Also, from a legal point of view, wouldn't it be prejudicial to Mr Tyson if he was recalled to duty before we even assembled the facts? It seems to me that would be premature and ominous. Truscott?'

Truscott answered, 'Well ... no more so than if a suspect were extradited from a foreign country. The government has to take certain steps in some cases to establish its jurisdiction. That shouldn't be construed as a presumption of guilt.'

Berg remained standing and sipped on his mineral water. His eyes unconsciously went to the window, and he stared at the White House. He looked away and said, 'Well, if we do that – recall Tyson to duty – it will make every newspaper in

93

the country. I'd still like to retain the option of keeping a lid on this.' He turned to Van Arken. 'Let's address the human element. What if Tyson spends six months or a year in the Army and it turns out he's innocent? You can't fool around with a man's life like that because of unfounded suspicions. Why can't we let this man go about his daily life until we are more certain there is reason to put him back in uniform?'

Van Arken replied, 'I told you why. And I don't think Mr Tyson is going about his daily life. A recall might be merciful. I'm human, too.'

Berg snapped, 'An Army induction notice in the mail is about as welcome and merciful as a public health notice regarding your last sexual partner.'

Truscott chuckled.

Van Arken's normally florid face turned redder. He moved to the centre of the room, as though he were on the verge of walking out. He seemed to be trying to control his voice as he spoke. 'We have sufficient information to suspect that a crime has been committed. We have a suspect. We either take steps to bring the suspect under our jurisdiction, or we drop the case. But keep in mind that if we turn our backs on two hundred alleged victims, as Tyson apparently did at the time, then we are as guilty as he is.' Van Arken added ominously, 'We can probably count on appearing before a congressional inquiry.'

Berg exhaled a long breath and said, 'I'll speak to the President personally about what we've discussed.'

Van Arken, still standing, said, 'Why don't you ask the President to sign an order as Commander in Chief recalling Tyson? It would be less subject to challenge than an Army-directed recall.'

Berg's tone was sharp. 'General, you know damned well the President does not want to do that. This is purely an Army affair, as we all agree. So let's leave the President out of it. This is a simple murder trial, not an international incident. All right? Now, how long do you think it will take the Army

94

to get Tyson back in the saddle?'

Van Arken drew a short breath, then replied curtly, 'I can't prophesy that. It depends on how hard Tyson fights the recall order.'

Truscott added, 'He can fight it all the way up to the Supreme Court.'

Berg sat back in his chair. He wondered if a long legal battle over recall and jurisdiction would be such a bad thing. It would take the pressure off the executive branch and put it into the judiciary where it belonged.

Truscott seemed to sense what Berg was thinking. He said, 'We can contact Tyson's attorneys or even Tyson directly.'

Berg looked at him. 'Why?'

'Sometimes,' said Truscott, 'the direct approach is best. If we informed him or his attorney that a recall was being considered in order for us to proceed with an investigation, we might get some indication of how he intends to ... respond.'

Berg glanced at Van Arken.

Truscott added, 'If I were Tyson's attorney, I'd urge him to try to make a deal. In exchange for not challenging a recall order, I'd ask the Judge Advocate General's office for ... well, something.' He turned to Van Arken. 'What would you offer?'

'Nothing.'

Berg said, 'Well, you'd offer him a fair court-martial, wouldn't you?' Berg wondered about Van Arken's actual motivations in pursuing this so aggressively. Berg had researched the General's psyche and philosophy, and on the surface the man appeared to be a staunch moralist and law-and-order advocate. Privately, he led a rather austere life, was unmarried, and lived in Army housing. It was rumoured he owned two civilian suits: summer wool and winter wool. Both blue.

Berg stood. 'All right, gentlemen, before we adjourn, I'd like to make a personal comment, and it is this: To some

95

degree, society feels a shared sense of guilt and culpability with their armed forces that they don't feel with the common criminal. So, if we eventually court-martial, convict, and imprison Benjamin Tyson, we should not expect to be national heroes.'

Van Arken's jaw hardened. 'I'm not concerned with my popularity in the Army. And I'm not running for public office.'

Truscott stood. 'Well, let's not have a row over this.' He turned to Berg. 'Basically, the General is correct, and you ought to tell that to the President. Cover-ups don't work anymore. I'd rather do something unpopular than face a charge of conspiracy.'

Berg nodded in agreement. 'I'm not suggesting a cover-up. I'm suggesting we balance whatever good a court-martial would do against the harm it will cause the nation.'

Van Arken replied, 'If we don't – or can't – see this through, then the system will have failed. And I can't think of a greater harm to a nation founded on law than that its justice system should fail – except perhaps that its public officials should have failed to try. I think, too, that if Mr Tyson were in this room and he were objective, he'd agree.'

Berg smiled without humour. 'Benjamin Tyson is fighting for his life, and he is not going to be objective. He is going to cause his government and his country great embarrassment. And I don't blame him.' Berg picked up his attaché case. 'This is going to open old wounds and those wounds will run with fresh blood. That fucking war is going to come home again. God help us.' Berg turned towards the door. 'Meeting adjourned.'

11

At 7:30 on a Tuesday morning, Benjamin Tyson walked into the clubhouse of the Garden City Golf Club, known unofficially as the Men's Club. The present building had been erected in 1899, the same year the women had been invited to leave, and the premises had developed, thought Tyson, that unique, ripe flavour peculiar to masculine establishments. Women, however, were invited to play the course once a year, though few availed themselves of this dubious honour.

Tyson surveyed the lounge area and saw a few men playing poker dice around a coffee table. He walked on, passed down the length of the bar, and entered the cathedral-ceilinged dining room. He walked through the room, nodded to a few people at the breakfast tables, and went out onto the rear terrace.

Phillip Sloan sat at a small round table under a blue-striped umbrella, reading a newspaper. Tyson took the chair opposite. Sloan looked up. 'Good morning.' He poured Tyson a cup of coffee from a pewter pot.

'Thanks.' Tyson drank the coffee black. He observed that Sloan's golfing attire contained all three primary colours, plus orange. Tyson looked out across the fairway. Men in bright plumage performed the repetitive rituals of ball and club. A hundred years before, when these acres had been pristine glacial outwash, the Carteret Gun Club had set up pigeon shoots, massacring a thousand birds at a shoot. And the Meadow Brook Hunt Club had also galloped through from time to time, hounds barking, horns blaring: 'the unspeakable in full pursuit of the uneatable.' Golf was tamer, but so were the times.

Golf was not Tyson's favourite sport, and neither was bird

shooting or fox hunting. But he felt somehow that these Elysian fields had been sanctified by a century of hedonism; that regardless of what social changes enlightened the world and defined American democracy, there ought to be a few acres set aside for gentlemen to make asses of themselves. At least until the next glacier came through.

Sloan looked up from his newspaper, apparently just noticing that his companion was wearing a suit. 'I thought you were going to play a round with me?'

'No, I'm catching the eight-forty-two. So let's wrap it up by eight-thirty.'

Sloan seemed disappointed, then regarded Tyson thoughtfully. He said, 'What is your status there?'

Tyson poured himself more coffee. 'Where? On the eight-forty-two?'

'Your *job*.'

Tyson sipped on his coffee. Women, he noticed, alluded to the strains on his marriage. Men usually inquired about his job. Nearly no one was solicitous of his psyche. Tyson replied, 'Hard to say, Phil. I mean, on the one hand you have the famous Japanese paternalism. On the other hand you have Japanese efficiency. I'm not very efficient these days. Added to that is the Nipponese obsession with appearances, face, and that sort of thing. I embarrass them.' He smiled and added, 'As a former samurai who has been disgraced, I should take the honourable way out. But American managers haven't yet embraced Japanese necrophilia.'

Sloan seemed uncomfortable with this line of conversation.

Tyson's tone was bitter. 'You know, if old man Stutzman were still in charge, he'd have offered me the corporation's law firm to fight this.'

Sloan waved a dismissive hand.

A waiter came to the table, and Tyson ordered eggs and orange juice. Sloan ordered sweet rolls and another pot of coffee. It struck Tyson that he had an irrational dislike for men who ate sweet rolls for breakfast.

Sloan reached into his briefcase and pulled out a folded newspaper page, handing it literally under the table to Tyson.

Tyson unfolded it and saw it was the front page of the *American Investigator*; not the one featuring Marcy, but the most recent edition of the weekly tabloid. One of the numerous headlines read: *MR PRESIDENT, WILL JUSTICE BE DONE?* That interrogatory headline, Tyson observed, was a sly way of suggesting to the *American Investigator*'s readership that the Chief of State received a copy of the rag on the White House doorstep. Tyson noticed another front page story titled *MARCY'S FRIENDS AND LOVERS TELL ALL*. Tyson refolded the page without reading the text and handed it back to Sloan. 'So?'

'Well, the story about Marcy goes beyond the bounds of common decency and journalistic ethics. Even for this scandal sheet. The fellow Jones who's been covering the story has interviewed some of Marcy's college friends and ... people who claim to have been intimate with her.'

Tyson poured cream into his coffee.

Sloan continued, 'The article is libellous. Filled with titillation, sarcasm, innuendos, and suggestions of radical activities of a violent nature. Marcy was radical, as we know, but to the best of my knowledge, never violent. There are also gratuitous remarks about drugs.' Sloan hesitated, then added, 'There is also a guarded mention of marital infidelity.'

Tyson didn't reply.

'Sleaze,' Sloan continued. 'Pure sleaze. And damned sure libellous. Look, this has gone on long enough. I think *she* ought to bring suit. I'm talking to you man-to-man, Ben. You don't have to get involved in the suit, but I thought I'd speak to you first. Now, we both know that Marcy is an independent woman, and she doesn't need her husband's permission to enter into a lawsuit. But tradition and common courtesy dictate that I speak to you first.'

'Don't let *her* hear you say that.'

Sloan affected a smile. 'Well, we'll keep this conversation

99

to ourselves. But she is my client, and I'm going to speak to her.'

'That's your prerogative.'

The breakfasts came, and Tyson buttered a slice of toast. Sloan bit into a sticky bun. Tyson asked, 'Good?'

Sloan nodded as he chewed. 'Want one?'

'No, thank you.' Tyson took a forkful of eggs.

Sloan lifted a packet of sugar from a bowl and emptied the contents into his coffee. Tyson said, 'They don't use sugar cubes anymore. Everyone uses those idiotic packets now. I'm going to speak to the manager.'

'These are more sanitary—'

'But you can't *build* things with packets. I was going to show you the battle of Hue. Here, I can do it with paper and pen.' Tyson took a pen from his inside pocket. 'Give me one of those yellow pads you people always carry.'

Sloan's eyes rolled slightly as he retrieved a legal pad from his briefcase.

Tyson began drawing as he ate.

Sloan glanced around the terrace and noticed a few people turn away. Both men ate in silence for a while as Tyson drew, then Sloan said, 'Let's speak about your suit for a moment. All right, you have been libelled in print and slandered on TV and radio. All the damage that could be done is done. You have suffered acute personal embarrassment, irrevocable harm to your career and your character, causing you great psychological damage—'

Tyson glanced up from his drawing. 'Are you sure? I feel okay.'

'Listen, Ben, if we delay any longer in initiating suit, we will be guilty of laches – that means sitting on our asses. The law specifically states that you may not unreasonably delay bringing suit for damages. The law recognizes that potential plaintiffs who do that are playing a game, trying to increase the harm—'

'*You* said to let my name get dragged through the slime so

we could sue for bigger bucks, Phil.'

Sloan cleared his throat. 'That's not exactly what I said. Anyway, the problem is, to avoid the appearance of laches we must begin now, today—'

'The problem was the layout of the city.' Tyson swivelled the yellow pad around on the table. 'See, within the Citadel, the old city was laid out in long, straight, narrow streets. There's no room for armour to manoeuvre. The ARVN tried, but the NVA easily knocked out their tanks with rockets. Okay, within the Citadel you also had the walls of the Forbidden City, which in turn held the emperor's Palace of Heavenly Peace. See? Then there were these watchtowers on the walls, which were seized early by the Viet Cong and North Viets. To complicate the situation, the Perfume River cuts the city in two. Right here. Further south of the city you have the area of the emperor's tombs, which were traditionally controlled by VC - tourists had to pay a VC tax. Crazy war. Anyway ... you see ... this is a difficult cityscape ... too difficult. The American commanders should not have chosen to fight the enemy on the enemy's terms. That's what caused so much death and destruction. Hue became a sort of Verdun, with everyone converging on the centre of the city to slaughter each other. Bad tactics. The Americans and South Viets should have withdrawn and established a *cordon sanitaire*. What do you think?'

'You know,' said Sloan, trying to control his irritation, 'because we're friends, I let you get away with jerking me around. And I know you're under a lot of stress. But it's time to cut out the nonsense and *act*.'

Tyson contemplated the map he'd drawn and added another detail.

Sloan leaned across the table. 'Here's the question – do we have a suit? Or is Andrew Picard, through his witnesses, telling the truth? Did you, Benjamin Tyson, or did you not, participate in any way in the murder of men, women, children, nuns, medical staff, et al., at Miséricorde Hospital?'

Tyson pushed the legal pad aside and chewed thoughtfully on a piece of toast, then met Sloan's eyes and said, 'I suppose you ought to know. Yes, I am, as suggested in Picard's book, guilty of murder.'

To his credit, Tyson thought, Sloan did not feign surprise or any other emotion that he did not feel. Sloan simply nodded curtly.

Tyson continued, 'So that's the end of the civil suit talk. Sorry to disappoint you and sorry to have jerked you around so long. But you understand.'

Sloan said a bit coolly, 'I'm not disappointed. Well, in a way I'm disappointed that you didn't confide in me earlier and disappointed that you don't think you're innocent—'

'I'm *not* innocent.'

Sloan stayed silent a moment before replying, 'That's up to the criminal justice system to decide. Look, in the event charges are brought against you and then dismissed, or otherwise disposed of, or if in fact you are tried, then found not guilty, then you can most probably win a civil suit for libel. Do you follow?'

Tyson nodded. The man *was* persistent and had obviously thought this through.

Sloan went on. 'But you must let me initiate the suit now. We can postpone and delay any resolution of the suit for as long as it takes to dispose of any potential criminal charges. That resolves your complaint about the possibility of the government monitoring a civil trial. That puts them in a position of having to try to outstall us. I can keep a civil suit alive for years without going to trial. They can't do that with criminal charges without violating your rights.'

Tyson thought legal strategies were more Machiavellian than even political strategies. Military strategy, if nothing else, was based on simplicity, speed, and commonly understood objectives. Tyson replied, 'I'm getting dizzy.

Anyway, as I said, with a few minor corrections, Picard has related the truth—'

'Oh, who gives a shit about the truth?' Sloan leaned further across the table and spoke in a low voice. 'Listen to me. I don't give a goddamn if you're guilty or not, and you've wasted a lot of my time trying to obscure that irrelevant fact. What I'm concerned with is what's happening *now*. You've been fucked around by the press, jerked off by your employers, snubbed by your peers, and held up to scorn on radio and TV by that schmuck Picard. Let's lay the groundwork for getting even.'

Tyson looked out over the greens. Fred Riordon, a semiretired pediatrician, was teeing off. He turned back to Sloan. 'Picard is not a schmuck. I've read his book, and I've seen him on TV. I wish he were a schmuck, but he's not. He's an arrogant twit, but nobody's fool. Secondly, getting even through civil suit, while civilized, is also wimpy and a poor substitute for kicking people in the balls or cutting their throats. If I ever sue, it won't be for revenge. Third, your points about our criminal justice system are well taken, but I've been doing a lot of reading, and I'm not so sure a military tribunal would find me innocent.'

'The rules of evidence still apply.'

Tyson shrugged. 'Go see a court-martial. Then we'll discuss it.'

Sloan drummed his fingers on the table. 'You know, it's time you made a public statement. Something ... something like you were saying before ... about the battle itself. Something to the effect that it was chaos ... but more than that ... that it was a military blunder ... gross stupidity, leading to unnecessary deaths—'

'What the hell purpose would that serve?'

'Oh, you'd be surprised. Allegations are not charges.'

Tyson watched as the shadow of an aeroplane passed over the links. Tyson turned his attention to Sloan. 'No, but there are allegations and then there are allegations. I'm not a lawyer, Phil, but let me tell you what I know of human nature. Here we have wide public knowledge of an alleged crime of some magnitude. Just as you see dollar signs, there are Justice Department lawyers and JAG lawyers who see glory and challenge.' Tyson lit a cigarette and added, 'Here we have a public spectacle with all the right elements: murder, conspiracy, Vietnam, sordid revelations, and exposés – a three-ring circus, complete with acrobats, jugglers, magicians, clowns, and tightrope walkers. You're right: Innocence or guilt has little to do with this.'

'That's cynical.'

Tyson laughed. '*That*, from a lawyer?'

'Cut it out, Ben. I'm trying to help you. And I didn't like that remark about money.'

'I know you're not in it just for the money, Phillip. You have an eye on press coverage, too. One man's misfortune is another man's fame and fortune. But that's okay. No sweat.'

'You're becoming paranoid.'

'Paranoia kept me alive once.'

Sloan poured himself and Tyson more coffee. He said, 'You certainly bring new perspectives to the legal system.'

Tyson seemed not to hear. He said, 'An important element, I think, in how I am ultimately going to be judged – either legally or in the eyes of my peers – lies in the ethnicity of the victims.'

Sloan eyed him closely but did not respond.

Tyson nodded to himself and continued, 'Some of them were Caucasian, Phil. White folk like us. The soldiers at My Lai had it easy. They had only to explain away two or three hundred slant-eyed gook bodies. I have to explain about a dozen dead Caucasians. In war, as in every facet of life, it's quality, not quantity, that counts.'

Phillip Sloan seemed to miss the sarcasm of the

observation and nodded agreement. He said softly, as if to himself, 'Catholics ... the Orientals were Catholic ...'

'Right, Phil. All the Vietnamese nuns were obviously Catholic. Probably many of the patients were, too. It was a predominantly Catholic suburb of Hue. Some of the Europeans may have been Protestant. Double trouble.' Tyson lit another cigarette. 'No priests, though.'

'Thank God for that.'

'A bunch of babies, however. Pregnant women, children, sick people, wounded people—'

'Jesus.'

'That's what you find in a hospital, Phil. In war, you have to take what you get.'

Sloan looked at him quickly. 'Are you crazy?'

'Now, there's an interesting question, fraught with many possibilities.' Tyson winked and stood. He handed Sloan the yellow pad. 'Do you see the mistake the Marines made?'

Sloan seemed momentarily confused, then glanced at the legal pad. 'Oh—'

'It's pretty obvious, isn't it? Look, instead of driving north across the river into the heart of the Citadel, they should have swept around to the west in an end run. *Then* north across the river to block the western gate in the Citadel wall.' Tyson tapped his finger on the yellow, lined paper. 'That was the key. The communists were pumping in supplies and reinforcements through the western gate. And no one was in a position to stop them. My company was moving toward the west wall, but we were understrength and spread thin. Picard glosses over this Marine blunder, which is interesting. You see, after all these years, there is a little part of him that is still a Marine. *Semper Fidelis.* Don't bad-mouth the corps. Even when you're supposed to be after the truth.'

Sloan said, 'He bad-mouthed you and your troops with no problem. That's what I was getting at before – command culpability at a level higher than yours. If you go before a

105

court-martial board, you can subpoena every commander who was within twenty miles of Hue that day. Make it clear to the Army that you were a small cog in a malfunctioning wheel, that you're not taking the rap alone. Go for the brass.'

Tyson stared at Sloan, then leaned down, close to Sloan's face. 'But don't you see, my friend? That's not fair. Any fool, including an ROTC lieutenant like me, can be a military genius at the breakfast table twenty years later, after having read a comprehensive history of the battle. But real genius is the ability to grasp the essence of a situation as it's happening. To think – not on your feet but on your belly, with five radiotelephones screaming at you, men dying and crying in pain, your pants full of piss, and the thump, thump, thump of mortar rounds walking toward you.' Tyson slapped the table three times. 'Thump, thump, thump!'

Sloan glanced around quickly and saw that people were looking.

Tyson straightened up and threw his cigarette on the terrace stone. He said in a quieter voice, 'Well, judge not, that ye be not judged. The Allied commanders at Hue killed more of their own troops through stupidity than the enemy killed through superior tactics. But I'd forgive those officers if they asked my forgiveness. Because, you know, buddy, in the heat of battle, there is no judgement to be made on anyone. When the battle ends and coffee is being served to the survivors, people ought to remember that. Thanks for breakfast, Phil.'

12

Benjamin Tyson lay naked on the ceramic tile edge and watched the steam rising to the ceiling.

The man on the tier above him waited until the steam stopped hissing, then said, 'I hope you understand why I wanted to speak to you here.'

Tyson felt the good sweat running over his body. He glanced up at the man sitting with his knees drawn up to his chest. Tyson replied, 'I assume it has something to do with recording devides.'

'Right.' He added, 'Everyone's paranod these days. Well, what with mini-transmitters, directional microphones, and all, I don't blame people. But this place is good. I have a lot of meetings in steam rooms. We'll swim later.'

Tyson sat up and propped his back against the wall. He had on past occasions discussed business here at the New York Athletic Club, but the place had been chosen to promote chumminess, not to put everyone at ease about tape recorders.

The man said, 'What are your clubs?'

'Book-of-the-Month.'

He laughed, then said, 'Don't you belong to two suburban clubs? The Garden City Golf Club – that's men only, isn't it?'

Tyson said, 'I'm afraid I'm not clear about who you represent, Mr Brown.'

'I represent the government.'

'The whole government? All by yourself?'

The man smiled slowly. 'Well, that's not important right now.'

'It is to me. Look, you convinced me on the phone you had

something important to say. That's why I'm here.'

Brown looked down at Tyson, but said nothing.

Tyson stared back at him through the white steam. Brown was somewhat younger than Tyson, and Tyson, like most men who've recently discovered they are middle-aged, disliked authority figures who were younger than themselves. The man was well built and well tanned, Tyson noted, except for the outlines of a brief bathing suit and a watch on his left wrist. He had curly blue-black hair and manicured nails, and his general appearance was that of a man who took some care with himself. Tyson noticed that he wore a wedding band and a religious medal. He didn't think Brown was military but felt he had once been. His accent hinted of private schools and an Ivy League college. Tyson said finally, 'What can I do for you, Mr Brown?'

'Call me Chet, okay?'

'Okay, Chet. What else can I do for you?'

The man smiled. 'May I call you Ben?'

'Sure.'

'Well,' said Chet Brown, as he massaged his sweaty calves, 'I want to speak to you about ... things. This conversation will be unofficial but authorized. We can come to some binding decisions here.'

Tyson remarked, 'Sounds like the government is in trouble.'

'Not at all. You are the one who is in trouble.'

Tyson did not reply immediately, then said, 'So why negotiate? What did old Ben Franklin say, Chet? "Neither a fortress nor a virgin will hold out long after they begin to negotiate."'

Brown laughed, 'I like that. I think I'm going to like you, Ben. You don't look like a mass murderer.'

Tyson resisted several responses, one of which was taking a swing at Chet Brown.

Brown continued, 'You see, Ben, justice has to be balanced with compassion. More to the point, there are popular cases

108

and unpopular cases. There is theory and there is reality.'

Tyson tuned out as the man went through his warm-up. Tyson rubbed the sweat from his eyes, then looked at the glass door. An attendant had stuck up a sign, and Tyson assumed it said something like 'keep out.'

Tyson yawned and stretched. No, he reflected, he certainly didn't feel awkward sitting naked with this man. Nor did he feel at a psychological disadvantage. He felt somewhat relaxed and somnolent as he suspected he was supposed to feel. He also felt he should keep in mind that he was discussing his fate with his enemy.

Brown was still speaking, and Tyson tuned back in. 'You see,' said Brown, 'this issue has obviously become too well known, nationally and internationally, to be ignored. We'd like to ignore it, but we can't.'

'Try harder.'

'You see, Ben, this has become a real emotional issue. We knew it would. All the old shit is being dredged up again.'

Tyson closed his eyes.

Brown went on. 'Public opinion is divided. Right? The national debate is following the old pattern – some columnists and commentators have pointed out that Picard's book discusses at length the infamous enemy atrocities at Hue. But, as usual, they say only America's alleged crimes are given media attention.'

Tyson liked that argument.

'But,' continued Brown, 'other people have pointed out that America is expected to behave better than its enemies. Double standard. Right? And in any case, carping about enemy atrocities doesn't get you anywhere. The perpetrators of the Hôpital Miséricorde massacre–' Brown pronounced it in good French '–those perpetrators are within US jurisdiction.'

'But actually,' replied Tyson, 'they aren't any longer.'

'Well,' said Brown musingly, 'that is the point, isn't it, Ben?'

'Yes, Chet, that is the point.'

Neither man spoke for some time. Then Brown said, 'People are beginning to talk publicly about court-martial. You may have read that in the newspapers. Or heard it on radio and TV.'

'I think I did read that somewhere. I don't watch much TV. I listen to tapes on my car radio. Fifties' sounds. Incredible stuff. Do you like fifties' music?'

'I love it. I could listen to the Everly Brothers all day.'

'How about the Shirelles?'

'They don't write them like that anymore. Listen, Ben, there are a lot of people on your side. Including me.'

'What is *my* side, Chet?'

Brown leaned down so his face was just inches from Tyson's. 'Please don't play games with me, okay?'

Tyson stared hard at the man until Brown returned to his sitting position on the tier above Tyson. The steam came on again, and Brown disappeared in the white vapour. Both men sat quietly listening to the loud hissing. Tyson closed his eyes. The steam stopped suddenly, and Tyson drew a breath through his nostrils.

Brown spoke in a soft voice. 'This is how it stands – the people who are on your side are mostly the civilians: the White House, the secretaries of the Army and Defense, the Justice Department, and others. It is the Army itself that wants your ass.'

'No gratitude.'

'Whatever. I think the Army and the Judge Advocate General Corps in particular are very anxious to redeem themselves. I'm speaking of the My Lai screw-up, of course. They can't retry that one, but they've been given another one.'

Tyson didn't reply.

Brown continued, 'Regarding this hospital incident, the Army wants to clean its own house, and the JAG is anxious to provide the broom. Fellow by the name of Van Arken.'

Tyson nodded. That name had been mentioned a few times in news stories.

Brown added, 'You see, the Army's memory of My Lai is long and clear. There is a continuity in the Army ranks that you don't have in the White House, for instance, where a half dozen administrations have come and gone since My Lai. And the folks in the White House can't seem to call the JAG Corps off or even get them to pull a few punches.'

Tyson nodded to himself. It made sense. The military would remain forever obsessed with honour lost and honour regained. Tyson suspected that somehow, in the collective psyches of the military, this case transcended Miséricorde Hospital and had to do with Vietnam as a whole.

Brown spoke slowly and deliberately. 'The Army has initiated the procedure to recall you to active duty.'

Tyson felt a tightness in his stomach, but his face revealed nothing.

'Do you understand you can't be tried except by court-martial?'

'I understand that.'

'You have an attorney named Sloan.'

'Right.'

'Do you have any other lawyers?'

'Do I need more than one?'

'Just checking. Look, I want to be honest with you—'

'Good.'

'The Army is going to have a hell of a time making that recall order stick in court. But you know what?'

'No, what?'

'They'll get you back. It may take two years, but they will. Do you have the *resources* to fight the government?'

'That's my secret.'

'Do you have the will?'

'What are you getting at?'

Brown swung his legs down from the ledge and leaned forward. 'I'd like to offer you some advice.'

Tyson construed that to mean a deal. 'Shoot.'

'Don't fight the recall order.'

Tyson slid off the tile ledge and stood. 'Great advice, Chet.' He bent down and touched his toes. 'Okay, what's in it for me?'

'A speedy trial.'

'You mean just like in the Constitution?' Tyson began a series of stretching exercises. 'You're wasting my time.'

Brown mused, 'God bless America, Ben. How many countries in the world are there where a suspected mass murderer can jerk around a government man who's trying to offer him a deal?'

'One, at last count. And here we are.'

'Right. But if this was someplace else, this white tiled room would be used for another purpose. Like me beating the shit out of you.'

Tyson straightened up. 'Try it, sonny.'

Brown seemed to be considering the offer, then shook his head. 'Look, let me get my business out of the way. Then if you want, we can go a few rounds. We'll both feel better.'

Tyson dropped into a push-up position.

Brown slipped down to the floor and came closer to Tyson. 'I'm prepared to make you an offer in exchange for your cooperation.'

Tyson jumped to his feet. He faced Brown, and the two men stood an arm's length apart. 'Is this legal?'

Brown shrugged. 'I'm not a lawyer. Neither are you. You said on the phone you'd meet me without a lawyer present.'

Tyson walked towards the door. 'Let's grab a shower.' They left the room and walked down a short passage to the showers.

Tyson felt his head clearing under the cool, pulsating water. Brown stood under a shower head a few feet away and said, 'You see, Ben, Van Arken believes he has sufficient grounds to recall you. But if you challenge this recall, then the President may have to sign an executive order recalling you. He'd rather not be put in that position.'

'Tell him I'd challenge his executive order.'

'He's not only thinking of himself. He thinks that if he got personally involved in your case, it would prejudice the case against you.'

Tyson shut off the shower and walked into the locker room. An attendant handed him a towel. Brown came up behind him and said, 'I've reserved two masseurs. My treat.' He led Tyson to a small massage room. Two tables sat side by side. Tyson jumped on the closer one and lay on his stomach. Brown sat on the table beside him. 'They'll be along in a while.'

Tyson closed his eyes and yawned. He felt relaxed despite the unpleasant subject of conversation. A dreamy lassitude came over him. He couldn't imagine what life would be like in jail, and in truth he was prepared to listen to anything that would keep him from finding out. He faced Brown on the nearby table. 'If you really want to be honest with me, you'll tell me on what grounds this recall will be made. Then I'll tell you how I'm going to beat it.'

'Once an officer, always an officer,' Brown said.

'I don't feel like an officer. You'll have to do better than that, Chet.'

Brown said, '"To all who shall see these presents, greeting." Sound familiar? That's what your presidential commission says. And mine too.' He continued, '"Know ye, that reposing special trust and confidence in the patriotism, valour, fidelity, and abilities of Benjamin James Tyson, I do appoint him a commissioned officer in the Army of the United States."'

Tyson stared at Brown.

Brown went on. '"This officer will therefore carefully and diligently discharge the duties of the office to which appointed by doing and performing all manner of things thereunto."' Brown smiled. 'The language is pretty archaic. But that's the kind of language that has some cachet in court. Sounds like it was handed down from George Washington's administration. Which it was. Anyway, here's the part that's of immediate interest to us – "This commission is to continue in force during the pleasure of the President of the United States of America."'

Tyson snorted, 'Nice performance, Chet.'

Brown continued, 'Your commission was signed by Lyndon Johnson, but any President could enforce it at his pleasure. And you accepted that commission. You raised your right hand and took a solemn oath.'

Tyson didn't reply.

Tyson hung his toes over the edge of the diving board, bounced, and dived into the swimming pool. He did a few laps, then swam to the middle of the pool and trod water.

Brown floated on his back close by. There were two other men in the pool, both elderly, some distance off. An uninterested lifeguard sat on a deck chair reading a paperback book. Brown said, 'I'm glad there are a few places left where a man can swim *au naturel*. How much longer can these private clubs hold out? I'm going to write a book someday called *The Feminization of America*.' Brown yawned lazily. 'Your wife, I understand, is an active feminist.'

Tyson said nothing.

Brown rolled forward and trod water beside Tyson. 'The last point in this recall business ...' Brown's eyes moved towards Tyson. 'Did you know you are still listed on the rolls of inactive reserve officers?'

'No, I didn't,' Tyson lied.

'Well, it's a fact. You were asked once by letter to indicate if you wished to remain on the inactive roles or be dropped from the rolls. You didn't check either box. Instead you wrote a nasty little note on the letter and sent it back to the Department of the Army. You're not supposed to do that Ben. You were supposed to check a box. A lot of modern life depends on what box you check.'

Tyson swam to the edge of the pool and rested his head on the tile rim. He closed his eyes, extended his arms and floated. He remembered that standard form letter from the Department of the Army. It had come in mid-April 1975.

114

Cambodia had fallen to the Khmer Rouge, Lagos was falling to the Pathet Lao, and the North Vietnamese Army and Viet Cong were about to enter Saigon. Tyson, like a number of men he knew who had served in Vietnam, was bitter and angry. He thought he'd got Vietnam out of his system years before, but the names in the news awakened old memories. City after city, camp after camp, fell to the enemy in rapid succession. Quang Tri, Hue, Da Nang, Pleiku, and one night, his former base camp, the First Cavalry headquarters at An Khe. And each name that he heard or read evoked images of blood, death, sacrifice, and bravery. He said aloud, 'That letter came at a bad time.'

Brown was standing beside him in the shallow water. He replied, 'It must have. You scrawled across the letter these words: "Fifty thousand Americans dead, one hundred fifty thousand wounded. For what?"'

Brown continued, 'That little impetuous note has been seen by everyone in the JAG office. There was, I understand, some discussion regarding the type of man who would write something like that for the posterity of the Army Records Bureau.'

Tyson opened his eyes. 'I resent the fact that people are analysing me and talking about me as though I were a specimen. I don't like people reading my Army records, though I know you have a right to do that. I'm getting pissed off, Chet.'

'Of course you are. I don't blame you. But remember, please, that though we're not discussing mass murder at the moment, that's what this thing is ultimately all about.'

Tyson glanced at the big wall clock across the natatorium.

Brown said, 'I won't keep you much longer. You probably have work piling up on your desk. I just wanted to inform you of this recall. If you fight it, the Army will counterattack. Eventually, you know, they will break through. You'll have bought some time, but at great cost.'

'That's better than going quietly to the slaughter.'

'It's not a slaughter. It's a trial. And I'll tell you something else, Ben. Even if you reach the Supreme Court with this and they find for you, you'll be beaten. You will never have had the opportunity to have these allegations resolved. Your entire fight to escape jurisdiction will appear as admission of guilt. If, on the other hand, you voluntarily come back to active duty, you will have gained an important psychological advantage, and you will have scored a tremendous public relations coup on your own behalf. The Army would look favourably on any such voluntary action on your part.'

Tyson said, 'What are you offering in exchange for my cooperation?'

Brown caught hold of the pool wall and rested his folded arms on the rim. 'Well, I can't promise you anything concerning the legal proceedings themselves. I'm not in the business of thwarting an Army investigation, or if it goes to trial, I can't tamper in any way with a military court-martial. But I can make a few guarantees in exchange for some promises from you.'

Tyson climbed the concrete steps of the pool and sat on the pool edge, his feet in the water. 'Let's hear the guarantees.'

Brown moved closer to him. 'First, if you voluntarily place yourself under Army jurisdiction, you will be assigned to a post within twenty-five miles of the metropolitan area.'

'Sounds like an enlistment pitch. How about a new uniform?'

'Sure. Also – and this is important – you will not be placed under restraint of any sort. You will be as free as you are now, within the parameters of your duties, if any. Okay so far?'

'No, but go on.'

Brown's tone was impatient. 'Look, Ben, if they get you back in after a court fight, it won't be so easy on you. They'll assign you to Fort Bumfuck in the Arizona desert, and you'll be confined to quarters.'

'Don't threaten me, junior.'

Brown stood in the shallow water on the concrete step and

clenched his right fist, cracking his knuckles. He said, 'You don't want to be confined, Ben. You won't like that. Neither will your family. Your wife. She'd probably have to stay in New York to work. It would get very lonely for her, buddy ... or maybe it wouldn't—'

Tyson drove the heel of his foot into Brown's solar plexus. Brown's eyes and mouth opened wide as he doubled over and stumbled back down the pool steps.

The two old men at the far end of the pool didn't notice, and the lifeguard kept reading his book. A young man in a nearby deck chair stood suddenly and made eye contact with Tyson.

Brown straightened up and caught his breath. His head bobbed quickly several times, and he motioned with his hand towards the young man. Tyson stood and took a step back from the pool as he kept an eye on the man. The man sat back in his chair.

Brown drew several deep breaths and stared up at Tyson. 'Okay ... okay ... I had that coming ...' Brown put his hands on the edge of the pool. 'I'm getting out. Okay? Truce.'

Tyson nodded.

Brown lifted himself out of the pool and turned from Tyson. He walked slowly to his deck chair and wrapped a towel around his waist. He sat on the edge of the chair and patted the chaise longue beside him.

Tyson walked to it, grabbed his towel, and put it around his waist.

Brown said, 'Feel better? Sit down.'

Tyson felt much better. He stretched out in the chaise longue.

Brown massaged his midsection. 'Christ ... you see, you *are* a violent man. You're normal.' Brown affected a smile.

Tyson relaxed but kept his eye on Brown. It came to him that since Vietnam he hadn't felt much deep passion, anger, or challenge. In a way, he realized, he was reverting, regressing in time and temperament, to the type of person he

117

had been before Marcy, suburbia, middle age and the corporate structure began limiting his aggressiveness. He was taking more control over his life, which in other ways was coming apart. He said to Brown, 'I'm sorry. But if you piss me off again, I'll hit you again.'

Brown forced a weak smile. 'Okay. Can I finish my business?' Brown leaned forward and rested his hands on his knees. 'Where was I? Restraint. Right. If you are actually court-martialled I can also guarantee that you won't be placed under restraint even during the trial. Therefore, if things don't seem to be going well in the courtroom, you at least have the option of removing yourself in the ultimate sense from Army jurisdiction. In fact, you can go now if you wish. No one is watching you.'

Tyson said nothing.

Brown added, 'Your passport will not be revoked or confiscated as is the normal procedure. But if you decide to go, now or at any time, please go some place where you won't embarrass the government with an extradition problem. Brazil is the choice of most, but you might consider Sweden.' He leaned closer to Tyson. 'Listen, everything I'm offering is within the power of the executive branch to do—'

'Sweden! Are you trying to tell me that eighteen years after I served my country and came home, I should run to Sweden? *I* should run to Sweden where—'

'Please lower your voice.'

Tyson sat up. '—where the deserters and draft-dodgers went? I should go to Sweden when all the draft-dodgers have been given a presidential pardon? Where's *my* presidential pardon?'

'It is rather ironic if you think about it—'

'Fuck you, Brown! Fuck you and whoever sent you.'

'Not so loud, please.'

'I'm not going anywhere, goddamn it! I'm an American citizen, and this is my country. Fuck Sweden and fuck the Army!'

Brown glanced around the pool area. 'Calm down.'

Tyson lifted himself out of the chair. 'Listen, Chet, or whatever the fuck your name is, tell your bosses this: I may be a suspected mass murderer, but I am also a certified war hero. I have two fucking Purple Hearts—' Tyson pointed to the white scar tissue that disfigured his right ear, then to the thick purple line that curved around his kneecap and ran down his shin. 'I have a fistful of medals and commendations. I am also a husband, a father, and a hardworking taxpayer. I am a respected member of my community, and I have never knowingly broken the law in my life. If something *did* happen in that shithole eighteen years ago, something that maybe lasted thirty minutes of my forty-year life, then ... then ...' Tyson found his heart was beating heavily and his fists were clenched. He glowered at Brown, who was sitting very still.

Brown spoke in a soft voice. 'This was the first war in our history that produced not one certifiable, media-anointed, publicly acclaimed war hero. Not one.' Brown stood. He stared at Tyson for some time, then added, 'Hey, you have to understand, my friend, there are no bad guys in this piece. Not me, not Van Arken, not the folks in the White House, not the media, and not even you. There is only the system. The law.'

Brown touched Tyson's arm gently and cocked his head towards the locker room. As they walked, Brown said, 'No one has anything against you personally. Everyone I spoke to wishes you well. But you have to understand, Ben, the military needs this one. You've read the Peers Commission report on My Lai, haven't you? Well, everything that General Peers said was wrong with that case, from beginning to end, will be right with this case. No cover-ups, no legal blunders, no undue command influence, no congressional whining, no journalistic Monday-morning quarterbacking, no fuckups. Just justice. Even if we have to script it and fake it. Okay?'

They reached the door that led to the locker room and stopped. Tyson said, 'Tell them I'm a fighter, Chet.'

'I will.' Brown rubbed his stomach. 'You are.' Brown glanced around. 'I'm going to do some laps. You have to get going.' Brown hesitated, then said, 'There's more. You see, Ben, you *can* hurt the Army, the government, and the country if you want. So if you're going to fight, fight fair. If you're going to run, run clean.' Brown continued, 'No swipes at the Army or the President or the system. No criticism of the Army justice system, no going on about the immorality of the war. No talking to reporters. No opening of old wounds.'

'That's it? Or that's not it?'

'Almost. We want you to accept a JAG-appointed defence counsel.' Brown glanced at Tyson, then continued. 'We don't want you retaining an F. Lee Bailey. You couldn't control a hotshot civilian lawyer. The deal wouldn't work with a civilian. You see, a civilian would drag it out, try to get all kinds of publicity for himself. We want the trial concluded before the reporters from the *Times* and the *Post* get their pens uncapped. We don't want the continuing saga of Ben Tyson on the nightly news. Neither do you,' Brown continued, 'though you can't plead guilty, you *can* at least refrain from calling witnesses, cross-examining government witnesses, and that sort of thing. There's nothing irregular about not offering a defence. In fact, military court-martial boards look favourably on that. They'll probably hand you one to ten for being a gentleman. And you won't do a day of it anyway. As long as you accept this offer. Okay? Do you understand what is required of you? We'll remind you of what is required from time to time as certain situations arise.' Brown added softly, 'It's not a bad deal, Ben. It guarantees you won't be imprisoned. Will you think about it?'

'Sure.'

Brown smiled, then gave Tyson a hard look. 'If you turn this deal down, there will be no hard feelings. But do *not* mention this conversation to anyone. Not your wife, your lawyer, or anyone. If you do and we find out, then ... then it becomes personal.'

120

Tyson nodded.

Brown said, 'I'll call you.' He extended his hand. 'No hard feelings.'

Tyson took Brown's hand. 'When I drove my heel into your solar plexus, it was not personal, Chet. I was acting out my rage against the system.'

Brown laughed. He turned and walked towards the pool. Tyson watched him jump in, then passed through the door to the locker room. *Yes*, he thought, *justice will be done, even if it has to be scripted and faked.*

13

General William Van Arken stood behind a podium that bore the crossed sword and quill pen emblem of the Judge Advocate General's Corps. He addressed the four officers seated before him. 'Although we have no authority at present to investigate the Tyson case, we may choose an investigating officer to contact Mr Tyson on the day he receives his recall orders, to inform him that charges are being contemplated against him, and to inform him of his rights.'

Van Arken looked at the three men and one woman seated in the row of writing desks in the small lecture room located in the third side of the Pentagon. Van Arken's adjutant, Colonel Sam Spencer, sat directly in front of him. To Spencer's right was Lieutenant Colonel Eugene Pellum, Van Arken's special legal counsel. To Spencer's left was Captain Lorraine Connelly from personnel. Next to her was Lieutenant Jack Gibbs, Van Arken's aide. Van Arken said, 'As you know, the Uniform Code of Military Justice recommends that in felony cases, the investigating officer be a major or higher rank. Therefore I've asked Captain Connelly to assemble the microfilmed files of approximately twenty-five such officers who may be suitable to conduct this investigation.' Van Arken motioned to the projection screen behind him.

'I'll remind you,' he continued, 'that in the interests of fairness, we should not discuss this case as such, but we can make references to certain facts that are relevant to the task of choosing an impartial investigator.' He looked at his legal counsel. 'Colonel Pellum?'

Pellum nodded. 'Let me also remind everyone that just as we have the sworn duty to choose an investigator who will not be prejudicial towards the suspect, we should also choose someone who will not be sympathetic towards him.'

Colonel Spencer added, 'As we know, any JAG officer should be impartial and acceptable. However, in this case it would be appropriate to consider candidates.'

Captain Lorraine Connelly said, 'We should perhaps first come up with a profile. Credentials, requirements, character traits, and so forth. Then we can narrow the field.'

Van Arken nodded in agreement. 'Well, what *are* we looking for?'

Colonel Pellum replied, 'Ideally, the investigating officer should be as free from negative or positive bias regarding the Vietnam War as possible.' He smiled grimly. 'That would either be someone who is young or someone who has spent the last two decades on the moon.'

Lieutenant Gibbs spoke. 'Maybe the investigating officer should be someone who has decided not to continue his military career.' He hesitated before adding, 'Someone who has nothing to lose and nothing to gain. An officer who won't feel ... pressured to come to a conclusion that he feels will please the Army.'

Van Arken didn't reply.

Colonel Spencer nodded. 'That's a good point. No one can accuse us later of bringing in a gung-ho hatchet man who's trying to make rank.'

Several heads nodded. The discussion continued for some

122

minutes before Van Arken said, 'In summation, then, everyone feels that this officer should not have served in Vietnam or even been in service during the Vietnam era. That would obviously be consistent with him not being a career officer. He should in fact be too young to have even been involved in college activities, pro- or antiwar, during this period.' Van Arken reflected a moment. 'There can't be many men in that age group who are majors and who are not continuing their military careers.'

Captain Connelly said, 'I think someone who is fulfilling a four-year tuition assistance obligation will meet these requirements.'

Van Arken mulled over these suggestions. This was not precisely what he had in mind. He said, 'I want a man who will project a good image for the Army and for the Judge Advocate General's Corps.'

No one responded.

Van Arken said, 'Well, let's begin going through the files.' He pressed a button on the podium to signal the man in the soundproof projection room.

'Excuse me, General.' Captain Lorraine Connelly spoke. 'May I make a suggestion?'

The lights dimmed, and the screen behind Van Arken brightened. The General looked at Lorraine Connelly in the reflected light of the screen. 'Yes?'

She said, 'I suppose it isn't proper for any of us to propose a candidate, but that's what I'm going to do.'

'Whom do you have in mind?'

She replied, 'Major Karen Harper.'

There was a stillness in the darkened room. Captain Connelly added, 'Some of you may know her. I met her when we worked together in Germany.' Connelly paused, then said, 'I included her file among the ones we're going to consider. Why don't we look at it first?'

No one responded.

Captain Connelly spoke into the silent darkness. 'Major

123

Harper fills the initial requirements that we've agreed on. In addition, she is very thorough. Good attention to detail. Fine judgement, shows outstanding initiative, and her personal appearance is always up to standards.' Lorraine Connelly could see in the dim light that the General seemed to respond positively to these military buzz words. Taking heart, she continued, 'Colonel Pellum made a humorous comment about finding someone who spent the last two decades on the moon. Well, more importantly, it would be favourably viewed if the investigating officer has spent the last month in a media vacuum. It so happens that Major Harper is recently returned from a thirty-day leave which she spent in the Far East. I doubt if she bothered to pick up any American papers there.'

Van Arken said curtly, 'Choosing an Army investigator is not like jury selection. I don't think a JAG officer believes everything he – she – reads in the papers.'

Colonel Spencer, Van Arken's adjutant, interjected, 'Still, General, I like that idea. So will the media.' He turned to Connelly. 'Do you know her personal history?'

Captain Connelly replied, 'Yes, sir, I believe she comes from a large family. Rural people. Farmers, I think. Ohio.' She was tempted to add 'heartland,' but resisted the overkill and went on. 'Her undergraduate work was at Ohio State, as her file will show. I believe her education was touch and go because of finances. She entered American University Law when she was in her mid-twenties, and Defence picked up the tab.'

Lieutenant Gibbs mumbled, 'In exchange for four years' hard time, like me.' He laughed to try to slough off the ill-considered remark.

Van Arken presided over the silence for a while, then abruptly pressed the intercom button on the podium and spoke to the projectionist. 'Let's have Harper, Sergeant.'

Within a minute the first page of the file was projected on the screen.

The five officers read the page on the screen. Colonel Spencer said, 'She's assigned to the JAG School in Charlottesville. That's close to us here, but not too close. And she can hop on a shuttle to New York whenever necessary.'

Colonel Pellum commented, 'Her ETS is July sixteenth. That gives her enough time to complete the preliminary investigation and not have to stick around for the consequences.'

Lorraine Connelly said, 'The file will show she's success-fully conducted Article 31 and 32 investigations. Also, she's a remarkable interrogator—'

'Meaning what?' asked Van Arken curtly.

'Meaning, sir, she gets at the truth. Suspects – men, I suppose you'd say – talk freely to her. She's not abrasive, officious, or intimidating—'

'I don't want anyone who's going to be soft on Tyson.'

Lieutenant Colonel Pellum said, 'General, Tyson is obviously a bright man. He knows he can cripple an Article 31 investigation in the two seconds it will take him to exercise his right to remain silent. I think, though, that if a woman called on him … Not to be sexist, but it may help. At this stage we're only empowered to conduct this informal inquiry. So we'd like to get the most out of it until such time as we can proceed further.'

Van Arken saw the others nod in agreement. He said bluntly, 'Tyson may not take kindly to being investigated by a woman.' He hit a button, and the next page appeared. The five officers read the pages of Harper's file as they rolled across the screen. Van Arken commented, 'She is unmarried.' This elicited no response. Van Arken said into the intercom, 'Sergeant, go on to the photograph.'

The film advanced quickly, then stopped at a blurry file photograph. The projectionist adjusted the focus, and the screen filled with a black-and-white picture of a woman with light, tousled hair. She had a wide smile, big eyes, and freckles. No one spoke until Lieutenant Gibbs commented,

'Looks like someone I'd let in the door.'

There were a few chuckles. Van Arken heard Gibbs say something else and caught the word 'wife.' There was some further laughter. Van Arken snapped, 'At ease.'

Captain Connelly regarded General Van Arken in the glare of the projector's beam. She could see Van Arken was deep in thought. Lorraine Connelly had heard that Van Arken was not amused by the off-colour jokes his junior officers were making about Tyson's wife. Lorraine Connelly strongly suspected, too, that General Van Arken was not favourably disposed towards a man with a wife like that.

Colonel Spencer's voice broke the stillness. 'General, I know the choice of a woman could cause some problems; but if it's image you're after, then there's a good image for you.' He pointed at Karen Harper's picture. 'Looks like she stepped out of a Coke ad.'

Van Arken rubbed his chin thoughtfully. Putting a woman in charge of the investigation, he understood, could very well enhance the image of the JAG Corps. It would also defuse recent criticism regarding the postings and promotions of female personnel in his command. The Pentagon would be pleased.

Lieutenant Gibbs seemed to read Van Arken's thoughts. 'This might give some credence to the recruiting slogan, "Be all you can be."'

Van Arken eyed Gibbs with some annoyance, then continued his ruminations. He realized that if Harper bungled the investigation, it might not reflect too unfavourably on the mostly male and mostly career officer corps. And if Major Karen Harper ran into trouble with the investigation, the White House could be pressured to quickly authorize the formal, grand jury type investigation, with subpoena powers, a working staff, and assistance from the Army CID and the FBI. There was, of course, the possibility that Major Harper would find no evidence to recommend that charges be forwarded to a grand jury. But Van Arken didn't think that was a strong possibility, given the nature of the allegations. Van Arken looked at the officers in front of him. He had the impression they favoured assigning this Harper woman to the case. The General said, 'Does anyone have any objections to this officer serving as the Article 31 investigating officer in the matter of Benjamin Tyson?'

No one objected.

Van Arken stared at Captain Lorraine Connelly in a way that suggested he thought she'd stuck her neck out and had better be prepared for the consequences. Van Arken said, 'All right. Major Harper it is.'

Van Arken turned and stared at the photograph of Karen Harper still projected on the screen. Beyond the fresh good looks and the warm smile, he thought he saw some strength of character, some keen intelligence; a result, he imagined, of the hard climb from rural poverty to an education, a law degree, a military tour of duty. He, too, had been born in rural poverty on a Pennsylvania farm not eighty miles from where he stood now. And like Karen Harper, he reflected, he had made the climb alone, without marrying. Dependents got heavy when you started so far down in the hole that it took half a lifetime just to reach ground level with everyone else.

General Van Arken turned back to the people in the small dark room. 'Captain Connelly, you will not communicate this decision to Major Harper. On the day Tyson receives his recall orders, Major Harper will receive her orders assigning her to temporary duty as investigating officer. No one here will divulge anything that was said. No one here will have any contact with Major Harper until her investigation is completed. If there is nothing further' … he met everyone's eyes … 'then thank you for coming. Dismissed.'

14

The old Volvo rolled east on Sunrise Highway, through Southampton, then Water Mill. Tyson turned left at the Methodist Church and headed up Scuttle Hole Road. The late afternoon sun lay mellow and pleasant over the well-tended and prosperous potato farms. Scuttle Hole Road intersected with the Sag Harbor turnpike, and Tyson swung north.

He turned his head and spoke to David, who shared the rear seat with cartons and suitcases. 'David, do you remember any of this?'

'Sort of. It's real nice.'

Within ten minutes they entered the old whaling village of Sag Harbor. Stately homes with widow's walks lined lower Main Street, then at the Civil War monument the street widened into the business district.

Tyson joined the line of slow-moving traffic. The sidewalks were crowded with a happy-looking mixture of families, singles, gays, townsmen, fishermen, farmers, and yachtsmen from distant ports.

The Volvo continued slowly. Tyson scanned the storefronts, looking for the bookshop. In the front window was a hand-lettered sign announcing BOOKS BY LOCAL AUTHORS. Tyson was surprised to see that there were nearly two dozen scribblers in local residence. There among the books he spotted the distinctive scarlet cover of *Hue: Death of a City*.

'Still a hot item.'

'What?'

Tyson cocked his head to the side.

Marcy looked. 'Oh. Sure. Five weeks on the *Times* bestseller list. Number twelve and climbing. Maybe you and Picard can do a little East End publicity together. Put a rocket up that book's ass, as we say in the business. I'll handle the PR.'

'Not funny.'

'No,' agreed David, 'not funny.'

Marcy shrugged. 'Just trying to kill time in traffic.'

The Volvo approached the traffic circle at the end of Main Street. In the centre of the circle rose a tall white flagpole. The stars and stripes snapped nicely in the wind that blew off the harbour, and the halyard slapped against the pole. Beyond the circle in a grassy patch was the windmill overlooking the harbour. To the right was the Long Wharf, thick with cars, people, and fishmongers. Sailing vessels swayed at their moorings, and Tyson could hear the creaking in the riggings.

David said, 'I remember this. A red seaplane landed there.'

Marcy said, 'We used to have lunch at that restaurant on the wharf. See it?'

'Oh, yeah. I helped unload fish from a boat.'

Tyson put in, 'Catch of the day. Red snappers. I paid nine dollars a plate for them an hour later.'

Marcy remarked, 'You have a selective memory.'

Tyson nodded, 'You ain't seen nothing until you see my selective amnesia on a witness stand.'

No one spoke. Tyson took the Volvo around the circle and headed to North Haven over the bridge crammed with joggers, bicyclists, and pedestrians. He turned left on Short Beach Road, then left again onto a small peninsula called Baypoint. 'Which way?'

'Right over there on Cliff Road, left on Bayview. There it is. The grey-shingled Cape.'

Tyson looked at the white-trimmed cottage as the car descended the curved road. The grass was brown and high, the mimosa hung in heavy bloom over the small portico. Wildflowers grew where they could, and untrimmed spruce and cedar darkened the left half of the property. Quite lovely.

He said, 'Does this place have electricity?'

'Don't get cute, Tyson.'

He pulled the car into the gravel drive and shut off the engine. There was a silence as the Tysons surveyed the property from the car. Tyson said, '*This* was nine thousand dollars for the summer?'

Marcy snapped, 'And we were lucky to get it. There's nothing left on the entire East End.' She added, 'It's quaint, and it's on the bay.'

David opened the rear door. 'I'm going to take a look.' He shot out of the car and disappeared around the side of the garage.

Marcy and Ben sat in silence. The engine ticked, and a locust clicked somewhere. Tyson said, 'You're right. This isn't far from the one we rented a couple of years ago.'

'It was eight years ago.'

'Was it? Time flies.' He looked at the house and the trees, and he thought of that summer. Each Friday after work he'd take the Long Island Railroad from Penn Station to Bridgehampton, an unpleasant three-hour run made barely more tolerable by spending it in the bar car. Marcy and David would meet him at the station, and they'd usually have dinner in a Bridgehampton pub whose name escaped him at the moment. On Monday morning, at dawn, he'd board the Hampton jitney bus with other men and women who were making the commute back to the front lines. Marcy had been between jobs then, and she'd spent the entire summer in Sag Harbor with David.

Marcy broke into his thoughts. 'Where are you?'

He looked at her. 'That summer.'

She nodded. 'You took most of August off.'

'Yes, I did. Things were slow at Peregrine. No one seemed to be building many fighter bombers or attack helicopters that year. That's all changed now.'

'Unfortunately it has.'

'How about you? No one needs any quick publicity fixes

130

this summer?'

She replied, 'I told you, I took extended leave. The job is there when I want to go back. Tom was very good about it. Very understanding.'

'Good old Tom.'

They sat in silence for a while, then Tyson opened his door. 'Well, let's see what sort of horror house you've rented this time.'

They walked across the high weedy lawn, and Marcy found the key. They entered directly into an all-white living room furnished in what Tyson thought of as East End rental chic: chrome, glass, moulded plastics, and beige cotton suede.

At the far end of the living room were sliding glass doors that let out onto a wooden deck. Marcy walked to the doors and slid one open. She took a deep breath. 'Smell that sea.'

Tyson slid the screen door open and walked onto the redwood deck. Marcy followed. Tyson looked out over the property. The yard dropped off and ended in a tangle of bramble and a heap of bulkhead rocks. Beyond was the body of water called Sag Harbor Cove. David was picking his way over the rocks. Tyson said, 'I hope there's some hot little number around here for him.'

Marcy leaned on the deck rail and watched their son. 'I hope he finds whatever he needs out here.' She stared out at a sleek yellow-sailed catamaran gliding west towards the narrows. 'A sailboat in the backyard. This is beautiful, Ben.'

'Yes ... but you'll miss the Big Apple. You may even miss Garden City.'

'I'll miss New York, but I won't miss Garden City. It was insufferable these last few weeks.'

'It's all in the mind.' Tyson gave her a sidelong glance. The wind blew her hair, and the sun shone fully on her face. Her eyes were closed, and she looked about ten years younger than she'd looked yesterday.

Tyson walked along the deck and peered into a second set of glass doors. 'The kitchen looks decent. But ... oh, God ... I don't see a dishwasher. There's no trash compactor or microwave oven. Marcy, is this the right house?'

'Don't be a wiseass, Ben. Anyway, I have menus from fourteen take-out places.'

'That's my girl. Resourceful in the face of privation. Well, hell, you may as well enjoy your vacation.'

She replied coolly, 'It is not a vacation, Ben. We're on the lam.'

Tyson didn't reply.

Marcy looked across the hedgeline into the adjoining yard. Two men in their twenties were sunbathing on lawn loungers. They had on matching yellow bikini shorts.

Tyson followed her gaze. 'They're probably gay.'

Marcy turned her attention back to the water and didn't respond.

Tyson said, 'Well, let's get the bags inside and unpacked.'

Tyson sat in a cane rocker on the back deck, a scotch in one hand, a thin cheroot in the other. He wore faded jeans, sandals, and a sleeveless sweatshirt with the ubiquitous Sag Harbor whale across the front. The remains of an improvised barbecue lay on the round picnic table. The sun was setting behind a line of cedars across the cove, and lighted boats made their way between the channel markers.

Tyson listened to his neighbours' radio and was happy to discover they preferred soft over hard rock. Tyson reflected again on Andrew Picard. He was not quite as certain of Picard's exact location in Sag Harbor at this moment as he was of their relative positions at Hue in 1968 – thanks to Picard's book with accompanying campaign maps. The night of Tet had found Picard in the South Vietnamese Army's First Division Headquarters, an enclave in the northeast corner of the Citadel. Tyson's platoon had been advancing eastward, and with a brief stop at *Hôpital Miséricorde,* had come a few kilometres from the Citadel walls. Their mission had been to link up with what was left of the ARVN First

132

Division which had broken out of their enclave and were driving west through the narrow streets of the Citadel itself. Tyson supposed that if he had accomplished his mission he might actually have met Picard, one of only a dozen or so Westerners who had taken refuge with the ARVN division. He supposed, too, that Picard would have been happy to see Americans and would have taken Tyson's picture and written a little piece about him. Perhaps they'd have shared a canteen cup of Japanese gin. And if Tyson could have seen into the future, he'd have put his .45 automatic to Picard's head and blown his brains out.

Tyson looked out across the cove at the bluff on the far shore. Backyards were strung with Japanese lanterns, and barbecue pits gave a distinctive charcoal smell and a chimerical glow. Someone who couldn't wait for July Fourth was sending skyrockets arching into the black eastern sky. The smell of the charcoal in the damp night air strongly reminded him of the pervasive smell in the Vietnamese villages at mealtime. He was reminded, too, of the coloured paper lanterns hung before Tet and the night sky lit with fireworks that were not fireworks. He fancied that the cove at the narrows was the Perfume River, and the lighted boats were sampans gliding down to the South China Sea. At night it was easy to imagine things, to create moods, fantasies, or nightmares, to find peace or to refight wars. But one thing was certain about that distant lantern-lit shore: Andrew Picard lived there, and sometime before the summer was done, he would knock on Picard's door.

Tyson drew on his cigar. The glass kitchen door slid open, and Marcy stepped out to the deck. She went to the rail and surveyed the cove. 'Do you remember the time we were swimming in the nude out there? It was a full moonlit night, and that cabin cruiser came up beside us, and the people insisted we come aboard for a drink?'

Tyson smiled and looked at her. She had on loose-fitting, blue cotton boating pants with a matching hooded jersey. He noticed she was barefoot and wore little makeup and no jewellery except for her wedding ring. The metamorphosis was nearly complete. Tomorrow she'd have colour in her cheeks and sand between her toes. She'd smell of brine and charcoal, just like that summer. But it was not going to be a summer just like that summer. Tyson said, 'How about the night we were screwing in the rubber raft and we floated through the narrows into the lower cove?'

'We fought that tide for two hours before we got back.' Marcy sat on the edge of the round table, her bare feet on a chair. She poured a glass of red wine and said, 'How did it go this morning?'

Tyson rattled the ice cubes in his drink. 'Well, I'm afraid I lost my temper. Most unfortunate. Greatly embarrass Kimura-san and Shimamura-san.'

'Cut the Mr Moto talk, Ben. Were you canned?'

'No ... oddly enough, I wasn't.'

Marcy said, 'So, did they offer you a raise?'

'Actually, they want me to request a transfer to Tokyo.'

Marcy looked at him in the light of the flickering citronella candle. 'Tokyo?' She thought for a moment, then said, 'I have a career, and I don't see why I should give it up.'

Tyson sat forward in the rocker, and his voice was sharp. 'To save my ass, lady. And besides, *I* have the career. You have a *job* – from which you've absented yourself for three months with no problem. Anyway, who said you were invited?'

The crickets chirped, and the water lapped against the stone. A breeze rustled the crab apple tree. Tyson said, 'I'm sorry.'

Marcy didn't reply.

'I didn't mean that.'

'Okay.' She poured the last of the wine. 'Are you going?'

Tyson had no intention of going to Japan but discovered to his surprise that he had no intention of telling her that. He said, 'I'm weighing the decision.' What, he thought, was the

134

purpose of the lie? Lying had become habit. He lied to his attorney, his employers, to Brown, to his friends and family, and now to his wife. He supposed he was in training for the main event, trial by general court-martial. He settled back into his rocker. 'Where's David?'

'He found some boys his age. They went night fishing down at the end of Whaler's Walk.'

Tyson nodded. 'Did you remind him his name is Anderson?'

'Yes.'

Tyson blew cigar smoke into the misty air. 'I feel like a criminal.'

'Do you?'

Tyson looked at her in the flickering light but didn't reply. She said, 'Anyway, I think the real estate agent knew who I was even though I used my maiden name.'

'Your maiden name and your picture, madam, are as prominent as my name and picture. You should have used a *nom de guerre.*'

'I don't think we'll be bothered out here.' She watched him make his way across the dark lawn toward the rocks and bushes. She suddenly felt an unspecified fear grip her and jumped down from the table. 'I'll go with you.'

They walked together in silence and picked their way down the white rocks until they found a wide, flat piece of shale at the water's edge. They both sat. Marcy said, 'It's cold here.'

'Go back and get a sweater.'

'Put your arm around me.'

He did so, awkwardly.

She snuggled closer to him. At length she said, 'What's bothering you?'

'Is that a joke?'

'No, it's a question. And I'll tell you what isn't bothering you. The massacre business isn't bothering you. Not today. You've coped quite well in recent weeks.'

Tyson didn't respond.

135

She said, 'It's me that's bothering you. Or rather what the schlock tabloids are saying about me, and the respectable media are intimating.'

He shrugged. 'It's not relevant. On the scale of one to ten, court-martial for murder is up there. Your past rates a one.'

'I don't think so.'

Tyson slipped his arm from her shoulders. 'Well ... I guess when they start interviewing a seemingly inexhaustible supply of ex ... boyfriends. ...' He threw his cigar in the water.

Marcy tucked her legs under her and wrapped her arms around her chest. 'Are you embarrassed by me?'

He didn't reply.

'None of this would have come out if it weren't for *your* notoriety. But I don't blame you.'

'Right. Okay. Look, I'm not trying to blame you for my predicament. I was the one who—' Tyson drew a deep breath. 'But can't you at least see that these steamy articles, the picture, and all this crap has kept the public interest alive in my case? It's had a sort of synergistic effect. You know? And David ... I took the time to explain to him ... I mean, my side of it. You never tried to explain to him that ... I mean that there was a sexual revolution or some damned thing. All he's getting is what he's reading. And he *is* reading that crap.' He looked at her.

Marcy threw a stone into the water.

Tyson listened to a frog croaking. Another skyrocket rose from the distant shore. Marcy stood. 'All right. I'll deal with David. But how do *you* feel about everything that's been written about me?'

He stood also. 'You seem to believe everything they are writing about *me*.'

Neither spoke, then Marcy said in a calmer voice, 'There are grains of truth in what has been written about each of us, I suppose ... but ... not infidelity, Ben. Not that.'

Tyson nodded. 'Okay.'

She forced a smile and touched him lightly on the arm. 'Hey, Tyson, one day we'll get roaring drunk and tell each other all our darkest, most intimate, most dangerous and embarrassing secrets. Then we'll file for divorce. Or fall in love again.' She laughed softly.

Tyson smiled in return but didn't feel appreciably better. Intellectually he knew that what he did in 1968 was far worse than what she did in that same year. Yet he and society seemed harsher toward her, the traditional scapegoat: the whore. He drew a long breath and said, 'Well ... anyway, it sounds like you had more fun than I did. Maybe I'm jealous.'

She took his arm in a firmer grip. 'I'm sure, Ben, we both got what we really wanted out of that time.' She hesitated. 'You wanted to be there.'

Tyson looked at her closely, then replied, 'Yes, I've had that thought myself.'

She ran her fingers down his arm and squeezed his hand.

He glanced out over the water. 'I'd like to be alone here.'

She hesitated, then said, 'Don't jump in.'

'No.'

'Promise.'

'See you later.'

'Promise!'

He was momentarily startled, then nodded quickly. 'Promise.'

She turned and climbed back toward the lawn.

Tyson watched her as she picked her way barefoot over the rock, her dark clothing against the bleached stone, graceful in the moonlight; a sight to store away, then conjure up someday when they were no longer together.

There was a chill in the night air, and the central heating didn't seem to be working. Marcy lay sleeping on the couch. David was in his room. Tyson knelt before the fireplace and touched a match to the paper and cedar kindling beneath the oak logs. The fire caught, and the smoke drew nicely up the flue. He leaned back against the armchair and focused on the flaming wood. He pulled out another cigarette and struck a wooden stove match, watching the phosphorus ignite in a white flame.

Tyson slipped out the door and walked down the short corridor. Tony Scorello was standing at the entrance to the maternity ward. Tyson saw that a white phosphorus grenade had been thrown into the ward. If it had been thrown by Scorello, Tyson thought, he looked now as though he wished he could take it back.

But there was no taking it back and no putting it out. White phosphorus had peculiar properties when ignited, sticking like napalm and burning with a white-hot intensity, which needed no air to support its combustion. Neither water nor smothering would extinguish it. Willy Peter, it was called, because GIs have to call everything something else. Willy Peter was splattered on the whitewashed walls of the crowded ward and Tyson noticed that a large crucifix on the far wall was burning.

Tony Scorello turned to him, tears streaming down his dirty face, his mouth moving to form words, but only moans came forth. Scorello's rifle lay at his feet, and his arms were flapping like an excited child's.

Tyson pushed Scorello aside and stepped through the arched entrance to the ward. About half of the two dozen beds were burning and melted mosquito nets hung in black strands like giant cobwebs. Most of the bassinets had collapsed in fiery heaps. A naked woman staggered up the aisle between the beds, but there was no other movement. The bed closest to Tyson was burning, and through the flames and smoke he saw the shape of a woman lying very still, like a Hindu woman, he thought, performing suttee.

Tyson noticed that the louvred shutters were open, and he saw the rain falling outside. Somewhere in the dying hospital a generator still put out electricity because the three paddle fans spun and a light burned over the nurses' station.

Tony Scorello suddenly ran into the burning ward and Tyson went after him. The stench of the ward was overpowering: flesh, hair, bedding, the phosphorus itself, and the charred bones as the phosphorus ate deeper into the bodies.

Tyson found Scorello sitting on the floor, his face buried in his hands. He began sobbing, 'Mother of God. Mother of God. I didn't do it. I didn't do it.'

Tyson left him where he was and returned to the door he had first come through marked *Salle de Contagion*. Tyson opened it and went inside, pulling the door shut behind him.

Sister Teresa, dressed in a white linen habit, sat on the edge of the single bed, her hands resting in her lap. Tyson thought she looked very composed. He was annoyed that she hadn't got under the bed as he'd instructed her. He said, *'Le feu.'* A Vietnamese phrase came to him. *'O day khong duoc yen* – It is not safe here.'

She nodded in acceptance but remained sitting.

Tyson said, *'Est-ce qu'il y ... une porte de toit?* A roof door?'

'Oui.'

'Où?'

She said in English, 'I do not wish to escape.'

'Like hell.' Tyson took her by the arm and raised her off the bed. They stood face-to-face for several seconds, and he could see tears welling up in her eyes.

She said, 'Why are they doing this?'

Tyson had a dozen explanations but no answers.

Sister Teresa put her head on his shoulder and wept.

Tyson glanced up and saw the single paddle fan slowing to a stop. Through his boots, he felt the heat from the fires below. The sound of gunshots penetrated the thick-walled room, and the familiar acrid smell of burning humans permeated the air. Outside, the rain still fell, and a distant thunder from the direction of Hue rolled across the grey, sodden landscape. Benjamin Tyson felt a greyness in his soul such as he'd never felt before or since. He found he was squeezing Sister Teresa in his arms, and he heard her sobbing softly. 'My God,' he said, 'My God, I thought I knew them.' And a voice in the dim place in his mind answered, *You knew them. You always knew them. You always knew. You knew what they would do one day.*

'No!'

Tyson dropped the match and looked at the black burn on his fingers.

'No, what?'

He stared at Marcy standing over him.

She said, 'Would you like a drink?'

'Oh, no thanks.'

She eyed him closely. 'You look like you could use one.'

'I always look like that.' He turned his head back to the fire and stayed silent for some seconds before saying, 'Afterwards, that night in the bunker, he looked normal.'

'Who?'

'Tony Scorello. Well, not really normal. None of us, I think, looked normal or acted normal for weeks ... but Scorello was brewing a canteen cup of coffee. His hands were wrapped in bandages. I suppose he was burned. Later he played cards. I watched him by the light of the flickering candle.'

Marcy looked puzzled.

Tyson stayed silent for a second, then added, 'You know, I just realized something. I might see him again. I might see them all again.'

She knelt beside him and took his hand. 'Ben ... please ...' she said with concern, 'please be all right.'

The next morning, Ben Tyson sat at the round table on the

140

back deck and sipped a cup of steaming coffee. The table was damp, and he took care not to get the sleeves of his suit wet.

The morning air had a chill to it, and he could see his breath. Tyson looked out over the cove where a mist lay gentle on the water. A red cloud-streaked sun sat close over the North Haven Bridge, and sea gulls cut the still air with that unexpected, early morning screeching.

Marcy came through the glass kitchen doors, wearing a short red robe. 'You're up early,' she said in a husky voice. 'I guess the living room floor wasn't comfortable.'

'You should have woken me.'

'I did everything but kick you.'

He stared toward the water. A twenty-foot inboard open whaler was manoeuvring between the fog-covered channel markers. The tide was out, and Tyson could see a man in the bow probing the bottom with a gaff.

Marcy said, 'I didn't know you were leaving this early. I thought you'd stay with David and me for a few days at least.'

He shrugged.

Marcy walked barefoot across the wet deck and looked out over the lawn. Tyson regarded her legs, the thin kimono drawn tight across her back and buttocks.

Marcy turned and studied his face in silence. At length she said, 'What's bothering you this morning? Your notoriety or mine?'

'Yours,' he answered before he had a chance to think.

'Oh, Christ, are you still on that?'

'What's changed?'

'Why can't you let it go?'

'I don't know why.' He stared into his coffee cup, then said softly, 'I thought I was beyond jealousy and possessiveness. Yet ... when my wife's complete sexual history is national news, I feel a little foolish. But I guess I'm not normal.'

She snapped, 'Men! My God, you're all so damned hung up on how many—' She drew a deep breath. 'Forget it. I'm not adding fuel to this.'

141

Tyson nodded. 'I'll try.' But he thought that Marcy's attitude towards the photograph and the stories had again become somewhat blasé. Tyson had discovered that the photograph had been reproduced in various pulp magazines where it had been presented without blackout. In addition, several more articles about Marcy Clure had developed. These were less sensational than the ones in the *American Investigator,* and purported to be serious examinations of the life and times of a young radical turned suburbanite, wife, and career woman. Still, Tyson thought, these pieces were little more than cleverly concealed titillation. Then, a week ago, Sloan had shown him a wall poster version of the *Life* photograph which someone had picked up for him in one of those funky card shops down in the Village. The poster was captioned, HAPPY DAYS.

Sloan had remarked, 'People of the eighties are often shocked by what people of the sixties did, and they are often the same people.'

Marcy's past history, he understood, was irrelevant to his past history. Yet he knew instinctively that the photograph and the stories would hasten his downfall. He also understood that he was becoming obsessed with his wife's past, and he wanted very much to make amends, but couldn't.

Tyson stood and discovered his legs were shaky. He saw that tears had formed in Marcy's eyes.

She shouted, 'I didn't do anything wrong! You knew, damn it! You knew all about *me* when we met. I never *hid* anything. I fucked. So what? You *killed.* You killed more people than I fucked.'

'Get the hell out of here!'

Tyson went back into the house, retrieved his attaché case, and left by the front door. He began the two-mile walk to Main Street from where he would catch the jitney bus to Manhattan. As he came out of Baypoint onto the beach road, an old red Ford Mustang drew up beside him, and a young man called out, 'Need a lift to town?'

Tyson nodded and hopped in. The driver, he saw, was no more than eighteen, dressed in jeans and a white T-shirt that had no message. Tyson thought he was a local. 'Thanks. Can you drop me at the movie theatre?'

'Sure. You going to catch the bus?'

'Right.'

The young man drove off. 'You out for the summer?'

'Yes.'

'Where you staying?'

'Baypoint.'

'Nice. You're on TV, aren't you?'

Tyson shook his head.

'Yeah, you are. A news show. Right?'

'A cooking show.'

'No kidding?' He gave Tyson a sidelong glance, then observed, 'Lots of famous people out here. I saw Norman Rockwell last week.'

'He's dead.'

'No, I saw him. I never read any of his books, but I saw him on TV a couple times.'

'Norman Mailer?'

'Right. What did I say?'

'Rockwell.'

'No, that's the Nazi.'

'That's George Lincoln Rockwell. He's dead, too.'

'Is he?' The young man seemed to be sorting this information. He said, 'What's your name?'

'Jack Abbott.'

'Right. You do a talk show.'

'No, a cooking show.'

'Right. My name's Chuck.'

They drove across the North Haven Bridge and entered Main Street. Tyson said, 'You can let me off here. I'll walk the rest.'

Chuck pulled to the side. 'You're early for the next bus. There's the Paradise Grill up the street. Good coffee.'

'Thanks.' Tyson opened the door.

'You going to do a show in New York?'

'Right.' Tyson climbed out.

'What time? What channel?'

'Noon today. Channel Thirteen. Fried snapper with dill.' Tyson patted his briefcase. 'Got 'em right here. So long, Chuck.' Tyson closed the door and headed toward the coffee shop.

He heard a horn honking behind him but didn't turn. The slow-moving car kept slightly behind him, and the honking became insistent. People on the sidewalk were looking. An old man motioned to him, then pointed to the car. Tyson kept walking. The last thing he wanted with his coffee was Chuck.

A voice called out, 'Tyson, get your head out of your ass.'

He turned. Marcy motioned him toward the car. He approached the open passenger-side window. She said, 'Get in here.'

He opened the door and slid in. She pulled away. They drove in silence through Main Street and out of the village, onto the Bridgehampton Road. She said, 'I'll take you to the station.'

'I felt like taking a bus.'

'You'll take the fucking train and like it.'

Tyson shrugged. The Volvo headed south through the outskirts of the village and into a forest of scrub pine and pin oak. There was little early morning traffic, and a ground fog crept through the stunted and misshapen trees onto the lonely road. To Tyson this landscape always seemed foreboding. He said, 'I'm sorry.'

'About what?'

'That remark.'

'What remark? Which one are you sorry about?'

'That one about ... forget it.'

'No. Which one are you sorry about? The one where you suggested that I fucked more than a hundred people?'

'Right. That one.'

144

'Well, what if I did? At least I left them smiling. How did you leave your hundred?'

'Let me out.'

Marcy accelerated, and the speedometer showed sixty miles per hour.

'Hey, slow it down.'

'Whores drive fast.'

'Cut the crap and slow down!'

She pressed down on the accelerator and took a curve on the wrong side of the road. Tyson reached out, shut off the ignition, and pulled the key out. The car began to decelerate. He looked at her and saw she was fighting back tears.

The Volvo slowed to a near stop on an uphill grade, and Tyson turned the wheel, putting the car into the sandy shoulder. He threw the car in to park, then got out and came around to the driver's seat. 'Move over.'

She slid into the passenger seat. Tyson got in and started the car. He threw it into low, and the wheels spun, then the Volvo lurched back onto the road, and he continued toward Bridgehampton.

Neither spoke until they reached the station parking lot. He said, 'I need some time to think this out.'

She seemed composed now and nodded. 'Me too.'

He said, 'Call me with the unlisted number when you get the phone.'

She kept staring out the windshield.

Tyson cleared his throat. 'I won't be coming out this weekend.'

'All right.'

He said, 'I've caused us a lot of pain.'

She didn't respond.

He hesitated, then opened the door. 'Will you be all right now?'

She nodded and handed him his briefcase.

He got out and closed the door, then put his head in the open window. 'Careful driving. Tell David I'm sorry I didn't have a chance to say good-bye.'

'Your train's coming.'

Tyson glanced back and saw the big diesel's headlamp far down the misty tracks. He turned back to her. She looked at him, and they held each other's eyes for a long time, then the train whistle blew, and Tyson turned away.

Part 2

He who does not prevent a crime
when he can, encourages it.

Seneca: Troades

15

Miss Beale looked pale, Tyson thought. He'd noticed, too, that over the weeks she had become drawn and fidgety. He supposed she was having personal problems of some sort, but the astonishing notion came to him that Miss Beale was worried about him. Tyson said, 'What is it?'

She handed him a large manila envelope. The first thing he noticed was that its shade of buff was darker than anything he'd seen in normal business correspondence. The second thing he noticed was the government franking mark. Lastly he noticed that the envelope was from the Department of the Army. But he knew where it was from when Miss Beale first came through the door.

Miss Beale said, 'It came registered mail. I signed for it...'

Tyson saw that the envelope was addressed to Lieutenant Benjamin J. Tyson. He placed it on his blotter. 'Thank you. Have you typed the Taylor contract?'

'It's almost finished ...' Miss Beale seemed reluctant to leave.

Tyson said, 'Anything else?'

'No ...' She started towards the door, then said, 'Will you be leaving us?'

Tyson replied, 'It would appear so.'

Miss Beale blurted, 'Oh, we all think this is terrible, Mr Tyson. Terrible. This isn't ... isn't right. We're all upset ...'

Tyson assumed she was referring to the lunchroom clique who obviously discussed this at some length. The boardroom group was not so sympathetic. He recalled that in the infantry, after every battle, some promotions opened up, and people scrambling for them did not care if they had become available because of 81 millimetre mortar fire or 122 millimetre rocket fire. The corporate world was not so much different. Tyson said, 'I appreciate your concern.' He saw that Miss Beale still seemed stuck to her spot and added, 'Incidentally, you will continue here as long as you wish. I've spoken to Mr Kimura about that.'

She nodded. 'Thank you.' Miss Beale finally turned and left.

Tyson was as touched by this display of concern as he was mystified. He didn't think he was particularly popular with the rank and file, but apparently they decided he was being ill-treated by the world. This was something they could identify with. In fact, from what he could determine from the media, there was a ground swell of man-in-the-street support taking shape. He'd read that someone in Virginia had begun a Tyson Defence Fund, though no one had contacted him or Sloan about it. Odd, he thought, how Americans react to publicized stories of woe. He wanted to believe that there was a genuine altruism and sense of charity in the country, and perhaps there was, and perhaps he'd learn to believe there was.

He stared down at the manila envelope, then pushed it aside.

'It's your wife,' said Miss Beale over the intercom.

'I'll take it.' Tyson pressed the blinking phone button. 'Hello.'

'Hi.' Marcy's voice sounded distant.

There was a short silence, then Tyson said, 'Let me have the phone number.'

She gave it to him and said, 'We've had rain the last two days. How is it there?'

Tyson glanced back through the window. 'Same.'

'Sometimes the weather here is different.'

'Sometimes it is. How's David?'

'Fine. He found some friends, and the rain doesn't seem to keep them from fishing. They found a hangout, too. A disco off Main Street.'

'In Sag Harbor? What's it called? The Wailing Whaler's Top Deck? What's the world coming to?'

'Who knows? There's a steel band on the Long Wharf at night.'

'Is there?'

'Yes, and that place where John Steinbeck used to hang out – the Black Buoy – well, it's got a new image.'

Tyson wondered how she knew. He said, 'Well, sometimes it's not a good idea to try to go back, is it? I mean, sometimes it's painful.'

'Sometimes.'

Tyson swivelled his chair around and stared at the rain-splattered window. He used to be ambivalent about rain, but after going through two monsoons, each of three months' duration, he had developed a deep dislike for wet weather.

Marcy said, 'Are we still friends?'

'Sure.'

'Good.' Her voice still had a tentative tone. 'Anything new at work?'

'No. The arms race is still making everyone here giddy with delight. Lots of work.'

She hesistated before saying, 'I was thinking . . . if . . . well, I'd consider going to Tokyo with you . . . I mean, I'd definitely go . . . if that's what you decided.'

Tyson replied, 'Tokyo is no longer an option.'

'Why not?'

'Because I'm in the Army now.'

'What . . .?'

Tyson glanced at the papers on his desk. 'The letter said, "Greeting." After that it was all downhill.'

'Oh . . . oh, Ben . . .'

'Well, anyway, I had a meeting with Kimura, and I informed him of my new status.' Tyson thought back to the meeting less than an hour before. There had been nothing inscrutable about Mr Kimura's visage, and Tyson had read him well. Kimura, he was certain, knew about the recall order, though he feigned otherwise. Tyson said to Marcy, 'Kimura offered me half pay during my time on active duty. I don't know if that includes gaol time.'

Marcy didn't reply.

Tyson continued, 'Plus all my vacation pay, sick pay, and some year-end bonus money.'

'That ... that was very generous.'

'Very.' But Tyson didn't think generosity had anything to do with it. The government was subsidizing this, one way or another. They didn't want to leave him destitute. And that was not altruism, that was public relations strategy. But he didn't think he wanted to play their game. He said, 'I don't know what first lieutenants make these days, and I really don't give a damn, but I figure with that pay and your salary we'll be broke within the year.'

'What do you mean? Didn't you accept the offer?'

'No. In fact, I'm thinking of resigning as a matter of principle.'

'Why? That's absurd, Ben. Take half pay. You've put in years of hard work for that company—'

'But how about principle? You're a principled person, so I thought you'd understand. I thought you'd back me up on this. And you're an antimaterialist. So it can't be money you're worried about.'

'Are you baiting me?'

'Quite possibly.'

Marcy stayed silent for some time, then said, 'What is the principle you're going to resign for?'

'The right to be financially ruined. The right to reject money you don't work for. The right to suffer the consequences of one's actions. The right to embarrass the government. How's that for antiestablishment rhetoric? Aren't you proud of me?'

'Look ... I didn't call to fight ... and I think I understand ... but you have a family ...'

'We'll get by.'

There was a silence, then Marcy said, 'Yes, we'll get by. Do what you think is best.'

Tyson nodded to himself. He had the feeling she meant it.

Marcy said, 'What does this recall mean? Do you have to go somewhere?'

'Well, yes. I also received assignment orders.' He glanced at the separate sheet of paper. 'Could be a lot worse—'

'Where?'

'Fort Hamilton. Brooklyn. You know where that is? Near the Verrazano Bridge.'

'Yes ... well, that's good. Can you ... are you confined or anything?'

'I don't know. I just have to report by fifteen July, as they say in the backassward Army.' He thought a moment. 'Hey, when's my shark trip?' He looked at his daybook. 'The fourteenth. Good. I can do that, then report in the next day. I'll bring the shark if I get one.' He paused, then observed, 'This sucks a mop.'

She didn't reply, but he thought he heard her stifling a sob.

Tyson lit a cigarette and put his feet on the windowsill. If he were unmarried, he reflected, he'd have already quit his job and been in Hong Kong by now, a city he remembered fondly from his R and R. Everyone, including and especially the government, would be glad to see him go. But not, unfortunately, to Hong Kong, a British colony. He'd have to go, as old Chet indicated, someplace where the government could make a pretence of being unable to get him back. That is what he would do if he were not a husband and father. But he was. Still, it was enticing. He watched the rain running down the big windowpane, then said, 'What do you think of the idea of me skipping out of the country? I mean, is that an alternative to this mess?'

'It is. But your ego and your overblown sense of responsibility will keep you here.'

Tyson thought that her voice sounded stronger, more like Marcy. She always bounced back quickly. He said, 'But I'd be

153

saving you, David and the government a lot of embarrassment and trouble. They're probably praying in Washington
that I fly away and bother them no more.'

'Well, if that's true, you should work out a deal of some
sort...'

Tyson thought Marcy and Chet Brown would get along
well. 'Right. Airfare and pension. Send for the family later.
Brazil has no extradition, but I don't care for the tropics.
Maybe Sweden. They have limited extradition. I'll get a job
with Volvo. I'll talk them into putting electronic rocket-
aiming devices in the four-door model. What do you think?'

Marcy forced a light tone in her voice. 'Get yourself a big
blonde Viking. You always liked blondes.'

Tyson smiled. 'Well... let's think about it. Fight or flight? I
have a few weeks.'

Neither spoke, then Marcy said, 'How are we doing?'

Tyson was surprised to hear himself saying, 'I love you.'

She replied quickly, 'I love you, too.' She added, 'But I
think you've decided not to come home.'

Tyson didn't reply.

She said, 'I suppose you have enough on your mind
without marital problems. Right?'

Tyson didn't offer an immediate reply, then said, 'I found a
place in the city. Paul Stein's. You know him. He's going to
the Hamptons. I pay the utilities, keep the burglars away,
forward the mail, and take phone messages.'

Again, there was a long, awkward silence, then Marcy
spoke. 'Will they let you live ... what is it called—?'

'Off-post. I hope so. Beats BOQ – bachelor officer's
quarters ... My horoscope this morning said, "You will
exchange a well-paying executive position for a job as a house
sitter. New careers in the armed forces will open up for you.
You may go on a long trip at government expense, or you
may go at your own expense to a place where the government
can't find you. Your mate will be understanding if she gets a
postcard from Rio de Janeiro signed Juan."'

154

'Just keep me informed.'

Tyson swung the chair around to his desk. 'Okay. You have Stein's number. I'll be moving in this weekend.'

'Well ... watch out for those horny working girls.'

'Best to David.'

'I'll tell him.'

'Okay. Take care.'

'I will. You too.'

'Good-bye.'

'Good-bye.'

Neither hung up, and Tyson said, ' 'Bye.'

' 'Bye.'

Tyson put the receiver in the cradle and saw that his hand was shaking. 'Damn it.' He slammed his hand on his desk, and the desk items bounced. 'Damn it!' He stood and kicked the wastebasket across the room.

16

Ben Tyson stood in front of the round barbeque grill, a scotch in one hand, a spatula in the other. He looked down at the single hamburger. There was something pathetic about it, he decided, and he scooped it up with the spatula, flipping it into the bushes. He finished his scotch.

The stillness of the backyard was broken by a sudden, sharp report that quieted the birds. Somewhere out on the dark street there was a series of hollow popping sounds, and a dog began barking. A few backyards down, he could hear the sounds of recorded music and laughter. July Fourth was not his favourite holiday, but spending it alone was no treat either. Most years, if he was home, he, Marcy, and David would go to the country club. The club went to great pains to create a traditional Fourth with striped tents on the lawn, hot dogs, hamburgers, balloons, and cotton candy. People sat on the veranda and drank beer, children's games were organized, and a brass band played Sousa marches. The only thing missing, thankfully, was speeches.

He had considered joining the festivities, but decided he was not in the mood to meet the public, nor did he feel like spreading awkwardness among his neighbours. His objective for the evening was to get too drunk to consider taking the rented car out to Sag Harbor.

Tyson opened the French doors and went into the den. He poured himself another scotch and took a few books from the shelf, dropping them into a carton. He intended to drive to Manhattan in the morning and move into Paul Stein's apartment.

The phone rang, but Tyson ignored it as he went through his desk drawers trying to find his pocket calculator. The phone kept ringing. Only about a dozen people had the unlisted number, and he couldn't think of one he wanted to speak to. He found his calculator and dropped it in his briefcase. The phone continued to ring. He suddenly realized it might be David, and he picked it up.

A female voice he didn't recognize said, 'Mr Benjamin Tyson?'

Tyson said, 'Who is this?'

'This is Major Harper—'

He felt his stomach give a turn.

'I'm from the Judge Advocate General's office. I've been assigned to conduct an investigation under Article 31 of the Uniform Code of Military Justice to look into the facts surrounding certain allegations of wrongdoing at Miséricorde Hospital in the Republic—'

'Are you serious?'

'Yes, Lieutenant, I am.'

Tyson sat in his desk chair. 'How did you get my number?'

Major Harper replied, 'It was given to me in my briefing papers—'

156

'This is an unlisted number.'

'I don't see what relevance that has. I do apologize for calling on a holiday evening—'

'Where are you calling from?'

'Washington, which is also irrelevant, *Lieutenant*.'

'I don't wish to be called lieutenant.'

'Did you receive your orders recalling you to active duty?'

Tyson leaned forward and doodled on his blotter. This call was not unexpected, yet he found he wasn't quite prepared for it. A few days ago he might have been able to leave the country legally. Today, he was an officer in the United States Army, and he did not have the freedoms that most American citizens enjoyed.

Major Harper said, 'I have a registered mail receipt here—'

'Yes, I got the damned thing.'

After a silence on the phone, Major Harper said, 'I would appreciate it if you would address me with the respect that is due my rank.'

Tyson rubbed his eyes and sat back in the chair. 'Do you expect me to call you ma'am?'

'That is the correct form of address for a female officer of higher rank.'

Tyson exhaled a long breath. His head was beginning to ache, and his stomach did another turn. He put a milder tone in his voice. 'All right. I suppose I ought to be as polite as possible, ma'am.'

Her tone was immediately conciliatory. 'I'm sorry if I came on a little strong.'

'No problem. What can I do for you?'

'Well, as I said, I'm conducting this informal investigation to determine if there is any substance to certain allegations put forth in a book called *Hue: Death of a City*. I assume you're familiar with the work.'

'It certainly sounds familiar.'

She said, 'I was going to begin my investigation in other areas, then call you. But then the thought occurred to me

157

that you may want to have the opportunity to give your side first.'

'That's thoughtful.'

Major Harper continued, 'I'm supposed to advise you of your rights under Article 31 of the Uniform Code of Military Justice. You have the right to remain silent and the right to counsel. Also, I'm to advise you of any possible charge contemplated ... which is ... murder.'

Tyson did not reply.

She continued, 'You also have the right to question witnesses, but we have none at this time. As I said, I called you first. Look, as an officer you know your rights. What I want to know is if you'd like us to meet.'

Tyson considered his reply. The woman was unusually open, admitting she hadn't done any preliminary work before calling. The usual procedure in an Army investigation, he recalled, was to suggest to the suspect that there were already battalions of witnesses against him, drawers full of signed depositions, and lockers overflowing with incriminating evidence.

He saw a faint possibility that this could be quashed at this stage. It depended to a large extent, he understood, on himself and this unknown woman. To be sure, there were other factors, but the recommendation of a preliminary investigating officer not to pursue the matter might kill it. Tyson said, 'All right. Let's meet.'

She replied, 'Fine. Do you want to come to Washington?'

'Not particularly.'

'Well, I'll fly to New York. How about tomorrow?'

Tyson thought a moment, then said, 'Okay.'

'What time would be convenient?'

'What *place* are we talking about, Major?'

'Well ... several choices ... the airport, Fort Hamilton—'

'No and no.'

'Your office?'

'I don't think that would be appropriate unless you come

158

in civilian clothes.'

'Well, I could do that, but ... can we meet at your home?'

He said, 'Take the nine A.M. shuttle. Any Long Island limo should be able to find the address. You'll be here before eleven.'

'All right, about eleven A.M., your house. And I assume that since we are meeting, you will waive your right to remain silent.'

'I wouldn't ask you to come all the way to New York so I can plead the Fifth.'

'Fine ... because there is a possibility we can ... I don't mean to hold out false hope, but perhaps if we just discussed this, we could get it into perspective. This matter may end after I interview you and the other members of your platoon whom we can locate.'

'Good.'

'May I ask if you're bringing civil suit against the author of that book? You don't have to answer.'

'I'm considering it.'

'Will you have an attorney present at our interview?'

'I'm considering it.'

She didn't reply immediately, then said, 'That's your right, of course. But as an officer and an educated man, you may not need one present.' She continued, 'You could have an attorney available by phone, but there's no use escalating this. If you have an attorney, then I may have to bring a stenographer, then—'

'Then I'll need a tape recorder, and before you know it we'll have TV cameras and a house full of people. Okay, no attorney.'

'I don't mean to talk you out of anything. Under the UCMJ, you have a right—'

'I know the UCMJ. I took a refresher course at the library.'

'Fine.'

'May I ask you a question?'

'Certainly.'

159

'If I'm a lieutenant and you're a major, why am I calling some of the shots? Now, you don't have to answer that. It's your right as a lawyer to dissemble.'

There was a short silence before Major Harper replied, 'Do you feel like an officer in the United States Army?'

'Not in the least.'

'Then, rank aside, I'll be considerate of your feelings. This must be disorienting for you.'

'It was disorienting the first time I was called to active duty. This time it just plain sucks.'

Major Harper didn't reply.

Tyson said, 'I hope this is a short tour of duty.'

'So do I.'

'Do you?' He asked abruptly, 'Do you drink coffee? I hate to make a whole pot if you don't drink it.'

'Coffee would be fine.'

'I'll see you tomorrow. Have a happy Fourth.' Tyson hung up.

He sat back and breathed deeply. He thought about the disembodied voice he had just heard and tried to picture a face. The voice was pleasant, soft, almost melodic, with a touch of the Midwest. She was, he thought again, very frank. Disarmingly so. And it wasn't because she was being particularly considerate. It was her interrogation style, and he'd be wise to remember that.

Also, the reason he had been able to call the shots wasn't because of any female deference or consideration for his feelings. It was because she had been ordered to take a soft approach. The JAG Corps, the Pentagon, and perhaps even the White House were handling him gingerly. 'Good,' he said aloud. 'I like being handled gingerly by powerful people.' He had been so engrossed in his own fears that he had forgotten they were afraid too.

Tyson stood and poured himself another scotch. He surveyed the partially packed boxes around the den.

He threw open the French doors and stared out onto the

dark patio with its glowing brazier. Fireworks echoed between the houses, and rockets from the county park lit up the eastern sky. He almost looked forward to the interview, to the prospect of having his fate hinge solely on his own resources. To hell with lawyers. Here was a challenge in a life that had become devoid of important challenges.

Tyson felt a long-forgotten flutter in his stomach: It is the night before the big Auburn-Navy game, it is the hour before the dawn attack. It is, he thought, the culmination of one life and the beginning of another. He said softly, 'Not one game, not one battle ever turned out to be half as bad as the anticipation. Let's get on with it.'

17

At ten minutes to eleven, Benjamin Tyson's doorbell rang. Tyson moved to the foyer and looked at himself in the full-length mirror. He regarded the navy blue blazer of summer wool, then fluffed the red silk pocket handkerchief. The crease in the beige trousers was, as they said in the Army, razor sharp. His black loafers were polished, and the white cotton shirt accented his tan. His intent was to look prosperous, self-assured, untouchable. This was his castle, the clothing his armour.

The doorbell rang again. Tyson moved to the front door, reached out, and opened it quickly.

Subconsciously, he'd expected to see a woman in a light-coloured uniform, but she wore what the Army called Class A greens: forest green skirt, matching tunic, light green blouse, and a crisscrossed black tie. On her head, at a jaunty angle, was a green garrison cap with officer's gold piping. A black handbag was slung over her shoulder, and she carried a black leather briefcase in her left hand. She smiled pleasantly. 'Mr Tyson?'

'No. I'm Lieutenant Tyson. I guess the mufti threw you.' He extended his hand. 'The gold oak leaf tells me you're a major, and your name tag says Harper. Hello, Major Harper.'

As she took his hand she said, 'There's no need for you to wear a uniform.'

'Good.' He looked her over quickly. Her hair was honey-coloured, her eyes pale blue, and she looked well scrubbed. He pictured cornfields and church socials. Somewhere beneath the unflattering uniform dwelt a good body. He stepped aside. 'Please come in.'

She entered, removing her garrison cap. They exchanged some words about the cloudy weather, her flight, and his home.

Tyson took her cap and laid it on the foyer sideboard. He said, 'Can I take your jacket?'

She hesitated, then said, 'Yes please.' She set down her briefcase and handbag, then unbuttoned the four brass buttons of the tailored tunic and slipped it off. Tyson saw that her light green blouse was also well tailored and fit more snugly than the Army might have liked. He put her jacket in the foyer closet and turned back to her. They looked at each other for a few seconds before he said, 'This way.'

He led her through the living room into the rear den. Tyson indicated a suede armchair and she sat, remarking, 'Nice room.'

'Thank you.' He'd removed the packing boxes and any other evidence to suggest he was removing himself from his primary residence. Tyson went to the wall unit that held a small bar, on which sat an electric coffeepot. He poured two cups and said, 'Would you like some cream liqueur cognac with this? Or don't officers drink on duty in the new Army?'

'They do. But I'll wait.'

Tyson poured some Irish cream into his cup. 'Hair of the dog.' He assumed she'd noticed his bloodshot eyes, but having made the self-observation, he thought he should

162

explain it. 'Drinking with some friends. After you called. Actually, it was sort of a fund-raiser. My defence fund,' he lied. 'They have this annual July Fourth bash-up at the club – my country club – and everyone was in a patriotic mood, so they passed the hat.' Tyson realized he was not making a good job of it, but added anyway, 'I've a good deal of support in the community. I also understand that a national defence fund is forming ... if I need one.'

Karen Harper took a small printed card from her briefcase and said, 'Let me get the formalities out of the way. Your rights and all that. I should do this again in person. Okay?'

'Cream?'

'Yes, please.'

'Sugar?'

'Yes ... I'd like to read you your rights now.' She glanced at the card.

'I'm listening.' He put cream and sugar into her cup.

'All right ... you have the right to remain silent—'

'Excuse me. One lump or two?'

'Just one, please. You have the right to question any witnesses. You have the right to be represented by Army counsel.' She continued reading from the card as Tyson placed a cup of coffee on the table in front of her.

Tyson considered sitting at his desk, then decided against it. He took the Eames recliner opposite her, across the coffee table, and put his cup down. He watched her as she read the short list of rights. He'd read that list to suspects at least fifty times, and each time he could feel the awkwardness, the tension, that hung in the air between him and the soldier standing before him.

Karen Harper looked up from the card. 'Do you understand your rights under the Uniform Code of Military Justice?'

'Yes, ma'am.'

'Do you wish to be represented by Army counsel?'

'No, ma'am.'

'Do you wish to have your own attorney present at this time?'

'He's playing golf.'

She looked at him and waited.

Tyson said, 'As I indicated on the telephone, I do not.'

She nodded perfunctorily, then continued, 'I'm to advise you òf the offences charged against you. As yet, there are none. But obviously what we are contemplating is murder.'

Tyson did not respond.

She went on. 'As I said, there are no witnesses as yet, but you will have the right to cross-examine them if there is a formal investigation. You have the right, at this time, to suggest witnesses who may provide you with statements of defence, extenuation, or mitigation. Do you have any such witnesses?'

'No, ma'am.'

'You have the right to make a statement. Do you wish to do so?'

'No, ma'am.'

There was a long silence, then Tyson said, 'I wish to answer questions. Shoot.'

She glanced at her notes. 'All right ... Have you read the book *Hue: Death of a City*?'

'Yes, ma'am.'

'You can drop that. Are you the Lieutenant Benjamin Tyson mentioned in the book?'

'It would appear so.'

'Were you in command of the platoon described in chapter six of said book?'

'Yes, I was.'

'Were there any higher-ranking officers present?'

'No. I was operating independently of my company and battalion.'

'Did you have radio contact with your chain of command?'

'Sporadically. The radio batteries were weak. Resupply was a problem at that time.'

She nodded, then asked several more questions. Tyson knew she was just getting him into the habit of answering questions, avoiding anything too close to the central issue of mass murder. *She's good,* he thought. But he himself had done this before, and it was coming back to him.

Tyson decided to interrupt her stream of questions. He stood and poured more coffee for both of them. 'Let's take a break.'

She smiled, as though this was a good idea, but Tyson knew otherwise. He said, 'Cigarette?'

'No, thank you.'

'Do you mind if I do?'

'Not at all.'

Tyson leaned back on the edge of his desk as he drew on his cigarette. He looked at Major Karen Harper. She must be, he thought, a bit anxious despite her calm exterior. She had a 180-pound fish on the line and he could break it anytime he wished.

She began to speak conversationally, as if this was not part of the interview, though Tyson knew it was. She said, 'I found something interesting in your personnel file – that note you wrote on the Army questionnaire. Do you remember that?'

He let a few seconds pass, then replied, 'Oh ... that ... I must have been in a mood that day.'

'I suppose. It was a rather strong note for an officer to have placed in his permanent file.'

'I wasn't an officer.'

'But you were. You are. You have always been, since the day you took the oath of office after college.'

'Would it have made a difference if I had checked the damned box requesting that I be dropped from the rolls?'

'I don't know. That's not my department. I was only interested in what prompted you to write that.'

'Do you have any recollection of the war? Of the fall of Saigon? I mean, you look very young.'

'I was about fifteen during the 1968 Tet Offensive—'

'Fifteen? Christ, I wish I had been fifteen. By the way, Tet was a time, not a place. Do you know that?'

'Of course I do. Anyway, I was twenty-two when Saigon fell in 1975. I recall thinking at the time that the war had gone on ever since I could remember. I was relieved it was over.'

'My wife was too. She proposed a toast to the National Liberation Front.'

She said, 'I think one of the reasons they picked me to conduct this investigation is my lack of involvement in the events in question.'

'Perhaps.' She exhibited, he thought, an ingenuousness beneath which was a certain cunning. Or maybe, he conceded, she really was simple and naive. He found himself studying her more closely. Neither the cut nor the colour of the Army uniform did anything for her, but her face, her hair, her voice, and her movements more than compensated for that. Her mouth, he noticed, was expressive and capable, he guessed, of sensuousness in other situations. He said, 'What are some of the other reasons they picked you? I mean, why *you*?'

She shrugged.

'Probably your experience in murder investigations.'

'I've never investigated a murder before.'

'I've never been suspected of a murder before. Small world.'

She picked up the bottle of cream liqueur from the coffee table. 'Do you mind?' She poured some in her coffee. 'Anyway, in regard to the note and the questionnaire, I was wondering if you were planning to challenge your recall to active duty.'

'Look, Major, once the government decides to start grinding you up, there's not much you can do unless you have unlimited resources.'

She leaned towards him, across the coffee table. 'You shouldn't feel as though you're being railroaded. If you think the recall was illegal, I suggest you find the resources, financial and otherwise, to fight it ... That's your first line of defence, as the infantry would put it.'

Tyson didn't reply.

They sat in silence for some time, then Tyson stood and walked to the bookcase, opened a drawer, and retrieved a cedar box. He spilled the contents out on the coffee table.

They both looked at the array of medals and ribbons, including the Purple Heart, the Combat Infantryman's Badge, the Air Assault Medal, and the Vietnamese Cross of Gallantry. Tyson picked up the brass cross by its yellow and orange ribbon and dangled it. 'This is a Vietnamese decoration. It was given to me at an awards ceremony in the ruins of the Citadel at Hue, on a blistering hot afternoon after the city was retaken. I'll never forget the little Viet colonel who gave out the medals. He was badly burned, smelled of fish, synthetic Japanese scotch, sweat, and putrid flesh. When he embraced and kissed me, I thought I was going to vomit.' Tyson stared at the medal. 'But he was a hell of a soldier. I'm sure he didn't survive the war. Neither did his government. So here I hold a useless medal from a defunct government.' He let it fall on the table. 'Does it count for anything?'

She nodded. 'Of course. A court-martial – if there is one – will take that sort of thing into consideration. Do you have the paperwork for that?'

'I seem to have misplaced it. But I remember that the commendation cites me for bravery ... for actions that took place on 15 February 1968, in and around the village of An Ninh Ha. The English is bad, and the language is general, but it may be that the Army will find it difficult to prosecute me for murders that allegedly took place at a battle for which I was decorated. What do you think?'

'Try to find the written orders.'

'There was no copy in my file?'

'No, and I don't think the present government in Saigon – or Ho Chi Minh City – will be helpful.'

'I was also supposed to receive a Silver Star for the same

action. The Viets usually read the lists of proposed American awards and matched their version of the medal with the American one. That's how I got the Viet Cross. But I never got the Silver Star.'

'Why not?'

He shrugged. 'I saw the recommendation made by my company commander, Browder, now dead. But it was probably misplaced. That was fairly common at the time.'

'Perhaps it was turned down.'

'Perhaps, but I don't think so.'

'Captain Browder, I assume, wrote up the recommendation based on verbal reports from your men. Browder, you indicated, was not at the hospital.'

'That's correct. Standard practice.'

'Which of your men made the recommendation?'

'Kelly, my radio operator, put me in for the star. Someone else would have had to corroborate Kelly's report of my valour. I don't remember who that was though. Not many of my platoon survived anyway. Did you locate any of them?'

'Yes.'

'How many? Who?'

'I'll send you or your attorney a list of names and addresses ... if necessary. You may not have to go to the time and trouble. And perhaps neither will I. We may just drop it.' She pulled her pad toward her. 'I'll make a note to check on the Silver Star.'

'You're being very helpful, Major.'

She said, 'Again, let me make it clear that I'm working for the prosecution. I'm here to gather facts.'

'Yes. I remember how it's supposed to work.'

She stared at the ribbons and medals lying on the coffee table. Tyson studied her face. She looked impressed, even a bit unhappy that it had come to this. *It's an act, of course*, he thought. He's acting, she's acting. *Souvenirs de guerre*, like mementos of the departed, called for a minute of respectful silence. Of course, he thought, both she and the Army would be highly sceptical of any medal proposed or awarded to him on 15 February 1968. But to suggest this aloud would be akin to sacrilege.

She said, 'I read the citations for the two Purple Hearts. I can see – I hope this doesn't make you uncomfortable – I can see the wound on your right ear.'

Tyson let the silence drag out, milking it for what it was worth, then replied, 'Yes, a village called Phu Lai, on the first day of the Tet Offensive. I lost nearly half my platoon that day. That bullet had my name on it, but ... an angel was sitting on my shoulder ... and pushed my head an inch to the left.'

She nodded. He went on, 'Then, as you probably read, I was wounded by shrapnel in the right knee. That was on February 29th – 1968 was a leap year. The battle of Hue was declared officially over on February 26th, but somebody forgot to tell Chuck.' Again she nodded.

Tyson decided to break the gloomy pall. He grinned suddenly. 'Do you want to see my knee wound?'

She smiled quickly in return. 'Not right now.' She added, 'Great line, though.'

'It used to work like a charm.' Tyson held his smile, but his mind returned to that extra day in February. The hot shrapnel had sliced in from the left side, and he'd fallen to the ground. When he looked down, not knowing what to expect, he saw his fatigues covered with blood. He'd ripped open the light cotton material, and there was a large piece of meat – fat, flesh, ligaments – flapped over, exposing his patella. He recalled staring at the bare bone incredulously. He'd never seen such a thing. And if there had been any lingering doubts concerning his mortality, they were dispelled then as he gaped at the stuff he was made of.

Tyson sat back down in his chair. 'Do you want to continue?'

Karen Harper leaned forward. She asked a few more warm-up questions, then, without any change in tone or expression, said, 'Can you describe for me, in your own words, the events of that day, 15 February 1968?'

Tyson regarded her closely. 'If I gave you a general account of what happened, I wouldn't want to be held to any of the details.'

She put aside her pencil and paper. 'I'm barely making notes, as you can see, and in any case this is not sworn testimony.'

'And do I have your word as an officer that you have no recording devices with you?'

She sat back and crossed her legs. 'Yes, you do.'

Tyson took a few moments to collect his thoughts, then began. 'We were dug into a defensive perimeter around a small clump of trees about five kilometres west of Hue. We had taken mortar and small-arms fire during the night and suffered two wounded. I had the wounded medavaced out at first light. It was rainy and chilly. It gets cold in February in the northern provinces. Anyway, we pulled out of the perimeter and began advancing on Hue, as per radio orders.'

There was a rushing sound on the radio speaker, then a crackling, followed by Captain Browder's voice. 'Mustang One-Six, this is Mustang Six. How do you hear me? Over.'

Tyson took the handphone from Daniel Kelly, his radiotelephone operator, and squeezed the handle lever. 'Six, this is One-Six. Weak but clear. How me?'

'Same. Orders from Big Six. Proceed in a Sierra-Echo direction toward Hotel Uniform Echo.'

Tyson replied into the mouthpiece, 'Solid copy. Anything specific?'

'Negative. Use your own judgement. Don't make the city today. We'll rendezvous tonight and advance on the west wall together.'

'Roger ... Maybe we should link up now. I'm down to one-niner folks, and there're signs that Chuck is all over the damned place. In strength. Saw hoofprints last night before sundown. Estimate five hundred or more. Heading toward the city.'

'Roger that, One-Six. Orders is orders. Everybody's spread thin, kiddo. Hey, are we having fun yet?'

Tyson glanced at Kelly, who had his hand around the radio aerial and was stroking it, which was Kelly's way of suggesting that the brass was jerking everyone off again. Tyson drew a deep breath and spoke into the radiophone. 'Let me know how my two wounded make out.'

'Roger,' Browder hesitated, then said, 'Keep to the open paddies. Avoid the bush and avoid the hamlets.'

Tyson didn't think that was consistent with search and destroy, or harassment and interdiction. It sounded more like avoid and evade. He wondered if the Army Security Agency or any brass was monitoring. Tyson cautioned, 'Big brother, big ears.'

'Fuck them,' snapped Browder, who was obviously on edge himself. 'Anything further?'

'I need C's. And I don't have a map beyond An Ninh Ha.'

'Ask at the next Chevron station. I'll get C's dropped in. I'll see about the map. Further?'

Tyson thought he should report that everyone had trench foot, fatigues were torn, boots and laces were falling apart, and the halogen-treated water they were drinking was making them all sick. But Browder knew that. Tyson said, 'Negative further.'

'Roger. Keep up the splendid work. Out.'

Tyson handed the phone back to Kelly. 'Let's move it. Order of march: one, B, three, A, then two.'

Kelly's voice boomed out over the perimeter. 'Saddle up! Movin'! Movin'! First squad on point.'

Tyson walked out of the entrenched positions to a wide dike and moved down it, surveying the terrain around him. Kelly came up beside him, joined by Specialist Four Steven Brandt, the platoon medic, who set his medical bag

171

down in the mud.

Tyson watched the men move at intervals out of the copse of willow trees and onto the dike toward him. First rifle squad consisted of five men out of the original ten, all pfc's. Normally led by a staff sergeant, the squad was now led by Bob Moody, a nineteen-year-old black kid who had been chosen by Tyson because he'd been in the country a month longer than the other four. He was also the only one who wanted the job.

Behind first squad was team B, one of the two M-60 machine-gun teams, consisting of a gunner, assistant gunner, and an ammo bearer.

Third rifle squad followed: three men, led by Pfc Larry Cane. Bringing up the rear was machine-gun team A and the squad leader of the two teams, Paul Sadowski, a twenty-year-old who had been a sergeant for five days.

Even as the platoon contracted, Tyson kept his machine-gun squad up to strength by assigning riflemen to the two teams. Conventional wisdom had it that the life expectancy of machine gunners in battle was shorter than that of officers and radio operators. And Tyson believed it. At Phu Lai, every one of the original fourth squad was killed or wounded. Men were understandably reluctant to be assigned to the machine-gun squad but were perversely proud when they were; only the best, the brightest, and the strongest men could be trusted with this gruelling and crucial job. The guns had to be manned and fed, and when a gunner was hit, someone else took his place, just as someone always picked up the fallen colours in the old cavalry regiments.

Personnel management, Tyson thought. *Just like they taught us in Personnel Management 401 at Auburn. Though it was a little more complex here.*

Tyson watched the last man come out of the copse of willows. Pfc Hernando Beltran, a hefty Cuban-American and the sole survivor of second squad. Beltran claimed he was now the second-squad leader and refused to be assigned to either of the remaining rifle squads or the machine-gun squad. Tyson could see his point and allowed Beltran to command his phantom squad, always in the rear guard.

Beltran carried a Browning automatic shotgun and slung an M-79 grenade launcher over his shoulder. He wore a Colt revolver, and judging from its ebony handles and chrome finish, Tyson doubted that it was standard Army issue. Probably West Miami standard, however. Also smuggled in from the States was Beltran's machete, made of gleaming surgical steel and with an ivory handle. Beltran said it had belonged to his late father, who had owned a sugar plantation in pre-Castro Cuba. Beltran also claimed that Nuestra Sěnora del Cobre had appeared to him one night in boot camp and instructed him to kill one hundred communists to avenge his family's misfortunes. Tyson was somewhat sceptical of this but saw no good reason to disabuse Pfc Beltran of this useful notion.

Tyson's platoon command group, usually five men, consisted of himself, Brandt, and Kelly. His second radio operator, Johanson, had been killed at Phu Lai, and the platoon sergeant, Fairchild, was in Japan by now, contemplating the flat bed sheets where his legs should have been. Losing Fairchild, Tyson thought, had been particularly unfortunate. Fairchild had been the only regular Army man among them. At thirty-eight years of age, he had been a stabilizing influence, a father figure to the teenaged platoon. This war, Tyson thought, had become a children's war. And children, as any school-teacher would tell you, were capable of astonishing acts of brutality if left unsupervised.

Tyson moved to the edge of the dike and watched the procession of men coming toward him. As each man passed by, Tyson laid a hand on him and said something. 'How's the jungle rot today, Walker?' 'Stand a little closer

173

to the razor next time, Scorello.' 'How short, Peterson? Eighteen days? Hang in there. I'll get you out of the field in a day or two.'

Brandt handed out malaria pills, and Tyson watched as each man dutifully placed his pill in his mouth. A few paces away, about half of them spat their pills out. In a choice between malaria and what had come to look like certain death or injury in combat, malaria seemed to be the preferred choice of half.

Tyson looked into each man's eyes as he passed and saw that too many of them had developed the Thousand Yard Stare.

But perhaps today or tomorrow would be the day Alpha Company rotated to the rear: rest, recreation, refitting and replacements. Not to mention a little debauchery, if the Quang Tri brothels had survived the enemy 'cleansing' programme. Tyson turned to his radio operator. 'Well, Kelly?'

Kelly nodded in understanding. He said softly to Tyson, 'I give them one or two more days, if things go right – no more mine fields, no snipers, no booby traps, and damn sure no more Phu Lais. A break in this shit weather would help.'

Tyson lit a cigarette and blew the smoke into the grey, rain-sodden air. Kelly, like most radio operators, was a notch above the average grunt. Officers picked their RTOs for their ability to think fast and talk quickly on the radio. RTOs observed their officers at close quarters, and ostensibly some leadership ability rubbed off. In fact, Tyson thought Kelly to be officer material.

Inevitably, Kelly had become almost a friend, though the Army frowned on officers fraternizing with enlisted men. This quaint custom extended into combat, and due to the fact that Alpha Company had only two officers left of the six authorized – Browder and himself – Tyson's circle of potential friends was limited to Browder. It was,

174

Tyson reflected, lonely at the top.

Kelly added, 'I don't think anyone is real anxious to reach Hue.'

Tyson considered a moment, then said, 'There are a lot of Marines there waiting for the cavalry to arrive.'

Kelly shrugged. 'This bunch won't do them a lot of good.' Kelly added, 'Besides, the Marines got themselves into that shit, they can get themselves out.'

Tyson threw down his soggy cigarette and glanced at Kelly, wondering how much more Kelly knew of the men's state of mind than he did.

'Orders is orders.'

Kelly snapped, 'Come on, Lieutenant.' Kelly hesitated, then said softly, 'I don't trust them anymore.'

'Who? The brass?'

Kelly snorted. 'I haven't trusted those assholes since I set foot in the country. No, I mean *them*.' He cocked his head toward the straggling platoon.

Tyson nodded. He had stopped trusting them a week before, when Fairchild stepped on a land mine. The thought occurred to Tyson, as it had undoubtedly occurred to his men, that Lieutenant Tyson was the last vestige of military authority in the platoon; that if he were removed from the picture, things might, in some dimly perceived way, get better.

But there was, he hoped, a lot of emotional territory between wishing for the elimination of an officer and actually eliminating him. For the most part he was trusted and respected. Even the Phu Lai debacle hadn't hurt his standing with the platoon; he got them into the mess, but he'd also got them out.

Kelly, who seemed to be reading his mind, observed, 'You're the only one in this platoon who knows how to read a map or call in artillery.'

Tyson didn't reply.

'If you weren't here, the colonel would have to let us join

up with the company. Or better yet, with Browder as the only officer left, he'd order us all to stand down.'

'They'd send some rear echelon lieutenant out to take over.'

'*He* wouldn't last long.'

Tyson nodded to himself. No, *he would not last long*. Tyson watched the last man, Beltran, move past him. At ten-metre intervals, the line of troops stretched nearly a quarter kilometre along the muddy, rain-splashed dike. Tyson scratched at a leech bite on his forearm and contemplated the watery blood running over his pallid skin. 'Damn it.'

Brandt looked at the arm. 'Still got teeth in there, Lieutenant. It's getting infected.'

Tyson squeezed the raised red circle and felt the sharp microscopic teeth in his flesh. The leech had joined him sometime in the night, and by the time he'd awoken, it had engorged itself into a grey, pulsating tumescence the size of a fountain pen. Leeches injected an anticoagulant into the blood, and Tyson knew it would be hours before the holes clotted.

The leech, he thought, was probably the sole remaining object of disgust among the hardened veterans who had grown accustomed to the repulsive flora and fauna of Southeast Asia, who picked lice out of one another's hair, and who found poisonous snakes in their sleeping bags on cold nights. The blood-sucking leech was metaphor; it was Vietnam sucking them dry.

Brandt splashed iodine on the bite. 'I'll give you a needle later so you can dig the teeth out. You shouldn't have squashed him. Heat their ass with a cigarette. They'll back off.'

'I know that.' But Tyson had smashed the obscene thing with his fist and had no regrets about it. He said, 'Let's go.' Tyson, Brandt, and Kelly moved quickly up the column to take their positions in the middle of the formation. Tyson turned to Brandt, who walked bent under the weight of his medical bag, the rain dripping from his camouflage net. Tyson asked, 'Did anyone come to you this morning?'

Brandt raised his head, and Tyson was struck by the colour of his flesh. Tyson had seen unhealthy skin that was chalky, mottled, yellow, greyish. But Brandt's face was actually deep grey, the colour of clay. Tyson suspected that the man had been eating some sort of nitrate substance – probably the propellant envelopes from a mortar round – to feign illness but had overdone it. *Bastard*. 'Any sick calls, Brandt?'

Brandt replied tonelessly, 'Only Scorello. Said his nerves were shot.'

Tyson replied, 'I told you to send those to me.'

Brandt shrugged.

Tyson regarded his medic as they walked. Brandt, the only other college graduate in the platoon, had been a premed student at Bucknell. Having failed to get quickly accepted into medical school, Brandt belatedly declared himself a conscientious objector and was drafted directly into the Medical Corps. Tyson said to him, 'Next time you eat an explosive, Doc, do me a favour and swallow a lit match.'

'What are you talking about?' Brandt turned his head away as he walked.

Tyson recalled that Brandt had been in the country about seven months. Many COs began refusing to carry a weapon, but within a month accepted a pistol for self-defence. Sometime later, depending on the depth of their belief and how frequently they brushed shoulders with death, they graduated to an M-16 automatic rifle. Some began requisitioning hand grenades and other nonpacifist ordnance. Brandt, on the other hand, had come to the field fully armed. Tyson made no moral judgement on that account. But, he had come to judge Brandt in other ways, and Spec/4 Steven Brandt was found wanting. Tyson

177

asked, 'No one had any physical complaints?'

Brandt shook his head.

Tyson reflected on this. There certainly wasn't a man in the platoon who was physically well. He didn't have to be a medic to hear the hacking coughs or see the effects of dysentry, fever, and vomiting. Blood and water blisters oozed into rotting boots, and there was barely a man who walked right. Yet no one had tried to go on sick call for at least a week. There was some message there, and Tyson thought it was this: The survivors of First Platoon, Alpha Company, were beyond pain; and that frightened him.

Tyson, Brandt and Kelly reached a point in mid-column and fell into file. Kelly remarked to Brandt, 'Someday, Doc, when you're sitting in your consulting office listening to some fat executive complain about his haemorrhoids, remember that you did something good here. Don't bug out on this platoon, Doc, or you'll never have that memory.'

Brandt's eyes met Kelly's. Brandt said, 'Fuck off.'

Tyson opened a cellophane packet of stateside Nabisco cream-filled sugar wafers that his sister had sent him and passed it to Kelly, then to Brandt. Tyson took one himself and put it in his mouth, letting it dissolve slowly like a Communion wafer, his mouth salivating in response to the aromatic essence of vanilla and the richness of the cream and sugar. *Bless you, Laurie*, he thought. *Bless you for the sugar wafers. When I get home I'm going to buy you ten boxes of sugar wafers.*

They trekked on slowly through the dead and quiet countryside. After an hour, Tyson pulled his plastic-coated map from his pouch pocket and opened it. He studied the map as he walked, glancing at the terrain features around him. He reckoned he was about equidistant between Highway One to the northwest and the Perfume River to the south. Hue was about three kilometres to the east, off the map. In fact, whenever the rain lightened and the wind blew from the South China Sea, he could hear the far-off rumble of war.

Intellectually, Tyson was fascinated by the chaos. He understood that he was a direct participant in an historic event. The national life of twenty million people had almost ceased to exist. The country's social fabric and institutions were in shreds, and its army was near collapse. Hunger and disease stalked the cities and villages. From his small perspective, and from radio and written briefings, Tyson knew that the situation was serious. And if Alpha Company was a microcosm of the American fighting formations in the field, then the Green Machine was barely holding together.

Kelly's radio crackled, and the voice of the point squad leader, Moody, came over the speaker. 'Hey, there's a bunch of gooks, about two o'clock, two hundred metres.'

Kelly handed Tyson the radiophone. Tyson looked out across the rain-splattered rice fields. He spoke into the phone. 'Roger. See them. Hold it up. I'll take a look. Cover me.'

The platoon came to a gradual halt, and the men knelt in the mud of the wide dike, facing alternately left and right for security. The two machine guns were set up facing the group of unknown Vietnamese who stood on a small bare knoll.

Tyson motioned to two riflemen, Farley and Simcox. 'Let's take a walk.'

Tyson, Kelly, and the two men moved further up the main dike, then turned right, onto a smaller dike, and headed out across the exposed paddies. Tyson drew a pair of field glasses from a plastic case and adjusted the focus. The people appeared to be civilians. 'ICs or good actors.'

Simcox remarked, 'Yeah. I haven't seen a real innocent civilian since I left San Francisco.'

They turned again onto a still smaller dike that was knee-deep in water and sloshed forward, toward the

Vietnamese. Tyson could see that the people were standing on a burial mound. In fact, they appeared to be burying bodies. He counted ten Vietnamese on the mound: five old men, one young boy, and four females, consisting of two women and two teenage girls. Typical of what was left in the villages. They appeared to be peasants, all dressed in black pyjamas and conical straw hats. Normally, there would be some mixture of Western clothing, but since Tet, the peasantry had reverted to traditional garb, undoubtedly, Tyson thought, to curry favour with the ascendant power. If the communist offensive failed, the peasants would be back in jeans and Hawaiian shirts. Being a peasant was tough.

A few of the Vietnamese glanced at the approaching Americans, but otherwise they went about their unhappy business. Kelly remarked, 'I can smell the stiffs from here.'

Tyson came within twenty metres of the earth mound that rose from the grey water. He called out, '*Dung cu don!*' The Vietnamese stopped moving and faced him. They seemed to know the drill because they separated so he could see them all and kept their hands to their front. The boy and a young woman dropped their shovels.

Tyson, with Kelly beside him, walked out of the water onto the mound. Farley and Simcox covered. Tyson stood directly in front of the group; then looked down at the bodies. He counted eight of them, wrapped in good, white cotton bed sheets, which made him think the bodies had come from Hue. One of the shrouded corpses was a small child. Tyson surveyed the burial detail and met their eyes, one at a time. He said, 'ID – *cho toi xem gian can cuoc*. ID.' The six males and four females produced plastic ID cards from their pyjamas. Tyson inspected them perfunctorily, then following protocol, addressed the oldest male, a bald, age-spotted man with a wispy, grey beard. '*Ong lam gi o day?*'

The old man looked at the young boy, who replied in

English, 'We bury mama-san, papa-san. VC kill beaucoup – VC very bad, VC number fucking ten—'

'Okay, cut the bullshit.' Tyson looked at the freshly opened holes and counted six finished graves and two more started. The Vietnamese had a strong prohibition against mass graves, and the holes must have taken hours to dig with the two shovels. Each body, he knew, had been wrapped first in black cloth, then in white. Grains of rice had been placed in the mouth. In the end, he thought, even a dying civilization tries to inter its dead properly.

Tyson could not imagine anything more depressing than this grey tableau of frightened villagers burying their families in the cold winter rain. He spoke again to the old man. '*Ong o dau den?*'

Again the boy answered. 'We from An Ninh Ha. Beaucoup VC come. Kill papa-san, mama-san, baby-san—'

'Okay, ace, cool it.' Tyson looked at his map and located An Ninh Ha. 'Which way is your village? *Con bao xa nua den lang?*'

The boy pointed to a mist-shrouded tree line in the far distance. Tyson estimated it at about a kilometre. He took a bearing with his compass, then looked at his map again and said to Kelly, 'According to the map, there's a hospital there.'

Kelly glanced at Tyson's map. 'Don't count on it.'

Tyson looked again at the white bed sheets and turned to the boy. '*Nha Thuong – hôpital?*'

The boy nodded vigorously. 'Beaucoup VC in *Nha Thuong.*'

Tyson's eyes met Kelly's, and Kelly observed, 'Good place to avoid.'

Tyson replied, 'The mission, Kelly. The mission of the infantry is to—'

'Make contact with and destroy the enemy. Fuck it, Lieutenant.'

Kelly cocked his head toward the two riflemen at the edge of the mound and said quietly, 'No one has to know about the beaucoup fucking VC. No one gives a shit.'

Tyson spoke to the boy again. 'VC in *Nha Thuong*? *Bac si* in *Nha Thuong*?'

The boy nodded again. '*Français. Français. Catholique. Catholique.*'

Tyson looked again at Kelly.

Kelly's expression conveyed that he could not have cared less if the pope were in the hospital. He suddenly turned and knelt beside one of the bodies. Blood had seeped through the white sheet, and Kelly stared at the red, rain-soaked blotch. 'Stinks.' He grasped the shoulder of the corpse and shook the body. 'Big sucker.' Kelly drew his Marine K-bar knife, and made a slice through the white sheet from forehead to chest. The Vietnamese began wailing. Kelly ripped open the double shroud and exposed the blue-white features of a young man, the slice from Kelly's knife bisecting his bloodless face. Kelly ripped further and exposed the khaki tunic of a North Vietnamese soldier.

The wailing stopped, and a tense silence hung over the burial mound. Kelly stood slowly and looked grimly at the group of Vietnamese. He said to Tyson, 'These bastards are burying enemy dead.'

Tyson thought he didn't give a damn. He said, 'Forget it.'

'Like hell.' Kelly levelled his rifle, and the Vietnamese immediately huddled together, clutching at one another. Kelly shouted, 'You die!'

One of the young women fell to her knees and began crying, 'No! No kill me!'

Tyson snapped, 'Knock it off, Kelly!'

Kelly lowered his rifle. 'Fucking gooks.'

Tyson turned and motioned to Farley and Simcox.

The two men climbed onto the mound. Tyson said, 'Cut

the wrappings open.'

The men hesitated, then drew their knives.

Kelly was staring at the two shovels. He said to Tyson, 'Look at this shit. A GI entrenching tool.' He picked it up and swung it at the boy, who ducked. Kelly shouted, 'Where did you get this, cocksucker? *O dau?*'

The boy was trembling, but like survivors everywhere, thought Tyson, not only could he speak the lingua franca of the occupying army and not only could he duck quickly, but he probably had a good answer for life-threatening questions. The boy cried out, 'Buy from GI! Black market. Buy. Eight hundred piaster.'

'You're full of shit,' said Kelly.

Simcox called out, 'Two more NVA.'

Tyson said, 'Throw them in the water.' He looked at the Vietnamese. 'No bury.' He made a cutting motion across his neck. 'Savvy? You *biet?*'

They all nodded in unison, affecting contrite expressions. '*Biet! Biet!*'

Tyson heard a splash and turned. The first enemy soldier floated face-down in the paddy. Farley and Simcox threw the second and third in after him. The floodwaters carried the corpses east, down toward the coastal plains, toward Hue, where they had begun their funeral journey. As he watched, a wake appeared at a right angle to one of the bodies, and Tyson saw a water rat scurry on top of one of the corpses. The rat probed at the winding sheets with its long grey muzzle. Tyson turned away.

Farley said, 'I hope those three fucks were at Phu Lai.'

Simcox nodded and looked thoughtfully at the civilians. He said tonelessly, 'Let's waste them.'

'At ease, Simcox.' Tyson was feeling petty. Even if they had been at Phu Lai, the three men had been soldiers and deserved a decent burial. But in the field, in the absence of a functioning judicial system, Tyson felt obliged to administer summary justice to the living and the dead. He was wondering what to do with the Vietnamese when Kelly called out, 'We ought to search this crew.'

Tyson shrugged. 'I suppose.'

Kelly barked an order in Vietnamese, and the villagers, hesitantly at first, then more quickly, as Kelly levelled his M-16, began to undress.

They stood there, naked in the cold rain, the five old men, the boy, the two older women, and the two young women, their silk pyjamas and conical hats lying in the mud. Kelly, Farley, and Simcox walked around them, kicking at their black pyjamas, trampling their laboriously woven straw hats into the mire.

Tyson turned away and lit a cigarette. The radio crackled, and Larry Cane's voice came over the speaker. 'One-Six, this is One-Three. What are you guys up to over there?'

Tyson took the radiophone from Kelly and looked out across the inundated checkerboard of rice fields, to the north where his platoon was strung out along the high dike. 'One-Six here. Saddle up and move out. Head toward that tree line at four-five degrees. Try to stay on the dry dikes. We'll intersect with you. Out.' He handed the phone back to Kelly, then stared at the miserable villagers standing over the open graves, naked and shivering in the winter rain. He remarked softly, 'My God, Kelly, we're Nazis.'

Kelly nodded in agreement, 'We're shits, Lieutenant. I mean to tell you, we are *shits*.'

Farley said, apropos of nothing, 'Fucking gooks.'

Simcox concurred, 'Cocksuckers.' He glowered at the pathetic wretches who had instinctively huddled closer to one another for warmth, despite their obvious embarrassment. Tyson noticed that the women were shielded by the old men. The boy was in the forefront, ready to do some fast negotiating if he smelled a massacre, Tyson thought.

Farley shouted, 'You're all fucking VC! VC!'

This standard accusation brought forth the standard exclamations of protest and shaking of heads. 'No! No! No VC! No VC!'

Tyson felt that if he turned his back, Farley, Simcox, and perhaps even Kelly would mow these people down with no more regard than they had for slashing a machete through a troublesome vine. And the incredible thing, he thought, was that Farley attended the company Bible study group, and Simcox was always giving little GI luxuries like soap and ballpoint pens to village school-teachers. Kelly had a good rapport with village elders and old mama-sans. But that was last month and the month before. That was when the sun was shining, before the green-grey body bags began filling with Alpha Company.

Today, Tyson understood, the war completely possessed their minds, had insinuated itself deeply into their hearts, and had sickened their souls. To say that war brutalized men was like saying that famine made people hungry.

Tyson felt suddenly old, tired, and demoralized. Surely, he thought, there was a spark of decency left in them. He said softly, with no expression on his face, 'Make them lie in the graves and shoot them.'

Kelly looked at him quickly. Farley's eyes widened, Simcox lowered his rifle. No one spoke, no one moved. A full minute passed, then Tyson snapped, 'Okay, heroes, confiscate the shovels. They can bury their dead with their hands.'

Farley picked up the Army entrenching tool, and Simcox, the long-handled gravedigger's shovel. Kelly motioned to the Vietnamese to get dressed, then said, 'Chao ong. So long, suckers. Look me up when you get to the States.'

Farley laughed.

Simcox kicked a clod of mud that splattered on the boy's groin.

The four soldiers moved down the opposite side of the

185

burial mound, and Tyson took the lead along a narrow, bush-choked dike. He saw the main body of his platoon moving onto a submerged path in order to intersect with them.

Kelly walked directly behind Tyson. He said softly so the other two couldn't hear, 'Are you going to that hospital?'

Tyson replied without turning, 'Maybe.'

'Don't push it, Lieutenant.'

'Don't push *me*, Kelly. In fact, shut the fuck up.'

They walked in silence awhile, then Kelly said, 'Hey, I'm looking out for your ass.'

'Look out for your own ass.'

'I'm doing that too. What would I do if you got greased? I'd be a rifleman again.' Kelly affected a laugh.

Tyson bent his head forward and lit a soggy cigarette with his Zippo lighter. He looked at the stainless-steel lighter, given to him at Christmas by his platoon. One side of it had the First Cavalry shoulder patch engraved on it. Etched on the other side was a ribald version of the Twenty-third Psalm: *Yea, though I walk through the valley of the shadow of death, I fear no evil, for I am the meanest motherfucker in the valley.*

Tyson dropped the lighter in his pocket and passed the cigarette to Kelly. Tyson said, 'We'll give it a peek. I'm curious. If it looks dicey, we'll bypass it or call artillery on it. If it looks okay, maybe we can set up there awhile. They might have showers, hot chow, toilet bowls, and who the hell knows what else. Hot and cold running French nurses.'

Kelly laughed. 'Okay. We'll take a peek. I'm not real anxious to get to Hue anyhow.'

'You said that.'

'And I'll say it again tomorrow.'

The four men intersected the other fifteen troops of the platoon at a place where two dikes crossed.

186

Moody said to Tyson, 'What the hell was going on there, Lieutenant?'

'Burial detail. Local gooks planting some NVA. We took their shovels way. Mission accomplished.' Tyson said to Kelly, 'Report to Browder later; three confirmed NVA bodies. Okay, let's move.'

The platoon began moving along the straight dike that pointed toward An Ninh Ha. Simcox called to Tyson as they walked, 'Where are we heading now, Lieutenant?'

'Hue, sonny. Hue.'

'Fuck Hue.'

'Fuck Hue,' agreed Tyson. He added, 'There's a little Frenchy café on Tihn Tam Street with half-breed honeys, Simcox. They serve Martell brandy and croissants.'

'Not anymore, they don't. What's a ...? A what?'

'A croissant. That's French for a blow job under the table. It comes with the brandy.'

'No shit?'

'No shit.' After a minute he said to Brandt, Simcox, and a few others within earshot, 'Intermediate objective: a hospital about two clicks from the Citadel's west wall. Pass that on.'

The platoon trekked slowly east through the rain and mud. The distant tree line loomed larger, and the muted sounds of explosions grew more distinct. *Hue*, Tyson thought. Hue sounded like a meat grinder. What other species of living thing on God's earth would go willingly or unwillingly into a meat grinder? There was a lesson to be learned here, he reflected, but he was damned if he knew what it was.

The bloated, putrid carcass of a water buffalo lay on the dike, its belly full of rats and its hide covered with wiggling maggots. The platoon detoured around it, into the chest-deep, leech-infested rice paddies, holding their noses and swearing at this further outrage.

Tyson climbed back onto the slippery dike, Kelly pulling

him up by his rifle muzzle. The platoon stopped for a leech check. Tyson glanced at his map and saw the little square with the cross nestled in the village of An Ninh Ha. *Nha Thuong*. Literally, house of love. He hoped so. They could all use some love.

Tyson looked at Major Harper. 'Excuse me?'

'To recap, you said you moved out at first light. You received radio orders from Captain Browder to proceed to the village of An Ninh Ha, a sort of suburb of Hue that was reportedly controlled by the enemy. An Ninh Ha was along the main enemy supply route into Hue. A helicopter spotted a large concrete structure in the village. The structure flew an enemy flag. Your radio orders were to assess the situation in An Ninh Ha and determine if the concrete structure was in enemy hands, and if so, to occupy it and pull down the flag. Correct?'

Tyson nodded. 'Correct.'

She thought a moment, then said, 'There's no way to verify that, of course.'

Tyson shrugged.

She continued, 'Picard's book says you heard of this hospital from some local peasants who were burying their dead; that it was *you* who decided to go to the village and to the concrete structure which you knew was a hospital.'

'Not true,' he lied. 'I was ordered to go there and make contact with the enemy. Intelligence reported that the ... the structure – I didn't know it was a hospital then – that the concrete structure was in enemy hands. No one said anything about a hospital.'

She nodded. 'So you were psychologically prepared to meet the enemy?'

Tyson thought a moment, then replied, 'Yes, that's a good way to put it.'

'You advanced on this village ...' She glanced at her notes. 'An Ninh Ha ... am I saying it right?'

'Close enough for government work.'

'Did you meet any resistance on the way?'

Tyson replied cautiously, 'No ... but we could see signs of them.'

'Who?'

'Chuck, Charlie, Mr Charles, VC, Viet Cong, Victor Charlie. Whom are we talking about?'

'What sort of signs?'

'Well, the usual stuff: strung-out commo wire, spider holes – those are gooksize foxholes – smothered cooking fires, hoofprints – what we called hoofprints: fresh VC sandal prints; they made their sandals out of old tyres. And North Vietnamese Army boot prints – actually black sneakers. There was evidence of a large number of enemy troops moving in the same direction we were. Toward Hue.' Tyson lit a cigarette. 'We also saw unburied dead – VC and North Viet. I think Picard confirms all of this. We were not in friendly territory.'

'Apparently not. And you knew the enemy was to your front?'

'Right. We suspected he was stalking us from behind as well. I think we all felt like lost lambs in a clearing, getting a little nervous about all those slanty yellow eyes staring out of the dark woods.'

She cupped her chin in her hand and regarded him for some time, then smiled. 'Did you? I saw a group photo of you and your platoon. To paraphrase the Duke of Wellington, I don't know what effect these men had on the enemy, but by God they frightened *me*.'

Tyson suppressed a smile. 'Well, they *looked* mean; but they were pussycats.'

'Anyway, you approached this village?'

'Yes. Like most villages, it was heavily treed, and we moved carefully across the dike to the tree line that marked the edge of the village. According to my map, the village was nestled in a bend of a small river: a tributary of the Perfume River. The

189

western wall of the Hue Citadel was about two kilometres further – off my map. At this point I called for air recon, but the weather was awful and whatever was flying was committed elsewhere. So we did what soldiers have done since the beginning of warfare – we called out to the inhabitants to assemble where we could see them. But no one appeared. Intelligence had indicated that the village had been abandoned in the first days of the offensive. So we began probing fire –'

'You fired into the village?'

'Yes. That was standard prodecure after a warning. But we drew no fire, so we moved cautiously along two parallel dikes, toward the tree line. This is always the worst part because when you come within, say, ten or twenty metres, if they're in there, then they chop you up.'

'But no one fired?'

'No. But then another trick they had was to suck you into the village, then spring the door shut behind you. That's what happened to us at Phu Lai on the first day of Tet.'

'So you were all … jittery?'

Tyson replied, 'Cautious, but not trigger-happy.'

'Please go on.'

'The village was quite picturesque. It was, as you said, sort of a suburb of Hue, and it had some Western influence. There were some French-style villas, paved paths, well-kept gardens, and a few shops around a market square. Very different from the really rural villages that were all bamboo and buffalo shit. Anyway, on the concrete walls were painted VC and NVA slogans –'

'In Vietnamese?'

'Most of them.'

'You could read them?'

'No …'

'Then how did you know they were VC and NVA slogans and not government slogans?'

'Well, they were painted in red. The enemy used red.

Commies – Reds. Get it?'

'You said *most* of the signs were in Vietnamese?'

'Yes, there were a few in English. Routine crap – "Throw out the imperialist running dogs of American adventurism," or something catchy like that.' He added, 'There were also these red silk banners strung between the trees with more slogans. It was obvious to me that the place had been under enemy control for some time.'

Karen Harper nodded, then asked, 'Were there any signs in English directed specifically towards American soldiers?'

Tyson replied, 'Yes, I remember one in particular. It said, "GI, who now sleeps with your wife?"' Tyson smiled. 'I think Charlie hired Tokyo Rose as a media consultant.'

Karen Harper nodded, then asked, 'Any threatening sort of signs?'

'Sure. One said something like, "GI, Death will come today."'

'Did that sort of thing have any effect on your troops?'

Tyson considered a moment, then replied, 'Sure, the signs and banners and brochures we found got to us a little. Why?'

'Just wondering. Anyway, notwithstanding the slogans and psy-warfare messages, the village was deserted? No civilians? No enemy?'

'No civilians to be seen. No sign of a government presence either. As for the enemy, he was usually unseen. Anyway, we saw this small concrete church and moved toward it. It was there we discovered another open square, a *place* as they say in French. It was paved with concrete slabs and surrounded by stucco buildings with red tile roofs. On the far side of the square, at about fifty metres distance, was a large concrete structure. It was two storeys high and had two wings projecting from the front, forming a courtyard. There were a few smaller buildings to each side in the same style and painted the same cream colour as the main building. I took it for a government complex of some sort. From the main building, on a flagstaff over the front doors, flew a Viet Cong flag, or perhaps a North Vietnamese flag. It was hard to tell the difference, and the difference didn't matter. Now, banners and slogans are one thing, but an enemy battle flag is another. They don't leave their flag behind any more than we do. An enemy flag equals enemy people.'

'Was there a Red Cross flag on a pole in the courtyard, as the book indicates?'

'There was no such flag. No red cross, only a red star flag.'

Karen Harper reached into her briefcase and took out Picard's book. Tyson looked at it but made no comment.

She said, 'I read the entire book. In fact, I just finished it on the plane.'

'Good for you.'

She opened the book to a marked page and, without preamble, read:

It was common at the time of the countryside offensive to run up the enemy flag as a sign of surrender, a gesture that the building and the people should be spared. In Hue, however, a number of students and Buddhist groups were sympathetic to the communist cause, and certain Europeans in the city had similar sympathies. Hue was cosmopolitan, sophisticated, liberal, and generally anti-war. When the enemy took possession of most of the city during the general offensive, these elements in the city's population sometimes hoisted the communist flag in a victory celebration. As the battle lines changed, however, so did the flags. To be fair and accurate, the North Vietnamese and Viet Cong often ran up their own flags over captured buildings. So in this case it was not known if that taunting red flag was raised over the hospital by the enemy or by the hospital staff. If by the staff, was it for reasons of protection, surrender, or in sympathy? Or was it perhaps some combination of the three?

Karen Harper looked up from the book and met Tyson's

eyes. 'Picard agrees that there was an enemy flag there, but he indicates that it might have been raised by the hospital staff for the reasons he indicates. Why did you assume, as you indicated, that enemy soldiers were there?'

Tyson stubbed out his cigarette and replied with a touch of annoyance in his voice, 'I didn't have Picard's book with me. I had no idea, Major, of what the hell was going on in Hue or its environs. When I saw an enemy flag, I made the logical assumption that I was approaching a fortified enemy position.'

'Yes, of course. Please go on.'

Tyson leaned back in his chair and thought. *She is playing dumb, and she is imploring me to educate her. I am responding to this dumb woman by trying to teach her about war. Only she is not so dumb. She is using a very sophisticated method of interrogation. Careful, Tyson.*

'Mr Tyson? You were saying something about the church and the square.'

'Yes, we deployed on the near side of the square. There were, as I said, no villagers around to question. But it never occurred to me that I was looking at anything other than a large concrete building, a former French admin building or something, currently flying an enemy flag and in fact being used as a fort.' Tyson leaned forward. 'You have to understand, Major, that you can't be ethnocentric if you're trying to understand this. Picard says hospital, and you think of a big, sleek building with nice blue signs directing you to visitor parking and all that. You think that mistaking a hospital for an administration building is hard to swallow, like mistaking a water buffalo for an elephant. Well, try to imagine, if you will, a country without neon signs, McDonald's, or corner gas stations, a country where suburb doesn't mean PTAs and lawn mowers but means a shithole village close enough to a rinky-dink city to have a few buildings with glass windows and no pigs in the street.'

Karen Harper did not reply immediately, then said

somewhat coolly, 'I just spent a month in Japan and the Philippines, a good deal of that time in the countryside. I've been all over the world in the last four years. I am not ethnocentric, but your point is well taken.' She added, 'Still, hospitals, especially in war zones, are somehow always well marked. But go on.'

Tyson stared at her for some time, and their eyes met and held.

She said with a note of near sarcasm, 'Do you need another break?'

Tyson stood and went to the side window. It was a soft grey day, damp and cool, an almost welcome relief from the bright sunshine and heat. He smelled rain in the air. Karen Harper, he decided, was ahead on points. He knew he should end the interview now, but his ego wouldn't buy that. Like his father, a gambler, he believed you couldn't win it back unless you kept playing. He turned from the window. 'I don't need a break.'

She nodded. 'You were saying you were on the near side of the square.'

Tyson moved back to his chair and sipped on his coffee. 'Yes. We moved into positions of cover and concealment around the church. Kelly, my radio operator, who had a good voice, shouted across the square in Vietnamese for anyone inside the concrete building to come out. No one replied. We fired a few probing rounds. No return fire. We waited, called out again, then fired again. No return fire. But we knew they were in there. We could smell them.' He looked at Karen Harper, but she did not challenge that statement.

Tyson continued. 'We increased our rate of fire, trying to get them to give themselves away. I was beginning to wonder if anyone was in there when it happened. Someone, probably some scared kid, fired back. Now we *knew*. We stepped up our fire, blasting the windows. The enemy began firing back, very intense fire. Mostly small arms, but a few rockets and propelled grenades. Then a machine gun opened up from the roof. We exchanged fire for about five minutes, then I decided to assault the building. The square was not completely exposed. There were trees and ornamental gardens, a few low walls, and also a pool and fountain. We began moving out, firing and manoeuvring. We took one killed and two wounded before we reached the front doors of the building. That's in the book –'

'Yes, but the book says the main enemy force had withdrawn sometime before you even got there. The three casualties were the result of a solitary sniper on the roof. Picard says through his two witnesses – two men in your platoon – that you never fired on the building, that civilians in the hospital signalled to you and hung out a white bed sheet. You believed the building held no enemy troops, and apparently so did the hospital staff. Seeing their signal to you, you advanced directly across the square, and the solitary sniper opened fire from the roof. So here we have a further divergence between your account and the account in the book.'

'Well, I'm telling you what happened as I recall it. The enemy force had not withdrawn. We met with intense fire and we returned it.'

'All right. By the way, did your field map indicate a hospital? What is the hospital symbol? A square within which is a cross with equal-length arms, like the Red Cross.' Her eyes met his.

He said slowly, 'Well, there was a hospital symbol on my map ... as I'm sure you know ... but old map symbols in a country at war for nearly thirty years are somewhat meaningless. Try checking into the hotel that you see on a Vietnam map, or crossing a bridge that's been down for twenty years.'

'I understand that, but —'

'More to the point, I was temporarily disoriented, and I thought I was on the other side of the village. I thought the building designated as a hospital on the map was to the north.'

'I see.' She seemed to be mulling this over, then reached into her briefcase and drew out a plastic-coated map.

Tyson felt his mouth go dry.

Major Harper stood and came around the coffee table. Unexpectedly, she knelt beside Tyson's armchair and unfolded the map.

Tyson looked down at the coloured Army ordnance map. The map was trilingual – French, Vietnamese, and English. It suddenly seemed very familiar: the rice paddies, the trails, the burial mounds, the rivers and streams, the woods and hills. After nearly two decades, he still knew the place. His eyes focused on An Ninh Ha.

Major Harper asked, 'This was the standard issue map, was it not?'

'Looks like it.'

She seemed to be studying it, her finger sliding across the plastic coating, stopping at An Ninh Ha. 'Here it is.'

'Yes. There it is.'

'You see here . . . you said you saw a church on the near side, the west side of the square. Here's the church on the map, a box clearly marked with a Christian, or Latin, cross. The only church in the village. And across the square on the east side is the hospital, marked with the cross of equal-length arms. That seems clear. What I'm wondering is where you *thought* you were.' She glanced over her shoulder at Tyson.

Tyson's eyes went from the map to her face, and they stared at each other in silence. Her proximity was somewhat unsettling. He could smell her scent, an unusual spicy fragrance. He saw that her hair had highlights he hadn't noticed. Between the buttons of her blouse, there was a gap, and out of the corner of his eye he saw the curve of her breasts and observed she was wearing a half-cut bra.

She said again, 'Where did you think you were?'

Tyson drew a deep breath through his nostrils and leaned over the coffee table. He scanned the small village quickly. In the north end, near the bend in the river, was a pagoda whose

196

symbol, a box with a projecting line, could conceivably be mistaken for that of a church. Some distance away, perhaps a hundred metres, was the symbol for a school: a black box with a pennant flag. Tyson said, 'There. I thought I was there.'

Major Harper nodded as though she accepted this. 'So you thought the Catholic church you passed was a pagoda, and the hospital across the square was a school? You said you thought it was an administration building.'

'Well ... I meant a public building ...'

'I see.' She looked at him with an expression meant to convey that she was a little confused. She said, 'But the juxtaposition of these two sets of buildings is quite different. Also ... here you have an open square, a *place*. Here, between the pagoda and the school, you have tiny black boxes which I presume are houses, and the distance is greater –'

'Look, Major, I don't need a course in map reading. You know, it's easy to sit here in a dry room with a nice new map and play devil's advocate. But *my* map was bent and folded so many times the plastic coating was cracked, and water had seeped into the paper. An Ninh Ha was nearly obliterated on *my* map.' Tyson's voice was sharp. 'Let's forget maps. Okay?'

Major Harper folded the map. Still kneeling, she handed it to Tyson. 'These are hard to come by. I assume you don't have yours. My compliments.'

Tyson took the map. 'Thanks for the memories.'

She stood. 'Look it over when you get a chance. It may jog your memory.'

Tyson did not reply.

She returned to her side of the coffee table. Still standing, she said, 'All right. Where were we?'

'I was attacking the building. Do you want a blow-by-blow account of the assault? Or do you want to wait until they make it into a movie?'

'Actually, I'd like us to back up to when you're deployed around the church. You're looking at the building, fifty

197

metres across the square. It's flying an enemy flag, and you're focusing on that. But did you see any written signs on the building, in English or in French? Do you know French?'

'As you know from my file, I have a working knowledge of it. There were no signs – written or otherwise.'

She handed him a slip of paper. 'What does that mean?'

Tyson looked at the Vietnamese words. *Nha Thuong*. He threw the paper on the coffee table. 'I told you I didn't know the written language. I spoke a few words and phrases, most of which had to do with getting me laid.' He smiled.

Major Harper smiled in return and sat. She said, 'Well, that means hospital, of course.'

'Does it?'

She pointed to the map on the coffee table and observed, 'The maps were trilingual and were therefore like a Rosetta stone.' She nodded to herself, as though arriving at a truth, then continued. 'The legend on that map included the words "*Nha Thuong, hôpital*, hospital." You saw this trilingual legend day in and day out as you consulted your map. So of course you know "*Nha Thuong*" when you see it written. The question is, Was it written on the concrete building?'

Tyson did not reply.

She seemed lost in thought for some time, stroking her chin with her finger. At length she said, 'The question of whether or not you knew that building to be a hospital is pertinent but not crucial to the central issue. Let's assume you did not know it was a hospital.'

'Right.'

'You deployed, fired at a building with an enemy flag, drew fire in return, and began an assault. Believe it or not, I rather like a good war story. I saw *A Walk in the Sun* about ten times. Please continue.'

Tyson leaned back in his armchair. He wanted a cigarette but decided this was not the time to display what could be construed as a nervous habit. He said, 'We began by laying down heavy suppressing fire. You know – we blasted all the windows and doors with automatic fire to keep the enemy down. Then we began our final assault –'

'Excuse me again. The book said someone hung a white bed sheet from a window to indicate surrender or all clear. Apparently the two witnesses told Picard they saw this.'

'Why the hell would the enemy hang out a surrender flag? They had an avenue of escape. Why the hell would I begin an assault if I or anyone in my platoon saw a white flag?'

'That goes back to the original point. The enemy had already withdrawn, according to the book. It was the hospital staff who hung the bed sheet from the window, also according to the book account. They waved to you from the windows. But you don't agree with any of that. So please continue.'

'Right. So we began to fire and manoeuvre, working our way toward the building. We continued to draw heavy fire —'

'I'm sorry. It's just that I've done some basic infantry tactics research. I spoke to an infantry colonel who was there. A friend of mine. I sort of anticipated that, if I had the opportunity to hear your version, it would probably be that some sort of firefight took place. Excuse the comparison, but that's what was said about My Lai —'

'What's your point?'

'The point is that this colonel said a frontal assault on a concrete building was not something he would ever expose his men to.'

'Maybe he's a wimp.'

'Hardly. He did say he would fire some sort of incendiary devices into the place and burn the insides, which would be mostly wood, I guess. Then, he said, he might move in for an assault.'

He regarded her for some time, then replied, 'We didn't have any incendiary ordnance that could be fired from a launcher. We had only hand grenades – fragmentation, white phosphorus, and concussion grenades. So we had to move in close.'

'Why didn't you call in air strikes, aerial rockets, mortars, or artillery? Isn't that standard operating procedure in American infantry tactics? Send bombs instead of men?'

'Yes, that's standard procedure. But there was no fire support available. Nothing was functioning right at that time. So we moved in for an old-fashioned frontal assault. Fire and manoeuvre. We broke into the ground floor, just like in the war movies that you seem to like —'

'Where and when did the casualties occur? Was it before or after you got into the ... the building?'

'I ... we took two wounded on the initial assault. Peterson had a sucking chest wound ... both lungs were involved ... the bullet passed from side to side ... he was drowning. The other man, Moody, was hit in the thigh ... he was all right ... The third man, Larry Cane, was killed inside the building.'

'Oh, I thought you indicated earlier that all the casualties occurred outside. That's what Picard's book said also, except he said they were caused by a single sniper. Anyway, there were remarkably few casualties for an assault on a fortified structure.'

'Everyone's allowed to get lucky once in a while. I'm sorry I can't report more dead and wounded.'

'I was just wondering. Please continue.'

'There was no one on the first floor and still no indications that the place was a hospital. There were offices, a chapel, a lobby, some sleeping quarters, and a kitchen and dining room. We found two staircases. We reached the second floor and got into a room-by-room fight. It was then that a few phosphorus hand grenades were tossed around. The place started to burn —'

'How many enemy do you estimate?'

'Maybe thirty or forty – we were outnumbered.'

'But you didn't know how many were in there when you attacked. There could have been two hundred.'

'Well, I could tell by the amount of fire coming from the windows that there weren't two hundred.'

'And you lost one killed in that room-to-room fighting? A

man named Cane?'

'Yes.'

'But a while ago you said all three casualties occurred outside, during the assault. Picard agreed, though his account of the severity of the fight is somewhat different from yours. Now you say Larry Cane was killed inside.'

Tyson lit a cigarette. He drew on it, then replied, 'Well, that's a result of having read Picard's book. You see, what's happening is that my memory is being jogged by all this, but Picard's book has put some false recollections in my mind. Cane *was* killed inside the hospital. I'm positive of that. I saw him get hit. Upstairs, in the main ward.'

Karen Harper nodded. 'I'm sure we can clear that up if it becomes necessary. And I understand what you mean about false recollections as a result of having recently read the book.' She added, 'Nonetheless, Mr Tyson, I find it all a little hard to believe. I mean, nineteen very fatigued men taking a frontal assault on a building held by a significant number of North Vietnamese regulars. And why didn't you surround the building so the enemy couldn't escape? That, I understand, would have been standard procedure. And what, may I ask, prompted you to such acts of heroism? If you couldn't get fire support to level the building, why not just bypass it? Pretend it didn't exist? Am I being cynical, or did American troops sometimes avoid a fight?' She leaned forward. 'I don't expect you to answer any of these questions because they presuppose that you are lying about the whole assault business.'

Tyson looked at her.

Karen Harper continued, 'In most murder investigations we look for motive. In cases of war-related massacres, investigators tend to overlook motive because motive, in the hands of the defence, becomes extenuation and mitigation. In other words, defence argues that the motive was a good one. For instance, you mentioned Phu Lai a few times, and I was wondering if perhaps your men were looking for revenge ...' She stared at him. 'That would be understandable.'

201

Tyson did not reply immediately, then said, 'I would be lying if I told you that all of us were not looking for revenge. Killing breeds killing, as you may know. But combat deaths do not – should not – breed murder. We were looking for revenge on the battlefield, and we found it at Hôpital Miséricorde. In fact, there's your motive for my assault on the building, and there's the reason my men followed me. A payback for Phu Lai. But it had to be paid quid pro quo. Slaughtering civilians would not even the score. But taking that concrete building from the enemy would. Did.'

She nodded. 'You're a very bright man.'

'Am I blushing?'

She said, 'Still, your account is ... not ... not a good war story. In fact, it's unbelievable.'

Tyson drew on his cigarette. He realized in retrospect just *how* unbelievable his story sounded from the standpoint of military tactics and logic. He saw that if even a JAG officer and a woman with presumably no knowledge of infantry tactics beyond an unlikely fondness for war movies and a friendship with an infantry colonel could punch holes in his story, then it would not stand up under closer scrutiny. Yet it seemed like a good story when it was first fabricated. It was standard Vietnam cover-up. Whenever a few ICs – innocent civilians – were killed by mistake – or in less blameless ways – you came up with a hair-raising story of a firefight. No one questioned you. No one said anything about your lack of casualties. And a good officer always made certain his men carried a few enemy weapons to turn in along with the bodies of old men, women, and children. It was that kind of war.

Tyson reflected: *The story sounded good at the time, because we'd told it to each other in a vacuum, without outside criticism, and because we wanted to believe it ... Damn her,* he thought. *Was the hospital marked? Why didn't you call in artillery? Why so few casualties in the assault?*

She broke into his thoughts. 'So, anyway, the hospital was burning now. You had killed a number of the enemy. The

202

rest, I assume, fled. How?'

'They jumped from the second-floor windows.'

She nodded, then asked, 'Did you see any patients, any hospital staff?'

Without hesitation he replied, 'Yes, we saw patients and staff.' *Stick to the damned story. Don't deviate. It's the only story we have. The only one we all know. It may sound improbable, but it's not impossible. Beyond a shadow of a doubt.* He said, 'Most of them were dead. I don't know if they were killed in the assault or if they were executed by the enemy.'

She said nothing.

Tyson continued his narrative. 'It was total confusion at that point. I mean, you wouldn't believe what chaos it was – wounded VC and NVA soldiers in uniform – you couldn't tell if they were patients, if they were armed, if they were surrendering, or if they were about to shoot you. There were a few women, but one of them was a VC nurse, and she fired a pistol at us. Someone killed her. It was incredibly confusing. I blame the goddamned VC and NVA for using a hospital full of people ... By that time we could see that it was a hospital ... Anyway, the place was burning by now, and we threw some of the patients – the ones in the maternity and paediatric ward – out of the window ... to save them ... There were bushes below ...' Tyson stopped. He realized he was trembling. He cleared his throat and continued. 'Well, I suppose in a way you could call it a massacre ... but certainly not an intentional one on our part. I could see how that Eurasian nun could misinterpret what she saw ... But most of the dead were a result of the assault or of the enemy executions that took place before we assaulted the building. I think they massacred the staff and the patients, including their own wounded, when they saw they were going to be overrun ...'

She said, 'And Dr Monteau?'

'I don't remember being introduced to anyone by name, Major.'

'But one of Picard's sources – one of your men – related an incident—'

'Which man?'

'I don't know. I told you I came here first.'

'By law you'd have to tell me who Picard's sources were, if you knew them. *That* is the reason you came here first.'

She didn't comment on Tyson's observation but said, 'And the Australian doctor—'

He said irritably, 'Damn it, I told you there was a hospital full of patients and staff. Yes, they were killed. Yes, some of them were probably killed by us. But they were killed as an unfortunate consequence of military operations against an armed enemy who made use of a place of sanctuary to conduct operations against American forces. Write that down. End of statement.'

She nodded and asked him to repeat it as she wrote. Then she said, 'Why are there such discrepancies between your story and the stories told to Picard by two of your men?'

'Maybe Picard distorted what they said.'

'Possibly.' She seemed to be lost in thought, then said, 'But Picard says in his book that he learned of this incident as a result of a chance meeting in France with this Sister Teresa. *She* apparently used the word massacre—'

'In what context? A massacre by whom? And how did she use the word? It is spelled the same in French and English, and the meaning in French is close to ours, but in French it has the added connotation of useless killing, the slaughter of battle – not solely wanton or premeditated killing of unarmed people. I did my homework, too—'

'So I see. Those are good questions. I'll call the Army language school and get an opinion on that.'

'Have you located this Sister Teresa?'

'No. Do you remember her?'

'I believe so. Will you interview Picard?'

'Of course.' She said, 'Your version is interesting because it is so subjective, whereas Picard's account seems so objective.'

204

'Meaning?'

'Meaning you've left room for interpretation of events, while he has been unequivocal in saying he has heard the story of a massacre and reported it.'

Tyson said nothing.

She added, 'If Picard was embellishing, then I can see very clearly from your version how he could do so. All the ingredients are there: a hospital, a large number of deaths, the flags, the shooting in the wards. Anyway, Picard was a novelist once. Did you know that? He's used to making up stories. Don't forget to advise your attorney of that.'

Tyson seemed not to hear her.

She continued. 'Then again, it might have been that the two men from your platoon were embellishing or lying when they spoke to Picard. But why would they do that? It certainly brings no credit to them.'

'It certainly does not.'

'But it brings discredit on *you*. Did you have any enemies in your platoon?'

'I'll tell you that when you give me the names of those two men.'

She nodded. 'Also, Sister Teresa may make the worst kind of witness. She may not have understood what she saw or may not have communicated it very well to Picard.'

'Probably.'

She leaned forward and said, 'I would imagine that at some point she made some sort of report to the Catholic authorities in Saigon or France who ran the hospital. Don't you think that's a possibility?'

Tyson had always thought that a distinct possibility. He replied, 'Maybe.'

She continued, 'But I understand that the South Vietnamese government, and to some extent the Catholic church in Vietnam, had a tendency to bury any stories unfavourable to their allies and champions. They did not want to embarrass the Americans. Saigon tried to kill the My

205

Lai investigation even as the JAG Corps was pursuing it. Foreigners don't understand why we insist on washing our dirty linen in public. So if this nun's report, if there was one, in any way reflected unfavourably on American soldiers, then it never would have got back to France. That's my theory.'

'To which, as I see,' said Tyson, 'you've given some thought.'

'I've given the whole incident some thought.'

'Me too.' Tyson stood and walked to the window. With his back to her, he said, 'You know, a month or so ago I would have related this incident at a drunken stag party as a good shoot-'em-up war story. I had nothing to be ashamed of. We did a brave thing. A lot of officers *would* have bypassed that building – like your infantry colonel friend. I mean, it was unfortunate that so many innocent people got killed, but the bad guys were the ones in black pajamas.' He turned toward her. 'Now I'm getting very defensive. I'm having second thoughts about what happened. But I shouldn't have second thoughts. My perceptions at the time were the correct ones.'

She nodded. 'I know. You start to second-guess yourself. Every commander since the beginning of time refights his battles in his mind. Also, it's been a long time.'

'A very long time.'

Karen Harper said, 'That's why we may need more statements. For instance, if Sister Teresa is found and her testimony turns out to be lucid ...' She looked at him. 'Would you like her to be found?'

Tyson did not reply.

She observed, 'It's odd that there were no other survivors.'

He sat down again. 'I told you we saved some people. But don't expect any long-distance calls from Nam.'

'No. This is difficult. Too many years and too many miles.' She commented, 'You say you may remember Sister Teresa. What do you remember about her?'

'I remember she was scared. Maybe hysterical. Someone got her out a window. That's all I remember at the moment.

I'll think about that.'

'Fine. You know, I was thinking that if the investigation were broadened, we might try to contact Vietnamese refugees through their representative organizations. That might lead us to another survivor.'

'It's a long shot that you'd find another survivor that way.'

'True. Do you think the present government of Vietnam would cooperate? They have the advantage of access to the scene of the incident, which we do not.'

Tyson began to feel that he had become her assistant, which was, he knew, another method of interrogation. He said, 'If they did cooperate I don't think anyone that they present as a witness would have much credibility in front of a court-martial board of American officers. Do you?'

'I guess not. That was foolish.'

Tyson nodded. Both suggestions were foolish. She was trying to shake him with the old unexpected-witness routine. What she didn't know – yet – was that there were absolutely no survivors. Except Sister Teresa.

Karen Harper poured coffee into their cups.

Tyson remembered a home-improvement salesman who felt that as long as he was drinking coffee, he wouldn't be tossed out. He was wrong. He said to Karen Harper, 'I think that's about it.'

She sipped her coffee. 'You've been very helpful. As I said, I'm trying to arrive at the truth, for your sake as well as in the interests of justice. You'd like this cleared up too, I suppose, so you can get back to your normal routine.'

'Major, I never again want to go back to my normal routine. But I would like to get this done with and resign my commission. This time I'll check the correct damned box. Double-check it. How long will this last?'

'Oh ... a few more weeks. I just need to contact Picard, then get the names of the two men who gave him his story. If necessary, we may contact other men from your platoon whose whereabouts we've tentatively determined.'

'Who?'

'I told you – I'll send you or your lawyer a list as soon as we decide whether or not we even need their statements. I really hope I just find that Picard was, well, bullshitting a bit.'

Tyson smiled in spite of himself.

She said, 'Do you feel good about this interview? Do you think it was conducted fairly and properly?'

'Absolutely.' He thought a moment, then added, 'You're a remarkable woman. Why don't you get a civilian job?'

She smiled. 'I'm getting out soon.'

'Are you? You're not a career officer?'

'No. I'm paying back my tuition.'

'I see … Do you mind if I ask you whether or not you're married?'

'That's not relevant … but no, I'm not. Why?'

'Just curious.' He saw she wasn't going to leave until asked to, and he wanted to end it before he said anything he'd regret. He stood. 'I have a tennis date in half an hour.'

She stood. 'Yes, of course.' She gathered her things and followed Tyson into the foyer. 'I'm going to Manhattan. I understand there's a train.'

'Yes.' He looked at his watch. 'The next one leaves in about twenty minutes. You can walk to the station.'

'I'd like to freshen up first.'

'Right. Up the stairs, to the left.'

She climbed the long, sweeping staircase. He watched her and thought, *Tuition assistance programme*. That's like admitting you're dirt-poor. He tried to imagine what sort of background she came from. Her accent was definitely Midwestern. She was well spoken and carried herself well. She had made major within her four years of active duty, so she must be on the ball. He wondered what line of convoluted reasoning had led the JAG to send her to his door. What Machiavellian logic was behind this? He shrugged. Military logic, which was to say nonlogic. Yet there had to be some method to the madness. In this case, he admitted, there was

208

definitely some method ...

She came down the stairs and walked towards the front door. 'I have enough to do to keep me busy for some days, but I'd like us to meet again. Is that all right?'

Tyson thought a moment, then replied, 'I'll have to think about that.'

'Well, if you decide you'd like to, let's make a tentative date for a week from today. Why don't you come to Washington?'

Tyson knew he could not be ordered to speak about this case. But he could be ordered to go to Washington, to Fort Benning, Georgia, to Nome, Alaska, or to anywhere they decided he should go. He could exercise his right to remain silent from one end of the continent to the other. But he'd rather play ball in New York or Washington than Nome. He said, 'I suppose I could meet you in Washington.'

'Good. I'll call you with the details of the meeting.' She handed him her card. 'Please call me if anything else occurs to you in the meantime, or if you need assistance or just want to talk.'

'That's what I used to say to suspects. It's trite, Major.'

'I know. But I get lots of calls.'

He took her jacket from the coat closet and helped her on with it, then he opened the door. Outside a light rain had begun to fall. He took an umbrella from the stand, and they walked together down to the street. She said, 'Thank you for being so cooperative. I feel I'm getting closer to understanding this.'

'Then you're a damned sight smarter than I am.' He considered a moment, then said, 'If charges are actually brought against me ... what is the current Army policy on ... restriction?'

She replied, 'Of course that's on your mind ... I'm fairly sure ... off the record ... that as an officer, and taking into account all the sensitive aspects of this case, you would have almost complete freedom ... I'm sure you can live off-post, within the confines of your duties, if any. They may impose one restriction—'

'Don't leave the country.'

'That's right.'

'Am I restricted to this country as of now?'

'Not as far as I know. You are on administrative leave until you report to Fort Hamilton. Do you have any plans to leave the country?'

'No.' He added, 'And you can tell them that.'

'Who?'

'Whoever is wondering, whoever is worried, or whoever is hoping. You've heard *that* sentiment expressed, I assume.'

She nodded. 'This thing has brought back so many bad memories of that time— Look, if you're innocent, I honestly feel that the Army, the nation, and others, including the media, will make full restitution to you. This is a country that knows how to say "I'm sorry."'

'Who's going to apologize to my wife?'

She looked into his eyes. 'No one. That damage is done, and no one can ever make that right again. We're also a country that is obsessed with ... with ...'

'Fucking.' He smiled. 'On second thoughts, you're too honest to be a civilian lawyer.' He paused, then said, 'Well ... it was good of you to come all the way here. I realize it could have been done differently. I think this informal format was best.'

'I think so.'

He looked around at the gently falling rain, then remarked, 'I'd offer you the umbrella, but I remember that military people can't carry umbrellas.'

'Silly custom ... or is it a rule? It's sillier to get wet. I'll take the umbrella, unless you need it for your tennis game.'

They exchanged smiles as he passed her the umbrella. She said, 'I'll return it next week.'

He looked at his watch. 'You'd better hurry. Right at the end of this block, five more blocks, and you'll see the station. I'm not going to salute. The neighbours are watching.'

She put out her hand and he took it. 'Good-bye.' She turned and walked away.

He stood under a tree and watched her moving down the street, carrying his umbrella.

His attention shifted back to the rain. It was a gentle rain, and when it rained in a certain way, he still thought of Vietnam: hot, steamy rain, vaporous ground clouds, and the steady, soft, susurrant sounds of water brushing the leaves. And the mouldy smells of the wet earth, which he smelled now, brought back the jungle.

Vietnam, he thought suddenly, *is here, in this village*. He smelled it on the damp, rotting vegetation, heard it in the falling rain, and saw it in the vaporous air. Tyson walked slowly back towards his house in the rain.

18

Benjamin Tyson walked unhurriedly across the broad lawns of Constitution Gardens. It was twilight, breezeless and humid, and he could feel the sweat seeping through his white knit shirt and sticking to his poplin trousers.

There were a good number of people about, flying kites, lying on blankets, strolling, listening to radios. To Tyson's left lay the Doric Parthenon of the Lincoln Memorial, and to his right, the long Reflecting Pool running due east towards the massive obelisk of the Washington Monument. The setting sun cast a mellow aura over the park, the pool, and the surrounding buildings. On the north edge of the park, across Constitution Avenue, stood a phalanx of august and commanding buildings, that Tyson thought looked familiar from photographs, though he couldn't identify them. He did not know Washington well, but even a stranger coming into this city by chance would know that he was in an imperial capital, a place of power, a new Rome.

It was no more than a black slash in the ground, a poignant contrast to the lofty white marble and limestone of this monumental city. It was cut into a gently rising slope of grass, and critics had complained that it was antiheroic and nearly invisible. Yet it was as easy to spot as the two presidential monuments that flanked it, because it was where all the people were.

Tyson approached slowly, and the nearer he drew, the quieter the park became, as if this were a protected zone, a place where it was understood that one did not fly kites, throw Frisbees, or play radios.

The atmosphere around the black memorial was not unlike that of a funeral home: silent, sombre, subdued. An al fresco mortuary.

Though he had been to Washington on business, he had never come here. Yet he felt he knew the place after years of media exposure. As he moved closer, however, he realized that no photograph could capture the essence of this vast headstone, no news film could convey the impact of its hushed presence. Unlike other shrines to the dead, this was a tactile and participatory memorial. People were passing their fingers over the etched names, reading them, pointing to them, making pencil rubbings of a name with any piece of paper at hand.

Tyson stopped some ten feet from the black granite wall. On the rising lawn behind and above the wall stood six men in jungle fatigues. They seemed to be a permanent part of the site, soldiers frozen in time at the vertex of the black wedges, standing precariously close to the precipice. Tyson had the impression they were young men, but that was because he associated jungle fatigues with young men. On closer scrutiny he saw they were men nearer to middle age, his age.

Tyson moved closer to the wall and stood on the paved walkway that paralleled it. Other men of about his own age had on bits and pieces of uniforms. A wasted man sat in a wheelchair; two men walked with canes. And there were those in good clothing, with no visible signs of wounds, who in some subtle way were nonetheless identifiable as veterans. Tyson saw in those faces something he had not seen in nearly twenty years – the Thousand Yard Stare. He felt he was among a gathering of wraiths, and he swore they stank of the jungle and were splattered with Asian mud. He had a sudden fear that he'd see a face he knew. He wanted to turn and walk quickly away, before the black arms of the outstretched walls engulfed him. He drew a breath, turned, and found himself facing the bronze statues of the three soldiers clad in jungle fatigues. They each seemed to be in a trancelike state, though it was not the Thousand Yard Stare, but an oddly lifeless look as though the sculptor had consciously tried to represent three ghosts.

He turned back and focused on the names in a tall black panel near the vertex: *James B. Alexander, Robert J. Betz, Jack W. Klein, David J. W. Widder, Lawrence W. Gordon.* There were no ranks, he noticed, no unit designations, no clue as to whether they were Army, Marine, Navy, Air Force, or Coast Guard, no hometown, age, or any vital statistic; just names arranged chronologically from the first deaths in 1959 to the last in 1975. And this, he thought, was as it should be, just names. The mothers, fathers, wives, children, brothers, and sisters knew all there was to know about the names.

Tyson saw flowers stuck between the stone panels, flowers strewn at the base of the monument, photographs set against the wall. Here and there were more impressive floral arrangements. To his right, lying on the black stone bordering the base of the wall, was a first baseman's glove.

'Can I find a name for you?'

Tyson looked to his left. Beside him was a young girl of about sixteen, in jeans and T-shirt. She had nice eyes and a good tan but was otherwise rather homely. She carried a pad and pencil. Tyson said, 'Excuse me?'

'I can find the location of a name.'

213

'Oh ... okay ... Browder. Roy Browder.'

The girl replied, 'That might be a common name. Do you have a middle initial? A date of death?'

'Date of death, February 21, 1968.'

'Okay. Be right back.' She walked quickly to the east end of the memorial, and Tyson saw her approach a woman in the green uniform of the National Park Service. The woman had a thick registry book and was looking up names for people. The young girl, Tyson realized, was a sort of free-enterprise link between the overworked civil servant and the visitors.

Tyson looked back at the polished wall and stared beyond the white etched names into the dark mirrored stone. The granite was reflective, he thought, in the sense that it reflected the living and that the living reflected on the dead. If that was its purpose, then the monument worked.

An attractive woman, a few years younger than Tyson, stepped onto the narrow grass border between the wall and the path. She touched her finger to a name, and Tyson looked at her reflection. He saw her lips pucker in a kiss, then turn up in a sort of wistful smile. She winked and turned. Tyson's eyes followed her, and he saw her join a man on the path. The man, Tyson thought, looked somewhat uncomfortable.

'Sir?'

Tyson turned to see the girl beside him.

'Panel 36 E. Line 95. That's over here.' She pointed.

'Thanks ...'

She handed Tyson a green and black brochure. 'This will help you locate other names if you know the approximate dates of death.' She added, 'If you'd like to make a donation to the memorial fund ...'

'Sure.' Tyson took out his wallet and gave the girl a five-dollar bill.

'Thank you.' She hesitated, then said, 'I like to know ... I mean, who ... a friend, relative ...?'

'A friend.'

'Were you there?'

'Yes.'

She nodded. 'My father was killed in 1967. Before I was born. He was a career NCO. Army. Panel 22 E. Line 91. Patrick Duggan.'

Tyson wondered if she was asking if he knew him. He said, 'I'm sorry.'

'Oh, it's not painful or anything. Just sad.'

He nodded. She didn't seem anxious to leave, and it occurred to him that this rather plain-looking girl was lonely. He found that he was curious about the life of a soldier's posthumous child. Did her mother remarry? Did she live here in Washington? Did the Army really take care of its own? Or did they take her father and leave her and her family to struggle on less than a family on public assistance as he'd once read? But he knew he wasn't going to ask her any questions.

Tyson's eyes fell on the sunlit wall again. Long before there were military death benefits and widows' payments there were grand monuments to the fallen, conceived and built by the lobbies for the dead. And in the regimental mess halls, toasts were offered to the missing. But for the survivors, he thought, there was precious little in the way of glory or sustenance. If he could design a single monument to all wars, it would consist of a statue of a woman with the Thousand Yard Stare.

The girl followed his gaze. She said, 'Do you like it? The wall?'

He nodded again.

'Lots of people don't. Well, most people come here thinking they're not going to like it. But it gets to them somehow. You know?'

'Yes. I do.'

'My mother said they should have put fifty-seven thousand gravestones on the west lawn of the Capitol.'

'Yes, with my statue of the woman standing among them.'

The girl didn't respond to this but pursued her own line of

215

conversation. 'They'd have to see them every day. The Congress. They should have done it while the war was going on. Each week they'd unload gravestones on the lawn. You know?'

'Sounds good.'

The girl smiled.

Tyson and the girl stood in companionable silence for some time, then Tyson said, 'Do you know who I am?'

The girl's eyes fell on his face, and she shook her head.

'Ben Tyson.'

She shrugged.

Tyson shrugged in return and smiled.

The girl stuck out her hand awkwardly. 'Pam Majerski.'

Tyson took her hand.

She said, 'My stepfather adopted me. Majerski.'

Tyson squeezed her hand before he released it. 'Thanks for your help. Panel 36?'

'Right. Line 95. Roy Browder. I think I had him before. Wife, I think.'

Tyson turned and moved down the wall. He stepped in front of the panel. He saw the year 1968 etched in a nearby panel and saw, too, that 1968 took a lot of panels. A bad year. The worst year. It would have been a good year to spend somewhere else.

He found Browder's name and stared at it a moment, trying to remember the man and conjuring up the slightly pudgy face with the perpetual cigar jammed in the left corner of his mouth. Browder's death had moved him deeply at the time, though Tyson had not particularly liked his company commander. But Browder had been the Old Man, the embodiment of gruff, fatherly discipline, the essence of authority, the place where the buck stopped in Alpha Company.

And, on Captain Browder's death, six days after Miséricorde Hospital, Lieutenant Benjamin Tyson, twenty-six years old and with an ROTC Commission, had become

216

commanding officer of Alpha Company. Had Browder lived, Tyson thought, he would have ultimately confessed to him. And in some way what was happening now would not be happening. The Old Man would have made it right.

Tyson moved to the next panel, then the next. He spotted the names of men he knew, men he'd seen die, men he'd seen evacuated with grisly wounds, and men he'd said good-bye to when he'd left Vietnam. He couldn't say for certain how many people from Alpha Company had contributed their names to this wall, but he thought there were at least fifty.

Tyson consulted the brochure, moved on to other panels, and saw the names of men he knew from other times and places: a childhood friend, two college classmates, men he'd trained with and served with in the States. He thought he knew an inordinate number of the 57,939 Americans listed here.

He walked slowly along the length of the wall until he realized the sun was nearly gone. He moved back to the panels that represented the year 1968. He saw the names Frederick Brontman and Irwin Selig, who had been alive when he left Vietnam, and it was the first he knew of their deaths. He found the names of Peter Santos and John Manelli, who had been killed at Hue on the same day Browder had died. He found the name of Arthur Peterson, who had been wounded in the chest and died at Miséricorde Hospital. He discovered the name of Michael DeTonq, the only man in Alpha Company to be reported missing in action. Following DeTonq's name was a cross, denoting that he was still missing, but Tyson strongly believed he was not MIA. DeTonq was MOP – missing on purpose. DeTonq, a Cajun from Louisiana, spoke passable French and had undoubtedly chosen to terminate his short military career before it terminated him. Tyson often pictured DeTonq in the arms of a sympathetic French woman. Good for him. Tyson hoped he'd survived the fall of Vietnam and somehow made it back to the States.

217

Tyson took out a handkerchief and wiped the sweat from his brow. He turned away from the stone and looked out over the park. Long purple shadows lay in the groves of trees. About a hundred yards away stood a solitary man in full camouflage fatigues and bush hat. Tyson thought for one uncomfortable moment that this was a true ghost, that no one but he saw the man. Then the man raised a bugle to his lips, and the last sunlight glinted off the polished brass. The air was suddenly split with the doleful, haunting sound of taps.

The dwindling crowd turned, watched, and listened. The final note hung in the hot, humid air. The man returned to a position of attention, turned smartly, and walked away.

The people around the memorial began moving off as well. Tyson stepped away from the wall, hesitated, then turned back. He ran his hand over the smooth black granite, feeling its radiant warmth, the grit-blasted names, the seams between the panels. His hand slid upward to a height of nearly eight feet, and his fingers rested on the name of Lawrence F. Cane. Killed in action at Miséricorde Hospital. Tyson had written the official letter of condolence to Cane's mother: *Dear Mrs Cane, You may take some comfort in the knowledge that your son Larry died in the service of his country.* Which was true, Tyson thought. People did take some comfort in that. Better than losing a son in a gang war. *I knew Larry well, and he was as fine a soldier and human being as I've ever had the honour to serve with.* Well ... but after all, speak only good of the dead. He wasn't a bad sort really. *Larry was a valuable and respected member of my platoon, and he will be missed by everyone who knew him.* All riflemen are valuable, and they're all missed. Nothing personal, just practical. *I was with him at the time of his death, and I assure you he died quickly and without pain.*

Which was, Tyson thought, the only absolutely true line in the letter. Tyson *had* been with him and *could* verify that

Larry Cane died quickly and without pain because Tyson had shot him through the heart.

Sincerely yours,
Benjamin J. Tyson,
First Lieutenant,
United States Army, Infantry

19

Benjamin Tyson sat in the Garden Terrace Lounge of the elegant Four Seasons Hotel located at the edge of Georgetown. The Four Seasons was where he stayed when he travelled for Peregrine-Osaka, so this, he reasoned, was where he should stay when he travelled for the Army. He doubted, however, that the Army was going to reimburse him. But really this was for Ben Tyson, he thought; this was for each of the three hundred and twenty-two nights he'd stayed awake in the jungles and swamps, in fear and discomfort. They owed him.

He hadn't changed his clothes and still wore the sweat-stained shirt and slacks he'd worn to the monument. The air-conditioning made his skin feel clammy, and he recalled those occasions when he'd come directly from the field into a frigid officers' club, the Vietnamese waitresses with blue noses and toes, coughing and sniffling, the Americans drinking cold beer and moving animatedly as though they'd just been revived with a bucket of ice water over the head.

He sprawled deeper in his armchair, put his feet on the cocktail table, and kicked off his loafers. He regarded his toes awhile, then drank the last of his scotch.

A waitress approached, and Tyson ordered his third drink. He was vaguely aware that he should be better dressed for this lounge and for this meeting. But his socioeconomic status being vague at the moment, he thought he could dress as he pleased.

Tyson glanced at his watch. She was late.

He reflected that he had not experienced survivor guilt to any great degree. But sitting here in comfort in the nation's capital, surrounded by memorials and mausoleums of one sort or another, he began to feel a certain unease, or perhaps it was a maudlinism brought on by a combination of the black wall and the alcohol. Tyson decided he ought not to meet her in his present state of mind. His drink came, and he paid the bill, then rose to leave.

He spotted her coming in from the lobby and felt an unexpected disappointment in seeing that she wasn't wearing civilian clothing. Her garrison cap was tucked in a side pouch of her black handbag, and she still carried the black briefcase.

Karen Harper looked around the dimly lit lounge, her eyes adjusting to the light. Tyson sat as she approached. She said, 'Good evening.' She extended her hand. 'I was afraid you'd left.'

'Would an officer and a gentleman do that?'

She smiled as he motioned her to an upholstered chair diagonal to his. Tyson signalled to a waitress, and Karen Harper ordered white wine. She said to Tyson, 'This is a very nice hotel.'

'Nothing but the best for our boys in uniform.'

'You were authorized to stay at the Presidential. Did you get your travel vouchers in the mail?'

Tyson swirled his glass and stared at the ice cubes. At length he replied, 'My attorney advised me not to accept any government funds. In any case, I stay at the Four Seasons when I'm in Washington.'

'If you got a haircut and dressed up a bit you could use one of the officers' clubs in the area. Cheap drinks.' She asked, 'Do you intend to report to Fort Hamilton as ordered, in uniform?'

'I'm not sure.'

220

'I'd strongly advise you to do so.'

'My status is not settled.'

'Your status is clear. You are on active duty.'

He shrugged.

She asked in a conversational tone, 'Did you get your business taken care of today?'

Tyson nodded. 'I met with a fellow who has done the legal groundwork to establish a nonprofit national defence fund for me. Then I met with a lawyer from the Reserve Officers Association, over on Constitution Avenue. Then I had lunch with some people from the Disabled American Veterans. I have a ten per cent disability as you know. Actually I think it's seven and a half per cent, but what the hell. Anyway, they asked me to join, and I did. After lunch I met with a delegation from the Veterans of Foreign Wars, and then I called on my congressman.'

'You've had a peripatetic day.'

'Right. And I moved around a lot too.'

She smiled, then said, 'It's good to keep busy.'

'Well, Major, you have to hustle when you're trying to beat a firing squad.'

'Don't be melodramatic.'

Tyson picked up his drink. 'I had the feeling today that I have a lot of support. That the government and the Army are following an unpopular course of action.'

Karen Harper replied, 'Well, that's the strength of a pluralistic society, Mr Tyson. Free people rally around a cause or issue and fight the government. I think that's very healthy.'

'Do you understand what I'm telling you?'

'Yes. The government is aware of all this. But to use a military expression, the Rubicon has been crossed.'

'Are they looking for a way to retreat with honour?'

'I don't think so. They can't.'

Tyson commented, 'Then the hell with them. They'll get a fight.'

She said, 'I've always thought that ninety per cent of wars, trials, and fistfights were started because no one knew how to back off while saving face. Perhaps if people didn't feel the *need* to save face, we could avoid conflict.'

Tyson snorted. 'That's a very feminine attitude. Face *is* important, and conflict is not necessarily bad.'

The waitress brought Karen Harper's wine.

Tyson raised his glass. 'To a short relationship.'

She touched her glass to his. 'Don't be sulky.'

They both drank.

She said, 'I forgot your umbrella.'

'So I see.'

'I think I left it on the plane.'

'It was a gift from my grandmother, right before she died.'

'Then she won't know I lost it.'

They stared at each other awhile, then smiled simultaneously. Tyson noticed she was in a somewhat lighter mood than last time. He wondered if this was because she had some good news for him. But based on the conversation so far, that wasn't likely. More likely she'd just got some good news for herself or had sex or bought a new shade of lip gloss.

She said, 'I'm to advise you again of your right to remain silent and to have an attorney present and of your other rights in regard to this investigation.'

'I'll waive that.'

'Okay.' She surprised him by signalling to a waitress. The waitress approached, and Karen Harper motioned towards the nearly full glass of wine. 'Please take this and bring me a glass of Principessa Gavia. Do you have that?'

'Yes, ma'am. Only by the bottle.'

'Fine.'

The waitress took the glass and moved off.

Tyson said, 'When in Rome ...'

She replied, 'It's actually a Piedmont wine from the Banfi estate at Gavia.'

'Really.'

'I visited the winery once.'

'Are you going to drink the whole bottle?'

'I only want a glass.'

'You wouldn't have ordered that at the Presidential.'

'Probably not.'

She continued, 'I've done some further work on this investigation. Mostly telephone calls plus some records research. I contacted Andrew Picard by phone. He was very reluctant to tell me the names of your two platoon members who gave him his story. But I persuaded him it would be in the best interests of justice.'

Tyson recalled that Picard was an ex-officer and might also be vulnerable. He replied, 'I'm sure you were convincing.' He lit a cigarette.

She stared at him awhile, then said, 'Well, aren't you going to ask me who they were?'

'No, I'm playing it cool.'

She replied, 'Well, I'll pretend you asked because then I have to tell you. One of the men who related the Miséricorde Hospital story to Picard was your former platoon medic, Steven Brandt.' She glanced at him. Tyson showed no reaction.

She continued, 'He's now a physician in Boston. An orthopaedist. I spoke to him by phone.'

'Did you?'

'Yes. And he reiterated and confirmed the story he gave to Picard about the massacre.'

'Did he?'

'And he elaborated on it somewhat. That is, he'd read Picard's book, of course, and he added some details.'

Tyson knew it was Brandt, hoped it was Brandt, and not one of the others. But there *was* another man, and Tyson had no idea who it could be.

Karen Harper continued, 'I'm obligated to tell you about Brandt; that is, the name of a possible witness against you. But because his testimony was unsworn, there was no transcript and no recording made. Therefore I'm not obligated to tell you precisely what he said. However, if we proceed to a formal investigation, you or your attorney will have the opportunity to cross-examine any sworn testimony Dr Brandt might give. Do you understand this point of law?'

'I remember.'

'Good.' She seemed thoughtful, then said, 'Was there any bad blood between you and Dr Brandt?'

'He wasn't a doctor then, only a scared punk kid like the rest of us. The title "doctor" has some cachet, and I don't want·it used in these proceedings. How's that for a point of law?'

'I'll make a note of it. How about the bad blood?'

'No.'

'Are you certain? Mr Brandt – Spec/4 Brandt – was a conscientious objector. There were often bad feelings between—'

'That's not true. The medics who were COs were as fine a group of soldiers as you could find. I respected their beliefs, their bravery, retrieving wounded under fire, carrying that huge medical bag that made them a better target than my lieutenant bar made me.'

She nodded, then said, 'But you're speaking in general terms. Did you feel that way about Brandt?'

'I'll think about that.' Tyson stubbed his cigarette into an ashtray. 'Okay, who was the other man who spoke to Picard?'

'Richard Farley.'

'Farley?'

'Yes. Do you remember him?'

'Vaguely.'

'What do you remember about him?'

'Nothing of any consequence.'

'Was he a good soldier?'

'Check his record.'

'I'm asking you.'

Tyson thought a moment. *Farley. Why Farley? Why not?*

'Mr Tyson?'

'He was ... not particularly bright, not particularly brave – somewhat below average in all areas.'

'Any bad blood between you? I ask that because if there was an incident it might be possible to show that Farley is not unbiased towards you.'

'I understand. But there was no bad blood between us. Neither was there any love lost between officers and enlisted men. Actually, it was a classical love-hate relationship.'

'You and Farley?'

'Me and them.'

A busboy brought a wine bucket and stand, setting it beside Tyson. A sommelier approached followed by the waitress. Tyson observed to Karen Harper, 'This is getting serious.'

The waitress set down two glasses and the sommelier displayed the label to Tyson. Tyson said, 'I only read scotch labels. The lady ordered the wine.'

The wine steward bowed his head. 'Very good, sir.' He pivoted smoothly and held the bottle towards Karen Harper. 'Major?'

She nodded.

He drew the cork and set it on the cocktail table in front of her, then poured a few ounces into her glass. She sipped the wine. 'Fine.'

'Very good, Major.' He filled her glass and turned to Tyson. 'Sir?' he said, with the expertise of one who recognizes an oenophobe when he sees one.

Tyson shrugged. 'Good chaser for the scotch.'

The sommelier filled Tyson's glass, submerged the bottle in the bucket, bowed, and left.

The waitress lingered a moment, looking at Tyson, then glanced at Harper, and recognition dawned on her face. She said, 'Can I get you anything else?'

'The bill,' said Tyson.

She turned and left.

Karen Harper sipped her wine in silence.

Tyson tasted his. 'Not bad. How would you describe it?'

She replied, 'It has a fresh, perfumy bouquet. It is clean, well balanced, with a light frizzante and a haunting aftertaste.'

'That's just what I was thinking.' He set his glass down and said, 'By the way, the waitress recognized me. Maybe you too.'

She nodded. 'I thought she might have.'

He said, 'In New York, there are waitresses and such who get paid by gossip columnists to report on newsworthy people having a tête-à-tête in a dark lounge.'

Karen Harper seemed a bit surprised by that. 'Well, I don't think—'

'I don't want to be here when a photographer from the *American Investigator* arrives.' He stood.

'We could go to a pub I know in Georgetown. About five minutes' walk—'

'I'm tired of bars. Room 618, if you want to come up. Five-minute intervals, sound and light security, three knocks, password is "lollipop" – the enemy can't say that. They say "rorripop." Did you know that?' He nodded towards the wine bucket. 'That's on the Army.' He turned and left.

20

Ben Tyson stood at his room bar and poured a miniature bottle of scotch into a glass of ice and soda. He looked around the room. A hanging lamp cast a soft glow over the sitting area. The triple-sized bed was lit by a table lamp, and Tyson switched it off, leaving the bed in darkness.

There were three solid raps on the door, and he moved towards the foyer. 'Password.'

After a moment of silence, he heard her say, 'Rorripop.'

He smiled, then opened the door.

She stood at the threshold a moment, then entered wordlessly.

He motioned her towards the couch on the far side of the room. She went to it but did not sit.

Tyson took a split of white wine from the bar refrigerator and filled a stem glass. He set the glass on the coffee table in front of her. 'Domestic. Okay?'

She didn't reply.

Tyson took his drink to an upholstered chair opposite the couch and sat.

After a full minute of mutual silence, she said, 'I really shouldn't be here.'

'Neither should I.'

'I have to put this in my report. I mean where we are conducting this interview.'

'You're free to leave.'

She said, 'I'm thinking of your interests too. You're a married man ...'

'That is the least of my problems. Listen, Major Karen Harper, I didn't ask for a female investigator, and I'm cooperating in this investigation. If I choose to conduct this interview in the privacy and comfort of my room, and if you're uncomfortable, we can reschedule this for another time and place. I can't promise I'll be as talkative then, and I may have a lawyer present.'

She seemed indecisive for a moment, then sat on the couch. 'Where were we?'

'Downstairs in the lounge. Farley and I.' Tyson settled back in his chair.

'Yes. Farley is a paraplegic. He was badly wounded by shrapnel in the spine about two months after you left Vietnam. Did you know that?'

'I seem to remember someone writing to me about that.' He'd maintained some contact with the platoon for a few

227

months. Then, through normal attrition – death, wounds, sickness, rotation back to the States, and transfers – there was no one left. The first platoon of Alpha Company had, like a college fraternity, metamorphosed into a different platoon, only the name remained the same – new blood in; old, tired, and dead blood out. A succession of new officers and new riflemen, who became old men if they lived longer than ninety days. Stories and myths were handed down: tales of cowardice and bravery, and the tales changed with each telling as the oral history of the platoon was transmitted like a compressed epic poem in the vernacular of the GI. He often wondered what legacy he'd left.

Karen Harper broke into his thoughts. 'Farley lives in Jersey City now. He spends a good deal of time in VA hospitals. He is drug-dependent and suffers from emotional disturbances.'

'Good witness for the prosecution.' Tyson added, 'Sorry to hear about that though.'

'I spoke to him briefly by telephone. His story seems to corroborate that of Brandt.'

Tyson kicked off his loafers and rubbed his feet against the thick rug. 'You can make yourself comfortable.'

'I'm comfortable.' She glanced around the softly lit room. 'Very nice. Your company does quite well with government contracts.'

'Those are not unrelated thoughts.'

'No.'

'I worked hard to get where I am – was.'

She nodded. 'I didn't mean to be offensive.'

'No, I don't think you did. We're from different worlds, Major.' He thought a moment, then said, 'To use a lover's expression, this is not working.'

She stared at him before replying, 'Let's try to make it work.'

He shrugged.

She said, 'Richard Farley is a potential witness for the

228

prosecution. You will have the right to cross-examine him if—'

'How did Picard find him? How did Picard find Brandt?'

'Interesting. It seems that Picard, after his chance conversation with Sister Teresa in France, placed an ad in the locator section of the First Cavalry Division newspaper.' She opened her briefcase and handed Tyson a photocopy of the locator section dated some two years before.

Tyson looked at the circled ad and read: *Historian looking for veterans of Alpha Co., First Battalion, Seventh Cav. who served during the first three months of 1968. Specifically would want to hear from anyone from the first platoon who was at the battle of Miséricorde Hospital at Hue. Researching same for private client. All replies kept strictly confidential, anonymity assured.*

Which, thought Tyson, was bullshit. He noticed a post office box address in Sag Harbor. He laid the ad on the coffee table.

She said, 'The First Cavalry Division informs me that they send *you* that newspaper.'

Tyson nodded. About the only thing he ever glanced at in that newspaper was the sometimes interesting locator section: men looking for lost buddies, women looking for wayward men, historians doing research – that sort of thing. But he'd obviously missed this one. Brandt had not. *Fate*. He said, 'Brandt and Farley answered this?'

'Actually only Brandt did. Sometime later, at Picard's urging, Brandt supplied a corroborating witness in the person of Richard Farley.'

Tyson nodded. 'How did Brandt know the whereabouts of Farley? Why did Brandt come forward in the first place?'

She shrugged. 'When I spoke to Brandt he confined his answers to what he saw at Miséricorde Hospital. If he's subpoenaed, we'll discover the answers to your other questions.'

'Was Brandt perhaps the medic who treated Farley after he

229

was hit?'

'Funny, but I asked that too. According to Farley, he was.'

'That's interesting. What else did Farley say?'

'Not much that was comprehensible. He seemed very distraught. He cried actually.'

Tyson's eyes met hers, and she turned away. Tyson stood. 'Want another?'

'I haven't touched this one.'

He walked to the refrigerator and opened it. 'Hey, here's a bottle of champs.' He popped the cork on a split of Moët and poured two glasses of the champagne, then carried the glasses back to the sitting area. 'Here. Join me in a toast.'

She took the glass. 'To what?'

Tyson raised his glass. 'To Richard Farley and the other two million, seven hundred thousand who returned to pollute our society with wasted limbs, damaged chromosomes, and sick minds.'

She lowered her glass. 'I won't drink to that.'

'Well, I will.' He raised his glass, then suddenly flung it across the room where it shattered against the bar cabinet. He strode quickly out of the room into the bathroom and slammed the door.

Karen Harper sat motionless and listened to the water running. She noticed her hands were shaking. She reached for her briefcase, then released it, then reached for it again and stood.

Tyson came back into the room, motioned her into her seat, and sat down without a word.

She noticed he'd splashed water on his face and combed his hair. She detected the faint scent of a good cologne.

Tyson said, 'Go on.'

Karen Harper cleared her throat. She said, 'May I have a cigarette?'

'You don't smoke.'

'Sometimes I do.'

He held his pack of cigarettes towards her, and she took

230

one. He lit it, noticing that she held it awkwardly and drew on it as though she were sucking through a straw. She exhaled and continued, 'As I indicated in our first meeting, I've located some members of your platoon. Two, to be exact. Since I last spoke to you I've spoken to them by telephone.'

Tyson did not reply.

She continued, 'One is a former squad leader named Paul Sadowski, who lives in Chicago, and the other is Anthony Scorello, who now lives in a suburb of San Francisco. Do you remember them?'

'Vaguely.'

'I thought men remembered who they served with in combat.'

'Macho myth.'

Karen Harper regarded him for some time, then asked, 'Do you want to know what Sadowski and Scorello said?'

'Sure.' Tyson felt his heart thumping, and his mouth went dry. 'Sure. What did they say?'

She leaned towards him and watched him, making no pretence of not noticing his unease. Tyson stared back at her, angry that she would play it out like this. He snapped, 'Well, what did they say, Major?'

'They said,' she replied evenly, 'exactly what you said.'

Their eyes met, and neither looked away. Tyson settled back in his chair. 'So. There you have it.'

'Have what?'

'*My* corroboration. Two against two. And if I offer sworn testimony in my own behalf—'

'Neither a grand jury nor a court-martial takes a vote of witnesses, Lieutenant. They would be interested, however, in who is perjuring himself.'

Tyson felt his confidence returning and said curtly, 'I would be interested in *why* Brandt and Farley would perjure *themselves*.'

She nodded appreciatively, drew on her cigarette, then stubbed it out. She said, 'Whether it is perjury or truth, Mr

231

Tyson, I think that ultimately only you can tell me why they told Picard this story. Only you can tell me why Sadowski and Scorello told me a different story.' She stared at him, but he did not reply.

She leaned across the cocktail table and lowered her voice. 'Lies are destructive and spread like malignancy to the innocent and guilty alike. I want the lies to stop. I want *you* to put an end to them, if not for your own sake, then for the sake of the innocent and for the sake of your country. End the nightmare for everyone. Tell me what happened on 15 February 1968. What *happened*?'

Tyson spoke with no inflection in his voice. 'If I know the truth, and I haven't told you, it's because I'm not convinced that you, the country, the Army, or anyone deserves to know the truth.'

'What can I do to convince you?'

'Probably nothing. Maybe just get closer to it by stages. Truth should be hard-won. The truth is only recognized as the truth after all the lies are told and discounted. You won't appreciate the truth or even begin to fathom it unless you take a tortuous road to find it.'

She nodded. 'But you *will* tell me? I mean, sometime after this is all over? You will tell me, personally and privately, if not publicly?'

'I may. I may very well.'

'But now I have to work hard.'

'Yes, I had to work hard.'

'Fair enough.' She sat back in her chair.

Tyson looked at her in the dim light of the lamp. He had the sudden impression that she was more obsessed with this thing than she ought to be. It occurred to him that if he could understand the source of her obsession he could outflank her and the Army.

Like every good interrogator, she had made a sudden switch from inquisitor to confessor. That often worked with the smug patriot or religious fanatic, happy in their martyrdom, or with the mentally deficient who didn't understand the consequences of confession. But since he didn't fit any of these types, he saw no reason to offer a confession. And it wasn't the truth they wanted anyway. The truth reflected more unfavourably on them, on the system, than it did on him. What they wanted was a final offering to Mars, a last scrap of flesh, because 57,939 sacrifices weren't enough, and the soothsayers had somehow divined that 57,940 was what was required to put the war to rest for all time. But, Tyson thought, since he didn't recall having started the war, he saw no good reason for sacrificing himself to end it. Marcy, he realized, would be pleased with that reasoning.

He said aloud but not to Karen Harper, 'I made it home. I'm standing on home base. You can't tag me out now. What is the statute of limitations on being tagged out?'

Karen Harper stood and moved to the large picture window. She looked up Pennsylvania Avenue towards the lighted White House. She said, 'There in that mansion lives a man who knows your name, who has memos on his desk with your name on them.'

Tyson looked at her dark profile against the window.

She continued, 'That man deals with issues of global importance and national survival every day. From time to time, because of the structure of our laws, he must personally deal with the cases of individual citizens. He is Commander in Chief of the armed forces, your boss and mine. He can grant clemency, immunity, and pardons. He can commission you into the armed forces, and he can rescind your commission. Somewhere along the line, he will have to make a decision regarding you – before, during, or after a court-martial.' She turned her head towards Tyson. 'Soon, in the next few days, he is scheduled to hold a press conference. Your name will come up. He, or his aides, have prepared a brief statement regarding your case.' She added, 'I strongly suspect that he wishes he'd never heard your name and hopes he never hears it again after that press conference.'

'That would make two of us.'

'The nation, Mr Tyson, wishes they'd never heard your name.'

'Then that makes all of us.' He asked, 'How about you?'

'I'm glad I met you. You are a remarkable man ...' She added self-consciously, 'A man by whom I will probably judge other men.'

He stared at her for a moment, then remarked, 'Having said that, you probably want to leave.'

'Should I?'

He rubbed his lip contemplatively, then replied, 'No. I don't think we will speak again like this, alone and without witnesses or counsel. We may as well both get the most out of it.'

'Yes, there are certain dynamics that take place when only two people are present ... It gets complicated and phony when there is even one more person. We couldn't speak like this.'

Tyson put his right leg on the cocktail table and abruptly pulled his trouser leg up, revealing his shin and knee. 'Come here. Look at this.'

There was something of the infantry officer in his voice that compelled her to respond quickly and automatically.

'Look. This is something I wouldn't do at a formal hearing. Closer.'

She stepped closer and looked down at the thick, curving purple scar.

'Not much as far as wounds go, Major. But when it happens to you, your stomach heaves and your skin goes all clammy.'

She kept staring at the old wound as if studying it for some meaning.

Tyson said, 'A shrink once spent two hours telling me about the synergistic effect of a physical scar on a mental scar. The great truth he revealed was this: The disfigurement and pain is a daily reminder of the traumatic episode.' Tyson pulled the trouser leg down. 'Well, no kidding.'

She looked up and said, 'A shrink?'

Tyson realized he should not have revealed that information. He replied, 'A friend. Cocktail party chatter.'

She nodded, but he saw she didn't believe that. She asked, 'Did Brandt treat you?'

Tyson glanced up at her but didn't reply.

'Did Brandt treat you?'

'No.' Tyson stood. He paced to the centre of the room, turned, and faced her.

'Why not? He was your platoon medic.'

Tyson did not reply.

'Was he there at the time you were wounded?'

'Ask him.'

'I'm asking you.'

'Ask *him*!'

She was momentarily startled, then said, 'All right. I will.' At length she said, 'In addition to the chapter in Picard's book that deals with the Miséricorde Hospital incident, Picard mentions you in two other chapters.'

She stooped down and retrieved Picard's book from her briefcase, placing it under the light of the hanging lamp over the cocktail table. She said, 'You are mentioned in an early chapter – the firefight at Phu Lai on the first day of the Tet Offensive. Then you are mentioned at the end of the book, the aftermath of the battle of Hue.'

She opened the book to a marked place and, still kneeling, read:

The battle was officially declared over on 26 February, and military communiqués spoke of 'mopping-up operations.' But the battle was not over just because the American military declared it to be. For the Marines and Army personnel still engaged in shooting matches with communist troops in and around the city, there was precious little difference between battle and 'mopping up.'

Ironically, one of the last American casualties at Hue was the man whose platoon had made one of the first contacts of the Tet Offensive, Lieutenant Benjamin Tyson.

Tyson's platoon, badly mauled in the market square at Phu Lai on 30 January, had gone on to Miséricorde Hospital on 15 February, then was helicoptered to a secure beach area for a few days of rest and refitting. But the battle of Hue raged on, and the barely fit platoon was helicoptered with the rest of Alpha Company, Fifth Battalion, Seventh Cavalry, to an area two kilometres north of Hue. The company, still under the command of Captain Roy Browder, patrolled south towards the city.

On 21 February, Alpha Company found themselves on the north bank of the Perfume River. Across the river was the Gia Hoi quarter of Hue, a triangle-shaped point of land nestled in a sharp bend of the river. Most of the Gia Hoi suburb was still under communist control.

Captain Browder, apparently on his own initiative, commandeered a number of flimsy watercraft from the local villagers and crossed the river at dusk. After they reached the opposite bank, the company came into contact with an enemy unit dug into the high ground above the riverbank. The two groups exchanged fire in the growing darkness. Several men of Alpha Company were wounded, and two men of Tyson's first platoon, Peter Santos and John Manelli, were killed. Also killed was Captain Browder.

At daybreak, Tyson, the last officer in the company, received radio orders making him Alpha Company's commander. The enemy had disappeared during the night, and Tyson moved Alpha Company away from the river into an area known as the Strawberry Patch. This was a semirural section of the Gia Hoi suburb of Hue, a place we would describe today as a gentrified exurb. There, in the Strawberry Patch, Alpha Company encountered thousands of wretched refugees. And there they also discovered the first of the mass graves that held the approximately three thousand citizens of Hue massacred by the Viet Cong and North Vietnamese.

Meanwhile, a South Vietnamese ranger battalion had also crossed the river and was making its way south. On 26 February, this unit, with supporting fire from Alpha Company, stormed the last stronghold in Gia Hoi, the Cambodian Pagoda across the street from the high school. It was then that Gia Hoi was considered clear, and the battle of Hue was declared over. But this was premature. Whether by design or circumstances, hundreds of enemy troops remained in Hue's main suburb of Gia Hoi.

On 29 February, Alpha Company was engaged in aiding refugees and searching for Viet Cong hiding among the masses of displaced civilians. Tyson had set up checkpoints on a road that led to the east gate of the Citadel wall. His men examined civilian ID cards, handed out C rations, and set up a medical aid station. Suddenly rockets streaked out of a nearby grove of fruit trees. Several soldiers and civilians were hit by flying shrapnel, and Lieutenant Tyson suffered a wound to the knee. As the refugees scattered, the enemy began firing automatic weapons at the Americans who had taken cover in a drainage ditch and were firing back. After ten or fifteen minutes, the enemy broke contact.

The wounded of Alpha Company, including its last officer, Benjamin Tyson, were medevaced to a hospital ship in the South China Sea.

Another irony of this tale is that Lieutenant Tyson, whose platoon had acted so inhumanely at Miséricorde Hospital, was wounded while on a mission of mercy. Alpha Company itself, now without a single officer and with over half its men killed or wounded, was finally ordered to stand down. They were helicoptered to Camp Evans, the First Air Cavalry Forward Base Camp, and given two weeks of relatively safe perimeter guard duty.

Replacements of officers, sergeants, and enlisted men filled the ranks of the decimated company, as the original men found increasingly ingenious ways of removing themselves from that ill-fated unit.

Hue, that smoking, burning cauldron where so many had died, was peaceful on the morning of March the first. The birds had returned, and no gunfire could be heard for the first time in over a month. But the proud city, often described as the most precious piece of Vietnam, lay devastated, its inhabitants totally demoralized, their once legendary spirit crushed for all time.

And yet the killing was not quite over. There was still the matter of revenge. This writer personally observed the National Police 'Black Squads' rounding up hundreds of men, women, and students accused by their neighbours of having aided the occupying communist invaders. These unfortunate people were taken to various places in and around the city and presumably executed since they were never heard from again.

As a young Marine officer, standing on a tower of the Citadel, I watched the endless funeral processions winding through the rubble-strewn streets. Hue, which had thumbed its nose at the war, would never be the same again, and neither would the American soldiers who fought there.

Vietnam's most celebrated songwriter at the time, a young man named Trihn Cong Son, was living in Hue during the battle. In March, with the Vietnamese spring in full bloom, he wrote a ballad, a stanza of which is translated here:

> When I went to the Strawberry Patch
> I sang on top of corpses
> I saw, I saw, I saw on the road
> An old father hugging the corpse of his
> Frost-cold child.

238

When I went to the Strawberry Patch of an
afternoon
I saw, I saw, I saw pits and trenches filled with
The corpses of my brothers and my sisters.

Karen Harper closed the book and looked up at Tyson.
The room was still, and neither spoke.

Finally Tyson said, 'I just realized that it must have been as
unsettling for Picard to write that book as it was for me to
read it. He smelled the same evil smell that I did.'

Karen Harper nodded. She said, 'I'd like to know what
happened to you during that ten or fifteen minutes of the
firefight.'

'I bled.'

'Yes, of course you did. And you were in pain. And a medic
should have got to you. But ...' She stood. 'Well, you said
there was no bad blood between you and Brandt, but I
strongly suspect there was.'

Tyson sat on the edge of the bed. He said, 'If you suspect
that Brandt did not tell Picard everything that happened at
the Strawberry Patch, why would you believe Brandt's
selective perceptions of the events at Miséricorde Hospital?'

'I never said I did. What did Brandt do or fail to do at the
Strawberry Patch?'

'You find out. Then you tell me. Then I'll tell you if you're
right.'

'All right.' She paused, then said, 'Picard lives in Sag
Harbor on Long Island. Did you know that?'

'That was on the book jacket.'

'Yes ... and it's an odd coincidence that you and your
family are summering there.'

Tyson rose from the bed and crossed to the cocktail table.
He picked up his drink. 'Partly coincidence, partly fate.
Partly ... reading that on the jacket reminded me of the place.
We used to go out there ... long ago.'

She said, 'You may run into him out there.'

'Right.' He reflected a moment, then said, 'People out there have these neat mailboxes by the side of the road with their last names on them.' He glanced at her. 'I guess you know about rural mailboxes. Anyway, you read all sorts of famous names. But there is an unwritten rule of privacy. Well, I used to see the name Picard, but I never associated it with Andrew Picard the novelist, probably because I never heard of him. Anyway, down the road from a house I rented some years ago was a mailbox with the name Algren. I found out it was Nelson Algren, the guy who wrote *The Man with the Golden Arm*. I loved that book, and I had a copy of it. I wanted to knock on his door and ask him to autograph it. But I didn't want to violate that rule of privacy. Then some months later I read that he died. So my book is unsigned. But I have this other book, by Andrew Picard, and I think I'd like his autograph, before something happens to *him*.'

She raised her eyebrows. 'Don't do anything ... that will get you into trouble.'

Tyson sat on the arm of the upholstered chair and stared out of the window.

She said abruptly, 'Are you separated?'

He was taken aback by the question, but answered, 'Yes.'

'Is there any chance of a reconciliation?'

'I suppose ... I don't think it's ... I mean I think we're just separated for the duration. Not legally. Why?'

'Just curious.'

'Are you?' Tyson lit a cigarette.

Karen Harper said, 'I'm sorry. I mean about your marriage. And your job.'

'Well, that's life though. You can't be suspected of mass murder without there being a few inconveniences attached.'

'It's easy to be bitter—'

Tyson suddenly jumped to his feet. He felt tired, angry, sick of the subject of murder. 'Oh, Christ, Major, I don't need any more damned sympathy. I've had enough of that today.'

'Sorry—'

'If I'm a mass murderer, then I don't deserve the sympathy. If I'm not, I'll sue the pants off everyone and retire to Switzerland.' Tyson continued, 'Do you know where else I was today? I went to the memorial ... I could stand here all fucking night and tell you what passed through my mind in ten minutes there. But it's all been said. I mean it's all there in that great big black fucking wall. Do me a favour. Go there. Look at yourself in the wall. Take your goddamned list of Alpha Company and find them in the wall. Listen, I don't care about myself. But how in the name of God can the government bring further discredit on those poor bastards? Go there, Major, and talk to the dead and explain your course of action to them.'

She nodded slowly. 'I *will* go there.'

Tyson suddenly felt fatigued and slumped back into his chair. He closed his eyes.

Karen Harper walked to the window and stared out of it. Finally she turned from the window and said, 'Can I make you a drink?'

He looked at her in the dim light and nodded.

She crossed to the bar and made him a scotch and soda, then carried it back and handed it to him. She said, 'I'm not feeling very well. Can we continue this another time?'

'No. Finish it up.'

'Are you sure? ...'

'Finish it. Tonight.'

She nodded and sat on the couch across from him. 'I'm not feeling sorry for you. I'm feeling sorry for myself.'

'Good. Press on, Major.'

Karen Harper looked across the cocktail table at Benjamin Tyson, then drew a typed sheet of paper from her briefcase and glanced at it. She said, 'Based on Picard's book and on Army records and on the statements of Brandt, Farley, Sadowski, and Scorello, I've compiled this list of five additional men who were present at the hospital and who we believe are alive today.' Harper read, 'Dan Kelly, Hernando

Beltran, Lee Walker, Harold Simcox, and Louis Kalane.' She handed the list to Tyson and said, 'Could you add any names to this list?'

Tyson took the list and scanned the names. 'No ... well, yes. Holzman and Moody.'

She replied, 'Kurt Holzman was killed in a motorcycle accident fifteen years ago. Robert Moody died of cancer two years ago. That's why they're not on the list.'

'I see ...' He put the paper on the cocktail table. Picard had mentioned the names of most of the platoon members in his book but had not included the usual appendix of 'Where They Are Now.' Picard obviously did not know where they were, or he'd have contacted them as he'd contacted Brandt and Farley and had tried to interview Tyson himself. Picard, though, when he'd had his photograph done at the wall, could have taken the trouble to look at the names behind him. Tyson said, 'I learned today that Brontman and Selig were killed in action after I left Vietnam.'

'Yes, they were. How did you learn that?'

'I saw their names.'

She nodded. 'Yes, of course.' She inquired, 'By the way, did you find your personal journal, or platoon log, or whatever you kept?'

'I didn't keep a log.'

Her eyebrows rose to indicate incredulity. 'I was told all officers kept some sort of logbook or journal. How could you remember radio frequencies, platoon rosters, promotions, guard duty, grid coordinates, and all that, without written entries in some sort of book?'

Tyson sat back and stared thoughtfully at a point above Karen Harper's head. In a steamer trunk in his basement, that held much of his war memorabilia, he'd found his tattered, water-stained log, bound in furry grey hide, which according to the itinerant Chinese stationer who'd sold it to him was elephant hide, though Tyson suspected the deceased animal to be a rat. The daily entries were written in GI-issue blue ballpoint pen, now turned light violet. The paper was yellowed and water-stained, and the writing was barely legible. It was, however, legible enough to spark his memory, and as he'd flipped the pages, names, places, and incidents returned to him in a way that Picard's book was not able to conjure up for him.

The entry for 15 February had begun in much the same way as other days: *BMNT* [Beginning of Morning Nautical Twilight] *0632 hrs. 68 F, rainy, cold, windy*. Then followed the platoon roster, people on sick call, notes regarding resupply, a change in a radio frequency, grid coordinate objectives, and other small details of infantry life in the field. He'd made one personal note that morning that read: *Morale awful*.

The next entry for that date was written in almost total darkness sometime after sundown, the words scrawled across two pages. It read: *Platoon on verge of mutiny. Overheard death threats. Filed false radio report re: hospital battle this A.M. Investigate. God—*

And there it ended. *God what?* he thought. *God forgive? God help us?* He'd forgotten what he was going to write.

He had slid the book into his waistband as someone drew close in the dark and spoke to him; they might not think to search his body for his logbook.

Investigate. And they were. But not, unfortunately, posthumously. The entry in itself was not revealing, but in light of recent developments it was incriminating enough; incriminating enough to put him behind bars. Yet he could not bring himself to destroy the book and had mailed it to his sister Laurie in Atlanta for safekeeping.

'Lieutenant Tyson? *Did* you keep a log?'

He looked at her. 'Actually I did. But I recall that after I was evacuated to a hospital ship it was lost.'

'Lost?'

'Yes, along with most of my personal effects. They helicoptered you onto the ship, pretty nurses stripped you

243

and scrubbed you, and injected you, and what personal effects you had were put into a small plastic bag. Government property was put into another bag. Give back to Caesar that which is Caesar's. You were damaged meat that needed processing and mending. And if you couldn't be mended, then *you* were put into a plastic bag. Give back to God that which is God's. Get it?'

She seemed to have some trouble following him, then said, 'So ... the logbook was ...'

'Probably put into the government bag and recycled or burned or whatever they did with bloody clothes and equipment. When my bag of personal effects was returned – watch, wallet, letters, and cigarette lighter – I noticed my diary was missing.'

She nodded, and Tyson had the impression she appreciated a well-constructed lie. She said, 'That would have been a nice keepsake, the basis for your memoirs.'

'I don't think anyone is interested in my memoirs.'

'But they are.'

Tyson lit a cigarette. 'So, these five – Kelly, Beltran, Walker, Simcox, and Kalane are unaccounted for?'

Karen Harper nodded. 'But we're looking for them.' She drew another piece of paper from her briefcase. 'I'll give you a rundown.' She glanced at the typed sheet. 'There were, we believe, nineteen of you who approached that hospital on the afternoon of 15 February 1968. Does that sound right?'

'I suppose. Except we didn't know it was a hospital.'

She looked annoyed. 'The building. Structure. Edifice.'

'Right.'

'Of the nineteen, we are in contact with five – Brandt, Farley, Sadowski, Scorello, and you.' She continued, 'Arthur Peterson was wounded by a bullet to the chest during the ... assault or approach to the hospital and died there. Correct?'

'Correct.'

'Moody was lightly wounded but was returned to duty the following week.'

'Correct.'

'According to what you told me, Larry Cane was killed in the room-to-room fighting. The Army death certificate lists a bullet through the heart. Correct?'

Tyson said nothing.

She looked at him a few seconds, then said again, 'A bullet through the heart.'

Tyson nodded.

She continued, 'Two men, Peter Santos and John Manelli, were killed at Hue in the incident described in Picard's book. Correct?'

'Correct.'

'That was the day Captain Browder was killed and you became company commander.'

'Right.'

'And Michael DeTonq disappeared in the city of Hue on 29 February, the same day you were wounded. He has never been accounted for.'

Tyson did not respond.

She added, 'And you were evacuated that day, leaving your platoon with thirteen men who had been at the scene of that incident. Later, after you'd gone back to the States, Brontman and Selig were killed as we know. Holzman and Moody died, as I said, in civilian life, leaving five possible witnesses: you, Brandt, Farley, Sadowski, and Scorello, whose whereabouts we know; and five witnesses who we believe to be alive but whose whereabouts are unknown at present: Kelly, Beltran, Walker, Simcox, and Kalane. Also one possible witness, Michael DeTonq, who is officially listed as missing in action and presumed dead. Is that correct?'

Tyson glanced at his copy of the typed sheet. 'Sounds right.'

'Have you ever heard from any of these men who are unaccounted for?'

Tyson shook his head. Men sometimes kept in touch after having shared the common experience of war. In fact, there

245

were reunions sponsored by the First Cavalry Division Association. *But*, he thought, *we shared something that would make it unlikely we would attend such reunions or that we'd send Christmas cards to one another*.

'What do you think happened to Michael DeTonq?'

'How would I know?'

'Do you think he deserted?'

'He's listed as missing. Why dishonour his memory?'

'If he deserted, there is no honour attached to his memory.'

Tyson replied curtly, 'Why cause pain to his family?'

'What sort of pain? If he deserted, he may be alive. That would give them some hope.'

'Hope is nothing more than deferred despair. Leave it alone.'

She said, 'This is important. He is a potential witness, perhaps a witness for you. The Army commission on MIAs will investigate his status, if even a shred of evidence can be found to suggest he may be alive ... perhaps a statement from you indicating why you believe he deserted, as opposed to the official conclusion of missing, presumed dead.'

'Even if he did desert I doubt he survived the fall of Vietnam.'

'He may have made it back to the States before then. If so, he could be back with his people in rural Louisiana. And the statute of limitations on desertion has run out.'

'Has it? Who writes these laws? And who gives a damn anyway? Not Michael DeTonq. Not me.'

She seemed deep in thought, then said, 'Under the category of silver linings, then. Okay? If nothing else comes of this, help the Army account for another one of its lost men. Tell me something I can transmit to the Army commission on MIAs.'

Tyson rested his chin in his hand contemplatively, then replied in a faraway tone, 'When I was wounded, as the helicopter was landing to take me away, Michael DeTonq knelt beside me, lit a cigarette for me, and said, "The war is over for you today. For me too. We'll meet again, back in the world. *Adieu, mon ami.*"'

Karen Harper leaned forward. 'May I write that down?'

'Yes.'

She took a notebook and pen from her purse and wrote, then read it back to him. 'Is that correct?'

'Yes.'

'And from what he said and perhaps how he said it and under the circumstances, you had the impression he was going to desert?'

'Yes.'

'Thank you.' She added, 'Back in the world – that was GI jargon for back in the States – he meant to make it back.'

'So did everyone.'

'Would you consider making a public appeal for these men – DeTonq, Dan Kelly, Hernando Beltran, Lee Walker, Harold Simcox, and Louis Kalane – to come forward?'

'No.'

'Why not? Won't they corroborate your story? If you line up enough witnesses for the defence, there may be no court-martial.' She added, 'I told you I would help locate witnesses for the defence. That's my job.'

'Then do it. Work hard.'

'I will. Why won't you help?'

Tyson contemplated his glass of scotch and soda, pressing an ice cube down with his fingertip. At length he said, 'I thought about what you're suggesting. I've decided that it would be unfair of me to make such an appeal. Each man has to be found by you or has to decide in his own way to come forward.' He looked at her. 'Do you understand?'

She nodded. 'But you will at least give me some clues? Some background?'

'Within limits.'

'All right, then let's continue. Have you ever heard from Dan Kelly?'

Tyson observed, 'This is beginning to sound like a class

247

reunion attended by only us two. Except you weren't in my class.'

'How long was Kelly your radio operator?'

'Want another cigarette?'

'I understand he was your radio operator for about seven months. I understand, too, that you had a close relationship. So I wonder if you heard from him recently.'

'No.'

'A long time ago, then?'

Tyson realized that as the scope of the investigation widened, as she spoke to more people, she would learn things or pretend to have learned things, and his chances of getting caught in a lie grew exponentially. For all he knew, Kelly had already spilled his guts into a tape recorder, and Karen Harper would pluck the recorder and tape out of her black bag of tricks and replay it for him. He said, 'Have you spoken to Kelly?'

'No. I'd have to tell you if I did.'

'But I have to ask.'

She shrugged. 'You make me ask the right questions.'

'I have more rights than you. I'm the suspect.'

'I have to work harder.'

'Right.'

'Have *you* heard from Kelly?'

'Actually I have. In about August of '68, then again about seven or eight years ago.'

She waited.

Tyson lit another cigarette. 'Kelly enjoyed soldiering. He enjoyed war. There are always a few like that ... Anyway, he wrote to me in August 1968 saying he was taking his discharge at an American installation in Ethiopia instead of back in the States. You probably know from his personnel file that he was discharged overseas.'

'Yes. I know that a soldier can take his discharge almost anywhere there is an American military installation. But I found it odd that he should pick Ethiopia instead of Rome,

248

for instance.'

'Well, there was no war in Rome at the time. But there *was* one in Biafra. Remember that one? Anyway, he wrote me saying he was going to join the mercenaries in Biafra. I figured he was killed there. Then ... yes, it was 1976 ... Bicentennial time, remember? ... he wrote to me again, from Portugal—'

'Excuse me. How did he have your address after so many years?'

'Well, he alluded to the fact that he was working for a civilian concern. In Nam this used to mean the CIA. And they have everyone's address, don't they?'

She asked, 'What did he write to you about?'

'About joining him in Portugal. Then taking a little trip down to Angola to look into the civil war there. A thousand a week, banked in Switzerland, and all expenses paid.'

'Were you enticed?'

Tyson thought a moment, then replied, 'I was married ... had a son by then. I remember thinking that the Army paid me eighty dollars a week as an infantry officer in Nam and that the CIA paid twelve hundred per cent more for the same shit work.' He smiled grimly, then added, 'And I'll bet the CIA never asked their people questions like the Army is asking me. If you want to investigate suspicious deaths, ask the CIA about their Operation Phoenix in Nam. They murdered, or caused to be murdered, about five thousand civilians who may or may not have been VC sympathizers. Go down to Langley tonight and ask them, Major. They're open all night. I'll go with you.'

'Did you respond to Kelly's letter?'

'No.'

'Did you hear from him again?'

'No. I remember seeing the published names of American mercenaries who were captured and executed by the leftist faction in Angola after they'd won the war. But Kelly's name wasn't among them.'

'I may be able to check on that.'

'Right. Go ask the spooks if they know of him or of his whereabouts. If you think I'm good at stonewalling, wait until you talk to those jokers. Maybe you'll learn something else about the law at Langley.'

'If you hear from any of these men as a result of the national publicity surrounding the case, will you let me know?'

'Perhaps.' Tyson stubbed out his cigarette.

'I'll let you know immediately if I locate any of them.'

'A little more immediately than you let me know about Sadowski or Scorello, please.'

'I have the right to question possible witnesses first.'

'So do I, if I find them first.' He looked at his watch.

'Just one or two more things.' Karen Harper regarded Tyson and said softly, 'Of course there is one more possible witness, someone whose testimony would be, I think, beyond reproach.'

'And who might that be, Major?'

'You know. The French government is cooperating in trying to find her. So is the Vatican.' Major Harper took a sip of her wine and continued, 'It should not have been difficult to locate a French-Vietnamese nun, but it is proving so. We believe she really exists, beyond what Picard has said and you have said. Actually the records of the Catholic Relief Agency list a Sister Teresa at that time and place, with other pertinent details of age and ancestry. What do you remember about her? Her age, for instance.'

Tyson said, 'The Eurasian nun I knew was then in her mid-twenties. She was strikingly beautiful, though the Catholic Relief Agency might not have that fact in their records. She worked at the dispensary attached to the Joan of Arc School. She lived at a convent nearby.'

'How did you know she was a nun?'

'Little clues. Like the nun's habit. A cross around her neck. Living in a convent. Didn't date much.'

'You're being sarcastic. I asked because the Vatican has no record of her having taken her final vows.'

Tyson remembered something Sister Teresa had said to him. *If we sin, it is not so great a sin as you think.* He said to Karen Harper, 'You know, over there, credentials were not carefully checked. If this woman had been educated by the Catholics, especially in a convent, and if she'd somehow acquired passable medical knowledge, then she could present herself as a nursing nun whether or not she was a nurse or a nun.'

Karen Harper nodded. 'So ... if she were an impostor then and continued to be when Picard met her in a French hospital, she might be lying low as a result of all this.'

Tyson shrugged. 'Possibly. But you should not use a pejorative word like impostor. Understand that Eurasians were outcasts in Vietnamese society. A woman like that would find protection, comfort, and a means of survival within the Catholic Church. I'm sure she earned her keep.'

Karen Harper replied, 'I'm sure she did. It's hard to comprehend that, isn't it? I mean being born into a society where the moment you are born you are an outcast with limited prospects. And you have to do something like impersonate a nun ... and lead a life of ... confined social opportunities ...'

'Celibacy.'

'Yes.'

'Well, most Eurasian women – those born of French soldiers and Vietnamese women – had the choice of the convent or the whorehouse. The whorehouse provided a similar sort of comfort and protection, without the celibacy requirement obviously.'

'Obviously.' She asked, 'Did you know Sister Teresa before this incident?'

Tyson did not want to lie about peripheral matters, but neither did he want to fashion a hangman's rope for the Army out of small threads of truth. The less said about Sister

Teresa, the better. On the other hand, she, like the others, might appear at any moment. He said, 'Yes, I knew her prior to that day.'

'How did you know her?'

'I met her briefly, in happier times, before Tet.'

'How?'

'By chance. At mass in the Phu Cam Cathedral.'.

'What were you doing there?'

'Looking for my dog.'

'I meant, you are not Catholic.'

'I went with a Catholic officer. To see the cathedral mostly.'

'When was the next time you saw her?'

'A week before Christmas. I was delivering some ... aid packages to the convent. She happened to be there. Then a day or so later there was a children's Christmas party at the Joan of Arc School in Hue. The MAC-V civic action officer was looking for someone to play the piano.'

'You play the piano?'

'As well as I speak French. But I can do Christmas carols. I'll play for you someday.'

'We'll wait until Christmas. So you met her then – at the Christmas party – and spoke to her?'

'Yes. A short conversation.'

'In what language?'

'French, Vietnamese, and English.'

'What was discussed?'

'Nothing that has any bearing on this case. We spoke of war, children, God's grace ... that sort of thing.'

'Are you a Christian?'

'Yes, it's fashionable now. Except at Peregrine-Osaka. There I'm a Buddhist from nine to five.'

'Were you a Christian then, in 1968, when it wasn't quite so fashionable?'

'I tried to be. Why?'

She shrugged, then asked, 'Did you see Sister Teresa again, after that Christmas party?'

252

'Yes.'

'How often?'

'Perhaps four times.'

'In what context?'

'What do you mean?'

'Did you see her officially? By chance? By design? Socially? How did you see her?'

'All of the above. What difference does it make?'

'I'm trying to pre establish her bona fides. Now that I see that you knew her, she may not be an unprejudiced witness as I was first led to believe. So I'd like to determine the extent of your involvement.'

Tyson didn't respond.

She asked, 'After the Christmas party, when and how did you see her?'

'I saw her twice more around Christmas. There was a truce, a cease-fire. I apparently made such a hit at the Christmas party that MAC-V requested that I do temporary civic action work in Hue.'

'Could Sister Teresa have had anything to do with MAC-V's request?'

'Ah, the plot thickens, does it not?'

'Well?'

Tyson shrugged. 'Possibly.'

'So you saw her twice more during the period of the Christmas cease-fire. How about after that?'

'Yes. In mid-January. I was asked to come to Hue to discuss job opportunities with MAC-V.'

'They offered you a job?'

'Yes.'

'Did you accept?'

'Yes. Frankly, I'd seen enough combat.'

'So how was it that you wound up still leading an infantry platoon?'

'Timing. I was to report to the MAC-V compound on or about January 30 to begin my new duties of winning hearts and minds. A staff officer said something about my arriving for the Vietnamese New Year party. He used the word Tet, but I didn't know what that meant. Anyway, when January 30 rolled around, Alpha Company was in the field, as usual. I decided not to take the morning resupply helicopter back to base camp, but to take the evening helicopter instead. I guess I was feeling a little guilty about leaving my platoon and company. Browder was razzing me about becoming a rear echelon flunky. So that morning I went out on what was to be my last patrol.'

She nodded. 'And the morning of January 30 found you in the market square at Phu Lai?'

'Yes. As I was lying there waiting to die, I thought it might have been better if I'd taken that morning resupply chopper. But as fate would have it, I lived, and by January 31, the MAC-V compound at Hue was surrounded by thousands of communist troops. They never broke through, but a lot of Americans died defending the compound, and a lot more were caught outside the compound walls, at Tet parties, and were found later with their hands tied behind their backs and bullets through their heads.' He lit a cigarette. 'So ... it's all written somewhere in God's daybook. Isn't it? "January 30 – A.M. – Tyson misses appointment with helicopter. Meets VC at Phu Lai instead. Bullet nicks ear. P.M. – Dinner with Alpha Company. C rations in the cemetery. Begin Tet offensive."' He looked at the smoke rising from his cigarette. 'But I wasn't fated to die at Phu Lai or at the MAC-V compound or Miséricorde Hospital or the Strawberry Patch. Instead, it was my fate to sit here with you tonight.'

She lowered her head in thought, and Tyson could see she was processing something. She finally looked up and continued her questioning in a neutral tone. 'So during the time you were in Hue in mid-January interviewing for a staff job, you had the opportunity to see Sister Teresa again. How many times?'

'I don't recall exactly. Once or twice. I was there only about two days.'

'And you didn't see her at any time after that, until 15 February at Miséricorde Hospital?'

'That's correct.'

'That must have been a surprise.'

'To put it mildly.'

'You didn't know she worked there?'

'I didn't know the place existed, Major.'

'Of course. But she never mentioned that she worked at another hospital?'

'No. I only knew she worked at the Catholic dispensary near the Joan of Arc School and Church.'

'Where did you meet her on those occasions after that Christmas party? What is there to do in Hue? I mean where does an American officer take a nun?'

'Are you being sarcastic or just nosy?'

'I'm intrigued.'

'Perhaps I *should* write my memoirs.'

'The locale is exotic, the unsuspecting city is on the eve of a great cataclysm, you are a young soldier about to return to the front. You meet a strikingly beautiful woman, a nun—'

'When you put it like that, it sounds like melodrama. A woman's story.'

'Don't be sexist. Where did you take her?'

'That's my business.'

'All right. How do you suppose she wound up at Miséricorde Hospital, outside the city walls?'

'Beats the hell out of me.'

'Fate?'

'Yes, fate.'

Major Harper nodded. 'And that was the last time you saw her?'

'Yes.'

'Did you ever wonder what became of her?'

'Often.'

'Picard's book, then, brought you some good news.'

255

'Yes, that was the good news.'

'Would you like to see her again?'

'No.'

'Why not?'

'For the same reason I don't attend class reunions.'

'Why is that?'

'I have nothing to say.'

'Reminisce.'

'The young have aspirations that never come to pass, the old have reminiscences of what never happened.'

'Who said that?'

'I did.'

'Originally.'

'I don't remember.'

'Did you speak to her then? At the hospital?'

'Just a few words.'

'Such as?'

'I don't remember. You can imagine what sort of words – hurried words, words of comfort. Then ... someone took her away. The building was burning.'

'That was the last time you saw her?'

'I said it was.'

'But where did she go? Certainly she would have stayed close by until the shooting was over. She would have put herself under your protection, or your platoon's protection. They were offering protection, weren't they?'

Tyson spoke softly. 'They were not ...'

She waited, then said, 'They were not?'

'I mean, they were not in a ... position to ...'

Her eyes met his and held contact. Finally she said, 'Did you look for her when the shooting stopped?'

'Well, yes, of course. But we had to move on. To pursue the enemy. I thought she'd died ...'

'Pursuing the enemy was more important than offering protection to the survivors of that hospital?'

'Unfortunately it was. They have a name for it. War.'

'But there were Europeans there, Vietnamese Catholics, wounded—'

'We didn't distinguish between types of refugees.'

'Didn't you? How often did you come across Europeans? Catholic nuns? Excuse me but that would have been a great feather in your cap to have rescued these people and got them to an American base camp. Where did they go, these survivors of the battle?'

Tyson saw she was tired and noted that her tone had become argumentative. He had the impression she was becoming frustrated and obsessed.

She snapped, 'Where did they *go*, Lieutenant?'

'They fled.'

'Why did they flee from you?'

'They did not flee *from* us. They just fled.'

'The wounded fled?'

'The wounded ... were carried away by the survivors.'

Karen Harper's voice rose. 'There *were* no survivors, Lieutenant! They all died there. That's what Sister Teresa told Picard. Your platoon murdered everyone. That's what she said. That's why the Catholic Relief Agency lists all those doctors and nurses as missing. They died at Miséricorde Hospital.'

Tyson stood and nearly shouted. 'They were killed by the goddamned communists, before, during, and after the battle. They panicked and fled and were killed by enemy troops in and around this village.'

'No! They died in the hospital.' Karen Harper stood also. 'The question is did Sister Teresa, in her hysteria, witness an ill-advised and perhaps blundered assault that led to the deaths of innocent people and the burning of the hospital? Or did she witness a cold-blooded massacre, followed by the deliberate burning of the hospital to cover the evidence?' She looked him in the eyes. 'If you just made a stupid blunder, for God's sake say so, and we can forget about murder. Forget your ego and your pride, and tell me if you made a dreadful

257

mistake that led to the deaths of those people. There *is* a statute of limitations on that sort of thing – on manslaughter – and it has expired. Tell me.'

'If I tell you that, will you return a report saying I admitted to manslaughter but not to murder and that this is your finding as well?'

'Yes, I will.'

'Will that be the end of it? For me? For my men?'

She hesitated, then said, 'I'll do everything I can to see that it is the end of it.'

'Will you? Why?'

She shook her head. 'I'm sick of it.'

'*You're* sick of it? Everyone is sick of it. But how about truth and justice?'

'The hell with that.' She rubbed her eyes with the back of her hand, the way a child would do, then composed herself. 'I'm sorry. I'm tired.' She looked at him and cleared her throat. 'Of course we'll pursue this with the intent of either clearing your name completely or forwarding charges to the proper court-martial convening authority, if necessary.'

He saw the moment had passed and had some regrets about it. 'I think you'd better go.'

'Yes.' She gathered her things and turned towards the door. Tyson watched her as she crossed the long room. She opened the door, turned, looked at him a moment, then left.

Ben Tyson surveyed the cluttered cocktail table – the ashtray, the glasses, the papers. His eyes wandered to the bar area where his champagne glass lay shattered on the floor. He looked around the room, like a detective wondering what had happened here.

Tyson stepped to the window and stared out into the city lights. He looked down at the sidewalk six storeys below and saw her walking up Pennsylvania Avenue. He watched her closely, noticing even from this distance that her gait was not jaunty or purposeful. Rather she walked like he felt: deflated and unsure. He was glad he wasn't alone anymore.

21

Benjamin Tyson turned off the lights of his hotel room, made himself a fresh drink, and sat in the armchair, his feet on the cocktail table. He felt drained and weary. He stared out the window at the summer sky and watched a succession of aircraft make the approach to National Airport.

The imperial city, a city of monuments. *Hue. Washington.* They were becoming confused in his mind. He closed his eyes.

Lieutenant Benjamin Tyson consulted the city map spread out on the passenger seat of his open jeep, held down by a .45-calibre Colt automatic.

Hue was divided into three parts: the old city within the Citadel walls, built on the north bank of the Perfume River; the Gia Hoi district, a new suburb outside the city walls; and the South Side, the European Quarter on the left bank of the river.

He turned cautiously into an unmarked street in the South Side and scanned the block. When he'd borrowed the jeep from MAC-V – Military Advisory Command–Vietnam – a motor pool NCO in the compound had instructed him on urban driving. 'Don't drive down no deserted streets,' drawled the big bony sergeant from South Carolina.

'Right.'

'Pick streets with lots of kids. Even Charlie don't shoot up a street with kids.'

'Can I bring my own kids?'

'Don't pick up no hitchhikers, includin' pussy, and watch for them motorbikes. Charles likes to flip you a little something from them bikes.'

'Maybe I need a tank.'

'Naw, Hue's pretty safe really. A whole lot safer than the streets of New York, Lieutenant.'

Well, perhaps. But Tyson thought he'd rather be on Third Avenue at the moment.

'Bring my jeep back in one piece. Okay?'

Tyson had pointed out that if the jeep were in several pieces, the chances were good that he would be, too.

Tyson now scrutinized the white stucco houses and courtyards. Looked okay. He headed up the long straight road.

As he'd left the MAC-V compound, he'd spotted the old French Cercle Sportif, with its verandas overlooking the Perfume River, its tennis courts and gleaming white concrete driveway, and he was reminded of an incident that took place on his first trip to Hue, a month earlier in November. He had gone alone to a French café on Tihn Tam Street and practised his French on an elderly half-breed bartender. A middle-aged Frenchman of slight build had moved down the bar and introduced himself as Monsieur Bournard, the proprietor of the establishment. Monsieur Bournard had unexpectedly invited Lieutenant Tyson to Le Cercle Sportif, *'pour jouer au tennis.'*

After a set of lawn tennis, they sat on the veranda, furnished with Art Nouveau pieces, and drank cold beer. Monsieur Bournard had remarked, 'Hue has changed little since I was a boy. In the Buddhist myth, Hue is the lotus flower growing from the mud. It is serenity and beauty amidst a sea of carnage. Hue is eternal because she is sacred to communist, Buddhist, and Christian alike. Hue will survive the war, Lieutenant. You may not.'

'And you?' Tyson had inquired.

The Frenchman shrugged. 'The communist cadres enjoy my little café.'

'You entertain communists in your café?'

'*Certainement.* They have been good customers long

before you arrived. You are shocked? Annoyed?' he'd asked in a tone that suggested he'd made this little confession before in similar circumstances. 'One must be *très pratique*. They will be good customers long after you and your countrymen are gone. Don't be naive.'

Tyson had replied, 'I grew up in a place where naivete is a virtue. However, Monsieur Bournard, I am not shocked, nor annoyed. But I may report you to the National Police.'

'As you wish. But most of them use my little place to do business with the communists. The National Police are also *très pratique*, you see.' Monsieur Bournard had leaned across the marble table. 'This was a nice manageable little war until you arrived.' The Frenchman made it sound personal. As Tyson considered pointing out that he hadn't come here by choice, the Frenchman made a sudden sound of exasperation and muttered, '*Les Américains*,' as though this said it all.

Tyson had risen from his chair. 'Thank you for the tennis and the beer.'

The Frenchman looked up, but did not stand. '*Pardon*. You are my guest. But I saw too many of my countrymen die here. In the end the Asians will have their way.'

'With you too.'

'*Non*. Me, I am like a little cork bobbing on a raging yellow sea. You and your Army are ... well, like the *Titanic*.' Monsieur Bournard turned his attention back to his beer.

As Tyson walked away he heard the Frenchman call out, 'Take care of yourself, my friend. I can't think of a worse cause to die for.'

Tyson had then gone into the changing room, showered, and returned his borrowed white tennis clothes. He received in exchange his combat fatigues, freshly laundered, and his boots, polished. The Vietnamese attendant had presented him with his holstered .45 automatic in the way a porter in an English club might give a gentleman his walking stick. To say that Le Cercle Sportif was an anachronism was to understate the extent of the establishment's improbable existence. Yet it existed the way his own club back home existed: as a bastion of cultivated lunacy surrounded by a justifiably hostile and suspicious world.

Riding now in another borrowed jeep from the MAC-V compound, Tyson recalled that incident of a month earlier and reflected on what Monsieur Bournard had said. He concluded that it was Monsieur Bournard who was naive in the extreme. Neither Monsieur Bournard nor his café nor his club would survive this war. The communists represented something new under the sun, and those like Monsieur Bournard and his sporting friends who thought they could accommodate those grim puritans had obviously not learned anything from life, history, or the daily news.

But in one respect, the Frenchman had been correct: The Asians would have their way. Tyson saw no possible victory in this war, and like the other half million Americans in the country, he was beginning to concentrate on the only victory that made sense: victory over death.

Tyson drove slowly through the busy tree-lined streets of the South Side, crowded with three-wheeled Lambrettas, Peugeots, cyclo-cabs, and motorbikes of every make and colour. Military traffic was light. The late afternoon air was suffused with pungent and exotic smells. A line of pretty high school girls crossed the street, dressed in their flowing silk *ao dai*. They stole glances at him, giggled, and chattered. Their teacher, a stern-looking old nun, reprimanded them. The procession passed, and Tyson drove on.

It was Christmas week, and so long as he saw no signs of Christmas in this tropical city, he was neither nostalgic nor homesick. But here in the mostly European and Vietnamese Catholic quarter, he saw little reminders: a Christmas tree in a window, a boy carrying a wrapped present, and from the shuttered loggia of a villa, he heard a piano playing 'O Holy Night.'

Tyson drove through the square in front of the Phu Cam Cathedral. On the north side of the square was a sandbagged machine-gun emplacement. A few ARVN soldiers were strolling, holding hands as was the custom of Vietnamese men. But otherwise, there was no sign that Hue was at war. Quang Tri to the north and Phu Bai to the south were desecrated by barbed wire, gun emplacements, and green vinyl sandbags. Hue remained unspoiled, a hauntingly attractive illusion, as Monsieur Bournard had suggested, its energy and charm heightened by the realities of the terror beyond its useless walls.

Tyson turned down a narrow lane and stopped in front of a fenced courtyard. He jumped down from the jeep, slung his rifle, then reached in the rear and lifted out a heavy box wrapped in PX Christmas paper.

He looked up and down the lane, then opened a rotting wooden gate and walked through the courtyard garden choked with hibiscus and poinsettia.

Tyson pulled at a bell rope, and a minute later the mahogany door was opened by an old servant woman. Tyson said, "*Allo. Toi dai-uy Tyson. Soeur Thérèse, s'il vous plait.*"

The old woman smiled, flashing an uneven set of teeth dyed reddish brown with betel nut. She motioned him into the dark foyer, then led him to a sitting room.

Tyson stood his rifle against a credenza and sat in a musty armchair, its threadbare fabric home to a few darting silverfish. The chair, indeed all the furniture, looked European, pre-World War II vintage. A lizard climbed up a dingy-white stucco wall and disappeared behind a cheap print of the Blessed Virgin. The mortar between the red terracotta floor tile was green-black with mildew, though the floor seemed to be freshly scrubbed.

263

The tropics, he thought, were not hospitable to man's creations. That, added to thirty years of war, made it a wonder anything still stood or functioned in this wretched country.

Tyson didn't hear her come into the room but saw her shadow pass along the wall. He stood and turned. She wore a white cotton *ao dai* with a high mandarin collar. The floor-length dress had slits up to the thighs, but she also wore the traditional silk pantaloons beneath the dress. She seemed, he thought, somewhat embarrassed that he'd called at the convent. Thinking about it, Tyson was embarrassed also. War was justification for much that was uncivilized, but a man calling on a woman ought to have a good reason for doing so. He said, '*Je suis en train de venir ... à MAC-V ...*' He thought that 'just passing through' sounded as trite in French as in English. '*Comment allez-vous?*'

She inclined her head. '*Bien. Et vous?*'

'*Bien.*' He hesitated, then lifted the box from the floor and set it on the credenza. '*Pour vous ... et pour les autres soeurs. Bon Noël.*'

She looked at the box but said nothing.

Tyson vacillated between leaving and pressing on with his unexpected visit. He knew that if his heart were pure, suffused with Christian charity and the spirit of Christmas, he would not be acting so awkwardly. But the fact was he had other things on his mind.

Sister Teresa took a step forward and laid her long fingers on the box.

Tyson drew his K-bar knife from its scabbard and sliced open the giftwrapped box, then pulled the corrugated lid open, revealing a potpourri of PX treasures: soap, stationery, tinned fruit, medicated talc, a bottle of California wine, and other consumer products whose nature and usefulness would probably have to be explained.

Sister Teresa hesitated, then reached into the box and withdrew a bar of Dial soap wrapped in gold foil. She studied the foil and the clock on the wrapper, then sniffed it, and an involuntary smile passed across her lips.

Tyson said, '*Pour tout le monde*,' attempting to further depersonalize the gift. '*Pour les enfants, pour le dispensaire. Une donation.*'

She nodded. '*Merci beaucoup.*' She placed the soap back in the box. '*Bon Noël.*'

They stood in silence awhile, then Tyson said, '*Je vais maintenant.*'

She said, 'Could you ... take me ... a ride?'

He smiled at the unexpected English. 'Where?'

'*Le dispensaire.*'

'Certainly.'

Tyson slung his rifle, and she led him to the door.

He followed her out through the garden and helped her into the jeep. He did a walk-around to see if any parts had been appropriated, or worse, if anything lethal had been added. Satisfied but not positive, he climbed in, unlocked the ignition, and pushed the starter button. The jeep didn't explode, and the gas gauge still read half full. The ubiquitous VC and local slicky boys were sleeping on the job. He decided it wasn't such a bad country after all.

They drove in silence along the Phu Cam Canal, crossed the An Cuu Bridge, and headed north on Duy Tan Street, a section of Highway One. The buildings here were mostly two-storey wooden clusters, with narrow fronts, wooden sidewalks, and alleyways between them. Tyson was reminded of an Old West town.

Here on the South Side of the river were the university, the Central Hospital, and the sports stadium, as well as the treasury, the post office building, and the French-style provincial capitol. None of these institutions or services had existed in the imperial walled city, but the French had grafted them neatly onto the South Bank while the emperors reigned in splendid isolation within the Citadel. But neither the emperor nor the French ruled here any longer. In fact, no one ruled here any longer. Instead the city was a collection of fiefdoms: the military, the civil government, the Catholic and Buddhist hierarchies, the students, and the Europeans. The Americans had found the place too perplexing, and Hue was the only city in Vietnam where no American combat forces were committed. The small MAC-V compound was like the Emperor's Forbidden Palace, secluded and forlorn. And everywhere, in every quarter of the city, in every government building, every school and pagoda, on every block, was the invisible presence of the communist cadres, Hue-born and educated, mingling easily in the cafés, lunching with Monsieur Bournard one day, the National Police commander another, and all the while waiting. Waiting.

Tyson picked up speed, checking the side and rearview mirrors, staying to the centre of the road, and keeping a close watch on the motorbikes that passed him. He found Hue more unnerving than the jungle. He glanced at Sister Teresa, sitting placidly with her hands in her lap. He said, 'Do the VC bother you? At the school?'

She remained staring straight ahead. 'They leave us alone.'

'Why?'

She shrugged. 'In Hue everyone leaves everyone alone.'

'They say there are many VC and sympathizers in Hue.'

'There are many intellectuals in Hue.'

'They also say Hue is very anti-American.'

'The Europeans in Hue are sometimes anti-American.'

Tyson smiled. 'Hue is very antiwar.'

'All the world is antiwar.'

'Hue reminds me of Greenwich Village. Even the people dress the same.'

She looked at him. 'Where is that?'

'In America.'

266

She nodded. 'There are riots in America.'

'So they tell me.' Tyson sometimes felt adrift between a once-familiar world that had become increasingly alien the last time he'd seen it and a true alien world that was becoming uncomfortably understandable. They said that if a day came when you completely understood the Orient, you should seek professional help.

The jeep approached the Joan of Arc Church, a yellowish stucco building with a colonnaded front and an impressive steeple. There was a school close by, and a small dispensary building marked with a red cross. Sister Teresa said, 'I will walk from here.'

Tyson pulled to the side of the busy street. Sister Teresa remained sitting in the seat beside him, then said, 'When do you leave?'

Tyson glanced at her. 'Vietnam? I'm leaving on 17 April. If not sooner. No later.'

She nodded slowly.

'Why do you ask?'

She shrugged, a very Gallic shrug, he thought. He wondered which parent was French. He said, 'Do you have family in Hue?'

'*Oui.* The family of my mother. My father, he is *un para.*'

'A French soldier. A paratrooper?'

'*Oui. Un para.*'

'In France?'

She shrugged again. 'I never knew him.'

'Have you ever been to France?'

'No. I have been only to Da Nang. To the convent school.'

'You speak French well. You are educated, a nun, you are half French. Why don't you leave here? Go to France.'

She looked at him. 'Why?'

Tyson thought he should tell her there was a war going on, that eventually, as Monsieur Bournard said, the communists would win, that she was a beautiful woman, and that she would do well anywhere. Instead he changed the subject. 'Why did you become a nun?'

'My mother wished it. My father was Catholic.'

'How old are you?'

She seemed somewhat surprised at the question but replied, 'Twenty and three.'

He nodded. She would have been born in 1945, the year the Second World War ended, the year the Japanese surrendered Vietnam and the French and the communists began their war to determine who was going to be in charge here. He looked at her, hesitated, then asked, 'Don't you find it difficult? Not being able to ... marry?'

She looked away from him.

He said quickly, 'That was not a proper question.'

She replied, 'I am content. There are many of us of mixed blood in Hue, and we are ... how do you say? ... *Les parias* ...'

'Outcasts.'

'*Oui.* Outcasts to our people. The Europeans treat us well, but we are not as good as them. We find peace in the Church.'

Tyson realized her view of the world was rather limited. He had a dislike for men who played Svengali or Professor Higgins with women of other cultures or lesser stations in life, so he dropped the subject for a more immediate one. 'When can I see you again?'

She turned towards him and looked him fully in the face for the first time. He met her eyes and held them. Seconds ticked by. Finally, she said, 'Tomorrow if you wish. There is a – *une soirée pour les enfants. A l'école. Pour Le Noël* ... Do you? ...' She made a fluttering motion with her fingers. '*Le piano.*'

'Oh ... sure. *Un peu.*'

'*Bien. Les chansons de Noël?*'

'That's about all I can play. Except for "Moon River."'

'*Bien. A onze heures. A l'école.*' She pointed.

'I'll try to be there.'

She smiled. 'Good.' She put her legs over the side of the jeep and looked back. '*Merci*, lieutenant.'

'*A demain, Thérèse.*'

She seemed surprised at being addressed that way, then said, '*A demain* ... Benjamin.' She slid down from the jeep and walked towards the dispensary in the church compound.

Tyson watched her. She looked back, smiled shyly, then hurried on.

He thought of the first time he had seen Teresa, a month earlier on his first trip to Hue. He had gone to the Phu Cam Cathedral with a Catholic officer and attended mass. Two dozen nuns were taking Communion together, and among them was this singularly beautiful Eurasian, hands pressed together, returning from the Communion rail to her pew. The officer he was with noticed her too, and so did most of the Europeans around him, or so he believed.

After mass he saw her again in the square speaking with a Vietnamese Catholic family. At Tyson's urging, he and the American officer he was with approached her. Tyson introduced himself and the officer in French.

Even then, he reflected, he couldn't imagine not seeing her again. And today he had. And now they both understood that any subsequent meetings were at their own peril.

Tyson sat in the jeep a while longer, then noticed it was nearly dark. Hue had a late curfew, midnight to five A.M., but MAC-V wanted their charges safely tucked into the compound by dark. Unless you'd made other sleeping arrangements and informed them of the lady's address.

Tyson threw the jeep into gear and travelled the few hundred metres to the MAC-V compound. The sentry waved him through the barbed-wire gate between the high concrete walls.

Tyson opened his eyes and saw by the illuminated clock on the night stand that it was three-fifteen. The city was darker now, and he could see stars high above the horizon.

Several images vied for attention in his mind: Teresa, Karen Harper, Marcy, the wall, the hospital, and Hue. It was as if the past was overtaking the present and about to become the future.

22

Benjamin Tyson entered Sag Harbor from Brick Kiln Road. He drove slowly through the narrow streets, past early eighteenth-century houses of white clapboard and grey shingle.

The drive in the rented TR6 had taken nearly three hours from his apartment in Manhattan, and it was already twilight here on the eastern end of Long Island. There was no streetlighting, and the tree-lined roads lay in darkness.

Tyson realized he was in a part of the town that he did not know. He pulled the Triumph to the kerb and got out. The air was damp and briny, with misty auras shimmering around the post lamps near the entrance to the tightly spaced houses.

Tyson reached back into the car and retrieved a book. He zippered his wind-breaker and began walking west, towards the setting sun. At length he recognized a street and turned into it, and within a few minutes he came to Main Street. There were a good number of people promenading to the Long Wharf and back, entering and leaving several taverns and restaurants. People sat on the veranda of the old American Hotel, rocking in their bentwood rockers, throwing back drinks on the aft roll and returning the glass to a rest position on the forward roll.

Tyson crossed Main Street and turned into a small lane,

following it downhill towards the water. He had remembered where he'd seen the mailbox so long ago and found the house, a very old cedar-shingled saltbox sitting on a small bluff above the body of water called the Lower Cove. A tilted picket fence surrounded the house and the unkept grounds. The mailbox still said Picard/Wells. The lights were on.

Tyson opened the gate and approached by way of a footpath paved with broken shells. With no hesitation – because he had not come this far to have second thoughts – he raised the brass knocker and brought it down hard on the black-painted door. He heard footsteps, and the door opened. 'Yes.'

Tyson did not reply.

Andrew Picard peered at his visitor in the dim light of the porch lamp. Finally Picard's eyebrows rose. 'Oh ...'

Tyson stared at him, and neither spoke for some time. Picard showed what Tyson thought was a good deal of cool, or perhaps it was the alcohol that Tyson smelled on his breath.

Tyson regarded the tall, lanky man standing a few feet from him. He was wearing blue jeans and a button-down oxford shirt with the sleeves rolled up. He was very tanned, and his longish hair appeared to be bleached by the sun and salt. Tyson knew him to be a preppie and a Yalie, and had heard his voice on radio and TV, so the words 'tweedy' and 'madras-covered marshmallow' entered his mind. But the reality belied this unkind prejudice, and Tyson reminded himself he was looking at an ex-Marine officer who by all accounts had done his duty.

Picard said simply, 'Come in.'

Tyson followed him into the foyerless room. A stereo was playing Paul McCartney's 'Hey Jude.' Tyson's eyes adjusted to the darkness of the room. It was, he saw, a large open space, created by the removal of all the interior walls where hand-hewn posts still stood. The simple painted furnishings all looked as if they had been bought at a Quaker garage sale.

271

Three hooked rugs sat on the rough floorboards, and a fireplace of round river stone dominated the left-hand wall. A small coal fire in the grate warmed and dried the sea air.

At the rear of the open room was a long countertop separating an enclosed porch that held what had once been called a summer kitchen. The rear windows of the kitchen looked out onto the cove, and Tyson saw the lights of Baypoint across the water and picked out the deck lights of his house. Shadows moved in front of the sliding glass doors, and he felt his heart give a sudden thump.

Picard said, 'Are you here to kill me?'

Tyson turned from the window. 'The thought never crossed my mind.'

'Fine, then how about a drink?'

'I don't need one, but if you do, go ahead.'

Picard did not reply. His eyes dropped to the book in Tyson's hand.

'I came for your autograph.' He held out the book.

Picard took it and smiled. '*The Quest*. One of my early ones. Did you like it?'

'Not bad.'

'Fiction is fun. Nonfiction sometimes gets people upset.' Picard placed the book on the oval dining table and opened it. 'Pen?'

Tyson handed him a pen.

Picard thought a moment, then wrote: *For Ben Tyson, Where have all the soldiers gone? Long time passing. Best, Andrew Picard.*

He handed the open book to Tyson, and Tyson read it, then closed the book. 'Indeed.' He laid the book back on the table.

Picard went to the stereo and turned it off. Both men stood in silence, though it did not seem to Tyson an embarrassing silence, but a time to reflect on a shared experience and to go through the mental leaps necessary to get to the here and now. Finally Picard said, 'If you wanted a drink, what would it be?'

'Scotch.'

Picard went into the open kitchen and put ice in two glasses. 'Neat?'

'Soda.'

He rummaged through the refrigerator, then held up a bottle of Perrier. 'Wimp water of the Hamptons. Okay?'

'Fine.'

Picard split a bottle of Perrier between the glasses. 'How'd you find me? I'm not listed.'

'Mailbox.'

'Right. Mailbox. Have to paint that out. Getting too much attention these days.'

Picard poured from the bottle of Cutty Sark, then came around the counter and handed Tyson his drink. Picard held out his glass. 'To those who met their fate at Hue, including us.' He touched his glass to Tyson's, and they drank.

Tyson's eyes wandered around the room. Under a side window was a writing desk cluttered with papers and pencils. 'What are you doing for an encore?'

Picard shrugged. 'Hard act to follow.'

'Well, you can do the court-martial of Benjamin Tyson.'

Picard for the first time seemed ill at ease. 'I don't think so.'

Tyson put his glass on an end table. He glanced at a steep open staircase that ran along the right-hand wall, up to the loft. He said, 'Are you alone?'

Picard replied, 'Yes, but I'm expecting company any moment.' He added with a smile, 'Five duck-hunting friends with shotguns.'

Tyson did not acknowledge the quick wit.

Picard swallowed more of his drink, and Tyson suspected he was a bit under the influence. Picard said, 'I almost called you a few times.'

'Did you? Actually you called me twice some years ago. I probably should have met with you then.'

Picard nodded. 'I found it easier to write about you because I hadn't met you. Had I met you, had we got drunk together, I might have chucked the whole chapter into the fire.'

'Then you'd still be an unknown author.'

'But a happier one. I'm not gloating, you know.'

'No, I don't think you are.'

Picard sipped on his drink thoughtfully, then observed, 'I assume you read the entire book, so you'll know I lost friends there, too. And most of my friends didn't even have the chance to die fighting. They were staff officers with MAC-V, like myself, and they were caught by the communists outside the compound, marched to a ditch, and were shot in the head. Or worse, some were buried alive.' Picard stared down at the floor for a few seconds, then added, 'Some men talk to their shrinks. Writers write.'

Tyson nodded. 'And how are you feeling now, Picard? Are the nightmares gone? How are your ghosts doing?'

Picard rubbed his chin contemplatively. 'Well ... I think about it more now. I opened the wrong door ... It started when I began researching the book, talking to survivors. That brought it back ...'

Tyson commented, 'You didn't do the survivors any favours either.'

Picard seemed not to hear. He went on, 'I didn't really see much action there ... until Tet. Then I saw things I was ill prepared to see. Things I could barely comprehend. I'd lived in Hue for nearly a year and become enchanted with the place. It was a city of light in a country where night had descended. I fully believed the myth that Hue was special. Then after the battle I walked through the grey ash and the black corpses, and I remember thinking, "Nothing is sacred," and I began feeling sorry for the whole fucked-up human race.'

Picard ran his fingers through his long hair, then continued, 'And sometimes now – you asked about ghosts – I have this dream. You remember the Army medical expression "the walking wounded"? An innocuous expression only meaning ambulatory cases. But in this dream I see these bandaged ... things ... part zombie, part mummy ... and they're walking through grey ash, their hands held out as though they were pleading, and they drop in their tracks, but more keep coming out of the white smoke ...' He looked at Tyson. 'I can tell you this.'

Tyson nodded.

Picard stared off into space awhile, then said, 'I saw a little boy about six years old wandering down the street naked. He had his genitals blown off ... but he seemed more concerned with the glass shards in his arms ... and ... I can't forget that face ... he was alone, with no one to help him, tears running down his cheeks ...' Picard looked at Tyson. 'But you must have seen worse ... I mean in the infantry.'

Tyson didn't respond for a while, then said, 'In the infantry, one is not just a spectator, but often the cause of the suffering, as you pointed out so well.'

Picard stared at the floor.

Tyson drew a long breath and said, 'You know, sometimes after you've shot first and asked questions afterwards, and the old mama-san or little baby-san is not answering, then you feel like the worst monster God has ever created. So the next time you react more cautiously to a perceived threat, and you take a bullet for your trouble. And your buddies vow to shoot first the next time, in memory of you. And the march of death goes on until everyone is in step, shooting first – blowing away anything that moves, cutting a grim swath, death's premature harvest, through the rice fields and fruit orchards ...' Tyson's eyes drifted to the coal burning on the fire grate. He watched the blue flames for a minute, then turned back to Picard. 'Did you help that little boy?'

Picard replied haltingly, 'I ... he ... he saw me ... he raised his arms ... like he was surrendering ... but he was showing me that he was badly cut ... There were still pieces of glass in his hands and arms. He said, *"Bac-si. Bac-si."*' Picard closed his eyes for a moment, then said, 'I wanted to scream at him,

"Not your arms, you idiot! Your balls! Your balls!" ... but he was a little boy. I took a step back as he came closer, then ... I levelled my rifle and shouted, "Go away! *Di-di*." Then I turned and ran.' Picard drew a breath. 'I couldn't let him get near me. I simply could not handle it.' His eyes met Tyson's.

Tyson nodded. 'It happens.'

Picard finished his scotch. 'Yes ... but other men around me did better than I did.'

'That day.'

Picard walked slowly back to the kitchen and made himself another drink. 'Right.' He seemed to come out of his dark mood and added, 'Some days were better than others. You had a bad day on February 15. On February 29 you were attending the sick and wounded. Later that day you were one of the wounded. *C'est la guerre*, as our little friends used to proclaim ten times a day.'

Tyson finished his drink and put the glass on the coffee table. It occurred to him that Picard was the first man he'd spoken to about this who had actually been there. Beyond their differences in experiences and perceptions there lay the same residual malaise, the little time bombs waiting to go off.

'Another?'

'No.'

'Have a seat.'

'I'll stand.'

Picard came around the breakfast bar and sat on a Boston rocker to the side of the fireplace. At length he replied, 'I told your friend Harper I would only offer impartial testimony – regarding my sources. Especially Sister Teresa. You can tell your attorneys that also.'

Tyson nodded. He also wondered why Picard had referred to Harper as his friend.

Picard added, 'I'm not looking to crucify you.'

'That's what I like about artists and writers, Picard. They're always doing this little dance around the shit pile, but they never step in it, never have to eat any of it, and by God

276

they don't even smell it.'

Picard leaned forward in his rocker. '*I* stepped in it up to my ears.'

'You fell in it by accident. And when the stink was gone two decades later, you decided to describe your brief combat experience to the world.'

Picard rocked slowly for some time, and the floorboards creaked in the silent house. He said, 'I reported what I saw and what I heard from witnesses ... But sometimes I think that I never should have written that chapter.'

'Why do you think that?'

'Well ... it wasn't ... well documented, and ... it leaves me open to a libel suit—'

'That's not why. Why shouldn't *you* have written that chapter?'

Picard replied without hesitation, 'Because I didn't help the little boy with his genitals blown off and because I didn't put that in the book. Because one night when the communists were storming the walls of the ARVN compound, I went to pieces in front of the ARVN soldiers, and a Vietnamese colonel punched me. And I didn't put that in the fucking book either. And I realize now that you can't put it behind you until you hold it up and show it to everybody.' He looked at Tyson. 'I may have done you a favour I couldn't do for myself.'

'Thanks, buddy. I'll return that favour first chance I get.'

Picard smiled grimly.

Tyson thought a moment, then said, 'You reported your own heroics, however. The day the ARVN broke out of their compound and began their counterattack into the Citadel. You were a hero that day, carrying wounded ARVN to safety through machine-gun fire. Is that true?'

'Oh, yes. Two little guys at a time. Bullets and rockets splattering all over the fucking street. Who can figure it? They weren't even Americans.' Picard crossed his legs and swirled his drink. He said, 'I suppose if you're an honest writer, you write about the times you pissed in your pants. I suppose your platoon did things that would make the Army proud. I suppose I should have dwelt on those things a bit more.'

'Well, Picard, maybe if you meet my men in some closed hearing, you'll recall the things you discovered tonight.'

'I'm sure I will. But I don't know what good it will do anymore.'

Tyson watched the smoke rising from his cigarette. He said, 'I didn't come here to coach the witness, Picard. I came here to see if we fought in the same war. I think we did.' Tyson tossed his cigarette into the fire. He continued, 'We all have secrets, and sometimes we tell them to each other, because we understand one another. But we usually don't tell these things to other people. We are embarrassed by some of the things we did and appalled by most of the rest. But among ourselves, we can speak without explanations or apologies.' He moved closer to Picard. 'I'm not saying the story of Miséricorde Hospital should not have come out, but I don't think *you* were the person it should have come from.'

Picard stood. 'But *you* were.'

Tyson nodded. 'Yes. And now that you broke the understood rule of keeping your mouth shut, I may very well tell my story.'

'But according to Dr Brandt, you all swore to lie. That was not an unspoken rule but a blood oath. What are you going to say to your men about telling the truth?'

'I will tell them that the truth shall make ye free.'

'Is the truth ... I mean is it close to what I wrote ...?'

Tyson smiled. 'You will find out in court.'

'Are you going to sue me?'

'Quite possibly.' Tyson looked around the room with a proprietary interest. 'Nice place. Do you rent or own?'

Picard laughed. After some reflection he said, 'You are not the sort of man to engage in blackmail. I am not the sort of man who will be blackmailed.'

Tyson looked at him appraisingly, then changed the

subject abruptly. 'Who is Wells?'

'Wells ... Oh, on the mailbox. Lady who used to live here. I should paint over the name.'

'You live alone?'

'Sometimes. They come and go.'

'Do they? You never married?'

'Once. I have a twelve-year-old daughter. Lives with her mother and stepfather in California. I miss her. Life ... I mean life in the good old USA ain't what it was when I was a kid. If there was someplace less fucked up I'd go there. Know anyplace?'

'I'm afraid I don't. Do you hang out with the local literati?'

'Christ, no. They're bigger assholes than I am.' Picard went back to the kitchen. 'One more, Tyson. Then you can go if you want.'

Tyson noticed Picard had trouble navigating. He said, 'Short one.'

Tyson lit another cigarette and tossed the match in the fireplace. He looked at Picard moving about the kitchen. He did not particularly like the man, but neither could he bring himself to dislike him. Picard was like a fraternity brother, and allowances had to be made. Picard had revealed two acts of pure cowardice. That may have been a way of making amends or a way of making Picard feel better about himself. In either case it had the effect of making Tyson feel like the recipient of an unwanted gift, the keeper of yet another appalling secret. Had they been friends, Picard would have hated him the next morning. Tyson said, 'You spent nearly a year in Hue before the Tet attack?'

'Right.'

'You knew the place.'

'Pretty well.' Picard came around the counter with the two drinks.

Tyson took his glass from Picard. 'Did you ever go to a café on Tihn Tam Street? *Le Crocodile?*'

Picard sipped his scotch. '*Certainement*. That little shit

279

who owned the place had a foot in every camp.'

'Bournard?'

'I think that was his name. Why?'

'I sometimes wonder what became of him.'

'Friend of yours?'

'No. I met him only once. He advised me to go home.'

'He should have taken his own advice.'

'Why?'

'Well, I can tell you what I heard, though it might not be true. You know what the VC did to Vietnamese who had any commerce with Americans, like barbers, prostitutes, cleaning women, and all?'

'I heard.'

Picard nodded. 'Well, Monsieur Bournard and the staff of his café, according to what I heard, showed up at the Central Hospital minus their hands.'

Neither man spoke for some time, then Tyson said, 'My father once said to me, about his war, "That was a war I would go to again."' He looked at Picard. 'I don't think we can say that about our war.'

Picard replied, 'No, we don't have that. And that, I think, is at the heart of this post-stress syndrome. Not what happened there – because all war is the same shit – but what happened here.'

Tyson finished his drink and set the glass down. 'Could be.'

Picard cleared his throat. 'By the way, a word of advice: Dr Brandt would like to see you in front of a firing squad. Don't ask me how I know, because he seemed cool, logical, and objective. But, Christ, Tyson, he indicted you for murder in no uncertain terms.'

'I'm sure he did.'

Picard seemed on the verge of asking why but apparently thought better of it.

A silence enveloped the room, broken only by the ticking of the mantel clock. Tyson glanced at it and said, 'I should go.' He zipped his windbreaker.

Picard hesitated, then said, 'Are you going home? I mean the place you're renting here.'

Tyson gave him a quick look. 'Perhaps. Why?'

'I met her.'

'Who?'

'Marcy. Your wife. She was here.'

Tyson nodded. Of course Marcy would have called on Picard.

'She's very nice.'

'Was she?'

'She was to me. No rancour, no hysterics. A remarkable woman. All she wanted to know was whether or not I told the truth in my book.'

Tyson didn't respond.

'So how do you answer a wife who asks you to reveal a truth about her husband? I told her I was not an eyewitness to the event. I was only a reporter. Typical writer – right, Tyson? Dancing around the shit pile again. Well, she let me off easy. Told me I probably did what I thought was right.'

'Very gracious. Now you can sleep better – despite your ghosts.'

Picard didn't respond directly but said, 'Why did she ask *me*? Why doesn't she ask *you*? Well, of course, she's asked you. But you're not talking. Not even to the woman who shares your bed.'

Tyson walked towards the door, then turned back to Picard. 'How did she look?'

'Marcy? Fine. Nice-looking woman.'

'No, I meant Sister Teresa. How did she look, Picard?'

Picard glanced at him quickly, then replied, 'Fine. Serene—'

'Physically. Good-looking?'

Picard considered a moment, then replied, 'She went through a very difficult time after the communist victory.'

Tyson nodded. She would be about forty now and not an American forty. A real world forty. 'What happened to her over there?'

'Bad things. Prison camps, forced labour, that sort of thing.' Picard regarded Tyson for some time, then said, 'She never mentioned you by name. Only referred to you as the lieutenant. But lately, after speaking to Karen Harper and thinking about all that Sister Teresa said and now after your questions about her ... I think I missed something ...'

Tyson opened the door. 'Thanks for the drinks.'

'You forgot your book.'

'I don't really want it. Good evening.'

'Go home, Tyson. She might actually miss you.'

Tyson closed the door and walked down the path of broken shells.

The door opened behind him, and a shaft of yellow light fell over the front yard. Picard's voice called out into the damp night air. 'What would you have done? If the situation were reversed, Tyson, what would you have done in my place?'

Tyson called back, 'I would have helped the little boy.'

'No, I mean about putting that chapter in the book.'

Tyson knew what he meant and did not reply as he opened the gate and passed through it. He stood on the sidewalk and looked up the path at Picard's silhouette in the lighted doorway. He said finally, 'I would have done what you did, Picard. And if you had been in command at Miséricorde Hospital instead of me, nothing would have been any different there either.'

'I know. I know that. Fuck Nam, Lieutenant.'

'Yes, indeed, Lieutenant.'

23

Ben Tyson left the dark road and made his way through the bulrushes down to the water's edge. The cove was misty, and the moon was obscured by haze. Yet he could see the lights of the far shore about a fifth of a mile across the gently swelling seawater. Red-blinking channel markers swayed about halfway across the cove, and a sailboat passed silently into the narrows. The tide was out, and the low-tide terrace was strewn with pebbles, shells, and marine life.

The lights of Baypoint seemed to beckon him, to draw him closer to the edge of the lapping water. He recalled clearly a night before the Tet Offensive, standing on the north bank of the Perfume River, staring at the mesmerizing lights of the European Quarter across the water. He felt soothed now, as he'd felt then at the water's edge, at peace with himself and enchanted by the colours on the water, beguiled by the rhythmic rippling of the swells. Impulsively he stripped down to his shorts and threw his clothing into a tangle of bayberry. He waded into the water. He began swimming, only in circles at first, the water cooling and cleansing his warm, sweaty skin. Then, without realizing it, he struck out across the cove for Baypoint.

The tide was running strong, pulling him east towards the outer harbour, and he compensated by angling in a northwesterly direction. The swells were higher than they looked from the shore, and he found he was becoming fatigued.

Reluctantly he made for a channel marker and held on to its bell cage.

He could see his house clearly now, less than three hundred

yards further to the north. Tyson drew a deep breath and headed out. About halfway to the shoreline he felt his right knee begin to throb, then suddenly the knee gave out, and his leg hung useless in the water. Tyson swore silently and turned over on his back. He floated east with the tide towards the North Haven Bridge inlet.

The water seemed warm, and the swells were undulating with a soothing rhythm. A hazy moon with its beautiful corona looked down on him, and Tyson felt strangely in tune with his world.

He was vaguely aware of floating beneath the North Haven Bridge, through the inlet, and past the lighted Long Wharf a few hundred yards to his left. He floated through the ship opening in the stone jetty and out into the great harbour. He tried to move his left leg but found that the knee had seized up. 'Damn it.' This had happened before, and it would pass if he let it rest.

After what seemed like a long time, he felt the tidal pull slackening. A while later he was conscious of a change in direction caused by the land breeze coming from Shelter Island to the north. He tried to picture a map of the coastal region around Sag Harbor and concluded that if the wind prevailed from the north and the tide began its flood, he should wind up at the disco on the Long Wharf. In his underwear. He laughed and swore at the same time. He tried to flex his knee, but it seemed tighter.

After a time Tyson noticed that the wind was picking up, and small but ominous whitecaps broke over his body. What was worse, the wind had come around and was blowing from the south and west now, taking him away from Sag Harbor, out to sea. The water that had seemed so warm was cooling him rapidly, and the wind, too, had a chill in it. He found he was having difficulty catching his breath now, diminishing his ability to stay afloat. 'No good.'

He righted himself and trod water with his arms and good leg. He scanned the horizons for boats, but his visibility was limited by the rising sea as the swells gave way to the first random breaking waves, and for the first time he was frightened.

Tyson was lifted onto the crown of a large swell and looked around quickly. There were boat lights on all horizons, but none of the craft seemed close enough to hail. The lights of Sag Harbor twinkled enticingly about a quarter mile to his southwest, but they might as well have been on the hazy blue moon. The changing tide was too slack to pull him back, and his drift was determined by the rising wind from the southwest. To the northeast Tyson saw the Cedar Point Lighthouse, beyond which was Gardiners Bay where he was headed, and beyond that the Atlantic, next stop France.

The swell flattened, and Tyson dropped into a trough. He tried to distance himself from the problem and think about it objectively as he'd done in combat. As for passing boats, they'd have to be passing damned close to see him at night with these waves. And if he was reading the wind and tide right, it didn't seem likely he'd be washed ashore anywhere. But if he was, it might not be on a sandy beach because too much of these coasts was bulkheaded with rock and timber. That was all the bad news except for sharks, which he wouldn't think about. The good news was that he was able to think at all.

As he expected, the waves began to build up, and floating on his back became impossible. He tried to ride the back of the waves, slipping down into the trough before the wave ascended and crested, then timing the next wave to break before it reached him so that he was lifted again on the back of that curling wave and dropped into the following trough. The wavelengths and periods of crest were still far enough apart to do that, and the heights were running only three to four feet. But this seemed to be changing for the worse.

Tyson thought he saw a boat's lights nearby as he was lifted onto a wave. But the sea had become too loud to waste his breath calling. And his field of vision and his own visibility were narrowly confined within the walls of the black and white water around him. The moon and stars had disappeared, and the night was darker. The smell and taste of brine began to churn his stomach, and he heaved up a mouthful of seawater.

He was fighting for his life now. He suddenly realized that if he didn't make it they'd think it was suicide. 'No. *No!*'

He pictured his house in Baypoint, its deck lighted in the distance, and he saw himself moving closer to it. David and Marcy were having a quiet dinner at the round redwood table. A candle lamp burned between them, and he saw their faces in the flickering light and heard the soft susurrant sound of the radio playing, Willie Nelson drawling out 'All of Me.'

As he'd feared, the wavelengths and the intervals of crest shortened as the heights rose. The troughs were shorter, less than ten feet from the back of one wave to the wall of the oncoming one. The curl of an eight-foot wave blocked the sky above him like an unrolling canopy, then crashed down around him, blinding and deafening him.

As he struggled to the surface, fighting for air, he knew there was no riding this out any longer. One or two more like that and he'd be gone.

Tyson concentrated on his numbed knee, trying to will it to respond, to move, to get his leg kicking. In his youth, before Vietnam, before the Purple Heart, he'd swum in worse seas than this, far out into the treacherous Atlantic, out of sight of land. *This is a goddamned harbour. Benjamin Tyson will not drown in a harbour, in moderately high seas, in the middle of summer. No.* He shouted 'FUCK NAM! FUCK NAM! FUCK NAM!' He shouted until the words were indistinct, even to his own ears. 'Fucknam, fucknam, fucknam, fucknam—!'

He marvelled at lights that could be so bright and hands that could be so clean. The white sheets felt cool against his naked body, and the hovering nurses were solicitous. The

286

USS *Repose*, he thought, was a halfway station between death and life, a salvage ship that collected the flotsam and jetsam from the ravaged shore.

You're going home, soldier.

You'll have complete recovery of that knee.

Oh, the nurses at Letterman are going to love this one.

Here are your personal effects, Lieutenant.

There will be no disability.

Seen some shit, did you, ace?

There's a movie in the lecture hall tonight, Ben. Would you like me to take you?

This war is obscene. Obscene.

Captain Wills and Lieutenant Mercado have been transferred to another ward. They're fine. No, you can't see them.

No psychological counselling recommended. This one has all his marbles.

Your brigade commander is coming aboard to pin medals on pyjamas. Some men fake sleep, then he pins it on their sheets. Your choice.

You're flying to Da Nang tomorrow. They want you at a special awards ceremony in Hue next week.

I don't know where they keep the corpses, Lieutenant. What difference does it make?

You'll be able to run, jump, swim, play tennis, even climb mountains.

No combat duty.

Good luck, Tyson.

Good-bye, Ben.

That knee will be good as new in a month. Swimming will be good for it.

The white life ring lay about ten feet to his left, then it moved far away in a backswell and disappeared. It surfaced again and shot across the churning waters directly at him as though it were homing in by remote control.

Tyson grabbed it firmly with both hands, ducked under it, and slipped up into the hole. The lifeline tautened and broke water. Tyson followed the dripping line with his eyes and for the first time saw the lighted boat not fifty feet from him. It was a cabin cruiser, about a forty footer, with a flying bridge. Tyson bobbed in the wake of the craft, then as he drew closer felt the churning turbulence of the propellers. As he was pulled closer he saw across the white transom the boat's name: *Tranquillity II*. Then everything went black.

Tyson opened his eyes. He was aware that he was wrapped in a robe. He tried to stand but couldn't.

A man knelt beside him. 'Dick Keppler.' He pulled aside the flap of the robe exposing Tyson's right knee. 'War wound?'

Tyson looked at him.

Dick Keppler said, 'They have a sort of signature – pockmarks where minute particles of debris were blown in by an explosive force. Don't get that from a football injury. Seen it before. Is this what's bothering you?'

Tyson realized the man must be an M.D. He replied, 'Just fatigued. Cramped.'

'Could be. You'll be back on the courts in a week.'

'No combat duty.'

The doctor laughed. 'No. Here, let me help you up.'

Tyson took his arm and stood. A woman who introduced herself as Alice handed him an eight-foot gaffing hook, and Tyson supported himself with it. He asked if they could take him to Baypoint, and within fifteen minutes they approached the Baypoint Peninsula. Tyson scanned the near shore and pointed. 'There.'

Keppler cut the throttle and swung to starboard, heading for the long dock. Tyson felt the keel scrape bottom once or twice before the boat eased alongside the dock.

Alice looped a line around a piling, and everyone shook hands. Tyson said, 'If you'll wait, I'll return the robe and gaff.'

Dr Keppler replied, 'Keep them as a souvenir. Do you need a hand getting up those rocks?'

'No, just get me started.'

Keppler jumped onto the dock, took Tyson's hand, and helped him ashore. 'Thanks again.' They exchanged farewells.

Tyson stood on the rickety dock and watched the *Tranquillity* ease back into the channel. They waved and he waved in return.

Tyson rested his weight on the gaff pole and turned towards the shore.

He climbed the rocks backward, in a sitting position, and reached the lawn. He stood and looked at the house set back a hundred feet. The deck was lit, and he could see someone reclining in a lounge chair. He moved across the lawn using the gaff as a walking staff. As he drew near he saw through the deck rail that there were in fact two people in the lounge chair, lying face-to-face groping at each other. The woman had her back to him, and he could see that her T-shirt was hiked up to her armpits. Tyson coughed and took a few more steps.

The man on the lounge chair jumped up and adjusted his trousers, then came quickly to the rail. 'Who's that?'

'Hello, David.'

'Dad! Dad!'

David vaulted over the rail onto the lawn and stopped short. 'What happened?'

'Where?'

David seemed confused. 'What ... why? ...'

Tyson could see the girl had got herself together and was standing at the railing. Tyson imagined he presented an odd appearance dressed in a white robe, barefoot, with his hair tangled, and leaning on a gaff pole. Tyson said, 'I was boating with friends. Went swimming, got a cramp, and they dropped me off. Introduce your friend.'

'Oh ... right.' David looked over his shoulder, then back to his father, then again to the girl. 'Right. This is my dad – Melinda. Dad, Melinda.'

Tyson said, 'Hello, Dad.'

Melinda laughed. 'Nice meeting you.'

Tyson started towards the steps, and David took his arm. 'Are you sure you're okay?'

'Just a bad cramp.' He walked up to the terrace and sat in a folding chair. 'Where's your mother?'

'Oh, out. Be back by ten.'

Tyson nodded.

David said, 'Are you staying? ...' He glanced quickly at Melinda.

Tyson yawned. 'I guess. I live here, don't I? How about getting me some kind of cordial? Straight up.'

'Right.' David darted into the house.

Tyson and Melinda regarded one another for some time. Tyson judged her to be older than David by a few years. She was a nice golden brown, a little pudgy but cute. 'Live here?'

'Just for the summer. We live in Manhattan.'

'Where are you staying?'

'Down the road. The grey-shingled house.'

'That narrows it down to twenty.'

She laughed. 'Green shutters.' She added, 'Last name is Jordan. My father comes out on weekends. My mother is having dinner with Mrs Tyson.'

Tyson nodded. That answered the question he would not ask David and also told him that the Anderson cover was blown. He supposed it didn't matter. 'And you and David are baby-sitting each other?'

She smiled with only enough embarrassment to show she knew she should be but wasn't. Tyson recalled the summer his father had discovered him in a beached skiff with a tarp over it. The skiff rocking on the sand must have looked suspicious if not ghostly. Tyson smiled.

David returned with a half-filled tumbler. 'Crème de cacao. Okay?'

It wasn't, but Tyson assured him it was. 'Sorry to butt in on your time together.'

David and Melinda made sounds of protest though Tyson knew they must be frustrated. Tyson sipped the liqueur. He felt an odd burning in his throat and stomach and thought he might get sick. He put the drink down on the armrest and took a deep breath.

David said, 'You don't look good.'

'I'm just tired. I'm not sick or anything.' Tyson added, 'I'm going upstairs to shower the salt off. Then I'm going to catch some z's.' He raised himself on the arms of the chair and grasped the gaff pole with his right hand. 'No, I don't need help. Just slide the door open.'

Melinda slid the screen back, and Tyson passed into the living room. He called back, 'David, I have a shark boat chartered for tomorrow. Be downstairs by five A.M.'

'Aye, aye, sir.'

Tyson climbed the stairs the way he'd climbed the rocks, buttocks first, then crawled into the large bedroom. He laid the gaff against the footboard, climbed into the low platform bed, and stretched out. He yawned. 'Shower.' He yawned again. The evening had taken on an unreal quality: the old town, the mist, Picard, the bay, the *Tranquillity* and her crew, the climb to his house, and finally David into some heavy petting. Little David. Time flies. He closed his eyes, and his last thought was that he should not be here. He should be, he knew, at the bottom of the sea.

24

'You smell like a fish.'

'I feel like a fish. A cod, I think.'

'What happened?'

Tyson yawned and rubbed his eyes. Marcy's face came into clearer focus above him. She was sitting on the edge of the bed close to him. He noticed that the gaffing hook was still at the foot of the bed. The window was open, and the breeze rustled the blinds. The night-table lamps were on, and the room was softly lit.

'Whose robe is that?' she asked.

'Dick's.'

'I think it's a woman's robe.'

'Then it must be Alice's.'

'Who is Alice?'

'She's married to Dick.' Tyson raised himself and sat up against the headboard. 'The people on the boat. Didn't David tell you?'

'Yes. Why were you swimming in the cove with these people, bare-assed?' She parted his robe, exposing his groin.

He pulled the robe back. 'I didn't start off bare-assed. Don't I get a hello?'

'Hello.' She asked, 'How do you know these people?'

'Met them while I was swimming. They took me aboard.'

'I see.' She glanced at his bare knee. 'How does it feel?'

'Fine. I've been soaking it in salt water.'

'Very funny. Can you move it?'

He tried to flex his knee. 'Not yet.' Tyson looked at his wife. Her normal olive complexion was nearly black, and the white of her teeth and eyes contrasted starkly against her skin. She wore a white jumpsuit, cut low in the front, revealing the curve of her tanned breasts. When she leaned over, Tyson could see she was braless and saw the white flesh an inch above her nipples. She looked at him. 'Are you staying or visiting?'

He replied, 'My shark trip is booked for tomorrow. I thought I'd stay here tonight.'

She smiled without humour. 'I think you've had enough of the sea.'

'We'll see how the knee feels.'

She asked, 'How did you get here? To Sag Harbor?'

'Rented a car.'

'Where's the car?'

'On the other side of the cove.'

'Where are your clothes?'

'In my pocket. Cut the inquisition. I'll need to borrow the Volvo in the morning and some money. I'll bring you a mako to clean and fillet.'

She seemed pensive, then asked softly, 'You didn't try to ... you know?'

Tyson began to reply in the negative, then said, 'I don't know ... I think I just wanted to swim. I was swimming here actually.'

She nodded dubiously.

He said, 'I came about as close as you can get and still get back. Now that I've caught a glimpse of the far shore my curiosity is satisfied. I don't want to go there. Not for some time.'

'I hope not.' Marcy stood and went to the French doors leading to the balcony. She looked out into the cove as she spoke. 'How are you making out in the big city?'

'Okay. Paul Stein has a nice apartment. You were there once before he got divorced.' He added, 'It's a little lonely. How about you?'

'I'm doing fine. Lots of people we know are here. Coincidentally, Paul stopped by, and we had dinner. He wanted to let me know he wasn't promoting our separation by loaning you his apartment.'

'That was thoughtful.'

She turned from the window and faced him. 'Also, Jim, my boss, came by. We went swimming. And Phil Sloan was out last weekend.'

'Sounds like a public rest house. I thought we were hiding out.'

'I'm not hiding.' She took a step towards him. 'It's idiotic and sneaky. And it doesn't work. Those two guys who are

293

renting next door knew who I was right away.'

Tyson didn't reply.

Marcy inquired in a neutral tone, 'What are you doing with yourself?'

Tyson shrugged. 'Not much. Reading, exercising, walking a lot. I've never been unemployed. What am I supposed to do?'

'Are you keeping out of trouble?'

He smiled.

She frowned in return, a mock-annoyed frown. 'I don't like you out of my sight, Tyson.'

He didn't respond, but he felt a little happier. Against his better judgement he asked, 'Are you keeping out of trouble?'

She shrugged.

Tyson waited.

Marcy moved to the side of the bed. She said, 'Jim came with his wife. So did Phil. Paul Stein had his girlfriend with him, and the two guys next door are married – to each other.' She laughed. 'God, it's true that all the men are taken, gay, mental basket cases, too young, too old, or sexual deviates.'

'Don't rule out the sexual deviates.'

She looked at him sternly. 'Anyway, I'm not available. Yet.'

Tyson sat up straighter. He said, 'It's best if you get used to not having me around ... I mean beyond the question of our recent problems is the possibility that I'll be in some sort of ... custody for some time ... so it's best if you get used to—'

'I want you here for just that reason. I want you to be with your family until this is resolved.'

Tyson didn't respond.

Marcy drew a deep breath, then said, 'Look, Ben, I understand why you left. Your wife became an embarrassment, the locker-room talk got smutty, people were laughing behind your back. So you did what all self-centred males do. You said, "Look, guys, I left the slut." Is that about it?'

Tyson said unconvincingly, 'I told you your past is your

294

business. My past is not. I left to save *you* embarrassment.'

'Bullshit.' Still standing beside the bed, she leaned closer to him. 'How do you feel about me? In your heart?'

'I love you.'

'Then fuck the world, and especially fuck the past. Let's go away from here.'

Tyson shook his head. 'I have orders to report to Fort Hamilton day after tomorrow.'

'Don't. Do you still have your passport?'

'Yes—'

'Then go, for God's sake. Go while you can. I'll tie up all the financial ends here. Give Phil power of attorney. We can clear a nice sum on our house. David and I will join you in a few months.'

'Where do you propose I go?'

'Who cares? Anyplace where they'll leave us alone.'

'I'm an American. This is my country.'

She snorted, 'The last refuge of a patriot is somewhere without extradition.'

Tyson smiled grimly. He stared at Marcy awhile, and their eyes met. He said, 'Fight or flight? That is the question. I think I'd rather fight.'

She sat again on the edge of the bed. 'Let me ask you something. If I was the one who was facing a gaol term, would you consider leaving the country with me?'

'Yes.'

'Well, I'm willing to go with you. You're not dragging me. I'm suggesting it. I won't ever hold it against you.'

'Easy to say now.'

'Ben, why are you staying?'

'I'm optimistic. I think I can win.'

'You once said to me, on the day this began, that this will be the Army's game, with their rules. That was good insight. Don't forget you said that.'

'I've come to respect military justice now that I see it and remember it.'

'You know what I think? I think the Army has already sent a memo to the commander of Leavenworth instructing him on the sort of accommodations they want for you.'

Tyson cleared his throat. He replied, 'Well, if that happens, when I get out I'll have paid my debt to society. And I can live a normal life.'

'*What* society? This society doesn't give a rat's ass about what you did or didn't do in some benighted non-country two decades ago. Half the nation doesn't care if you're guilty or not, and the other half is ecstatic that you bagged a hundred gooks in one day.'

'No, that's not my country you're talking about.'

She looked at him curiously, then replied, 'I'm afraid it is. It's poor Picard's blood the country wants, not yours.'

'Nonsense.'

'Is it? You're out of touch.'

'You sound like me when I was a member of the silent majority twenty years ago.'

'I've woken up a bit. In fact, a curious incident happened to me about a week ago. I was in the American Hotel bar with Gloria Jordan, Melinda's mother. Now, this is not one of your blue-collar reactionary pubs. Not at four bucks a pop. There are city people and local gentry in there. And what do you think the subject of conversation was at the bar?'

'The resurgence or decline of the Broadway stage?'

'No, sir. The subject was you.'

'No kidding?'

'And the consensus was "guilty, but who cares?" Also, "guilty with loads of extenuation and mitigation." A few people suggested that you might be innocent as a result of temporary insanity.'

'There's nothing temporary about it. I'm still married to you.'

'One gentleman suggested you be given a medal, though he didn't specify which one he thought appropriate.'

'I already got the Vietnamese Cross of Gallantry for that

action. Let's not overdo it.'

'One lady seriously doubted that such a good-looking man could do anything like that.'

'Did you get her name and phone number?'

'Point is, Tyson, the public, if that was an accurate sampling – and I think you'd find even more support at the Sandpiper – the public thinks you're getting a raw deal whether or not you and your soldiers murdered a hundred men, women, and children. They think Picard is a shit.'

'Poor Picard. What were you doing in a bar?'

'Getting drunk.'

'You're supposed to say, "Looking for my dog." How did you vote?'

'I was very tempted to deliver my standard lecture on the immorality of the Vietnam War, but I remembered I couldn't testify against my husband. So I took Gloria's arm, and we slipped out.'

'Before they recognized you and carried you down Main Street on their shoulders.'

'It was very embarrassing. With Gloria there, I mean.' She rubbed her chin contemplatively, then said, 'But public opinion will not get you acquitted any more than it will get Picard indicted. It's not *that* kind of democracy.'

'I guess not.'

She glanced at her husband, then said, 'Someone told me that federal agents are watching Picard's house – to protect him. Did you know that?'

'No. How would I know that?' But he should have known, he realized. He should have suspected that Picard's coolness in inviting him in was a result of having some heavy artillery on call. Interesting. He had to keep reminding himself that this was not a personal problem but a national one; that there were unseen players in the wings and people like Chet Brown who entered the stage for a moment, then faded back into the shadows, and their numbers were legion. He said, 'Is anyone watching us?'

She shrugged. 'If they are, it is not to protect us from an angry lynch mob. We have not been harassed by anyone except the media, and we've been threatened by no one. What does that tell you about your country?'

'It tells me I am innocent until proven guilty.'

'Yet Picard is guilty. Guilty of smearing the name of a war hero. You, my friend, like your former boss, Westmoreland, are a sacred cow. You fought for your country, you were wounded in battle, and you are being persecuted by an ungrateful Army and a biased press. Well, that is the perception. The truth, as we both know, is that the government is actually doing its job in spite of the unpopularity of its course of action. The press, for all its faults, is seeing that the government doesn't lose its nerve.'

Tyson said, 'Whose side are you on?'

'Yours, damn it.' She thought a moment, then said softly, 'The test of how we feel about our convictions is whether or not we stand up for them when we are personally involved. If your case was one that I was reading about, I'd be inclined towards wanting to see you tried and convicted. But you are my husband, and I love you. So I say you ought to run, to become a fugitive from justice, because ... because I'm afraid you may be guilty ...' She turned away from him, and Tyson could see she was near to tears.

He waited, then said, 'Somehow I don't see Marcy Clure Tyson aiding and abetting a suspected war criminal. But you're right: If the suspected criminal is the man you love, then you have to make a choice. Well, lady, I'm damned flattered. But I'm not running. I've run and run for nearly two decades, pursued by a hundred bloody ghosts. And they would have let me run until the day I died. That was my punishment on earth. I don't know what they have in store for me when I finally join them, but I hope to God they are merciful when we meet.'

'Stop it. Stop that.'

'Well, anyway, the least I can do now is face this imperfect system of justice we've created. As I said, I've already had my punishment, and anything the Army does to me now is inconsequential.'

'To you. Not to me.' She put a cool tone in her voice and informed him, 'I will not wait for you.'

Tyson felt a tightening in his stomach but replied lightly, 'That's my girl.'

She added, 'I will not wait for a fool.'

He said nothing.

Marcy lowered her head in thought then spoke. 'You said fight or flight. But there are people who do neither. People who wait for the state apparatus to knock on their door in the middle of the night—'

'Oh, spare me your Kafka nightmares. I have enough nightmares of my own. This is America. The only people who knock on your door here in the middle of the night are drunks. And I'm not waiting like a paralysed rabbit. I'm fighting.'

'In your mind perhaps. But no one else sees any sign of it. Phil Sloan—'

'Fuck him.'

She drew away from him and said, 'Why are you optimistic? Has Major Harper said anything?'

Harper's name caught him by surprise, though it shouldn't have. He said, 'Well, no. But I have a feel for the Army's case against me. It isn't strong. I think she may recommend that no charges be forwarded.'

'Do you?' Marcy stood, went to the dresser, and opened the top drawer. She moved some underclothes aside and took out a newspaper. 'I didn't want this lying around for David to see.' She held up a copy of the *American Investigator*. 'Have you seen this one?'

'Actually the supermarket was out of them. I bought toilet paper instead.'

She laid the newspaper across her knees. 'I know it's a rag, but this stuff seems to find its way into more respectable publications. Worse, other publications dig deeper for any grains of truth.'

Tyson looked at the inside page to which she had opened. The story was headlined: *Splitsville for Tysons?* A subline announced: *Major Karen Harper Not the Cause, Say Friends.* Very sly, thought Tyson.

Tyson looked at the head-and-shoulders photo of himself and Marcy together. They were wearing evening clothes, and both had rather silly smiles. Tyson recognized it as the photo taken at the hospital charity ball. There was also a photograph of Karen in uniform, probably an Army PR handout.

Marcy said, 'Can I get you something?'

Tyson looked up. 'How about a glass of ice water?'

Marcy left.

Tyson scanned the article. He read a few lines at random: *Marcy has taken up residence on the chic East End of Long Island, while Ben is living in a bachelor pad on Manhattan's fashionable East Side. Friends say they are not legally separated but 'just living apart.'* He read another line further down the column: *He was seen having drinks with her in the cocktail lounge of Washington's exclusive Four Seasons Hotel. A hotel spokesman would not confirm that Tyson was registered there, but employees of the hotel said he was. We don't know who picked up the bill for Tyson's room or for the cocktails with Major Karen Harper, but we hope it wasn't the taxpayer.*

'Me neither,' said Tyson aloud. 'The nerve of those people flaunting their looks and money in exclusive cocktail lounges.' He read a few more lines, getting the subliminal message that the *American Investigator* was trying to get across, and it had less to do with the American taxpayer getting screwed than with the possibility that Tyson and Harper were getting it on. He threw the paper aside, then opened the night-table drawer and found the pack of cigarettes he'd left there. He lit one with a paper match.

Marcy came into the room with a tray on which was a glass of ice water and a glass of white wine. She passed him the water and said, 'I'm taking you to Southampton Hospital.'

'Why? To get me neutered?'

'That's not a bad idea either.' She picked up the newspaper and dropped it back in the drawer. She sipped on her wine, then said, 'Interesting piece.'

Tyson shrugged.

Marcy said, 'I didn't know that investigations for capital crimes were conducted in cocktail lounges.'

Tyson replied, 'Better than a holding cell.'

Marcy said, 'I suppose you're trying to smooth-talk her. Turning on the charm.'

Tyson knew there was no sarcasm or rebuke in that statement; only an appreciation for a possible explanation of his interest in Karen Harper. He said, 'I'll tell you something you'll never read in that rag or anyplace else, and it is this: If by compromising that woman I could weaken or kill the government's case, I still would not do it. Not to her, not to you, and not to myself.'

Marcy nodded. 'Still, the story, for what it's worth, hints at some impropriety. You'll see that suggestion again in the *Washington Post* in a more genteel form.'

She added, 'Anyway, if you want to try that route, I give you my conditional permission.' She smiled.

'Conditional on what?'

'Conditional on results.'

Tyson drank most of the water.

Marcy said in a carefully neutral tone, 'Is she nice?'

Tyson had heard that loaded question enough times to know the correct response. 'From the standpoint of looks, you can see for yourself, though she's certainly not my type. Her personality is abrasive, bitchy, and entirely too officious. Typical . . . of some people with newfound power.' He glanced at Marcy surreptitiously over the rim of his glass.

Marcy seemed to be mulling this over, and if it had a ring of

301

familiarity she didn't say so. She said, 'Well ... anyway, as long as it's only business, do what you have to do. I do in my business.' She smiled mischievously.

Tyson put down his glass and finished his cigarette, throwing the butt in the glass. He said, 'What prompted you to pay a visit to Andrew Picard?'

Marcy shrugged. 'Curiosity.' She added, 'I could see his house across the cove, and one day while I was out alone in the skiff, I just came ashore in his backyard. He was cutting the grass. I introduced myself. We talked, then I left.'

'I suppose if he lived inland that meeting never would happened.'

She looked across the bedroom at him. 'Is that where you were tonight?'

'Yes. And I felt damned silly finding out you'd been there. He probably thinks all the Tysons are going to drop by to check him out. Maybe I can get my mother to fly from Florida. She'd rap him over the head with her cane.'

'I'm allowed to call on whomever I please. This concerns me too, you know.'

'I trust you didn't ask him to do me any favours regarding testimony.'

She shook her head. 'I didn't.'

'Good.' He adjusted the pillow behind his head. He didn't like this feeling of physical disability. He could see why permanently disabled people were sometimes cantankerous. He said to her, 'Picard's testimony is not that important. So you don't have to be nice to him if you see him downtown. You can snub him if you want.'

'All right. But I doubt if I'll run into him.'

Tyson glanced at her. Her response was somewhat out of character, he thought. But perhaps his perceptions were getting cloudy with fatigue.

Marcy sat in the dresser chair and kicked off her sandals. She regarded her toes awhile, her wineglass held in her lap.

Tyson decided he wanted to be alone. He managed a

convincing yawn. 'I'm going to get some sleep. Could you shut off these lights for me?'

Marcy remained seated. She said, 'I want to speak to you about David. He's involved with that girl.'

'Good. She seemed nice. Great tits.'

'I think he's having sex with her.'

'Terrific.'

'That's not ... I mean, how are we to react to that?'

'Well, if we had a daughter, we're supposed to get upset, angry, and frantic. With a son you say, "terrific."'

'You're baiting me. And this is serious. The boy is just sixteen. Aside from any moral issues, there are practical issues here. Psychological issues.'

'Right.' Tyson was aware that sometimes a call to perform some sort of parental duty was a spouse's way of trying to get an errant partner back into the fold. He said, 'Have you spoken to him?'

'Well ... no. It's more a father-son thing.'

Tyson said straight-faced, 'What does that mean?'

'You know. That's something a father should discuss with his son. It would be awkward for him and me if I spoke to him about it.'

'It might be awkward for me too if I had to ask him if he's fucking the socks off his girlfriend. Why, by the way, do you think he is?'

'Well ... sometimes you can sense these things,' she said.

'Really? How?'

'Oh, stop being an ass, Ben. You can tell when people are doing it.'

'Now you're getting me nervous.'

'Will you speak to him?'

'Yes. Tomorrow. On the boat.'

'We'll see about the shark trip.'

'I'm going.'

'Why is this important to you?'

'My grandmother was eaten by a shark. And on the subject

303

of sex, close the door.'

Marcy hesitated, then stood and moved to the door. 'I thought you were tired.'

'I was, but you were talking dirty.'

She smiled. 'Get Melinda Jordan off your mind, Tyson.' She closed the door and moved towards the bed. 'Do you want to see *really* great tits?'

Tyson pulled off the robe and threw it on the floor. 'Do you want to see my war wound?'

Marcy smiled slowly as she unzippered the jumpsuit and pulled it down to her waist. Her breasts stood erect from her dark bronze torso.

Tyson felt his penis move as it hardened.

She said, 'Want to see any more?'

'All of you.'

She slid the jumpsuit and panties down to her ankles and kicked the bunched clothing to the side. Tyson stared at her black pubic hair which seemed to cover more area than the bathing suit she'd worn when she'd got her tan. She came beside the bed. 'How do you want to do this?'

'Female superior, as they call it in our manual. I don't think I can get my leg moving even for this.'

'Are you sure you want to do this?'

'Sure. Thought about it while I was drowning.'

She came into the bed and straddled him with her knees. 'Too heavy?'

'I'm fine.' He reached out and massaged her breasts, then let one hand slip down to her crotch and ran his fingers between her labia. 'Long time, Marcy.'

She nodded. 'Feels good.' She cupped his testicles with one hand and stroked his stiffening penis with the other. 'If we can get this as stiff as your knee, we'll be in business.'

He smiled as he felt her getting moist on his fingers.

She leaned forward and kissed his lips. 'Salty.'

He put his moist finger to his mouth. 'Very salty.'

'Pig.'

Tyson felt her hand guiding him, and he slipped into her easily. She wiggled her groin until she fully enveloped him, then still in the kneeling position began a slow rhythmic movement. 'Ben ... oh, my ...'

He stroked her back and buttocks, then massaged her feet.

Marcy stretched out, covering him with her body, and they embraced. She picked up the tempo, and Tyson heard her deepening breath in his ear. She murmured, 'Oh, God, Ben. I missed your cock.'

'My cock missed you.' He felt her coming – not all at once, but in small rippling tremors with rests between each series of undulating waves; like the sea, he thought, the primeval seas from which we came, the salty moon tides that still surge within us. She took in a short, deep breath of air, then her body stiffened a moment and went limp. He thrust upward hard and felt a sharp pain in his knee shooting up and down his leg, but he thrust again, the pain fighting for attention with the pleasure. He came and almost passed out.

Tyson breathed slowly and steadily. His fingers ran through the cleavage of her buttocks, and he felt the sweat that always formed when her orgasm was intense.

She whispered in his ear, 'Are you all right?'

He nodded. 'Yes.'

'Hurt?'

'A little.'

She rolled off carefully and lay on her side. 'You're pale.'

'All the blood went south. Just give me a second.'

Marcy slid out of the bed and walked to the bathroom. She returned with aspirin and a tube of liniment.

Tyson took the aspirin, and Marcy rubbed the liniment into his knee. He felt drowsy but was aware of her leaving again and returning with a basin and sponge. She washed his groin, then sponged the salt from his body. She lay down beside him and covered them both with the sheets. 'Shock and exposure. You need rest and body warmth.'

'Wake me at four.'

'Okay.' She snuggled up to him, and he fell asleep with her arms around him.

Marcy waited, then got out of bed. She put the clock radio on the floor, turned off the table lamps, put her robe on, and walked to the door. She turned back and looked at her husband in the shaft of light coming from the hallway. He never slept in a supine position, and that he was doing so now was vaguely disturbing. She watched the rise and fall of his chest, thinking how much she felt for him and wondering why the best man she had ever known had to suffer for the past sins of an army and a nation. She left the room and closed the door softly.

Tyson opened his eyes and saw that the ceiling had lightened almost imperceptibly. He could hear gulls and jays screeching, and a boat's horn echoed over the cove. A faint touch of dawn lightened the window, and he could see the tree outside.

'I'm alive,' he said. 'I'm home.'

25

Ben Tyson drove west on the Shore Parkway. The Triumph's top was down, and the afternoon sun shone brightly in the southwest sky. To his left he saw the parachute towers of Coney Island, and beyond, the deep blue Atlantic. It was a fine afternoon for a drive.

Tyson had chosen a nice tan suit of summer-weight wool in which to report for duty, though the Army had requested something green: a uniform actually. 'Well,' he said aloud, 'maybe they won't notice.'

The radio was turned to WNBC-FM, golden oldies, and Bobby Darin was belting out 'Somewhere, Beyond the Sea,' and Tyson hummed along.

Tyson thought about the first time he'd reported for active duty, September 15, 1966. The draft was sweeping up young men by the thousands, and the procedure in his draft board was to report to a parking field on the campus of Adelphi College. From there, chartered buses took the draftees to the induction centre on Whitehall Street in lower Manhattan. Reporting time at the parking field, recalled Tyson, had been 6 A.M. And Tyson never knew if that was simply because the Army liked to begin the day at dawn or because the Army thought it wise to take away these suburban boys under the cover of morning darkness.

He looked down now at the dashboard clock. He would arrive at Fort Hamilton before 5 P.M., early enough to report directly to the post adjutant, but late enough not to have to begin the processing procedure of getting a physical, ID card, payroll records, and all the other details of in-processing that he vaguely remembered as clearly distasteful.

He looked at his hands on the steering wheel, then he looked at the speedometer. He was doing sixty-five, but since he was in no hurry, he slowed down and slipped the Triumph into the right-hand lane. The song on the radio was 'Mr Tambourine Man,' Bob Dylan's version.

A half mile ahead, the massive Verrazano Bridge spanned the Narrows from Fort Hamilton to Fort Wadsworth. Traffic sped by in the outside lane, and gulls circled overhead. The Fort Hamilton exit approached. Tyson downshifted the Triumph, cut the wheel sharply, and exited into the ramp. He came off the ramp, made a series of right turns, and approached the main gate that sat under the bridge's elevated approach road. He stopped in the middle of the road, took a deep breath, and pulled up to the MP booth.

The MP, a woman of about twenty with short red hair and a pug nose, stepped from the booth. Tyson handed her his orders. She glanced at them, then handed them back. 'You have to report to post headquarters. Do you know where that is?'

307

Tyson thought he detected a note of snippiness in her voice, and had he been a civilian, he would certainly have let it pass. He looked at her name tag, then said, 'The next time I pass through this gate, Pfc Neeley, I will have an officer bumper sticker on this car, and you will salute as the car passes. If I should stop to address you, you will address me as sir.'

The young woman came to a position of attention. 'Yes, sir.'

Tyson didn't feel the least bit petty. It's like riding a bicycle, he thought. Once you learn, you never forget. He snapped, 'Carry on.'

She saluted. He returned the salute, his first salute in nearly two decades, and drove through the gate onto Lee Avenue. To his right was a row of vintage artillery pieces on display. To his left stood an old white wood frame building with a sign on the lawn informing him that the house had once been home to Robert E. Lee. As he drove he realized he didn't know where the headquarters building was but knew he'd eventually find it. He remarked to himself on the extraordinary neatness of the place, the lack of even a scrap of paper on the grounds, and he remembered those prebreakfast police calls, the entire garrison turned out to scour the post for offending litter.

He noticed, too, that the uniforms had changed; male and female soldiers wore camouflaged battle fatigues somewhat similar to the ones that in his day had been authorized only for Southeast Asia. He tried to picture himself dressed like that now but could not.

Tyson came to a building marked with a sign that said, *Headquarters NYAC Command Group*. He pulled into a visitor parking slot and shut off the engine. The building was a two-storey rectangular red-brick affair, nearly indistinguishable from a 1950s elementary school.

Tyson straightened his tie, took his attaché case, and got out of the car. His knee was stiff, and he was aware that he was dragging his leg. He entered through glass doors into a hallway of painted cement block, further reinforcing his impression of an institution of lower education. The asphalt tile floor, however, was polished to a lustre found only in military establishments.

Tyson approached a sort of ticket window on the right-hand wall. A duty sergeant, another young woman, looked up from her desk and came to the window. 'Yes, sir?'

Tyson passed his orders through the opening. The young sergeant looked at the name. 'Oh ...'

'Am I expected?'

'Yes, sir, we've been expecting you.' She hesitated and noted his civilian attire but said nothing. Tyson thought the reporting without uniform was the least of his problems today. The woman slid a sign-in book across the counter along with a black government ballpoint pen. Tyson hesitated, then took the pen and signed in. The pen clotted and skipped.

The duty sergeant said, 'Welcome to Fort Hamilton, Lieutenant.' She handed him back his orders. 'Please proceed to the adjutant's office, up the stairs to the right.'

'Thank you.'

'Yes, sir.'

At least, he thought as he walked, no one here said, 'Have a good day.' That alone might be recompense for this whole mess. He climbed the stairs and came to an open door above which was a sign that said *Adjutant*. He entered a small outer office staffed by four young soldiers: two male, two female. He found the sight of all these female personnel more than slightly disorienting. Still, the presence of women lent a little reality to what he remembered as an unnatural environment.

One of the young men, a specialist four, stood at his desk. 'Can I help you?'

'Lieutenant Benjamin Tyson to see the adjutant.'

He looked over Tyson's shoulder as though trying to spot the officer, then looked at Tyson. 'Oh! Yes.'

'Right.' Tyson was aware that the other people in the room

309

were stealing glances at him. Tyson handed the young man his orders. The man said, 'Please follow me, Lieutenant.'

Tyson followed him into a small office that was marked *Captain S. Hodges, Assistant Adjutant.* The office was sparsely furnished and sparsely populated. In fact there was nobody there.

The soldier said, 'I'll let the adjutant know you're here. You can wait here in the captain's office.' The man went through a communicating door into another office.

Tyson went to the window behind the desk. He could see the great bridge, its massive grey steel piers rising up from the north end of the post and completely dominating the skyline. Across the Narrows, a mile away where the bridge was anchored on the far shore of Staten Island, was Fort Wadsworth, which, like Hamilton, held an old coastal artillery battery, built to protect the sea approaches to New York Harbor. National defence, reflected Tyson, had been simpler in the last century; an enemy warship sailed towards the Narrows, and just in case there was any doubt if it was friend or foe, the ship considerately flew the enemy flag. The coastal guns fired. The ship fired back. The stone forts were picturesque, and so were the ships. Defending New York Harbor, he thought, must have been a piece of cake.

The communicating door to the next office opened, and an officer strode into the room. 'Tyson?'

Tyson turned from the window. His eyes took in the pertinent information to be gleaned from the uniform: The name tag said Hodges, rank of captain; branch, Adjutant General Corps; awards and decorations, none. Tyson noticed the West Point ring. The man was in his middle twenties, his bearing was too stiff, and he wore a rather unpleasant, almost nasty expression. Tyson did not like the way the man had addressed him and had the urge to bury his fist in the captain's supercilious face. Tyson hesitated, then with great and obvious reluctance, came to a position of attention and saluted.

'Sir, Lieutenant Tyson reports.'

Hodges returned the salute peremptorily, then ruffled the papers in his hand. 'It says here you are to report in uniform.'

'I don't own a uniform.'

'Do you know a barber?'

'Yes ... yes, sir.'

'How dare you report like *that?*' He jabbed a finger in Tyson's direction.

Tyson did not reply.

'Well?'

'No excuse, sir.'

'I should think not.' Captain Hodges seemed to realize that Tyson was actually standing behind Hodges' desk while Hodges was standing in front of it. He said, 'Stand over here.' He switched places with Tyson, then sat in his swivel chair. He said, 'Before you report to the adjutant, I want you in proper uniform and your hair cut to regulation length.'

'I'd like to see the adjutant now.'

Hodges' face reddened. *'What?'*

'Captain, I have until midnight to report for active duty. This is an unofficial call. I would like a word with the adjutant.'

Hodges seemed to be processing the protocol of such a request. He stared at Tyson.

Tyson stared back.

Hodges nodded to himself as though coming to the conclusion that it might not be a bad idea for Tyson to make a negative impression on the adjutant. He stood. 'Wait here.' Hodges disappeared into the adjoining office.

Tyson let out a long breath. He had sudden and vivid fantasies of perpetrating ingenious acts of violence on the person of Captain S. Hodges. But in a way he had provoked the man by his appearance. Tyson may as well have shown up barefoot in dirty jeans and wearing shoulder-length hair and a T-shirt that said *Fuck the Army*. Still Hodges had not displayed even a modicum of the military courtesy that was due an officer of lower rank.

Tyson looked around the sparse office. Hanging on the walls were Hodges' West Point diploma, his commission, and a few certificates of completed courses. Tyson also noticed a framed paper with typing on it and came closer to it. It was headed, 'An Excerpt from General MacArthur's Farewell Speech at West Point.' Tyson read:

The shadows are lengthening for me. The twilight is here. My days of old have vanished tone and tint; they have gone glimmering through the dreams of things that were. Their memory is one of wondrous beauty, watered by tears, and coaxed and caressed by the smiles of yesterday. I listen vainly for the witching melody of faint bugles blowing reveille, of far drums beating the long roll. In my dreams I hear again the crash of guns, the rattle of musketry, the strange, mournful mutter of the battlefield.

But in the evening of my memory, always I come back to West Point. Always there echoes and re-echoes Duty – Honour – Country.

Today marks my final roll call with you, but I want you to know that when I cross the river my last conscious thoughts will be of The Corps, and The Corps, and The Corps.

I bid you farewell.

Tyson turned away from the wall and stared through the window. 'Yes, all right. I see.' Captain Hodges, young West Pointer, about ten years old at the time of the Tet Offensive, considered Benjamin J. Tyson a disgrace to the Corps, to the nation, and to humanity.

Tyson thought about that, putting himself in Captain Hodges' place, and found himself disliking Benjamin Tyson. *I understand*, he thought. *And I'm relieved to have finally found some overt moral outrage.* He suspected he would run into more professional soldiers like Captain Hodges before

312

this was ended. The Army was much tougher on its own than civilians could ever be.

The door opened and Hodges snapped, 'The colonel will see you now.'

Tyson replied, 'Thank you, Captain.'

Hodges stood at the door as Tyson entered the adjutant's office. Tyson strode in and stopped, as was customary, in the centre of the room facing the desk. He saluted. 'Sir, Lieutenant Tyson reports.'

The colonel returned the salute from a sitting position but said nothing.

Tyson heard Hodges' footsteps retreating behind him and heard the door close. Tyson, while keeping head and eyes straight ahead, managed to see the person to whom he was reporting. The adjutant was a rather stocky man, about fifty years of age, and what was left of his hair was grey. His face was doughy, and his jowls hung like pancake batter. Tyson realized he didn't even know the man's name, and what was more he didn't care to.

At length the colonel said, 'Sit down, Lieutenant.'

Tyson sat in a chair opposite the desk. 'Thank you, sir.'

Tyson did not overtly look around at the office, nor would he do that in civilian life. He did note, however, that the room was spartan: a steel-grey desk, a number of vinyl chairs, blinds on the windows, and grey asphalt tile on the floor. The walls were the same cream-painted cement block as the rest of the building. Tyson recalled his office at Peregrine-Osaka with more fondness than he'd felt for it while he was there. This office, however, did have something his did not: The wall behind the desk was covered with military memorabilia, photos, certificates, and other symbols of recognition and accomplishment. Tyson realized that he could finally hang his framed military certificates in his new office. He also realized he wasn't going to.

The adjutant inquired, 'Have you been to Hamilton before?'

The man's voice was gravelly, and the stink of cigar smoke that permeated the room was a clue why. Tyson replied, 'No, sir.'

'Had no trouble finding us, did you?'

'No, sir.' Tyson looked at him. He saw that the man wore the silver oak leaves of a lieutenant colonel, not the eagles of a full colonel. Tyson's eyes went to the black name tag over the right pocket: *Levin*. Tyson looked at the desk nameplate. *LTC Mortimer Levin.*

Colonel Levin said bluntly, 'Are you surprised to find a Jew sitting here?'

Tyson thought of several possible replies but none that would do him any good, so he said, 'Sir?' which was the military way of responding to a superior officer without responding.

Colonel Levin grunted and stuck an unlit cigar in his mouth. 'This, I take it, is a social call.'

'Yes, sir. I meant to report in. But I had second thoughts after meeting Captain Hodges.'

'I'm sure he had second thoughts after meeting you.'

Tyson cleared his throat. 'Colonel, I'm considering registering an official complaint, under ... I believe it's Article 138 of the Uniform Code of Military Justice, with respect to my treatment by Captain Hodges.'

'Are you?' The colonel nodded appreciatively. 'A good defence is an aggressive offence. Well, don't try to confuse the issues, Tyson. Why don't you just invite Captain Hodges to meet you in the basement of the gym? That's where I like to see officers talk over their differences. Five rounds, sixteen-ounce gloves, referee must be present.'

Tyson looked the colonel in the eyes and saw the man was not being glib or facetious. Tyson replied, 'I may do that.'

'Good. Listen, Tyson, it is my duty as adjutant to say welcome to Fort Hamilton and to arrange for you to meet Colonel Hill, the post commander. But in candour, Lieutenant Tyson, Colonel Hill does not want you here and would rather not meet you. So don't embarrass everyone by

314

asking to meet him. And don't show up at social events that by custom you will be invited to. Please arrange to mess separately. Do I make myself clear?'

'Yes, sir.'

Levin tugged at his jowl and seemed to be thinking. He looked at Tyson. 'Let's say you are reporting in now so you don't have to come back later in uniform. Okay?'

'Yes, sir.'

Levin shuffled some papers on his desk and found what he was looking for. 'Your special instructions said you were to bring your passport. Did you do that?'

Tyson hesitated, then replied, 'Yes, sir.'

Colonel Levin extended his hand across the desk. 'May I see it?'

Tyson reached into his breast pocket and drew out his passport. He put it in Colonel Levin's open hand.

Levin laid it on the desk and flipped through it. 'You've been around.'

'Yes, sir.'

Levin dropped the passport into his top drawer and shut it. He folded his hands on the desk and regarded Tyson.

Tyson said, 'By what authority are you taking my passport?'

Levin shrugged. 'Beats me. Those are my orders. Take it up with the State Department or the Justice Department. You can have it back for authorized travel.' He added, 'I have instructions from the Pentagon assigning you temporarily to my office. So for the time being I am your commanding officer. However, I don't think you will want to share space with Captain Hodges, so I will try to find something for you to do away from this building.'

'Yes, sir.'

Levin took a deep asthmatic breath and said, 'Is there anything you might be interested in doing on this post?'

Tyson found himself replying in an irritated voice, 'Not a thing.'

Levin's doughy face seemed to harden, then soften again. He finally lit his cigar and blew a puff of smoke into the air. 'The Army,' said Levin, 'gave me a few special instructions. I am to assign you a duty commensurate with your abilities and experience.' Levin tapped the thick personnel file. 'You were an infantry officer.'

'For less than two years – a long time ago. Most recently I was a vice-president of a large aerospace corporation.'

'Is that a fact?' Levin tapped his cigar into a coffee mug. 'We'll find something for you. By the way, do you know how much you make? Now, I mean.'

'No, sir.'

'You make $1,796 a month. Does this recall to duty impose an undue financial hardship on you?'

'One might say that. In fact, sir, if this tour of duty lasts very long I may have to sell my house.'

Levin rubbed his jowls, then said, 'I don't think this tour of duty will last very long. But please keep me informed regarding your financial situation.'

'For what purpose, sir?'

'Well, the Army will help in any way it can. There's a credit union for one thing. All right?'

'Thank you.' Tyson knew that Levin's concern was not personal; it was the government that was concerned about his economic welfare, which was why Levin had brought it up, to see what Tyson would say. In America, he'd learned, the worst thing that could befall a citizen, short of going to jail, was the ruination of his credit rating. Ruined reputations and ruined marriages and crises of the soul and psyche were small tales compared to a bad TRW rating. Tyson was happy to see that the government was concerned, that they were worried.

Levin said, 'I'm confident you will figure out a way not to have to sell your house. Which reminds me, I have been instructed to offer you post family housing, though we're a bit tight here.'

'Thank you, Colonel, but I don't think my family will be

316

joining me here, and I wouldn't want to put another officer and his family out on the street. In fact, if the Army has no objections, I'd like to continue living off-post, and I will not require bachelor officer's quarters or any other Army accommodations.'

Levin leaned across his desk. 'Let me be a little more precise, Lieutenant. The Army orders you to take a family housing unit. Frankly the Army does not want to give the media or the public the impression that you are being put into a hardship situation. There is a nice two-bedroom brick row unit assigned to you, and it will have your name on it by morning. It is partly furnished, and you are authorized to move your household goods into it at government expense. You are also authorized to move your wife and son into it, though of course you do not have to do that. Clear?'

'No, sir, it's not. Do I have to live on post or not?'

Levin said, 'I'm afraid you do.'

'That,' said Tyson strongly, 'is most irregular. That would constitute an undue hardship, and there is no justification for that type of restriction.'

Levin cleared his throat. 'Unfortunately there is. A preliminary investigation into your case is being conducted under Article 31 of the Uniform Code of Military Justice, and it is the right of the Army to restrict its personnel to ensure your continued availability for this investigation. Restriction, as you know, is a moral rather than a physical restraint, and it is enforced only by your moral and legal obligation to obey this order.'

Tyson nodded. 'I know all that, Colonel. What are the limitations of this restriction?'

Levin looked at a sheet of paper on his desk. 'You are to be in your post quarters between twenty-four hundred hours and six hundred hours – that's midnight to six in the morning. You may, though, stay away overnight on the evening preceding your off-duty days. Your off-duty travel, however, is restricted to fifty miles from this post.'

Tyson said nothing for a long time, then remarked, 'My family is on the East End of Long Island. That, as you know, is about a hundred miles from here.'

'Then obviously you cannot visit them.'

'That would present an undue hardship.'

'I hardly think, Lieutenant, that the Army's refusal to allow you to summer in the Hamptons is a hardship. You will have some duties here, and it is not reasonable that you should attempt to travel a great distance every day after work and be back here by midnight. Fifty miles, and you may not travel by boat or plane unless it is first cleared by me or the post commander.' Levin hesitated, then added, 'I was under the impression you were not living with your wife.'

'I was not, but I intended to do so again.'

'Well, then ...' Levin looked at Tyson's orders. 'You have a principal residence in Garden City. That's well within fifty miles of here, isn't it?'

'Yes, sir. That's the house I may have to sell.'

'Well, Lieutenant, until that time comes, your wife can move back to that house in Garden City. As a practical matter, you can spend weekends at home there. Also your wife and son may want to spend some weeknights with you here in your family housing unit.'

'Colonel, I do not think my wife will set foot on an Army installation.'

Levin said irritably, 'You'll have to work out your conjugal visits yourself, Lieutenant. It is not my duty to become involved in that.'

'No, sir.'

Levin tapped his fingers on his desk. After a time he said, 'I realize this is very difficult for you, but if it will make you feel any better, this will all be over soon.'

'Will it?'

'Yes. Actually the imposition of restrictions on you makes it necessary for the government to dispose of your case one way or the other without delay. In fact, your right to a speedy

318

trial or the Army's decision not to pursue the case must come within ninety days of any sort of restriction. The civilian courts may not know what a speedy trial is, but a trial by court-martial is, if nothing else, speedy. So this restriction is a blessing in disguise. The clock is running for the Army as of now. Before mid-October this will be finished one way or the other.'

Tyson nodded. 'I see.'

Levin said in a kinder tone, 'Also the restrictions are not very onerous. And no one is watching you. But be careful, for your own sake.'

'Yes, sir.'

Levin asked, 'By the way, are there any other addresses I should know about?'

'Yes, sir. As you may have read in the papers, I'm currently living on the fashionable East Side.'

'You've got more addresses than I've got bathrooms.'

'Yes, sir.'

'I want that East Side address and the Sag Harbor address. Give them to Hodges.'

'Yes, sir.'

Levin turned another page of Tyson's file. 'Two Hearts. Where and where?'

'Right knee and right ear.'

Levin nodded, and his eyes focused on Tyson's scarred right ear. He said, 'I noticed you were limping. Is that a result of your wound?'

'Yes, sir.'

'Are you fit for active duty?'

'No, sir.'

'Well, you're fit enough for what they have in mind.'

Tyson did not reply.

Levin said, 'I half didn't expect you, Tyson.'

'I was ninety per cent sure I wasn't coming.'

Levin smiled.

Tyson added, 'My attorney has filed a motion in federal

319

district court to have this recall to duty rescinded.'

'That's none of my concern. You're here now, and you were right to report as ordered, uniform or not.'

'Yes, sir. That's what my lawyer said.'

'One last thing. Your oath of office. They require you to do this again, and they asked me to administer it upon your arrival.'

Tyson nodded. Levin was being open with him, revealing to him the fact that the Army and the government had thought this out. Pull the passport, assign family housing, administer the oath. Slam bang, we got you coming and going. Only you're not going anywhere.

Levin picked up a piece of paper and handed it to Tyson. 'No need to do it aloud. Just read it to yourself and sign it.' He drew on his cigar.

Tyson read: I, Benjamin J. Tyson, having been appointed an officer in the Army of the United States, in the grade of First Lieutenant, do solemnly swear (or affirm) that I will support and defend the Constitution of the United States against all enemies, foreign and domestic, that I will bear true faith and allegiance to the same; that I take this obligation freely, without any mental reservation or purpose of evasion; and that I will well and faithfully discharge the duties of the office upon which I am about to enter: SO HELP ME GOD.

Tyson looked up from the paper and saw that Levin was extending a pen across the desk. Tyson hesitated, then took the pen and noticed irrelevantly that it was a good Waterman fountain pen. Tyson said, 'I have some mental reservations.'

'Is that so?'

'So ... can I make a note of that on here? Cross that out and initial it?'

'You'd better not. Look, Lieutenant, this is the Army, and that is your oath of office, not a home improvement contract. You will sign it as it is, or you may refuse to sign it.'

'Then I refuse to sign it.'

'Fine. Give it back.'

Tyson handed the paper back with the pen.

There was a silence in the room, then unexpectedly, Levin said, 'You been fishing, or loafing in the sun?'

'Both.'

'There's good fishing at Sheepshead Bay, not too far from here.' He glanced at his watch. 'I take it you were not warmly received by Captain Hodges. That is not a presumption of guilt.'

'Then what was it, Colonel?'

'It was an anticipation of problems: media nosing around here, maybe demonstrations, curiosity seekers. This is a nice quiet little post. Less than five hundred military. People like it here. Actually I was born and raised a few miles from here. Brighton Beach.'

'I didn't ask to come here, Colonel.'

'No. But the Army assigned you here as a courtesy to you; however, it is no big treat for us. I personally believe you should have been stationed at one of the larger bases, perhaps down South. A place like Bragg which dominates the community around it, instead of vice versa as it is here.'

Levin continued, 'We are ill equipped to provide the necessary logistics and security in the event a ... a judicial proceeding takes place here. It would be a media circus. And you see, Tyson, the careers of several officers like myself and Hodges who are responsible for you and for maintaining good order and discipline here, could be jeopardized.'

'I appreciate your problems. I won't add to them.'

Levin nodded and stubbed out his cigar, then looked down at the papers spread across his desk. When he spoke again, he spoke as the post adjutant delivering the required advice to the newcomer. 'I don't know how you've been treated by your civilian peers these last few months, but here you are an officer, and if you act like one, eventually you will be treated like one – even by people like Captain Hodges.' He added, 'Do the best you can in the time you are here. Whether you leave here a free man or under guard, you should be able to look on this time with a sense that you acted correctly and with honour.'

'Yes, sir. I understand that.'

'Good.' Levin said more lightly, 'I'd like us to have dinner. Maybe talk about things. Meet me at the O Club at eighteen hundred hours.'

Tyson had a dinner engagement with his accountant in Manhattan and began to decline automatically, then recalled that he was in the Army, and in the Army the colonel's wish was a direct command. He said, 'Yes, sir, Officers' Club at six o'clock.'

'You say it your way, Lieutenant, I say it my way. Be there then.'

'Yes, sir.'

'See Captain Hodges on your way out, and he will give you some orientation literature. Give him those addresses. That will be all.'

Tyson stood. 'Yes, sir.' He saluted, turned, and left the adjutant's office, closing the door behind him.

Tyson stood near Hodges' desk, but the captain was bent over paperwork and did not look up at him. Tyson drew his notebook from his breast pocket and scribbled the addresses Levin had asked for. He laid the paper on Hodges' desk. 'Colonel Levin asked me to give you these—'

'Fine.' Hodges added without looking up from his desk, 'Take that packet. Familiarize yourself with the post and its facilities.'

Tyson picked up a large brown envelope stuffed with papers and put it in his attaché case.

Hodges said, 'Begin your in-processing tomorrow.'

'Yes, sir.' Tyson headed towards the door.

'Tyson?'

'Yes, sir?'

Hodges looked up at him. 'We didn't need this.'

Tyson wasn't certain if the 'we' referred to Hodges and

Levin or Fort Hamilton or the Army or the officer corps or the nation. Probably all of the above. Tyson replied, 'No, sir.'

'If you should ever have reason to come into this office again, and I hope you don't, I expect you to look like a soldier.'

Tyson took a step towards Hodges' desk. He wanted to ask this young staff officer what the hell he knew about being a soldier. Tyson took a deep breath.

Hodges glared at him.

Tyson said, 'Good afternoon, sir.' He turned quickly and left.

He was vaguely aware of passing between the desks in the outer office, striding quickly through the corridor, down the stairs, past the reception window, and out of the glass doors into the sunlit parking area. He walked to his car and flung his attaché case into the front seat. He kicked the car door and put a dent in the panel, then shouted, 'Damn it! Damn—' He suddenly looked back at the headquarters building. In an open second-storey window he saw the stocky figure of Lieutenant Colonel Mortimer Levin, his hands behind his back, a cigar stuck in his mouth, watching him.

Tyson composed himself, got into his car, and pulled away from the headquarters building. As he drove through the narrow streets of the small post, he came to the belated realization that he was in the Army. He said it aloud. 'I'm in the Army. I am *in* the Army.'

His first tour of duty and subsequent release from active duty had always had a feeling of tentativeness, of unfinished business, an unfulfilled obligation to the Army, to his country, and to himself.

But this time, he understood, was the final muster, the last call to arms. In reality, this recall to duty was but a continuation of his service after a long furlough. He did not know how this would end, but for the first time, here at Fort Hamilton, he saw the end in sight.

323

26

Benjamin Tyson climbed the steps to the Officers' Club, housed in the grey granite artillery fort.

The foyer and the hallways that ran to the left and right were arched and vaulted, constructed of stone and brick, and covered in places with stucco. The floor was made of flagstone, and the lighting fixtures were black wrought iron. Because it had been a fort, there were few openings to the outside world: only small gun ports, and these were bricked over.

A man in his twenties, dressed in a grey suit, was sitting at the reception desk. 'Your name, sir?'

'Tyson. Where is the bar, please?'

The man ignored the question. 'May I see some identification?'

Tyson replied, 'What for?'

'Club regulations.'

Tyson showed the man his driver's licence, and the man checked the name against a list, then asked Tyson to sign in, which he did. The man said, 'Thank you, sir. Bar is to the right.'

Tyson walked down an arched corridor. Shorter arched cul-de-sacs extended at right angles in the direction of the Narrows. These were, he knew, the casemates, the places where the big guns had sat overlooking the Narrows. The gun ports here were bricked up also.

He entered a long windowless chamber that might have been the magazine where powder and shot had been stored but which now was the lounge. A long mahogany bar ran along the left side of the room, and tables sat along the right wall. A hand-painted sign said *Patriots' Bar*.

The bar-room was full, and Tyson was surprised to see more civilian-attired people than uniformed officers. He supposed the clientele consisted of retired military personnel, government workers, civilian guests, and spouses.

The decor could have been East Side pub, but the patrons were not. For one thing, he noticed, despite the crowd, there was not that raucous noise that you hear in an after-work place. Rather, there was a subdued tone to the room, punctuated by an occasional laugh of the type a lieutenant gives when his captain has said something witty.

Tyson spotted Colonel Levin sitting by himself at the far end of the bar. Tyson walked down the length of the room and joined him. 'Good evening, Colonel.'

'Good evening, Lieutenant. Have a seat.'

Tyson sat on the barstool beside Levin.

Levin said, 'Did you get a chance to explore the club?'

'No, sir. I just got here.'

'It's an interesting place. They don't make them like this anymore. It's a national historic landmark.'

'Is it?'

'Yes, that's in the post information book. I suggest you read it.'

'Yes, sir.'

'Do you want to become a member here?'

Tyson lit a cigarette. 'I'm not certain.'

'Every officer is urged to join.'

'Yes, sir, I know.'

'In fact, I took the liberty of signing you up.'

Tyson drew on his cigarette. 'Thank you, Colonel.'

Levin regarded him. 'What's your drink, Tyson?'

Tyson thought that Levin put the question the way someone might ask, 'What's your religious affiliation?' as though each man were born with or chose a drink for life. He looked at Colonel Levin. The man was an odd amalgam of U.S. Army and New York Jewish. Tyson would rather have had to deal with either of those two types but not both in the

325

same personality.

'Tyson? Something to improve your hearing?'

'Sorry, Colonel. Dewar's and soda.'

Colonel Levin said to the barmaid, 'Sally, meet Lieutenant Tyson, a new member.'

The middle-aged woman gave a friendly smile. 'Welcome to Fort Hamilton ... Lieutenant.'

'Thank you, ma'am.'

She looked at him curiously, taking in his longish hair and probably, he thought, wondering about a lieutenant in his forties. Sally suddenly brightened. 'Oh, police.'

This, thought Tyson, was a logical deduction. A police lieutenant would be in his forties, and that was how Sally fitted Tyson's age to his rank.

Tyson waited for Levin to say something tactful. Levin said, 'No, this is Lieutenant Benjamin Tyson, United States Army, who is the subject of a murder investigation.'

Sally's mouth dropped open. 'Oh ... yes.'

Tyson thought that was probably the best way to do it. He decided he liked Levin.

Colonel Levin informed Sally that Lieutenant Tyson's drink was Dewar's and soda, and Tyson knew he'd be unwise to order anything different next time he came in.

Levin ordered another Manhattan for himself, then said to Tyson, 'Did you get over to finance? You're entitled to some pay.'

'No, sir. My attorney advised me not to accept any money.'

'Did he? Well, try not paying *him* and see if he gives you the same advice.'

'Yes, sir. You see, that's also why I don't know about joining the club. I've signed in as ordered, but there are certain things I can't or won't do on advice of counsel. On the other hand, as you suggested, I would be well advised to act like an officer, to become part of this post and its community. So I'm in somewhat of a quandary, and I hope you understand if I don't appear as gung-ho as most newly assigned lieutenants.'

Levin replied curtly, 'I'm sure it isn't only the advice of counsel that's making you less than eager to fit in here.'

'That's correct, Colonel. No offence, but I was doing okay as a civilian.'

Levin lit a new cigar and didn't reply.

Tyson continued, 'As you just witnessed, I'm a little old to be wearing a first lieutenant's bar, Colonel.'

The barmaid set down the drinks and added them to the colonel's chit. Levin raised his glass. 'Welcome.'

Tyson raised his glass also but did not touch it to Levin's. 'Thank you, Colonel Levin.'

Both men drank, then Levin said, 'Tomorrow you will get your ID card, your physical, your uniform, and all that. Start early. I expect you firmly established in the Army and ready for duty by eight hundred hours, day after tomorrow.'

'Yes, sir. What sort of duty?'

'The Department of the Army has instructed the post commander to instruct me to assign you casual duties so that you have ample time to attend to any personal problems that may have arisen as a result of your unexpected recall to duty. Also to allow you time to attend to any legal necessities that may arise as a result of this ongoing investigation.' Levin ate the cherry from his Manhattan. 'In other words, you are attached to my office as I said, and I'm supposed to find something for you to do that won't take up any of your time.'

'Why can't I just report to you every morning, then knock off for the day?'

'I thought about that, Tyson. But that's not consistent with the Army work ethic and, I suspect, not consistent with your own work ethic. Casual duties are often boring, demeaning, and demoralizing.'

'Yes, sir.' Tyson remembered being on casual duty once and concluding the same thing: It was stressful to be pretending to be doing something when you weren't. But that was then. Now he'd just as soon spend the time before the final disposition of his case with his family and lawyer.

Levin said, 'Did you notice that granite triangular-shaped building as you came into the club?'

'Yes, sir.'

'That was the old fort's caponier.'

'I thought so.'

'Don't be sarcastic, Lieutenant. A caponier is a fortification to protect the landward side of the coastal battery. Anyway, that's where the Harbor Defense Museum is housed. Did you know we have a museum here?'

'Yes, sir. There was a booklet in the orientation literature.'

'Right. The curator is a fellow named Dr Russell. Nice eccentric sort of chap. He's civil service. In fact there he is over there.' Levin cocked his head towards a table in the corner. 'The guy with the glasses.'

Tyson looked towards the cocktail table and saw a tall lanky man not more than thirty years old sitting with three other civilians.

Levin said, 'I spoke to him earlier about taking you on as an assistant.'

'Assistant *what*?'

'Museum curator.'

Tyson said nothing.

Levin asked, 'What's wrong with that?'

'Well ... I don't ...'

'Look, Tyson, I'm doing you a favour. First of all, it's a job that won't take up much of your time or mental energies. Secondly, it has dignity, as opposed to some other jobs I could cook up for you. Finally, it's outside the normal activities here, and it will keep you segregated from your brother officers, which is desirable for all parties. And your immediate supervisor will be Dr Russell, who's a civilian and an okay guy. And four, it's across the lane from the O Club so you can hang out here if you get bored. Also it's a nice little museum and sort of interesting. So what do you say?'

'I ... don't know ... Do I have to wear my uniform?'

'Only on certain occasions. Like when dignitaries come to visit or school groups come.'

'School groups?'

'Yes, you'll give tours to school kids. And senior citizen groups.'

'Tours? …'

'Do you need another drink to improve your hearing?' He called to the barmaid. 'Another round, Sally.' He looked back at Tyson. 'Well?'

'Look, Lieutenant, I'm under orders to walk on eggs with you. That's between us. And I'm becoming media conscious. The museum job is good. It *looks* good. Take it.'

'I'll take it.'

'Fine.' Levin held up his glass, and Tyson took his fresh drink and touched the glass to Levin's.

Levin said, 'I'll introduce you to Dr Russell later.'

'Yes, sir.'

Levin finished half of his drink, and Tyson could see he was feeling the effects. His unhealthy pallor had turned a nice ruddy colour, and his wheezing seemed less stertorous. Tyson suspected that Colonel Levin looked good every night around this time.

Levin said, 'The public affairs office has been handling news people all day.'

Tyson looked up from his drink. 'Sir?'

'This is an open post. We really can't stop the press from coming through the gates unless we have special orders from higher up to keep them out.'

'I see.'

'We can, however, keep them out of *here* because this is a private club.'

Tyson nodded. 'I had trouble getting in.'

'So did a lot of other people tonight, thanks to you. Point is, you can get waylaid by the press anyplace else on post that isn't a restricted area or isn't your place of work, like the museum. That's the instructions the Department of the Army

329

is giving to the media. So you're safe in the museum and the club. You have about ten yards to run between the two places and twenty yards to the parking lot. So it's up to you to use your good judgement in dealing with these people. From what I read, you've displayed good judgement in the past.'

Tyson said, 'Is that your personal opinion, Colonel, or is that a compliment you've been asked to relay to me?'

'Both. Subject closed.' Levin said, 'Take your drink.' He rose and made his way a bit unsteadily towards the table at which Dr Russell was sitting. Levin said, 'Dr Russell, may I present Lieutenant Tyson?'

Dr Russell stood and took Tyson's hand warmly. 'Has Colonel Levin told you I'm in need of an assistant?'

Tyson replied, 'Yes, he has.' Tyson noted that Dr Russell had a pleasant professorial accent. The man was taller than Tyson, very thin, and wore the sort of rumpled suit one might expect of a museum curator, not to mention a civil servant.

Dr Russell introduced Tyson to the three men he was drinking with, and they seemed genuinely happy to make his acquaintance, as though they'd been introduced to a celebrity. Tyson had come to expect a wide range of reactions from people who knew who he was, and there was always that interesting few seconds as people processed the name and face and decided if they were happy to meet him or not.

Levin, Russell, and the three other men were making small talk, and Tyson tuned back in as Dr Russell addressed him, 'I've always thought it desirable to have a uniformed officer conduct some of these tours. I'm glad this opportunity came up.'

Tyson replied, 'So am I.'

Dr Russell's brow knitted as though he were thinking about what he had just said. He added, 'Of course I realize this won't be a lengthy arrangement. You won't be here long, will you?'

'I think not.'

Colonel Levin took Tyson's arm and announced, 'We have a table waiting.'

330

Tyson and Levin left the bar and went into the main corridor. Levin observed, 'Dr Russell seemed happy to have you aboard.'

Tyson responded, 'He'll be sad to see me leave.'

They entered a medium-sized dining room that looked fairly new. Large windows let in the red light of a beautiful sunset. Levin explained, 'This is a recent addition. The exterior is built of granite to blend in with the old fort, but Dr Russell is nonetheless appalled. Everyone else is happy about the room.'

Tyson saw that about half the tables were empty, and Levin asked the hostess to seat them away from the other diners. They were shown to a table near one of the large windows looking out towards the Narrows.

Tyson said, 'You could do a nice court-martial here.'

Levin didn't reply immediately, then said, 'I thought of it, but it would inconvenience people who normally have lunch here.'

Tyson put his blue napkin on his lap. 'Still, it's a great view.' He asked, 'Where do you hold trials now?'

'Oh, we have a small room in the JAG building. But that wouldn't do.'

'I've sometimes wondered why there are no courthouses in the Army.'

Levin shrugged. 'Maybe because there is no permanently convened court. Military justice is ad hoc, Tyson, unlike civilian justice. Therefore, anyplace will do.'

A young waitress came to the table and greeted Levin. She said, 'Manhattan, sir?'

'Right. Ann, this is Lieutenant Tyson who's been in the news recently. Dewar's and soda, and I'd appreciate it if you told the staff not to talk to reporters.'

The waitress took a second to digest all of that, then quickly looked at Tyson. 'Oh. Hello ... hello.'

'Hello.'

'Soda and water?'

'Dewar's and soda.'

'Yes, sir.' She dropped two menus on the table and hurried off to get the drinks. Levin lit a new cigar.

Tyson perused the menu. 'How is the food, Colonel?'

'Compared to what? The Four Seasons or the mess hall?'

'The Four Seasons, sir.'

'Never been there. Hey, I guess I should stop baiting you. It's not your fault you were a successful civilian. I recommend the steak. Good meat, and they have a charcoal grill.'

Tyson put his menu down. 'Fine.' He lit a cigarette. Neither spoke. A new waitress came with the drinks and left with their dinner order. Levin observed, 'We'll have the whole staff come and check you out by dessert.' Levin raised his glass, and Tyson realized the colonel was one of those men who felt that alcohol was a sacred nectar that needed to be offered to some worthy sentiment before it was imbibed. He realized Levin was getting a little rocky. Levin said, 'I wish you a happy stay here.'

They drank, and they spoke in general terms for a while, discussing the post and how the Army had changed in the last two decades and how it had remained the same.

Levin had another drink, and Tyson admired his capacity. Levin said apropos of nothing, 'I told you I was raised in Brighton Beach. My father used to work here at Hamilton. He was a maintenance supervisor, a government employee. My brother and I used to tell everyone he was a G-man.' Levin laughed.

Tyson stirred his drink. He didn't know where this was heading, but he was fairly sure he didn't want to get there.

Levin continued, 'Anyway, I used to come to work with him sometimes on weekends – when I was in high school – this was during the Korean conflict.'

'War.'

'Whatever. Anyway, I guess I was very impressed by the officers strutting around. They had nicer uniforms then, and

332

some of them carried swagger sticks. I was very impressionable.'

Tyson said, 'My father claims he saw Lindbergh take off for Paris, and that inspired him to be a flier. He was a Navy pilot. When was this addition to the club built?'

Levin seemed intent on his own narrative. 'And I would sweep the floors and change the light bulbs. Right here ... well, I mean in the original section. This was the O Club then, too. Anyway, I would see these gentlemen at their mess on Sundays, and I guess it stuck with me, being from a hard-up family. So in college I joined the ROTC programme, and here I am.' Levin drank some water and cleared his throat. 'You can put a Jew in the Army, Tyson, but you can't put the Army in the Jew. I don't know why I stayed. I guess there must be something about it I like.'

Tyson commented, 'A military career can be very rewarding.'

'I guess the officer corps is a quick way to achieve genteel respectability. It's always been for southerners. Why not a Jew from Brighton Beach, Brooklyn? Right, Tyson?'

'Why not?'

'Look, I'm not that drunk, and there is a point to this. We are all equal in social standing, we are all gentlemen by act of congress.'

'Yes, sir.'

Levin leaned across the table. 'But I want to reveal to you an inequity in the system. Even though the Army does not care about your background, breeding, or social standing for purposes of promotions, assignments, or career advancement, they do care about that when they court-martial you. Follow?'

'Sort of.'

'Let me make an unfortunate but necessary comparison. Lieutenant Calley, the platoon leader of My Lai fame, was an underprivileged kid, as I recall, lower-middle-class background. You were quite the opposite type of officer and

333

gentleman.' Levin drew on his cigar and lowered his voice. 'Now, I don't know what the *fuck* happened at that hospital, Lieutenant, but let's assume *something* happened that was not entirely kosher, not precisely in keeping with "The Rules of Engagement" or "The Rules of Land Warfare." Okay? Then you, Benjamin Tyson, were supposed to be able to make finer distinctions of morality than a man like Calley. Follow?'

Tyson did not respond.

Levin continued, 'You are more accountable and more liable than the poor schnooks around you who are firing their rifles into helpless people. No one will be sympathetic or understanding or offer the defence that you were just an underprivileged, teenage draftee who was as much a victim as a victimizer. You were an educated, mature man, a volunteer, and an officer.' Levin pointed his cigar at Tyson. 'You may not have pulled a trigger, but if you did nothing to stop it – *even at the risk of your own life* – then God help you.' He jabbed his cigar towards Tyson. The two men stared at each other, then Levin said, 'That's the point.'

Tyson replied, 'Social rank, too, has its problems.'

'Right.' Levin settled back in his chair. 'I've been following this in the news. And I'm trying to put myself on the court-martial board. I'm sitting there listening to testimony and looking at you. Maybe I'm envious of your good looks, your advantages in life. Also maybe I'm a little awed. I'm thinking to myself as I sit on that board – that jury – that you are supposed to represent the culmination of our civilization, the final product of the great American experiment. And I look at you in the defendant's chair, and it's hard for me to comprehend how you could have been a party to what they are saying happened there. And that would frighten me, Lieutenant Tyson, because if you were capable of that, then what hope is there for the rest of us?'

Tyson said, 'To be honest with you, Colonel, after Vietnam I never again thought there was any hope for any of us.'

Levin looked sad.

Tyson finished his drink and lit another cigarette. At length he said softly, 'And regarding your estimation of me as a product of our country you are partly right. My concept of right and wrong and of duty in that year of 1968 was influenced less by what I learned in the Army than by what I saw happening in America. I found it difficult to do my duty to a country that wasn't doing its duty to me. The essence of loyalty, Colonel, is reciprocity. A citizen or a soldier owes allegiance to the state in exchange for protection, for the state's allegiance to and duty towards the individual. That is an implicit social contract. I may not have put it so well in 1968, but in my guts I felt my country had abandoned me and my men and in fact the entire Army in Southeast Asia.'

Levin nodded in understanding. 'Heavy stuff before a beef dinner. Here's our food. Bon appétit.'

The two men ate in silence, then Colonel Levin began speaking in a pleasant tone as though the previous conversation had been entirely amiable. 'Do you want to sign your oath now?'

'Do you have it with you?'

'Right here.' Levin tapped his side pocket. 'Want to sign it?'

'No, I just wondered if you had it.'

'Be careful, Lieutenant.'

'Sorry, Colonel.'

Levin shrugged. 'Doesn't matter. I called the JAG school in Virginia for a legal opinion. They said the one you signed in 1967 is still good. Be advised that you're still bound by that oath of office.'

'I understand.'

Levin chewed thoughtfully on a piece of bread, swallowed it, and said, 'Do you want some advice?'

Tyson thought he had had enough advice over the past weeks to last him twenty years. He replied, 'I don't think it would be appropriate for you—'

'Let me worry about that. You've been assigned to me, so I

335

can give you advice as your commander.'

'Yes, sir.'

Levin sipped on his water, then said, 'In case you don't know it, the Army is very nervous about this. They're afraid of you.'

Tyson nodded. 'So there's some advantage after all to being a respected member of society?'

'Right. And I'll tell you what scares the Army – they're like organized religion in this respect – the Army is scared of scandal.'

'Scandal?'

'Right. Listen to what I'm saying, Tyson. It might save your neck.' Levin looked around the dining hall, then leaned forward and spoke in a confidential tone. 'As far as the Army is concerned, any officer who fucks up is ipso facto a renegade, atypical of the officer corps, no matter how fine a background he comes from. The officer corps is like the priesthood. It is a calling, and when you answer the calling, you leave your world behind and enter a new one. It's not like being vice-president in charge of whatever you were in charge of at whatever that company was you worked for. When you are an officer in the United States Army your conduct reflects on the Army and the officer corps. Like a priest and his church. So it is not only you who are being judged but all of us: you, me, Captain Hodges, and the Joint Chiefs of Staff. Follow?'

'Yes, sir. But Captain Hodges was about ten years old at the time of the incident, and the Joint Chiefs of Staff have turned over a few times.'

'But there is a continuity in the military, an institutional memory. If they can claim honours from the past, then they must accept the guilt as well. Your old unit, the Seventh Cavalry, is still trying to live down the Little Big Horn. Conversely, when you finally get your uniform on you'll wear a presidential unit citation given to the Seventh Cav long before you were even born. Point is, you have to somehow convince the Army that you are a *typical* product of the fucked-up state of the whole military system – not now, perhaps, but certainly at that time. And that you, who used to be a sensitive boy, a boy who got upset when his little pet canary croaked, became really psychotic during all that infantry training. You were a victim of a system that issued little plastic cards called "The Rules of Engagement" telling you whom you were allowed to kill in less than a hundred words, then turned you loose with an undertrained, undisciplined, and demoralized platoon of seventeen-year-old armed savages from the Ozarks and the slums and made *you* liable for *their* actions. Ha, ha, what a laugh! Right? You had as much control over them as I have over the weather. Right?'

Tyson didn't reply.

Levin continued, 'If you can threaten to bring the whole temple down around their heads, if you can hint that not only did American boys kill indiscriminately, but got killed in great numbers because of bad training, bad leadership, bad tactics – are you following me, Tyson? This isn't easy for me to say. But I *know* what it was like then. I was there, Tyson. Not in the infantry, but close enough to the front to see and hear all I wanted to see and hear.' Levin looked at Tyson closely and said, 'Tell them that if they stand you in front of a court-martial, you will testify for a week, indicting the Army, and that you'll give lots of interviews to the media. Tell them you'll take them with you.'

Tyson pushed his plate away and lit a cigarette. He thought about Chet Brown telling him not to do exactly what Colonel Levin was suggesting he do. Apparently everyone thought he had great secrets to reveal. But Tyson did not recall thinking at the time that the Army was the cause of Miséricorde Hospital. He did not at that time blame them for his actions or the actions of his men. He had not protested the bad training, the immaturity of the troops, the vague guidelines of conduct, or his own unpreparedness as a combat infantry leader. If he had one scrap of evidence that he'd had such thoughts then – a letter home or a memo to his superiors – then, yes, he might reverse the blame for Miséricorde Hospital and indict the Army. But he'd accepted the blame then, and it was not justifiable to rewrite history in order to escape the blame now. He said to Colonel Levin, 'I think I have to take this walk alone, Colonel.'

Levin sighed. 'Yeah. You and Jesus Christ, Tyson. Wise up.' Levin hunched over the club chit with a pencil and tallied it. 'How many drinks did you have?'

'Four.'

'You drink too much. But at these prices you might as well.' He looked at Tyson. 'Listen, I'm not saying you should indict the Army. I'd never say that. But you should mention the fact that if they indict you, you'll return the favour. They'll back off.'

'I'm not much of a bluffer. But thank you for the advice.'

'We talked baseball.' Levin stood. 'One parting piece of advice, Lieutenant. Get the best goddamned certified military lawyer money can buy. Don't take one of those assigned yo-yos from the JAG office. They cost nothing, and that's exactly what you get.'

Tyson stood also. 'I've heard of certified military lawyers, but I'm not certain of what they are.'

'Civilian lawyers certified by the military to serve as defence counsel at general courts-martial. There are only a few of them. Check the bar association.'

'Could you recommend one?'

'No way.' Levin picked up the chit and flipped it to Tyson. 'You sign for it, Lieutenant. Your club number is T-38. I wrote it in. Thanks for dinner.' He left.

Tyson picked up the chit and saw, written in pencil in the signature space, the name *Vincent Corva, Esq. N.Y.C.* He erased the name and signed his own.

338

27

Benjamin Tyson stood in front of the tunnel-like opening of a large artillery casemate and faced a group of about twenty senior citizens crowded around waiting expectantly for his next piece of useless information. There was no one else in the museum except this group, and he suspected that very few people came on their own.

The museum itself was interesting, as Levin had said. The caponier was a nearly perfectly preserved specimen of mid-nineteenth-century military architecture. The red-brick pillars rising into the arched ceilings were an appropriate setting for the martial displays. The displays themselves – cannon, muskets, sabres, uniforms, and such – were not unique or particularly good examples of their type, but set in the old fort, *in situ*, so to speak, they took on a more immediate significance. Still, Tyson thought, as someone once said, museums were the graveyards of the arts – in this case the martial arts, which were themselves inextricably tied to graveyards.

Tyson laid his hand on a four-foot-high section of black wrought iron fence that ran the six-foot width of the casemate opening. He smiled at the group. 'This fence has a personal significance for me.'

He saw several sets of perfect white dentures smile back. For the life of him he could not understand why people that age would want to hear any of this. Yet they were attentive and polite. Conversely, the Boy Scout group of the day before, who were supposed to show the curiosity of youth, not to mention some hormonal interest in the subject of war, were bored and restless. Tyson thought perhaps he didn't have the hang of it yet. He said, 'This fence dates back to about the 1840s. You can see here among the finely scrolled ironwork, the federal shield and American eagle, which was a common motif in those days.'

Tyson badly wanted a cigarette and/or a breath of fresh air. The massive walls of the caponier held out some of the afternoon heat, but by the same token, the air was stagnant and redolent with cloying floral perfume and dusting powder. Also the modern track lighting was hot. He supposed it was difficult to vent or air-condition such a structure. No, they didn't build them like that anymore.

A man said, 'What personal significance does that fence have for you, Lieutenant?'

'What? Oh, yes. I did say that, didn't I? Well, this fence section is not from Fort Hamilton. It was salvaged from the old Federal Building on Whitehall Street before it was torn down. Now, to most men in the New York metropolitan area the words Whitehall Street are synonymous with induction into the armed forces.' He smiled and saw a few of the old men nod and smile back.

'Anyway,' he continued, 'I remember this old fence from when *I* reported in for active duty, and I was surprised to see it *here*.' He smiled again. In truth he didn't remember the fence at all. He'd had other things on his mind that morning than the architecture of that gloomy old processing facility that had sent a million men to the battlefields. He looked to his right to see the next station of the cross and caught a glimpse of himself in a glass display case. He was honest enough to admit he rather liked the way he looked in uniform. Most men did. He straightened his tie.

A woman's voice asked, 'Did you see combat in Vietnam?'

He turned towards the voice. She was standing at the back of the group, somewhat taller than the generation born at the beginning of the century. Tyson wondered how long she'd been there. Most of the white heads were turned towards her.

Karen Harper added, 'What are all those medals for?'

He cleared his throat and replied, 'Mostly good conduct. I

340

got one every time I was good. I have seven medals.'

A few people laughed.

Tyson said to his tour group, 'Why don't you look around on your own awhile? I'll be right back.' He moved through the group, took Karen Harper's arm, and led her towards the front door. Outside, on the lane between the museum and the Officers' Club, she disengaged her arm from his hand. She said, 'Lieutenants do not take the arm of female majors like that.'

'Do you want a drink?'

'No. The last time I had a drink with you it got in the papers.'

He smiled. 'That caused me some trouble ... at home.'

'Did it?' She stood silently a moment, then said, 'Me too. I mean ... I have that friend I told you about. The infantry colonel, in Washington. But I shouldn't be telling you this.'

Tyson felt just a twinge of jealousy. He'd somehow assumed she had a boyfriend, but he didn't particularly want it confirmed. He forced a smile. 'I'll write him a letter explaining. You write one for me.'

'Sure. Listen to me, Lieutenant, I think you're becoming a little too familiar.'

'Sorry. I missed you.'

'Stop that. Secondly, you're a lousy tour guide.'

'I know.'

'Third, I have some important things to tell you.'

Tyson drew a deep but discreet breath. He said in a light tone, 'So you've finally reached a conclusion in your investigation?'

'I've reached many conclusions.' She turned towards the Officers' Club. 'Follow me.'

Tyson followed her into the club, through the foyer area to a steep and narrow stone staircase that wound up to the second floor of the club. As they walked Tyson said, 'Observe that this level is built of brick not granite, indicating it was built afterward. The big guns originally sat here when this

341

was an open parapet and—'

'I know all of that. I've had this tour. What is going to become of your tour group?'

'They'll get back on the bus and talk about us all the way back to the home.'

She suppressed a smile. 'You're being mean. I thought they were cute.'

'It's mean to call them cute too. I don't want to get that old.'

'You may not.' They came to a long, roofed terrace whose seaward side was walled-in glass. Bright sunlight flooded through the glass, casting prismatic colours over the floor. Tyson said, 'I found two reception rooms up here, either one of which would be perfect for a court-martial. Want to see them?'

'The Washington room and the Jackson room. I know them.'

'Good. What do you think? The Washington has a really neat cathedral ceiling, but the Stonewall Jackson room is rather more *intime*, if you know what I mean.'

'You're in a flippant mood this afternoon.'

Tyson looked through the glass. Below he could see the new dining wing to his right, the Shore Parkway beyond that, then the Narrows, spanned by the Verrazano Bridge. A mile away was the Staten Island shoreline. Tyson could make out the grey artillery fort called Battery Weed which was the sister fort to the one he was standing in. 'Nice view.' He lit a cigarette and asked, 'Do I look as good in uniform as you imagined?'

'I assure you I never gave any thought to how you would look in uniform. But, yes, you look fine. You didn't get much hair taken off.'

'I did. It grows back very quickly. By the way, did you ever find my umbrella?'

'No. I told you I left it on the plane. Do you want me to pay you for it?'

'It was a gift. Why don't you just buy me a similar one? Black.'

342

'All right. Black.' Karen Harper said, 'I've been instructed to submit the report of my findings within five days.'

'Good. Then we'll all know where we stand.'

'Yes, the waiting is the tough part. I didn't mean to drag this out, but my resources have been limited by the provisions of Article 31 of the UCMJ, which, as you know, stipulates only a preliminary inquiry. Anyway, I'm to recommend one of two things: that the matter be dropped or that there is probable cause to believe that there was a violation of the Uniform Code of Military Justice and that charges be drawn up and forwarded to an Article 32 investigating body for consideration.' She continued, 'My recommendation would not be binding, as you know.'

'But still it carries some force, and you're wondering what the Army wants you to recommend.'

She replied strongly, 'I don't care what they want—'

Tyson went on, 'You're trying to figure out if they want you to be the heavy. If Harper says go with it, then the machinery is set in motion to take the investigation to a grand jury, and it will be you who prodded them into it. But if Harper says "No go," then they shrug and reluctantly drop the case even though your recommendation is not binding. Then the media flak is diverted towards you. I don't envy you.'

Karen Harper let out a short breath. 'Can I speak to you in confidence?'

'Of course.'

She hesitated, then began, 'Well, I always thought this thing was partly staged, partly a put-up job. I mean why would the Army place so much responsibility on one individual? Why me?'

'Now you're thinking.'

'This investigation should have been handled from the beginning by a trained staff – CID, FBI, Justice Department, and so forth. It should have lasted only long enough to determine if the facts warranted a grand jury investigation.'

'True. But they've done nothing illegal so far.'

343

'Well … perhaps not illegal. Just … unusual.' She looked directly at him. 'Let me ask you something. Has anyone … anyone from the government approached you … with an offer?' Karen Harper waited, 'Well? Has anyone other than I been speaking to you?'

'No.'

'You see, Lieutenant, I don't like being played for a fool any more than you like being a scapegoat.'

'I certainly know how you feel.'

'And I don't think either of us likes being pawns in a game that we know nothing about.'

'No, we do not. Listen, Major, if you thought this was a straight case of seeing that justice was done, then you were naive in the extreme. This case has gone beyond anything we said to one another and any evidence you may have gathered. Don't be surprised if someone approaches *you* and recommends to you what you should recommend to the Army.'

She turned toward the glass wall and stared off into the distance. Tyson, too, looked out the windows. An ocean liner, the *Rotterdam,* cut through the Narrows and slid beneath the central span of the bridge, rocking the small pleasure craft in its wake. A jetliner approached from the south, making its descent into Kennedy Airport. Tyson recalled the vacations he'd taken with Marcy, the places where they'd been happy together. And it struck him with full force that that life was gone, that the life to come was shrouded with images of jail, divorce, financial troubles, and the stigma of criminality, proven or unproven.

Karen Harper broke into his thoughts. 'I must tell you, Lieutenant, and you already know, that I've found sufficient facts to recommend that a grand jury consider the charge of murder.'

'Then do it.'

'But I've also begun to … suspect that the government is tampering with this case. And if that is true, then your rights may have been violated somewhere in this process—'

'Oh, look, Major, my rights were violated from the day the obstetrician slapped my ass without provocation. But sometimes the authorities have to do certain things for the general good of society and even for the good of the individual they are slapping around. Where did you get your legal training? In a convent?'

'You sound as though you're defending the government.'

'I'm certainly not doing that. But I do understand that they're engaged in damage control.'

'Did you make some sort of deal with the Army or the Justice Department?'

'No.'

'Would you consider any sort of deal?'

'Depends on the deal. You never take the first one.'

'So someone did approach you? That's illegal during an Article 31 investigation. Only I may approach you and only with your permission.'

'You may stand on ceremony. I'm trying to stay out of Leavenworth.'

'How were you approached? What were the circumstances?'

'Is this still off the record?'

She replied, 'No. I can't hear anything like that off the record. I would have to report that.'

'Then drop it.'

She nodded reluctantly, then said, 'Can I give you some basic advice?'

'You'll have to take a number.'

She ignored this and said, 'Get a qualified lawyer. Not Sloan. I've spoken to him, and he's out of his league on this. Get a good JAG lawyer or a certified military lawyer.'

'That's excellent advice, Major. A little odd coming from my investigator but excellent nonetheless. I assume that means you're through with me.'

'Yes. I'm going back to Washington tomorrow to finalize my report. That's one of the reasons I wanted to speak to you.

345

To see if you want to include a written or oral statement in the report.'

Tyson thought she could have asked that over the telephone. 'I'll think about it.' He inquired, 'Aren't you due to be released from active duty?'

'I was. But I'm not being released. After I submit my report I am officially through with this case. However, if they need any clarifications they'd rather not have to subpoena me from civilian life. So I'm being held until the final disposition of this case.'

'Tough break. I suspect, also, that the Army doesn't want you making any clarifications to the press, which is the real reason they're holding on to you. In other words, you've seen and heard too much to be allowed to go free. That should have occurred to you when you accepted this case. Well, they'll let you out eventually.'

'I'm not upset about being held on duty ... it changes my civilian plans a bit though. I was supposed to join a law firm ... here in New York.'

'I'll look you up if I need a new will.'

'But my problems are insignificant compared to yours.'

'Your problems will be a lot more significant if you pursue your theory or suspicions that the government is tampering with the case. They'll eat you alive, Major. So take some advice from an older man who's survived many corporate jungles as well as the Asian jungle. Don't try to be a hero. Let me worry about what the government is up to.'

'I'm not concerned about you personally, you understand. I'm only concerned that justice—'

'Please. That word stimulates my gag reflex these days. Look, just play the game, keep your back to a solid object, and watch out for anyone heading for the door or the light switch.'

She snorted, 'That's nonsense.'

'There are times, Karen, I wish you were a man and other times I'm glad you're not.'

346

'That's sexist and entirely too personal. You may not use my first name.'

They both stayed silent, then Tyson asked, 'Other than the trouble you had with your friend, was there any official trouble?'

She rubbed her lower lip, then replied, 'Well, yes. That's why they wanted me to wrap it up.'

He laughed.

'It's not funny.'

'Men and women are funny.' He added, 'Who's giving you a hard time? That stuffed shirt, Van Arken? I've heard and read a few things about that character.'

She didn't respond but said, 'I think they may have you under some sort of surveillance.'

'That's all right. I'm not skipping the country, meeting with foreign agents, or sleeping around.'

'Good. May I have a cigarette?'

'Another one? You had one last week.' He took out his pack and shook one loose. She took it, and he lit it. She drew on it and exhaled, then coughed. She caught her breath and said, 'You should quit.'

'You're the one who coughed.'

'Listen, Lieutenant ... to deny ... well, to pretend that ... there has not been some ...' She drew on her cigarette again, then looked at her watch. 'I have to go.'

'Finish the sentence.'

She nodded. 'Well ... some words and feelings, I guess you would say ... that have passed between us ... that were other than professional or germaine to the inquiry ...'

'I'm losing the subject and object of the sentence. Do you mean that you think we've developed a personal rapport?'

'Yes, that's what I meant.'

'An attraction of sorts.'

'I suppose.'

'Well, me too.' He looked at her and reminded her, 'You said on our first interview that wouldn't happen.'

347

'Did I?'

'Yes. Well, anyway, I like you very much, and now the air is clear.'

'Yes.'

He could see her hand with the cigarette shaking, and he realized his mouth had gone dry. 'Well ... so ... what should we do about that?'

'Nothing.' She cleared her throat and threw the cigarette down. 'If you want to include a statement in my report, notify me before noon tomorrow.'

'Where are you staying?'

'The guest house. Here.'

'Can we have dinner tonight?'

'Certainly not. Not unless you want to get me into more trouble than I'm already in.'

'Sorry about that. It wasn't intentional.'

'If it were anyone but you, I'd say it was an intentional ploy to gain some advantage. Anyway, it was as much my fault as yours.' She extended her hand. 'Good-bye, Lieutenant.'

He took her hand. 'I'll be in my quarters tonight.'

'And I'll be in mine.' She turned and walked away.

Tyson watched her moving briskly down the bright sunny terrace. He said to himself, *Well, there is flesh and blood there after all.* He knew that he would see her again, and he knew, too, that nothing would come of it – not in a carnal sense anyway. But he understood, just as she must, that if the circumstances were different, then the outcome would be different. And when the time came that they parted for the last time, they would both be content in the knowledge that they had changed each other's life for the better.

28

Ben Tyson lay stretched out on the couch of his darkened living room. The small room was stifling hot, and he wore only a pair of running shorts. A cold bottle of beer dripped onto the coffee table. He sat up and took a deep breath. His two mile run around the post had left him exhausted. 'You smoke too much, you drink too much, and you're old.' He recalled the gruelling infantry training he'd once accomplished with relative ease: thirty-mile forced marches with full combat gear, a hundred push-ups at a time, rock climbing a five-hundred-foot waterfall during jungle training in Panama. 'My God, you were tough then.'

He stood slowly and walked to the small window fan. He didn't know what the policy was on air conditioners, and he didn't care because he'd decided to rough it out though his resolve was weakening. 'Pussy, Tyson. You're a pussy.' He did fifty quick jumping jacks, then began a series of bends. As he did he looked around the room. It was freshly painted and judging by the size of it, a half gallon would have done the job. The rest of the ground floor consisted of a small dining area and a kitchen. Upstairs were two bedrooms and a small bathroom. All the units in the row of red-brick attached houses were similar. Families with one and even two children were his neighbours. 'Tyson,' he said aloud, 'you've been out of touch.'

Cheap maple furniture, government property, was placed here and there, but he could bring his own, he was told. He tried to picture his furniture in this place and decided he'd have to stand it on end to make it fit. He'd have much preferred bachelor officers' quarters, which were more motel-like and efficient than this pretence of a home. But somewhere in the bowels of the Pentagon some bright half-wit had decided that Ben and Marcy should be given the opportunity to cohabitate. Presumably this decision was made in the spirit of the zookeepers who decide when and where the prize pandas should be allowed to mate.

There were no rugs or carpets on the wood floors, but in Army tradition the floors were highly polished. There were blinds on the windows but no drapes. His bedroom furniture consisted of a box spring and double mattress on a steel frame, one nightstand, and a mismatched chest of drawers. The second bedroom had a single bed, presumably for David. He'd had to sign for linens and towels but was expected to eventually get his own.

The kitchen held a stove and refrigerator and little else. There was no dishwasher, but he had no dishes so it worked out well. He wondered if he should get a coffeepot and invite the colonel and his lady for coffee. Medals will be worn. Bring your own cups and spoons.

Tyson straightened up and took several deep breaths. The sun was fully set now, and the only illumination in the room came from the street lamps casting stripes of light and dark through the blinds. He hadn't been given a television and hadn't bothered to buy a radio. American primitive. He understook how fragile and statistically beyond the norm had been his existence in the magic suburb.

This wasn't exactly house arrest, he reminded himself. He only had to be here between midnight and 6 A.M. He could even drive into Garden City and go to his club or to his house and turn on the air conditioner, watch television, or jump into the Jacuzzi. But that wasn't what he wanted to do. He wanted to stay here, sweat, be bored, be alone, think, suffer, and get tough. 'Tough,' he said aloud.

Tyson ended his exercises and stood in front of the window fan again. A movement outside caught his eye, and he peered between the blinds. On the small lane that cut between the facing row houses he saw a figure approaching: a woman dressed in light slacks and dark top. She was carrying something in each hand, looking at the nameplates on the houses. She stopped in front of his unit, hesitated, then strode up the path. In the light of the porch lamp, Tyson saw it was Karen Harper, carrying a furled umbrella.

He saw her lean the umbrella against his door, then the mail slot opened and a folded Army-tan envelope began to appear. Tyson stepped quickly to the front door, knelt, and pushed the envelope back outside. The envelope reappeared, and Tyson pushed it back but this time met with some resistance. Karen Harper called out softly, 'What are you doing? Get away from there.'

He spoke through the mail slot. 'Is this a bill?'

'Don't be an idiot. Take this.'

He yanked on the envelope and pulled it in through the slot. He stood and opened the door, and the umbrella fell at his feet. He looked up the path and saw Karen Harper halfway to the lane. He picked up the umbrella, noticing it had a PX tag on it, and threw it back into the living room. He pulled the door shut and followed her, the envelope still in his hand. He caught up with her as she turned onto the lane. They walked side by side in silence. She finally said, 'Get some clothes on if you intend to walk next to me.'

'It's hot. What's in this envelope?'

'You'll see when you open it. When are you going to get a telephone?'

'When I think of someone I want to call.'

'You were asked to put in a telephone to facilitate this investigation.'

'I have telephones in Garden City, Sag Harbor, and my borrowed apartment in Manhattan. I don't think I can afford another one on my salary.'

'Well, no one can order you to install a telephone in your quarters, but it would be more convenient for everyone, yourself and your family included, if you did.'

'I'll give it some consideration. Come on back. I'll give you a beer.'

'I've got work to do.'

'I want to discuss your request for a statement.'

She slowed her pace. 'All right. But we can't talk in your quarters.'

'I'll get some clothes on, and we'll walk. Come and take a look at my accommodations.'

She hesitated, then followed him back. He showed her in and turned on the table lamp beside the couch. He looked at her in the light, noticing the simple blue short-sleeve blouse and the light cotton slacks. She wore white tennis shoes.

Karen Harper glanced at him a few times, keeping her eyes focused on his, taking care not to drop them to his mostly bare body.

Tyson thought she looked rather good in civilian clothes. He noticed, too, that she was actually thinner than she appeared in uniform – smaller breasts and hips, more lithe, and longer limbed. He waved his arm around the room. 'Not bad for an officer and a gentleman.' He added, 'I think it needs a mirror to make it look larger.'

She didn't reply but looked at him oddly. He said, 'Oh yes. Bugs. Not cockroaches, to be sure.' He smiled. 'Ben Tyson is wising up. I had a private security firm here this morning, and they pronounced the premises bug free. Cost me a bundle. I'd have liked for them to have found something. Then you could have seen the stuff hit the fan.'

'You're a thorough man.'

'I'm becoming so. Also if I had a phone, I wouldn't discuss anything sensitive on it.' He added, 'As for *me* having a bug here to record you or anyone, you have my word again, as an officer and a gentleman, that there is no recording or transmitting device here.'

She replied, 'You didn't have to say that.'

'No, we're beyond that. But just to be sure, can I check you for recording devices?'

She smiled. 'Certainly not.'

Tyson shrugged. 'Can't hurt to ask. Anyway, this game is

getting damned serious, isn't it? I mean they've lifted my passport, I'm fairly certain I'm being watched, and I've been placed on restriction.'

'The restriction is not very onerous.'

'This house is onerous. Do you want to see the rest of the palace?'

'No.' She added in a less than cordial tone, 'If you think you are a martyr, you need to get some perspective.' She looked around the room. 'Most people have never had the kind of house or life you had. I don't know why anyone is supposed to feel sympathetic when we hear about someone who has lost his manor and now lives in the gatehouse. Half the world would give their left arm for the gatehouse.'

Tyson did not respond.

She stayed silent a moment, then said, 'You know, your real problem is that you may be charged with murder. Your problem of reduced life-style is minor. I'd advise you to give more thought to the murder charge and less to your creature comforts.' She paused. 'I'm sorry, I shouldn't be lecturing you.'

'But you're right. And I've come to the same conclusion. I mean to spend as much time here as possible until this is resolved. If I wind up in Leavenworth the transition will not be so shocking. If I wind up home I will kiss my garbage compactor.' He smiled.

She smiled in return. 'I admit it *is* hot as hell in here.'

'Want a beer?'

'All right.'

Tyson went into the kitchen and came back with two opened bottles of beer. He handed her one and said, 'I got these glasses at Bloomingdale's. They look just like Budweiser bottles. *Très chic.*' He added quickly, 'I'm not whining. I like beer out of a bottle.'

'I doubt it.'

Tyson hoisted his bottle and gulped down half the beer. She drank from her bottle. Tyson said, 'What's in the envelope?'

353

'Just some forms for you to sign.'

'I don't sign Army forms.'

'I heard.'

'Did you? Word travels fast.'

'You're the subject of many people's attention these days. Don't let it go to your head. Anyway, these are just forms stating the times and locations of our meetings and confirming that you were read your rights. You can discuss them with your attorney before you sign them, but I'd like to have them before I leave tomorrow.'

'And if I can't reach my attorney?'

'Well ... then mail them to me in Washington.'

'You need them to include in your report?'

'Yes.'

'The one that's due five days from today?'

'Well ... I thought I'd get this taken care of while you were here. Also there was the umbrella—'

'It was good of you to walk across post to deliver these forms and the umbrella. Especially considering you could have had everything delivered to the museum tomorrow morning. But I like the personal touch.'

'Yes, it was good of me.' She changed the subject. 'Will your family be joining you here?'

Tyson replied, 'I think that given a choice between a beach resort and here, they'll opt for the beach.'

She didn't respond, but he knew what she was thinking. He added, 'It's not a matter of loyalty or being a fair-weather family or being supportive. It's simply a practical matter. I don't want them here, and I've told them so. I'll see them on weekends.'

She nodded.

He added, 'Tight quarters can lead to unnecessary stress. My son wouldn't have any friends. Marcy might be subject to some harassment – by the media. That sort of thing.'

Karen Harper nodded again.

Tyson cleared his throat. 'Of course I realize they could go

354

back to Garden City, and we'd be much closer. But I think everyone is better off staying where they are for the summer at least.'

'I think so.' She put her beer on the coffee table and looked at her watch. 'We've been here about ten minutes. That's about as long as we should be here.'

'In case someone is watching.'

'Yes, in case someone is watching. As it turns out, they knew I went back to your room that night. So I'm glad I put it in my report. But I don't want to have to do any more explaining.' She moved toward the door.

Tyson set down his beer bottle and slipped on his sandals and a T-shirt. He opened the door, and they left together.

They walked down to Sterling Drive, which overlooked the Shore Parkway. Tyson gazed out over the water. There was something undeniably magical about harbour lights and boats on a summer evening.

She said, 'I suppose you think I came to your quarters because I wanted to see you. Well, I'm not sure if that's true or not. When I got there and saw the lights were out, I thought you weren't in. And I felt ... I felt ...'

'A combination of relief and disappointment.'

'Yes. I thought about taking a walk and coming back with that envelope and the umbrella, but then ... then I decided to just drop them off...'

'And the thought crossed your mind that I might be at the guest house looking for you and that we'd miss one another.'

She nodded. 'Why don't I feel foolish?'

'Because you know I don't find it foolish.' He stopped walking but did not face her. Instead he looked out at the indistinct horizon where the black ocean met the black sky. He said, 'The circumstances under which we met were intense and emotional, and so we could have expected one of two intense and emotional reactions: hate or ... well, repulsion or attraction might be better words.'

'I know that. I'm wondering if I'd met you under normal

circumstances if I'd have given you a second look.'

Tyson smiled. 'If I'd met you under other circumstances, I'd have taken notice.'

She began walking again, and he followed. She said, 'Let's talk about something else. I wanted to give you some pointers regarding any statement you might choose to include in my report.'

He replied, 'I gave you a statement you could use when we first met. What would be the purpose of another one?'

'Well, in that statement you said you were conducting military operations against an armed enemy. It was fine as far as it went. But what you have to do is to categorically deny the allegations of the witnesses against you. Brandt and Farley. You see, those witnesses are all that the government has against you. Picard's interview with Sister Teresa is hearsay and not admissible. Also there is no documentary evidence against you and no physical evidence. So the Army's case, if there is one, revolves around Brandt and to a lesser extent Farley.'

Tyson nodded. He'd figured that out by himself. 'So I should directly contradict what they said?'

'Yes. Or show why they would lie or why they would not be impartial witnesses for the prosecution. In other words, weaken their credibility by revealing whether or not there was any bad blood between you. As we say in law, impeach the witnesses.'

'That's good of you to tell me that.'

'Any lawyer would tell you the same thing. But when it comes from me, it is a hint that if you discredit Brandt – and Brandt is the key – then the Army may very well drop the investigation.'

Tyson nodded.

'Can you discredit Brandt?'

'Perhaps in a sense I could. But that would mean saying something about what he did over *there* of course. Not how he's led his life since then, because I don't know anything

356

about him except what I read and that seems to indicate he's a fine doctor, married for sixteen years, with a son my son's age and two daughters. Why would I want to tell a tale that happened nearly two decades ago? Is saving my own skin that important?'

'I hope so.'

'But that would be contrary to what I believe, which is that the past ought to be forgiven. If I want to be judged by how I've lived my life since Vietnam, how could I justify dragging up the past and throwing it in Brandt's face?'

'He threw it in your face.'

'That's his problem. I won't make it mine.'

She shook her head. 'Colonel Levin was right.'

Tyson gave her a sidelong glance. He said, 'It's not that I have no sense of self-preservation. It's that I do. Every piece of advice I've had so far has been somehow repugnant to me. I'm the one who has to live with Ben Tyson after this is over. I'm going to try to beat this thing, but not by deception, compromise, or name-calling. I want a clean verdict on this, even if the verdict is guilty.'

She nodded. 'You're entitled to do it your way.' She added, 'But given the facts I've assembled and given the fact that you won't make a statement impeaching Brandt's statement, then I hope you understand that if I recommend that charges be served on you, I have no choice.'

'I won't take it personally.'

She walked off the drive onto the sloping grass and stared at the traffic passing on the Shore Parkway, her hands in the pockets of her tan slacks. She said as if to herself, 'What else can I do?'

Tyson stood to one side and looked at her. A land breeze was coming up, and her hair began to blow. Tyson thought she looked very at home out-of-doors, very at ease in the elements. He said, 'Why don't you believe Sadowski and Scorello? Are you calling them blatant liars? And me a liar?'

She turned her head toward him. 'No. But as a practical

matter, allegations of wrongdoing are given more weight than denials of wrongdoing.'

'Why?'

'It's obvious. It's common sense. Steven Brandt is a respected physician and—'

'Never mind. I understand that too.' He looked to his left. About ninety miles east along this same shore was Sag Harbor, and he felt some anger and bitterness that he wasn't there with his wife and son on the back terrace of his summer home. But he felt, too, that if he were with them at Thanksgiving, he would be with them in a better way. He said, 'Ninety days?'

'Yes, that's the law.'

'Can the Army wrap this up in ninety days?'

'They can wrap it up next week if they choose to drop it. But if they choose to press on, then all that remains to be done in a case like this is to contact the remaining witnesses and determine whose witnesses they will be.'

'Did you find any of the remaining witnesses?'

'I put a memo in the envelope.'

'What did the memo in the envelope *say?*'

She looked at him. 'You'd have heard it on the news tonight. It will be in tomorrow's papers. Harold Simcox was killed in an automobile accident. Near his home in Madison, Wisconsin. His car hit a bridge abutment at a very high speed. There was a high alcohol level in his blood.'

Tyson contemplated the shimmering water for a while and tried to conjure up Simcox's face but was surprised to discover he could not. Even his recent perusal of his Army photo album did not help. Simcox was always somewhere else, or his face was turned from the camera or covered with grotesque camouflage makeup or in deep shadow under the Australian bush hat he liked to wear. Harold Simcox. Tyson felt bad about that, but he also felt a sense of foreboding: spooky actually. He said to Karen Harper. 'Accident?'

'I don't know.' She added, 'He was divorced, out of work,

358

alcoholic and sort of a loner from what I've been told. He left no note.'

'Well, sometimes there's nothing to say.' And, he thought, *sometimes there is too much to say that is better left unsaid.* Harold Simcox, he reflected, *a possible suicide. Moody dead of cancer.* He recalled the patrols through the defoliated areas. That was a war that would not stop killing and maiming. Richard Farley would be next. He said slowly, 'I'm not superstitious ... but the Army has bad-luck outfits like the Navy has bad-luck ships. I always somehow felt that the Seventh Cavalry was an ill-fated unit. The Little Big Horn was not the only bad day that outfit had.' He drew a deep breath. 'Well, perhaps it's not luck or fate but a matter of the collective psyches of military units, an institutional memory, as Colonel Levin suggested.'

She didn't respond, and they both stood in silence. The wind was picking up, and heat lightning flashed over Staten Island. After some time she turned and began walking back the way they'd come. Tyson followed. She came to a park bench and sat. Tyson sat on the opposite end. He said, 'Did you go to the monument?'

She nodded.

He waited, then said, 'It's the sort of monument you put off seeing. I did.'

'Yes, so did I. Because it's a gravestone.' She added, 'But seeing that wall with all those names gave me some perspective. I kept thinking that each man there did not die alone but died in combat among his friends, and those friends had the means to avenge those deaths, which is so unlike civilian death. And I thought that the chevron shape of that wall, which could stand for Vietnam, could also stand for vengeance. I thought that war, which is conceived in terms of global strategy, is ultimately fought by men who take it personally. And I tried to use that perspective to help me understand what may have happened at Miséricorde Hospital.'

359

Tyson did not respond.

At length she said, 'Well, anyway, regarding the witnesses. Precluding any more deaths, there will be at least four witnesses present at any judicial proceeding. There will be the two witnesses for the prosecution, Brandt and Farley, and the two for the defence, Sadowski and Scorello. Louis Kalane, Hernando Beltran and Lee Walker will eventually be found. Dan Kelly and Michael DeTonq may never be accounted for. And then there's Sister Teresa.'

He looked down the length of the bench at her.

She said, 'No luck there. I'm beginning to wonder why she hasn't turned up.'

Tyson replied, 'I'm beginning to wonder if she ever existed. I mean this whole thing has a strong sense of unreality about it. I can't believe it is happening, so I can't take any of it too seriously. This is very much like my first combat experience. It was so unreal – people firing rifles with live ammunition at *me*. Do you know what I did? I laughed. It was too ludicrous. It was a war movie. So, now, nearly two decades later, people are asking me to relive an experience that I didn't believe was happening *while* it was happening. Am I making sense?'

'Yes. I've heard that before, including the part about laughing in combat.' She looked away from him and said, 'That reminds me. The Army will want you to see a panel of psychiatrists before too long. That's standard these days for capital crimes investigations.'

'Is it? What does that say about us as a nation? Why, I wonder, don't they order me before a board of chaplains to test if I am morally healthy? If my moral health is unsound, then I need religious and ethical therapy, not a court-martial.'

She smiled. 'Somehow that's not as absurd as it sounds. Nevertheless, you will be extensively tested – psychologically.' She added, 'I suppose you resent all of this. I mean being ordered here and there to do this and that.'

'That is an understatement. I resented having to take a physical, having my picture taken for an ID card, being assigned to post housing, being told to get a haircut, being told what the uniform of the day is, and so on, and so on.'

Karen Harper said, 'You're a real civilian. But if you recall, you get used to it.'

'That's what I'm afraid of. I'd like not to get used to it. I'd like to retain my personality and my sense of myself.'

'You have to bend a bit in the service. Don't be angry or bitter. Or if you are, don't show it. It's not productive.'

He nodded. 'You're right. I don't want to hate the Army or my country or anyone associated with this investigation. There are no evil geniuses out there looking to crucify me. There are only paper-shufflers who are doing their jobs according to the law as it is written. The fact that many may be guilty, but only one is indictable, should not make me question the wisdom of the law.'

'You *are* angry.'

'Anyway, the way to beat the legal system is with lawyers. So with your advice in mind to get a better lawyer, I called one whose name was given to me. He called me back after I returned to the museum this afternoon.'

She inquired, 'Have you retained him?'

'I think I may. He sounded fairly bright. I have a meeting scheduled with him tomorrow morning. But I have a group of summer-school kids coming in for the tour. What do you advise?'

She smiled. 'Go see the lawyer. By the way, did your group of senior citizens wait for you?'

'Oh, yes. They have nothing but time. They asked me embarrassing questions about you. Wanted to know what my intentions were actually.'

She smiled again but did not respond. She said, 'If you retain this lawyer, let me know so I can enter his name and address in my report.'

'I'll tell you his name now. It's Vincent Corva.'

She nodded slowly. 'Yes, I know him. He's certified by the JAG office.'

'So he said. But is he good?'

'Well, that's not my place to say. But I saw him in court once at Fort Jackson.'

'Who won?'

'The Army. Well ... it was a tough case. The accused – a captain – was charged with manslaughter.' She added, 'He'd found his wife in bed with her lover.'

'Ah! This sounds good. Continue.'

She shrugged. 'Well ... this captain was officer-of-the-guard one night, and while he was driving his jeep checking the sentry posts, he detoured back to his house. I guess he had a suspicion. Anyway, he found them ... his wife and a young lieutenant ... together ... *in flagrante delicto* ... drew his forty-five, fired, and killed the lover.'

Tyson leaned towards her, feigning more interest than he had in the case. 'How close was he when he fired? How many shots? Who was he trying to hit?'

She smiled again, and he could see she thought him amusing. She replied, 'It's funny you should ask that. Corva, in his summation, said something like, "Any soldier who can hit a ... moving target with an Army forty-five, with one shot, at twenty-three feet, without injuring the person ... directly beneath the intended target, should be commended for his marksmanship, regardless of his inability to exercise the same sort of control over his emotions" ... or something like that.' She added, 'It was an absurd statement and rather idiotic ... but you know, it worked.'

'Did the court find it amusing?'

'Yes. There was laughter. That statement appealed to all that was ... macho ... on that board of officers.'

'So how did the defendant do?'

'He received one to ten ... for the manslaughter. But they slapped him with two years for leaving his post and dereliction of duty.'

'Typical Army,' commented Tyson. 'He would have been in more trouble if his pistol had misfired because it was dirty.'

Karen Harper stretched her legs out and settled back on the bench. 'That's a bit of an exaggeration. But your point, I assume, is that the military gives different priorities to some offences than do civilian courts. That's something you and Mr Corva ought to keep in mind. I'm sure you both will. Anyway, I understand he's rather good though his record is not so good. He takes mostly hopeless cases.' She looked out towards the ocean. 'There's a storm coming. See it?'

Tyson turned from her and gazed out over the water. He could see whitecaps forming on the dark blue expanse of open sea, and the stars on the horizon were obscured by a blurriness that he knew was rain.

She stood. 'I'd better get back. I have work to do.'

He stood also, and they began walking. A few drops of rain began falling, and the hot blacktop steamed. He said, 'I'll lend you my umbrella again if you promise not to lose it.'

She picked up her pace. 'Well ...' The rain became heavier. Ahead were the lights of the officer family housing. The guest house was a quarter mile away. She said, 'All right,' and began moving quickly towards his housing unit. The rain became heavier. They both broke into a run.

They reached the front door soaking wet. Tyson hadn't locked the door, and he threw it open. They ducked quickly inside, out of breath. Tyson wiped the rain from his eyes and cheeks. He said, 'Let me get you a towel to dry off.'

'If you don't mind.'

'No, I have three Army towels. Do you want to stay until this passes over?'

'No. I'll just take the umbrella.'

'I can drive you to the guest house.'

'I'll walk.'

'Beer?'

'No thanks. A towel.'

He looked at her, rainwater running down her face, and he reached up and wiped her brow and cheeks with his fingers. Their eyes met and held. He put his hands on her shoulders.

She stood perfectly still, then put her left hand on his side, then hesitantly her right hand rested on his forearm. Tyson could hear his own heart beating and saw that a vein was fluttering in her throat. He felt his hands and her hands shaking. He drew her closer.

A footstep on the stairs broke the silence, and they stood apart. Around the corner of the landing appeared Marcy. She said, 'Hello. I thought I heard voices.'

Tyson said, 'Marcy, may I present Major Karen Harper?'

29

General William Van Arken sat in the rear of the lecture hall and listened to the instructor, Colonel Ambrose Horton, deliver the final words of his talk to the two dozen military students sitting in the front row. Horton's deep, Virginia-accented voice, unaided by a microphone, echoed through the nearly empty amphitheatre of the United States Army's Judge Advocate General School. The school, located within the Charlottesville campus of the University of Virginia, was a three-hour car ride from the Pentagon.

Colonel Horton's eyes drifted up into the rear rows and rested on General Van Arken, who was wearing a civilian suit of dark blue. It would have been correct to introduce the Army's Judge Advocate General, the boss, to the JAG school students, and indeed they would have been honoured. But Colonel Horton's instincts told him that the General wanted to remain anonymous. Horton directed his attention back to the first row and spoke. 'It has been said by combat commanders that the battlefield is the most honest place in the world. It has also been said by legal types such as that, regarding war crimes, there are unique complexities in discovering the truth about a combat soldier doing his duty in the field.'

General Van Arken listened to the echoes of Colonel Horton's words die away in the open spaces around him. The chimes of the clock tower struck eight, but the students did not move. The sun was fading from the large vertical windows, and the interior lighting seemed to grow harsher.

Colonel Horton concluded, 'The next time we meet, we will examine those two statements and attempt to reconcile them. Specifically we will discuss atrocities, how they happen, and how we, as Army lawyers, must ultimately deal with them. Thank you.'

The students stood in unison as Colonel Horton moved from the lectern up the centre aisle. General Van Arken met him halfway. Horton said, 'Good evening, General. An unexpected pleasure.'

They shook hands. 'This is not official,' General Van Arken said. 'Let's walk.'

The two men left the lecture hall and went out into the hot night, walking through the nearly deserted campus. Van Arken said, 'I'd like your opinion on the Tyson case.'

Colonel Horton nodded. 'Unofficially?'

'Of course.' Van Arken gave Horton a sidelong glance. The man was well into his seventies and had the distinction of being the only man still in the Army who had been involved in the Nuremberg trials. He was considered by many to be the dean of Army jurisprudence and taught the philosophy of law and ethics to civilian as well as military students. Notwithstanding Horton's stature, he had been passed over for promotion to brigadier general twice, and in almost any other branch of the Army he'd have been asked or forced to resign. Van Arken said, 'Would you like to sit awhile?' He indicated a wooden bench.

Horton nodded and lowered himself heavily onto the bench. He commented, 'I've had a busy schedule today.'

Van Arken sat on a facing bench and replied diplomatically, 'This heat has drained me too.' He looked into the old man's eyes. 'Can I speak to you in confidence?'

Colonel Horton unbuttoned his green tunic and loosened his tie. He replied in a slow drawl, 'As long as we don't stray into prohibited areas, General.'

Van Arken regarded Colonel Horton for a moment. Horton caused him some measure of unease. The man was a maverick and a nuisance. He lectured widely on the Nuremberg trials, the Calley-Medina case, and on other controversial areas of military law. The Army did not always appreciate his views. Neither did Van Arken, which was one reason Horton would remain a colonel. But Van Arken needed straight answers, and Horton gave them. Van Arken said, 'There is some talk that Major Karen Harper has inadvertently damaged the Army's case against Tyson.'

'Well,' said Colonel Horton, 'what happened between Tyson and Harper as far as I can determine was magic. There is the doctrine in law which says we cannot enjoy the fruits of the poison tree. But we know they taste as good. Better. So, consider the Article 31 investigation a success, General. And end it. Soon.'

Van Arken said, 'I have.'

'Good. Do you have any guesses as to what Harper will recommend?'

Van Arken shook his head. 'It is really up to Tyson to impeach Dr Brandt's testimony. If he does and if there is some substance to whatever he says about Brandt, then it doesn't much matter what Brandt has said about Tyson. I would not want to go into a courtroom with no evidence beyond two shaky witnesses. And neither would an Army prosecutor.'

'But as it stands now,' asked Colonel Horton, 'Dr Brandt is unimpeachable?'

'To the best of my knowledge. I have no contact with Major Harper of course.' Van Arken looked at Horton. 'Do you want to walk?'

'Yes.' He stood and buttoned his tunic. They walked on a path that cut diagonally across the Great Lawn. The multipaned windows of the buildings cast light patterns on the dark grass. Van Arken said, 'During the Calley business, there was little sympathy for the accused within the JAG. We have a different situation here. Certain people at the top – in the White House and the Justice Department – are beginning to waver. I believe we owe it to the Army and to the nation to press on. And I was wondering if you felt the same way.'

Colonel Horton looked around at the lighted buildings. He loved this old university founded nearly two centuries before by Thomas Jefferson. It was a magnificent showplace of neoclassical architecture: colonnades, cupolas, rotundas, and balustrades. But more than that, it was a place of mellow moods, an institution that still placed some value on chivalry, honour, and tradition. Horton mused, 'What would Jefferson advise us, General?'

Van Arken took the question to be rhetorical and did not reply. Colonel Horton answered his own question. 'Jefferson did not see the law as a narrow vocation but as a means of understanding the history, culture, morals, and institutions of a society. I think if we ran into him on this path now, he'd ask us how it came to pass that the American government is not certain it has the right to judge its citizens.'

General Van Arken responded, 'The question I put to you is do we owe it to the nation to press on despite our ... well, our shared culpability in the events of 15 February 1968?'

Colonel Horton smiled wryly, then said, 'Are you looking for me to put something in writing, General? A memo to the White House or the Justice Department?'

'Well, yes. A sort of white paper from you as a respected jurist. Legally, we are on the right track. But people have raised these moral and ethical questions on both sides of this issue. We'd like to address those, to put this legal framework on a firm philosophical foundation.'

Colonel Horton rubbed the side of his nose with his bony index finger and spoke contemplatively. 'You know, General, when I was a young lieutenant working the prosecution side

367

of the bench at Nuremberg, virtually the entire world was on our side. The press corps covered every minute of the trial, but there was no real scrutiny as we know it today. Consequently, we got away with a great deal. Errors in procedure, that sort of thing. But more importantly, we got away with making up the law as we went along. We hanged who we wanted to hang and were amazed at ourselves when we actually handed out prison terms instead of the death penalty. And there was no appeals process. Death meant death.'

Horton reflected a moment before continuing. 'There were only a handful of voices raised against the Allied tribunals. I was not among those who had the wisdom or foresight to see that what we were meting out was not justice but revenge. And even if I had understood that, I would not have had the moral courage to raise my voice.' He looked at Van Arken. 'I mean, my God, Hollywood blessed us with Spencer Tracy and *Judgment at Nuremberg*. There was not even the slightest doubt that we were not wholly on the side of the angels.' They continued on in silence awhile, then Colonel Horton said, 'General, when you were a young captain working on the prosecution side in the My Lai cases, you were operating in a different world, a different moral climate. The media did their own investigations and in fact forced the Army investigation. The President did not see it as something to be proud of, and national opinion polls showed a majority in favour of letting the accused go free.'

'Yes, I recall that clearly.'

'Yes, so here we are today, both of us veterans of two of the most important military trials of this century, and I hope we'll keep in mind the lessons we both learned. We have no excuses for errors in judgement.'

Van Arken replied with a touch of impatience, 'What I learned from the My Lai trials, Colonel, was that the nation and the world will not tolerate barbarism in the armed forces of the United States no matter how that barbarism tries to disguise itself as battle.' Van Arken drew a breath, then continued, 'And Nuremberg, for all the faults, showed the world that civilization will not tolerate barbarism even when it becomes the national policy of a sovereign state. It is my considered opinion that if we are ever again to judge our enemies, legally or morally, we must first judge ourselves no matter how painful it may be to do so.' Van Arken continued, 'Any contemplated trial of Benjamin Tyson must serve as a warning to every combat officer in future wars that he will be held accountable for his actions until the day he dies.'

Colonel Horton wondered how much of what Van Arken said was in the interests of justice, humanity, the Army, or the nation and how much was in the interests of General Van Arken and his career. But he did not want to be uncharitable toward the man. He might well be sincere. Horton spoke in a conciliatory tone. 'Certainly, General, what you say is correct. But on a less theoretical level, I want to point out to you those unique complexities in discovering the truth about a combat soldier who was doing his duty in the field. Tyson was sent to Vietnam to kill. Any court-martial that is convened will not have to determine whether or not he killed but if he killed the right people in the right way.'

Van Arken replied tersely, 'My concern is that the entire question of the morality of the war will be raised as a defence. At Nuremberg you operated from a position of moral certainty.'

'So did the Nazis. If you raise philosophical questions and try to drag me into it as an apologist for the government, you will give the case more stature. And that will play into the hands of the defence. That is my advice to you, though I give it grudgingly because I quite frankly don't believe that justice is being done.'

'Why not?'

'Because the climate that existed in 1968 allowed not only the crime but the cover-up to flourish. Something had gone fundamentally wrong with the ethics and standards of the

369

officer corps, the Army, and the nation. We've corrected much of that. But we can't go back and start court-martialling lieutenants until we call the generals to account. *And* the civilians in those past administrations. That's another thing I learned at Nuremberg.'

Van Arken nodded. '*That* is what I'm afraid the defence is going to say. I'm afraid they're going to offer what has come to be called the Nuremberg defence.'

'Good for them,' snapped Horton. 'I often have fantasies of convening a national inquisition and subpoenaing every son of a bitch who got us involved in Vietnam.'

They continued in silence, then came to a crosswalk. Van Arken stopped. 'Can I buy you dinner, Ambrose?'

Colonel Horton shook his head. 'Thank you, General, but I have to work on tomorrow's lecture.' He stared at Van Arken awhile, then said, 'You know, Bill, you've been a force in getting this case under way, and I'm not certain that is your function. I'm not being critical. You've filled a vacuum left by the Justice Department, who should be pursuing this, and I congratulate you on your devotion. However . . . you see, I feel our civilian bosses are setting us up. They learned something from My Lai, too. As our enlisted men would say, we've pulled some shit duty.'

Van Arken nodded. 'I've figured that out. But that doesn't alter our obligation. My obligation.'

Colonel Horton said impatiently, 'You're rather sure of yourself, aren't you? I mean you're sure you're on the side of truth and morality. Well, I'm not so sure.'

'Just what does that mean?'

'I mean, Bill, you've spoken of accountability. And I'm thinking that if Lieutenant Benjamin J. Tyson did in fact command a platoon that massacred approximately one hundred men, women, and children, then where is the moral justification, sir, in offering the platoon survivors – the actual triggermen – immunity?'

Van Arken didn't reply.

'So you see, General, don't tell me you want to pursue this because of some moral absolute, because there is none. *That* is the main lesson I learned at Nuremberg.'

Van Arken began to reply, but Horton interrupted. 'At Nuremberg, I often wondered why the SS guards and the hangmen and the torturers were not called to account in greater numbers. Then I came to realize that had they been called, they would have simply said, "I was only following orders." ' Horton added, 'As you well know, General, the military constructs a unique subculture whose teachings supersede everything a man has learned in church or Sunday school, everything he has been taught by parents, teachers, and the community – indeed everything he knows in his own heart. So when a soldier says "I was only following orders," he has offered a formidable defence and an embarrassing one for his superiors. He has offered the Nuremberg defence.

'And so, the buck is passed onward and upward, and at every echelon of command we hear the same thing – "I was only following orders" – direct orders, inferred orders, implied orders, standing orders, and so on. Until we finally come to the top where the sewerage begins flowing downhill again, as I saw at Nuremberg. The top Nazis would say, "I could not possibly know how my orders were being misconstrued." Or the line I heard over and over again, "I had no idea this was happening among my subordinates." '

Van Arken drew a short breath and said slowly and deliberately, 'You've taught the philosophy of the law too long, Ambrose. You ought to get down to cases, as we say. But as I indicated, it wouldn't be altogether proper for us to discuss this case.'

Colonel Horton smiled, then replied in a thoughtful tone, 'Then let me discuss the fictional case of Lieutenant X who is court-martialled for murder. Everyone assumes that even if he is found guilty, he will not suffer the ultimate penalty – will not stand in front of a firing squad. And that's a safe assumption since a firing squad has not been constituted to shoot an American in the armed forces for over two decades. But *my* philosophy of law is this – if you try a man for a capital crime, be it murder or sleeping on guard duty in time of war, then you should fully acknowledge that you may in fact send him to his death. Do not assume that judicial reviews of the sentence will reduce the penalty or that an executive pardon will stay the execution. That's a game, and the law is not a game. So if you cannot justify-in your own conscience a firing squad putting ten bullets into a man – if you have no stomach for that, then you must reduce the charge.'

'There is no lesser charge for which the statute of limitations has not run out.'

Colonel Horton's eyes narrowed. 'Ah, I see. We are down to cases. So whereas Mr Tyson at some previous point in time might be more correctly charged with, let's say, conspiracy to conceal a crime, at *this* point in time, it must be first-degree murder or nothing.'

Van Arken nodded slightly.

Colonel Horton nodded too, as if he were just discovering an interesting fact. He said, 'Well, I must be going. I think I have an idea for my lecture tomorrow. Thank you, General.' Colonel Horton saluted, turned on his heel, and walked off.

General Van Arken watched him for a few seconds, then turned and walked in the opposite direction. For the first time he began to feel less confident about the justice of his own position. Privately he thought Tyson was guilty; but as Horton had pointed out, he would not want to see the man shot down by a firing squad. He only wanted to hold him up as a bad example for the rest of the officer corps. However, in his zeal to promote the ethical revolution that was sweeping the armed forces since Vietnam, he had reopened issues and debates best left in the past.

Nevertheless, the thing was started, and there was almost no way to stop it. Like a shout that begins an avalanche, this was growing and gathering force and momentum and thundering with deadly energy toward Benjamin Tyson.

30

Ben Tyson regarded his wife standing on the bottom landing. She wore shower clogs, cut-off jeans, and a white T-shirt. In blue letters across the front of the T-shirt was the Army reenlistment slogan: *Keep a Good Soldier In*. He wondered where the hell she had found that. He noticed her hands were red, and he smelled ammonia. She'd been cleaning.

Marcy Tyson crossed the small living room and extended her hand to Karen Harper. Marcy said, 'I'm so glad we finally met.'

Karen Harper took Marcy's hand. 'So am I.'

Both women regarded each other for a few seconds longer than Tyson considered necessary. He said, 'Well, I'm glad too.' He addressed Marcy. 'Major Harper and I were walking and talking.'

Marcy looked from one to the other, then remarked, 'Perhaps you'd like to go upstairs and dry off.'

Karen Harper replied, 'I'll just borrow an umbrella, if I may. It's a short distance to the guest house.'

'Stay awhile,' said Marcy.

'No, thank you.'

'I've brought a bottle of champagne. Help us drink it.' She took Karen Harper's arm and led her to the staircase.

Karen Harper seemed to sense that to insist on leaving would be more awkward than staying. She said, 'Thank you.' She went up the stairs.

Marcy looked at her husband, smiled sweetly, then went into the kitchen without a word.

Tyson mumbled to himself, 'Typical Tyson luck these days.' He headed up the stairs, passed the closed door to the bathroom, and heard the hair dryer running. He entered the master bedroom and was surprised to see the bed covered with garment bags and the floor crowded with suitcases. He slipped off his running shorts and wet T-shirt, dried himself with his terry cloth robe, and put on a pair of jeans, a tennis shirt, and sandals. He combed his damp hair and went out into the tiny hallway where he bumped into Karen Harper, whose hair and blouse were now dry. She had touched up her makeup and looked, Tyson thought, rather good.

She said, 'I'm finished in the bathroom if you want to use the dryer.'

'That's all right.'

They looked at each other, and Tyson said, 'Please stay for a drink.'

'I'd rather not.'

'I sense that my wife is upset about something, and if you had a drink with us, she might feel better.'

'I doubt that, but if you mean you'd like ten minutes of calm before the storm, I'll stay.'

Tyson smiled. 'I guess that's what I meant.' He motioned toward the stairs. 'After you.'

They descended the stairs in tandem, and Marcy greeted them in the living room. 'There, you both look much better.' She popped the cork on a bottle of champagne and filled three plastic champagne glasses that sat on the coffee table. She said to Tyson, 'When you told me there was no dishwasher, I brought lots of plastic and paper with me.'

'Good thinking. Where's David?'

'The Jordans are looking after him. Melinda is only too happy to have him as a house guest.'

Tyson explained to Karen Harper, 'She's my son's girlfriend. The Jordans are summering in Sag Harbor. The Tysons are apparently now summering in Brooklyn.'

Karen Harper addressed Marcy, 'Will you be staying here then?'

Marcy handed her a glass as she replied, 'Yes. I thought Ben was probably lonely here.' She smiled and turned to

Tyson. 'Are you surprised? You looked very surprised.'

'Did I?' Tyson picked up his glass. 'I suppose that surprise is as good a word as any to describe my joy.'

Marcy added, 'David will join us shortly.'

Tyson replied, 'I don't think that's a good idea.'

'Nevertheless,' said Marcy, 'we're cutting our vacation short to be with you.' She looked at Karen Harper. 'When will this be resolved?'

'By mid-October. The law—'

Tyson interrupted, 'Why don't you and David just return to Garden City? We'll be close, and—'

'No, darling, we want to be *with* you. Here.' She motioned around the room with her glass. 'It's ... cute. Like our first apartment.'

Tyson didn't see any comparison with their first apartment. He said, 'Major Harper thinks it will do me some good to experience a reduction in my life-style.'

'I'm happy to see Major Harper is interested in the development of your character.' She added, 'I sublet the Sag Harbor house for August and got a nice price. So there's no turning back there. As for Garden City, I don't think the climate is quite right for David or me to return.' She looked directly at Karen Harper. 'David has suffered far more peer persecution than he's let on. Children are such savages. Do you have children?'

'No, I've never been married, as you may have read.'

Marcy held up her glass, 'Well, before it goes flat – here's to our new house.'

They drank. Tyson put his glass down on the coffee table. 'Anyway, I'm glad the two women in my life had this opportunity to meet. So—'

Karen Harper addressed Marcy, 'I want you to know, Mrs Tyson – I told your husband this – that I personally feel very badly about the way the press has carried on regarding your ... your counterculture activities and other forms of protest during the Vietnam War. I myself was not old enough at that time to comprehend much of it, though I think I can understand your commitment to the peace movement as well as the forms of protest you chose to exhibit ... to demonstrate that commitment. And I want to assure you that the negative publicity you are receiving is in no way influencing the Army's handling of this case.'

Marcy Tyson regarded Karen Harper for some time. The sound of the rain outside filled the small room. At length Marcy responded, 'I would have guessed you to be old enough to recall the war. But I'll take your word for it.'

Tyson thought he ought to change the subject, but some perversity in his character made him want to hear more.

Karen Harper replied coolly, 'It's good of you to say that. I wish others could be as mature.' She put her glass down and with her hand out approached Marcy.

'Thank you for the wine.'

Marcy took her hand and held it. She looked into Karen Harper's eyes and said, 'But I'm also not so foolish or naive as to believe that you and Ben have not established a close rapport. I'm sure you've discovered that my husband is a remarkable and decent man and if the law is at all compassionate, he is deserving of that compassion.'

Karen Harper held Marcy's gaze and replied, 'That is precisely what I've discovered, Mrs Tyson, and unfortunately not much else. Good evening.'

Marcy released her hand.

Karen Harper retrieved her handbag and briefcase. Tyson picked up the umbrella that was propped beside the front door. Karen Harper walked to the door, then she turned back to Marcy. 'I had an image of you that was quite different and probably influenced by the media. In fact, I thought you were a liability to your husband's cause, but I see you are an asset. He needs all the assets he can get now.' She turned to Tyson. 'The best of luck to you.'

Tyson smiled, 'Alas, the Tyson luck has run out. But the

Tyson wit, charm, and intelligence will suffice. Good night, Karen.'

'Good night, Ben.'

Tyson handed her the umbrella and opened the door. He watched her raise the umbrella and walk off in the gusty rain. He was reminded of the first day they'd taken leave of each other in front of his house, another house, long ago in the May rain, with his borrowed umbrella above her head. He closed the door and turned to his wife. Marcy's eyes were fixed on him, and he knew from long experience that she would not speak unless he did. He said, 'Women are very stiff and formal with each other when they first meet, but they can still get some good zingers in. All in all, I'm happy to see you finally learned something from the ladies in Garden City.'

Marcy peered at him through narrow eyes.

He cleared his throat and added, 'There are times when savoir faire is preferable to salty language and emotional outbursts. You are, after all, an officer's wife. I'm quite proud of you.'

'Go fuck yourself.'

'Now, now—'

'You were both here *before* you took a walk, weren't you? That's when she said something about this place being good for you or something. How long were you here?'

'Not long enough for a man my age to consummate the sexual act.' He poured himself more champagne and added, 'Look, I'm flattered that you're jealous. But I'm being extremely faithful to you and chivalrous to her.'

Marcy seemed to have calmed down somewhat. 'All right ... but things sometimes happen even when we don't want them to.'

He drank the champagne. 'What the hell is this stuff?'

'Cordón Negro.'

'What? African champagne?'

'No, idiot. It's Spanish. It's not bad, and it's cheap.'

377

'Spain is off the boycott list?'

'Yes, since Franco died. Didn't I tell you?'

'No. Can I buy sherry now?'

'Absolutely. And real Spanish olives for your martinis. And I think you fucked her. Psychologically, I mean. She's old enough to understand a man like you but still young enough to be spiritually seduced.'

'How much a bottle?'

'Less than seven dollars. Incredible. The dollar is strong against the peso. She wished you luck with some finality. Does that mean your official relationship is over?'

'Yes. I don't think champagne is the place to cut corners, though.'

'You have domestic beer in the refrigerator.'

'Don't tell anyone. By the way, I didn't see the Volvo outside.'

'I guess not, or you two wouldn't have charged in here hot as three-dollar pistols.'

'That's hardly the way I would characterize our taking shelter from the rain. Where's the Volvo?'

'It died, and I gave it a Viking funeral. That new Toyota outside is ours.'

'*What?* You bought a Nipponese automobile? Are you crazy? I won't drive it. How could you do that knowing how I feel about Japanese products flooding the country, and—'

'Don't try to change the subject. Will you have any occasion to go to Washington to see her again?'

'None. The preliminary investigation is concluded. And I'm not speaking to anyone again without counsel present.'

'All right.' Marcy drank her champagne. 'You do have taste. She's quite good-looking. A natural wholesome beauty. She even looked good wet. I wonder why she never married. Did you ask her?'

Tyson didn't think this was a subject he wanted to discuss any longer. He said, 'She's engaged to a colonel. The papers never tell you that.'

'I didn't see an engagement ring.'

'Well ... engaged to be engaged. Anyway, are you really moving in?'

'Yes. David is coming as soon as we're set up.'

'Why?'

'Because we had a family council and decided you couldn't be trusted alone. Also your mother called *again*. This time to inform me that a wife's place is with her husband. I didn't know that. Did you know she lived in a converted chicken coop near Fort Stewart, Georgia, while your father was training in the Army Air Corps?'

'I believe she mentioned it a few hundred times when I was growing up. In fact, I was conceived in that chicken coop. Born in a private hospital on Park Avenue, to be sure, but conceived in a chicken coop.'

'That explains a lot. Anyway, if she can do it, I can damned well do it.'

'Don't put yourself out on my account.'

Marcy looked at him. 'Actually David was coming with or without me. He decided he loves you and is willing to give up his first lay in order to be here with you. Knowing men as I do, I would say that is a supreme sacrifice.' She added, 'Sometimes adolescents act like adults. Sometimes it's vice versa.'

Tyson said, 'I do miss you both, but it's ... embarrassing ... I mean for you to see me like this...'

She replied, 'You're not on the Bowery. You are an officer in the United States Army. And that's nothing to be embarrassed about.'

Tyson tugged on his ear. 'I must be hearing things.'

'I'm not as subversive as you like to think,' she said. 'Anyway, the point is the minister said for better or worse, and I said yeah, okay, and we've had it mostly better for our whole married life, and what the hell, it could be even worse. And I love you and missed you like hell.'

Tyson put his arms around his wife, and they embraced.

379

Marcy said, 'You are a proud man, Benjamin Tyson. Entirely too proud and too macho to survive in this sort of world. You have to show your weaknesses, let your friends and family share your pain.'

He squeezed her tighter. 'You know, Marcy, I've been a careless husband, indifferent father, shallow friend, and undedicated employee. I haven't shown any commitment to you, David, my job, or anything. And it started sometime before this mess.'

'I know. Other people noticed. But don't be too hard on yourself.'

'Why not? I'm glad I got this kick in the ass to wake me up. I'm not going to romanticize how things were before this started, but life *was* good. It was my perceptions of home, family, job, and friends that had gone wrong. I don't know why it did, but it did.'

'It was partly my fault. I needed this, too, Ben. Our marriage, our life together, had become unnecessarily pointless. We're going to be one hell of a happy couple when this is behind us.'

Tyson stayed silent for some time, then said, 'I may be away awhile.'

She dug her fingers into his back. 'No! No, you won't be!'

He kissed her, and they clung tighter to each other. She put her head on his shoulder, and he could tell she was crying. He said in a light tone, 'Where'd you get that idiotic T-shirt?'

She spoke without looking up, 'Oh ... I had it made at that shop in Southampton. It struck me as a double entendre. Keep a good soldier in.' She laughed. 'Get it?'

'No. And I don't find it very funny.'

She drew away from him, and he saw her eyes were moist. She said, 'Then I'll remove the offending article.' She pulled the shirt off and threw it on the floor. 'Better?'

Tyson found he was staring at her bare breasts. 'Yes. Oh, yes.' He smiled.

She cleared her throat and wiped her eyes with her hand.

'Well, what am I supposed to do as an Army wife? I mean, besides cleaning the upstairs latrine?'

He poured the last of the sparkling wine into their glasses. 'Well, get a dependent's ID card first, a bumper sticker for the car, join the officers' wives' club, volunteer for something worthy, get the downstairs squared away, and invite some of the officers' ladies for tea, familiarize yourself—'

'Whoa, Tyson. Let's just start with the bumper sticker so I can park.'

'That reminds me—'

'Oh, I didn't buy a Toyota. Just pulling your chain a little. I bought a Jeep.'

'A what?'

'Jeep. Very practical. Good for your image. It's out front. Take a look.'

Tyson looked out the window and saw a light-coloured vehicle glistening in the rain.

'Jeep Cherokee. Four-wheel drive. It's got a CB radio and a gun rack.'

'Are you serious?'

'It's only a year old. Bought it from a local out east. It's also got a winch so you can pull in fishnets or small boats or pull yourself out of mud or snow. That's neat. Go look at it.'

Tyson turned from the window. 'Maybe later.'

'Can I see you give a tour of the museum tomorrow?'

'If you wish.'

'Great. Hey, put on your uniform.'

'No.'

'Yes. I want to see how you look.' She held his arm and pulled him toward the stairs.

'No, really—'

She rubbed her breasts against him. 'Come on. I've never done it with a soldier.' She winked.

'Well, if you put it like that...'

They climbed the stairs and went into the master bedroom.

Marcy sat on the edge of the bed and crossed her bare legs.

381

'Okay, soldier, strip off those civilian duds and get into uniform.'

Tyson found he was self-conscious as he began undressing. Marcy whistled.

'Cut it out.' He stood before her, naked, and drew a deep breath. 'Warm up here.'

'Turn around. Let me see your body.'

Tyson turned around, then faced her again. She said, 'Good officer material. Come here.'

He approached the bed. She reached out and cupped his testicles in her right hand. 'Turn your head and cough.'

He did as she said.

She pronounced, 'Okay, you're in.' She reached around and slapped him on the buttocks. 'Get dressed.'

He went to the closet and began putting on his greens without underwear. 'This is silly—'

'Speak when you're spoken to.'

He mumbled something, knotted his tie, and slipped on his tunic, buttoning it as he turned to her.

She nodded. 'Not bad. Good fit. Brass all shiny. Ribbons straight. Okay, take a shower. Then report to me here.'

'Yes, ma'am.'

He undressed again and walked naked to the bathroom. He showered the sweat off, dried himself, and came back into the bedroom. The bed was clear of luggage, and Marcy lay on the rough white sheets, her legs spread and a pillow under her head. She was wearing his fatigue shirt which was hiked up to her waist, and his forage cap sat on her head. She said, 'Let's clip those horns, Lieutenant, before you get into trouble.'

He got into the bed, on top of her, and slipped in easily, finding her wet.

They made love in the small, hot, airless room, and they both knew this was a sort of parody of what could have happened with Major Karen Harper. Marcy whispered in his ear as she neared orgasm, 'I don't usually do this with married men.'

'My wife's a bitch.'

'I know. I know.'

'Keep a good soldier in,' he said.

She wrapped her legs around his back and locked her ankles together. 'I am. I am.'

31

Marcy and Ben Tyson sat across from each other at the small table. Tyson was dressed in a maize-coloured linen suit. Marcy wore a yellow cotton-knit sweater and matching skirt.

Marcy said, 'This was a fort?'

'Not this part. This is the new dining room. Most forts don't have picture windows.'

'Don't get smart.'

Tyson picked up the menu. 'The steak here is good.'

'I don't see any quiche on the menu.'

'Nor will you ever.'

'You say that with relish.'

'With steak sauce.'

'I'll bet you stay in if you're acquitted.'

'The military has a certain masculine appeal.'

'Don't get carried away.' She looked at him. 'Would you ... would you ever go back in – I mean under other circumstances – if they called you in a national emergency? Another war?'

Tyson replied, 'Yes, I would serve my country again.'

'Even after what the Army has done to you?'

'They've done nothing to me. They think I've done something to them.'

'Would you go back in for an unpopular, Vietnam-type, undeclared war?'

'Mine is not to reason why. I didn't even fight this recall as hard as I could have.'

'Boy, once they've got you, they've got you forever, haven't they?'

'I'm afraid so. Military service exerts a lasting influence on a man far beyond the short number of years he was on duty. Just like jail time. Ask anyone who was in – jail or the Army.'

'I believe you. I just don't understand. I never understood how millions of men could clash on the battlefield, leaving piles of corpses, then do it again and again.'

'Men love war. They love fucking the enemy, and when they withdraw, there is a postcoital depression that lingers for the rest of their lives.'

'Scary, Ben. Scary.'

'Don't I know it?'

They sat in silence for a few minutes. Marcy looked out over the nearly empty dining room and saw a couple turn their faces away. She said, 'Why do you suppose people are staring at us?'

'They are absolutely dazzled by the dashing new officer and his lady.'

She smiled grimly. 'As long as they're not saying, "There's that war criminal and his whore." '

'My dear, in the officer corps all the brothers are courageous and all the sisters virtuous.'

'I didn't know that.' She sipped her gin and tonic as she looked out the window. The night sky had cleared as suddenly as it had darkened earlier, and a stiff wind from the south fluttered the illuminated Stars and Stripes on the lawn. On the patio a barbecue was in progress, and she heard the sound of a steel band and saw the flames of the charcoal pit and the Tonga torches. She said, 'There's something vaguely anachronistic about this place.'

'That's what you say about Garden City. In truth, *you* are the anachronism, a time-traveller from the sixties.'

'Perhaps you're right. Still, this is a very closed society, isn't it?'

'It's supposed to be. It has its own internal reality which is based in part on its own history, exclusive of the society outside the gates.'

'Now that I'm here in this environment, I'm beginning to understand you better.'

'I'm beginning to understand me better too.'

She asked, 'Were you invited to that party out there?'

He glanced out the window. 'All members are invited to all club functions. But I'm supposed to send my regrets.'

'I see.'

The waitress came, and they ordered their food and a bottle of Mouton Cadet. They chatted pleasantly, just like old times, they agreed. They held hands across the table, and the waitress smiled at them as she brought the food. Marcy and Ben ate in companionable silence.

Tyson finished his steak and poured himself and Marcy more wine. He looked across the dining room and said, 'We're about to have company.'

Marcy turned and saw a large ruddy-faced man with sandy hair, about fifty years old, making his way toward them from the direction of the patio. The man wore casual slacks and a rather silly flowered shirt. She said, 'Who is that?'

'That is the Reverend Major Kennard Oakes, a Baptist chaplain. He has befriended me.'

'Well, you need all the friends you can get.'

The Reverend Oakes drew up to their table and smiled widely. He drawled in a deep southern accent, 'Ben, are you drinking the devil's brew again?'

Tyson shook hands with the minister. 'I'm Episcopalian. Drunkenness is a sacrament.'

'Blasphemy. Is this Mrs Tyson?'

Tyson made the introductions. Reverend Oakes sat without an invitation and took Marcy's hand across the table, patting it. 'You are a very beautiful woman.'

Tyson said, 'I'd offer you a glass of wine, but I don't want to tempt you.'

385

The minister smiled. 'Why aren't you two outside?'

Tyson replied, 'Marcy and I just made wild passionate love, and we wanted to be alone.'

Marcy's eyebrows rose, and there was a silence at the table. Finally the Reverend Oakes smiled and said lightly, 'So Ben, how was your day?'

'Fine.'

'Are you free tomorrow morning? I have to drive down to Fort Dix, and I'd like the company.'

Tyson lit a cigarette. 'I have a group tomorrow morning.'

'Then perhaps tomorrow afternoon. I can reschedule my appointment at Dix.'

Tyson exhaled a stream of smoke. He said to Marcy, 'Major Oakes is on temporary duty here like I am. But unlike me, he's not awaiting court-martial.' He addressed the minister. 'What did you say you were doing here?'

He turned to Marcy. 'I'm here on special orders from the Army Chaplain School to evaluate the Bible classes given to young people at the various posts and installations in the New York metropolitan area.'

Marcy said, 'How interesting.'

Tyson said, 'You won't be conducting any services at the post chapel then?'

'No, I'm afraid not. The Reverend Perry is an excellent preacher if you want to see a good Baptist service.'

Tyson nodded. 'I'm glad you're here.' He put his hand firmly on the minister's arm. 'I had an argument with a fellow in the lounge last night, padre. He insisted it was John who said, "The Pharisees also came unto him, tempting him, and saying unto him, 'Is it lawful for a man to put away his wife for every cause?'" I say it was Luke. So who was it?' He stared at Reverend Oakes.

'John.'

'No, it was Mark.'

'That's right.'

'No, that's wrong,' said Tyson. 'It was Matthew. You fail

Bible class.'

The Reverend Oakes smiled and replied, 'Who gives a shit, Tyson?'

Marcy's eyes widened.

The man pulled his arm away from Tyson, and they both stood. Tyson said, 'Beat it, bozo.'

The man glared at Tyson for a second, then nodded. 'Chaplains are hard to do. I told them that. You're good though.' He turned and left.

Tyson sat.

Marcy said, 'What in the name of God? ...'

'In the name of God indeed. What swine!'

'Who?'

'That is the question,' said Tyson.

'That man was spying on you?'

'I suppose you'd call it that.' Tyson finished his glass of wine. 'Well, there's a lesson for you. Be careful who you speak to.'

Marcy drew a deep breath. 'This is bizarre.'

'Amen.' Tyson looked at his watch. 'I have to make a phone call. This new lawyer, Corva.' He stood. 'Be about ten minutes. Order coffee and dessert.'

She said, 'I want a telephone installed.'

'Call about it tomorrow.'

'I can't. I don't have a telephone.'

He smiled and walked out of the dining room. Tyson passed the pay phones and headed towards the exit. He'd made his phone call earlier in the day, and it wasn't his lawyer he'd called but the *American Investigator*.

Tyson walked across the cobbled drive, still wet with the earlier rain, and opened the heavy oak door of the museum with his key. He entered, leaving the door partly ajar. Dim security lights illuminated uniformed mannequins with sabres and rifles, giving the impression of an evil place. Tyson glanced at his watch again. He heard a sound at the door, then a weak rap, and the door swung in. Tyson said, 'Come in.'

A figure stood on the cobbled drive, then stepped up into the lobby area. 'Mr Tyson?'

'Right. Mr Jones?'

'Yeah.' Wally Jones stayed near the door and peered into the shadowy room.

Tyson looked at him in the doorway, silhouetted against the lights of the Officers' Club on the far side of the drive. He was heavyset and wore an ill-fitting bush jacket with matching light trousers. He had a leather bag slung over his shoulder. Tyson couldn't see his face clearly, but he appeared to be a man in his early fifties. Tyson said, 'Come on in and shut the door.'

Jones took another step into the museum's lobby but did not close the door. 'Is this where you want to talk?'

'Yes. I have an office in the rear.'

'You want to give me your side of the story?'

'That's what I told your editor.'

'Okay. That's good. That's what we always wanted. Your side of the story. We never want to be unfair. Nobody wanted to do a hatchet job on you. Least of all me. I was in Korea. Most of our readers are the patriotic type. You know? So this is good.'

'I want to tell you how the Army shafted me. But if your readers are the patriotic type, maybe you won't print that.'

'Oh, we'll print it! We'll print anything you say.'

'Okay. Follow me.' Tyson turned and took a few steps. He looked back over his shoulder. 'This way.'

Jones chuckled nervously and said, 'Hey, are you alone?'

'Yes. Are you?'

'Yeah. Look, why don't we step outside? Someplace sort of public but private. Like take a walk down to the water.'

Tyson replied, 'I can't be seen talking to you. But ... okay. Let me get my notes.' Tyson walked off into the dark recesses of the museum, slipped off his loafers, and, carrying them, circled back and stood at the doorway behind Wally Jones. 'Ready?'

Jones gave a start and spun around. 'Oh ... Christ, you scared—'

Tyson delivered a powerful blow to Jones' solar plexus. Jones doubled over, and Tyson brought his knee up into Jones' face, hearing and feeling the man's nose break. Jones stumbled around, bent over, one hand on his midsection and the other over his face. Tyson slipped his shoes on and planted a savage kick to his rear, and Jones sprawled across the stone floor, moaning in pain.

Tyson heard a sound behind him and turned. A flash blinded him, followed by another. He charged out of the museum towards the photographer, who got off another shot before he turned and ran. Tyson followed.

Suddenly two men in jogging suits appeared from around the side of the museum. One grabbed the photographer around the arms, and the other pulled the camera from his hands, smashed it on the pavement, then came at Tyson. Tyson crouched in a defensive stance and waited.

The man drew abreast of the open museum door and shone a flashlight on Wally Jones lying inside on the floor. The light revealed a small puddle of blood forming around Jones' face. The man swung the flashlight toward Tyson and shone it in his eyes. He said, 'Just stay where you are and keep your hands where I can see them.'

'Who the hell are you?'

'The man with the forty-five automatic pointed at you.'

Tyson heard the metallic double click of the hammer being cocked.

The headlights of an approaching vehicle rounded the side of the museum, and the vehicle drew up beside Tyson. A man poked his head out of the rear window. 'You *are* a violent man.'

Tyson clearly recognized the voice of Chet Brown. Brown said, 'Get in the car, killer.'

The car sped over the Verrazano Bridge. Tyson lit a cigarette.

The driver, a young man with a hard look, called back, 'Would you mind not smoking?'

Tyson exhaled a stream of smoke towards the front. Brown laughed softly. Tyson looked at Brown at the far end of the rear seat. He was wearing a white tennis outfit. Brown said, 'How's your new job?'

Tyson drew on his cigarette and looked out the side window at the Statue of Liberty standing tall in its eerie green splendour.

Chet Brown said, 'By the way, someone will escort your lady back to your quarters with an explanation.'

Tyson inquired, 'Was Oakes yours?'

'Maybe. Chaplains are hard to do.'

'I know.'

'We'll have to set up a special class for that now.'

'Who? Who are you?'

Brown replied, 'You wouldn't recognize the name. We're so shadowy even the CIA doesn't quite believe we exist.'

'Sounds like bullshit to me.'

Brown changed the subject. 'As for Wally Jones, I don't blame you, Ben. That bastard had it coming. If he'd written things about my wife like that, I'd have done the same thing. Anyway, that one was free – on us. But if you do anything like that again, you can deal with the police yourself. I can't obstruct justice more than once a month or so.'

'Don't do me any favours.'

'Well, that's my job, Ben. I'm your assigned guardian angel. That's why I'm wearing white.'

Tyson retreated into a moody silence.

The car went through the far right lane of the toll plaza without paying, swung around to the right, and approached the main gate of Fort Wadsworth. The MP waved them on, and the car wound its way through the dark, deserted streets of the mostly unused fort. They drove down an incline towards the Narrows, passed a dock, and pulled up to the foreboding granite walls of Battery Weed.

Brown got out of the car and motioned Tyson to follow. They walked to a set of huge double doors on the landward side of the three-tiered artillery battery. Brown pulled a door open and entered a cavernous chamber partially lit by small hanging light bulbs. Iron staircases ran off in different directions, and Tyson followed Brown to one of them, their footsteps echoing in the damp, still air. Brown led the way through a wide arched corridor that was lined on one side with wooden doorways. He said, 'Pick any door.'

Tyson indicated one, and Brown opened it. Tyson followed him into a room illuminated only by the light coming from two open gun ports.

Brown stood at one of the openings and looked out across the Narrows. 'Some view. Hamilton, the Shore Parkway, Coney Island, Kennedy Airport, the bridge, and the harbour. Smell that salt air.'

Tyson's eyes adjusted to the weak light, and he noticed that the stone walls were covered with grotesque depictions of animal-like creatures painted in fluorescent colours.

Brown followed his gaze. 'Cult stuff. The CID says they're Satanists. They find slaughtered dogs, cats, and chickens in these rooms.'

Tyson didn't respond but moved to the far right gun port and stared out across the Narrows. Brown, he admitted, had a flair for choosing interesting places to chat. 'How long have you been snooping on me?'

'Long enough to deduce that you and Harper are on the verge of something wonderful.'

Tyson leaned out over the three-foot-thick sill of the gun port. It was about thirty feet to the embankment below.

'You came close tonight, lover. But you didn't count on your wife showing up. I literally held my breath when you and Karen ran into your digs. You must have done some fancy footwork because an hour later there you were holding hands with the missus over dinner. What a man!'

Tyson lifted himself onto the sill and sat lengthways in the

391

big gun port, his back to the stone wall and his knees drawn up. He lit a cigarette and looked out over the far horizon. He noticed that Brown's manner was somewhat less cultured than it had been at the Athletic Club. Brown seemed more the tough guy here, and Tyson suspected the man had the chameleonlike ability to blend into his surroundings. He wondered which one was the real Chet Brown. Probably neither.

'You've had a hell of a day.' Brown moved closer to Tyson. 'Hey, are you practising? I mean sitting in a stone room and staring forlornly out the window.'

Tyson flipped his cigarette towards Brown. 'Keep your distance.'

Brown retreated a step. 'I'm just so thrilled to see you again. Anyway, as a guardian angel I can do certain things or not do them to alter the fate of mortals. But you control your own destiny on my days off. So watch the fucking and the fighting and don't call journalists unless you intend to beat them up. Okay?'

Tyson yawned. 'Are you finished?'

'No. Does the name Colonel Eric Willets mean anything to you?'

'No.'

'Well, your name means something to him. He's Karen's lover, and he'd like a piece of your ass.'

'Tell him not to believe everything he reads in the papers. That's what I tell my wife.'

Brown laughed. 'I'll pass that on.' He said, 'You know, Ben, I like you. But you are the cause of much unhappiness. There is a black cloud following you, and everyone near you gets rained on. And on a national level, you have caused unhappiness in Washington. Did you read this morning's *Times*?'

'No.'

'Well, you're the subject of a congressional inquiry. Also the U.N. Commission on Genocide has expressed interest in

392

the case. They're talking about sending a fact-finding mission to Hue, and Hanoi says they're quite welcome to do that. I mean who needs this shit, Ben?'

'Not me.'

'Not your country either.'

Tyson stared at Brown in the pale light. Things were becoming more clear. He felt his mouth going dry. He swung his legs around and slid down from the gun opening.

'Now you keep *your* distance.' Brown continued, 'We could get mad at Brandt too, I guess. He had the big mouth. If he weren't around, the case would collapse.'

Tyson slipped his hand in his jacket pocket and found his Swiss Army knife.

Brown went on ruminatively, 'I voted for Brandt to go, but ...' He shrugged. 'There are those who think justice would be better served if it were you.'

His hand still in his pocket, Tyson worked the clasp blade out of the handle, slicing his fingers as he levered it open.

'We offered you a deal.'

'Offer it to me again.'

'Okay. Will you take it?'

'Shove it up your ass.'

Brown smiled tightly. 'You are a cool one. I'll give you that.' Brown glanced around the room, then his eyes focused again on Tyson. He drew a small automatic from an elastic band on his waist, and Tyson saw the black dull silencer in sharp contrast to the silvery nickel plating of the pistol. Brown said, 'Climb out on the sill.'

Tyson remained still. The distance between him and Brown was about ten feet, or about five feet too many according to his old hand-to-hand combat manual.

Brown snapped, 'Get up there.'

'Go fuck yourself.'

Brown said coolly, 'I want to help you do what you tried to in the bay. This is easier and faster than drowning, Ben. Just get up there, close your eyes, and roll back.'

'What the hell are you talking about?'

'What the hell do you think I'm talking about?'

Tyson stared at Brown. 'I didn't try to commit suicide, you asshole.'

Brown seemed confused. He snapped, 'Well, too bad. They really hoped you'd be honourable about it.'

'Don't talk to me about honour. If you want me dead, do it yourself.'

Brown shook his head and lowered the pistol. 'At this point in time, I am authorized only to encourage you to terminate yourself. But please believe me when I tell you termination has been discussed. And if you do meet an untimely death, it will be a suicide or an accident, as happened to Mr Harold Simcox. If you want to reach me, post a lost-and-found notice on the O Club bulletin board. "Found – Copy of Camus' *The Stranger* – pick up at club office." I'll contact you. In the meantime, keep alert, Lieutenant. You're on patrol.'

Tyson said, 'I don't need you to tell me that.'

Brown stuck the automatic back into the elastic band and opened the door. He looked back at Tyson. 'You can call for a taxi at the main gate. Enjoy the day.'

Tyson watched the door close, then went to it and listened to Brown's footsteps echoing away in the damp corridor. He drew his hand from his pocket and saw it was covered with blood, and there were deep gashes in his fingers. He wrapped his handkerchief around his fingers and opened the door. The corridor was empty. He thought, *With a guardian angel like that, who needs the grim reaper?*

As he walked slowly through the dark corridor, Tyson suppressed the feeling of gratitude that he was still alive, which was the feeling Brown had wanted to leave him with. He also fought back the feelings of anger and outrage; Chet Brown and company would have no effect on his emotions or decisions. Chet Brown did not exist.

'Enjoy the day.' *Oh, Christ*, he thought, *is that going to be the new variation of "Have a nice day"*? He hoped not. Things were bad enough.

32

Benjamin Tyson sat across the desk from Vincent Corva.

Corva said, 'Coffee?'

'Fine.'

Corva spoke to his secretary over the intercom.

Tyson regarded the small man in the morning light of the east-facing window. Corva was perhaps a few years younger than Tyson, very thin, with pale sunken cheeks and bulging eyes, giving an appearance of malnutrition. His black hair was swept back from his forehead, and his Adam's apple bobbed, moving the knot on his tie. The suit was very much Brooks Brothers, though Tyson suspected it had needed much alteration to fit so slight a frame.

Tyson lit a cigarette and held it clumsily with his bandaged fingers. Corva looked at the wrapped bandages but said nothing. He leaned forward, his arms on the desk, then inquired, 'Who did you say referred you to me?'

Corva's voice, Tyson noticed, seemed much stronger and deeper than he'd expected from a man who couldn't have weighed a hundred and forty pounds. Tyson replied, 'I didn't.'

'Well, who did?'

'I called the bar association, and they gave me a list.'

'So you picked Vincent Corva because the name sounded good.'

'Something like that.' Tyson looked around the office. It was an off-white room with acoustical ceiling tiles, grey carpet, and furniture that looked like it had been carried out of Conran's that morning. The wall decorations were a series

395

of sepia prints that might have been named 'Great Moments in Law,' and Tyson was surprised there were more than two of them. On the windowsill sat a single plant that looked suspiciously like marijuana.

'Basil.'

Tyson looked at Corva. 'Excuse me?'

'Sweet basil. Smell it? Can't get fresh basil, even in New York. Do you like *pasta al pesto*?'

'Love it.'

'You have to pick it fresh and make the sauce within fifteen minutes. Captures the essence of the basil. Makes all the difference.'

'I'm sure of it.' Tyson was briefly nostalgic for Phillip Sloan and his woody, leathery office.

'My father used to put a sprig behind his ear – some kind of superstition. Never got it clear though.' Corva straightened up and drew a yellow legal pad towards him. He made a notation, and Tyson wondered if it had to do with sweet basil or murder. Corva said, 'The press has reported that you are on restriction. Is that correct?'

'Yes.' Tyson gave him the terms of his restriction.

Corva nodded thoughtfully. 'That's odd, because that began the ticking clock. The Army may not have time to perfect a murder case in ninety days. But someone – higher up – has ordered restriction as a means to move the Army along. I suspect the government theorizes that the longer this is unresolved, the more harm it will cause.'

'That's my theory too. Can you perfect a defence within the time remaining?'

'Well, they've had a few months' jump on me, but I'll see what I can do.'

Tyson drew on his cigarette and looked over Corva's head at the framed diplomas and various professional accreditations on the wall behind the desk. He noticed a framed colour photograph of soldiers in jungle fatigues standing on a desolate plain with black smoke rising in the distance. Tyson said, 'You were in Nam?'

'Yes. Here's my background, Mr Tyson: I was admitted to the New York State bar in 1967 and was shortly thereafter drafted directly into the Judge Advocate General's Corps and went to the branch school at Charlottesville. I was with the Staff Judge Advocate at Fort Benning. I used to watch the infantry OCS guys training sometimes. I never saw men pushed so hard. Then one day as I was walking past one of those full-length mirrors in the lobby of the JAG building, I saw this pale, skinny nerd with a briefcase that was pulling him over like a listing ship. So in a moment of pure lunacy, I decided I wanted to be an infantry officer.' He looked at Tyson.

Tyson smiled and said, 'Perhaps it was a moment of crystalline sanity.'

'No one else thought so. Anyway, after months of red tape and bureaucracy, I got out of the JAG Corps and got assigned to the infantry school at Benning. I died six times during the first month of training. But I never let them know. I graduated, and shortly thereafter I shipped out for Nam and was assigned to the Twenty-fifth Infantry Division, down near Cu Chi.'

Tyson nodded.

'I was a platoon leader like you and saw action, and went through the Tet Offensive like you. Unlike you, I wasn't wounded. Any questions?'

'Not at the moment.'

'All right, on my return I was assigned to the Pentagon and performed various legal duties. Actually I was sort of a JAG mascot, and they liked to show me off – a JAG lawyer with a Combat Infantry Badge, living proof that even lawyers have balls.'

Tyson smiled.

Vincent Corva added, 'When you're five-six and scrawny, the infantry has a certain appeal that a man like yourself might not appreciate. I would not have been much of a warrior before gunpowder, but God gave us little squirts M-16 rifles and lightweight field gear and made us all equally deadly. But up here' – he tapped his forehead – 'there are still vast differences among men. And up here is where this fight is going to take place.' He rose. 'I'm going to take a piss, Mr Tyson.'

'Okay.'

'If you're not here when I come back, that's okay, too.' Vincent Corva left his office.

Tyson stubbed his cigarette into an ashtray. He stood and went to the framed photograph behind Corva's desk. It was a posed shot, like a sports team, front row kneeling, back row standing. There were about forty men, armed with the basic ordnance of the rifle platoon. The background appeared to be a flat, endless expanse of black ash or soot, running out to the horizon of black smoke. It was a colour photograph, but there was little colour in it.

Standing in the middle of the back row was Lieutenant Vincent Corva. He looked almost comical sandwiched between two huge black men. But Tyson looked closer and saw something in Corva's features, in his eyes, that he understood. It was not the Thousand Yard Stare, but the look of a hungry predator, a man who knows he is dangerous.

Tyson went to the window and plucked a dark green leaf from the basil plant. He crushed the leaf between his thumb and forefinger and sniffed its unique fragrance.

The door opened behind him, and he heard Corva say, 'Smells jog the memory in a surprising way. Sweet basil always brings back my parents' house in early fall, canning tomatoes on the sun porch.' He handed Tyson a mug of coffee. 'They make coffee, but they won't bring it anymore.'

Tyson said, 'Well, why should they?'

'She's my wife.'

'More reason not to.'

Corva sat in his chair. Tyson remained standing. Corva said, 'After I was released from active duty, I forgot about military law. But then came the Calley case, and I followed it closely. There is something uniquely fascinating about a court-martial. Don't you think so?'

'Absolutely.'

'You were involved with special courts-martial, I assume.'

'About a dozen.'

'Well, I missed that – I do mostly real estate law – so I boned up on military law and got certified. I've done about fifteen general courts-martial in the last fifteen years.'

'I heard of one at Fort Jackson. Army captain. Shot his wife's lover.'

Corva smiled.

Tyson looked at him, wondering what sort of impression he made on a court-martial board of officers. At least, Tyson thought, Corva didn't have shifty eyes like Phillip Sloan.

Corva leaned forward. 'Look, Mr Tyson, we could waltz around all morning, me pretending I'm sort of interested in taking your case and you pretending you might take your business elsewhere. I don't have time for that, and neither do you. I know every detail of this case that's been reported and some things that haven't been reported. Also I've read Picard's book. Twice. And I want the case. And there are only two certified military lawyers as good as me on the East then a weak rap, and the door swung in. Tyson said, 'Come in.' you picked me from the list the bar association gave you.'

Tyson said, 'Okay, you're hired.'

'Fine. I get two hundred dollars an hour. Double for courtroom time. This will cost you a small fortune.'

'I'm broke.'

'Who isn't these days? Do you have a rich aunt?'

'Lots of them. But I also have some defence fund groups here and there.'

'I know,' replied Corva. 'I'll contact them. Or more likely they'll contact me. Don't worry about money. If there's not enough of it, I'll make up the difference. *Pro bono publico*.

That's Latin, not Italian. Means for the public good.' Corva stood. 'Deal?'

'Deal.' They shook hands.

Corva said, 'I don't have time to go into any details, but the first piece of advice I'm giving you is not to speak to Major Karen Harper again. Not under *any* circumstances. Understood?'

Tyson nodded.

'I'd like to contact your personal attorney. Sloan. Garden City.'

'Right.'

Corva seemed deep in thought, then said, 'I knew Van Arken, by the way. At the Pentagon. Not personally, but I knew of him. After My Lai hit the fan, I saw his name mentioned a few times. He's an uncompromising son of a bitch.'

'The whole Army, Mr Corva, is made up of uncompromising sons of bitches. I wouldn't want any other type of Army.'

'Me neither. And the JAG is not much different than the infantry in that respect. There is no plea bargaining as we know it in civilian law.'

'I'm not interested in plea bargaining.'

'Nor am I, Mr Tyson. But sometimes the government jumps over the Army's head and approaches you with a deal. Has that happened to you?'

'No, it hasn't.'

'Let me know.'

'Of course.'

Corva opened the door. 'Well, go meet my wife. Linda. She's the brunette with the pink dress in the outer office. She thinks you are handsome. She'll work hard for you, too. Sometime down the line, you and your wife will come over for dinner. In the early fall, when the sweet basil is at its best.'

'If I'm available I'll be there.'

'You'll be available, Mr Tyson.'

Tyson stopped at the door and turned back to Vincent Corva. 'You understand, don't you, that a violation of the Uniform Code of Military Justice did take place on 15 February 1968? A violation for which there is no statute of limitations.'

'Is that so?'

'You understand that most of what Andrew Picard wrote in his book is true.'

'Is *what*?'

'*True.*'

'How do you know?'

'I was *there*.'

'Were you?' He stepped closer to Tyson and lowered his voice. 'Let me tell *you* something – let me reveal to you the one great truth about war, Mr Tyson, and it is this: Ultimately all war stories are bullshit. From a general's memoirs to an ex-pfc's boasting in a saloon, it is all *bullshit*. From the *Iliad* to the Grenada invasion, it is all *bullshit*. I have never heard a true war story, and I never told one, and neither have you. And if we do enter a courtroom, we will shovel the bullshit faster and higher than the Army, and by the time we are ready to walk out of there, we will all be up to our eyebrows in spent shell casings and bullshit. Don't burden me with the truth, Mr Tyson, I am not interested.'

Tyson looked into Corva's eyes. 'You mean you don't want to know what—'

'No. What the hell do I care what happened there? When you have heard one war story, you have heard them all. Keep the details to yourself. And if I should have to ask you for a detail or two in order to form a strategy for the defence, do me a favour and bullshit me.' Corva pointed his finger at Tyson. 'The only story I want from you is the cover story, my friend. The one Mr Anthony Scorello and Mr Paul Sadowski are putting out. You see, Mr Tyson, I am not much of a courtroom actor, and when Brandt and Farley get on the stand and start their version of the bullshit I want to look

401

appropriately incredulous. You know the Japanese play *Rashomon*? Read it. See you tomorrow. Fort Hamilton. Buy me dinner, seven P.M. Coffee at your place. I want to meet your wife.'

Tyson remained standing in the doorway. At length he said, 'I once heard a true war story. A Confederate officer's account of Gettysburg. He wrote, "We all went up to Gettysburg, the summer of sixty-three, and some of us came back from there; and that's all except for the details."'

Corva smiled appreciatively. 'Yes, except for the details. Good-bye, Mr Tyson.'

'Good-bye, Mr Corva.'

33

Benjamin Tyson said, 'Pass the cucumbers, please.'

David passed the cucumbers.

Marcy said to Vincent Corva, 'More iced tea, Vincent?'

'No, thank you.'

Tyson sat in his rolled-up shirt sleeves and loosened his black uniform tie. 'Hot.'

Marcy rose and closed the blinds, blocking out the noon sun from the small dining room.

Tyson surveyed the room, a ten-foot-square area, opening onto the living room. Marcy had purchased a dinette table from the post thrift shop and carried it home in the Jeep along with some framed pictures, including a scene of Mount Fuji painted in iridescent colours of black velvet. Tyson regarded the picture as he picked at his cucumbers. On the opposite wall of the dining room hung his commission.

Marcy said to Vincent Corva, 'More chicken salad?'

'No, thank you, Marcy. That was a good lunch.'

Tyson snorted, 'Bullshit.'

'No, really—'

'Protestant food, Vincent. You are what you eat. Today you're cool cucumbers and chicken salad made with Miracle Whip on white bread. By tonight you'll be speaking in aphorisms and lose your sex drive.'

Corva smiled embarrassedly.

Marcy gave Tyson a look of mock scorn. 'Ethnic slurs are not welcome at my table.' She turned to Corva. 'Wasn't that a good lunch for a hot day?'

'Yes.'

David said, 'Dad, I'm taking the bus and subway to Sheepshead Bay this afternoon. I'm going to hang around the boats and help out. Okay?'

Tyson said, 'Why not?'

Marcy said, 'Because I don't think I want him taking a bus and subway.'

'How are we ever going to live on West Seventy-something Street if he can't take buses and subways?'

'Well ... he has no experience with public transportation, and—'

'I had no experience with combat until a machine gun opened up on me one day. You talk about suburban turkeys—' He turned to Corva. 'What do you think, Vincent?'

'Well ... how old is—'

Tyson interrupted, 'What's the kid going to do around here all day?'

Marcy snapped, 'What do *I* do around here all day?'

Tyson snapped back, 'What do *I* do all day? I have a two-minute commute to work, I give guided tours to geriatrics and stare at the damned cannon the rest of the day. Don't I take you to the club for dinner and lunch?'

'I know the damned menu by heart, including the printer's name and address.'

David cleared his throat. 'Well, can I go or not?'

'Yes.'

'No.'

Tyson slammed his hand on the table. 'Yes!' He turned to Corva. 'Italian wives aren't like this.'

'Well—'

Marcy addressed Corva. 'Would you let your fifteen-year-old son—'

'Sixteen,' said Tyson and David simultaneously.

'Sixteen-year-old son take a subway?—'

'Subways are safe,' declared Tyson. 'Don't believe everything you read in the papers. That's the trouble around here. Everybody believes what they read in the papers.'

David said, 'Maybe I'll just go down to the baseball field.'

'Okay,' said Tyson. 'Why don't you go now?'

'Right.' He stood, grabbed some plates, and disappeared into the kitchen, calling out good-byes. The kitchen screen door opened and shut.

Marcy looked at Corva. 'Why do you and Ben have to see Colonel Levin today?'

Corva replied, 'Some administrative matter, I suppose.'

Marcy stared at him for some time. 'Bullshit.'

Tyson said, 'Let's stop browbeating our guest.' He turned to Corva. 'The food may be dull, but the company isn't.'

'I really like chicken salad.'

Marcy laughed without humour. 'Oh, God, sometimes I think we're going stir-crazy in this place.' She addressed Corva. 'It has been three weeks since you've been on this case. What have you done or discovered or whatever?'

'Well, I've spoken to Phillip Sloan, filed various motions in the Federal District Court, sent telegrams to the Department of the Army, Justice Department, the JAG, and the White House. I've held a press conference, and I've got my picture in *Newsweek, Time, US News*, and the *American Investigator*.'

Marcy smiled, then turned to Tyson. 'I haven't seen Wally Jones' byline for the last three weeks.'

'Really? Probably on vacation.'

Marcy turned back to Corva. 'And you've contacted the witnesses?'

404

'Well, the government's witnesses' attorneys. And Karen Harper. She wasn't obligated to give me the fruits of a preliminary investigation, but she was most helpful.'

'Yes, she was helpful to Ben, also. But what do you think she recommended?'

Corva glanced at Tyson, then said to Marcy, 'Based on the expected testimony of the two government witnesses she probably recommended pursuing the case.'

'Further investigation? A formal hearing? More months of this?'

'I'm afraid so.'

Tyson said, 'Anyone want a drink? Gin and tonic, out on the patio?'

Marcy stood. 'There is no patio, Ben. And I have no tonic or limes.'

'Well, call Gristedes and have them deliver tonic and limes and a patio. On the double.'

'How about wine spritzers on the front stoop instead?' suggested Marcy.

'Fine.' Tyson stood. He came around the table and kissed his wife. 'Good lunch.'

Marcy patted his cheek. 'Bullshit.'

Corva stood also. 'I'll be out front.' He took his suit jacket from the back of the chair and walked through the living room, leaving by the front door.

Marcy said, 'Do you have faith in him?'

'Do you?'

'I'm not the one facing murder charges. Answer the question.'

Tyson considered a moment before replying. 'He has an unusual philosophy of the law. Sometimes I think truth and legality are Protestant obsessions. Mr Corva takes a more subjective view of life. He's not interested in the crime but in the law's perception of it, the witnesses against me, and why they are against me. Sloan was always quoting the law, asking what happened at that hospital. Corva wants to know all

405

there is to know about Brandt and Farley and is trying to determine what they *think* happened at the hospital. Different approach.'

She nodded. 'But it makes sense, especially after all these years have gone by.'

Tyson said, 'On my first meeting with him he asked me to read the Japanese play *Rashomon*. So I did. Do you know it?'

She shook her head.

'Well, it was about a rape and a killing. And it was four perspectives of the crime, told by four people at a trial. No two people reported the same thing. The bandit said he killed the husband, the wife said she killed the husband, the ghost of the husband said he killed himself, and a woodcutter said the husband fell on his own sword by accident. Obviously at least three people were lying, perhaps all four. The point is that truth is in the eye of the beholder, and no single objective explanation for a human event can ever be found.' He smiled grimly. 'Of course everyone on the receiving end of what happened at that hospital had the same ultimate experience. But if they were around to testify I think they would relate different perceptions.'

Marcy nodded. 'So Vincent Corva's defence is based on a Japanese play?'

Tyson shrugged. 'Why not? Better than an Aesop's fable where everyone gets his just deserts.'

Marcy looked doubtful. She looked into his eyes and said, 'Ben, what is happening today?'

'Don't know, love. But I don't think it's an award ceremony.' Tyson said, 'Why don't you and David go back home?'

'We are home.'

He let out a breath. 'Well, why don't you go back to the big air-conditioned house we own with the patio out back?'

'You mean the house in Garden City where our country club is and all our friends are and where we have membership to the swimming pool and where all the nice stores and shops are, and the MPs don't ticket me every day for not having a parking sticker? That house?'

'Right. That's the place.'

'Why would I want to go there if it meant leaving you?'

'Be still, my heart. Look, have you thought about David starting school?'

'Yes. I don't think he can go back to public school. Not here or in Garden City or anywhere. They would make his life miserable.'

Tyson nodded.

Marcy said, 'Your mother has a room for him, and he could stay with her in Florida and go to school under another name, or have a tutor—'

'No. He's staying here. With me. And if there's a court-martial he will attend.'

'No, he will not.'

'Yes, he will. Find a private school or a tutor in the area.'

They stared at each other. Tyson looked at his watch. 'Forget the spritzers. I have to go. Get this table cleaned up, then go down to the laundromat and—'.

'Buzz off.'

Tyson grabbed her and kissed her hard on the lips. 'I love you.'

'Me too. Good luck.'

Tyson walked into the living room and took his tunic from the sofa. He left the house and found Corva sitting on the front stoop looking through his briefcase. Tyson said, 'Sorry to keep you waiting. I couldn't find the wine.'

'That's all right.'

'How about a drink at the club? It's on the way, sort of.'

'Thanks, anyway. We should get moving. We should be there by now.' He closed his briefcase and stood.

Tyson ignored him and asked, 'Did you ever play stoopball when you were a kid in the slums?'

'Actually I grew up in a nice section of Staten Island.' He motioned across the Narrows. 'Right over there. Big house

407

and garden.'

'Your father grew sweet basil and tomatoes and all that?'

'Right. Zucchini and eggplant. We had fig trees. Had to wrap and insulate them every winter. You ever taste a fresh fig?'

'No. But I saw them once at Gristedes for fifty cents apiece. My father grew roses and boxwoods. My mother couldn't cook.'

'Why would anyone want to cook roses and boxwoods?'

'I don't know. Protestants eat funny things.'

Corva smiled. 'Listen, I'll take you and Marcy and David to the Feast of San Gennaro next month. Down on Mulberry Street. You can get fresh figs for a quarter.'

'Good. Looking forward to it.' Neither man spoke. Finally Corva glanced at his watch. 'Well, I think it's time.'

Tyson nodded. 'Right.'

Corva said, 'Remember, it's only words. It's not incoming rounds.'

Tyson smiled. 'Right.'

'And if we don't like the words they're saying, we can just beat the shit out of them.'

'Can we do that?'

'Sure. Article 141. Let's go.'

They began to walk to post headquarters.

Benjamin Tyson and Vincent Corva sat in the office of the assistant adjutant, Captain Hodges. Tyson glanced at the communicating door that led into Colonel Levin's office. He said to Corva, 'Levin was the person who recommended you.'

Corva nodded.

'Do you know him?'

'No, but I had a manslaughter case at Fort Dix about a year ago, and Levin was on the court-martial board. He asked me a lot of questions.'

'Good questions?'

'Too good.'

'You lost?'

'Well ... the accused was found guilty.'

'Is that the same as you losing?'

'I guess so.' Corva yawned.

Tyson inquired, 'Do you win any?'

Corva was leafing through his notebook. 'What's that?'

'Do you *win* any?'

'Oh ...' He seemed to be searching his memory. 'A few.' He leaned towards Tyson. 'How many did *you* win? I mean when you were defence counsel at special courts-martial.'

Tyson said impatiently, 'That's not relevant. I wasn't a lawyer. And nearly everyone I defended was patently guilty.'

'Right. Or they wouldn't have been there.'

'That's right,' said Tyson.

Corva added, 'The Army rarely convenes a court-martial unless they know the accused is guilty. If there's any doubt, they usually dismiss the charge, or they offer the accused nonjudicial punishment and see if he bites. Occasionally they'll order further investigation. But they don't enter a court-martial room with their fingers crossed the way a civilian DA does.' He looked at Tyson and smiled. 'So how many did you win when you were the *prosecution*? All?'

'Most of them pleaded guilty. The rest were pretty much open and shut. I mean like AWOLs. Either you are there when you're supposed to be or you are not. But this is not a special court-martial. This is a general court-martial, involving a capital crime, a very complex case. So I don't see any analogy.'

'But there is a similarity. Most of the people I defend are as patently guilty as an AWOL soldier. By the time they call me they've fired their free Army attorney, and they are desperate. In this rather limited field I am known as Saint Jude, patron saint of hopeless causes.'

'Now you tell me.'

Corva smiled. 'Be of good cheer, Benjamin. I'm due for a miracle.'

'Me too.' Tyson stood and went to the window. He stared out over the small post, watching the activity of military life below. 'Sometimes I remember the faces of the accused men who were marched into a court-martial room. I don't like to see that look on men's faces. It's demoralizing to me to see men who are so frightened. It's embarrassing to everyone in the courtroom. I don't want to have that look on my face, Vince.'

Corva said, 'You're allowed to *be* frightened. But you will not *look* frightened. Not in front of a court-martial board. You know that.'

'I know it. I won't even flinch when they hand me twenty to life.'

'Twenty to life? Christ, *I'll* flinch.'

Tyson turned from the window and stared at Corva.

Corva said, 'By the way, when we get in there feel free to speak your mind. You say you have a good relationship with Levin, so you don't have to let me do all the talking. Also he doesn't represent the prosecution. He's just your immediate commander, and he's only doing his job.'

'What's his job today, Vincent?'

'Being a prick.'

The door opened, and Captain Hodges stuck his head in. Tyson said to Corva, 'Speaking of which.'

Corva laughed.

Hodges looked both annoyed and confused. He cleared his throat. 'The colonel will see you now.'

Corva stood and led the way into Levin's office. Corva stepped aside to the right, Hodges to the left. Tyson went straight to the desk, saluted, and said, 'Lieutenant Tyson reports, sir.'

Levin returned the salute, then stood to shake hands with Vincent Corva and introduced Corva to Captain Hodges, who also shook hands with Corva. Colonel Levin sat, Corva sat in the chair indicated by Hodges, and Hodges sat. Tyson remained standing at attention. He was sure every facet of protocol was satisfied, but somehow he felt left out. He thought he should remind them that he was the reason they were all there.

Colonel Levin said, 'Have a seat, Lieutenant.'

Tyson sat in the only empty chair, between Corva and Hodges.

Levin let a moment go by before saying, 'I have here a copy of Major Harper's preliminary investigation report, conducted under Article 31 of the Uniform Code of Military Justice.' He opened a legal-sized file folder on his desk and addressed Tyson. 'I've asked Captain Hodges to be present as a witness, owing to the fact that you have legal counsel present.'

Tyson nodded.

Hodges said, 'Please respond verbally, Lieutenant.'

Tyson said, 'Yes, sir.'

Levin looked down at the folder. 'I have been instructed, as your commanding officer, to make you aware of certain aspects of the investigation.'

Corva said, 'May I have a copy of the preliminary investigator's report, Colonel?'

'No, you may not. You and I know, Mr Corva, that unlike an Article 32 investigation report, this is an internal communication. This report is between Major Harper and General George Peters, post commander of Fort Dix, who has general court-martial convening authority in this case. However, I have been instructed by General Peters, on advice of his Staff Judge Advocate, to read to the accused pertinent sections of this report.'

Corva said, 'May I request, Colonel, that you begin with the end? What is her conclusion?'

Captain Hodges stirred in his chair and made a sound that clearly indicated he did not like to have his colonel interrupted or otherwise annoyed. Under other circumstances Tyson might have enjoyed Hodges' frustration in dealing with a civilian.

411

Colonel Levin seemed to take Corva's suggestion well. He nodded. 'Of course. I don't mean to drag this out and cause Lieutenant Tyson any unnecessary anxiety.' He looked directly at Tyson and said, 'Major Harper did not recommend that the case be dismissed.'

Tyson nodded. He never expected that she would. Yet somewhere in the back of his mind he thought she might.

Corva said, 'Then we are to have an Article 32 investigation?'

Colonel Levin seemed not to hear. He drew a typed sheet of paper towards him. 'I'll read you certain parts of this as I've been instructed.' He cleared his throat. 'She states: "My preliminary investigation did not uncover any documentary evidence or physical evidence of a crime, nor was it likely to, considering the locale of the alleged crime and the length of time that has elapsed since the crime allegedly took place. Further investigation for this type of evidence is not likely to be fruitful. Therefore, I have considered only the statements of the witnesses in reaching my conclusion. The statements of Dr Steven Brandt and Mr Richard Farley, if taken at face value, clearly indicate that a violation of the Uniform Code of Military Justice took place at the time and location in question. Further, their statements indicate that this violation would come under Article 118, murder, for which there is no statute of limitations. Further, the government has established its jurisdiction over the suspect but has not established such jurisdiction over other possible suspects. Therefore, though there appears to be testimonial evidence that would incriminate other former members of the United States Army, this report is confined to the subject of Lieutenant Benjamin Tyson."'

Colonel Levin looked at Tyson briefly, then at Corva. He said to Corva, 'Any questions so far?'

'No, sir.'

Levin nodded and continued reading. '"The statements of Paul Sadowski and Anthony Scorello, on the other hand, are in almost direct contradiction to those of Brandt and Farley and refute the most damning points of those two statements. During extensive interviews with Lieutenant Tyson, as noted in some detail earlier, he made statements which were strikingly similar to those of Sadowski and Scorello. It should be further noted, however, that Lieutenant Tyson did not impeach the statements or character of either of the potential witnesses against him; he merely told a different version of the events in question. There is, though, some evidence based on various statements made by Paul Sadowski that Dr Brandt may harbour some hostility or bias towards the accused. This hostility or bias would have had its genesis during the time Lieutenant Tyson and Dr Brandt served together, as there is no evidence to suggest they saw or communicated with each other since the day Lieutenant Tyson was medically evacuated from the Republic of Vietnam."' Colonel Levin looked at Tyson, then at Corva. 'Okay so far?'

Corva turned to Tyson. 'Okay?'

Tyson shrugged. 'I guess. Am I supposed to add anything or question anything?'

'No,' said Corva. 'Just listen closely because we're not entitled to see this, only to hear it, and that only as a courtesy.'

'And,' interjected Hodges, 'in the interests of justice.'

Corva turned to Hodges and smiled. 'Thank you, Captain. We know that.'

Hodges' face reddened.

Levin cleared his throat. 'Okay. Major Harper further states: "This preliminary investigation has noted the existence of five additional witnesses to this incident: Daniel Kelly, Hernando Beltran, Lee Walker, Louis Kalane, and Michael DeTonq. The status of these witnesses is covered in a separate section of this report."' Levin looked at Corva. 'They have not been located.'

Corva nodded.

Levin continued reading: '"There is in addition to these

eyewitnesses, the author Andrew Picard, whose role in this matter is well known. Mr Picard's statements to me on the telephone confirm that any testimony he would offer would be no more than hearsay. Mr Picard, however, is the link to the last known and possible eyewitness, Sister Teresa. This matter is also covered in a separate section."' Levin flipped a page and read, '"In conclusion I believe that the evidence I have uncovered to date indicates that there is probable cause to believe that a violation of the Uniform Code of Military Justice occurred. Therefore, I recommend that this matter be referred to further investigation under Article 32 of the Code."' Levin looked up from the report.

No one spoke. Finally Corva said, 'And has General Peters acted on that recommendation?'

Levin took a cigar from his drawer and peeled off the cedar wrapper. Tyson noted irrelevantly that Levin had switched to a better brand. Levin said, 'General Peters, on receipt of this report, forwarded it to his Staff Judge Advocate who in turn made his recommendation to General Peters regarding the disposition of this case. The Staff Judge Advocate concurred with Major Harper that an Article 32 investigation be initiated. General Peters in turn concurred with his SJA.'

Corva observed, 'That's a lot of concurrence. I hope there is no command influence present in those concurrences.'

Levin replied, 'Command influence would be illegal, Mr Corva. This matter is being judged wholly on its legal merits.'

'Really? I wonder if the decision not to dismiss this rather weak case is not a result of some sort of subtle command influence or the perception of same. In other words, to name titles, if not names: the Judge Advocate General, the Attorney General, the secretaries of the Army and of Defense, and the President of the United States. If I were General Peters, I'd hear those drums beating cadence, and I'd damned sure march to that beat.'

Levin finally lit his cigar and drew on it until the tip glowed red. He said, 'That is a serious allegation. And I'm not the one to hear it.'

'No,' said Corva, 'but until I put it in writing and send it off to everyone I can think of, would you be kind enough to pass on my thoughts to General Peters?'

'If you wish.' Levin handed Tyson a sheet of paper. 'These are the orders convening the Article 32 hearing. The date, as you can see, is 9 September, which gives you sufficient time to locate any additional witnesses for the defence as may exist. The place is here, at Fort Hamilton. Specifically the Stonewall Jackson room on the second level of the Officers' Club. The hearing will be closed to the media and the public. Any questions?'

Tyson glanced at the orders. He replied, 'No, sir.' He handed the paper to Corva.

Corva examined the convening orders with some care before putting them in his briefcase. He addressed Colonel Levin. 'I'd like you to pass on another comment to General Peters and his Staff Judge Advocate. I wish to remind them that the accused has a specific right under the UCMJ to request of the Army their assistance on his behalf. Therefore, if we are to have a formal investigation and hearing, I want the Army, at the Army's expense, to continue their efforts to locate missing witnesses and to advise the accused of the steps taken to accomplish that.'

Colonel Levin nodded. 'I will pass on your reminder to the convening authorities.' Levin glanced at Captain Hodges, then made eye contact with Corva and said, 'But my advice to Lieutenant Tyson and to you is that you should expend some effort yourselves in locating these witnesses if you believe they are going to be witnesses for the defence.'

Corva replied, 'There is no doubt in my mind that they are, Colonel. And in the interests of justice I'm certain the government will use its considerable resources to assist me in finding them and that the government will do so with the same zeal they've shown thus far in pursuing this case. And if they don't, I am going to take appropriate steps to have this case dismissed. I'll put that in writing, and you can forward it to General Peters.'

Levin drew on his cigar. 'Anything further, Mr Corva?'

'No, Colonel.'

The intercom buzzed, and Levin picked it up. He listened, then said to Captain Hodges, 'Sergeant Wolton needs some orders signed. We'll take a five-minute break here.'

Hodges stood and left the office.

Colonel Levin leaned across his desk and looked at Tyson. 'Real crock of shit, eh, Tyson?'

Tyson was momentarily taken aback by the sudden shift in tone and manner. He replied, 'Yes, sir. Real crock.'

Levin glared at Corva. He said gruffly, 'Save the legal razzle-dazzle for the hearing. You're giving me a headache.'

Corva smiled. 'You gave me a headache at Fort Dix.'

Levin looked again at Tyson. 'Smoke if you like.'

Tyson shook his head. The thought occurred to him that Levin had contrived to send Hodges out of the room.

Levin said to Tyson, 'You understand that, as your commanding officer, this is my job.'

Tyson replied, 'Of course. That's what I used to say to the men I was screwing.'

Corva laughed.

Levin glowered at Tyson, then he smiled wryly. He said, 'Just keep remembering that for the rest of this session.'

'Yes, sir.'

Corva said, 'Colonel, as Lieutenant Tyson's commanding officer, I would like you to offer testimony as to his character if this ever gets to the sentencing stage.'

Levin chewed ruminatively on his cigar. He finally replied, 'I hope this doesn't get that far. But if it does I don't know if my brief association with Lieutenant Tyson would count for much.'

'I think it would help for a court-martial board to hear that Lieutenant Tyson performed his duty here satisfactorily. Yes or no, Colonel?'

416

Colonel Levin put his cigar in the ashtray. He looked at Corva. 'You may have noticed that I'm a little old to be a lieutenant colonel. You may also have noticed that Fort Hamilton is not the Pentagon or NATO headquarters. The long and the short of it is that I've been passed over once for promotion to full colonel, and I've got shit duty-to boot. Be that as it may, *I* like Hamilton, even if the Army considers it the waiting room to oblivion. I'm up for full bird again, and there's talk I will be post commander when Colonel Hill leaves in October.'

Levin looked at Corva closely. 'Maybe you can understand, Mr Corva. My father was a maintenance man here. And this will be my last duty station, seeing I've got nearly thirty years in. From here I'll go home, back to Brighton Beach, down the Shore Parkway a bit. And I'll have come full circle. And once in a while I'll return here and bring my wife to dinner at the club and appear at a few functions as the former post commander and do whatever old soldiers do who retire around Army installations. And it will have been a good life.' He looked at Tyson.

Corva said, 'Does that mean the answer is no?'

Levin turned back to him. 'No. It doesn't. The answer is actually yes. I'd be happy to testify as to Lieutenant Tyson's good character. I just wanted you to appreciate it.'

Corva smiled.

Tyson said, 'Thank you, Colonel.'

Levin grunted. No one spoke for the next few minutes. The door opened, and Captain Hodges took his seat without a word.

Levin shuffled some papers on his desk. 'All right ...' He drew a long wheezy breath. 'All right ...' He turned to Tyson and cleared his throat. 'Lieutenant Benjamin Tyson, I have been instructed to read to you the charges that have been preferred against you.' Levin drew a long form from the folder, held it up so it hid his face, and read: 'Lieutenant Benjamin J. Tyson, you are charged as follows: Violation of the Uniform Code of Military Justice, Article 118, murder. Specification One: In that Benjamin J. Tyson, First Lieutenant, United States Army, presently assigned to the adjutant at Fort Hamilton, Brooklyn, New York, then a member of Alpha Company, Fifth Battalion, Seventh Cavalry, of the First Air Cavalry Division, did, in or about the city of Hue, in the province of Thua Thien, in the former Republic of Vietnam, in or about the vicinity of Hôpital Miséricorde, on or about 15 February 1968 engage in acts which were inherently dangerous to others and evinced a wanton disregard of human life, causing the murder of an unknown number, not less than ninety, Oriental human beings, males and females, of various ages, whose names are unknown, patients and staff of said hospital, by means of shooting them or causing them to be shot, or ordering them to be shot, with rifle and/or pistol fire, or causing their deaths with incendiary hand grenades, and/or by other lethal means and devices not yet known.'

Levin looked over the charge sheet, and his eyes passed briefly over Tyson's face. Tyson sat with his chin in his hand, his eyes focused on the wall behind Levin, his mind on some distant time and place. The room was absolutely still.

Levin cleared his throat again and continued, 'Specification Two: In that Benjamin J. Tyson did, in or about the city of Hue, in the province of Thua Thien, in the former Republic of Vietnam, in or about the vicinity of Hôpital Miséricorde, on or about 15 February 1968 engage in acts which were inherently dangerous to others and evinced a wanton disregard of human life, causing the murder of approximately fourteen Caucasian human beings, male and female, in the manner stated in Specification One, whose names are as follows: Jean Monteau, male, physician, French national, age forty-six; Evan Dougal, male, physician, Australian national, age thirty-four; Bernhard Rueger, male, physician, German national, age twenty-nine; Marie Broi, female, nurse, French national, age twenty-five; Sister Monique

(Yvette Dulane), female, nurse/nun, French national, age twenty-one; Sister Aimee (Henriette La Blanc), female, nurse/nun, French national, age twenty-one; Sister Noelle (Rèine Mauroy), female, nurse/nun, Belgian national, age twenty-three; Pierre Galante, male, nurse, French national, age thirty; Henri Taine, male, nurse, French national, age thirty-one; Maarten Lubbers, male, laboratory technician, Dutch national, age twenty-three; Brother Donatus (full name unknown), male, staff assistant, nationality unknown, age forty-one; Sister Juliette (full name unknown), female, nurse/nun, nationality unknown, age fifty-three; Susanne Dougal, female (wife of Evan Dougal), Australian national, age thirty-five; Linda Dougal, female (daughter of Evan and Susanne Dougal), Australian national, age fifteen.'

Colonel Levin stared at the charge sheet for a few more seconds, then put it down. He relit his cigar and puffed on it.

Tyson could hear the typewriters in the outer office. Through the open window came the sound of the Twenty-sixth U.S. Army Band practising on the drill field. They were playing 'Sweet Georgia Brown.'

Levin drew a copy of the charge sheet from his folder and handed it directly to Tyson. Tyson, without looking at it, gave it to Corva, who dropped it into his open briefcase without a glance.

Levin handed Corva several stapled sheets of paper. 'These are the names and brief biographies of the alleged Caucasian victims specified in the charge sheet. They were supplied to Major Harper by the Catholic Relief Agency in Paris and represent that agency's missing personnel – plus two dependent family members – who were assigned to duty at Miséricorde Hospital at the time of the alleged incident.' Levin said to Corva, who was flipping through the pages, 'Questions, Mr Corva?'

'Dozens of them, Colonel, but unfortunately you could not answer any of them.'

'No, I probably couldn't.' Levin ground out his cigar.

Corva said, 'Will that be all, Colonel?'

Hodges answered, 'The colonel will let you know when that is all.'

Corva smiled and leaned towards Hodges. He said in an amiable tone of voice, 'How would you like to spend the rest of the day in the hospital?'

Hodges jumped to his feet. 'How dare you threaten—'

Corva stood. 'That was no threat. That—'

Levin bellowed, 'At ease! Sit down, Captain!' He turned to Corva. 'Please take your seat, Mr Corva.'

Hodges and Corva sat. Tyson stared out the window in pointed disinterest. The Army band had struck up George M. Cohan's 'Over There,' and Tyson tapped his foot to the lively tune.

Levin said to Hodges, 'Captain, you will address Mr Corva with the courtesy which an officer in the United States Army extends to all civilians. This is not Prussia, and you are not in the Prussian Army. Loosen up, man.'

Hodges' face had gone from red to livid. He snapped, 'Yes, sir!'

Tyson smiled absently as his foot beat faster to the quickening cadence of the song.

Levin said to Corva, 'I'll let your remark pass seeing it was provoked.' He said to Tyson, 'Lieutenant, if you're going to break into a tap dance, could you wait until you're clear of this building?'

Tyson stopped tapping. 'Yes, sir.'

Levin picked up a piece of paper and read it to himself with some concentration as though he were trying to make sense of it. Finally he put down the paper and turned to Tyson. 'Lieutenant Tyson, I have been instructed by Colonel Hill, the post commander, to place you in arrest.'

Tyson made brief eye contact with Corva, then stared at Levin.

Levin looked away. He continued, 'You may know from your prior service that military arrest is a moral and legal

420

restraint not a physical restraint. However, it is a greater restraint of freedom of movement than the restriction which you are now under. Please don't interrupt, Mr Corva. Just listen. Lieutenant Tyson, the conditions of your arrest are as follows: You are not required to perform your full military duties, and in fact your duties at the museum are herewith terminated, and your name has been removed from all post duty rosters. You will not leave this post without permission from me or an officer designated by me to grant such permission. You will report in to this office at nine hundred hours each day, to me or to Captain Hodges or to the weekend duty officer. You will sign in, in a book provided for that purpose, every three hours until twenty-one hundred hours. You will be in your quarters after that time and remain there until you report in the following day at nine hundred hours. You will not bear arms. You will confine your post activities to the PX, the commissary, the Officers' Club, your quarters, and the gymnasium if you wish to use it. The provost marshal has been instructed to monitor the period when you are restricted to quarters.' Levin handed Tyson a sheet of paper. 'This is the arrest order. Do you have any questions?'

Tyson shook his head, which normally would have provoked Hodges into telling him to answer the colonel verbally. But Hodges seemed permanently rebuked, albeit content with the ultimate outcome of this session.

Corva said, 'I intend to protest this arrest to Colonel Hill. It is onerous, unnecessary, and it is most irregular to treat an officer in this manner. Also it sucks.'

Levin nodded as though in agreement. He said, however, 'You have no legal remedies concerning an arrest order. But if you want a meeting with the post commander, I can arrange that.'

Corva stood. 'Is *that* all?' He glared at Hodges.

Levin nodded. 'That's all *I've* got to say. How about you or your client?'

Corva said, 'My client requests permission to leave the post at eighteen hundred hours for the purpose of getting drunk with me.'

Levin replied, 'Permission granted.' He said to Tyson, 'You will report here to me at nine hundred hours tomorrow.'

'Yes, sir.'

Levin stood, followed by Tyson and Captain Hodges. Levin looked at Tyson, then with a barely perceptible shrug said, 'That will be all, Lieutenant.'

Tyson saluted, did an about-face, and walked smartly out of the office.

34

Ben Tyson passed through the corridor and down the stairs, vaguely aware of where he was going, and less aware of the footsteps following him.

Corva caught up with him. Tyson lit a cigarette as he left the headquarters building. He said to Corva, 'Did you know that was going to happen?'

'Sort of.'

'Why didn't you tell me?'

'You knew, Ben. Let's stop pretending this is some sort of silly bureaucratic screwup. These people are serious. They are charging you with *murder*. You knew that from the first day your friend handed you Picard's book.'

Tyson drew on his cigarette. He replied, 'I knew long before then.' Tyson said, 'Well, Vince, why didn't we beat the shit out of them?'

Corva smiled. 'You're sounding like a hot-headed dago now.'

They walked along Lee Avenue, past the antique cannon display, and approached the main gate.

Corva said, 'Where are you going? You can't leave post until eighteen hundred hours.'

'Fuck 'em. I don't even know what time that is.' He passed through the pedestrian walk of the gates, absently returned the MP's salute, and turned left, under the elevated bridge ramp towards the Shore Parkway.

Corva said, 'That's six o'clock. Come on. Let's go back. I am responsible for you.'

'No one is responsible for me but me. They can take their arrest order, roll it up, put a light coat of oil on it, and shove it up their ass. And if you don't want to be responsible, leave.'

Corva drew a deep breath but said nothing. They made their way through a small park down to the shore. Tyson walked east along the water's edge.

Corva followed a few feet behind. He said, 'People who are accused of a heinous crime often delude themselves into thinking they didn't do it. So when the law starts to inconvenience them, they get outraged. Listen to me, Ben. I haven't asked you for many details of what happened, but *you* know, *I* know, and the *Army* knows that a terrible slaughter of innocents took place at that hospital. You heard the roll call of the dead, as the prosecutor will undoubtedly say. Not to mention "not less than ninety Oriental human beings."'

'I liked that. The way they neatly divided the white folk from the Oriental folk.'

'They had the Caucasians' names, that's why they did that, not because of any racial bias, or—'

'Oh, bullshit. Would I be here now, twenty years later, if it was just a village of a couple hundred gooks? Slopes? Dinks? Zipperheads? Slants? What else did we call them, Vince? What did *you* call them? Anything but Oriental human beings. But I fucked up good. I zapped fourteen real people.'

'Okay, you don't have to tell me all that. I know what we did and how we behaved. Christ, if I could go back ...'

'Yeah.'

423

Corva kept up with Tyson's brisk pace. Corva said, 'The point is that you, I, and the Army also know that this slaughter was perpetrated by men directly under your command. Furthermore, there is probable cause to suspect that you were present and witnessed all or part of that slaughter. And they're going so far as to suggest you may have even pulled the trigger yourself a few times.'

'I didn't.' Tyson stopped and stared out over the water. Small ripples ran up to the pebbly beach. He drew in a deep breath of salt air. 'I did not,' he repeated.

Corva came up beside him. 'Who cares? Not me. You know and I know that the Army does not care if you shot anyone or not. They do not care why it happened or if you tried to stop it or if your troops mutinied and held you at gunpoint or if you just stepped out a minute to take a piss and missed the whole thing. They only care that you did not report that massacre which was your legal duty, not to mention, if you will, your Christian duty. For reasons known only to yourself you did not wish to see those murderers brought to justice. The irony here is that the men under your command most probably committed a crime of passion. Perhaps they were suffering from battle fatigue, which the Army recognizes under Article 118 as extenuating circumstances for murder. And undoubtedly your men were suffering from a fatal sickness of the soul. Fatal, that is, to others. But you, on the other hand, committed a crime of dispassion each and every day you did not report what you witnessed. You've had nearly two decades to set things right, Ben, and you did not. So now the Army is going to set things right not only for them but for you. As for the murderers, they have many defences, but they don't even need them in a court of law. The peculiarities of this imperfect system pretty much assure they won't be called to account. Their crime was of the moment, a moment of madness. Your crime is an ongoing one. Army justice may not be perfect, but it is instinctive, unclouded by civilian hocus-pocus and often uncannily just. You know that. And

424

you also know and I know and the Army knows you are guilty. The charge sheet may not precisely reflect your role in that massacre. But I assure you that after all the witnesses testify and lie, that court-martial board, made up of men like Colonel Levin, men who as officers and leaders see and evaluate the human condition daily, will arrive at the truth. The verdict is a foregone conclusion. You might as well accept that. The only thing I can guarantee you is that when you walk out of that courtroom, even if you are in handcuffs and under armed guard, you will be free. You understand what I mean by free?'

'Yes.'

'Good. So am I fired?'

'No. But I'd like to beat the shit out of you.'

'Later. Do you want to get drunk tonight?'

Tyson nodded distractedly. He said, 'Why don't we plead guilty?'

'Another quirk of military law. You are not allowed to enter a plea of guilty to a murder charge.'

'Right. I remember that. Good rule.'

'So to recapitulate, I'm not fired, and you want to get drunk with me tonight?'

'Right. Anything to get off this post. Even drinking with you.'

'Fine. Let's walk back before the post Gestapo realizes you're missing.'

They turned back towards the bridge and began walking slowly. Corva said, 'When we are both very drunk we are going to swap peace stories. R and R stories. I have to tell you about this whorehouse located in an old French villa outside of Tay Nihn, run by a very crazy half-breed madam.'

Tyson smiled. 'Sounds like the same one we had outside of Quang Tri. Must have been a chain.'

They passed under the bridge. The traffic overhead made a constant low humming noise, and seagulls circled beneath the huge superstructure. Tyson said, 'I was a damned good combat leader. But by the time I reached the hospital, I was a burnout case. I stopped doing my job. I really didn't give a shit anymore. I didn't even care if I lived or died.'

Corva said, 'Then eventually you would have died. But you were lucky and got wounded first. In the Strawberry Patch. And Brandt tended your wound. War is full of ironies.'

'So I've heard.'

They were back on 101st Street now, a commercial street of two-and three-storey brick buildings. Tyson looked at the fort's gates beneath the bridge. 'It's like jail.'

'No. Jail is like jail.'

'I always thought,' said Tyson, 'that if lawyers take a third of what they win for you in a civil case, they should do a third of the time their clients get in a criminal case.'

'They would be permanently in jail,' Corva pointed out.

Tyson stopped on the sidewalk outside the gate. 'You took the subway here?'

'Right. Didn't want to run up your bill with a taxi. I'll walk to the station from here.'

Tyson nodded.

Corva said, 'I'm ready to talk to the witnesses for the defence. Sadowski and Scorello. I'm going to go at Army expense. You are authorized to come along. Sadowski lives in Chicago. Scorello lives in a suburb of San Francisco. Get you off post for a few days. Nice reunion.'

Tyson shook his head. 'I don't want to see them.'

'Why not?'

'They don't want to see me. We don't want to see one another.'

'Okay. I understand. It's not important. Do you want to see Brandt and Farley? You have the right to be present at a cross-examination, to confront them before a hearing or court-martial.'

'Can we beat the shit out of them?'

'You bet.'

Tyson smiled. 'You're all talk, Corva.' He lit a cigarette. 'I

426

considered killing Brandt.'

'Did you? That would put a quick end to this business. That's the Nam solution to an annoyance. Blow it away.'

'But now I'm under tight scrutiny. Couldn't get away with it.'

Corva smiled slowly. 'WASPs don't know anything about these things. You put out a contract. I'll take care of it if you want.'

'Are you serious?'

'Are you?'

Tyson shook his head. 'No.'

'Well, don't talk about it if you're not. Do you want to see him? And Farley?'

'Just Brandt. Sometime before the court-martial.'

'Good. Did you ever fuck what's-her-name? Harper?'

Tyson looked at him quickly. 'No.'

'Too bad.' Corva looked at his watch.

Tyson threw down his cigarette. 'By the way, I read *Rashomon*.'

'Did you learn anything?'

'Is this a test? Well, the answer is that an act – killing – can be legal or illegal, can be interpreted as battle, self-defence, murder, and so forth. And the odd thing is that not even the *victim* is always sure of his absolute innocence in the act. Such was the case of the samurai in *Rashomon*. Similarly, as Dr Jean Monteau lay dying on the floor of Miséricorde Hospital, the thought must have crossed his mind that he contributed to his own death.' Tyson stared at Corva.

Corva said, 'And the perpetrators?'

'Yes, that's odder still. A man engaged in intercourse or killing is not always certain even in his own mind if he is making love or committing rape, waging war or committing murder.'

Corva nodded again. 'That's what juries are for.' He added, 'Your case is a bit simpler than *Rashomon*, however, because there are no surviving witnesses to give their impression of

427

what they thought happened to them. And unlike *Rashomon*, I doubt if the ghosts of any of the victims will be called to testify at the trial.' Corva added, 'However, there is that one surviving witness. Did she see much?'

'Enough.'

Corva thought a moment before speaking. 'I said before that the verdict was a foregone conclusion.'

'Right. That's what a defendant likes to hear from his attorney.'

'Well, I was trying to set you up for the worst scenario. That's an old lawyer's trick. The real situation is more in the balance. What you have here is a bunch of tainted soldiers giving self-serving testimony. It's quite possible a court-martial board will be so confused and frustrated that they will decide the government hasn't proven its case beyond a reasonable doubt. Therefore, they'll have no choice but to return a verdict of not guilty though they know you are. But let me tell you something. It's the nun that concerns me. If she appears out of the blue and takes the stand, they will accept her testimony as gospel. And I'm assuming that testimony will be very damning for you.'

'Do you want to know what she'll say?'

'Not particularly. If they find her, you can give me a few details. If they don't find her, it doesn't matter. Point is, nuns don't lie. At least that is the conventional wisdom in trial law. And defence counsels don't try to browbeat or attack the testimony of nuns, priests, rabbis, or ministers, except at their own peril.'

Tyson said, 'I wonder why she hasn't been found or hasn't come forward?'

Corva rubbed his chin reflectively. 'If I were paranoid, I'd say the government already knows the whereabouts of not only Sister Teresa, but also of Hernando Beltran, Lee Walker, and Louis Kalane. Kelly and DeTonq are another matter. Your former heroes are lying low on advice of counsel. They may never have to be called. But if they are, they will probably be your witnesses. Correct?'

'Probably.'

'Because you all made a blood oath to lie. You all gave your word of honour that you would stand by one another. Correct?'

'Very astute, Vince.'

'Oh, astute, my ass. Even a JAG lawyer could figure that out. What did Harper say in her report? Lieutenant Tyson made statements which were strikingly similar to those of Sadowski and Scorello. What do you think she was saying? You concocted a story nearly twenty years ago, rehearsed it, until finally you almost believed it. Christ, even if the government presented me with three or five more witnesses for the defence, I doubt if I'd march them all up to the stand to say the exact same thing. But no one can accuse *me* of coaching them. *You* coached them, Ben. Twenty years ago. You were their leader, you had the imagination to turn a massacre into an heroic epic. That's how you saved your life afterwards.'

Tyson's eyes met Corva's. Tyson said, 'Don't be humble, Vince. You *are* astute.'

'You're right,' agreed Corva. 'Point is, all war stories are bullshit. Did I tell you that?'

'You know you did.'

'Don't forget it. See you tonight. Meet me at my office.'

Tyson turned towards the fort. Every time he came away from a meeting with Corva, he felt just a bit more frightened yet paradoxically more at peace with himself. Freedom was just down the road, though it looked suspiciously like the walls of Leavenworth from here. He reentered the post without returning the MP's salute.

35

Benjamin Tyson stepped off the train at Garden City Station. It was one of those hot, dry August afternoons when everything seemed to move in slow motion, and there was an odd quietness in the still air. Tyson loosened his tie and slung his sport coat over his shoulder. He walked down from the platform and headed toward the taxi stand.

Three black Cadillacs sat empty in their spaces. Three black drivers sat under the shade of the station house overhang, reading newspapers and drinking canned soda. Tyson approached, and one of the men stood and smiled widely. 'Mr Tyson. You get off that train?'

'Hello, Mason. Just in for a few hours. Can you drive me around?'

'Sure can.'

Tyson fell in step beside Mason, a heavyset man in late middle age, dressed in black chauffeur livery. 'Hot today,' observed Tyson.

'Sure is. Least it's dry.' Mason opened the rear door of his Cadillac, and Tyson entered. Mason got in and started the engine. 'Get that AC workin'.'

'How have you been?' inquired Tyson.

'Fine, sir. Fine. How you been keepin' yourself?'

'Not bad.'

'You lookin' good. Gettin' your exercise?'

Tyson smiled. 'Doing five miles a day now.'

'That's real good. When you gonna stop smokin'?'

'New Year's Day.'

Mason laughed. 'Where we headin'?'

'My house first.'

Mason put on his billed cap and pulled out of the small

parking field. He drove slowly through the tree-shaded residential streets lined with imposing homes. The town seemed deserted. Tyson inquired, 'Had a neutron bomb attack while I was gone?'

Mason laughed again. 'August. Folks pulled out. I get a few runs a day. Airports. Couple out east. Slow.'

'Why don't you take the month off?'

'The bills don't stop in August.'

'That's true.' Tyson said, 'How is Mrs Williams?'

'Gettin' old. Just like me. Can't get up those stairs no more. I been lookin' at a place with an elevator. Air-conditionin' too.'

Tyson considered inviting the Williamses to house-sit at his place for the next few months. But his experiences in social engineering were limited, and he didn't know if it was a good idea. He suspected that Mason and his wife would rather be home, wherever that was. Tyson looked around the immaculate car interior. He said, 'You remember that Lincoln you had?'

'Sure do. Sixty-four. Block and a half long, wide as my mama-in-law's butt. They getting smaller. Can't find nothin' big enough no more. What those turkeys in Detroit thinkin' about?'

'The world's getting smaller and tighter, Mason. Just do me a favour and don't buy a Japanese car.'

'Hell no! You seen them things? I got a 'frigerator bigger than them.'

They talked cars for the next few minutes. Mason pulled up to the kerb in front of Tyson's house.

Tyson said, 'Come on in.' He opened his own door and stood on the sidewalk, staring at his house. The gardener had kept up with it, and no doubt the maid had too. The pest control men did their scheduled spraying, and the seven-zone sprinkler system was on timer, as were all the outside lights. The burglar and fire alarms were hooked up to central station monitoring. The house, in effect, was on automatic pilot. It

431

didn't need the Tysons. Tyson often envisioned a perfect upper-middle-class suburb, devoid of redundant residents, tended to by machines and service people.

He walked up the brick path, deactivated the alarm with a key, and stepped inside, followed by Mason.

The house smelled unfamiliar, not like his house. There was an odd mixture of odours, dominated by the smells of various cleaning products. The maid, Piedad, probably thought it was amusing to clean an empty house every week. Anglos were *loco*.

Tyson hung his sports coat on the clothes tree and went to the parsons table in the foyer where the mail was stacked. He leafed through it. Phil Sloan had a key and took care of small details such as sorting the mail and sending the important items to Tyson at Fort Hamilton. There was a stack of junk mail, a bundle of letters that looked like fan mail, and some bills that Sloan hadn't got around to forwarding. There were also a few parcels on the floor that Sloan had probably picked up from the post office. Tyson lifted one of them, a shoebox-sized package marked 'Fragile.' He opened it with his pocket knife, fished around in the Styrofoam packing, and drew out a particularly hideous Hummel of a boy and girl that looked as though it had been designed by Norman Rockwell for Hermann Goering. He placed it on the table and read the enclosed card: *Dearest Baby Brother, I've treasured this since Aunt Millie gave it to me five years ago, but remembering how much you always admired it, I'm thrilled to send it to you in your hour of need. Keep your nose up. Love to Marcy and David. Love Laurie.*

Tyson smiled as he placed the card on the table. He dug deeper into the packing foam and extracted his platoon logbook, which he slipped into his hip pocket.

Tyson turned to Mason. 'Can you give me a hand with something in the basement?'

'Sure can.'

Tyson went down the basement stairs to the storage room

and knelt in front of an old black steamer trunk. The padlock was still shut, but it was obvious by the disturbed dust in the area that someone had been there. *Bastards.* They'd got through the burglar alarm and the supposedly unpickable door locks. And they'd undoubtedly been through the entire house, every drawer, every closet, his desk, photo albums, diaries, chequebooks, address books, investment portfolios – every nook and cranny. They had penetrated into the very core of his privacy and had probably catalogued, photographed, and photocopied everything. 'Bastards!'

'Sir?'

'Nothing.' He was fairly certain they were opening his mail, too. But the heavily taped parcel from his sister had shown no sign of tampering. He felt somewhat good about beating them at their own asinine cloak-and-dagger game. Tyson said to Mason, 'Let's get this trunk upstairs.'

They each took a handle and carried the trunk into the living room and set it before the fireplace. He took a box of firestarter candles from the log bin and threw it onto the grate, lighting the entire box with a match.

Mason looked around the living room. 'Some castle you got here, Mr Tyson.'

'Yes, it is.' He stood and went to the kitchen, coming back with two frosted mugs filled with beer. He passed one to Mason. Tyson raised his mug. 'To liberty and justice for me.'

'Amen.' They touched glasses.

Tyson finished half the beer in one swallow. He took a key from his wallet, knelt, and opened the trunk.

On the left-hand side of the divided trunk were neatly folded jungle fatigues and khakis, plus a pair of canvas jungle boots, a bush hat, and a powder blue infantry fourragère. On the right was a photo album, maps, R and R brochures, and bundled letters from Hope Lowell, the girl he'd been seeing before he shipped out. There was also a metal ammunition box that held an Army compass, Army watch, Army flashlight, and other purloined government issues.

It didn't appear that anything had been disturbed, but when he looked through the photo album, he saw a few photos missing. Also missing were his orders for the Vietnamese Cross of Gallantry awarded for actions on 15 February 1968. Missing, too, was his logbook, but he'd lifted that himself.

Tyson turned to Mason and saw he was eyeing the contents of the trunk. Tyson said, 'I don't know why men keep junk like this.'

Mason said, 'I had a brother in Korea. Durin' that war they was havin' there. Only thing he came home with was underwear. Stole three duffle bags of underwear.'

'Sounds like a practical man,' observed Tyson. He took a tied bundle of letters. 'Well ...' He hesitated, then threw it on the blazing mass of wax and watched as the flames licked around the edges. Item by item, beginning with the most combustible, he fed the fire until all that remained were the metal items, the boots, and the photo album. He picked up the boots and crumpled the dried mud in his fingers. 'Southeast Asia. Instant Nam; just add water.' What a peculiar slime it was, he thought. Three thousand years of intense recycling: rice, dung, blood, rice, ash, blood, rice, dung. And so on. He dropped the boots back into the trunk, then leafed through the photo album. He extracted a single picture, a snapshot of him and Teresa standing in front of the Hue cathedral. There had been two more, but they were gone. He slipped the picture into his breast pocket and threw the entire album into the fire.

Sweat ran down his face, and the smell of mustiness and ash clung to his nostrils. He closed the trunk, locked it, and gave Mason the key. 'You can have the trunk if you want. The flashlight and the other odds and ends too. I'd like you to throw the boots and the rest in the garbage.'

'Yes, sir.' Mason put his beer carefully on the coffee table. He stared at Tyson. 'You feelin' better, or you feelin' worse?'

'I'm not feeling.'

Mason nodded.

'Can you take the trunk by yourself? I have a few more things to do.'

'Yes, sir.' Mason hefted the nearly empty trunk onto his shoulder.

Tyson said, 'I'll meet you outside.' He reached into his hip pocket and drew out the small hide-bound logbook. He sat cross-legged on the floor and opened it, leafing through the pages with his sweaty fingers. A drop of perspiration rolled from his chin and fell upon a page already stained by sweat and water twenty years before. He came finally to the entry for 15 February and read the last lines: *Platoon on verge of mutiny. Overheard death threats. Filed false radio report re: hospital battle this A.M. Investigate. God—*

He tried to recall how he felt after the massacre but could only remember the fear for his own life. He tried to imagine that he gave serious thought regarding the best way to report his platoon to Captain Browder or to the battalion commander. But his mind wouldn't play the game. In reality he knew he had never once seriously considered swearing to murder charges against the men of his platoon.

Tyson continued to turn the pages, noticing that the days after 15 February were represented by only a line or two of insignificant details, mostly grid coordinates and radio frequencies. He came to 29 February, the day he was wounded, and noted the only entry for the day read: *Refugee assistance. Battle for Hue officially closed, as per radio message.*

The next entry was for 3 March. He read: *USS Repose; South China Sea. Logbook returned today by orderly. Did anyone read entry for 15 Feb? Who cares? Nice to be alive. My hands look very clean. Knee giving me pain. Darvon only. No morphine. Doctor said, 'You don't take morphine well.' He wouldn't take it well either if he'd been given a triple dose.*

Tyson lowered the logbook and let his mind go back to the Strawberry Patch.

435

Ben Tyson lay on his back in a drainage ditch, actually the local honey pit, the place where offal was collected for sale to vegetable farmers. Green tracer rounds streaked over the ditch, lustrous against the dull grey sky. He could hear the muted chatter of automatic weapons and the occasional explosion of small rounds: 50-mm rifle grenades, 60-mm mortars, an occasional rocket. It was a desultory firefight between two spent armies, like two exhausted boxers, moving leaden limbs, taking a few obligatory swings at one another. A month before, he'd have taken this very seriously. But today, 29 February, he would describe the incident as light contact. The only remarkable thing about the day's contact from his point of view was that he'd finally been hit.

As the shock wore off, the pain became more severe, until finally it dominated his entire consciousness. The stench around him didn't matter, neither did the bone-chilling water or the occasional thump of the enemy mortar trying to put a round into the ditch where dozens of civilians were leaping for cover.

Within a few minutes the ditch had become crowded with Vietnamese: old men, a few young men who were ex-ARVN amputees, women, and children who did not cry. Only the babies cried.

A pig had got into the ditch, and it sniffed around him, then licked the blood from his knee. Tyson kicked the pig in the snout with his other foot. About ten of his men had withdrawn toward the ditch, and they slid in, cursing the muck and the Vietnamese refugees. One of his men, Harold Simcox, spotted him and called, 'Medic! Lieutenant's hit!'

Of the two remaining company medics, it was Brandt who answered the call. Brandt worked quickly and professionally, first examining Tyson for wounds more serious than the obvious knee injury. He checked Tyson's pulse, felt his forehead, and looked at his eyes. It was only then that Brandt cut away the trouser leg and squeezed a tube of antibiotic ointment onto the open would. He folded the flaps of flesh and stringy pink ligaments over the exposed patella. Tyson picked up his head to watch, but Brandt reached out and casually pushed his head back into the muck. 'No peeking,' said Brandt as he always said when dressing a wound. 'Don't want you getting sick on me.'

Tyson said irritably, 'I've seen worse than this.'

'Not on yourself. Just relax.' Brandt applied a pressure bandage, tying the strings loosely. 'Pain?'

'Some.'

'Do you want morphine?'

Tyson wanted something for the pain, but he didn't want to become drowsy while there was still enemy contact. 'Maybe just some APCs.'

'Right.' Brandt put two of the aspirin compound tablets in Tyson's mouth and placed the remainder of the bottle in Tyson's breast pocket. He pulled out a red grease pencil and wrote on Tyson's forehead, *NM*. No morphine given. He said, 'They'll give it to you on the chopper.'

'Right.'

The gunfire had slackened, and Tyson noticed more of his men rolling into the ditch as they made their way across the exposed area where they'd been pinned down. Brandt found a helmet in the water and put it under Tyson's head.

'Thanks.'

Brandt stared at him, then lit a cigarette and put it in Tyson's mouth. Brandt lit one for himself as there didn't seem to be any more customers for him at the moment. Brandt said, 'It's a good wound. A good-bye wound.'

'Million dollar?'

'Eight hundred thousand. You're going to limp. But you'll be limping in New York.'

'Right.' Tyson propped himself up on one arm and looked along the wide, shallow trench. About a dozen

437

soldiers were kneeling, firing short bursts at the far-off line of fruit trees from where the rockets and gunfire had originated. But Tyson didn't think they were drawing return fire any longer. The rest of Alpha Company had decided not to participate in this particular firefight and were hunched down, smoking cigarettes, eating C rations, bantering and bartering with the civilians. Farley had a chicken perched on his head, and the Vietnamese thought that was comical. Michael DeTonq was talking very seriously to a young girl, and Tyson guessed the subject without hearing a word. Lee Walker had the pig in a neck lock and was writing or drawing something in grease pencil on its face. The men around him thought it was pretty funny whatever it was. Tyson was glad everyone was relaxed.

Tyson lay back on the helmet. The thought occurred to him, not for the first time, that he would miss this, miss the ability to indulge in eccentric if not actually atavistic behaviour. Now that it was nearly over for him, he admitted to the excitement of combat, of living on the edge, of being free to release without constraint all of his aggressive energy. And he would miss too the sense of community offered by combat, the sense of bonding between men that was as profound as any between lovers, if not more so. It was a bond, unlike marriage, that could never be broken by divorce or separation or by anything other than death.

As he lay there in the slime, he thought again about that hospital and what they had done there. And again he felt no sense of failed duty, though by all legal, rational, and moral standards, he had failed miserably.

Tyson turned his head toward Brandt. 'Who else was hit?'

Brandt replied, 'Two guys from third platoon. Not bad.'

'Did anyone call medevac?'

'I guess Kelly did.'

'Where is Kelly?'

'Out there somewhere. But he's okay. I heard his voice over the squawk box down the line. How'd you get separated?'

Tyson had never been more than an arm's length from his radio operator, and he felt strangely powerless without Kelly and without the reassurance that personal radio contact with the outside world gave him. Tyson said, 'When the firing broke out, a mob of panicky Viets got between us. You're sure he's okay?'

'Yes, sir. No bullshit. You're not hit bad enough for me to lie to you.' Brandt drew on his cigarette and threw it, still lit, to a Vietnamese boy a few yards away. The boy fielded it with expertise and had it in his mouth before Brandt exhaled his smoke.

Tyson said, 'You know ... I feel a little better. Maybe I should take charge of this herd.'

'No. You lay there. Your pulse is a little off, and if you could see the colour of your face you wouldn't be thinking about taking charge of anything.'

Tyson tried to remember who the ranking man was, but his head felt strangely light. He said, 'Do me a favour, Doc. Find out who's the senior sergeant. Tell him to report here to me.'

Brandt replied without interest, 'Okay. But I don't think anyone wants the honour of leading Alpha Company.'

Tyson said, 'Also find Kelly. And if I don't get a chance, tell everyone I said *adiós*. Okay?'

'Okay.' But Brandt made no move to follow orders. Instead, he said, 'We're finished. Not an officer or senior NCO left. They'll pull us in. Right?'

'I guess so. Hey, good luck, Brandt.'

'Thanks.'

Tyson said, 'I'm feeling kind of funny.'

'Shock.'

'No ... very funny ... woozy ...'

439

'Really?'

'Did you ... you give me something? ...'

His mind was becoming clouded, and things seemed to free-float around him. Michael DeTonq appeared from somewhere and was telling him something about deserting. Tyson thought he was hallucinating at first, but he realized DeTonq was real. Then Bob Moody, recently returned to duty from his wound at the hospital, was looking down on him. Moody said, 'You'll be back in a week, Lieutenant, just like me.'

Tyson thought he answered him, 'No, not me,' but he couldn't be sure he spoke.

Kelly was suddenly at his side, but he didn't say much. Kelly called the battalion commander, Colonel Womrath, on the radio. The colonel spoke to Tyson, telling him what a fine job he had done and how good it had been to have him as Alpha's acting company commander. Tyson replied in similar stock phrases, though somewhat disjointed, telling the colonel that it had been an honour to serve under him and to be part of the Seventh Cavalry and that he'd do it again if he was able. DeTonq said, 'Bullshit.' Kelly said, 'Amen.'

Then a line of men came at him in a low crouch, each one taking his hand and shaking it, then, against field regulations, saluting him; Richard Farley was first, the chicken still on his helmet, then came Simcox and Tony Scorello. Scorello said, 'Thanks for saving my life,' though Tyson didn't recall saving the man's life. Hernando Beltran came up to him and said, '*Adiós, amigo.* Watch out for those hippies in Frisco.' Selig said his good-bye, then Louis Kalane, then Paul Sadowski gave him a religious medal, and Kurt Holzman accidentally bumped his knee. Finally Lee Walker, a black man, came up to Tyson, still holding the pig. He turned the pig's face toward Tyson, and Tyson saw that Walker had drawn slanty eyebrows and a mandarin moustache on the animal's face. Walker said,

'Charlie says good-bye too.' The pig squealed and tried to get away, but Walker held it tightly. Tyson's eyes became clouded, and all he could see was the pig's malevolent red eyes squinting at him, then everything went black.

Tyson looked down at the book in his lap, then shut it. Sitting cross-legged on the floor had caused his knee to stiffen, and he stretched out his right leg. He vaguely recalled being carried to the medevac helicopter and the ride, like a floating dream, out to sea.

After, when he woke on the hospital ship, he was told by the ward physician that he'd gone into shock, possibly morphine shock, and nearly died. The doctor questioned him about whether or not he'd received morphine in the field. Tyson had replied that he didn't think so. But blood and urine tests showed high levels of morphine. He overheard a doctor using the words 'therapeutic accident.' The consensus was that Tyson, who as an officer sometimes carried a Syrette of morphine, had injected himself to relieve the pain. Then one or both of the company medics, not aware of any previous dose being given, injected him again, and finally the helicopter medic had inadvertently given him the near fatal overdose. But that didn't fully explain the *NM* on his forehead, they agreed. Tyson had the impression that they wanted to let the unfortunate incident pass without official inquiry since it had not happened before. Tyson had considered giving the doctors his own conclusion, which was that medic Brandt had tried to murder him. But why rock the *Repose*? Brandt had nearly committed a perfect crime, and it was no less perfect for Tyson having survived.

Tyson stared down at the small logbook in his hands, then without further thought he threw it in the fire. He picked up a bellows and pumped air onto the fire until it blazed furiously, consuming the last scraps of his wartime reminders.

Tyson stood and began walking through the house. There were memories here too; ghosts in every chair, friends and family around the dining room table, people around the piano, bridge games in the den, making love to Marcy in front of the fireplace. There was the living room chair where his father had always sat, the place near the front windows where the Christmas tree always went, the corner in the kitchen where David's high chair had been, and the place in the foyer where David took his first step.

He went upstairs and wandered into David's room and stood there awhile, then looked into the two guest rooms and the spare room used as a second-floor sitting room. On the third floor was the garret with another whole suite for the maid's quarters which were standard when this house was built. But these days, as Tyson was fond of saying, the live-in help slept in the master bedroom, so the third floor was totally unused. 'What did we need all this space for? Were we trying to avoid each other?'

He recalled the house where he grew up, ten blocks away. It was about the same size as this one, but it was filled with people: his parents, his three sisters, his mother's mother and occasionally a spinster aunt, and a succession of mongrel dogs. 'We are too selfish to have children anymore. We farm out the elderly, and indigent relatives know better than to ask for a place to stay. No wonder we're all alone at the end.'

He went into the master bedroom and picked up the telephone. He dialled. Marcy answered, 'Hello.'

'It's me.'

'Hello you.'

'I want a baby.'

Marcy replied, 'Okay.'

'Maybe two. And a dog.'

'Whoa. How's the house?'

'Empty. Lots of nurseries.'

'Are you all right?'

'I'm fine. Mason is with me. I like Mason.'

'He's probably a Democrat.'

'He'd be a fool not to be.' He said, 'I don't think either of us

442

is a nominee for the spouse of the year award this year. But I want you to know I love you.'

Marcy said, 'I love *you*. Very much. Hurry home. You're to be back at nine o'clock. I think I like the Army keeping you on a short leash.'

He hung up, bounded down the staircase, and took his sports jacket from the foyer, activated the alarm, and left the house.

Mason opened the door of the running car, and Tyson got in. Mason slid behind the wheel. Tyson said, 'We have a lot of stops. Got the time?'

'If you got the stops, I got the go.'

Tyson laughed. 'Okay. First stop, the country club.'

Mason drove to the club, Tyson got out, went inside to the club secretary's office, and resigned his membership. They stopped next at the Men's Club, and he did the same. He got to his bank before closing and withdrew most of his savings in cash. He glanced in the side-view mirror a few times and said, 'Mason, we're being followed.'

'Know that.'

'No sweat. Just my guardian angels.'

'Okay.'

The limousine went up Franklin Avenue and stopped at the suburban branches of Bloomingdale's, Saks, Lord and Taylor, Abraham and Straus, and smaller chain shops in between. At each place, Tyson paid his charges off in real money, which caused some consternation, and he cancelled all his accounts, which gave him a sense of acting out a long-held fantasy.

He directed Mason to some of the local merchants where he settled up all house accounts and cancelled them. He took care of the last merchant, a florist, and got back in the limousine with a box of long-stemmed roses. He passed the box over to the front seat. 'These are for Mrs Williams from Mrs Tyson and me. Tell her we hope she's feeling better.'

Mason lifted the lid of the long box. 'Why, thank you, Mr

Tyson. Thank you.'

Tyson sat back in his seat. 'Let's just drive around town for a while. Fifty-cent tour.'

'Yes, sir.'

Tyson lit a cigarette and watched the familiar landscape from his window: the cathedral, the hotel, the churches, the clubs, the parks, the wide tree-lined streets, the shops, the schools, and the little railroad stations. He said, 'Do you know what this is called, Mason?'

'No, sir.'

'In the military they call it burning your bridges behind you so you can't retreat but are forced to advance. Civilians might say it's just a last farewell.'

Mason said, 'You not ever coming back?'

'I have to act as though I'm not. If I do come back, well, that's the way it was meant to be. If I never see this place again I want to remember it as it was when I was happy here, long ago, and happy here again on a late August afternoon.'

Mason glanced at his passenger in the rearview mirror. He said, 'In your head you never leave the place where you was born and raised. I ain't been back to Dillon, South Carolina, since I was seventeen. But I still has the place in my head. Strange, 'cause I wasn't none too happy there. Oh, some of it was happy. I remember we used to go to this little church, and ... aw, hell, ain't nothin' left there. 'Cept an old aunt.'

'Go see her. See the place where Mason Williams walked the streets and went to school and church.'

'Might do that.'

Tyson lit another cigarette. He said, 'Mason, are you following all this in the news? Of course you are.'

'Yes, sir.'

'And? What are your thoughts?'

'Well ... hard for me to say, Mr Tyson.'

'How long have we known each other? I remember you driving me places when I was in grade school. My father used to put me in your car and say, "Take this fathead to school.

He missed the bus again."'

Mason laughed.

'Or, "Take him and his juvenile delinquent friends to the movies." And a few times you took me into the city to meet my parents for dinner.'

'Yes, sir. Them was good days. I liked your father.'

'Me too. So give it to me straight. What do you think about all this?'

'Well ... I think, Mr Tyson ... you could have found some friends ... could have stuck closer to your friends ... and they would've stuck closer to you. You got a lot of friends in this town.'

'Do I?'

'Yes, sir. There was people who was on your side. There was talk of honourin' you at the Fourth of July party at the club ... I hear things when people sit back there, 'cause they don't think I hear nothin'.' He chuckled. 'The other drivers talk too. Anyways, I never heard of nobody sayin' nothin' bad about you. Mostly they was unhappy for you.'

Tyson nodded. 'Maybe I got real paranoid.'

'Maybe. Maybe you was unhappy in a lot of ways so you took it out on everybody.'

'Could be. I'm happy now though.'

'I know that.'

'Do you?'

'Yes, sir, I seen it in your face and in your walk. I hear it in your voice. Ain't seen you like that in lots of years now.'

'A few other people have told me that. Why do you suppose I'm happy? I'm about to go on trial for murder.'

Mason drove for a while before answering, 'You're startin' over. Lots of folks don't get that chance. You goin' to get that thing squared away, then you goin' on, and this time you goin' to get things right. You got a fine missus, and she'll stand beside you.'

Tyson smiled. 'I hope to God you're right. Listen, drive past my father's house.'

Mason nodded and swung into Whitehall Street. He stopped in front of the house where Tyson grew up, a brick and stucco Tudor. Tyson couldn't recall the name of the people who lived there now and didn't care. He stared at the second-floor window that had been his room. He said, 'When my father died, the cortege detoured past this house on the way to the cemetery. All the neighbours were out front. I didn't know that was going to happen. Took me by surprise. I cried.'

'I know. You was in my car.' Mason pulled away from the house. 'Now you done thinkin' about the past, Mr Tyson. Where you want to go now?'

'I don't know. I don't have to be back until nine. They don't let me out that often.' He glanced at his watch. It was a few minutes to seven, and the shadows outside the car were lengthening. Commuters were home by now, and he could visit any one of a number of people. But on what pretext? Did he need a pretext? 'Drive over to Tulamore.'

Mason headed west, and Tyson directed him to a white clapboard colonial, the home of Phillip and Janet Sloan. He couldn't tell if anyone was at home and realized he didn't really want to see Phil Sloan. 'Go on to Brixton.'

They drove past the McCormicks' house without stopping, then the houses of a few more friends, some of whom were in, some apparently not. Mason said, 'You wantin' to stop anywhere?'

'I don't think so. I just feel like an outsider who wants to look in. Do you think I should stop?'

Mason tipped his hat forward and scratched the back of his head. He said, 'I guess you know what's best.'

'Well, I'm a little shy these days.' Tyson looked at his watch. 'I guess I can catch the eight-ten to Brooklyn.'

'Yes, sir.'

The black limousine pulled up at the station. Tyson said, 'Mason, if you were a betting man what odds would you give me?'

Mason opened Tyson's door. Tyson got out, and both men looked at each other. Mason replied, 'I said you looked happy. No man who done what they sayin' you done looks happy about it. You just tell them the truth. Let them see your eyes.'

'Okay, I'll do that.' Tyson held out a fifty-dollar bill.

Mason shook his head. 'You been overtippin' me since you was a boy. This one's on me. You take care now.' They shook hands. 'Hurry on. I hear the train.'

Tyson walked up to the platform and saw the train approaching from the east. A soft breeze was blowing, and it was from the north in contrast to the usual southerly ocean breeze. A harbinger of autumn. The sun was below the horizon, and the large houses on the south side of the station plaza sat in deep shadow. A few cars remained in the parking field, a few wives waited for the city train. Further down the tracks were tennis courts, and he saw a couple he knew, the Muellers, playing doubles with another couple. The station plaza, the new hotel, the library, and the parks formed a sort of old-fashioned village common. This was the kind of place people pictured for themselves if they ever got nostalgic for the type of town that used to typify American life. Like many of the other commuter enclaves strung out along the great commuter rail lines radiating from New York, this was the best of worlds and the worst of worlds. It was both insular and part of the main. Marcy was right, and Marcy was wrong. It depended, he realized, on what was on your mind and what was in your heart.

He liked Robert Frost's definition of home: the place where, when you have to go there, they have to take you in.

But home was also the place where, when you strayed from it, they came looking for you.

That was not this place anymore.

The train stopped, and he boarded. He thought, There *is* something evocative about trains and railroad stations. The tracks and trains *do* run both ways. But there is a time in your

447

life – and you don't always know which time – when you are going only one way.

He took a seat in the empty coach and drew from his breast pocket the picture of him and Teresa in front of the Hue cathedral. He stared at it a moment, trying to reconcile the all-American boy in the photo with the man who had turned into a monster less than four weeks later. He stared at Teresa and marvelled that even after a lifetime of warfare and death she looked very naive, very shy and innocent. But perhaps that was the answer. She'd been inoculated at birth against the sickness of the soul that follows on the heels of war. His mind and soul had no immunities whatsoever, and he'd become sick the day he went out on his first patrol through the countryside and seen the massive destruction of lives, property, and family.

He put the picture back in his pocket and closed his eyes. He realized that Fort Hamilton might be the last place he saw before an armed escort took him to a federal prison. He opened his eyes and looked out the window. Everything was looking better than he'd ever seen it. If he passed this way again, he'd have to remember that.

36

The early morning sun slanted in through the venetian blinds of Tyson's living room. The rented television was balanced unsteadily on a folding snack table pushed against the staircase wall. Dressed in a warm-up suit, Tyson sat at the edge of the couch with a mug of coffee, watching a PBS news show. Marcy was in the armchair with coffee and a buttered corn muffin. David, sitting cross-legged on the floor with a glass of orange juice, said, 'Can we rent a VCR?'

Tyson replied, 'Not on my salary.'

'Well, then, can we get one of the ones from home?'

'No.'

David grumbled something.

Tyson glanced at his son. The boy was becoming surly. Perhaps he was just bored or maybe nervous about starting school.

The news commentator said, 'The House Judiciary Committee is meeting to discuss the Tyson case. Lieutenant Tyson's attorney, Vincent Corva, stated that any such inquiry would only serve to further prejudice his client's legal and civil rights since the case has not yet been tried. But the House appears to be responding to outside pressure. The agenda for the House Committee includes studying legislation that would clarify jurisdiction in such cases. The Justice Department in past cases has taken the position that an honourably discharged serviceman cannot be tried for a war crime committed prior to his discharge, either by courtmartial or in a federal court. Tyson's status as an ex-officer, however, made it possible to return him to active duty for the purpose of investigating charges against him stemming from this incident.'

Tyson glanced again at David. The boy was reading a car magazine and seemed to have little interest in this. Bizarre, he thought. Adults give children too much credit. That, too, was a story of the sixties: adults seeking the wisdom of shallow adolescents.

The PBS commentator continued, 'In another development, Colonel Ambrose Horton, an instructor at the Judge Advocate General School at the University of Virginia and a respected jurist, has directed a memo to General William Van Arken, the Army's Judge Advocate General. The contents of that memo have been revealed through an unidentified source. The memo reads in part: "As you know, General, under the Geneva Convention of which the United States is a signatory member, the United States is obligated to enact any legislation necessary to provide effective penal sanctions for persons committing grave breaches of the laws of war."' The commentator continued, 'Colonel Horton further points out that in the nearly four decades since the U.S. signed the Geneva Convention treaty, Congress has failed to enact such legislation though most other signatories have. His conclusion to General Van Arken is that the Army should not take it upon itself to selectively prosecute Lieutenant Tyson while not prosecuting other suspects over whom Congress has failed to establish federal or military jurisdiction. It would appear then that no one in Lieutenant Tyson's platoon will be or can be charged with a crime. And so it is that at the Army hearing, one week from today, at Fort Hamilton, Brooklyn, only one man will face indictment for that crime: Benjamin J. Tyson.'

Tyson leaned forward and turned off the television. He didn't know who Colonel Ambrose Horton was, but he knew that the man ought to put his retirement papers in if he hadn't already done so.

Tyson sipped his coffee. He avoided news stories about himself. But when he did watch or listen, he tried to be objective to determine how he felt about this fellow Tyson. Generally the stories seemed to be slanted in his favour. The stuff about Marcy popped up once in a while, but even that seemed to be handled with more sympathy than sleaze recently.

Marcy said, 'Is that going to affect anything?'

Tyson shrugged. 'I don't think it will for me.'

Marcy nodded. 'Sometimes it takes a landmark case to restructure justice in this country. Even the Civil Liberties Union is behind you on this. That's comforting.'

'To *you* perhaps.'

David looked up from his magazine. 'Dad, why is it if everybody's on your side ... I mean all those people who are contributing money and coming out on your side and all – why is the Army going to court-martial you?'

Tyson thought about that a moment. He replied, 'Because I

450

violated a trust, I broke my oath of office. So they want to . . . to set an example for the other Army leaders, now and in the future.'

'But it happened so *long* ago. Why can't they just forget something that happened thirty years ago?'

'Twenty.' Tyson had read a front page story once in the *Wall Street Journal* about how unaware college and high school students were of the war. A professor reported that a senior asked him what napalm was. Another instructor claimed three-fourths of his students had never heard of the Tet Offensive. Tyson said, 'The Army has the memory of an elephant, and for the first time in our history, the Army failed in its mission, and they will discuss the defeat forever.' He drew a long breath. 'Deep down inside, the Army wants a rematch. They would like to be sent again to Vietnam, to regain their lost honour—'

Marcy interjected, 'Oh, God, Ben, don't even think that.'

'It's true, Marcy. I know it's true.' He looked at David. 'But until then, anytime something about Vietnam comes up, they are going to overreact to it.'

David stayed silent, digesting this. He said, 'But you didn't kill anyone. You said you didn't kill anyone. The other guys did it, didn't they?' He looked at his father. 'Didn't they?'

Tyson met his son's eyes. He said, 'If you were hanging around with a bunch of guys and they got really wild one day and beat up a bunch of younger kids – really beat them badly – and you saw all this but did nothing to stop it, and afterwards didn't tell your mother or the police – would you be as guilty as the rest of the guys? Less guilty? More guilty?'

'More guilty,' David said softly. 'If I couldn't stop them, then I should have told on them.'

'Would it make any difference if the guys were very sorry for what they did? I mean if they didn't brag about it but were ashamed of it?'

'I . . . I don't think so. They hurt people.' David stood. 'I'm going out.'

Marcy asked, 'Where are you going?'

'Out. I'm bored. This place is driving me nuts.'

Tyson inquired, 'Have you made any friends here?'

'No.'

'Do you want to go to Sag Harbor this weekend?'

David hesitated a moment. 'No ...'

'Don't you miss Melinda?'

'Yes. But ... if you guys can stick it out here ... Dad, as long as you're under arrest I'm staying here.'

'*You're* not under arrest.' He turned to Marcy. 'Look, why don't you and David drive out east today? You can find a place to stay. I have a lot of work to do with Vince.'

Marcy shook her head. 'We made this decision already, Ben. I'm staying here until this is finished. Anyway, the damned media comments on every move we make. If I go out to the beach, the *American Investigator* will say something like ... Marcy enjoys the sun while Ben stews under house arrest.'

Tyson replied, 'Okay. That's your decision. I was looking forward to not having to wait to use the bathroom.' He smiled. 'But you'll notice the *Investigator* has not been too hard on us recently.'

'I noticed that. And Wally Jones' byline is completely gone. Why is that?'

Tyson looked at David, who was hovering impatiently by the door. Tyson said, 'David, you have stuff in my gym locker, right? I'll meet you there in about an hour.'

'Okay.' David left.

Tyson turned to Marcy. 'I've got into incredible shape. It's my mind that's shot now.'

'Sound mind, sound body – take your pick. So why do you think the *Investigator* dropped us?'

Tyson poured himself more coffee from the carafe. 'Well ... perhaps having reached new lows of journalistic depravity, they couldn't follow their own act. Especially with Major Harper out of the picture.' Tyson added, 'Also, I beat the shit out of Wally Jones.' He stirred his coffee.

She laughed. 'I bet you'd like to. By the way, I didn't think you handled David's questions very well.'

'Why not?'

'I don't know ... it's just that you press him too hard.'

Tyson lit a cigarette. He could see this was going to be a bad day. The strain of this confinement and inactivity, coupled with uncertainty, was beginning to tell on Marcy and David. He rifled through some envelopes on the coffee table.

Marcy said, 'The mortgage payment is late and there's a notice there from the village saying they're going to list the house for a tax sale unless we pay up.'

'Is that so?'

'You see? The Tysons have paid taxes in that fucking village since year one, but miss one goddamned payment – you see what I mean?'

'No.'

'I mean, damn it, that it doesn't matter how you've lived your life, brought up your kids, paid your stinking bills for twenty years. You miss a few payments, and you got to the top of the shit list. You're a nobody. A deadbeat.'

'Yes, that's what I keep saying about my situation. Just one lousy massacre, and everybody gets on your case.'

'Poor analogy.'

'Anyway, take heart. I heard from Phil Sloan yesterday that our bank is suspending our mortgage payments and paying all property taxes for us. It's a loan of sorts which we will eventually have to repay.'

Marcy looked doubtful. 'Are you sure?'

'Yes. Now, isn't that a nice bank? Doesn't it restore your faith in humanity?'

'I guess it does.'

'Well, don't be too reassured. Near as I can figure it, someone went to the bank and twisted their nuts.'

'Who?'

'Who cares? A guardian angel, I think. A G-man. Someone

from this shady cabal that has been reading our mail and dogging our every movement. The point is, even if we wanted to commit economic suicide, declare bankruptcy, and all that, we couldn't. The Army doesn't want that in the news before the trial. What if, God forbid, I'm innocent, and they've ruined me? Well, this is an enviable position in which most Americans will never find themselves.'

She stayed silent for some time, then announced, 'I don't like this.' She raised her voice. 'I do not *like* being watched, being—'

'Sh-h-h! You'll damage the microphones.'

She stood, took a heavy glass ashtray from the coffee table, and flung it at the front window. It went through the blinds, smashed a windowpane, and ripped the screen. 'Fuck the Army!'

'Calm down.' He stood and surveyed the damage, then looked at her and said seriously, 'We *are* being watched, you know. I do *not* want them to see us cracking up. Okay? Steady on, soldier.'

She put her arms around him and laid her cheek on his shoulder. 'Okay.'

Tyson's eyes moved around the small room as he held her. It cost him a good deal of money each week to satisfy himself that the place didn't have electronic plumbing, but still he wondered. He said, 'Did you get David enrolled at the local stiletto high?'

'It's actually supposed to be a good school according to the mothers I spoke to on post. The bus will pick him up on Lee Avenue. I spoke to the principal, and she's aware of the special problems involved.'

'All right. How is David reacting?'

'Ask him.'

'He always gives me the macho line. Takes after his old man. What did he say to you?'

'He's nervous.'

'Understandable.'

'Also he misses his friends.'

'So do we all. But they're probably not his friends anymore.'

'He says the school looks junky. Actually it is old but well kept.'

'Well, he shouldn't compare a city high school with that suburban country club he got used to.'

'It's good for his character. That's what you said.'

Ben Tyson smiled. 'Right.' He held her tighter. 'You know, without sounding too macho, a man likes to give his family the best. And when he can't he doesn't always feel like a man. Is that too patriarchal?'

'Yes, but I know how you feel.'

'The private schools were just too expensive, Marcy—'

'Don't worry about it. We'll all make do.'

'This might hurt his chances for a good college.'

She shook him gently by the shoulders. 'Stop that. You went to a lousy college, why shouldn't he?'

'Hey, there's nothing wrong with Auburn. Columbia was a pigpen.'

She laughed, and they held on to one another.

Tyson cleared his throat. 'Have you considered what you will do if I go up the river for a few years?'

'Sing Sing is up the river. Leavenworth is in Kansas. Across the river.'

'Answer the question.'

'I don't think about it. I *won't* think about it. So I can't answer your question.'

'Okay ... no use worrying about that now.'

'Are you worried about the hearing?'

'No. Corva said not to waste energy worrying. I'll be indicted for sure.'

'Oh ... Are you worried about *Corva*?'

'A little. Yes, a little. He's erratic. Sometimes I think he's a genius. Other times I think he's a dolt. He's fatalistic too. Well, maybe realistic is a better word.'

She moved away from him and poured coffee for both of them. 'He seems to really care about you, Ben. That's a good thing.'

Tyson took his mug of coffee. 'Corva and I were both infantry commanders, and our tours of duty coincided. I don't even have to say to him, "Look, Vince, Nam sucked, the leeches sucked, the homecoming sucked, so don't let them make the peace suck, too." He knows that, and I think if I went to jail, he knows that a little bit of him and all the rest of us would go to jail, too.'

She stared into the blackness of her coffee, then looked up. 'I think I understand that. I can see it when you're both together. Just promise me one thing.'

'What's that?'

'When this is over, don't invite him and his wife over so you can bore us with war stories.' She smiled.

He smiled in return. 'Mercifully, he doesn't tell or listen to war stories.'

Tyson thought a moment, hesitated, then asked, 'So what's happening Tuesday? Are you going back to work?' He glanced at her, and she turned away.

Marcy sat on the arm of the upholstered chair. 'Well ... if I don't, I think I'm fired.'

'I thought you were irreplaceable there. I thought Jim liked you.'

'Don't let's get into an ugly scene, Ben. Jim has to fill the job.'

'He could hold it another week until we see if I'm indicted or not.'

'He's been very patient. A lot more patient than *your* employers were. And *you* were supposed to be irreplaceable.'

'No salary slave is irreplaceable. That's what I learned. I wouldn't work for anyone again if my life depended on it. I'd rather be a self-employed handyman. *I* learned how the bosses treat you even if *you* didn't. I *was* a boss, and I let people go who had personal problems. There's no room in

456

corporate America for personal problems. If this guy can't give you a little more time, the hell with him.'

'We need the money, Ben. Get off your high horse. You are so damned hubristic about *everything*. You have to kiss some ass once in a while.'

'No, I do not. But I do need you ... I need your companionship. And your support. And David needs you more than ever.'

'I realize all of that,' she said in measured tones. 'But quite frankly, Ben, I am going out of my fucking mind here. You may have noticed.'

'No. I see no change.'

'And I'll be a better companion to you and David at night and on weekends if I can get out of here for a few hours a day.'

Tyson slammed the coffee mug on the end table. 'Oh, bullshit. It was never a few hours. It was, and will be, long hours and paperwork at home and business trips and your mind on the job at dinner and phone calls in the evening – do you realize, lady, that I'm facing murder charges? How much more time do you think we might have together?'

She stared down at the floor and said softly, 'I told him I'd be there Tuesday.' She added, 'We have new clients in Atlanta, and I have to fly down with him Thursday. I'll be back Friday night.'

'Good. You can read in the paper whether or not I was indicted Friday afternoon.'

'I'm sorry, Ben.'

Tyson went to the door. 'I'll be at the gym.' He hesitated a moment, then said, 'Look, I understand. Try to understand what it's like for me to be confined here by law. Maybe I'm just envious of free people.' He waited for a reply to his conciliatory statement, but there was none, so he left.

37

At 7:30 P.M. there was a knock on the door, and Tyson opened it. Vincent Corva said, 'Traffic was awful.'

Tyson showed him in. 'Thanks for coming on a holiday night.'

Corva walked into the living room carrying a briefcase. He wore jeans and a polo shirt and looked, Tyson thought, more diminutive than he did in a suit. He wondered how Corva had carried the basic seventy pounds of field gear, food, water, and ammunition in hundred-degree heat.

Corva said, 'I dropped my wife and kids off in Montclair.'

'Oh, is that where you live? That's Jersey, isn't it?'

'Yes. And we spent the weekend at our summer place in Ocean City.'

'Where is that?'

'The Jersey shore.'

'Oh ... I didn't know people went there.'

Corva smiled. 'Maybe not your people.' He placed his briefcase on the floor near the sofa.

Marcy came into the living room. 'Hello, Vince.' She gave him a peck on the cheek. Tyson watched her. She had an easy way with men and put men at ease. He could see Corva was taken with her. Apparently Picard had been, too.

Corva said, 'I'm sorry I couldn't get Ben released for this weekend. They are being real hardnoses. Usually an officer can give his word as his bond that he won't skip out.'

Marcy observed, 'This officer-and-gentleman routine is only for when it suits them. When it doesn't suit them, an officer's word is not enough.'

Corva said, 'Well, I think this has to do with keeping Ben clear of the media.'

Tyson had the impression he was some sort of invalid whom relatives talked about as though he weren't there.

Corva continued, 'Which reminds me. I've got a six-figure offer from a publisher. Christ, I've had to hire extra staff to keep up with these phone calls. Anyway, this is a respectable publisher. You want to tell your story for about a quarter million?'

Tyson looked at Marcy, and she looked back at him. Marcy spoke to Corva. 'No, he does not. We both decided long ago that we will not make one penny from this mess. All we want at the end is to cover your legal expenses.'

Corva nodded. 'Okay. I'll never mention these offers again.' He smiled. 'Even saints can be tempted.'

Marcy said, 'Sit down. I bought a bottle of that awful stuff you said you drink. *Strelger?*'

'*Strega. Significato* witch.'

She shrugged and disappeared into the kitchen.

Corva sat at the far end of the sofa. He said softly to Tyson, 'I want to speak to you alone.'

Tyson nodded. 'She and David are going to the post movie.'

Marcy came back with a tray on which were three fluted glasses and a long, slender bottle filled with a yellow liquid. She set the tray down and poured. They each took a glass, and Corva said, 'Careful. They don't call this "witch" for nothing.' He poured the drink down his throat, followed by Tyson and Marcy. They all looked at one another, and wiped their eyes. Tyson cleared his throat. '*Mamma mia*. This is paint remover.'

Corva explained, 'It takes getting used to.' He lifted a mason jar from his briefcase and put it on the coffee table. 'I promised you pesto sauce.' He spoke to Marcy. 'Don't open the jar until you're ready to use it. Don't heat it, or you'll lose the bouquet. Spoon it at room temperature on hot pasta. Okay?'

She examined the jar suspiciously. 'Looks like the paint the strega took off.' She stared at Corva. 'Is all this Italian stuff an affectation? I mean, you don't do this as a shtick, do you?'

'Certainly not. It's my heritage.' He winked at her.

She smiled in return. 'You could use a good PR lady when this is all over. I'll make you into an Italian F. Lee Bailey. What's your middle name?'

'Marcantonio.'

'Oh, I love it! V. Marcantonio Corva. Or Vincent Mark Anthony Corva. Or—'

Tyson said, 'Won't you be late for the movie?'

Marcy looked at her watch. 'Oh!' She stood and said to Corva, 'They're showing *Creator*, with Peter O'Toole.' She went to the stairs and called up, 'David! Show time!' She turned back to Corva. 'Image is important, but unlike a lot of PR people, I believe in substance too. That comes across with you.'

Tyson said to Corva, 'Lift your feet; the stuff is getting deeper.'

Marcy looked at him icily.

Tyson added, 'She's getting into practice. She's going back to work tomorrow.'

Corva sipped on his drink. He'd noticed that the Tysons weren't speaking directly to each other, and there was something in Tyson's voice that sounded strained.

David came downstairs. 'Hello, Mr Corva.'

'Hi, David. All ready for school tomorrow?'

'I guess.'

'Just remember, kids are the same all over, even if they have Brooklyn accents.'

David forced a laugh.

Marcy and David went to the door. Corva said, 'Enjoy the movie. If I don't see you later, good luck to both of you tomorrow.'

Marcy and David left, and Corva noted that no one offered any good-byes. Corva looked at Tyson awhile before speaking. 'This is not a personal question, it is a professional concern. Are you having domestic difficulties?'

Tyson nodded as he lit a cigarette. 'I've had them for seventeen years of marriage. So don't let it concern *you*. It doesn't concern *me*.'

'What is the nature of these domestic difficulties?'

'Are you a divorce lawyer?' He poured himself another strega. 'Well, since you won't drop it – it's Marcy's decision to return to work.'

'You don't like that?'

'I guess not.'

'You'll be home all day with the housework and trying to defend yourself against a murder charge, and she'll be having lunch with interesting people.'

'You got it, Vinny. Boy, you *are* quick.'

'Now, don't take it out on me.'

'And I doubt if her clients are interesting. And I don't intend to do any housework. Fuck it, I'm getting a maid.'

Corva stroked the bridge of his thin nose with his index finger. He said, 'You may be right. I mean, to feel hurt and angry and abandoned. However, that is not going to help your defence of the murder charge.' Corva leaned across the coffee table towards Tyson. 'Let me tell you something that I think you will agree with: This murder case against you is more important than your marriage. Get some perspective, my friend, and stop being so fucking self-indulgent.'

'Don't swear at me.'

'I'd like to beat the shit out of you.'

'You're all talk.'

Corva stood and pointed at Tyson. 'Look, you don't have the luxury to brood over your marriage or your life-style. If you don't keep your mind on this case, I'm walking out on it.'

Tyson stood too. His voice became loud. 'I'm not a goddamned robot. I'm angry. I feel betrayed.'

'So *what*? You can't do a thing about it. Before this is over, *everyone* will betray you in some way. Your duty is to yourself now. And that duty is to keep out of gaol. And when you are free of all this, then you can settle up the scores. *Capice?*' He stared at Tyson.

Tyson nodded slowly. 'Yeah, *capisco.*'

Corva stuck his hand out. 'Friends?'

Tyson took his hand. 'You're one of the scores I'm going to settle, you little wop.'

Corva laughed.

They sat and drank in silence awhile. Tyson commented, 'This stuff grows on you.'

Corva poured another round. 'The old men where I grew up made a home-brewed version of this. The government bought the recipe, and that's what Agent Orange is.' He let loose a slightly alcoholic laugh, followed by a belch.

Tyson asked, 'Did you hear or read that thing that Colonel Horton said?'

Corva nodded. 'I know of Horton. Everyone respects him. Like they respect God. He has about that much actual influence on Army justice too. But he did pull the philosophical rug out from under Van Arken. What this all means to you as a practical matter is minimal. But at least there are people out there – not just your VFW fans but intellectuals – who are saying you are being shafted. None of this will stop the Army juggernaut, but you can take some comfort in knowing your case has raised some important constitutional issues.'

'That's what martyrs are for, Vince. To suffer so mankind can progress into a more perfect society.'

Corva said, 'You may think you are being sarcastic. But I'll tell you, there will be millions of words written about the United States versus Benjamin Tyson. You will become case history. Did you know that the present French code of military justice was instituted as a direct result of the French Army's gross mishandling of the Dreyfus court-martial?'

Tyson lit another cigarette and sank back onto the sofa. 'Ask me if I care.'

'Someday,' continued Corva, warming to his subject,

'when you pass on to that great courtroom in the sky, your obit is a sure thing for the *Times*. Mine too.'

'Really?' Tyson blew smoke rings. 'What will they say about you? Never won a case?'

Corva was looking at the window. 'What happened there?'

Tyson explained, 'She went screwy a few days ago. You see, she's opposed to violence and is not completely understanding of how those poor bastards in my platoon cracked up and went on a rampage. But, out of ennui, she blasts an ashtray through the window. But I'm not being judgemental. I'm only pointing out that people who live in small houses shouldn't throw glass ashtrays.'

Corva nodded. 'Speaking of screwy, the Army intends to give you a battery of psychological tests. Any objections?'

'Yes. We can't offer an insanity defence two decades after the fact, and we're not going to claim that I'm incompetent to stand trial at this time. So, I'm not going to be a guinea pig for a bunch of crackpot shrinks.'

'All right. I'll do what's necessary to block the testing.' Corva inquired, 'Have you ever seen a psychoanalyst?'

Tyson stubbed out his cigarette. 'Briefly.'

'Would his notes help us?'

'I don't know. How?'

'Will his notes indicate that you felt remorse and guilt for covering up the hospital incident?'

'I don't think so. I never told him.'

'How can you go to a shrink and not tell him what is bothering you?'

Tyson smiled. 'That's what he wanted to know.'

'Would you have any objections if I contacted him?'

'Not at all, but you'll need a Ouija board.'

'Oh …'

'Suicide. If you contact him, tell him I didn't forget the last bill.'

'You're drinking too much.' Corva considered a moment. 'What happened to his files?'

'Don't know. They're privileged information, aren't they?'

'While the therapist is alive. Afterwards … well, I'll look into it.' He took out a pen and yellow pad, and Tyson gave him Dr Stahl's name and last address.

Corva extracted a folded page of the *New York Times* and held it up. 'Did you see this?'

'I don't read the papers anymore. I'm reading Agatha Christie.'

'Well, this is a story dealing with the international implications of this case.' Corva scanned the page. 'There is some talk of Vietnam taking the United States to the world court in The Hague. The moves towards normalization of relations between us and them have suffered a setback. That's another reason some people in Washington don't like you. Of course there are others who like you just fine for screwing it up.'

'That's no concern of mine. Fuck Hanoi and Washington.'

'Right. Also it seems that the governments whose nationals were alleged to have been among the victims – France, Belgium, Germany, Holland, and Australia – have taken a formal interest in the case. They are our allies, as you may know.'

Tyson shrugged. 'Last month there was talk of the U.N. Commission on Genocide investigating. *Genocide*? Christ, that hospital was a virtual U.N. itself. We didn't discriminate. Why is everyone trying to crucify us?'

'They don't like us, Ben. Anyway, the Vietnamese ambassador to the U.N., according to this article, has stated that the People's Republic would be favourably disposed towards allowing an international fact-finding team, including an American, to visit the site of the alleged incident – Miséricorde Hospital and environs. The Vietnamese ambassador also suggested there may be witnesses available. Also Hanoi has sent out a photograph of the former hospital which the *Times* has reproduced.' He handed the full-page story to Tyson.

Tyson looked at the photograph. It showed a two-storey white stucco building without a roof. Its walls were remarkably whiter than when he'd last seen fire licking out of the windows. But it couldn't have been repainted because it was obviously just a shell. Perhaps the monsoon had washed it, and the sun had bleached it like a bone. There were vines climbing up the sides, and he could see through the windows to the sky beyond.

The hospital blazed in the dirty winter rain. The men of the first platoon of Alpha Company stood close, within ten metres, warming their sodden fatigues by the fire. Tyson noticed the steam rising from their uniforms and saw the red flames reflected in their wet, shiny faces.

In the distance, artillery shells exploded, and a war plane streaked overhead, only its jet flame visible through the overcast. Tyson became aware of the crackling sound coming from the hospital as its teak timbers ignited and began splitting. There were noxious odours drifting out of the fiery windows – medical supplies, bedding, flesh.

Without orders the men had formed a cordon around the walls of the rectangular building. They had shown good initiative, Tyson thought, an instinctive deployment without verbal orders, an understanding that the horror inside that hospital had to be kept inside.

A figure appeared at the front doors, a young woman in a white dressing gown carrying an infant. The baby was heavily wrapped in what looked like a GI-issue olive-drab towel. The woman gently pitched the infant into a tangle of ground vines to the side of the entrance just as a burst of gunfire slammed her back through the doors.

Tyson looked at where the shooting had come from and saw Richard Farley loading another magazine into his M-16.

Another figure appeared from a set of French doors at a second-storey balcony on the east side of the building.

Tyson saw it was a naked boy about twelve years old with an amputated leg. The boy hesitated, looked quickly back through the French doors, then closed his eyes and vaulted over the balcony railing. He dropped into a kitchen garden, landing on his knee and amputated stump. As he struggled to right himself, Tyson saw he had a white handkerchief that he was waving. Tyson heard the dull pop of Lee Walker's grenade launcher and saw the boy's chest explode in a mass of flying blood.

Suddenly a man with his head swathed in bandages burst out of the front doors of the hospital and raced across the courtyard at full speed, barefoot and wearing only pyjama bottoms. He passed within twenty metres of Tyson, and Tyson realized he'd actually made it through the cordon.

Hernando Beltran swung his machine gun around and began firing furiously as the man approached a thick hedgerow at the edge of the plaza. The man was obviously a soldier because he moved like a broken field runner, avoiding the bursts of gunfire. Beltran was swearing in Spanish. The man reached the hedgerow and jumped, but his body suddenly contorted as a burst of bullets hit him, and he landed, tangled in the hedges. The probing red fingers of the tracer rounds found him and tore into him, mowing the hedges down until the man lay lifeless in a tangled clump of twigs and leaves.

Tyson turned away, back towards the hospital. He noticed a movement on the pitched roof. About six people had come up through the louvred dormer that acted as an air vent to the attic and were clinging to the red terra-cotta tile. One of them, a man wearing the white pants and shirt of the hospital staff, moved cautiously towards the branches of the huge overhanging banyan tree. He chinned himself on a branch and began making his way towards the tree trunk, disappearing into the dense foliage. A Vietnamese nurse followed him. Tyson watched with mixed feelings, wanting them to escape, but knowing if they did, they would eventually make contact with the Vietnamese or American authorities.

Tyson's mind raced ahead. The platoon would be called back to base camp. As soon as they got off the helicopters, they would be surrounded by MPs, disarmed, and marched en masse to the stockade. He'd seen that happen once at Camp Evans, though he never learned what it was about. But the image of that once-proud fighting unit, hands on their heads, being ordered around by a platoon of spit-polished, sneering MPs, had affected him deeply.

Tyson kept staring at the spreading banyan tree. He saw that it was possible to escape that way. And that was comforting because that was the way Teresa had gone earlier, before his men had left the burning hospital and surrounded it.

Paul Sadowski said, 'What do you see, Lieutenant?'

Tyson turned away from the tree and didn't answer.

Sadowski's eyes widened. 'Oh, shit! Oh, Christ!' He called out to Beltran, 'Put some fire in that tree.'

Beltran picked up the M-60 machine gun and, firing from the hip, began spraying the banyan tree with long bursts of rounds, while Brontman fed the ammunition belts from a metal box. The second machine gun, manned by Michael DeTonq and Peter Santos, began raking the sloping roof. The red tile cracked and splattered into flying fragments. Tyson saw what they were shooting at on the roof: Partly hidden by branches of the tree were two female patients in hospital gowns, an old man, and a little girl with bright red legs, burned legs, the colour of the tile. DeTonq's machine gun got the range quickly, and the four bodies, one after the other, tumbled down the roof, hit the rain gutter, bounced, and dropped along the wall to the ground. The machine gun followed them even in death and spewed burst after burst into the bushes where they'd fallen. Infantrymen, Tyson reflected, had seen too many

467

kills suddenly get up and run away or shoot at them as they approached. As the expression went, 'They're not dead until they're dead.'

Beltran's machine gun, which was still firing into the tree, was now joined by DeTonq's and by a few M-16s and shotguns. The banyan tree was losing branches, dropping leaves, and shedding bark rapidly. The nurse fell out of the tree first and dropped to the ground by the far side of the hospital where Tyson could not see her. Harold Simcox ran towards the base of the tree, and Tyson saw him raise his rifle and empty an entire magazine at the ground.

Tyson looked back at the top of the tree. He could make out the white clothing of the man trying to hide in the foliage. The man seemed to be hit, and Tyson thought he saw red stains on the white clothing, but the man hung tenaciously to the trunk. Lee Walker fired a grenade which burst on a branch over the man's head. Tyson heard a long mournful cry as the man released his grip and fell, bouncing through the branches. Again Simcox, still under the tree, finished the job.

There was no sound for some time except for the rain and crackling fire, and no one else appeared at any of the hospital doors or windows. Tyson saw several men glancing at him and figured it was his turn next. They had taken his rifle and .45 automatic pistol in the hospital, and he felt oddly naked without his weapons which he'd carried and slept with for nearly a year.

Kelly was beside him now, his PRC-25 radio on his back, the radiophone in his hand. He was speaking to someone. Kelly gave the phone to Tyson. 'Captain Browder.'

Tyson took the radiophone. He was aware that several men had moved closer to him. He squeezed the transmit button and spoke. 'Mustang One-Six here. Over.'

Browder's voice came across weak. 'Roger, One-Six. Need a sit rep and hawkeye,' he said, using the radio code word for grid coordinates.

'Roger. Situation ... sniper fire. Village of An Ninh Ha–Hawkeye of Yankee Delta, seven-two, five; two-one, six. How copy?'

Browder read the coordinates back and asked, 'Need help? Artillery or gunships?'

'Negative. Light, ineffective fire. Vicinity of stucco buildings. We'll take a look-see.'

'Roger. I haven't monitored any radio traffic from you in a while. I thought you'd all gone to sleep or died.'

Tyson licked his lips and replied, 'Nothing to report. You still drawing fire?'

'Roger. We're going to move closer.'

'Okay, be careful. Keep me informed. Hey, are you all right?'

Tyson was momentarily thrown off guard by the question. He replied, 'We're all okay. Tired.'

The radio was quiet a few seconds, then Browder said, 'Roger that. Take care of the snipers and proceed towards Hue.'

'Roger.'

'Out.'

Tyson gave the radiophone back to Kelly. He looked at the men around him but showed no fear. He looked back at the hospital and saw it was fully ablaze now, and every window had bright orange flames curling out of it.

The remainder of the platoon had assembled in the open plaza in front of the hospital, knowing there was no one left alive inside. Nobody spoke, and the only sound was the rain in the palm fronds, the rain on the plaza, the rain in the puddles, and the rain on their helmets, heavier now, washing away the sound of the burning hospital and the movement of boots and rifles.

A sudden loud report caused everyone to turn, and a few men dropped into firing positions, aiming towards the hospital. The heated roof tiles were exploding, scattering hot shards of clay over the plaza. The men moved back. They waited. Finally the roof sagged and caved in, dropping onto the second floor which in turn collapsed onto the ground floor, leaving the hollow concrete shell of the building standing like a giant glowing oven. As if that were the signal they had been waiting for, the men began picking up their field gear and ammunition.

They divided up into their decimated squads, ready to move out. A few men looked at Tyson, waiting out of habit for an order, a signal, though Lieutenant Tyson was clearly not in charge any longer. Kelly pulled a .45 pistol from his web belt – Tyson's .45 – and handed it to Tyson. Tyson slipped it into his holster, noting that no one came forward with his rifle. Kelly said quietly, 'Get them moving.'

Tyson didn't respond.

Kelly said more urgently, 'Let's get the hell out of here.'

Tyson looked around the plaza, beyond his assembled platoon, and scanned the picturesque houses and neat gardens bordering the open area. He wondered where she had gone, if she was watching them from some hiding place. He realized now that she would tell what happened, and he realized also that there might be other witnesses in this apparently dead and abandoned village.

Kelly seemed to understand at least part of what he was thinking. Kelly said, 'Don't worry about the villagers. They can't say for sure what happened. The people in there' ... he nodded towards the hospital ... 'they won't say a thing. Let's put some distance between us and this place. Before a command chopper comes by and asks what's going on.' Kelly looked at Tyson awhile, then raised his arm and called out, 'Saddle up! Movin' out!' He brought his arm down and pointed east towards a wide village lane that opened onto the plaza. Kelly gave Tyson a nudge, and the platoon began moving. Kelly said to him loudly, 'Hell of a firefight. Right?'

Tyson looked down the line of men and saw Bob Moody

being carried by Brontman and Simcox on a stretcher that they must have got from the hospital. Moody was smoking a cigarette and talking animatedly, the way the lightly wounded always did when they realized what could have happened to them and hadn't.

Further down the line, Holzman and Walker were carrying a bamboo pole on their shoulders. Slung from the pole was a green-grey rubber poncho, and in the poncho was the foetal-curled body of Arthur Peterson, who had died sometime during the time his platoon had been killing the doctors and nurses who might have saved him.

Behind him, Richard Farley was trudging under a heavy weight: Strapped to his A-frame, in place of his pack, like a deer, was the body of Larry Cane. Cane's head bobbed above Farley's left shoulder, his face covered with a big olive-drab handkerchief as was the procedure. But the tied handkerchief had slipped, and Tyson saw Cane's face, one eyelid still open. Someone had wiped the blood that had gushed from his nose and mouth, but there was still a smear of it on his chin, and his parted lips revealed red teeth.

Tyson stared at the white face as Farley drew nearer. Then Tyson looked at Farley's face in bizarre juxtaposition to the dead face behind him. Tyson's and Farley's eyes met and held. Farley's lips formed words, but Tyson heard nothing. Tyson reached out and retied the handkerchief firmly around Cane's face, feeling the cool clammy skin.

Tyson turned and began walking with his platoon. At least, he thought, they had two KIAs to back up a story of a battle. He hoped no one back at graves registration could tell that Cane had been shot at point-blank range with an Army .45-calibre pistol.

Kelly said, 'Where we heading?'

Tyson looked at him. 'Hell.'

Kelly nodded. 'Well, get out your map, Lieutenant, and show us the way.'

'Ben? Are you listening to me?'

Tyson's eyes focused on the photograph of the hospital. The banyan tree was still there, bigger now, its branches dropping into the roofless hulk. He handed the newspaper page back to Corva. 'Don't recognize the place.'

'Nevertheless, the Hanoi government states this is Hôpital Miséricorde. Or was.'

'Commies lie. Everyone knows that.'

Corva continued, 'I wonder if a team of experts could tell by the bullet pocks on the concrete what sort of shooting took place there. I mean I assume the shot groups or shot patterns of a massacre might look different from those of a firefight.'

Tyson didn't respond.

'Also the Hanoi government is excavating the ground-floor rubble, though I imagine the bodies must have been removed sometime after the Tet Offensive ended.'

Tyson lit a cigarette.

Corva said, 'Whatever was left there would have been used as ash fertilizer by the villagers. The vultures, beetles, and worms got the rest. Still, the concrete shell may reveal something, and this is the first possible physical evidence we've had to deal with.'

'Should I be concerned?'

Corva thought a moment. 'The *Times* story doesn't indicate that anyone in our government has accepted this invitation.'

Tyson observed, 'This invitation comes from the same people who massacred two thousand men, women, and children of Hue on the other side of the city. Where the hell do they get their nerve? I'd like to take an international commission to the Strawberry Patch and show them where I found the mass graves.'

Corva said ironically, 'That's not the way it works, Ben. American atrocities are more atrocious than communist atrocities. You know that.' Corva added, 'Anyway, this mess is making our government unhappy.' He sighed deeply.

472

'Damn it. I always knew this thing would make us look bad. Why do we always do this to ourselves?'

'Because,' replied Tyson, 'we do it better than anyone else could do it to us.'

Corva shook his head absently. 'Anyway, in answer to your question, it is my guess that the White House will tell the North Viets to take their kind invitation and shove it up their asses. Diplomatically.'

'But the other countries *will* send people to Hue.'

Corva rubbed his lower lip. 'Yes, and they may discover something. But I've already informed the Justice Department that if they think they are going to introduce at an American court-martial any evidence gathered in a communist country by foreigners, they'd better be prepared for a ten-year legal battle, not to mention public outrage. I think they understood. We'll see.'

Tyson commented, 'You place a lot of faith in American public opinion.'

'You should too. There is not much we can do about negative world opinion. But did you see that poll that indicated that an incredible seventy-eight per cent of the American public thinks you are being made a scapegoat?'

'I missed that one.'

'I have a clipping service that sends me anything with your name in it.'

'Good.'

'You've become a focal point, Ben, for a lot of pent-up feelings here and abroad.'

Tyson shrugged. 'Not my fault. I'd as soon drop the whole thing.'

Corva added, 'Like the Dreyfus court-martial, this is perceived as a case that transcends Benjamin Tyson and the first platoon of Alpha Company.'

'Is that so?'

Corva pulled a sheet of paper from his briefcase. 'Enough of international diplomacy and the state of the Union. Let's

473

move on to more important business. I had a pleasant chat with Major Harper last week. In my office.'

Tyson said casually, 'Did you?'

'Nice piece of goods, Ben.'

'I hadn't noticed.'

'Well, I did. Anyway, she's too tall for me.'

'Actually you are too short for her. What did she want?'

'Oh, just wanted to brief me on a few items. The most significant of which is that the FBI has located Hernando Beltran, Lee Walker, and Louis Kalane.'

Tyson said nothing.

Corva went on, 'That was quick work. Of course they knew all along where these men were. But the Justice Department wanted to see if you were going to be charged before they told you that.'

Tyson said, 'I never really understood why they weren't found sooner.'

'And the government never released the names of the men in your platoon because if they had, people who knew these men would have blown the whistle to the media.'

Tyson nodded thoughtfully. 'But you know, Karen Harper wanted me to make a public appeal for them to come forward.'

'Karen Harper was operating in a vacuum. For every hour she put in on the investigation, there were bureaucrats, JAG people, Justice Department lawyers, and FBI agents who were putting in hundreds of hours. She was the visible tip of an iceberg she didn't even know was attached to her. I think she knows that now. Doesn't matter though. Point is, she was asked to contact Beltran, Walker, and Kalane by telephone. And she did.'

Tyson stood and walked to the window. He stared out at the headlights of the traffic crossing the bridge.

Corva said, 'Harper reports that she spoke to each of the three men briefly by phone. Beltran and Kalane put her in touch with their respective attorneys. Walker did not have a lawyer. He is a mechanic, someplace outside of Macon, Georgia. Anyway the attorneys for Beltran and Kalane indicated that their clients would not make any statements unless they were subpoenaed. Beltran is a successful Miami businessman. Kalane is involved somehow in the tourist business in Honolulu. Harper asked these two attorneys if their clients' prospective testimony would characterize them as witnesses for the defence or the prosecution.'

Tyson lit a cigarette and continued to stare out the window.

Corva said, 'Harper informs me that they are your witnesses.'

Tyson exhaled a stream of smoke.

'So,' observed Corva, 'it seems you engender some sort of loyalty in your troops, Lieutenant Tyson.'

Tyson said, 'They kept the faith, Vince.'

'So they did. I'll tell you something though. If I had been the attorney for either of them, I would have advised them to jump on the government side.'

Tyson turned from the window. 'Why?'

'Well, they will never be charged with murder even if they get on a witness stand and give a blow-by-blow account of a massacre. On the other hand, if they tell the altered version of the hospital incident but you are convicted anyway, they may then be liable for charges of perjury.'

Tyson said, 'I'm sure their attorneys advised them of that.'

'I'm certain they did. Yet they want to stand up for you, Ben. I'm deeply touched. But not too deeply.'

'Meaning?'

'Well, meaning that if this case had come to trial in 1968 or anytime before these men had been honourably discharged, then *they* would have been charged with the actual murder. Also, whether or not they are immune from prosecution, they are still not going to stand up in a public trial and admit to mass murder. I'd like to think they are going to stand up for you totally out of loyalty, but they have other motives as well.'

475

'Perhaps, Vince. Perhaps. But it's not up to us to judge their motives.'

Corva stood. 'Do you have any loyalty to them?'

'Meaning?'

'Would you protect their reputations on a witness stand?'

'I suppose I would. But I do feel ambivalent towards them. They did something for which I'm now left holding the charge sheet, as you pointed out.'

'That's your fault, Ben. I can see why you didn't prefer charges immediately. But afterwards ... when you were safely on that hospital ship and had time to think – what was that if not loyalty?'

'I suppose I felt loyal. The Army engrains in you the concept of loyalty between an officer and his men. But when something like this happens, that loyalty can cause a miscarriage of justice.'

'I know that.'

Tyson went on, 'When I was wounded, they all said goodbye. And they were truly sorry to see me go. A small thing, but it loomed large while I was lying on the hospital ship, a writing pad in my hand, wondering if I should write a love letter to my girlfriend, or a memo to the battalion commander.'

'I understand.' Corva poured two more glasses of strega and handed one to Tyson. Corva said, 'What I meant by my question about loyalty is this: If you are convicted, it is *essential* that you take the stand and offer true testimony in extenuation and mitigation before the board votes on a sentence. True testimony – in as much as any war story can be true – would obviously be very damning towards Messrs Sadowski, Scorello, Beltran, Walker, and Kalane. And it might leave them all open to perjury charges which the Justice Department might well pursue in a federal court. And perjury is a very bad rap.' He looked at Tyson.

'Why don't we cross that bridge when we come to it?' He put down his drink. 'Tell me about Lee Walker.'

476

'Oh yes.' Corva took a sheet of paper from the coffee table and perused it. He said, 'Karen – Major Harper reports that Mr Walker's initial statements to her led her to believe he was a witness for the defence.'

Tyson nodded. Somehow he'd had no anxieties about Walker's testimony.

Corva continued, 'Unlike when she questioned you, Sadowski, and Scorello, she was obligated to end the interview with Walker as soon as she determined that he was a witness for the defence, because you have now had charges preferred against you, and you have an attorney. So, Major Harper turned Mr Walker over to me. I spoke to him by telephone. What do you remember about him?'

Tyson finished his drink and noticed the bottle was nearly empty. He put his glass down and lit another cigarette. 'I don't know ... a simple man. Honest. Kept out of trouble. Rural Southern black. You know the type.'

Corva said, 'He was a little jumpy. Kept saying you didn't do anything wrong.'

'Put him on the stand.'

Corva smiled. 'Well, that is the question. Which of the five do we put on the stand?'

'All of them.'

'No, I told you why we can't do that. It would sound like they were all reading from the same teleprompter. What I have to decide is not only who will do the best acting, but who will stand up under cross-examination. That is very important.'

Tyson observed, 'You haven't gone to see Sadowski or Scorello yet.'

'No, I have not.'

Tyson said with a touch of sarcasm, 'I've heard of armchair detectives. Now I've met an armchair lawyer.'

Corva looked at him awhile. 'There is such a thing as overpreparing for a case. I've seen that.'

Tyson laughed despite himself. 'Okay, you're the lawyer.'

'That's right,' agreed Corva. 'Anyway, in conclusion, Major Harper also advised me that neither Daniel Kelly nor Michael DeTonq has been located. Nor has Sister Teresa.'

Tyson nodded. The blinds rattled as a breeze blew in off the water. Tyson spoke musingly. 'It's cooling off. It was a hot summer. Summers are sort of memory markers of the mind. I'll remember this summer for quite some time. I recall the summer of 1966, before I reported for duty. I was out of college, and I took the entire summer off. It was one of those perfect times in one's life: no obligations, no pressures, a sense of accomplishment at having graduated, and the prospect of a new adventure in front of me.' He looked at Corva. 'At times like these, it's normal to return to the past. But not particularly healthy, is it?'

'It's all right. If there is a refuge in the mind, Ben, hide out there awhile.'

Tyson sat again and poured the remainder of the liqueur into his glass.

Corva shuffled through his papers. He said, 'I was impressed with her.' He looked at Tyson. 'You were too. And she was impressed with you.'

'Maybe if she gets out of the Army before my court-martial, I'll fire you and hire her.'

Corva finished his drink. 'Well, she won't get out of the Army while this is going on. They want her where they can keep an eye on her.'

Tyson went into the kitchen and came back with a bottle of port. 'Real Portuguese stuff. Thirty-five bucks a bottle. Float a little of this on top of the strega.' He filled Corva's glass to the brim, then filled his own. They both drank the port, then drank another. Corva mumbled something about having to drive. He suppressed a belch, then said, 'Also, Harper would not take the job of defending you, Lieutenant—'

'Cut the Lieutenant shit.'

'Because she believes you are guilty.'

Tyson slumped into the armchair and poured himself

478

another. 'How about you?'

'I would not have taken this case if I did not totally believe you should not pay for what happened there. I was there, buddy, and *I* would not want to pay again.'

'You didn't say *you* thought I was innocent.'

Corva shook his head several times. 'Of course I didn't say that. I think you are guilty. I only said you should not have to pay.'

Tyson leaned forward and stared at Corva. 'You said you would not want to pay *again*. Are *you* indictable? What did *you* do over there?'

Corva stood but did not move from his spot. He swayed slightly, and his eyes seemed to be focused on something a long way off. At length he said, 'Pretty much what you did, Ben. Looked the other way. Oh, it wasn't as grand as a massacre ... but it was more than one incident.'

'Tell me,' prompted Tyson out of perverse curiosity. 'Picard told me. You tell me.'

'Fuck Picard.' Corva seemed to forget what it was he was going to say, then blurted, 'My machine gunner mowed down three enemy soldiers who approached us under a white flag. I was sick for a week over that. Three kids who'd had enough and wanted to surrender. He cut them down like they were nothing ... nothing.' He glanced at Tyson. 'I had a sharpshooter, Ben, with one of those fancy hunting rifles and high-powered scopes ... he used to like to check the rifle's aim by shooting peasants running through the fields to get to their villages before curfew. He said his watch was fast. Get it? His watch was fast. He did it three times before I put a stop to it. Another time, we approached a village bomb shelter where a few villagers had taken cover, and—'

'All right!' Tyson stood. 'All right, Vince. Enough. For God's sake, enough.'

Both men stood in silence for some time. Then Corva walked over to Tyson, and to Tyson's utter amazement, embraced him.

Tyson stiffened, not knowing what to do. He hadn't been embraced by a man or embraced a man since ... Vietnam. He moved his arms awkwardly and patted Corva on the back.

Corva stepped away. 'Sorry ... you know how Italians are.'

Tyson cleared his throat. 'Oh, it's all right. I was getting ... emotional too.'

Corva took a deep breath. 'And those were only the offences that are indictable today – the murders. There were other things – the beatings, the sexual ... well, you know.' He looked at Tyson. 'Why did I let him do it *three* times before I put a stop to it, Ben? Why?'

Tyson replied, 'Because you didn't believe what you were seeing the first two times.'

Corva nodded quickly. 'Yes. Yes, that was it. I guess ...'

Tyson rubbed his face and said wearily, 'Is that about it? I mean are we finished here?'

Corva began packing his briefcase. He said, 'This is Monday night ... the Article 32 hearing convenes Friday morning. I guess we ought to talk about that next time. See what we can do about not getting you indicted.'

Tyson said, 'I might be a free man by Friday afternoon.'

Corva nodded. 'Might be.'

'And they will probably release me from duty the following week.'

'Probably.'

'Except none of that is going to happen, is it?'

'Probably not.'

Tyson could see that Corva was both upset and drunk and had become taciturn.

Corva picked up his briefcase and walked to the door. He said, 'I tried to get you a pass to meet me in the city tomorrow. But I think Colonel Hill thinks if you skip out, his career will be over. And he's right.'

'I'm not running.'

'I know that. But they don't know you. So I'll be here tomorrow, sometime before noon. Will you be here?'

Tyson forced a smile. 'Call my secretary, and she'll give you my schedule for the morning.'

'Right.' Corva opened the door and drew in a long breath. He looked back at Tyson. 'I broke my rule. About war stories. Sorry.'

'It's okay.'

'Won't happen again.' He stepped onto the stoop. 'Kiss your wife good-bye when she leaves for work tomorrow. Kiss your son too.'

'Can you drive?'

'No. I'll take a cab.' Corva walked unsteadily down the path.

Tyson watched him turn towards the main gate. He said softly to himself, 'God, do we *all* have blood on our hands? Did anyone return from that place with his honour intact?'

Corva, he thought, like so many of them, had seemed to come through it without a scratch until you looked inside his head.

38

The rain beat heavily against the windows. Tyson threw the morning newspaper aside and turned on the television, then shut it off. He poured himself another coffee but did not drink it, then lit another cigarette and stubbed it out. 'Damn it!'

He stared at the broken windowpane and smelled the damp cool air that blew in. He paced the length of the living room: five paces, turned around, five paces. He dropped to the floor and did thirty push-ups. He stood and wiped his face with the sleeve of his grey sweat suit. The sweat suit was grimy, and he wondered if he was allowed to go to the post laundromat, or if he had to send his son after school or his wife after work.

His eyes focused on a bud vase atop the TV in which was a single yellow tea rose. Somehow the idea of that flower in this dismal place offended him. Marcy's efforts to make the place a home angered him. He picked up the vase and went to the front door as the doorbell rang. He stood motionless, resisting the urge to answer it quickly. It was probably Corva, and he could stand in the rain awhile. Good for his character. The doorbell rang again. Tyson waited a full minute, then opened the door.

Vincent Corva hurried in and closed his umbrella. He looked at the vase and tea rose in Tyson's hands. 'For me?'

Tyson opened the door again and threw the bud vase out on the lawn.

Corva said, 'Hell of a day for the first day of school. I had to march my kids to the bus at gunpoint.' He took off his black raincoat. 'Reminds me of a monsoon I once walked in for two months. Did you have the monsoon up north?'

'I don't remember.' Tyson took Corva's raincoat and hung it in the minuscule coat closet.

Corva observed, 'Everything is small here. This place is so small you have to go outside to change your mind.' Corva moved into the living room.

Tyson looked at his watch. 'It's noon. What kept you?'

Corva put his briefcase on the coffee table. 'Traffic. I said before noon.'

'It's after noon. Five past.'

'Your secretary said for lunch.' He looked at Tyson. 'Are you stir-crazy?'

Tyson didn't reply.

Corva opened his briefcase and took out a brown paper bag. 'My wife made sandwiches. Italian cold cuts, provolone, and caponata. I want you to taste this.'

'I'm not hungry. I'm bored. I can't even take a walk in this fucking weather.'

'Well, you have to walk to post headquarters to sign in.

482

That's a nice break in the day.' Corva began unwrapping the sandwiches.

'Fuck post headquarters. I haven't signed in for three days.'

Corva looked at him. 'Hey, don't break the rules of your arrest, Ben, or they will put you in confinement. That means the slammer. All they need is an excuse.'

'At least there are people to talk to in gaol.'

Corva shrugged. He spotted the coffee carafe and a clean mug on the end table. He poured himself some coffee. 'I want you to sign in after we are done here.'

'Fuck them. They're not going to throw me in the slammer, and you know it.'

'Why not?'

'Because they're worried about their image, that's why.'

Corva put cream in his coffee. 'I wouldn't count on that.' He added, 'And if you wind up at the Fort Dix stockade, I damn sure don't want to drive down there to see you. And that place is grim, buddy. Also it's in New Jersey, and you wouldn't be caught dead in New Jersey.' He smiled.

Tyson didn't acknowledge the humour.

Corva sat in the armchair and opened his briefcase. 'Did you and Marcy and David kiss this morning?'

'No.' He lit a cigarette. 'No one was in a kissing mood. David was sulky. Marcy was trying to contain her exaltation at going back to the office. She almost floated out of here. Also, I slept on the couch. It sucks, Vince.'

'Oh, I know.'

'What am I supposed to do when she goes on a business trip? It will only be David and I here. And I can't even take the kid anyplace.' He picked up his metal ashtray, filled with cigarette butts, and heaved it at the opposite wall.

Corva pretended not to notice as he rifled through his papers.

Tyson sat down on the far end of the couch. He said, 'I told them to stay in Sag Harbor, then go home to Garden City. But, no, they wanted to share my martyrdom and mortification. Now they're as screwed up as I am.'

Corva picked up a piece of paper and said absently, 'Sorry about last night.'

'Oh . . . tell you the truth, I was so drunk, I don't remember much.'

Corva nodded. 'My wife was pissed off because she wanted the car today. I had to promise to stay sober and drive it home.'

'Don't let her push you around. You fought a war.'

'I don't think anybody gives a shit, Ben.'

'Right.'

Corva slid a wrapped sandwich across the coffee table and unwrapped his own.

Tyson opened his wrapper and lifted the long piece of Italian bread. 'What the hell is this?'

'It's eggplant, capers, olives, tomatoes, and some other good stuff. Beneath that is provolone. Then Genoa salami, prosciutto, capocollo, mortadella—'

'This will put a hole in my stomach. I could taste that fucking strega when I woke up.'

Corva bit into his sandwich. He spoke between mouthfuls. 'Anyway, the hearing convenes at nine A.M. in the Jackson room. It has some of the features of a grand jury except there is no jury – only the Article 32 investigating officer, this fellow who took over from Harper, Colonel Farnley Gilmer.' He peered at Tyson.

'Where do WASPs *get* these names?'

'Family names. Had a friend at school named Manville Griffith Kenly.'

'Christ. What did you call him?'

'Shithead.' Tyson picked up his sandwich and bit into it. He chewed cautiously, then nodded. 'Not bad. . . .'

Corva glanced at his notes. 'Anyway, Colonel Gilmer is supposed to be impartial, like Harper. He is not supposed to be perfecting a case for the government. But he knows who pays him every month. Also he is conducting a different sort of investigation than Harper did. Mostly he's reading her report, coordinating the efforts of the Army CID and the FBI in locating witnesses, using government resources to try to turn up any documentary evidence in the Army records bureau, and writing letters abroad regarding Sister Teresa. In addition, he's speaking to the newly appointed Army prosecution team and calling me when the mood strikes him. On the phone he sounds like an all-right guy, but you can tell he's nervous about fucking up. He's so cautious that when I say, "How are you?" he says, "Allegedly fine." '

Tyson smiled for the first time that day.

Corva continued, 'In the hearing itself, Gilmer is sort of a judge, jury, and moderator. However, there are instances when he performs some of the functions that are performed by a district attorney in a civilian grand jury. He does not have to literally change hats for this, but I always thought it would be good comic relief if that were required.'

'Christ, Vince, no wonder they won't let the press in.' Tyson sprawled out on the couch. 'I'm practising my military bearing for the hearing. Continue.'

'Right. There will also be a court reporter present. We will be present, and most importantly, the prosecuting team will be present. We will have an opportunity to see the face of the enemy. There are three of them.'

'There is one of you.'

'I could ask for one or two Army-appointed lawyers, if you'd like.'

'Do you want them?' asked Tyson.

'I prefer to work alone.'

Tyson considered a moment. He said, 'Wouldn't it be better from the standpoint of appearances and psychology if we had JAG lawyers in uniform present?'

Corva picked a piece of cheese out of his sandwich and chewed on it. 'Well, it would look good to Colonel Gilmer and to any court-martial board that is convened to hear your case. However, the presence of Army defence lawyers in uniform will give the subtle appearance that we concur with this whole travesty of justice. You have to be in uniform, of course, but I want you to somehow look and act like a civilian, with a civilian lawyer, who is being tried by a military tribunal. That is very un-American looking, and that's the way I want it.'

Tyson rubbed his jaw in thought. 'Okay, just you and me, Vince. Do you know anything about the prosecution team?'

'Yes, I know they are a very tough bunch. Their names are Colonel Graham Pierce, Major Judith Weinroth, and Captain Salvatore Longo.'

Tyson put his head back on the couch's armrest and stared up at the ceiling. He observed, 'The Army is an equal opportunity employer.'

'So it seems,' Corva said. 'The real problem is Colonel Pierce.'

Tyson lit a cigarette and blew smoke rings into the air. He flipped his ash on the floor. 'What do you know about him?'

Corva thought a moment. 'You want it straight?'

'Sure.'

'Okay. . . . First, he does mostly murder cases. He, like Van Arken, was on the prosecution staff in the Calley case. Before that he was an Army prosecutor at Long Binh. He tried capital cases there too. Sent a good many GIs home early. To Leavenworth. He is a protégé of Van Arken and therefore, a prick. He may one day be the next Judge Advocate General.'

Tyson sat up on the couch. He looked closely at Corva. 'Tell me more.'

'All right ... he is an accomplished trial performer but no buffoon, and the jury will never sense what a performer or a prick he really is. Only another lawyer can spot those sterling qualities. Also he is a genius in the true sense of the word. I've seen him introduce pages of documentary evidence, then without looking at it, quote long sections verbatim. He could be a stage actor.'

Tyson leaned forward, his eyes on Corva.

486

Corva went on, 'When he approaches the bench over some point of law, he can quote from the Manual for Courts-Martial, the UCMJ, and case law, chapter and verse, the way a Holy Roller can quote from the Bible. But he's not pedantic. He's quick-witted and has an analytical mind. He can switch tactics when he senses something isn't working, like a good battlefield tactician. Thinks on his feet.'

Corva went on in a quickening voice. 'He smells the weak points in the defence and attacks those weak points until he breaks through. Then when he's behind your lines, he blows up your ammo dump, pisses in your water wells, and eats your food. Then if you try to retreat, he blocks you, turns you around, and pushes you into the arms of an ambush. If you attack he makes a strategic withdrawal, then outflanks you and surrounds you. And he doesn't let up until you raise the white flag. Then he's magnanimous, like it was all just a jousting tournament, and he comes over to you wanting to shake hands and buy you a drink.'

Tyson said, 'Sounds like he might be a bit of a problem.'

Corva drew a deep breath. 'Well, I didn't mean to scare you.'

'Not at all.'

'I mean,' continued Corva, 'he is not invincible. He can be beaten.'

'Has he been?'

'No. He's never lost one.'

'Then you both have perfect records.'

'Right. But I'm due for a miracle.'

'That's right.' Tyson stood, went into the kitchen, and came back with a bottle of Sambuca. He poured a few ounces into his and Corva's coffee mugs. 'This is the first and last drink you're getting here.'

Corva lifted his mug. '*Salute.*'

'Cheers.' Tyson drank and put down his mug. 'That's not bad. Like drinking a liquorice stick.'

'This is good for digestion.'

'I think two fingers down my throat is what I need.' He sat on the arm of the couch. 'So, have you ever faced Colonel Pierce?'

Corva nodded. 'Once. At Fort Bragg. Eighty-second Airborne major. Violation of Article 114. Duelling.'

'Doing what?'

'*Duelling.* You know – ten paces, turn, and fire. That's been outlawed in the Army for over a hundred years. Takes a lot of fun out of garrison life. Anyway, I tried to show the jury that my client was defending his honour as an officer and a gentleman. It was a very unusual case.'

'But with the usual outcome.'

'Be fair, Ben. They had this major dead to rights. He slapped a young captain who he suspected was diddling his fiancée, then invited the captain to a clearing in the woods for a duel – forty-five automatics, no seconds to be present.'

Tyson waited. 'Well?'

Corva was picking up stray pieces of the sandwich from the wrapper and putting them in his mouth. 'Oh . . . well, the captain showed up with six seconds – all MPs – and they dragged this major off. The captain was no fool. Anyway, Colonel Pierce decided he wanted to prosecute this one even though duelling is not a capital offence. Even if someone gets killed. That's quaint. Anyway, you don't get many Article 114s.'

'What's the Army coming to? I was thinking of committing an Article 114 with Captain Hodges.'

'You are not allowed to bear arms. That's quaint, too. Lots of quaint customs in military life.'

'Right. So, what did this chivalrous major get?'

'Well, the rounds in the forty-five were short-loaded. Not enough powder to kill anyone according to my expert witness. The major was no fool either. Anyway, the jury loved this guy. I got him off with one year suspended and not even a separation from the service. Colonel Pierce was very upset. That was the one and only time he failed to get jail time awarded.'

'He's after you, Vince.'

'No, Ben, he is after *you*.'

Tyson smiled grimly.

Corva said, 'But I'm ready for the son of a bitch.' Corva seemed lost in thought for some time. He said, 'So that is how the hearing will stack up Friday. Colonel Gilmer officiates, Colonel Pierce and his two cohorts listen and watch.' Corva leaned forward. 'Your demeanour should be one of cool detachment.'

'Like the bloodless upper-middle-class WASP that I am?'

'Yes, that's right. Stay in character.' Corva reached for the Sambuca bottle, but Tyson moved it away. Tyson said, 'I need this to unplug the sink.'

Corva continued, 'Well, anyway, there are two theories regarding how the defence ought to proceed at a hearing. One: We can go into that hearing room prepared to fight every inch of the way to get the case dropped. Or two: We can assume that they mean to indict you even if we bring in six Carmelite nuns and the Archbishop of Hue, who swear you were taking Communion with them in Da Nang that day.'

'Where are the six nuns and the archbishop?'

'Doesn't matter. Point is, I believe they are going to indict you based on Brandt's statement, which, by the way, Colonel Glimer had Brandt swear to in writing. Farley's statement is also a sworn statement now. I have a copy of both. Do you want to see them?'

'No. But what makes you certain they are going to indict me?'

'I guess you're not following this case much.'

Tyson shrugged. 'If they're not going to indict me anyway, do I have to show up?'

'Only in body,' replied Corva. 'You see, Ben, I could drag in Sadowski, Scorello, Beltran, Walker, and Kalane. And they might just make one hell of a case for you. But this guy Colonel Gilmer will say to himself, "Why are these guys saying one thing, and Brandt and Farley are saying another?"

And he'll answer himself, "Let's have a court-martial to find out. Let's have a seven-person jury decide." Or words to that effect. You see, Ben, unlike a civilian grand jury where a lot of people vote in secret, Gilmer has the only vote. And if that vote is cast to not indict, everyone will guess that was his vote because he's the only one voting. *Capice?'*

Tyson nodded.

'And,' continued Corva, 'this obscure colonel will be suddenly well known to his superiors. So let's suppose Gilmer reads all the testimony, examines the facts, and we let him talk to our witnesses, and he does recommend that no indictment be forwarded. His decision, unlike a civilian grand jury's decision, is not binding.'

'Then why bother with this farce?'

'Because some years ago the Army was forced to institute a grand jury system in order to protect the rights of the accused who were subject to too many discretionary command decisions. So the Army came up with this watered-down Article 32 hearing that still lets higher commanders reverse any decision of the make-believe grand jury type of hearing. The President at that time bought the goods and signed it into law. And so far the Supreme Court has been reluctant to hear any challenges to it. You see, the federal courts try to avoid this land mine of military justice. The premier of France, after the Dreyfus case, commented, "Military law is to law as military music is to music." If the federal courts had legal jurisdiction over you, you would still be a civilian. I would have raised three hundred legal questions by now, and eventually I would have plea-bargained this down to a fifty-dollar fine. But that's not the case. You are going to sit in a room with some scared colonel who wants you out of that room as quickly as possible. If Colonel Gilmer goes home that night and prays for guidance from above, he will not be praying to God, but to General Van Arken. And even if Colonel Gilmer for some reason does not vote to indict you, then General Peters, post commander at Dix, will. And if

490

Peters doesn't vote to indict you, it can go right up to the Secretary of the Army, then Defense, then the Commander in Chief of the Armed Forces, who happens to be a politician. But the government does not want those people to have to stick their necks out and make an unpopular decision. And I strongly suspect poor General Gilmer senses that and would not want to cause anyone above him such anguish. So he will forward the indictment to General Peters, who, on the advice of his Staff Judge Advocate, will concur. General Peters will then issue orders convening a general court-martial.'

Tyson stood and walked to the window. He watched the rain awhile. 'The script is already written.'

'No, never written. Just understood by everyone who plays.'

'I used to respect military justice.'

'I still do. I told you I'd beat this in a federal court. But I'm having a hell of a time beating military justice. Point is, you are guilty. So you had better still respect it.'

Tyson continued to stare out the window. 'I don't like not putting up a fight, even if it's a losing fight.'

'If we put the defence witnesses on the stand, they will be subject to cross-examination. We will have prematurely revealed to Colonel Pierce our positions, our strengths and weaknesses,' Corva added. 'But the decision is yours.'

Tyson regarded the gloomy, rain-sodden landscape. 'Okay, we'll hold the witnesses for a court-martial. Will Brandt and Farley testify for the prosecution?'

'Colonel Pierce will not call them for the same reasons I won't call our troops. Colonel Gilmer will consider their sworn statements. I do have a lot of questions for Brandt and Farley, but I'll have to ask them in front of a court-martial board.'

'What sort of questions?'

'Well, I'm glad you asked. Maybe you can answer a few of them ahead of time.'

Tyson turned from the window.

'You see, Ben, there *is* one way of convincing Colonel Gilmer that he doesn't have to forward an indictment. And if his reasons are sound, the chain of command will concur, and you will be free.'

Tyson said nothing.

Corva fixed his eyes on Tyson's and asked, 'Is there something you can prove, either through Army records or through witnesses, that would show Colonel Gilmer and everyone that you and Brandt were enemies?'

Tyson stayed silent a moment, then replied, 'No.'

Corva continued staring at him. 'Why does Brandt hate you?'

'I didn't say he did.'

'Do you hate him? I don't mean because of this. I mean because of something that happened over there?'

Tyson considered the question. He replied, 'No, I don't hate him. I personally despise him. He was morally corrupt.'

'Will the accused expand on that?'

'Not at this time.'

'Can I tell you what Sadowski said to me? What he hinted to Harper and what she mentioned in her report?'

'What did Sadowski say?'

'He said you once beat the shit out of Brandt in front of the whole platoon. You kicked him and punched him repeatedly in the face. Then you threw him into a flooded rice paddy and wouldn't let him out until he was covered with leeches.' Corva stared at Tyson. 'He was half hysterical from the leeches, crying and begging you to let him come onto the dike.'

Tyson lit a cigarette and exhaled a long stream of smoke. 'I seem to remember something like that.'

'Why in the name of God would an American Army officer beat and humiliate one of his own men? A medic, of all people.'

'I guess I was having a bad day.'

'Don't be facetious, Ben.'

'Oh, look, Vince, you don't want to hear it. It's a war story.'

'I'll listen to this war story.'

'Some other time. It's not pertinent.'

'Not *pertinent*? It's very pertinent to why Brandt has come forward and told this story.'

'It doesn't change the *story*. Or the facts.'

'I'm not interested in *facts!* I'm only interested in showing that Brandt, in his hate for you and his desire for revenge, is not a credible witness.'

Tyson replied evenly, 'Brandt is a respected doctor. And he has a corroborating witness.'

'What does Farley have against you?'

'I'm not sure.'

'Why did Brandt know to tell Andrew Picard that Farley was the one who would back up his story? He didn't give Picard any other names. Only Farley.'

Tyson shook his head. 'Maybe Farley was the only one whose whereabouts he knew. Maybe they kept up their wartime acquaintance.'

'A medical doctor and a strung-out paraplegic junkie? I doubt that. Were they good friends over there?'

'Not that I recall.'

Corva sat. 'This is like pulling teeth. You are not going to tell me what motivates Brandt and Farley, though I think you know.'

'Maybe later, Vince, if it gets down to that.'

Corva snapped his briefcase shut. 'Okay. So Friday it will be you and I and Colonel Gilmer and the prosecution team, a court reporter, and no witnesses for the defence or prosecution. Also, there will be two other people present.'

'Who?'

'Karen Harper, for one. She is in an advisory capacity to Colonel Gilmer.'

Tyson didn't respond.

'Also, Colonel Gilmer has subpoenaed Andrew Picard.'

'Picard?'

'Yes. Not for the defence or prosecution, but as Gilmer's

own witness.'

'What does Gilmer want Picard to testify about?'

'Well, apparently Mr Picard told Karen Harper a few things that didn't appear in his book or in subsequent interviews, and Gilmer feels that oral testimony is the best way to discover more about those things.' Corva added, 'You had a chat with Picard yourself.'

'Yes.'

'Was it pleasant?'

'It was revealing.'

'Will he help us or hurt us on the stand?'

Tyson replied, 'We actually hit it off all right. But you know how writers are. They think they have a special relationship to the truth. I'm sure even Wally Jones believes that, or he'd have gone to court to have himself legally declared a cockroach.'

Corva said, 'Things are so rigged against us, Picard's testimony can't hurt. I don't want an eyewitness up there who can be cross-examined. But I'll take a chance with Picard and not raise any objections to his testifying. It should be interesting if not enlightening.'

'Could be.'

Corva went to the closet and got his raincoat. 'I'll speak to you tomorrow. If you recall why Brandt would like to see you in Leavenworth, please let me know.'

'I'll think about it. What amazes me is why you and Harper don't just accept the most logical explanation for Brandt's actions. He was tired of living with the damned thing.'

'Did he participate in the incident?'

'No. No, he didn't. But like me, he was a little ahead of the rest of the boys in education and maturity. And he was not infantry like the rest of us. He was trained as a healer. So he was particularly sensitive and upset. And now he wants to do the honourable thing. He wants justice.'

Corva nodded thoughtfully. 'That is what he will say, won't he?'

'Yes, that is what he will say. He will also say he respected me and I respected his work and having to testify against me is the toughest thing he has ever done in his life and he feels very badly for me and wishes it didn't have to be this way. But it's best for everyone if the truth is finally told. And so forth.'

Corva buttoned his raincoat. 'But deep down he hates your guts so bad that when he thinks about you he can taste the bile in his mouth. He has wished you dead a thousand times, and at the Strawberry Patch, he did something . . . something . . . and in the last twenty years, he has fantasized about smashing your face with a rifle butt or throwing you in a tank full of leeches. Right?'

'Most probably.'

'And one day . . . he sees this inquiry in the locator section of the First Cav newspaper and takes it as a sign. He throws caution to the wind, doesn't consider the ultimate consequences to himself if this comes to light, because his judgement is completely obscured by hate. And he spills his guts to Andrew Picard. And I'll bet by now he feels very ambivalent about what he did. It got a little bigger than he thought. He's ecstatic, of course, to see you being crucified, but he realizes there is some danger to himself as well. Right, Ben? He was an accomplice to this cover-up too. Meanwhile, Ben Tyson has figured out a way to finally settle the score. Right, Ben?'

'What do you mean, Vince?'

Corva pointed his finger at Tyson. 'You know fucking well what I mean. I mean that you intend for the trial of Benjamin Tyson to also be the trial of Steven Brandt. Right?'

'You're very bright, Vince, even if you are Italian.'

'And you're very, very vindictive for a coolheaded WASP, Ben. Christ, a Sicilian would wait twenty years to carry out a vendetta, but . . .' He shook his head. 'I think you're nuts. But if this is what you want . . . you must want it bad. Bad enough that you did damned little to fight your recall to duty, damned little to show Harper you were a victim of a man who

495

hates you, and damned little to try to make a deal with the government. Now I see *your* motive.'

Tyson handed Corva his umbrella. 'You may be partly right, of course. But it's all rather complex. I need this court-martial for me too. *Capice?*'

'Sure.' Corva opened the door. 'Well, it's still two hundred dollars an hour and double for court time even if you are nuts and even if you are enjoying yourself.'

'Hardly that, Vince, and I'm still counting on you to save me in the end.'

Corva laughed without humour, turned, and left, calling back, 'Sign in at post headquarters. Now!'

'Thanks for lunch.' Tyson closed the door, turned, and stared at the empty room. 'Yes, Brandt and I will take each other down together; but only one of us will rise again.'

39

Ben Tyson put his coffee cup on the white tablecloth and looked out the picture window of the Officers' Club dining room. White seagulls soared against the grey sky, dived, and skimmed the whitecaps of the choppy Narrows. 'Birds are free.'

'Very profound,' observed Corva as he helped himself to Tyson's toast. He looked up from his omelette and commented, 'That uniform is hanging a little loose on you, Lieutenant.'

'I'll see my tailor.'

Corva pointed at Tyson's ribbons with his fork. 'What is that there? Is that the gook cross?'

'Yes, the Vietnamese Cross of Gallantry. We don't say gook anymore, Vince.'

'I know that.' Corva swallowed a forkful of eggs. 'Odd, isn't

496

it? Wearing an award given by a country that no longer exists. Does that mean the award no longer exists? Makes you think.'

'About what?'

'About the transient nature of things we think are forever. About Babylon and Rome, Carthage and Saigon.'

'Ho Chi Minh City.'

'Precisely.' Corva went back to his breakfast.

Tyson poured more coffee. He asked, 'Did you get a medal for valour?'

Corva nodded slowly. 'Bronze Star.'

'Tell me a war story.'

Corva said, 'There are two versions of that story. One version got me the Bronze Star.'

'And the other version?'

'Would have got me . . . well, anyway, it had to do with tunnels. Tunnel complex near Dak To. Gooks would narrow the tunnels at some points so only gooks could get through. Well, I'm gook-sized. So I belly into this tight fucking hole, slithering like a worm, a silenced forty-five in one hand. Dark as hell, right? So I snap on my miner's lamp to take a quick look, and I'm face-to-face with Charles.' Corva put sugar in his coffee.

Tyson said, 'You're not going to tell me the rest, are you?'

Corva smiled mischievously. 'No. No war stories.' He leaned toward Tyson. 'Do you know why the Italian Army lost in World War II?'

'No, Vince, why did the Italian Army lose in World War II?'

'They ordered ziti instead of shells.'

Tyson lit a cigarette. 'I don't get it.'

Corva shrugged. He looked around the dining room. 'Do you know who's behind you? Don't look.'

'How many guesses do I get?'

'Having breakfast on the far side along the wall are Colonel Pierce, Major Weinroth, and Captain Longo.'

'What are they eating? Babies?'

Corva observed, 'We're going to have to share this dining room with them for some time if they hold the court-martial here at Hamilton. If you run into them in the club, be aggressively sociable – "Good morning, Colonel. Captain, do you have a light? Major Weinroth, may I suggest you visit the post beauty parlour."' Corva laughed. 'Well, don't say that. But you know what I mean. The Patriots' Bar is a little tight, and so are the urinals in the men's room, and you're going to be rubbing elbows with these people.'

'Maybe they'll take a liking to me. Do you think Major Weinroth will use the men's room urinal?'

'Quite possibly. And I think Pierce and Longo squat to piss. Point is, Army facilities for courts-martial are such that I've seen a lot of awkward encounters. I mean here's this guy Pierce trying to put you away for life, and you find yourself squeezed into a corner of the bar with him. Same goes for the prosecution witnesses and our witnesses. You and the dirty half dozen might run across Brandt or Farley.'

Tyson nodded.

'Farley is in a wheelchair so you can't touch him.'

'Can I beat the shit out of Brandt?'

Corva rubbed his nose thoughtfully. He said, 'Do what you feel you have to do to Brandt if your paths cross. I can't tell you what to do.'

Tyson looked towards the dining room entrance. Corva followed his gaze. Standing at the door waiting to be seated was Karen Harper. With her was a handsome older man in uniform.

Corva said, 'That's the Article 32 investigating officer, Colonel Gilmer. And the broad looks familiar too.'

'We don't call them broads anymore.'

'Right. What's wrong with me this morning?'

The hostess was escorting them to a table near Tyson and Corva's, but Colonel Gilmer said something to the hostess. She pointed to another table near Pierce. Gilmer shook his head, and after some discussion he and Harper found a neutral corner.

Corva said, 'Christ, somebody ought to brief the staff here.'

Tyson watched Karen Harper sit in the chair pulled out for her by Gilmer. As Gilmer came around to his chair, she looked at Tyson, and their eyes met across the room. She smiled first: the sort of brief but intimate smile old lovers pass to each other in restaurants when they are with their new lovers.

Tyson put on a smile he hoped was passable, though he didn't know how he felt towards her.

Corva nodded to Karen Harper and Colonel Gilmer. Corva said, 'He looks as uptight as he sounds on the phone. I'm going to have fun with this guy.' He added. 'She *is* a beautiful woman. I wonder why she never married. Probably fucks her brains out.'

Tyson said coolly, 'You really are a Neanderthal this morning.'

'I know. I'm psyching myself.'

Tyson glanced at his watch. 'It's a few minutes after eight. What are we supposed to do for the next hour?'

'I've arranged to have a conference room at our disposal. Here in the club. We'll sit and chat. And at precisely five to nine we will enter the fittingly named Stonewall Jackson room. By noon we will be back here for lunch.'

'Why don't you get fat? You eat like a horse.'

'I weigh two hundred pounds. But it's all muscle.' Corva stared across the room at Colonel Pierce for a while.

Tyson said, 'I want to see what they look like.' He turned in his chair at the same time Pierce looked towards him. Tyson didn't turn away, but Pierce did. Tyson looked back to Corva and commented, 'They look grim.'

'That's how prosecutors are supposed to look; like they are doing society's dirty work.' Corva asked, 'Did you hear from Marcy this morning?'

Tyson shook his head. 'She never calls when she's

travelling on business. I don't call her when I'm travelling either. It's a rule.'

'What kind of rule is that?'

'The kind of rule some couples who travel eventually discover.'

Corva bobbed his head slowly. 'I don't know if I would want my wife travelling. Is that insecure?'

'Yes.'

'I'm an old-fashioned dago.'

'That's your problem.'

'Is your mind on this hearing?'

'Absolutely.'

Corva finished his coffee. 'Let's go.' He motioned for the waitress, and for some reason got all five of them, plus three busboys and the hostess.

There was a stillness in the dining room as the hostess stepped forward and spoke. 'Lieutenant Tyson, we all would like to wish you the best of luck and to let you know it has been a pleasure serving you, your wife, and son these last few months. We want you to know that we all think you are an officer and a gentleman.' She led the small group in a brief round of applause.

Tyson stood and to his surprise felt a lump form in his throat. He reached out to the woman and gave her a spontaneous hug and a peck on the cheek. She blushed and said, 'Oh … my …'

Tyson said hoarsely, 'Thank you all so much.'

Corva started another round of applause, and this time a few of the diners joined in. The staff bowed in unison, turned, and left.

Tyson remained standing. His eyes fell on the table where Pierce, Weinroth, and Longo sat. They were eating their breakfast with exaggerated obliviousness. On the opposite side of the room, Colonel Gilmer studied the breakfast menu with intensity. Karen Harper gave him a quick wink.

Corva stood. 'How does such a snob like you inspire such

loyalty in the masses?'

'I'm handsome.'

'Yes, like Billy Budd. They hanged him, though.' Corva picked up his briefcase. 'Well, I don't see a chit, so I guess there is such a thing as a free breakfast.' He led the way out of the dining room.

They made their way to the northeast corner of what had been the old fort and approached a heavy oak door. Corva said, 'I have to go upstairs and pick up some paperwork. Go on in. There is supposed to be coffee and pastry laid on. I'll be back in a few minutes.' He turned and walked quickly away.

Tyson stepped up to the door. He didn't know who or what was behind the door, but it wasn't just coffee and pastry. He glanced back and saw Corva disappear around the corner. He opened the door and recognized the room.

It was an old powder magazine with walls of reinforced concrete, painted a nice beige now, with a royal blue carpet on the floor.

The room was dimly lit by a floor lamp, but an odd glow emanated from the ceiling which Tyson knew was a result of the ceiling being constructed of glass rods embedded in thick concrete; a means to let the daylight in so oil lamps did not have to be used in the powder room.

They were all sitting at a round table, drinking coffee, eating, and talking in low voices. A miasma of cigarette smoke hung in the air, enhancing the feeling that he'd stepped into a dream.

Tyson shut the door behind him. The talking had stopped, and the men sat self-consciously in silence, fidgeting with cigarettes and coffee cups.

Paul Sadowski smiled and stood. He bellowed, 'Ten-hut!' The other four rose hesitantly and stood, not at attention, but not at ease either.

Tyson took a few steps into the room. Sadowski, he saw, had grown huge. His hair was thinning, and he sported a moustache that looked like two arched caterpillars. He was

501

wearing what had to be the last leisure suit in the country.

Tony Scorello was thin as ever, but had sprouted a thick black beard to replace the hair that was missing from his nearly bald pate. Tyson wouldn't have recognized him except for the big brown doe eyes. He was well dressed in grey slacks and navy blazer but wore in place of a tie, a heavy gold chain.

Louis Kalane looked remarkably the same, his Polynesian features having become, if anything, more handsome. He had a full shock of jet black hair and wore a taupe-coloured suit of worsted wool in a style that Tyson had never seen in New York.

Lee Walker hadn't changed much either, though the seventeen-year-old that Tyson had known was now a little taller and a little more muscular. Walker wore a maroon polyester suit with a spread-collar shirt.

Hernando Beltran looked very old, and it took Tyson by surprise. His face was puffy, and beneath the finely tailored pearl grey suit lurked a fat man. Beltran sported gold rings and a Rolex oyster. He was smiling from ear to ear, showing a gold-capped tooth.

My God, thought Tyson, *how do I look to them?*

Sadowski stepped forward as if this had been rehearsed. He came to an exaggerated position of attention, sucked in his stomach, puffed his chest out, and saluted. 'Sergeant Sadowski reports, sir!'

Out of old habit, Tyson wanted to remind him that the 'sir' came first in the American Army, and last only in old British war movies. Instead Tyson returned the salute without comment. He said, 'At ease.'

Sadowski reached out and took Tyson's hand, grasping it firmly and pumping his arm.

Tyson wished Corva was in the room – not so Corva could share this moment with him, but so Tyson could beat the shit out of him. Tyson gave Sadowski a warm look. 'How you doing, Ski?'

'Fine, Lieutenant.'

502

'Ben.'

'Ben.' He laughed. 'Sounds funny.'

Tyson walked to the table, and Beltran grasped him by the shoulders. 'You borrowed twenty dollars from me, *amigo*. With compounded interest that is now two million dollars.' He laughed deeply.

Tyson took his hand. *'Cómo está, amigo?'*

'Oh, you speak Spanish now?'

'No, Puerto Rican.' He patted Beltran's stomach. 'How are you going to carry an M-60 with that?'

Beltran laughed as he patted his own stomach. 'Good living. I own half of West Miami. You come down, and I show you a hell of a time.' He winked.

Tyson turned to Lee Walker. 'How you been, Ghost?'

'Not too bad, Lieutenant – Ben. I don't own half of nothing, but if you come down to Macon, I'll take you bird shooting. You still good with a shotgun?'

'We can find out. I'd like that.' Tyson moved around the table to Louis Kalane and took his hand. Tyson pulled at the lapel of his elegant suit. 'You dealing dope again, Pineapple?'

Everyone laughed.

Kalane smiled abashedly. 'Just got lucky with them turkey mainlanders. I run tours. Come check it out.' He added, 'You look pretty nifty yourself, Lieutenant.' He grinned. 'Where'd you get all those medals?'

'You don't remember that war?' Tyson moved to Scorello. They shook hands, and Scorello mumbled, 'Nice seeing you again.'

Tyson replied, 'Same here, Tony. You're living in Frisco, right? Great town.'

'Right. I work for the city.'

'How long have you had that pussy tickler?'

Scorello forced a smile. 'Long time.'

They all stood in silence awhile, then Tyson said, 'Thanks for coming,' though of course they had little choice. He said, 'I didn't know any of you would be here.' He thought that

503

Corva must have switched tactics. He asked, 'Are you testifying today?'

Beltran spoke. 'No, no. Mr Corva just asked us to come and say hello to you. A little reunion.' He added, 'But we will be back for the court-martial to testify.'

Again, no one spoke. Tyson said, 'There may be no court-martial.'

'Good,' said Beltran.

Sadowski said, 'Sit down. Have some coffee. Hey, this fort is something else. Looks like those old Frenchie forts around Quang Tri.'

Tyson sat at an empty place, and everyone sat. He drew coffee from a silver urn.

Beltran looked around the table as though he were at a board meeting. He said, 'So this is it. Out of forty-five men, this is what is left of the first platoon of Alpha Company, Fifth Battalion of the Seventh Cavalry. *Mi Dios*, Custer had more survivors.'

A few men laughed halfheartedly.

Sadowski said, 'Don't forget Kelly and DeTonq. They're out there someplace.'

Scorello snorted, 'DeTonq is dead, Ski. He never made it back. Kelly is probably dead, too.'

No one spoke until Walker said quietly, 'There's Doc and Red, too.'

The room was silent again until Beltran smashed his fist on the table. 'Those *maricones*! Doc I could understand. He was not one of us. But Red – that I cannot understand.'

Tyson watched them through the haze of blue smoke caused by Beltran's cigar. He searched their faces for something, though he didn't know what. Perhaps there was a little guilt there, but mostly there was defiance, self-justification. If you couldn't justify the cold-blooded murder of babies, children, and women, then you died inside, or you died like Harold Simcox – inside and outside. Tyson said, 'Smallpox was almost here.' He looked at Scorello. 'He was a

504

buddy of yours, wasn't he, Tony?'

Scorello played with his beard. 'Didn't hear from him much the last few years. He got fucked up.'

Tyson took out a cigarette, and Kalane lit it with a gold Dunhill. Tyson said, 'I guess you know how Moody died.'

No one replied. Tyson had the impression that everyone was ambivalent about this reunion. Tyson asked, 'How did Brontman and Selig die?' He looked around the table.

Sadowski answered, 'Freddie died at Khe Sahn. Got hit by one of those little sixty-millimetre mortars the gooks liked so much. Selig was killed in the A Shau Valley. What a fucking mess that was, Lieutenant! Fucking gooks had armour, quad fifties, all kinds of bad shit. Selig stepped on a land mine. They sent him home in an envelope.'

Tyson drew on his cigarette.

Kalane added, 'You thought Hue was bad. Let me tell you, the A Shau sucked major cock. Khe Sahn was no picnic either. You missed the good stuff.'

Tyson nodded. 'I've always been lucky.'

Sadowski continued the oral history of Alpha Company. 'After you left, we got sent to Evans for rest and refitting. Some dork named Neely became CO. Then they sent four new second lieutenants out; bunch of fucking cherries right out of OCS; looked about sixteen years old. Then they send us a hundred replacements, all pfc's, not a sergeant among them, and they're still pissing water from infantry school. Well, fuck it, by that time I got transferred to the rear, and Hideaway rotated home. Ghost ... where'd you go?'

Walker replied, 'Unloading ships at Wonder Beach.'

'Right. And Tony ...'

Scorello said to Tyson curtly, 'I shot myself in the fucking foot. Got court-martialled and did a month in Long Binh.'

Tyson didn't respond.

They settled into a more relaxed atmosphere, telling a few war stories, talking about family and jobs.

Beltran took a cigar out of his breast pocket and handed it

505

to Tyson. 'Real *Habana*. Got contacts there.' He winked in a conspiratorial way. Beltran liked to wink, Tyson remembered. Beltran expanded on the wink. 'I still fight communists. I finance anti-Castro groups. I know how to fight those godless pigs even if the *maricones* in Washington don't.'

Tyson put the cigar in his inside pocket.

Beltran said, 'We killed a lot of communists at Hue, so what the hell are they complaining about now?'

No one seemed to have an answer.

Finally Walker spoke. 'Lieutenant, we want you to know we ... we were talking, and like we decided, it's nobody's business what happened. We'll stand up for you, like you did for us.'

Kalane said, 'When you got evacuated ... I told the guys you were going to squeal. But the MPs never came, and we're not going to forget that.'

Beltran looked around the table and declared, 'If they tortured me, roasted me on hot coals, I would not betray this man.'

Sadowski said, 'When that Major Harper called me on the phone, I nearly shit.' He laughed and looked at Tyson. 'My lawyer explained why they're nailing your ass to the wall and not ours. My fucking lawyer said to cooperate with the government.'

A few heads nodded.

Sadowski continued, 'But I told him where to put that idea.'

Tyson had the impression everyone wanted him to know they were doing him a favour. Or repaying the favour he did for them. But if they hadn't obliterated a hospital full of people in the first place, there would be no favours to repay. Tyson looked at Scorello, who hadn't offered any favours so far.

Scorello looked away and said, 'Let's stop the bullshit here. We're not going to talk because ... because we have jobs and families and all. I work for a liberal city government. And

506

things have been a little tough for me since this thing broke and my name got mentioned. Yeah, we'll help the lieutenant. But we're here to cover our own asses again, too.' He looked at Tyson. 'I had a kid when I was sent to Nam. I'm divorced now, but that kid – a son – is twenty-one. He's heard all the wild whore stories and all the times I shot it out with Charlie. Now he wants to know what the fuck I did there on February 15th.'

Sadowski said, 'I have a kind of sensitive wife. She cries a lot when she sees this shit on TV. When they say we killed the kids ...' Sadowski cleared his throat. 'This sucks.'

Beltran rubbed his double chin. He said, 'It does no good to speak of this. We all know what we have to do. Maybe you are doing it to save your reputations. In Miami I get no flak. So I am doing it only for Ben Tyson.' He nodded with finality.

Tyson marvelled that this was the same man who wanted to machine-gun him in the hospital. Well, he thought, people grow up.

Sadowski suddenly blurted, 'I'd like to kill that fucking Doc. And that shithead Red.'

Everyone looked at Tyson as if they wanted a second to the motion. Tyson said nothing.

Sadowski continued, 'I know guys in Chicago who would break their fucking legs and arms ... but I want them ... wasted.' Sadowski turned to Beltran. 'You got any guys who can do something about those two fucks?'

Beltran sat back with his hands on his paunch. He nodded slowly and winked.

Tyson looked at them, each in turn. Any five men who had not been to war would have been shocked at the turn the conversation had taken. But these were not any five men.

Walker said, 'Only Doc. Not Red.'

Scorello cleared his throat. 'It should happen before the court-martial.'

Kalane looked at Beltran. 'I'll pay for it. You arrange it.'

Tyson thought he ought to say something sane. 'I don't

507

think that will make us feel any better.'

Kalane leaned across the table. 'We gave our word, Ben, on pain of death. We weren't fucking around then. We're not fucking around now. That fuck Brandt gave his word. What the *fuck* makes him think he can break it without something happening to him?'

Tyson didn't think this was the time to mention that Corva wanted him to tell the whole story if he were convicted.

Kalane added, 'Listen, Ben, I wanted you dead that night after the hospital thing. Not because I didn't like you. I liked you a lot. But I liked me more. If *I* had shot my mouth off like Brandt, I would deserve to get wasted, too.'

Tyson looked around the table. He spoke in a voice that he hoped still had some of the old command authority in it. 'I covered for you *once*. I failed to do my duty *once*. But not again. If anything happens to Brandt or Farley, you might as well put me on your list, too, because by God I'll see to it that you all go to jail this time.'

No one met his eyes and no one spoke. Finally, Scorello said, 'Enough of this, for Christ's sake. Enough of this kind of talk. We're not killers.'

No one seemed to know how to reply to that remarkable statement. Tyson stared at the blue smoke hanging above the table, and his eyes drifted upward to the concrete ceiling with the small circles of thick glass, like blue-green bottle bottoms.

Tyson looked up at the pinpoint of light on the domed ceiling of the bunker and was reminded of a bright star in the night sky of the Hayden Planetarium. He guessed that an armour-piercing shell had once made a direct hit on the foot-thick rounded concrete top of the pillbox, probably during some long-forgotten engagement between the French and Viet Minh.

Someone struck a match, and the sudden phosphorus flare gave several of the men a start. A candle was lit, and its wax was puddled on the floor, then the candle was stuck

508

in it. The small flame seemed inordinately bright and cast shadows of the men along the round wall.

Tyson lit a cigarette with the lighter his platoon had given him. *Yea, though I walk through the valley of the shadow of death, I fear no evil for ... for I am the meanest ... for Thou art with me.*

Tyson leaned back against the clammy concrete and drew his knees up to his chest. He smelled, as much as saw, the wet canvas field gear strewn around the bunker. In the half light he picked out each of his men: Kelly to his right, Brandt to his left, both sitting with their backs to the wall. Spaced along the wall, also sitting, were Beltran, Scorello, Sadowski, Holzman, Brontman, Selig, Walker, Simcox, Kalane, Santos, Manelli, and DeTonq. Opposite him, about fifteen feet across the floor, was Richard Farley sitting between the poncho-wrapped bodies of Cane and Peterson. Moody lay on the floor in front of him and Brandt, moaning softly. Tyson leaned over to Brandt and said softly, 'Is he going to be all right until morning?'

Brandt replied in a whisper, 'I'm just afraid of blood poisoning. Otherwise he's okay.'

Tyson leaned forward and spoke to Moody, 'How you doing, kid?'

Moody took a few seconds to answer, then spoke through a morphine-induced haze. 'Oh ... Lieutenant ... feeling bad and good ... send me home ... checking out ...'

'Okay,' replied Tyson. 'Home.'

'Sign the orders.'

'Okay. Doc and I will both sign the orders.'

'Browder too.'

'Browder too,' said Tyson.

'No fuckups.'

'No fuckups.' Tyson whispered to Brandt, 'Home?'

'No,' replied Brandt. 'Fit for duty in a few weeks. Superficial. Just worried about the blood poisoning.'

Tyson leaned back against the wall again and drew on

his cigarette. There were four long narrow gun slits at eye level, and DeTonq was now peering out of the one facing Hue, Sadowski out of the opposite one facing An Ninh Ha. Tyson could see the flames and flares of night battle flickering at the gun slits, and he heard the rumble of impacting artillery and air strikes. He thought it was a bad sign that the only two sergeants in the platoon were doing what they should have ordered their men to do.

Scorello spoke softly, 'Doc?'

'Yeah.'

'Are they going to stink?'

Brandt replied, 'Yeah. They're dead.'

'Can't we put them outside?'

Farley's voice cut through the damp air. 'No! The animals'll get them.'

Brandt said, 'Double bag them. Two ponchos each, twist-tie them at both ends. No guarantee though.'

A few of the men moved towards the two bodies and did as Brandt instructed.

Tyson stubbed out his cigarette on the floor and felt for the handle of his .45 automatic in his holster. He wondered if they knew Kelly had given it to him. He wondered, too, if he'd use it or if he'd even have a chance to use it. He heard whispering around him and had the feeling that the whispering could end in the crack of a rifle shot. He worked his logbook out of his back pocket, drew his legs up further, and made an entry, then slipped the book under his shirt into his waistband.

The night passed slowly. Boots came off, feet were dried, socks changed, and boots were put back on. A few heat tablets were lit, and canteen cups of water were boiled over them. The smell of tea, coffee, and cocoa competed with the noxious fumes of the tablets, the mouldy concrete, and the stink of fear given off by seventeen bodies.

A card game started but broke up quickly. A few other men took turns at the gun slits. A few men went out into the rain to urinate or vomit. The radio speaker, its volume turned to the lowest setting, still filled the bunker with a continuous electronic crackling. Every half hour, Browder's radio operator would call the platoons for a situation report.

Tyson noticed the acrid smell of the local marijuana, but he didn't think he was in a position to make any arrests. In fact, he thought ironically, the more they smoked, the better he liked it. He pulled his fifth of scotch from his rucksack, took a short pull, and passed it to Kelly. Kelly drank some and passed it to his right. By the time it went around the wall and reached Brandt beside him, it was empty. Someone said, 'Hope Charlie don't hit us,' then laughed. A few other men laughed, but Tyson thought the laughs sounded shallow.

The radio came alive again. 'Mustang One-Six-India, this is Six-India,' the voice said, identifying itself as Browder's radio operator. 'Put your Six on for my Six, please.' Kelly hesitated, then handed the radiophone to Tyson. The bunker fell silent as Browder's voice came on in those low, distinct tones used at night in the field. 'One-Six, this is Six. I need some details of your contact for Big Six.'

Tyson licked his lips and spoke into the phone, 'Roger. Can't it wait until morning? We're trying to be quiet here.'

'Roger, that. I'll advise Battalion. You people okay?'

'Roger. But I've got listening posts out there. Hear lots of movement. If we make further contact, you'll hear from us loud and clear. Meanwhile, negative sit rep,' said Tyson in what he hoped sounded like an impatient tone.

'Roger. Keep cool. Dawn's coming.'

'Right, over.'

'Roger, out.'

Tyson handed the phone back to Kelly. Kelly said, 'As we approached the hospital, we took heavy fire. Peterson and Moody were hit. We took cover and returned the fire.

511

There was a sizable enemy force in the building. We didn't know it was a hospital. Lieutenant?'

Tyson spoke in the quiet bunker. 'There was a sizable enemy force in the building. I decided on an assault. We fired and manoeuvred towards the structure. We got inside and engaged the enemy in room-to-room fighting. Sadowski?'

'We got inside and engaged the enemy in room-to-room fighting. DeTonq?'

'We got inside and engaged the enemy in room-to-room fighting. Beltran?'

'We got inside and engaged the enemy in room-to-room fighting. Kalane?'

The litany continued as Tyson listened. When it came around to him again he added another line and again the congregation responded.

The hours passed, partly in silent thought, partly in restructuring the details of what had happened inside the hospital. Tyson noticed that the ponchos that shrouded the two bodies were bloating like balloons. He noticed, too, that the men had become lethargic – a natural result of fatigue, marijuana, and post-stress behaviour. They also seemed receptive to anything he said. Hour by hour he was regaining control.

A false dawn, peculiar to the tropics, broke through the east-facing gun slit, then it became very dark, the darkest hour. Tyson said, 'The structure was completely burned, and there are no weapons or bodies to turn in. But I estimate an enemy body count of twelve.'

Kelly said, 'That sounds about right. Ski?'

Sadowski actually seemed to think about it before replying, 'Are you counting the two that Kalane killed with the frag?'

Kalane said, 'I reported those two, didn't I, Lieutenant?'

'Yes,' replied Tyson, 'I have those two.' Tyson lit his cigarette and drank some tepid canteen water. He said,

512

'We pursued the fleeing enemy towards Hue but lost their trail.'

'Right,' said DeTonq. 'I spotted this old bunker half covered with growth, and we decided to check it out.'

'We moved towards it carefully,' said Beltran. 'Walker, he throws a concussion grenade inside, then we rush it.'

'It was empty,' said Walker. 'So we decided to hole up here 'cause we were pretty beat.'

Tyson watched the gun slits. The fires of the night faded as the sky lightened with the new dawn. The rain had stopped, and there was an odd stillness outside as the enemy made their usual dawn withdrawals.

Tyson stared at the sputtering candle awhile, then moved in a crouch to the centre of the bunker near the candle. Kelly, then Sadowski, drew towards him, followed by DeTonq, then the remainder of the men. Tyson put his hand out, and Kelly put his on top of his lieutenant's. Tyson watched as each man put his hand into the circle, and Tyson looked at each face in the light of the wavering candle. He did not know precisely what he felt for these men, but the overpowering emotion seemed to be pity. Tyson spoke in measured tones. 'We give our word as soldiers, as brothers, as comrades-in-arms, as men, as friends, as fellow sufferers, and maybe as Christians. And we know what we are giving our word about. And it is forever. Kelly?'

'I give my word. Doc?'

'I give my word. Sadowski?'

'I give my word. DeTonq?'

'I give my word. Beltran?'

Hernando Beltran said, 'Any one of us could have gone running to the colonel and told on the others. But we gave our word that night. And our lips were to be sealed to our death. I told no one, not even a priest. So I have this mortal sin on my soul ... this killing of nuns ... And I must pray each day that

God will forgive me when I meet Him. If He does not, then I am damned for eternity. This I did for us.'

Tyson listened for a while as they spoke, then said abruptly, 'Enough. We'll discuss Brandt at another time.' He switched to a mundane subject. 'Where are you all staying?'

Sadowski answered, 'The Army put us up at the guest house here. We got in last night. But your lawyer told us to make it a surprise.'

Beltran added, 'I want to take you all to a Cuban restaurant in the city, called Victor's. Then we go to another place for something else.' He turned to Tyson, but Tyson winked at him first and Beltran laughed. 'Yeah! You coming, okay?'

Tyson said, 'I'm under house arrest. But I can take you to dinner here at the club tonight.'

Kalane smiled. 'They don't let pfc's in here, Lieutenant.'

Tyson said, 'They do if pfc's means private fucking civilian.'

Everyone laughed. They made small talk for a while. The door opened and Corva entered. He looked around the table, and his eyes rested on Tyson's.

Sadowski called out, 'Another fucking officer. Right, Vince?'

Corva smiled. 'Right, Ski. First Lieutenant, infantry. The Twenty-fifth Division – Jungle Lightning. Best outfit in the fucking Nam.'

There were groans and jeers from the five men. Beltran said, 'The Cav was the number one ass kickers, and you know that if you were really in the Nam.'

Kalane added, 'Charlie shit when he saw the Cav coming.'

Corva pointed at Tyson's First Cavalry shoulder patch, a shield-shaped emblem with a black horse's head above a diagonal black stripe against a colour known as cavalry yellow. 'See this?' He tapped the horse's head. 'This is the horse that you never rode ...' He ran his finger along the diagonal stripe. '... this is the line you couldn't hold. And the yellow speaks for itself.'

'Oh, bullshit!' snapped Sadowski.

'Fuck you!' said Kalane.

'Eat shit,' suggested Walker.

Corva held up his hand. 'Just joking, men. Old Army joke. Everybody was jealous of the Cav.'

'Fucking-ay-right,' said Kalane.

Corva glanced at his watch. 'Well, time to go.' He said to the five men, 'I'd appreciate it if you'd hang out here, though I don't think I'll be calling on you.'

Tyson stood, and the other men rose also. Beltran produced a fifth of rum from his attaché case and emptied it into seven fresh coffee cups. 'A little toast, gentlemen.' He raised the delicate cup in his beefy hand with the style of a man who is used to presenting toasts. He said, 'A toast to the dead – God forgive me, but I can't remember all their names, but He knows who they are.'

They all drank. Walker said, 'And good luck to you, Lieutenant.'

Corva put down his cup and picked up his briefcase. 'Well, into the valley of death rode the First Cavalry.'

Tyson shook hands with each man and left with Corva.

Out in the corridor Corva said, 'Good to see unit pride.'

'It's remarkable after nearly two decades.'

'Yes, isn't it?' He added, 'It can't hurt us at the court-martial either.' Corva asked, 'Were you happily surprised?'

'I wanted to beat the shit out of you.'

'But you looked like you were having a good time.'

'Well ... I *was* glad to see them again after the initial awkwardness.'

'They seem like a fine bunch of men.'

Tyson walked in silence awhile, then said, 'They are all murderers.'

'Yes, but they are our murderers.'

They climbed the stairs and stopped at the door of the reception room marked 'Stonewall Jackson.'

Corva said, 'Look everyone in the eye when you enter. It's

515

not necessary to salute Colonel Gilmer. Our table is on the right as you walk in. Any questions?'

'How did I get here?'

'You took the long way.' Corva opened the door, and they entered.

40

It was a large handsome room with a highly polished wood floor, used for informal receptions and stag smokers. The front wall was brick with a fieldstone fireplace. The other walls were panelled in dark wood. Flanking the fireplace towards the ends of the brick wall were French windows with fanlights. Above the fireplace, appropriately enough, was an oil portrait of Thomas 'Stonewall' Jackson, who once served at Fort Hamilton before heading south.

In front of the fireplace was a podium, and behind the podium stood Colonel Farnley Gilmer. To Gilmer's right was a bridge table at which sat Major Karen Harper.

Tyson and Corva took their places at a long banquet table along the right-hand wall. Directly across from them along the left wall was another banquet table at which sat Colonel Pierce, Major Weinroth, and Captain Longo. To the prosecution's left front, Tyson noticed, was a court reporter, a pretty young pfc with blonde hair, freckles, and a sexy overbite, sitting at a portable olive-drab field desk of the type Tyson remembered from Vietnam. Other than the uniforms, that desk, and perhaps the oil painting of Jackson, there was nothing in the room to suggest a martial event was taking place.

The banquet tables were covered with floor-length white linen tablecloths. Tyson detected the faint odour of beer and stale smoke in the air.

In the far rear of the room were stacked about a hundred folding chairs. One of them had been opened and placed between the defence and prosecution tables, facing the podium. This, Tyson assumed, was the witness chair. An American flag on a stand had been positioned behind Karen Harper's table.

Between the flag and the door, standing at a modified position of parade rest, was a young black sergeant in dress greens. Tyson assumed he was the sergeant at arms, though he was not armed and wore no helmet as he'd seen at courts-martial he'd witnessed.

Tyson noticed that the defence, prosecution, and investigating team were spaced far enough apart so that private talk carried on in a low voice could not be heard by the other parties.

Colonel Gilmer looked at his watch.

Tyson looked at Karen Harper, but she was reading something in her lap.

Pierce, Weinroth, and Longo had their heads together and were conferring.

The court reporter hit a few keys on her stenotype.

Vincent Corva was making notes on some typed papers. He put his pencil down, leaned towards Tyson, and whispered, 'Ziti instead of shells. Why don't you get that?'

Colonel Gilmer said, 'Good morning. We are here to conduct a formal investigation into certain charges against Lieutenant Benjamin J. Tyson, ordered pursuant to Article 32b of the Uniform Code of Military Justice.'

Colonel Gilmer looked at Tyson. 'Lieutenant, you were informed of your right to be represented by civilian counsel at no expense to the United States or by military counsel of your own selection if reasonably available or by military counsel detailed by the Staff Judge Advocate at Fort Dix. You stated that you desire to be represented by Mr Vincent Corva of New York City.'

Tyson regarded Gilmer a moment. He was about sixty,

with short grey hair, a pleasant square face but a vacuous expression.

Gilmer continued, 'Let the record show that Mr Corva is present here with you.' Gilmer looked towards Corva. 'Mr Corva, I will ask you to step forward and enter your appearance by filling out item three on the official Investigating Officer's Report.'

Corva stood and walked to Harper's table. They exchanged a few words that Tyson couldn't hear, and Harper slid a form towards Corva.

Tyson looked across the room and saw that Colonel Pierce was looking at him pensively. Tyson continued to stare at Pierce. He was not more than fifty years old, a young colonel. He had dark red hair and wore it longer than the Army would have liked. He affected a pair of reading glasses, but Tyson had seen him reading with and without them at the same distance. His complexion was strikingly red, and Tyson couldn't tell if he'd been out in the sun too long or had dangerously high blood pressure.

Corva returned to the table and took his seat.

Colonel Gilmer referred to a procedural guide and began reading, glancing at Tyson from time to time. 'Lieutenant, I want to remind you that my sole function as the Article 32 investigating officer in this case is to determine thoroughly and impartially all of the relevant facts of this case, to weigh and evaluate those facts, and determine the truth of the matters stated in the charges. I shall also consider the form of the charges and make a recommendation concerning the disposition of the charges which have been preferred against you. I will now read to you the charges which I have been directed to investigate. They are as follows: Violation of the Uniform Code of Military Justice, Article 118, murder. Specification One.' Gilmer began reading the long, convoluted sentence of the first specification. Tyson tuned out and focused instead on Major Judith Weinroth.

She was about forty, he guessed, and he saw no wedding

518

ring, though that meant nothing anymore. The uniform looked awful on her, and Corva was right about recommending her to the post beauty parlour. Her expression was serious, all business-like, the expression of the professional woman. But as he looked at her, Pierce whispered something in her ear, and she smiled one of the brightest, prettiest little-girl smiles Tyson had ever seen, and her whole face radiated beauty. But then the smile faded, and the face looked forbidding again.

Gilmer finished reading the second specification and said, 'Lieutenant Tyson, I will now show you the charge and specifications.'

Karen Harper stood and walked across the polished floor. She stopped in front of Tyson and presented him with the charge sheet. Tyson took it with his outstretched hand as he turned to Corva and said loud enough for everyone to hear, 'Don't we have one of these?'

Corva said, 'You can always use an extra one.'

The court reporter giggled, and Gilmer looked annoyed. Harper, too, seemed annoyed and gave Tyson a look to show it before she turned and went back to her chair.

Gilmer let a full minute pass, during which time Tyson was supposed to read the charge sheet to himself. Instead, he looked at Captain Salvatore Longo. He was young, perhaps in his late twenties, and probably not too long out of law school. His uniform seemed perfectly tailored, and his curly blue-black hair was perfectly styled. His skin was deeply tanned in the way that Tyson had seen only on people who did a lot of boating. Tyson didn't think he was handsome, but he had no doubt Captain Longo had no trouble with women.

Colonel Gilmer again referred to something hidden behind the podium and said, 'Lieutenant Tyson, I advise you that you do not have to make any statement regarding the offence of which you are accused and that any statement you do make may be used as evidence against you in a trial by court-martial. You have the right to remain silent concerning the offences with which you are charged. You may, however, make a statement either sworn or unsworn and present anything you may desire, either in defence, extenuation, or mitigation. If you do make a statement, whatever you say will be considered and weighed as evidence by me just as is the testimony of other witnesses.' Colonel Gilmer poured himself a glass of water.

Corva said into Tyson's ear, 'What are the first five words a black guy hears after he puts on a three-piece suit?'

'What?'

'Will the defendant please rise?'

Tyson put his hand over his mouth. 'Cut it out.'

Gilmer was looking at the defence table with impatience. He said, 'Lieutenant Tyson, do I have your attention?'

'Yes, sir.'

'Good. Your defence attorney, Mr Corva, and the government attorneys, Colonel Pierce, Major Weinroth, and Captain Longo, have previously been given a copy of the investigation file which has thus far been compiled in your case. It contains the sworn statements of Dr Steven Brandt—'

Corva stood. 'Objection, sir.'

Colonel Gilmer's eyebrows rose quizzically. '*What* is your objection, Mr Corva?'

'My objection is to the use of the title "Doctor" in regard to Steven Brandt.'

'Isn't … Steven Brandt a medical doctor?'

'He may well be, Colonel. That has no bearing on this case. At the time of the alleged incident, nearly twenty years ago, Steven Brandt was a specialist four. If we have frozen my client's rank as lieutenant, then we can freeze Brandt's rank as well. Or we may call him "Mister" in these and any subsequent proceedings. I think you see my point.'

Colonel Gilmer seemed to be trying to see the point.

Colonel Pierce rose. 'Mr Corva … is that all right? *Mister* Corva? Or would you prefer *Signore*?'

Weinroth and Longo laughed.

Corva replied, 'You can call me Vince, Graham.'

The court stenographer giggled again.

Gilmer looked as though he wanted to bang a gavel, but he had no gavel. He said, 'There is a certain informality at an Article 32 hearing, but let's not overdo it, gentlemen. Colonel Pierce? Your point?'

'My point, Colonel, is that Mr Corva's point is pointless and petty. If he's suggesting that the use of Steven Brandt's title is somehow prejudicial to his client, then I suggest he's too infatuated with medical doctors. I, for instance, might think medical doctors are arrogant, insensitive, and avaricious.'

Gilmer turned to Corva.

Corva said, 'I wonder if Colonel Pierce would repeat that in the presence of his star witness?'

This time Gilmer smiled. Karen Harper stood and came up beside him. They conferred in low tones. Colonel Gilmer said, 'Major Harper informs me that Lieutenant Tyson made this point to her before he was represented by Mr Corva. So we'll assume the accused has a real objection to the use of Steven Brandt's title in these proceedings, and I can appreciate his point. Therefore, from here on we will all use the term "Mister" in referring to Steven Brandt. The issue is closed.'

Colonel Gilmer began again. 'The investigation file contains the sworn statements of Mr Steven Brandt, Mr Richard Farley, Mr Paul Sadowski, Mr Anthony Scorello, Mr Hernando Beltran, Mr Lee Walker, and Mr Louis Kalane. The file also contains the unsworn statement of Mr Andrew Picard. There is also in the file relevant documents, letters, and other incidental materials too numerous to identify individually.' Gilmer looked at Corva. 'Do you agree?'

'Yes, sir.'

Gilmer continued, 'I do not intend to call as witnesses Mr Brandt or Mr Farley, but intend rather to consider their

521

sworn statements as contained in the file, in reaching my recommendation.' Gilmer addressed Tyson and Corva. 'Even though I do not intend to call Mr Brandt or Mr Farley, whose sworn statements I intend to consider in arriving at my recommendation, it is your right to have an opportunity to cross-examine the witnesses on matters limited to their written statements, if those witnesses are available. If you wish, I will arrange an appearance of those witnesses for that purpose. Do you want me to call Mr Brandt and/or Mr Farley as witnesses?'

Corva conferred with Tyson. 'We could ask for them to be present, but that might take a week.'

Tyson said, 'I thought the prosecution was supposed to call prosecution witnesses.'

'No, Gilmer slipped on his DA hat. Didn't you see that? He calls prosecution witnesses or doesn't call them. Of course he confers privately with the prosecution first.'

Tyson said, 'I keep looking at that American flag there just to be sure.'

Corva smiled. 'I thought I'd let you see a little of this so you can reconsider our strategy if you want. A few minutes ago Gilmer told you that you could present evidence in extenuation or mitigation. Did you catch that?'

'Yes. That's like assuming I'm already guilty, and would I like to make excuses for what I did.'

'That's about the size of it. I'm glad you're paying attention. Also if I call Brandt or Farley I can only cross-examine them based on what is contained in their written statements. At a court-martial I can get into the real issues.'

Tyson nodded. 'I don't want to delay this a week. Let's get on with it.'

Corva stood. 'Sir, for the record we do not accept the sworn statements of Mr Brandt or Mr Farley in lieu of their presence. However, we will waive our right to cross-examine them for the purposes of this hearing.'

Colonel Gilmer addressed Karen Harper. 'Mark Mr

Corva's statement as an exhibit under item 6A.' He turned to Corva. 'I may consider *your* statement in arriving at my recommendation.'

'I hope, Colonel, you will also consider that the nature and seriousness of these charges is such that one would have expected you to call the government witnesses or have them present for cross-examination. It is most unusual to consider written statements alone in a case such as this.'

Gilmer's face reddened slightly. 'Well, then, do you want to call them for cross-examination or not?'

'No, sir. I think *you* should have called them so you could have examined them here in the presence of the accused. But if the written statements are cogent enough for you to consider how to proceed with an indictment for murder, then so be it. I only wish to register my utter amazement for the record.'

Gilmer glared at Corva.

Pierce stood. 'If it please the Colonel, I would like to register my own amazement that the counsel for the defence is questioning you on matters that are no concern of his.'

Corva smiled at Pierce. 'And no concern of yours. The colonel can take care of himself.'

Tyson sat back in his chair. He was actually enjoying himself even if no one else was. He glanced at the court reporter and saw she was having fun too. She looked up from her machine and caught his eye. She smiled.

Colonel Gilmer tapped his fingers on the podium. 'Will you both please take your seats?' He looked at Corva and said bluntly, 'Do you want Brandt and Farley here? Yes or no?'

'No, sir.'

Tyson leaned towards Corva. 'Why are you busting everyone's balls?'

Corva was staring across the room at Pierce, and he replied without taking his eyes off Pierce, 'I want to let Pierce know Vinnie Corva is back in town. As for busting Gilmer's balls, I want him to know we are not sitting still for any of this; that if there is to be a general court-martial, the counsel for the defence is going to attack the very form and substance of Army justice. That may give the people upstairs some second thoughts about a public trial.'

Tyson said, 'Can I smoke?'

'Why not? Gilmer and Pierce are blowing smoke.'

Tyson produced the long fat cigar Beltran gave him and lit it. Great billows of blue-grey smoke rose in the air.

Gilmer regarded Tyson a moment, apparently trying to decide if he should tell Tyson to put it out. Gilmer let it go with a look of annoyance. He continued with the procedural manual. 'Lieutenant Tyson, you also have the right to call available witnesses for my examination and to produce other evidence in your behalf. I have arranged for the appearance of those witnesses previously requested by you. If you desire additional witnesses, I will help to arrange for their appearance or for the production of any available evidence relating to your case.'

Tyson noticed that Major Weinroth had a folder in her hand and was fanning the smoke away from her face. She stood. 'Colonel Gilmer, may I request that there be no smoking allowed in here?'

Gilmer looked at Tyson. 'Do you need that cigar, Lieutenant?'

Tyson stood. 'I'm afraid so, sir.'

'Well, let's take a ten-minute break then. Smoking in the corridor.'

Tyson and Corva walked into the corridor, followed closely by Major Weinroth, who hurried off towards the rest rooms. Corva said, 'That was insensitive of you.'

'You said I could smoke.'

'I thought you smoked little cigarettes.'

'Beltran gave this to me. So how are we doing, Vince?'

'Not too bad. Gilmer is pissed off, and I even got to Pierce a little.'

'That's swell, Vince. Do you want to see now if you can get

524

me free?'

'First things first.'

The door of the hearing room opened, and Karen Harper came out. She hesitated, then walked up to them. 'Hello, Mr Corva, Lieutenant Tyson.'

Tyson said, 'Aren't you sick of this case?'

She didn't reply but said, 'Are you both quite pleased with yourselves?'

Corva answered, 'Oh, really, Major, farcical proceedings call for farcical behaviour.'

'This is a very serious matter and ... I think you are doing your client a disservice.'

'Let me worry about my client. Your relationship with him is terminated.'

Tyson's eyebrows rose.

She turned to him, and they looked at each other awhile. She said finally, 'I insisted that Andrew Picard testify today. I hope my insistence helps clear up this matter.'

Tyson dropped his cigar to the floor and ground it out with his heel. 'Sometimes I think that you're the only one who wants the whole truth and nothing but the truth.'

'I'm not sure *that's* true either. But if it is, then everyone else is wrong. Also, if you decide to take the stand yourself today, you might want to clear up the matter of how Larry Cane died.'

Tyson drew a deep but discreet breath. 'I told you how Larry Cane died.'

'Well, think about it.' She turned and walked towards the rest rooms.

Pierce came into the corridor, turned down the hall, stopped, and walked back. He stood in front of Corva, and Tyson saw he had at least a head on Corva and about sixty pounds. Pierce smiled unpleasantly. 'You see, what I forgot to establish is at how many *paces* the major intended to conduct the duel. After the trial I learned that within ten paces those bullets *would* have killed, and therefore, the weapons to be used *were* deadly weapons. Your analogy about duelling with ripe tomatoes impressed the board, but it was faulty.'

'I suppose it was, Colonel, now that you bring up the question of distance. How forgetful of me.'

'No, Mr Corva, it was forgetful of *me*. But I'll be more attentive to omissions on your part this time.'

'I'm sure you've learned something useful from that case.'

Colonel Pierce gave Corva a look that was not friendly. He fixed his eyes on Tyson a moment, smiled at some secret delight, turned, and walked down the corridor.

Corva watched him go. 'Very obsessed man. He ought to watch his blood pressure.'

'What is he obsessed with, Vince?'

'Unlike Van Arken, who may be an idealist, Colonel Pierce is an egotist. He has the temperament of a star tennis player. If he ever lost a case, he'd be impotent for months.'

'Well, that would be tough on Mrs Pierce.'

'Probably not. Point is, prosecuting is an individual sport, and if he lost he'd have no one to blame but himself. But he picks and chooses his cases carefully. None of them are cakewalks, but he doesn't pick cases that he thinks are too weak to win either.'

'Not like you, Vince.'

'No.'

'But he picked my case and picked it probably at a time after he knew you were the defence counsel. I thought you scared him off last time.'

Corva smiled and looked at his watch. 'Let's go back in. And stop ogling that little court reporter. Harper is annoyed at you.'

They entered the hearing room and took their seats. Within a minute, Karen Harper, Major Weinroth, and Colonel Pierce returned and took their places.

Colonel Gilmer said, 'Let's resume.' He looked around the room and said, 'In addition to the sworn statements for the defence and the prosecution, we have an unsworn statement from Mr Andrew Picard, whose role in this case is well known to all parties. It is within my power as investigating officer to call Mr Picard to testify under the category of an additional witness. This is done in the interests of justice, fairness, and a complete investigation.' He looked at Corva. 'Do you understand that Mr Picard is my witness and not the government's witness?'

Corva stood. 'I fail to see the distinction between you and the government, Colonel, but I'll play ball.'

Colonel Gilmer seemed to want to explain the difference but had second thoughts and went on to the next required point. He looked at Tyson. 'Would you please rise, Lieutenant?'

Tyson stood.

Colonel Gilmer read from his guide. 'Lieutenant Tyson, before proceeding further, I now ask you whether you have any questions regarding your right to remain silent concerning the offences of which you are accused; your right to make a statement, either sworn or unsworn, if you choose to; the use that can be made of any statement you do make; your right to cross-examine witnesses against you; or your right to present anything you may desire in your own behalf; and to have me examine available witnesses requested by you either in defence, mitigation, or extenuation.'

Tyson wondered who made up these endless sentences.

Corva replied, 'My client has asked me to explain to him why he is being offered the right to present statements or evidence in mitigation or extenuation. He says this is like being asked to give an excuse for something you never said you did. I admit to you, Colonel, I'm stumped by my client's question, and I thought that maybe somebody in this room could answer him.'

Colonel Gilmer cleared his throat and referred again to his procedural guide. At length he said, 'I may not proceed further until I am convinced that the accused understands what I have just read. It is general practice in these cases, Mr Corva, that if the accused is represented by counsel – and he apparently is—'

The prosecution desk chuckled.

'Defence counsel generally indicates that he has explained these matters to the accused beforehand, and they are understood.' He added, 'I have never had any other experience after reading that statement to the accused.'

'Nevertheless,' said Corva, 'my client, who is as innocent of the law as he is of the charge, has asked a commonsense question that I, as a lawyer, am not qualified to answer.'

Colonel Pierce rose and said, 'If it please the colonel ... I am not in the habit of assisting the defence or the accused in comprehending what their rights are. But in the interests of fairness and justice, I would like to explain the meaning of extenuation and mitigation as it relates to this hearing.' He looked directly at Tyson. 'In commonsense language, Lieutenant, suppose you were called in to the school principal and accused of hitting Tommy Smith. And you say, "I never hit him, and he deserved it anyway." That is a statement in defence, extenuation, and mitigation, all in one.'

Tyson replied, 'It sounds a lot like an admission of guilt to me, Colonel.'

Colonel Pierce smiled.

Tyson leaned towards Corva. 'Is this guy serious?'

'We are on the wrong side of the looking glass. Everyone here is nuts, and if we stay much longer we will start believing them. Tell the asshole you understand.'

'Which asshole?'

'Oh ... Gilmer.'

Tyson looked at Colonel Gilmer. 'Colonel, I fully understand and accept Colonel Pierce's explanation and example of how I may offer excuses for something I don't admit I did.'

Gilmer nodded, pleased that the matter was resolved.

Tyson took his seat, and Corva sat also. Corva said to

Tyson, 'We made our point.'

'We're making lots of points, Vince. But when I got here, the scoreboard showed they'd started without us and won.'

'No sweat.'

Colonel Gilmer said to Corva, 'You have indicated that you wish to call as witnesses the following individuals whose sworn statements are in the files: Mr Paul Sadowski, Mr Anthony Scorello, Mr Hernando Beltran, Mr Lee Walker, Mr Louis Kalane. I have arranged for the appearance of those witnesses at government expense, and they are present. Mr Corva, you may call the first witness by instructing Sergeant Lester' – Gilmer nodded towards the sergeant at arms – 'as to their whereabouts and which of them you want called first.'

Corva stood. 'I do not wish to call any witnesses.' He sat.

Colonel Gilmer leaned forward across the podium. 'Is it not your intention, Mr Corva, to call the witnesses for the defence?'

'No, sir, that is not my intention.' Corva doodled on a sheet of yellow paper.

Colonel Gilmer said, 'Mr Corva, these five men were brought here at your request. They were transported, lodged, and fed at government expense. If you did not intend to call them to testify in your client's behalf, why did the government, at taxpayers' expense, go through the trouble of bringing them here?'

Corva looked up from his doodling. 'Colonel, the government sent these five men to Vietnam for a year at the taxpayers' expense. They can send them to New York for a reunion at taxpayers' expense too. Small recompense.'

Colonel Gilmer's voice rose. 'Mr Corva, I've been quite patient with you. If you had no intention of calling those witnesses, there was no reason to bring them here.'

Corva replied, 'Colonel, the decision to call or not call defence witnesses is solely mine and the accused's and can be made at any time. I choose not to call these witnesses.'

Colonel Gilmer nodded tersely. 'That is certainly your right.'

Tyson looked at Sergeant Lester, who seemed disappointed, then at Colonel Pierce, Major Weinroth, and Captain Longo. They were concealing their disappointment much better. He looked at Karen Harper and caught her eye, but she looked away, so he turned to the court reporter, who smiled at him again. They held eye contact for a while until Colonel Gilmer said, 'Lieutenant Tyson, do I have your attention?'

'Yes, sir.'

'In lieu of defence testimony, I will consider the sworn statements of the five named defence witnesses, if that is your wish.'

Corva answered, 'That is our wish, Colonel.'

'Fine. Do you want me to call any witnesses whose names have not been entered as witnesses? If so, give me their names and organizations or addresses.'

Corva replied, 'We would like to call the following witnesses as either defence witnesses or impartial witnesses: Daniel Kelly, Michael DeTonq, and the French-Vietnamese nun known only as Sister Teresa.'

Colonel Gilmer seemed prepared for this. He said, 'Do you have their organizations or addresses, Mr Corva?'

'I have last-known addresses, Colonel. I believe you have those too.'

'Yes, I do. And I've made every effort to contact these people but have been unsuccessful.'

'Then we must consider the investigation incomplete.'

Colonel Gilmer shook his head. 'Mr Corva, since there is no way you can convince me or anybody that the appearance of these witnesses would aid your client's defence, it would not prejudice your client's rights if they were not present. The prosecution could just as easily claim they are government witnesses. The witnesses being absent and having shown no sign of life for approximately ten, eighteen, and two years, respectively, we might assume they are dead.'

Corva replied, 'I know government workers who have shown no sign of life for decades but are promoted nevertheless—'

Sergeant Lester stifled a laugh and wound up coughing.

Corva continued, 'But for purposes of this investigation and hearing I will table this request if you will assure me that the government will continue looking for these witnesses until these charges are finally disposed of in one way or the other.'

Colonel Gilmer thought a moment, and Tyson wondered if he was thinking about the taxpayers again. Gilmer said, 'That is a reasonable request, and you have my assurances on that.'

'Thank you, Colonel.'

Tyson said to Corva, 'I never said I wanted them found.'

'Don't worry about it. Adds to the drama.'

'What if they *do* turn out to be witnesses for the prosecution?'

'Sh-h-h – Colonel Gilmer wants to speak.'

'Vince!—'

Colonel Gilmer cleared his throat. 'Lieutenant Tyson, if you are aware of any military records which you want me to consider and which you have been unable to obtain, give me a list of those documents at this time.'

Corva said, 'We have been trying for some time, through Major Harper, to obtain the orders authorizing Lieutenant Tyson to wear the Silver Star for valorous acts performed in the line of duty in connection with military operations against an armed enemy, on 15 February 1968 in the vicinity of Hue City.'

Colonel Pierce said to his assistants, loudly enough for everyone to hear, 'What the hell does he think this is – an awards ceremony?'

Colonel Gilmer looked briefly at Pierce and then turned to Karen Harper. 'Major.'

Karen Harper stood. 'Mr Corva, I have with me

Lieutenant Tyson's orders authorizing the Silver Star.'

Tyson glanced at Corva, then turned back to Harper.

She continued, 'The orders were apparently never forwarded, or they were believed to be forwarded. In any case they are in my possession.'

Corva stood. 'May I put them in my possession?'

She replied, 'Certainly.' She came around her table and carried a large manila envelope to Tyson. She said, 'In addition to the orders, the envelope contains the actual medal and a ribbon.'

Tyson replied, 'Thank you, Major. That was thoughtful of you to procure the medal itself.'

'Not at all.' Her back to the room, she smiled at him, turned, and returned to her chair.

Corva said, 'She's got it for you, lover.'

'Fuck off.'

Corva said to Gilmer, 'May I take a moment to look at this?' He opened the envelope and slid out the contents. He read the citation proposed by Daniel Kelly and endorsed by Captain Roy Browder. It was a description of the action and the heroism that led to the award. It was general, describing the usual valour, self-sacrifice, and actions above and beyond the call of duty. But there were few specifics, and there was no mention of a hospital. Most importantly, the citation stated the date of 15 February and mentioned daylight action to distinguish it from something that might have happened before dawn or after sundown that day.

Corva drew a small blue box towards him and opened it. Inside, on a piece of white satin, lay the Silver Star. Beneath it was the small red, white, and blue rectangular ribbon. Corva took the ribbon from the box. 'Turn this way.'

'I can't wear that, Vince.'

Colonel Pierce stood. 'This is *not* an awards ceremony, Mr Corva.'

Corva paid no attention and pinned the ribbon over Tyson's two rows of existing ribbons. 'There, it's the first one you wear, so we don't have to move any.' Corva patted the rows of service ribbons. 'Good. Real hero.' He stood and turned to Pierce. 'Colonel, Lieutenant Tyson has waited eighteen years for the Army to find this. You can damned sure wait thirty seconds while I pin it on him.'

Pierce seemed about to say something, thought better of it, and sat down.

Corva turned to the front of the room. 'Thank you, Colonel, and thank you, Major Harper.'

Gilmer said to Tyson, 'Congratulations. Now if we may—'

Corva interrupted. 'Excuse me, Colonel, but I would like to point out to you that this award should be considered by you as evidence as you weigh and evaluate the facts in determining the truth of the matters stated in the charge sheet.'

Colonel Gilmer didn't reply.

Corva continued, 'I don't have to point out that the citation for this award and the charge sheet are two completely different documents which address themselves to the same event.'

'No,' said Gilmer, 'you don't have to point that out. I figured that out for myself.'

'Good,' said Corva. 'One can't be too careful when defending a man charged with murder.'

Colonel Gilmer let out a long breath. He turned a page in the book before him and said, 'Lieutenant Tyson, if you have any physical or real evidence which you have not introduced, you may introduce it at this time.'

Corva replied, 'We have no such evidence.'

'Are you aware of any other evidence that you want me to consider and which you have been unable to obtain? If so, let me know now.'

Corva stood. 'We have no such evidence. And, I should point out, neither does the prosecution. I would like you to consider, Colonel, that the government has not even established that any deaths, legal or illegal, took place as specified in the charge sheet. Specifically, there are no corpses nor any photos of corpses nor any death certificates nor anyone who personally knew any of the alleged victims who can testify as to that alleged victim's present condition. I realize that it is not mandatory for the government to produce a corpse to substantiate a charge of murder, but a corpse or two is not too much to ask, if they are alleging over a hundred deaths.'

Colonel Pierce stood and said sharply, 'Mr Corva, the government has no corpses to provide in order to satisfy your ghoulish sense of curiosity or your inane suggestion that there were no deaths at that hospital. If you—'

Corva's voice cut him off. 'I am not saying there were no deaths! I have here a citation for a Silver Star that speaks of deaths. And if the government has no corpses, the defence does: Larry Cane and Arthur Peterson. Killed in action against an armed enemy, Colonel Pierce. And I have death certificates giving time, place, and cause of death. And until recently, I would have said I even knew *why* they died. Now that the government is trying to strip these men – living and dead – of their honour and their dignity, I can no longer say why.' Corva sat.

The room was very still. Pierce sat slowly. Tyson was impressed by Corva's expression of outrage. And Corva, as he'd said himself, was no courtroom actor. Corva *was* outraged, because Corva had kept himself purposely ignorant of the actual events of February 15. Corva believed every word of the Silver Star citation.

Colonel Gilmer looked around the room. He said, 'Does the defence have anything further to present?'

Corva shook his head. 'No, sir.'

'All right,' said Gilmer, 'I would like to call the additional witness, Andrew Picard.' He turned to Sergeant Lester. 'Please show Mr Picard in.'

Sergeant Lester snapped to attention, turned smartly, and strode out the door.

Tyson lit a cigarette. Corva drank water. Corva leaned close to him and asked, 'How *did* Larry Cane die?'

Tyson replied, 'I shot him through the heart.'

Corva didn't seem particularly surprised.

The door opened, and Andrew Picard entered. Picard was dressed in brown tweeds, and Tyson thought he was rushing the season a bit and playing author a lot. Sergeant Lester showed him to the front podium, facing Gilmer.

Colonel Gilmer said, 'Mr Picard, will you raise your right hand, please?'

Picard raised his hand.

Gilmer said, 'You swear that the evidence you shall give in the case now being investigated shall be the truth, the whole truth, and nothing but the truth. So help you God.'

'I do.'

'Please take your seat in the witness chair.'

Picard walked towards the back of the room and sat in the chair facing Gilmer.

Colonel Gilmer said, 'Please state your full name, occupation, and residence address.'

'Andrew Picard, writer, Bluff Point, Sag Harbor, New York.'

'Do you know the accused?'

Picard looked at Tyson. 'We've met once.'

Gilmer said, 'I have an unsworn statement made by you in the presence of Major Karen Harper. My purpose in asking you here is to have you expand on this statement and to answer other questions I might have regarding your part in this case. And also to answer such questions as may be asked of you by the counsel for the defence or the prosecution.'

Picard crossed his legs.

Colonel Gilmer said, 'I am going to ask Major Harper to conduct this examination.'

Harper stood and walked towards the witness chair. 'Mr Picard, we can dispense with a good deal of the background and so-called establishing questions because I don't think

535

there's a person in this room who doesn't know the background on the case and your part in it.'

'Fine with me, Major.'

'Mr Picard, did you make any efforts to substantiate what Mr Brandt and Mr Farley told you?'

'I did look for more witnesses but couldn't find any. They corroborated one another's story. For my purposes that was fine.'

'Did you set out to expose alleged American atrocities during the battle of Hue?'

'Not at all. I wanted to – and did – expose communist atrocities. Lots of them. I was an eyewitness to some of them.'

'But not to the Miséricorde Hospital incident?'

'No. I was trapped in the Citadel during that time.'

'Did you *hear* anything about that hospital while you were there?'

Corva stood. 'We really can't allow hearsay evidence, Major.'

Colonel Gilmer said, 'Mr Corva, there is no jury present, and the strictest rules of evidence and examination do not apply. This is an informal format. If it weren't, I would have thrown you out long ago.'

Picard laughed, joined by a few other people.

Corva made a mock bow towards Harper. 'Please continue.'

'Thank you.' She addressed Picard. '*Did* you hear anything about the hospital while you were in Hue?'

'Yes, but only that it had been destroyed in the fighting and that Caucasian civilians and Vietnamese Catholics had been killed. That was the kind of news that made the rounds. The gooks – Viets – Buddhist-type Viets – were about as important as the local leech population. Not nice but true.'

'Do you recall any sort of investigation at the time?'

'No. You have to understand the conditions in Hue. The destruction of one hospital was not remarkable in any way. Plus, we had our own casualties.' He thought a moment, then

536

said, 'Also … the type of Westerner who was in Hue was …
how shall I put this? …'

'Any way you like, Mr Picard.'

'They were considered by the military to be mostly pinkos,
wimps, and bleeding hearts.'

'So this story of a possible massacre did not make the
rounds among the troops the way, for instance, My Lai did?'

Picard shook his head. 'This was not an open secret. Not to
my knowledge anyway. Notwithstanding what I said about
the type of Caucasians that were in Hue, I think the men in
Tyson's platoon knew they screwed up pretty bad. I think—'

Corva stood. 'Mr Picard was not *at* that hospital. I really
must object.'

Harper answered, 'I'm trying to establish the provenance
of what Mr Picard wrote.'

'Then ask him where he got the story, and let's not give the
witness free reign to engage in hearsay testimony.'

Harper turned back to Picard. 'From whom did you hear
this story, and when did you hear it?'

'I heard it from Sister Teresa. In a hospital in Orléans,
France. Nearly two years ago. I had pneumonia. There is a
record of that.'

'What hospital?'

'Mercy Hospital. Known in French – can you believe it? –
as Hôpital Miséricorde.'

'How did the subject of the alleged massacre come up?'

'I had my manuscript with me. She saw the word "Hue".
That was all it took to start her talking about the war. I told
her I was there. One thing led to another, and pretty soon I
had an inkling that something very dark had happened at
Miséricorde Hospital.'

'You followed up on it?'

'Yes. When I got back to the States, I told my publisher I
was on to something and the manuscript would be delayed. I
knew about locator ads, so I got the address of the First Cav
newspaper and placed an ad. A month passed. I placed it

537

again. Then I received a letter from this Dr Brandt in Boston. I went to interview him.

'Brandt at first refused to give me the names of anyone who could corroborate this story. He did give me the name of the platoon leader, Ben Tyson, who he said lived in a Long Island suburb of New York. I went through the suburban phone books and called a Benjamin Tyson. He said he wasn't the man in question. At this point I wasn't going to include this incident in the final draft, and I wrote a note to Brandt to that effect. Then Brandt came back with the name of Richard Farley, who he said could be contacted through the VA hospital in Newark. Brandt also said that the Benjamin Tyson I located in Garden City on Long Island was the man I was looking for. He said he was certain of that, but he wouldn't say how he was so certain. I phoned Tyson again, but again he said I was mistaken. Anyway I interviewed Farley. He was a little strung out. But he corroborated Brandt's story in substance and also the nun's story. I figured if it was all bullshit I'd know soon enough after it was published. I half expected about a dozen lawsuits from the platoon's survivors. But, as you see, no one is suing ... Though I suppose if Tyson beats the rap, they may all sue me then.'

Harper asked, 'Are you covered by insurance?'

'No ... but that isn't making me try to get Tyson convicted, if that's what you're getting at.'

Major Harper asked, 'What do you think Mr Brandt's motive was in contacting you and telling you this story?'

Picard smiled. 'He had the idea from the locator ad I was on to it anyway. I suppose I led him to believe I already knew all there was to know. Doctors are kind of naive. Also I think he wanted to get it off his chest. Hell of a secret, right?'

'You never suspected him of ulterior motives?'

'Such as wanting to screw up Tyson? Yes, I did. But I don't know what would have prompted these motives, and I don't care.'

'Why did Brandt give you Farley's name and no one else's?'

'Farley was the only man whose location he knew – except for Tyson's. I suppose he was able to clear it with Farley. He couldn't do that with the others because he didn't know where they were. He never gave me another name.'

'How did Brandt know Farley's location and Tyson's location?'

Picard shrugged.

The reporter looked up and said, 'Colonel, should I show that the witness shrugged?'

Picard laughed. 'No, you can show that I said, "How the hell should I know? Ask Brandt."'

Major Harper inquired, 'Have you found your notes yet, Mr Picard?'

'I told you, all my written notes and taped interviews were transferred to a word processor disc and were accidentally erased. They are in that great data bank in the sky along with everyone else's erased tapes and discs. Christ, I'd like to tap into that.'

'You didn't keep the printouts?'

'No one with a word processor stores reams of paper. Why is the military always ten years behind everyone else?'

Major Harper said, 'One or two more questions. I was never clear on how Sister Teresa was able to identify the unit involved in the alleged incident.'

Picard replied, 'She identified the division ... by their shoulder patches – *Ky binh* – cavalry. Everyone knew the First Cav patch. That's why I put the locator ad in the Cav paper, of course. Marines don't wear unit patches. We had the crazy idea that we didn't want to give the enemy any free field intelligence about the locations of units.'

'What I'm getting at is this: Did Sister Teresa know any of the men ... by sight?'

Picard nodded slowly. 'As I said on the phone, she recognized the officer – Tyson – but only referred to him as *dai-uý* – lieutenant. I couldn't get her to remember his name.'

'What did she say about him?'

Picard let a long time go by, then replied cautiously, 'She said – now this is in a combination of Vietnamese, English, and French – she said he came into a room where she was hiding. He saw her and he spared her life.'

'Spared?' asked Karen Harper. 'Not *saved* her life? According to Lieutenant Tyson's account and the other five witnesses, the platoon saved some lives by throwing people from the burning hospital.'

'Is that so? Well, the hospital *was* burning, according to the nun.' He paused. 'I'm not trying to crucify Tyson ... I can't think of the word she used. It was French, though. *Sauver*? To rescue or to save? Or was it *épargner* – to spare or to save? ... It's a matter of translation, I guess.'

'It's an important point, I should think. But not important enough to include in your book.'

Picard glanced for the first time at Tyson. 'An error of omission. It didn't fit Brandt's description of what happened, or Farley's. Sorry.'

Harper let some time go by, then said, 'You also told me that Sister Teresa mentioned the *bac si*.'

Picard nodded. 'Another point I overlooked in the book. But for good reason. However, I do want to tell you about that ... I've been a bit remiss. I wish I had my damned notes. My memory has been jogged by all this ...'

'What about the *bac si* – the medic? Steven Brandt?'

Picard leaned forward. 'She said that she also recognized the *bac si* ... from what we would call the Medcap programme. Medics went around to the schools, churches, villages, and all that. Anyway she described Brandt as ... *"un homme qui viole les jeunes filles."* You don't need a lot of French to translate that.'

Harper said, 'Nevertheless, I will translate. A man who violates or abuses young girls.'

Picard nodded again. 'Of course there are many, many interpretations of that. What medical person hasn't been

540

accused ... I couldn't possibly include that in my book. Talk about a lawsuit. Christ!'

Karen Harper looked at Andrew Picard a moment, then said, 'Did Sister Teresa say anything else to you about her relationship with Lieutenant Tyson?'

Picard glanced again at Tyson before replying, 'Sister Teresa told me she had met the *dai-uý* earlier, at some function at Hue Cathedral. She knew that the *bac si* was in the *dai-uý*'s unit, and she took the opportunity to speak to him about the medic's predilection for underage virgins.' He looked around the room. 'I don't think any of this detracts from the central issue. I'll tell you what the nun and Brandt and Farley *did* agree on. They agreed that American soldiers wilfully and with malice murdered a hospital full of unarmed and defenceless people.'

Major Harper said, 'We may be able to establish that, beyond a reasonable doubt. But there is only one man accused of that as it turns out – the officer in charge, Lieutenant Tyson. Now we have some reason to believe that his role in the alleged crime may not have been as great as we were led to believe – or as you suggested in your book—'

Picard said, 'You know, Major, I was a Marine officer, and I know what Tyson's responsibility was. If he failed to discharge that responsibility he ought to be called to account for it. But not this way. This is a goddamned travesty—'

Colonel Pierce stood, but Corva stood as well and said loudly across the intervening space, 'If the witness can give hearsay evidence, he can damned sure give his opinion.'

Gilmer said curtly, 'Please be seated. Both of you. Go on, Mr Picard.'

Picard continued, 'I just want to add that I think Dr Brandt lied to me about one important thing. I don't think Tyson ever gave a direct order to shoot anyone in that hospital. I think Tyson's troops mutinied. I think he was as much a victim as anyone else in that hospital. In fact, I think his platoon were victims too. Victims of war, combat fatigue, and shock. I think if you find Sister Teresa, she will tell you more about Lieutenant Tyson's actions that day than anyone else can.'

Harper waited a moment, then asked, 'Why did't you include some of these things in your book, Mr Picard?'

Picard replied, 'I've asked myself that question. I have no answer.'

'All right.' She asked, 'Did Sister Teresa tell you *how* Lieutenant Tyson saved or spared her?'

'No. You must understand that we had not only a language problem, but I was rather ill and not in the best of form. I often wish I had another chance to conduct that interview.'

Karen Harper observed, 'So do we all.' She drew a breath and said, 'I have no further questions.'

Colonel Gilmer addressed Colonel Pierce. 'Does the government wish to cross-examine the witness?'

Colonel Pierce seemed unprepared for the question. He conferred with his assistants, then stood and said, 'We have no questions.'

Colonel Gilmer turned to Corva. 'Does the defence wish to cross-examine the witness?'

Corva stood. 'I have one question for Mr Picard.' He looked at Picard. 'You were not an eyewitness to the events in question, and therefore neither the defence nor the prosecution has seen fit to claim you as their own witness. But you are the only link to Sister Teresa. I ask you this: Did the story you heard from Sister Teresa coincide with the story you heard from Steven Brandt in respect to the role of the accused in the hospital incident?'

'No, it did not.'

'Thank you.' He looked at Karen Harper. 'I have no further questions.'

Karen Harper said to Colonel Gilmer, 'I have no further questions.'

Gilmer said to Pierce, 'Do you wish a recross?'

'No, I don't.'

Colonel Gilmer said to Andrew Picard, 'The witness is excused.'

Picard stood and walked to the defence table. He said to Tyson in a soft voice, 'You're a little old to be dressed like that, aren't you?'

'Tell it to the Army.'

Picard smiled, 'Luck.' He walked towards the door held open by Sergeant Lester and left.

Colonel Gilmer drank from a glass of water. Karen Harper returned to her table. The room was still.

Corva said into Tyson's ear, 'Why did the monkey fall out of the tree?'

'Why?'

'He was dead.'

Tyson drew a deep breath. 'I don't need any more jollying.'

Colonel Gilmer addressed Tyson. 'Lieutenant, will you please rise?'

Tyson stood.

'Lieutenant Tyson, earlier in this investigation, I advised you of your rights to make a statement or to remain silent. Do you want me to repeat this advice?'

Tyson said, 'It is my understanding that if I make an unsworn statement, I may only be cross-examined on what I've said and not about other matters pertaining to this case.'

'That's substantially correct. Do you desire to make a statement in any form?'

Corva stood. 'No, sir.'

Tyson said, 'Yes, sir. I intend it to be unsworn, so I'll just make it from here, and I'll keep it short. Now that I understand all about making statements in extenuation and mitigation without incriminating myself, I'd like to make one. I want to say to you, Colonel Gilmer, that I am quite prepared to face a court-martial board in order to clear myself if you believe these charges can be disposed of in no other way. But if you choose not to forward these charges to a general court-martial, then I think you must recommend a way for the Army to publicly restore my reputation and my honour. The dropping of charges will not be sufficient to undo what has been done.' Tyson sat.

Corva whispered to him, 'I don't think that asking for a public apology will endear you to the Army or to General Van Arken. I think they would rather court-martial you, which is what you seem to want.'

Tyson replied, 'This court-martial is eighteen years overdue.'

Colonel Gilmer turned towards the prosecution table. 'Do you wish to cross-examine Lieutenant Tyson on anything he said?'

Colonel Pierce replied, 'No, I do not, but I can't let that statement pass without comment.' He looked at Tyson. 'Contrary to what you said, the dropping of charges is all that the Army has to do to restore your honour and reputation in the eyes of the Army. If you have problems in civilian life that is no concern of the Army.'

Tyson stood again, but Corva pulled him into his seat.

Colonel Gilmer looked at Corva. 'Does the defence have anything further to offer?'

'No, sir, it does not.'

Colonel Gilmer glanced at his watch, cleared his throat, and said, 'The purpose of this investigation was to determine if there was any substance to the charge and specifications initiated against the accused and to determine if that charge and those specifications were in proper form. The recommendation of this investigation is advisory only and is in no way binding upon the authorities who ordered it.'

Gilmer referred to a sheet of paper. 'In arriving at my conclusions, I will consider not only the nature of the offence and the evidence in this case, but likewise the military service record of the accused and the established policy that trial by general court-martial should be resorted to only when the charges can be disposed of in no other manner consistent with military discipline.'

544

Colonel Farnley Gilmer looked around the quiet room. 'My report and my recommendation will be forwarded to the authorities who ordered this investigation. A copy will be forwarded to the accused. These proceedings are closed.'

41

Benjamin Tyson began the last leg of his run, across the large open athletic field that lay behind the post headquarters.

The field was shrouded in a late September evening ground fog that obscured all but the lights of the surrounding buildings. Tyson moved at a slow pace through the clinging fog, realizing he'd lost his way in the disorienting white haziness.

He saw the tall white flagpole rising like a ship's mast above the vapour and altered his course, passing to the left of the pole. He crossed a concrete sidewalk and found himself on Lee Avenue. He slowed his pace and turned towards post headquarters.

An MP jeep drew up beside him, and the man in the passenger seat called out, 'You still at it, Lieutenant?'

Tyson recognized the voice. He turned his head towards the jeep, which was keeping pace with him. 'This wouldn't do you any harm either, Captain.'

Captain Gallagher grunted. He called out, 'As long as you're heading that way, why don't you sign in at HQ? It's nearly twenty-one hundred.'

Tyson didn't answer. He changed his speed a few times making the driver brake and accelerate to keep abreast.

Captain Gallagher added, 'Then it's back to your room, sonny. No kidding. You've been making us look bad, and we're cracking down on your all-night runs.'

Again Tyson didn't answer.

Gallagher inquired in a sarcastic tone, 'Doesn't your wife miss you?'

'Go fuck yourself.'

'Watch it, Lieutenant. I'll haul your ass in.' He added in a conciliatory tone, 'I'm trying to be helpful.'

Tyson said to the MP captain, 'There must be a felony in progress somewhere, Captain. Why don't you go find it like a good flatfoot?'

Captain Gallagher said something to the driver, and the jeep sped away.

Tyson slowed to a walk and turned up the path of the headquarters building. He wiped the sweat from his eyes and shouldered the glass door open.

The duty sergeant behind the ticket window was Sergeant Lester of recent Article 32 fame.

The young buck sergeant looked up from his desk in the small duty room. 'Hey, Lieutenant, how you doing?'

'Not bad, for a pack-a-day man.'

Lester laughed and stood. 'You here to sign in?'

'No, Sergeant, I'm looking for my dog.'

'No dogs allowed on base.'

'That's what I told him. Where's the book?'

'Oh ... yeah ... yes, sir. Colonel Levin has it. He's upstairs, and wants you to report to him.'

'Is that like him wanting to see me?'

'Same shit. Only you got to do the hand jive.' Lester whipped off a snappy salute and laughed.

Tyson took the steps three at a time, shadowboxed down the corridor to the amusement of two female clerks, and entered the adjutant's outer office. He walked to Colonel Levin's door and knocked sharply.

'Come in,' called Levin.

Tyson opened the door, stepped to his desk, and saluted. 'Sir, Lieutenant Tyson reports.'

Levin returned the salute. 'Sit down. You look bushed.'

'Yes, sir.' Tyson sat in a chair facing the desk. The room

was in almost complete darkness, lit only by a gooseneck desk lamp that illuminated the papers in front of Levin but left his face in shadow.

Levin spoke from the shadows. 'You've missed a good number of sign-ins.'

'Yes, sir.'

Levin observed, 'You were running again.'

'Yes, sir. Practising for my escape.'

Levin laughed. He stood and went to a file cabinet, returning with a bottle of premixed Manhattans and two water tumblers. He poured two drinks and handed one to Tyson.

Tyson put his drink on the edge of the colonel's desk. He regarded Levin's hands in the pool of light. The fingers of his left hand were nicotine-stained. Tyson waited, then broke the silence himself. 'Working late?'

'Yes, tomorrow is a holiday. Yom Kippur. The day of atonement. I want to finish up by noon tomorrow.'

'Right. My son has the day off from school.'

'How are things going at home?'

'As well as can be expected. Child care and child amusement are a bit of a problem.'

'I know. I have three sons. But they're grown now.'

'Career Army?' Tyson smiled.

'No, no. They saw too much of it. It's very tough on family life. I had three hardship tours. One was for a year and a half in Korea. It takes a special woman to be an Army wife. It takes a lot of trust, too, when people are separated for that length of time.'

Tyson wondered if there was supposed to be a message there for him. He drank some of the warm Manhattan.

Levin observed, 'Autumn is here. I used to like the season, but as I get older, it's the spring and summer that I look forward to. "Now it is autumn and the falling fruit and the long journey towards oblivion ... have you built your ship of death, oh have you?"'

547

Tyson finished his drink. 'Is that a direct question?'

'No, that was D. H. Lawrence.' Levin picked a half cigar from the ashtray and lit it, his match briefly illuminating his face. Billows of smoke disappeared into the dark. Levin said, 'What angers me is that the Army doesn't really *want* a trial. They feel obligated in some way to the press, the White House, the Congress who approves their budgets, the Army and Defense and even their own legal branch.'

Tyson unwrapped a piece of foil in which he kept a cigarette and a pack of matches. He lit the cigarette without permission. 'There's something obscene about carrying a cigarette in your jogging suit.'

Levin seemed not to hear, intent on his own thoughts. 'If this case had come to light eighteen years ago, while you were still on active duty, the Army would have a dozen options open to them and to you. But ironically the passage of time has worked against you.' He added, 'The options are limited to indicting or not indicting for murder.'

Tyson stubbed out his unsmoked cigarette in Levin's ashtray. 'I gave them the option of a public apology.'

Levin smiled weakly. 'The Army does not accept apologies from its officers and men, so I don't think you can expect to receive one.'

'Quaint custom.'

Levin said, 'I have some business to conduct with you.' He lifted a manila envelope from the right-hand drawer and laid it on the desk, then drew a sheaf of legal-sized paper from the envelope and said, 'The courier from Fort Dix arrived a while ago. This' – he handed Tyson a printed form with typed papers attached – 'is your copy of the Investigating Officer's Report. If you go to the bottom of page three, item seventeen, you will see that Colonel Gilmer recommended trial by general court-martial.'

Tyson put the papers on Levin's desk without looking at them.

Levin continued, 'General Peters, on the advice of his Staff Judge Advocate, agreed with the recommendation. Here' – he handed Tyson a single sheet of typed paper – 'is your copy of the orders convening a general court-martial.'

Tyson held the paper near the lamp and read the short document:

From: Major General George Peters, Post Commander, Fort Dix, New Jersey.

A general court-martial is hereby convened. It may proceed at Fort Hamilton, Brooklyn, New York, on 15 October, to try such persons as may be properly brought before it. The Court will be constituted as follows:

Military Judge: Colonel Walter Sproule.

Members of the board: Colonel Amos Moore, Lieutenant Colonel Stanley Laski, Lieutenant Colonel Eugene McGregor, Major Donald Bauer, Major Virginia Sindel, Captain Herbert Morelli, Lieutenant James Davis.

Trial counsel: Colonel Graham Pierce, Major Judith Weinroth, Captain Salvatore Longo.

Defence counsel: Vincent Corva.

[Signed] George Peters, Major General, United States Army.

Tyson placed the sheet of paper atop the others. He looked at Levin awhile, then inquired, 'Who do you think is the person who may be properly brought before this court-martial?'

Levin replied, 'You may ask for a postponement. Speak to your lawyer.'

Tyson shook his head. 'October 15th sounds fine.'

Colonel Levin handed Tyson a printed legal form. 'The charge sheet.'

'I have several of these. Do I need another?'

Levin explained, 'As you can see, at each stage of the process, more boxes are checked, more lines filled in. This is signed by Colonel Pierce now, and he will formally serve you

549

with a copy of this tomorrow at a time and place to be arranged. You may have your lawyer present, but it's not necessary.'

Tyson placed the charge sheet on Levin's desk. 'So that's it? Indicted, charged, and ready to be tried. All tidied up. I know that justice delayed is justice denied, but as Corva said, the JAG Corps ought to wear his old Jungle Lightning patch.'

Levin did not respond.

Tyson stood and rubbed his neck. 'My God, I was a commuter in May.' He laughed. 'I'm glad it's happening fast. Not much time to brood over it.'

Levin said, 'There is one item on that charge sheet that disturbs me.'

'What is that, Colonel?'

'The endorsement.'

'What endorsement?'

'On page two,' said Levin, 'where it says "subject to the following instructions." It is here that the convening authority usually gives special instructions to the court.'

'What sort of special instructions?'

'Usually a limit to the punishment that the court can impose. It is within the power of General Peters or the chain of command right up to the Commander in Chief to state a maximum punishment that can be awarded. For instance, in a capital crime, this space' – he pointed to a line on the charge sheet – 'will often state something like ... the death penalty may not be imposed ...'

Tyson picked up the charge sheet. There was nothing written in the place provided for special instructions. He looked at Levin. 'Are you telling me I could be shot?'

'Well ... that's highly unlikely. An impossibility actually ... But I'm disturbed that General Peters didn't exclude the death penalty as a possible—'

'You're *disturbed*? Colonel, I'm outraged.'

'Well, of course you are. It's a threat. I'm really surprised ... usually the government, the Justice Department, or someone will offer the accused some sort of guarantee in a capital crime – in exchange, of course, for something else. But I'm not qualified to talk about that. I do know, however, that no court-martial board is going to impose the death penalty.'

'How do you *know* that, Colonel? If the chain of command didn't instruct General Peters to exclude it, this court-martial board which has been constituted' – Tyson tapped the convening orders – 'may take that as a sign that the death penalty is precisely what the chain of command wants.'

'That's an interesting observation,' admitted Levin. After a moment, he added, 'But any sort of command influence, even subtle influence, is illegal.'

'That's reassuring. I'm sure Colonel Gilmer's recommendation to indict was based solely on the facts.' Tyson gathered the paperwork and stuffed it into the envelope. 'If there's nothing further, I'll leave you to your work.'

Levin cleared his throat. 'There is one thing further. You are, as of now, confined to your quarters. Confined means confined. You may not leave unless there is a medical emergency. If you feel you have a need to leave your quarters for any other reason, you must put a request in writing directed to General Peters at Fort Dix.'

'He's the guy who wants to shoot me. And I don't even know him.'

Levin poured Tyson another drink. 'It's not personal. There is nothing personal in any of this.'

'That's the horror of it, Colonel.'

Levin swallowed half his drink. 'Yes. I'm sorry about the confinement. I put in a good word for you, but when the honchos came here from Dix and looked at all the blanks in the sign-in book, the shit hit the fan.' Levin finished his drink. 'Could have been worse. Could have been jail.'

Tyson took some of his Manhattan. He said quietly, 'May I walk in my backyard?'

Levin looked down at his desk a long time. 'I'm sure no one will mind that.' He added, 'The confinement to quarters

551

won't be too long – only until the conclusion of the trial.'

Tyson nodded. 'Then I go home. Wherever that may be.'

'Yes, then you go home.' Levin went to the window and contemplated the white clinging mist that carpeted everything below the second floor of the building. He said, 'I've seen so many wonderful places in my life. I found peace once in a Swiss village. A peace that I never felt before or since.' He sipped his drink, then drew on his cigar. 'At the end of the Book of Numbers, chapter thirty-five, there is a mention of creating six cities of refuge, places where a suspected killer may go to live in peace until passions cool and justice may be done. "Then the congregation shall judge between the slayer and the revenger of blood." Between the murderer and the man who killed for justifiable revenge or in the heat of the moment.'

Tyson didn't reply.

Levin turned, put his glass on the desk, and put his cigar in the ashtray. 'Your passport is in the middle drawer of my desk. I'll be back in five minutes. You'll be gone by then so I'll say good night now. No need to salute.' He extended his hand, and Tyson took it.

Levin turned and left the room. Tyson came around the desk and opened the middle drawer. His blue and gold passport lay on top of a cigar box. He looked at it awhile, then closed the drawer.

Tyson left Levin's office with the envelope of legal documents. He walked out into the vaporous night and headed back to his quarters. A pair of headlights appeared out of the fog behind him and lit the way. The vehicle stayed with him as he walked slowly down to the officer housing units.

He reached his front door, and the vehicle stopped at the kerb. Captain Gallagher's voice called out in the damp air, 'Good night, Lieutenant Tyson.'

'Go fuck yourself, Captain Gallagher.'

Tyson entered the house and pulled the door shut behind him, realizing he would not open it again until the morning of his court-martial.

Part 3

I shall tell you a great secret, my friend. Do not wait for the last judgement. It takes place every day.

Camus

42

Ben Tyson opened the front door of his housing unit and walked down the path. The MP driver saluted, and opened the rear door. Tyson took off his billed officer's cap and slid in beside Vincent Corva.

Captain Gallagher, in the front passenger seat, turned his head, smiled, and said, 'Where to?'

Tyson didn't reply, but Corva said, 'Take us to church.'

The driver pulled away from the kerb. He drove slowly towards the U.S. Army Chapel on the corner of Roosevelt Lane and Grimes Avenue.

Within two minutes they approached the large red-brick chapel, with a long adjoining office wing. The extensive chapel complex had been built during the brief period when Fort Hamilton was the Army Chaplain School. As the staff car approached the chapel from the south, Tyson regarded the wide lawns and maple trees now a rich golden yellow. Beyond the chapel's single spire rose the grey suspension tower on the Brooklyn side of the Verrazano Bridge. Tyson noticed that there were nearly a hundred people milling around the chapel steps.

The staff car jumped the kerb and drove across the lawn, stopping directly in front of a small doorway in the north office wing of the chapel. Captain Gallagher turned to Corva and Tyson. 'They want you to use this door.'

Corva replied, 'Is that why you drove across the lawn and stopped right in front of it?'

Gallagher bit his lip. 'Yes, sir.'

Corva opened his door and slid out. Tyson followed. They stood in the crisp October morning sunlight, between the parked car and the door. Tyson looked over the roof of the car. 'Why are all those people standing there?'

'Because they can't get in. It's by invitation only. But they'd like to say they were part of it. So they stand there.'

Tyson didn't reply.

Corva added, 'In fact, they must be military or military dependents, because this base has been off limits to all civilians as of last night. Except those who work here, of course, and those with trial passes.'

'We should have charged for the trial passes, Vince.'

'Right. Would pay my fee.'

Tyson realized the people on the chapel paths were looking at him. Some waved, some took pictures. They would have got closer, but there were about a dozen MPs cordoning this section of the lawn.

Corva said, 'Enough photo opportunities. Let's get inside.' Corva reached for the door, but it was pulled inward by an MP wearing a polished white helmet and a white pistol belt from which hung a holster and .45 automatic pistol. Corva waved Tyson through the door.

Tyson removed his hat as he entered the long white corridor. There were doors on either side, and above each door was a wall bracket from which hung red signs: *Chapel Activity Specialist; Captain Smythe; Blessed Sacrament*; and finally a sign that was marked *Rabbi Eli Weitz, Major, Chaplain Corps.*

Corva stopped at the door. He said to Tyson, 'When I drove in, there were literally thousands of people around the main gate with signs proclaiming everything from "Free Tyson" to "Shoot the Bastard."' He paused. 'There are a lot of emotions running loose out there, Ben. Lots of old questions, but I don't see anyone with any answers.'

'That's because the questions are wrong.'

Corva knocked on the rabbi's door, then opened it.

Rabbi Weitz, a heavyset man with grey curly hair, rose from his desk. He was wearing civilian clothing, a brown flannel suit. 'Good morning, gentlemen.' He shook hands with Tyson and Corva.

Corva said, 'It was good of you to offer us your office, Rabbi.'

'Offer? I didn't offer anything. They said, "The court needs offices." We drew lots, and mine said "defence." So I'm saying good-bye. But I wanted to say hello first.' Rabbi Weitz picked up his attaché case. 'How long will this last?'

Corva shrugged. 'Can't say. Today is Monday... It may be wrapped up by Friday.'

'I need the office Friday night before services. That's the Sabbath.'

'Yes, sir. I know that.'

Tyson asked, 'Will you be in the spectator seats?'

Major Weitz walked to the door and turned. 'They offered me passes as compensation for commandeering my office. But there is nothing here that I want to see. But good luck, and may the Lord bless you.' Rabbi Weitz left his office.

Corva put his briefcase on the rabbi's desk, and Tyson threw his hat beside it. Corva said, 'The physical layout here lends itself to a court-martial.'

'I still think it's bizarre.'

'Where else on post could they do this? We didn't want it at Dix.'

Tyson said, 'What the hell difference does it make?' He went to the window and peered between the slats of the blinds. There were vehicles, including television vans, parked end-to-end along Roosevelt Lane. MPs were directing traffic.

Corva said, 'They had to call in two MP platoons from Dix, and the city put on a hundred cops outside the gates.'

Tyson turned from the window. 'I've never been the centre of a public spectacle before.'

'Oh, you get used to it.'

Tyson asked, 'Wasn't there any way to do this in private?'

'I'm afraid not, Ben. I would have liked just enough press and civilian spectators to keep everyone honest. But once the Army bowed to pressure and announced an open trial, then

557

the list of people who absolutely *must* be there seems to get bigger. The post commander's wife, Mrs Hill, asked for thirty passes.' Corva added, 'The chapel holds about two hundred people, but out of common decency the Army is trying to limit the number of actual spectators to about one hundred.'

Tyson smiled grimly. 'I never saw a hundred people at Sunday services.'

Corva commented, 'The room they used for the Calley trial held fifty-nine people, and every seat was filled every day of the trial.'

Tyson saw that Major Weitz had brewed a fresh pot of coffee and helped himself to a cup. He said to Corva, 'Want some?'

'No. You have to consider your bladder. Lawyers get windy.'

Tyson put the cup of coffee down untouched and lit a cigarette. He looked at his watch, then picked up a book and flipped through it for a few seconds until he realized it was in Hebrew.

Corva said, 'Everyone has stage fright. Within ten minutes after you're in there, you'll be all right.'

'I'm all right now.'

'Good.'

Tyson said, 'I keep waiting for someone to call this off.'

Corva didn't respond.

Tyson looked at his watch again. He searched for an ashtray, couldn't find one, and dropped his cigarette in the coffee cup.

Corva was flipping through a yellow pad of notes.

Heavy-booted footsteps sounded in the corridor. They stopped, and there were three knocks on the door. The door opened, and a tall young MP sergeant addressed Tyson. 'Sir, will you accompany me, please?'

Tyson picked up his hat, and Corva picked up his briefcase.

The MP, whose name tag read Larson, said, 'You can leave your cover here, sir.'

'What? Oh ...' Tyson put his hat back on the desk, straightened his tunic and tie, and walked into the corridor, followed by Corva. The MP, Sergeant Larson, overtook them with long strides and led the way.

They came to a cross corridor and turned left. Sergeant Larson opened the door at the end of the corridor, and Corva went through it, followed by Tyson.

Tyson walked behind Corva, across the red carpet of the altar platform. He was aware of the murmur of a large number of people in the pews to his left. Corva indicated a long oak table on the far side of the raised altar floor, and Tyson went around the table and sat in a hard wooden chair. Corva sat to his left.

The first thing Tyson noticed was that the altar table had been removed. Across the red carpet from the direction he'd entered sat the long table that would hold the members of the court-martial board – the jury. Seven empty chairs faced him. Tyson looked to his left. The rear wall of the chapel, panelled in light pecan wood, rose two storeys to the arched cathedral ceiling. In the centre of the wall hung gold drapes stretching from ceiling to floor. Behind the drapes, Tyson knew, was a large recessed area, the presbytery, where the high altar sat beneath a large cross. The drapes were closed for Jewish services and for nonreligious events such as this one. In fact, he noticed, there was no longer anything visible to make this altar area look sanctified; it could have been an auditorium stage, and was no doubt designed to be transformed from religious to secular by the switching of a few stage props.

The wooden pulpit had been moved from its usual place and was now standing on a higher platform in front of the closed drapes, to be used, he assumed, as the military judge's bench. To the left of the pulpit was an American flag on a stand. And, hung on the panelled wall above the flag, where a religious tapestry usually hung, was the prescribed photograph of the President, flanked by photographs of the Secretary of the Army and the Secretary of Defense. But why anyone present cared in the least what the chain of command was, was anyone's guess. Tyson supposed that every institution needed its symbols, and the symbols of Army justice were less intrusive than those of the institution that normally used the premises.

To the right of the military judge, as he faced the pulpit, was a witness chair as in a civilian courtroom. To the left front of the pulpit was the court reporter's desk, also as in a civilian court.

Tyson turned to his right. Towards the edge of the raised platform, near the Communion rail, was the prosecution desk, its chairs arranged with their backs to the pews facing the judge's bench, or pulpit. Sitting at the desk were Colonel Pierce, Major Weinroth, and Captain Longo. Their table was covered with paperwork, whereas Corva had not yet opened his briefcase.

Corva checked the desk microphone to be certain it was off, then said to Tyson, 'Looks like more than a hundred to me.'

'I haven't looked yet.' He turned his head to the right and looked into the nave. The pews, which he'd never seen more than half full for services, were completely occupied now, and there were people standing in the aisles. 'Somebody must be counterfeiting tickets.'

Tyson heard a subdued, almost sombre murmur from the assembled court spectators. They'd come to see a play, but they behaved as though they were in church.

Tyson looked over the pews, above the front doors where the choir loft hung, running the width of the nave. At the rear of the loft were three slender lancet windows of stained glass that let diffused light into the dark loft. Corva had told him that the loft was reserved for General William Van Arken and his staff, other Army and government VIPs, including the Fort Dix post commander General Peters and a few local politicians and security people. By the light of the windows, Tyson saw figures moving around the loft. No doubt his old pal Chet Brown was up there too. He said aloud, 'The night gallery.'

Corva followed his gaze. 'No one is supposed to know they are there. That might be construed as command influence.'

'I saw the secret staff cars outside with flags and stars.'

'Right.'

Tyson looked along the walls of the nave. There were four tall stained-glass windows in each of the walls, and the morning sun poured through the south windows, casting a multi-hued luminescence over the pews. The depictions on the windows were somewhat abstract, designed like the rest of the chapel to satisfy all Christians and Jews, but ultimately satisfying no one. Most of the windows had patriotic or military themes, in red, white, and blue. Two windows had Old Testament motifs.

Tyson finally looked into the pews themselves. About three-fourths of the spectators were uniformed men and women. A whole block of pews had been reserved for a group of JAG students from Charlottesville. The civilian-attired people seemed to be middle-aged and well dressed. The type of people one saw at Wednesday matinees.

Marcy had made the arrangements for the Tysons' friends and family to be present, and she had handled the challenge in a way that only a public relations person could. Most of the people he knew seemed to be seated in the left front rows, including John and Phyllis McCormick sitting with a few other people from Garden City.

Conspicuous by their height were Messrs Kimura, Nakagawa, and Saito. Tyson had to look twice to be sure it was them. He knew he should be amazed, but nothing amazed him anymore. With the gentlemen from Japan was his former secretary, Miss Beale, looking like she'd lost some weight and found a decent dress shop.

He spotted Andrew Picard, who had somehow made the acquaintance of Phil and Janet Sloan and was chatting with them.

561

He saw Paul Stein, in whose apartment he had sojourned too briefly. He spotted Colonel Levin and a woman he took to be Mrs Levin. They were sitting with Tyson's boss of short duration, Dr Russell. He saw Captain Hodges, who was looking at his watch. Tyson wondered who was running the post.

He kept scanning the pews looking for Karen Harper and finally saw her sitting in the last row. Beside her was a good-looking man in officer's uniform, speaking to her in a way that led Tyson to believe they were more than professional acquaintances. In fact, he thought, that was probably the man that Brown had mentioned – Colonel Eric Willets. Tyson somehow suspected that Colonel Willets would like to see him draw a life term, and he was there to witness it, if it happened.

Tyson had received a letter a few days before, a letter of support and sympathy from Emily Browder, Captain Roy Browder's widow. And she was out there in the pews somewhere, though there was no way for him to know who she was.

In the front left pew he saw his mother talking with the Reverend Symes, his minister and her former minister. It looked as if they were gossiping about the congregation which was the only reason his mother used to speak to the man.

To his mother's right were his sisters, Laurie, June, and Carol, without their husbands. And to his sisters' right were Marcy and David. Marcy caught his eye, smiled, and blew a kiss. Tyson contrived a smile in return. He turned to Corva. 'Is your wife here?'

'No. I get nervous when she's in the spectator benches.'

'Really? Should I be nervous that everyone I know, including my sixth-grade teacher, is out there?'

'Not at all,' Corva assured him. 'You don't have much to say. Just watch me make a fool of myself.'

Tyson looked at the right front pews which had been

reserved for the media. You could always tell the members of the press, he thought; they looked like reluctant refugees from the sixties.

Corva poured water from a glass pitcher into two paper cups.

Tyson noticed a metal ashtray and lit a cigarette.

Corva said, 'You ought to quit, you know.'

'Let's see first if I'm going to be shot.'

'Makes sense.' Corva took some papers from his briefcase and began laying them out on the table.

Tyson looked down at a copy of the charge sheet and read: *Jean Monteau, Evan Dougal, Bernhard Rueger, Marie Broi, Sister Monique, Sister Aimee, Sister Noelle, Pierre Galante, Henri Taine, Maarten Lubbers, Brother Donatus, Sister Juliette, Susanne Dougal, Linda Dougal.*

Tyson did not think he was a man with any mystical leanings, yet somehow he felt the presence of the dead in this quasi-chapel, the presence of Captain Browder, the dead of Alpha Company, and the dead of Miséricorde Hospital.

Tyson looked at Corva. He thought his lawyer seemed a little anxious, which was understandable. But the bottom line was that if Corva lost the case, Corva was not going to gaol. Tyson said, 'I think I got the joke about the ziti and the shells.'

Corva smiled. He laid a row of pencils beside a yellow pad. He said, 'An oddity of the court-martial procedure, as you'll see, is that the prosecution performs some procedural functions that would be done by the judge at a civilian trial.' Corva glanced at Pierce. 'That bastard tried to confuse me on procedural matters in that duelling case. Most military lawyers will give the civilian defence lawyers a little slack on military procedures. But Pierce plays it tough.'

Tyson said, 'He's playing to a lot of civilians this time, and to the press. That might throw him off balance.'

Corva nodded. 'I think it might. See how his hands are shaking?'

Tyson looked at Pierce closely, but all he could see was a

picture of composure. 'No.' Tyson drew a deep breath and stubbed out his cigarette. The spectators seemed to be getting restless. The door in the wing of the altar area opened, and a man in uniform strode across the red carpet. An expectant hush fell over the pews. Then the man, a middle-aged sergeant, took his seat at the court reporter's desk. After everyone was satisfied that his appearance did not augur anything important, the talking began again.

Tyson commented, 'Typical military. Hurry up and wait. Right, Vince?'

'Right.'

The side door to the corridor opened again, and an MP stood at attention beside it. The MP, Tyson noticed, was unarmed, no doubt so as not to give the civilians or the press the impression that Tyson was dangerous. Through the door filed the seven-member board, led by Colonel Amos Moore, who was the president of the board, a sort of jury foreman but with far more power.

Colonel Moore walked directly to the long table and stood at the middle chair, facing Tyson. The other six members of the board followed in descending order of rank and peeled off to take their places. To Colonel Moore's right stood Lieutenant Colonel Stanley Laski, Major Donald Bauer, and Captain Morelli at the end. To Moore's left stood Lieutenant Colonel Eugene McGregor, Major Virginia Sindel, and the junior member, Lieutenant James Davis, who walked to the far left chair.

Tyson watched with some curiosity. He studied the faces of the seven members, but they had probably practised impassivity in front of a mirror all morning. Corva knew something about each of them, but all Tyson knew for certain was that they were career Army officers. Some of them wore the branch insignia of the infantry and the combat infantryman's badge. All of them, except Virginia Sindel and Lieutenant Davis, were heavily beribboned.

The unarmed MP walked to the centre of the floor where

the missing altar table had crushed the nap of the red carpet. The MP faced the spectator pews and announced in a loud voice, 'All rise!'

Tyson and Corva stood as did the prosecution and the court reporter. The spectators rose noisily, and Tyson could now see the silhouettes in the choir loft against the lancet windows. Several people from the press section came forward and Tyson could see they were sketch artists. They came right up to the Communion rail, but no one was passing out wafers.

Through the open door behind the board table strode Colonel Walter Sproule, the military judge. He wasn't wearing robes, but wore the Army green dress uniform with colonel's eagles, and the branch insignia of the Judge Advocate General's Corps.

Colonel Sproule walked to the pulpit and took his place behind it. Tyson thought that the juxtaposition of Sproule, the high pulpit, and the gold drapes looked either magisterial or theatrical.

Colonel Sproule, a man nearing seventy, Tyson guessed, looked around briefly, noting that everyone was in place. There was no gavel, Tyson knew; and none was needed at a court-martial. Colonel Sproule didn't bother to adjust the pulpit microphone, but his strong voice carried over the silent pews. 'The court will come to order.'

43

Colonel Pierce remained standing after everyone sat. Pierce adjusted his microphone and spoke. 'This court is convened by court-martial convening order one-thirty-nine, Headquarters, Fort Dix, New Jersey, a copy of which has been furnished to the military judge, each member of the court, counsel, and the accused.'

Tyson looked into the spectator section. He wasn't imagining it; he had never seen so many enraptured expressions.

Pierce continued, 'The following persons named in the convening orders are present.' Pierce read the seven names of the court-martial board, the military judge, the three trial counsels including himself, and the defence counsel. Pierce addressed Colonel Sproule. 'The prosecution is ready to proceed with the trial of the case of the United States against Benjamin James Tyson, First Lieutenant, United States Army, Fort Hamilton, New York, who is present in court.' Pierce took his seat.

Colonel Sproule surveyed the court, his hands on the sides of the pulpit, and said, 'It is my duty at this time to give the court preliminary instructions regarding your duties concerning the proper conduct of this trial.'

Tyson looked closely at Sproule. He was a crochety-looking old man with a powder pale face, a few strands of grey hair combed neatly over his bald pate, and eyes that seemed unfocused. Tyson suspected he was nearsighted, but he wore no glasses. Tyson did see a hearing aid behind his right ear. Here was a man, Tyson suspected, who had seen about forty years of courts-martial and had little patience left for posturing lawyers, inarticulate witnesses, and guilty men. Tyson didn't think that even this trial impressed Colonel Sproule much.

Sproule glanced briefly towards Corva and said, 'It is the duty of the defence counsel to represent the accused in a manner consistent with the special requirements of military justice. It is the defence council's right and obligation to ensure that the rights of the accused are maintained throughout these proceedings. It is not the duty or right or obligation of the defence council to wilfully obfuscate the facts of this case or to engage in any courtroom tactics which may compromise the dignity of this court or delay or obstruct justice.'

Colonel Sproule surveyed the prosecution team opposite him and said, 'It is the duty of the trial counsel to prove to the members of the board, beyond a reasonable doubt, the truth of the charge and the specifications that you have forwarded to this court as stated in the charge sheet. The government has had ample time to investigate this charge and to put it into proper form. I will assume that the case you are presenting here has close relevance to the charges you have sworn to. I want to remind you that in trial by court-martial, the trial counsel's primary duty is *not* to convict; it is to see that justice is done. I have no wish to quell the natural desire of counsel to win a case. However, this zeal must be tempered with the realization of your responsibility for ensuring a fair and impartial trial, conducted in accordance with not only proper legal procedures, but in accordance with the needs, customs, and traditions of the United States Army.'

Colonel Sproule turned towards the seven-member board. 'It is your duty to hear the evidence that is presented.' He paused. 'To hear only the evidence that is presented in this courtroom. You must remove from your minds, as much as is humanly possible, anything you have read or heard about the case now before you. Your ultimate purpose here is to decide whether the accused has violated the Code as charged and, if so, to adjudge an appropriate punishment, if any, for the offence.' Sproule looked at Colonel Moore. 'Colonel, you have served as president of the court on previous occasions, and I trust you will offer guidance and knowledge to those members who may not have had experience in sitting on the board.'

Colonel Sproule faced the front and said, 'It is the wish of this court that the spectators to this trial will conduct themselves in the quiet and dignified manner which is consistent with the seriousness of the matters being decided here.'

Tyson thought about Sproule's preliminary statements to Corva and Pierce. What Sproule had done in effect was to tell the rabbits not to run.

Colonel Sproule turned to Colonel Moore. 'President and members of the board, I will now introduce to you the other participants to this trial.' Sproule formally introduced Sergeant Reynolds, the court reporter, then Corva, then the prosecution: Pierce, Weinroth, and Longo.

Colonel Sproule addressed Colonel Pierce. 'The members of the court will now be sworn.'

Colonel Pierce stood and announced, 'The members will now be sworn. All persons please rise.'

Everyone stood, including the spectators, though Tyson noticed many of the press corps did not stand, but continued to sit, taking notes. Apparently Colonel Sproule noticed as well. He said, 'When the instruction is given by any member of the court to all rise, that instruction should be interpreted to include everyone who is not crippled.'

There were a few chuckles in the pews as the press rose.

Colonel Pierce, still standing behind his desk, turned and faced the board. 'As I state your name, please raise your right hand.' Without referring to notes, Pierce began, 'Do you, Colonel Amos Moore ... Lieutenant Colonel Stanley Laski ... Lieutenant Colonel Eugene McGregor ... Major Donald Bauer ... Major Virginia Sindel ... Captain Herbert Morelli ... Lieutenant James Davis ... swear that you will faithfully perform all the duties incumbent upon you as a member of this court; that you will faithfully and impartially try, according to the evidence, your conscience, and the laws applicable to trial by court-martial, the case of the accused, Benjamin James Tyson, Lieutenant, United States Army; and that you will not disclose or discover the vote or opinion of any particular member of the court unless required to do so in due course of law, so help you God?'

The seven members of the board replied in unison, 'I do.' They lowered their hands but remained standing as Pierce turned to Colonel Sproule, who raised his right hand. Pierce said, 'You, Colonel Walter Sproule, do swear that you will faithfully and impartially perform, according to your conscience and the laws applicable to trial by court-martial, all the duties incumbent upon you as military judge of this court, so help you God?'

Sproule replied, 'I do,' and lowered his hand. Sproule then addressed the prosecution bench, who now raised their hands. Sproule said, 'You, Colonel Graham Pierce, Major Judith Weinroth, Captain Salvatore Longo, do swear that you will faithfully perform the duties of trial counsel in the case now in hearing, so help you God?'

The prosecution team replied in the affirmative and lowered their hands.

Sproule next turned to Corva, who raised his right hand, and Sproule swore him in.

Colonel Pierce said into his microphone, 'All be seated.'

Colonel Sproule announced, 'The Court is assembled.'

Tyson said to Corva, 'I see what you mean about the trial counsel. I've never heard of a DA swearing in a judge.'

Corva nodded. 'It's a subtle way for the Army to put the judge in his place. The Army instinctively mistrusts an independent judiciary, especially since no one in the chain of command can write efficiency reports on them.'

Colonel Sproule looked out over the pews and announced, 'Unless they are required to be present for other reasons, all persons expecting to be called as witnesses in the case of Benjamin Tyson will withdraw from the courtroom.'

Tyson noticed that the spectators were looking around to see if there was a witness among them. Tyson spotted an MP walking up the aisle. The MP stopped and pointed to Andrew Picard. Picard pointed to himself in that idiotic way people do. *Who, me?* Picard rose reluctantly, said something to Phillip Sloan, and made his way clumsily out of the pew, all eyes on him.

Tyson leaned towards Corva. 'Is Pierce going to call him?'

Corva covered his microphone. 'No. I subpoenaed him. I may or may not call him. Let Pierce think about it.' Corva added, 'I have a subpoena waiting for Picard when he's brought to the head chaplain's office. He can cool his fucking heels there for a few days. Why should he see the trial?' Corva smiled.

After Picard was led out the main doors by the MP, Colonel Sproule said to Pierce, 'Will the trial counsel distribute copies of the charge sheets to the members of the board, and will the members please take time to read these now?'

Captain Longo stood and approached the jury table, carrying a stack of papers. Beginning with Colonel Moore, and moving left to right like a shuttlecock, in descending order of rank, Longo set down before each member, not only the charge sheet, but a yellow pad and several pencils. Pierce remained standing as the board read the charge sheets.

Corva said to Tyson, 'In a few minutes we'll be asked if we have any challenges against any of the board. Do you recognize any of them?'

'I recognize the type.'

Corva smiled. 'Not sufficient grounds for a challenge. We also have one peremptory challenge, and if we use it, I'd like to use it wisely.'

'Wisely meaning what?'

'Meaning whose face don't you like?'

Tyson looked at the board reading the charge sheet. 'I don't like any of their faces. Can we challenge the president of the court – Colonel Moore?'

'Yes. But the judge has already indicated to me and Pierce that he would not look favourably on that.' Corva explained, 'Before, in his preliminary statement, that reference to Moore's experience was for me and Pierce.'

'Oh. I'm glad you understand the language spoken here.'

Corva pulled a piece of paper towards him and said rapid-fire, 'Colonel Moore commanded a company of the Fourth Infantry Division. You can see he was highly decorated. Next, Lieutenant Colonel Laski was an infantry platoon leader, like us, Ben. He served with the American Division,

Calley's former unit. His tour of duty coincided with the Tet Offensive and with My Lai. Next is Lieutenant Colonel McGregor, also a former infantry platoon leader. He was with the Cav, and if you look, you'll see why he wears the Purple Heart.'

Tyson looked at McGregor and noticed now that a good piece of the man's left ear was missing, and there was a scar that ran down the side of his neck and disappeared under his collar. 'I see it.'

'Okay, then we have Major Bauer, who is old enough to have caught the tail end of the war. He was a MAC-V advisor and saw action with a Vietnamese Ranger Battalion. So those are the four who have tasted blood. Next, Major Sindel is a public information officer at Fort Dix. She was a newspaper reporter before joining the Army. She will probably listen closely and ask too many questions for clarification. Captain Morelli is in the Adjutant General's Corps, and is stationed at Dix also. He is about thirty years old, so he was about twelve at the time of the incident we're here to discuss. Who knows how he'll react when the witnesses start getting into blood and gore?'

Tyson said, 'I'm not sure how anyone is going to react. This has got to be painful for those old troopers.'

Corva glanced at Tyson, then concluded, 'Lieutenant Davis is a West Pointer, who is awaiting orders for Germany. He is a product of the new Army, and has had more courses in ethics and morality than he's had in calling in artillery fire. He has no idea where you're coming from. He was about three or four years old at the time of the incident, and the date on the charge sheet looks to him like D-Day, June 6, 1944, looks to us.'

Tyson nodded. The composition of the board was supposedly random. But with four Vietnam infantry veterans it was obvious to Tyson that the majority of the board had some expertise in evaluating the sort of testimony to be presented.

Colonel Moore looked at the board members to either side and saw they were finished reading. He announced, 'The board has read the charges and specifications.'

Colonel Pierce nodded and addressed the open court. 'The general nature of the charge before this court is violation of the Uniform Code of Military Justice, Article 118, clause three, murder, in which the accused is alleged to have engaged in an act which was inherently dangerous to others and evinced a wanton disregard of human life.' Pierce paused shortly for effect before adding the mandatory statement, 'The charges were prepared by General George Peters, post commander, Fort Dix; forwarded with recommendations as to disposition by Colonel Farnley Gilmer and investigated by Colonel Gilmer under Article 32; and investigated by Major Karen Harper under Article 31 of the Code.' Pierce added, 'Neither the military judge nor any member of the court will be a witness for the prosecution.'

Tyson said to Corva, 'I hope not.'

Corva smiled. 'There was a time when that was possible. But everything is fair now.'

'Right.'

Pierce gave the defence table a look of impatience. He waited a moment longer as if to see if Corva and Tyson were quite through talking, then said, 'The records of this case disclose no grounds for challenge to the military judge or to any member of the board.'

Sproule and Pierce began a series of procedural questions and statements, and Tyson thought they harmonized well. Tyson looked at Colonel Sproule. 'Do you know him?'

'I know of him. He's a bit stuffy but not above a little sarcasm, like most judges. He doesn't put up with courtroom antics as you heard him suggest. Basically he's fair. If he jumps on Pierce, he'll look for an opportunity to jump on me and vice versa. Someone told me he keeps a little score sheet in front of him for that purpose. But none of that really concerns you. He does not have the power of a civilian judge.

The real power, as it has always been in courts-martial, lies there.' He nodded towards the board of officers.

Tyson said, 'I remember a bit of this. I told you I sat on a general court-martial board once. Right where Lieutenant Davis is sitting. I had to sharpen pencils, count ballots, and arrange for coffee.'

Corva continued, 'You know that unlike a civilian trial they don't have to be unanimous for a verdict. They only need two-thirds for a conviction. With seven members, they need four-point-six members to convict you. Call it five. If we exercise our one peremptory challenge, then they need four. Or, the other way to look at it, with seven members, we need three to vote not guilty. So, from the standpoint of a numbers game, our number is three. And we don't want to bump anyone who might be one of those three.' Corva looked at Tyson. 'So now that you've seen their faces, do we want to bump one of them? And if so, which one?'

'What do *you* think?'

Corva studied his yellow pad of handwritten notes. He said, 'Morelli is a *paesano*, Sindel is a woman, Moore is the designated president. They're already accustomed to Davis running their errands. So that leaves the lieutenant colonels, Laski and McGregor, and Major Bauer. The Veterans of Foreign Wars. My vote would be for one of them to go. They know too much. They feel qualified to judge you.'

Tyson nodded.

Corva said, 'Let's see if Pierce exercises a peremptory challenge first.'

Colonel Sproule said to Colonel Pierce, who was now sitting, 'Does the prosecution have a peremptory challenge?'

Pierce answered from his chair, 'The prosecution has no peremptory challenge.'

Sproule looked at Corva. 'Does the defence have a peremptory challenge?'

Corva stared across the twenty feet of open space that separated the defence table from the facing jury table. He

573

looked each member in the eye, and each met his stare and held it. He wrote something on a scrap of paper, folded it, and said to Tyson, 'Write a name.'

Tyson, too, looked at each member of the board. He wrote a name and slid the paper towards Corva. Corva opened his folded paper, and they both looked at the names they had written, which were the same name: Laski.

Corva stood and addressed Colonel Sproule. 'The defence challenges Colonel Laski peremptorily.'

Colonel Pierce stood. 'If it pleases the court, let the record show that Mr Corva responded as required that it was the accused, not defence counsel, who exercised the peremptory challenge.'

Colonel Sproule looked at Pierce for some time, then said, 'That will be noted by the reporter.' Sproule turned and addressed Lieutenant Colonel Laski. 'The challenged member may be excused.'

Lieutenant Colonel Laski stood, almost reluctantly, thought Tyson. He turned and left through the side door.

Captain Longo approached the board table and assisted in reseating everyone according to rank.

Corva stood and addressed Colonel Sproule. 'If it please the court, I would like to suggest that any errors I may make in the future be brought to the court's attention by your honour. I only suggest this in the interest of freeing Colonel Pierce's mind so he may concentrate on presenting the government's case.'

A few spectators tittered, and Colonel Sproule looked out over the pews, which fell silent. He said to Corva, 'It is the proper function of Colonel Pierce to raise procedural points.' He looked at Pierce. 'However, I would appreciate being given the opportunity to make these points myself.'

Pierce bowed his head but said nothing.

Colonel Sproule added, 'One of these points being that the prosecution should now remove the empty chair from the board table.'

Captain Longo sprang to his feet, went back to the board table, and moved the chair into the wing, out of view.

Colonel Sproule now turned to Tyson. 'Will the accused please rise?'

Tyson stood.

Colonel Sproule said in a voice louder than he'd used previously, 'Lieutenant Benjamin Tyson, you are charged with violations of Article 118 of the Uniform Code of Military Justice. How do you plead to the charge and to the two specifications?'

Benjamin Tyson replied in a clear voice free of any emotion, 'To the charge, and to both specifications, I plead not guilty, sir.'

There was the expected murmur from the spectator pews. Sproule ignored it and turned to the board. 'President and members, your task then is to hear evidence and return findings.' Sproule looked at Pierce and said, 'Does the prosecution have an opening statement?'

Pierce replied, 'Yes, your honour, I do.'

Sproule said, 'I remind the prosecution that in trial by court-martial, opening statements are not required and not customary. But when they are made, they are brief, and they should serve to clarify how you propose to present this case.'

Pierce did not acknowledge the admonition. He stood and Tyson noticed that Pierce's red hair was now military length, perhaps to make points with the board.

Pierce moved around the table and stood in the centre of the floor where the altar had been. He faced the board, so that his profile was to Sproule and to the spectator section. He began, 'President and members, the accused is charged with two specifications of murder under clause three of Article 118 of the Code. We are not charging premeditated murder, but we are charging that the accused, by his actions, engaged in, or allowed others to engage in, acts which showed a wanton disregard for human life leading to and causing mass murder.'

Pierce spoke in even, measured tones. 'These murders took place nearly eighteen years ago. The victims in Specification One are unnamed, and I cannot give you their names. I cannot give you their ages, nor can I tell you how many there were of either sex. I can produce for you no bodies, no death certificates, no pictures, no graves. I can, however, produce two witnesses who can attest to these deaths.' Pierce paused in thought.

Tyson looked out at the pews. He realized that without a microphone, Pierce's voice was not carrying well, but the effect was to make everyone strain to hear every word, and there was not even the sound of breathing from the hundreds of men and women out there.

Pierce continued, 'In Specification Two we have names and ages and sexes. We have this information from the Catholic Relief Agency for whom these people worked at Miséricorde Hospital. These people, fourteen of them, according to that agency, simply disappeared one day during the Tet Offensive in the month of February, in the year 1968. They were never heard of again. Now we think we know what happened to them.'

Pierce paused again and turned his head towards Colonel Sproule, then glanced briefly over his shoulder and looked at Tyson. Pierce faced the board again. 'In order for the government to prove a charge of murder against the accused, we must establish several connecting points: We must first establish that Lieutenant Tyson was in command of the platoon involved in this incident. We must establish that Lieutenant Tyson's platoon was at Miséricorde Hospital on 15 February 1968. We do not have to establish that Lieutenant Tyson was physically present at the scene of the alleged murders, but we will do so. We will also establish that wilful and wanton murder took place there. And we will establish that Lieutenant Tyson ordered those murders, *or* did nothing to prevent those murders, *or* conspired to conceal the facts of those murders from his superiors. It is not necessary to establish that Tyson himself committed any of those murders with his own hands; and in fact the government will not try to establish that.'

Pierce looked at each member of the board. 'As officers, you understand and appreciate the fact that Lieutenant Tyson, as the officer in charge of the body of men at Miséricorde Hospital, had the lawful responsibility to either anticipate, prevent, stop, or report the unlawful actions of his men. If the government can prove that he failed to carry out any one of his lawful responsibilities, then the law and Army traditions and customs clearly indicate that Lieutenant Tyson is guilty of wilful and wanton murder.'

Colonel Pierce drew a thoughtful breath and went on, 'I would like to draw to the attention of this court the Department of the Army's own Law of Land Warfare. Specifically, Article 501, a copy of which will be submitted to the court. The article is headed "Responsibility for Acts of Subordinates" and reads as follows.' Pierce quoted without reference notes, '"In some cases, military commanders may be responsible for war crimes committed by subordinate members of the Armed forces, or other persons subject to their control. Thus, for instance, when troops commit massacres and atrocities against the civilian population of occupied territory or against prisoners of war, the responsibility may rest not only with the actual perpetrators but also with the commander."'

Pierce, still facing the board, half turned and pointed behind him to Tyson. 'Lieutenant Tyson, as an officer, had direct knowledge of the "Law of Land Warfare" and in fact was required to instruct his troops in the provisions of this law. He carried with him at all times, as per MAC-V orders, a plastic card on which was printed a condensation of the Law of Land Warfare.' His voice rising, Pierce said, 'This should have been a constant reminder to him, if indeed one was needed, that the massacre of unarmed, unresisting, and in this case, sick and wounded nonbelligerents was a violation of the

577

Law of Land Warfare, not to mention a violation of the Uniform Code of Military Justice and of the Geneva Convention. And it was also in direct contradiction to his training and to what he learned and was required to teach his men on the subject of the rules of engagement in Vietnam. In point of fact, as an officer and a troop commander, who had served ten months in Vietnam, the accused knew full well what his lawful responsibilities were in regard to command and control of his troops.'

Pierce moved a step closer to the board and said, 'You members of the board, as officers, are fully aware that an officer with command responsibilities may commit a violation of the code through the actions of his men, that an Army officer may commit murder without having personally murdered. That indeed, many of the most infamous and brutal acts of murder perpetrated by soldiers against civilians have been committed in the manner set forth in the charge and specifications.'

Pierce added, 'The testimony you will hear should leave no doubt that the accused did in fact commit acts of murder as defined by the total body of military law, rules, regulations, customs, and the traditions of the officer corps. Thank you.' Pierce walked back to the prosecution table, glancing briefly at the spectators for the first time.

Colonel Sproule turned to Corva. 'Does the defence have a preliminary statement?'

Corva stood behind his table. 'Yes, your honour. And the defence will keep in mind the court's instructions regarding such statements.'

'Proceed,' said Sproule.

Vincent Corva surveyed the court, then said, 'The defence, in the interests of justice and keeping in mind that a trial by court-martial ought not to be a vehicle for obfuscating self-evident truths, has made several pretrial stipulations. The first stipulation was that Lieutenant Tyson was in fact the platoon leader of the first platoon of Alpha Company, Fifth

Battalion of the Seventh Cavalry. The second stipulation we made was that his platoon was in fact engaged in operations in or about the area in question. We further stipulated that these operations led to an engagement in the vicinity of a building that was discovered to be a hospital or infirmary. We even went so far as to stipulate that, though no one at the time knew the name of this facility, we would be willing to assign it the name of Miséricorde Hospital for the purposes of this case. The fourth stipulation was that Lieutenant Tyson was present when the alleged events occurred. Therefore, the prosecution's contention that it must establish those connecting points is in error. The defence has stipulated to those points, and any questioning of the witnesses that makes it appear to the court that the prosecution is uncovering new and incriminating truths would be ... misleading to the court.'

Corva looked at Pierce for a moment, then continued, addressing the board directly, 'At some length, the prosecution has appealed to you as officers to understand what you undoubtedly already knew: that an officer is responsible for his men.' Corva paused as though reluctant to pursue the point, then said, 'I do not mean this in a pejorative way, but it is the sort of thing that an officer of the Judge Advocate General's Corps might think it necessary for you to be reminded of, though you, as career officers in the mainstream of Army life, live that fact every day.'

Tyson glanced at the prosecution table and saw that Pierce's face was quite red, though it wasn't embarrassment that caused the interesting colour, but anger. Tyson looked at the board, but again he saw nothing beyond the impassive expressions that are peculiar to juries.

Corva cleared his throat and said, 'I had the honour of serving my country as a combat infantry officer in Vietnam. And during that time, I had no difficulty remembering my duties or responsibilities or the rules of engagement or the Law of Land Warfare or that I was ultimately responsible for the actions of my men. I assure you that Benjamin Tyson as a combat leader knew his duties and responsibilities as well. Yet, the prosecution has asked you to keep all these things in mind as though they were the central issues for you to consider as you hear this case. However, the issue is not whether or not Benjamin Tyson was responsible for the actions of his men. He was. The issue is what did his men *do*.' Corva stroked the bridge of his nose in thought. 'And,' he added, 'what did Lieutenant Tyson do.'

Tyson suddenly realized that Corva had prepared no preliminary remarks; that Corva was extemporaneously rebutting what Pierce had said and was doing a fine job of it.

Corva again met the eyes of each member of the board. He said, 'The prosecution has appealed to you as officers to understand the unique circumstances of command culpability and command responsibility. I appeal to you as *soldiers* – soldiers who have seen combat or have heard of combat from your fellow officers and from your men. I appeal to you to keep in mind that whatever you hear in this case, including the testimony of the defence's own witnesses, is the testimony of an event that took place eighteen years ago. But more importantly, it is the testimony of an event that was seen through the eyes of men who had already seen too much of war. Through the eyes of men who were themselves confused and frightened. Through the eyes of men who were, at the time of the alleged crime, caught up in the heat of battle. It is the intention of the defence to show that whatever deaths took place at Miséricorde Hospital, including the deaths of two American soldiers, took place as a result of hostile action and hostile action only. But if the accounts of that action seem to differ, I ask you to remember your own war stories or those you have heard. I ask you to consider that when the soldier comes home, what he remembers is a fraction of what he forgets, and what he forgets is what he chooses not to remember. Ultimately, all war stories, all the war stories you

580

will hear in sworn testimony, are as true as they are false. The details are as clearly remembered as they are fabricated. And the motive for all testimony is as noble as it is self-serving. Thank you.' Corva lowered himself slowly into his chair.

Colonel Sproule stared fixedly over the heads of the silent spectators. There was no movement in the chapel for some time, then Sproule looked at Pierce. 'The prosecution may call its first witness.'

Pierce stood and turned to the sergeant at arms standing at the side altar door. 'The prosecution calls its first witness, Mr Richard Farley.'

44

Richard Farley came through the door in a battery-powered wheelchair, guided by Sergeant Larson. Pierce himself moved aside the witness chair and indicated Larson where to position Farley's chair. The MP turned Farley towards the pews. Pierce said solicitously, 'Is that all right, Mr Farley?'

'Yes, sir,' replied Farley in a weak voice.

Corva grumbled, 'Next comes "Are you comfortable?"'

Pierce asked Farley, 'Are you comfortable?'

'Yes, sir.'

Tyson stared at Richard Farley. His complexion was unhealthy-looking and his trousers hung loosely over his wasted legs.

Colonel Pierce seemed to be trying to think of another solicitous question when Colonel Sproule said, 'The witness will be sworn in.'

Pierce adjusted the floor microphone so it was closer to Farley, then said, 'Please raise your right hand.'

Farley raised his right hand, and Pierce recited, 'You swear that the evidence you shall give in the case now in hearing shall be the truth, the whole truth, and nothing but the truth, so help you God?'

'I do.'

Pierce said, 'Please state your full name, occupation, and residence.'

Farley's thin voice barely carried, even with the aid of the microphone. 'Richard Farley ... unemployed, and I live on Bergen Street in Newark, New Jersey.'

'Could you also please state your former grade and organization?'

'Yes ... I was a pfc with Alpha, Fifth of the Seventh, First Air Cav.'

'What were your duties in this unit?'

Farley thought awhile, then replied, 'I was a soldier.'

'A rifleman?' prompted Pierce.

'Yes.'

Tyson looked at Farley and said to Corva, 'This is pathetic.'

Corva nodded.

Pierce asked, 'Do you know the accused?'

'You mean Lieutenant Tyson?'

Pierce hid his annoyance and said patiently, 'Yes, do you know him?'

'I did.'

'Will you, Mr Farley, point to the accused and state his name?'

Farley looked at Tyson, pointed, and said, 'Lieutenant Tyson.'

Tyson and Farley looked at each other for a moment, then Farley dropped his hand and turned away.

Corva stood. 'Your honour, now that the dramatics are over, I wish to object. Pointing and naming are not necessary unless the question of identification is at issue.'

Colonel Sproule said, 'Objection sustained. Colonel Pierce, you can omit that if you call additional witnesses.'

Tyson thought that Pierce had the chagrined look of a man

who had tried to pull a fast one and got caught.

Pierce asked Farley a series of preliminary questions, and Farley seemed to be responding better as he got used to the format. Pierce said to Farley, 'On the morning of the incident in question, before you reached the village of An Ninh Ha, did you see any Vietnamese civilians?'

Farley nodded before the question was finished, and Tyson knew they were into the rehearsed part of the testimony, though he didn't know why Pierce would ask that question.

Farley said, 'There was 'bout ten civilians on a burial mound.'

'What were they doing?' asked Pierce.

'Burying gooks.'

Pierce looked at Farley sharply, and nearly everyone guessed that Pierce had instructed Farley not use this pejorative term. But, thought Tyson, a gook was a gook was a gook. He began to feel sorry for Farley.

Pierce said to Farley, 'Did you approach these Vietnamese civilians?'

'Yes, sir.'

'Who approached them?'

'Me, the lieutenant, the lieutenant's RTO, Kelly, and Simcox.'

'You, Lieutenant Tyson, Daniel Kelly, and Harold Simcox.'

'Right.'

'Can you tell us in your own words, Mr Farley, what happened as you made contact with these ten Vietnamese civilians?'

'We never made contact with them. They were civilians.'

Pierce looked confused and tried to rephrase the question, then realized the problem was one of semantics and not the witness's memory. 'I meant contact in the sense of . . . you met them.'

'Yes, sir.'

'In your own words, Mr Farley, tell us what happened.'

Tyson wondered whose words Farey would use if not his own. As Farley related the story of the burial mound, Corva whispered to Tyson, 'What's this all about?'

Tyson shrugged. 'Beats me.'

Corva said, 'Neither Farley nor Pierce mentioned this in our pretrial conference.'

'I barely recall the incident. I'm surprised Farley can.'

Farley continued his story, and Tyson leaned towards Corva. 'I think I know what he's getting at.'

Pierce said to Farley, 'And it was Lieutenant Tyson who ordered these people to remove their clothes?'

'Yes, sir.'

'Was this common practice?'

'Well ... sometimes. Not like this though. Usually it would happen in a hootch. The medic, maybe an officer. Maybe an older guy. A sergeant. One at a time. In a hootch.'

'But Lieutenant Tyson ordered them to strip there?'

'Yes, sir.'

'People of different sexes?'

'Yes, sir.'

'What happened next?'

'He told us to make them lay in the graves, then shoot them.'

Pierce straightened up, as though shocked and surprised. He looked briefly around the silent court, then turned back to Farley. 'And did you?'

'No, sir. They hadn't done nothing wrong except burying the ... the NVA bodies.'

'No one complied ... no one followed this order?'

'No, sir.'

'But you clearly heard Lieutenant Tyson give the order?'

'Yes, sir. He said something like "Make them lay in the graves and shoot them." The peasants got the idea of what was going on, and they got real frightened and started begging.'

Pierce delved further into this, then said, 'So, after no one

584

responded to the order, what happened?'

'Lieutenant Tyson told us to get going, and we went back towards the platoon.'

'Where were you heading?'

'I'm not real sure. But somewhere around Hue.'

'What was your mission?'

Farley shrugged. 'Just get on to Hue. Marines were in heavy contact there.'

Pierce said, 'Did you have as an intermediary objective the village of An Ninh Ha and/or the hospital there?'

'Yes, sir. The gooks at the grave told us about a hospital. Lieutenant Tyson passed the word that this was an intermediate objective. He told one of the men ... I think Simcox, that there'd be broads there.'

'Women. At the hospital.'

'Right. And showers and hot chow. Everyone got real anxious to get there.'

'Did you have the impression that Lieutenant Tyson meant to commandeer this hospital?'

'Well, I guess so. We usually took what we wanted.'

'And you're quite sure that Lieutenant Tyson and everyone knew they were headed towards a hospital?'

'Yes, sir. Like I said, we couldn't wait to get there. But once we got there we wished we never went.'

Pierce let that sink in a few moments, then said, 'Mr Farley, in your own words, please tell what happened as you reached the village of An Ninh Ha. Spare no details, no matter how unimportant they may seem to you.'

'Okay.' Farley began a long disjointed narrative. He seemed confused and unsure, but Pierce never once interrupted, though he prodded often with 'Go on' and 'What happened next?' Tyson thought Pierce was quite clever to let an inarticulate witness tell it his own way.

As Farley began relating his story of the massacre, Tyson glanced around the court and looked into the pews. People were actually bent forward, listening with the sort of rapt attention that no minister, rabbi, or priest was ever able to elicit in this place.

Farley stumbled through it, groped for words, forgot names, contradicted himself a dozen times, showed no remorse, and even inadvertently made points for the defence. But the overall effect of this, the first testimony, was damaging. More than that, Tyson thought, when Farley finished, there probably wasn't a person in the chapel who didn't conclude that the first platoon of Alpha Company massacred an entire hospital full of people.

An hour and fifteen minutes after he began, Farley said, 'By dawn, we all got it straight. Then one of the guys – I think it was Louis Kalane – made everyone put their hands in a circle ... you know ... we put our hands in the middle and swore we would all stick up for each other. They were good guys like that. We always stuck up for each other.' Farley wiped the sweat from his forehead with his hand.

Pierce looked at his witness, torn between inquiring about his present mental and physical state and inquiring about more important matters at hand. Finally Pierce said, 'And did the accused join hands with you and the others and swear to cover up the facts of the massacre?'

'Yes, sir. He's the one who straightened our story out. He had a lot on the ball.'

'Really?' Pierce allowed himself a smile. Feeling good, he asked, 'Do you want a drink of water?'

Farley's mind was not yet in the present, and his brows knit in concentration at the question.

Pierce said, 'Do you want to take a rest?'

Farley nodded.

Pierce said to Sproule, 'Your honour, we don't need a formal recess. Perhaps five minutes right in place.'

Sproule replied, 'Take what you need.'

Pierce motioned to Captain Longo, who brought Farley a glass of water.

Corva leaned toward Tyson. 'Do you have an explanation

for the incident at the burial mound?'

Tyson thought Corva's tone was a bit sharp. He replied, 'Yes. Vietnam.'

'That won't do. Did you order those peasants to be shot?'

'Yes.'

Corva unconsciously drew away from him.

Tyson said, 'Look, Vince, I'll tell you what happened, then you can decide if you're defending a monster or not. Okay?'

Corva nodded. 'Tell me before I cross-examine him.' He added, 'I'm ... I'm sure there's an explanation. You see what Pierce is doing?'

'Yes. Suggesting that I was prone to ordering massacres that day.' Tyson thought a moment, then said, 'Farley is believable, isn't he?'

Corva replied, 'Inarticulate witnesses frighten me. But on the cross, they always fall apart. I'll take Mr Farley apart piece by piece.'

Tyson looked at Farley. 'I'm not enjoying that man's discomfort.'

'Don't worry about him. He might put you in jail.' Corva asked, 'If I had to assign a motive to him, I'd say that Brandt has some sort of hold on the wretch. Maybe drugs. But I don't think we'll ever know.'

Tyson replied, 'I remembered something after you asked me about motive. I never knew too much about the interpersonal relationships of my platoon – an officer doesn't. But I do recall now that Farley and Cane were best buddies. Funny thing was that after the incident, I never put two and two together. But now it's making sense. Yet Farley never said a word to me afterward. Probably brooded about it, then forgot it. Then perhaps Brandt put the bug in his ear again. Farley looks and sounds like a guy who hasn't had a close friend since the day the shrapnel severed his spine. He may romanticize the past, though God knows there's not a thing to romanticize.'

'There is if you were able to walk on your own two legs in

the past.' Corva thought awhile then said, 'We'll keep this motive in mind. Meanwhile, I want enough information from you during the lunch recess to completely demolish him. I want him so demolished that Pierce will not call him back on a redirect exam to try to, as they say, rehabilitate the witness. *Capice?*'

'Right.'

Pierce said to Colonel Sproule, 'I think we're ready, your honour.' Pierce turned to Farley. 'Mr Farley, you stated that you were in the operating room of this hospital when Lieutenant Tyson got into an argument with a French-speaking Caucasian whom you took to be a doctor. The argument concerned the doctor's apparent refusal to treat one of your wounded, Arthur Peterson. Is that correct?'

'Yes, sir.'

'And you personally observed Lieutenant Tyson strike this doctor in the face?'

'Yes, sir.'

'And you stated that you then struck the doctor with your rifle.'

Farley hesitated, then said, 'Yes, sir.'

'Why did you strike the doctor with your rifle?'

'I ... thought maybe he was going to swing at Lieutenant Tyson. The lieutenant didn't put him out, only pissed him off. So I hit the guy with my rifle.'

'Where did you hit him?'

'In the stomach.'

'With your M-16 rifle? You were carrying an M-16?'

'Yes, sir. It's real light. It has a plastic stock. I only gave the guy a tap really. Doubled him up a little.'

'Did you knock him down?'

'No, sir. He was on his feet and chattering again a few minutes later.'

'You thought Lieutenant Tyson might be assaulted by this man.'

'Yes, sir. The guy was really hot. So I cooled him down a

little.' Farley seemed to be remembering a time when he could do such a thing.

Pierce asked, 'Did you think it was wrong to hit this man with your rifle?'

'You should never have to hit anybody without a reason. But I figured there was a good reason, because the lieutenant belted him first.'

Pierce nodded, then said to Farley slowly and distinctly, 'After this incident, you say that Lieutenant Tyson ordered Hernando Beltran to pull a patient off one of the operating tables – there were six or so in this large operating theatre – and put Arthur Peterson on it.'

'Yes, sir. The lieutenant was looking out for his man, but this led to a big argument with the other doctors there. Then this one doctor who spoke English goes after one of our guys, and the guy just reacted and pulled the trigger, and this doctor goes down.'

'Did Lieutenant Tyson say or do anything at that point?'

'No, sir.'

'He didn't say anything to the man who shot the English-speaking doctor?'

'No, sir.'

'Then, you say someone shot the French-speaking doctor.'

'Yes, sir.'

'And you don't remember who shot these doctors, except that you think it was the same man?'

Farley licked his lips. 'Well ... I hate to say a guy shot someone if he didn't, but I think it was Simcox.'

'Harold Simcox.'

Corva stood. 'If it please the court, I would like the record to show that Harold Simcox is deceased and can obviously not defend himself against this allegation.'

Colonel Sproule said, 'Let the record reflect this. Continue, Colonel Pierce.'

'Why do you think the man who shot the first doctor shot the second?'

'Don't know. The first one sort of had it coming. The second one was the French guy who wouldn't help Peterson.'

'The doctor whom Lieutenant Tyson struck.'

'Yes, sir.'

'What did Lieutenant Tyson do or say upon the shooting of the second doctor?'

'Nothing.'

Pierce asked, 'Did he approve? Did he say "Stop that"? Did he make any statement?'

'No, sir. He didn't seem to care. You see, Brandt had yelled out that Peterson was dead. And I don't think Lieutenant Tyson cared about the doctors anymore. I think he was very angry.'

'You stated that Lieutenant Tyson at some point gave an order – a direct order – to locate the wounded and sick enemy soldiers in the hospital and shoot them. He said, "Waste them."'

Farley's lips curled up in a smile that looked almost wistful. 'Yes, sir. That's what we used to say. Waste them.'

'Meaning what?'

'Kill them.'

'Lieutenant Tyson said to waste enemy soldiers who were in the hospital for wounds and sickness.'

'Yes, sir. So a bunch of guys went out and did it.'

'Did you see this?'

'No, sir. I was still in the operating room. Well, I saw two of them get wasted. Somebody drew a forty-five and found two NVA on the tables there – one was really on the floor where Beltran put him – and this guy shot the two NVA in the head.'

'Did Lieutenant Tyson observe this?'

'Sure. He was right there.'

'Did he say anything? Do anything?'

'No, sir. He just stood there most of the time.'

'You stated earlier that there was no resistance, armed or otherwise, inside the hospital.'

'Yes, sir.'

'What then, in your opinion, led to the shooting of other patients who were *not* enemy sick or wounded? And to the shooting of other staff members after the initial two doctors were shot? In other words, Mr Farley, how did the general massacre that you described begin?'

Farley replied, 'Everybody just got carried away. They found seven or eight NVA in the beds and shot them. Then some people – nurses and doctors – started to run, and the guys started shooting at them. Then one thing led to another. I don't know. I never moved from the operating room. All I saw was what happened there.'

'Did you yourself fire at anyone in the hospital?'

Farley licked his lips. Then he said, 'A couple shots ... but only the people who were trying to get away.'

'After the men began shooting other patients and staff, after they'd gone beyond Lieutenant Tyson's orders to shoot wounded and sick enemy soldiers, did Lieutenant Tyson do anything to stop them at this point?'

'No, sir.'

'Were you near him most of this time?'

'Yes, sir. We mostly stayed in the operating room. I did leave there once for a few minutes. After all the shooting stopped, and when I came back, he was gone. I didn't see him again until outside. The guys had surrounded the building now. I told you some of the guys had thrown white phosphorus grenades and the place was burning. So we all went outside. Some people inside tried to get out, but the guys shot them. Lieutenant Tyson waited until the roof caved in, then ordered us to move out. Then we got to a bunker near Hue, and we put up for the night. Lieutenant Tyson called Captain Browder a few times and told Browder we'd got into a fight. Well, there was the sniper who killed Peterson and wounded Moody, so that was a fight. Lieutenant Tyson came up with a body count of ten or twelve, I think.'

'And Cane had been killed by the sniper, too,' Pierce reminded him.

'Right. I think that's what caused the whole thing. This sniper firing at us from the hospital. Everybody was hot. So when we got in there, we went a little crazy. I mean, here's these NVA soldiers and all, laying in beds, and these doctors – white guys – saying they can't help us, sorry about that. So, sure, we got hot. And I want to say I don't really blame the lieutenant for saying "Waste the gooks." But I think a lot of guys didn't understand the order.'

'The order to shoot North Vietnamese Army personnel who were patients in the hospital?'

'Yes, sir.'

'Did Lieutenant Tyson do anything to clarify his order?'

'No, sir. But I don't think he wanted all them other people killed. But once it started, he sort of got scared and just let it unroll. It was sort of payback time anyway.'

'Payback time?'

'Yes, sir. What we used to call payback. Like getting even. Everything had to have a payback. Like once – before Lieutenant Tyson took over the platoon – we lost some guys in a mine field outside of Quang Tri. So we rounded up the gooks from the closest village and made them walk through the mine field ahead of us. That's payback. But that's another story.'

Pierce turned away and raised his eyebrows, affecting a look to show everyone that Farley might be his witness, but he wasn't his good friend. Pierce cleared his throat and said, 'So this was payback for the sniper?'

'Yeah, the sniper. And for the mortar fire the night before. And for Phu Lai. And for everything. And because we were going to Hue. And because the people in that hospital treated us like shit. Excuse me.'

'And that's why Lieutenant Tyson ordered the NVA soldiers killed and didn't stop anyone who went beyond his orders,' said Pierce, trying to bring the subject around again.

'Yes, sir. That's why.'

'And that's why Lieutenant Tyson fabricated a cover-up story.'

'Yes, sir.'

'Payback.'

'Yes, sir.'

'Thank you. Your honour, I have no further questions, but I reserve the right to recall the witness.'

Colonel Sproule looked at Corva. 'Does the defence wish to cross-examine the witness?'

Corva stood. 'Yes, your honour, but as it is approaching the lunch hour, may I recommend we recess at this time?'

Sproule replied, 'I would not want to keep you from your lunch, Mr Corva. May I take a minute to instruct the witness?'

A few people laughed, including Pierce, Weinroth, and Longo. The board, caught unawares by the sudden humour, smiled.

Corva smiled good-naturedly, but replied somewhat tersely, 'Your honour, I'm quite prepared to forgo my lunch in the interests of justice. If the witness, who appears somewhat befuddled, is able to continue, I will begin my cross-examination this very moment.'

Colonel Sproule regarded Corva closely for a few seconds, then said, 'We will recess for lunch, Mr Corva.' Sproule looked down at Farley and said, 'Mr Farley, thank you for testifying. You are excused temporarily. As long as this trial continues, do not discuss your testimony or knowledge of this case with anyone except the counsel who are now present or the accused. You will not allow any witness in this case to talk to you about the testimony he or she has given or intends to give. If anyone other than counsel or the accused attempts to talk to you about your testimony in this case, inform Colonel Pierce, Major Weinroth, or Captain Longo. Do you understand the instructions, Mr Farley?'

Clearly Farley didn't but he was already reaching for the power switch on his wheelchair. 'Yes, sir.'

Sproule said, 'The witness is excused subject to recall.'

Farley's chair made an electrical whirling sound as it

moved forward. Pierce had to step aside as Farley swung around and made his way past the board table towards the side exit.

Sproule waited until he was through the door, then said, 'The court will recess until fourteen hundred hours.'

Tyson and Corva stood, and Corva collected his papers. Tyson said, 'This is depressing.'

'No one said it would be uplifting. Where do you want lunch?'

'Paris.'

The MP car dropped them off at the bachelor officers' quarters located in the north section of the post. Tyson recognized the modern three-storey red-brick structure. 'Does this place swing?'

'Actually, it does. I worked late here one night, and all I heard were stereos and giggling women.'

They entered a plain vestibule and climbed the stairs to the third floor. Corva opened a door marked '3F' and showed Tyson into a good-sized living room/dining room area, furnished in passable Swedish Modern. The reddish carpeting looked like basement rec room quality, and there was nothing on the walls but notes, Corva's notes, taped all around the dining area. Tyson said, 'I'll take it.'

Corva showed him to a round blond-wood table on which were heaped books, yellow pads, and reams of typed material. On the floor were stacks of newspapers, more books, and cartons of files. Tyson said, 'I thought you worked out of your hat.'

'They gave me this as accommodation. This is where we will conduct our sessions from now on. I told the post commander we could not prepare a proper defence if we had to work in your quarters with your wife and son there. So, you are authorized to come directly here anytime I call you. Okay?'

'Okay.'

'And if things get a little tense at home, call me at my office or home and I'll come here, and we'll meet and cool out awhile.'

'Thanks.'

Corva went to a small bar refrigerator and came back with two beers and two wrapped sandwiches. Corva sat on the far side of the table. Tyson popped the top on his beer and unwrapped his sandwich.

Corva bit into his sandwich and said as he chewed, 'Payback.'

Tyson nodded. 'Did you call it that?'

'I guess. I don't think we institutionalized it, but I remember the philosophy.'

Tyson sipped on his beer. 'I guess it *was* payback. What did the Nazis call it? Reprisals.'

'Right. Reprisals are outlawed under the same Rules of Land Warfare that Pierce was going on about. I'm glad war has rules. Can you imagine how dangerous it would be without them?'

Tyson lit a cigarette and said, 'The one thing Farley seemed to grasp in his befuddled mind was the fact that the people in that hospital didn't like us. And in fact did not treat us as well as they undoubtedly treated the enemy who'd been there before us. I don't know if they were enemy sympathizers or if they just feared the enemy more than us. But they didn't fear us. Which I guess was good. Our reputation was not that bad. But this show of contempt on their part ... they didn't understand we were itching to pay back for what we got in the past few weeks.' He looked at Corva. 'Sounds like self-justification, doesn't it?'

Corva shrugged. 'I'll reserve my moral judgements.' Corva drank some beer. 'Tell me about the burial mound incident.'

Tyson related the incident as he remembered it and concluded, 'Farley was an uncomplicated man, as you may have noticed. He took things literally. One time when he was complaining about something, I told him if he didn't like being a rifleman, I'd ask the battalion commander to take him on as an intelligence analyst. The next day he actually asked me about it. It was very frustrating having to deal with people who didn't understand my wit.'

Corva smiled.

Tyson added, 'But thinking back on that incident, I think he *did* understand that I was telling them to put up or shut up. I got tired of these idiotic threats they'd make towards the Vietnamese. I wouldn't have let them do it, of course.'

'You don't have to say that. Sorry if I got a little worried back there. Point is, this was not a good story. It shows you in a bad light. Let's discuss the cross-examination.'

'There won't be any cross-examination,' said Tyson.

'What?'

'I don't want you to take him apart.'

'Why not?'

'Because if you pull apart his testimony, by the time you face Brandt, Pierce will have rearranged the parts of Brandt's story that he sees won't hold up. Farley is the gook in the mine field, Vince. Pierce wants him to show where the mines are, the hard way, so he can make a map for Brandt. *Capice?*'

Corva chewed awhile on his sandwich. '*Capisco.*' Corva bit and chewed again thoughtfully. He said, 'For instance, if I try to get Farley to admit that you shot Larry Cane in order to try to stop the massacre, then Brandt is forewarned that we are going to reveal that, and he can be prepared.'

'Right.'

'And the more I take Farley apart, the more Brandt will be able to come up with versions that hew closer to the truth, even if it contradicts some of Farley's testimony, and you don't really want that, because you want to expose Brandt as a total liar. Right?'

Tyson didn't reply.

Corva said, 'Well, your reasoning may be screwed up, but the tactics are sound. I don't want to tip off Pierce, who will tip off Brandt. And you want payback. So, okay, we will skip the cross on Farley, subject to recalling him if we have to. As for the burial mound incident, I could cross-examine him for a month, and I could not get across to the board what you just told me and what I believe. I'll let that rest until or if we decide to put him on the stand again. They can have that round. The only thing I am wondering is this: Where, when, and how are we going to expose Steven Brandt as a liar?'

'Sometime after he gets on the stand and lies.'

'I can do that through my cross-examination of Brandt, or I can do it through one of our sterling witnesses. Or I can try to do it through your testimony.'

'We'll see. Stay fluid.'

Corva snorted. 'Yeah, fluid.' He leaned across the table, his hands on a pile of books, and said to Tyson, 'I just want to remind you that it is *you* who are on trial, not Steven Brandt. You are what we call the accused. I often defer to the wishes of my clients, which is why so many of them are in gaol. But your wishes are not all coinciding with my needs. You're the one who has to live with the outcome, Ben. If you perceive this trial as a rite of exorcism and you'll feel better about yourself while you're making scratches on the wall of your cell in Leavenworth, then we'll try to do it your way.'

'Good. I'm glad we see eye-to-eye.'

'Right. You want that sandwich?'

'No.'

'Neither do I.'

The court reconvened at 2 P.M., and Colonel Sproule said to Corva, 'Your witness, Mr Corva.'

Corva stood and said, 'The defence has no questions for the witness, your honour.'

There was a stir in the court, and Colonel Sproule glared at the spectators. He turned back to Corva and said, 'You do not wish to cross-examine?'

'No, your honour. But we reserve the right to recall the witness at a later time.'

Colonel Sproule seemed to resist shrugging, then turned to Colonel Moore. 'Are there any questions by the board?'

Colonel Moore replied, 'The board has questions, your honour.'

Corva leaned towards Tyson. 'There are times when I like the idea of a jury who may ask questions. There are other times when I don't. Let's see if I like this bunch or not.'

Colonel Sproule was instructing the court. 'The format that I have decided is proper for these questions has already been explained to you in pretrial instructions. You may ask your questions individually or through the president of the board, Colonel Moore. I remind you, however, that your questions to the witnesses must not be misleading, must not show bias, must relate to the testimony, must serve to clarify a point in your mind, and should be short and succinct. If you have any doubts as to the admissibility of your questions, you may reduce them to writing and show them to me. If you ask a question that is improper, I will not allow the witness to respond. Colonel Moore?'

Moore referred to his notes and said, 'Major Sindel would like to put the first question to the witness.'

Pierce stood and said to Farley, 'Mr Farley, you are reminded that you are still on oath.'

Farley answered from his wheelchair, 'Yes, sir.'

Tyson had the distinct impression that Farley, after nearly two decades, was still intimidated by the trappings of military authority. Tyson had the urge to shake him and remind him that he was a civilian.

Major Virginia Sindel leaned in Farley's direction and asked, 'Mr Farley, you indicated you fired a couple of shots at people who were trying to get away. Did you hit anyone?'

Farley chewed on his lower lip a moment, then replied, 'No, ma'am.'

'Thank you. I have one further question. You stated several times that Lieutenant Tyson did nothing and said nothing in response to a variety of events that occurred. You also stated

598

that he was frightened. What was he frightened of?'

Farley thought for some time, then replied, 'He was frightened of us.'

'Thank you.'

Tyson looked at Major Sindel. She was about forty years old, with dark blond hair and blue eyes. The eyes were intelligent, and her voice had a touch of the South. She had beautiful hands that played with a pencil in an almost sensual way. She wasn't attractive, but Tyson thought she had enough going for her to be desirable.

Lieutenant Colonel McGregor asked, 'Mr Farley, you stated that Lieutenant Tyson gave an order to shoot any enemy sick and wounded that were in the hospital. I realize a great deal of time has elapsed, but could you recall the words he used?'

Farley tapped the fingers of both hands on the armrest of the wheelchair. Finally, he replied, 'Something like ... "go find the gooks" ... no, he said, "NVA" and maybe "VC" ... "Go find them and waste them."'

'He meant the NVA and VC in the beds?'

'Yes, sir.'

'Did he say that?'

'I think so.'

'How do you know he meant the NVA and the VC in the beds?'

'There was no other NVA and VC around.'

'There were no armed enemy troops in or around the hospital?'

'No, sir. They ran off.'

Captain Morelli, the Adjutant General's Corps officer, asked, 'Mr Farley, just a point to clarify language. The word "gooks". Does this mean the enemy? Or civilians? Or both?'

Farley seemed glad someone posed an easy question. 'Gooks could be both. Slants and slopes were civilians. Dinks could be both. It depended a lot on where you were and what you were doing. Charlie was always the enemy.'

'Charlie was always a gook? But a gook wasn't always Charlie?'

Farley smiled for the first time. 'You never knew when a gook was Charlie.'

'I see. Thank you.'

Colonel Moore asked, 'In the hospital, did Lieutenant Tyson ever give you a direct order of any sort?'

Farley shook his head, 'No, sir. He only gave the one order. To kill the sick and wounded. He shouted it to everybody.'

'He did not personally supervise the carrying out of this order?'

'No sir. He stayed in the operating room.'

'Did you personally see his order being carried out?'

'No, sir. I was in the operating room.'

'But there were two wounded enemy soldiers in the operating room whom you did see get shot.'

'Right, I saw that.'

'What came first, Mr Farley, the shooting of the two doctors in the operating room or Lieutenant Tyson's order to kill the sick and wounded enemy soldiers?'

Farley replied, 'I think the shooting of the two doctors. I can't remember. It was too long ago.'

'How could you or the men of your platoon identify who of the patients were enemy soldiers?'

Farley thought about that for some time, then replied, 'I don't know.'

'Did Lieutenant Tyson instruct the men on methods of identification?'

'No, sir.' Farley seemed to sense an opportunity. He said, 'That's why the order was crazy. Once he gave it, you could shoot anybody. Women were VC, too. Old men were VC.'

'But the women and babies in the maternity ward were not VC.'

'I guess not.'

'And the hospital staff were not VC or North Vietnamese Army.'

'No, sir. But they were taking care of them.'

'Did you ever observe anyone in your platoon trying to stop the shooting?'

'No, sir. But some guys didn't shoot. At least I never saw them shoot.'

'Can you name anyone who didn't shoot?'

'Only one I know for sure was Doc Brandt. He never fired his rifle.'

'Thank you.' Colonel Moore said to Colonel Sproule, 'The board has no further questions.'

Colonel Sproule looked down at Richard Farley. 'The witness is excused subject to recall.' Sproule looked at his watch and said to Pierce, 'Do you wish to call your next witness?'

Pierce stood. 'No, your honour. The next witness's testimony may be lengthy. I would prefer to begin tomorrow morning.'

Sproule said, 'The court will adjourn until ten hundred hours tomorrow.'

Everyone stood as Colonel Sproule left the pulpit and exited the court.

Corva said to Tyson, 'Bunch of amateurs.'

'I thought they asked pretty good questions. Could you tell anything by their questions?'

'Yes. They've bought the story of the massacre. Nobody as stupid as Farley could make up over an hour of testimony about something that never happened. Tomorrow, Brandt will fine-tune the story. All the board wants to discover is your precise role, if any, in the massacre. They do not want to hear about firefights and room-to-room fighting.' Corva picked up his briefcase. 'I had a feeling this would happen. And as soon as Farley got into it, I felt that everyone in this place knew that what he had read in Picard's book was basically true.'

'Well,' said Tyson, 'it was.'

Corva watched the pews emptying and noticed that Marcy

hadn't stayed behind. He turned back to Tyson. 'Where do you want to go now?'

'Paris.'

'My BOQ or your quarters?'

'Your place.' Tyson looked around the chapel, empty now except for a few MPs waiting for him, and Colonel Pierce obsessively putting his papers in order. Tyson walked over to him, and Pierce looked up from his chair.

Pierce said, 'Yes?'

Tyson said, 'Yes, indeed.'

'Can I help you?'

'Yes. You can. You can tell Richard Farley for me that I bear him no ill will. Will you do that?'

'Yes.'

'And tell Dr Brandt that it's payback time. Will you do that?'

Pierce, still in his chair, replied, 'I think Dr Brandt knows that.'

Corva put his arm on Tyson's shoulder and moved him away. Corva said to Pierce, 'You've improved quite a lot, Graham. I'm very impressed.'

Pierce smiled tightly. 'The best is yet to come.'

'I think you should spend the night holding Dr Brandt's hand,' Corva said. 'Two aspirins, see him in the morning. Good day.' Corva turned and walked with Tyson out the side door into the corridor.

45

If one were walking from Building 209, also known as Gresham Hall or the bachelor officers' quarters, and one were going to the officer family housing quarters, one might choose Pence Street, a quiet lane with few buildings, cutting through more of the flat treeless terrain of Fort Hamilton. And if one were coming from the Officers' Club and walking to the guest house, one might also use Pence Street, heading the other way. So, it was not completely fate, Tyson thought, that put him on the same street with Steven Brandt.

Tyson spotted him long before Brandt spotted Tyson, though they were the only two people walking on the grass that verged the narrow street. And, oddly, he knew it was Brandt long before he could discern his features in the widely spaced street lighting.

It was a few minutes after 10 P.M. and he'd just left Corva's accommodation at the BOQ where the main topic of conversation had been the man who was less than fifty feet from him now. Tyson was still in his uniform, not having gone home to change. He saw that Brandt was wearing a bulky overcoat against the chill night air and his hands were thrust deeply in his pockets, his chin resting on the front of his coat which was probably why he didn't see Tyson approaching him.

Tyson looked around but didn't see his usual MP escort. Tyson was within fifteen feet of Brandt now, and Brandt, sensing someone approaching, veered a few more feet onto the grass to allow room for the man coming towards him.

Tyson saw that not only was the overcoat bulky, but so too was the body it covered. Brandt had puffed out like a biscuit, and his face seemed to have the same appearance and complexion as flour and buttermilk. And he was quite bald except for a fringe of ludicrously long hair that fell on the collar of the dark blue overcoat. Tyson wondered how he'd recognized him from that distance; he barely recognized him now.

'Doc.'

Brandt stopped, though froze might be a better word, Tyson thought. They were less than five feet apart, hand-shaking distance if anyone had the inclination.

Brandt didn't seem surprised, nor did he seem

uncomfortable. If anything, he looked as if he'd just run into a dimly remembered patient, and he regarded Tyson with a cool clinical detachment, actually looking him up and down. Tyson had the urge to break the man's neck right there and then. Literally grab him as they'd taught him in the hand-to-hand class and snap the neck at the third and fourth cervical vertebrae. 'Out for a walk?' inquired Tyson.

Brandt nodded, 'Yup.'

'Coming from the club?'

'Yeah.'

'Small post,' observed Tyson.

Brandt remained in the position in which he'd frozen, one foot in front of the other, body slightly turned towards Tyson. 'I'm not allowed to talk to you.'

'On the contrary, Doctor, a witness may talk to the accused. If you don't *want* to talk to me, that's another matter.'

'I have nothing to say.'

'Save your voice for tomorrow.'

Brandt neither moved nor responded. He seemed to sense that this chance meeting had to have a resolution.

'Hey, when's the last time we saw each other, Doc?' said Tyson as though the response should be, 'The party after the Princeton game.' In case Brandt thought the question was rhetorical,Tyson said, 'When?'

'The ditch at the Strawberry Patch.'

'Right. Right. What a day that was. What happened later?'

Brandt shrugged. 'Don't remember.'

'You did a nice job on me in that ditch.'

'Thanks,' said Brandt.

'The surgeons on the hospital ship said it was a professional wrap job.'

'There's not much I could have done right or wrong with a wound like that. I'm glad to see you're walking well.'

'Gives me a little pain in this damp weather.'

'It'll always do that.'

'Really? I thought I'd grow out of it.'

Brandt straightened up and looked around.

Tyson said, 'You're married now.'

Brandt nodded.

'Children?'

'Two. Boy and a girl. Sixteen and twelve.'

'Perfect family.'

'Yes.'

Tyson said, 'Hey, I saw some of the old crew about a month ago. Beltran, Scorello, Sadowski, Walker and Kalane. They asked about you.'

For the first time Brandt smiled, but it was more of a grimace. 'Did they?'

'Yes. They inquired about your future health.'

Brandt didn't respond.

'See much of Farley?'

'Now and then.' Brandt yanked his hand from his pocket and looked at his watch. 'I have to go.'

Tyson didn't acknowledge the statement. 'What happened to the pictures?'

'What pictures?'

'The pictures, Doc. Your field study in female anatomy.'

Brandt took a step, and Tyson took a step to intercept him. They were closer now, about three feet, swinging distance if anyone wanted to. Tyson said, 'It's not even safe to hide them. You could die or something, and they'll turn up in your possessions. Maybe one of your children will get Daddy's war souvenir trunk and open it ten years from now. Bad for your posthumous reputation. Better to burn them, no matter how painful it may be to do so.'

Brandt replied, 'I don't know what you are talking about.'

Tyson continued, 'The ones I saw you take are classics, though. Hard to part with. You remember the one with the net hammock? That was clever of the National Police tying her in the hammock like a sausage. Every time they gave her a jolt of juice to the vagina, that hammock jumped, didn't it?

Hard to capture that with snapshots.'

Brandt looked around, but the long flat road was deserted.

Tyson said, 'Look, Doc, everybody is a little kinky, but those people in the villages we cordoned were in *pain*. Do you remember that woman who aborted after the National Police nearly drowned her in the well? And what was really *disgusting* was that you showed your corruption in front of the Vietnamese. It was one thing for us to all be crazy, but you compromised yourself with those people.'

All Brandt could manage was, 'Racist.'

Tyson smiled. 'I guess. And on the subject of morphine, I don't mind that you gave me more than my share, but I'd like to know what happened to the stuff that was missing.'

Brandt said almost indistinctly, 'Let me go.'

'Yet, you were a good medic. You were no hero, but you were no coward, either. You knew your business. Lousy bedside manner, though. Those men who got hit were just meat to you. Just like the woman in the hammock with the electrode up her vagina. You are one of the *least* human beings I've ever come across. What do you do now? Orthopaedic surgeon? Can I make any inferences from that? I guess not. That would be too psychoanalytical for me.'

Brandt looked directly at Tyson for the first time. He said, 'You never liked me from the beginning.'

'I guess not.'

'And I'll tell you why. Because you didn't like the competition. You liked being the honcho, the big college grad, with all your little adoring peons around you. I was an outsider, another college grad, and I had my own job separate from you and your lunatics. You all made such a thing about being infantrymen – First Cav troopers. What a laugh. If that was an elite unit, I shudder to think about the rest of the divisions.'

Tyson looked into Brandt's eyes. 'You may be on to something there, Doc.'

'You see, I thought about that while I was there. I had a

functioning brain, unlike the rest of them. You fancied yourself a knight, a tall handsome chivalrous knight with forty armed warriors at your side. I was the wizard, you see, the healer, whose presence you had to suffer and who reminded you – and your men – of death. And I watched for eleven months as men got chewed up and never said a word. But back in the aide stations and the hospitals, where *my* people were, they could at least cry together over the carnage. While I was with you I shut my mouth. You hated me because the men looked up to me. But I wouldn't have competed for the approval of that bunch if they were the last human beings – or whatever they were – on the face of the earth.'

Tyson nodded, 'Doc, I'd be a liar if I said you were all wrong. But that doesn't change what *you* did or what you were. Or what I did or what I was, for that matter. But I did my duty up until that day. There's no stigma attached to me before February 15.'

'You did your duty after you defined it for yourself. There were not many officers who would have reacted like you did to the – cordon incident. That was your white knight complex. You liked being morally superior to everyone. I saw you once, by the way, coming out of a whorehouse in An Khe.'

'How did you know it was a whorehouse?'

'Well,' said Steven Brandt, 'the past is past, and we shouldn't stand here in the cold and talk about things that happened nearly two decades ago.'

'No, and we shouldn't talk about them tomorrow either.'

Brandt said nothing.

Tyson said, 'We are all flawed, Dr Brandt.'

Brandt said, 'I'd like to go.'

'In a minute, Doc. I'm still the warrior, and you're not in the best of physical shape, as far as I can see. I want to ask you one question while I have this opportunity. Why didn't *you* report what happened at Miséricorde Hospital?'

Brandt said, 'Don't you know?'

'No, I thought about it. But I never understood why you, who had nothing to do with it, didn't report it.'

'Well, then, I'll tell you. When I first realized you were actually going to cover up that massacre, I felt my fingers closing around your balls. And every morning I woke up with a smile, wondering if I should make that the day I gave them a yank. And every day that passed, without you making a report, I knew you were in deeper trouble. The first few days were a little edgy for me, because I thought you would finally come to your senses and beat me to it. I thought perhaps you'd made a secret report, and that we'd be taken into base camp one day for R and R and find ourselves under arrest. But I gambled and waited, and by the end of February, I was going to yank you by your nuts off your high horse. I was going to see you in gaol and me back in Saigon spending the rest of my tour of duty with the JAG people at MAC-V headquarters. But then fate stepped in again at the Strawberry Patch.' Brandt shrugged and smiled, 'So here we are.'

Tyson stayed silent a long time, then said, 'You could still have reported it and reported me. Men have been served charges in hospital beds before.'

'Yes, but after ... the morphine ... I was a little jumpy. I waited a week to see if we got a communication about your death. Then we got word that you were being sent to Japan and wouldn't be back. I thought about it. I decided that you were bright enough to figure out what I'd done to you and bright enough to know you didn't have a shred of evidence. So I considered us even. Or even enough for the time being.' He stared at Tyson a very long time, then said, 'I came from a good family, like you did, and I was always told I was special, like you were. I developed a big ego, like yours. So, to have you throw me in a leech-infested rice paddy and humiliate me in front of all those people, then have to face them and you every day – and you wonder why I answered that locator ad?

608

You find it hard to believe anyone can hate so charming a man as Ben Tyson. I assure you, I hate you.' Brandt's eyes met Tyson's. 'I still have nightmares about those leeches. I wake up sometimes feeling them pulsating against my skin.'

'Do you? I'd recommend my shrink, but he killed himself.'

Brandt said, 'Can I go now?'

Tyson nodded, 'Sure, Doc. But you have to remember one thing. Payback. Tomorrow won't end this.'

'Well, it might for ten or twenty years. Good night.' He took a tentative step, saw Tyson wasn't going to stop him, and hurried off.

Tyson continued on his way without looking back.

46

'Steven Brandt,' said Colonel Pierce, 'you swear that the evidence you shall give in the case now in hearing shall be the truth, the whole truth, and nothing but the truth, so help you God?'

'I do.'

'Could you state your residence and occupation?'

'I live in Boston, Massachusetts, and I am a medical doctor.'

'Could you state your former grade, organization, and duties while you were a member of the armed forces serving in Vietnam?'

'Yes, I was a specialist four, with the Fifteenth Medical Battalion, and I served as a combat medic with Alpha Company, Fifth Battalion of the Seventh Cavalry, First Air Cavalry Division.'

Tyson looked at Brandt as the preliminary questions continued. Brandt was dressed in the expensive bad taste that

609

seemed to be common in the medical profession. He wondered if they all bought their clothes from an AMA catalogue.

Tyson looked into the first pew and made eye contact with Marcy, who smiled somewhat enigmatically, he thought. They had been strange to each other for some weeks now, but there had been no open arguments. He had taken Corva's advice and put the marriage on hold while the trial was on fast forward.

As he scanned the pews, he observed that everyone who had come for act one had returned for act two. The weather was still nice, too, and that always brought people out, he thought.

Brandt's testimony began to move to more specific, though still peripheral, matters. Tyson turned his attention to the board. The combat veterans – Colonel Moore, Lieutenant Colonel McGregor, and Major Bauer – looked more relaxed with Brandt's testimony than with Farley's going on about gooks and human minesweepers and soldiers who took what they wanted. Of course, Brandt was saying similar things, but his choice of words was better.

Tyson looked again at Pierce and Brandt and listened. Pierce was proceeding very slowly, very logically, and very cautiously, unlike he'd proceeded with Farley. Brandt was articulate and answered the questions well, as though he were used to this sort of thing, and Tyson suspected he'd probably been involved in some way in civil cases of compensation claims or medical malpractice. Tyson glanced at Corva, who was scribbling notes as he listened to Brandt and Pierce sing their duet. Corva hadn't objected to anything so far, and there was little to object to, except that Pierce was referring to Brandt as 'Doctor' in violation of a pretrial agreement. But Tyson thought Corva was smart not to draw attention to the point.

Pierce said, 'How far were you from the burial mound, Doctor?'

'About two hundred metres.'

'And you saw these people taking off their clothes?'

'Yes.'

'Did you observe any actions on the part of Lieutenant Tyson, Farley, Simcox, or Kelly that you would construe as threatening gestures towards these approximately ten civilians?'

'Yes, though I couldn't say with certainty who made the gestures. But there was some pushing of the civilians, rifles were pointed at them. And I saw one of the soldiers kick mud at them.'

Tyson glanced out over the pews again. The spectators were attentive, but it was not the rapt attention that Farley's testimony had engendered. Farley had laid the rough groundwork, now Pierce and Brandt were building on it, block by block, mortar and brick, until an unshakable structure would stand for Corva to try to take apart.

Pierce asked, 'Were you often called on to assist in these strip searches of civilians?'

'Always. It was general policy. This type of search could only be done under the direction of an officer or senior NCO. They were to be conducted with as much tact as the situation allowed. It was my duty to perform the intrusion aspect of the search.'

'What is the intrusion aspect?'

'The intrusion into the anus and vagina. Enemy documents were sometimes rolled into an aluminium tube and transported in that manner.'

'Based on past experience, do you believe that what you observed was a necessary or legitimate search?'

'I don't think so. It seemed to me to be nothing more than ... how shall I put this ...? A quasi-sexual event.'

Corva and Tyson simultaneously looked at each other. Corva said, 'This guy has more balls than a bull.'

Pierce glanced sharply at the defence table, then said, 'I'd like to ask you now your opinion of the desecration of the

611

dead bodies of the enemy soldiers who were wrapped for burial.'

Corva stood, 'Your honour, the defence objects.'

Colonel Sproule turned towards Corva with the look of a man who was rudely interrupted while listening to something interesting. 'What is the nature of your objection?'

'Your honour, the defence fully understands that the prosecution is attempting to show a link between the alleged events at the burial mound and the alleged events later in the day. We have not objected to some of this testimony, but I think it has gone on long enough. It is, in fact, taking on a prurient aspect which might hold some interest to some people, but has little relevance to the case at hand.'

Sproule thought about this a moment, then said to Pierce, 'Colonel, we've spent nearly an hour at the burial mound listening to the testimony of a witness who was two hundred metres from the scene. Now, I will allow you to go on, but I expect, as I told you in an earlier session, that what you present has some relevance to the charges you have sworn to. Objection overruled.'

Pierce nodded as though Colonel Sproule had made an interesting point, then turned around and continued the questioning of Brandt on the desecration of the bodies of the enemy soldiers.

In excruciating detail, the first platoon of Alpha Company continued its patrol towards the village of An Ninh Ha and Miséricorde Hospital. Tyson's own recollections of that rainy day coincided with Brandt's, and he was surprised at how good a memory Brandt had. And when Brandt didn't remember, he said so.

Pierce said to Brandt, 'Doctor, the events that I am about to question you on concern your platoon's approach to this hospital. These events are discussed at some length in a book titled, *Hue: Death of a City*, by the author Andrew Picard. Did you, in fact, supply any information for that book?'

'Yes, I did.'

'Have you read the book?'

'Yes, I have.'

'Generally speaking, how much of Mr Picard's reporting was based on information that you gave him?'

'A good portion of his written account was based on my oral account to him, though I saw details and facts that I could not have given him.'

'Such as?'

'The names of some of the hospital staff. He told me that he had interviewed a survivor of the incident – a nun named Sister Teresa, whom he later credited in the book.'

Pierce pursued the provenance of the story for a while, then asked, 'As the platoon medic, what was your physical location in the platoon formation?'

'Normally, on patrol, I travelled with what we called the platoon command group. This would consist of the platoon leader, one or two radio operators, and the medic. When the platoon halted for the night, the platoon sergeant would join us in the centre of the defensive perimeter and form the command post.'

'So you were usually close to the platoon leader, Lieutenant Tyson, day and night?'

'Yes.'

'You knew him well?'

'As well as you can know a man you spend ten months with, night and day. There was, of course, a barrier to any real intimacy due to the fact that he was an officer and I an enlisted man. But we did at times confide in each other.'

'How would you describe your relationship with him?'

Brandt turned and looked at Tyson. He gave Tyson a smile that Tyson and anyone who saw it would think idiotic.

Brandt turned back to Pierce and said, 'There were differences between us, but we generally respected each other. He often praised my work.'

'Did you often praise his?'

Brandt smiled again. 'I was sometimes impressed with his ability to lead. He seemed a natural leader. I may have praised him on occasion.'

Tyson listened to Pierce eliciting Brandt's opinion of him, and Tyson was surprised at what a high opinion Specialist Four Brandt had of Lieutenant Tyson.

Pierce went on in this vein for some time, and Tyson thought it was smart of Pierce to sandwich this personal element in between the burial mound incident and what was to come.

Pierce said, 'Doctor, one final question before our expected recess. As the platoon's medic, did you feel that Lieutenant Tyson was adequately concerned with the mental and physical condition of his men?'

Corva stood. 'Objection, your honour. The witness has no psychiatric training, to the best of my knowledge, and I should point out that, at the time we are discussing, he was a twenty-three-year-old medical corpsman, not a middle-aged doctor.'

'Objection sustained. Colonel Pierce, do you wish a recess at this time?'

Pierce had no intention of breaking for lunch on that note. He repied, 'I would like to rephrase the question, your honour.'

'Please do.'

Pierce turned to Brandt. 'Doctor—'

Again Corva was on his feet. 'Objection, your honour.'

'To *what*?'

'Your honour, I didn't mind when Colonel Pierce addressed the witness as "Doctor" the first thirty or forty times. But now that he's trying to elicit some sort of retrospective medical opinion, I think he's trying to give that opinion more worth than it has by referring to the witness as "Doctor."'

Sproule thought a moment and said, 'Objection sustained.

Colonel Pierce, perhaps you'd like some time to rephrase your question. This court will recess until thirteen-thirty hours.'

In the BOQ, Tyson and Corva sat across from each other in the Swedish Modern armchairs, a light-wood coffee table between them. Corva had the Officers' Club send over box lunches and explained to Tyson, 'It's on your bill. I gave them your number.'

'Thanks.' Tyson added, 'Short recess.'

'Yes. Sproule could see that Brandt and Pierce will be at it for some time. I've seen testimony at courts-martial go until ten at night. No one has to worry about the jurors getting annoyed. Or overtime for the court reporters or guards.' Corva dug into a plate of pasta salad. He said, 'Tell me all about the good doctor's moral corruption. Was that the reason for the incident of the leeches in the rice paddy?'

Tyson nodded. 'Did you ever participate in any of those cordon operations with the Vietnamese National Police?'

Corva nodded. 'Just one. That was one too many.'

'Right you are. My company did about four or five of them. Well, after we cordoned off the village before dawn, the National Police – the fucking Gestapo – would arrive in American choppers. Then they would go strutting in with their crisp uniforms to conduct search and interrogation operations. Is that the way they did it where you were?'

'Pretty much.'

'No Americans were allowed in the village. What went on between the police and villagers was not for American eyes. But American officers could sometimes enter to discuss coordination with the Gestapo commander. I entered a few times. Brandt, as a medic, could get in, too.'

Corva nodded. 'He enjoyed himself, did he?'

'Did he? He was in heaven. Talk about tactless strip searches. These police did some strip searches and intrusions that weren't in any field manual I've ever seen. And, of

615

course, there was the torture – the whippings, the water treatments. I myself was disgusted by what these sadists were doing in the guise of a counterinsurgency operation. Brandt, on the other hand, was ecstatic. It was strictly forbidden to take pictures, of course, but Brandt had a cosy relationship with these National Police pigs. On the particular operation that led to his leech bath, I saw him snapping away with his camera. He didn't see me. Kelly was with me, and we followed him into a hootch. I caught him with two National Policemen, raping three young girls.'

Corva shook his head. 'Hearts and minds.'

'You want to hear all the details, or do you want to finish your lunch first?'

'What do you think?'

'Have your lunch first.'

The court reconvened at one-thirty, and Colonel Pierce said to Brandt, 'You are reminded that you are still under oath.'

Brandt nodded an acknowledgement.

Colonel Pierce apparently had not thought of a way to rephrase his last question because he asked instead, 'Dr Brandt, you have testified that your platoon had knowledge that they were approaching a hospital in the village of An Ninh Ha, a western suburb of Hue.'

'That is correct.'

'What was the platoon's reaction to this?'

Corva stood. 'Objection, your honour. How is the witness supposed to gauge the reaction of nineteen men strung out over a distance of perhaps a quarter kilometre?'

'Objection sustained.' He looked at Pierce. 'Could you rephrase the question.'

'Yes, your honour.' He looked at Brandt. 'Did you hear any reaction to the information that you were on your way to a hospital?'

Brandt crossed his legs, and Tyson saw he wore light grey

loafers with little tassels on them. His socks were almost sheer, and Tyson could see his white skin underneath.

Brandt replied, 'During the rest breaks, I would often walk up and down the file to check on the physical condition of the platoon. During this time I heard reactions from several men about Lieutenant Tyson's decision to make this hospital an intermediate objective on our march to Hue.'

'How would you characterize these reactions that you heard?'

'Mostly positive. The men seemed excited by the prospect of encountering some civilization.'

'So they had no preconceived negative feelings about this?'

'On the contrary. I heard Lieutenant Tyson give a few of the men incentives. He spoke about hot chow, showers and women.'

'Could you be more specific?'

'I heard him speak to a man named Simcox and tell him that he might get a blow job at the hospital.'

A few people in the spectator pews gasped. A man laughed, then became abruptly quiet.

Pierce waited a moment, then said, 'Did you take this to mean that Lieutenant Tyson was suggesting to Simcox that he ... Simcox ... how do I phrase this ... ' Pierce smiled self-consciously.

Dr Brandt volunteered a clarification. 'A blow job, of course, is slang for fellatio. Lieutenant Tyson was telling Simcox that there was a chance of having this performed on him – Simcox – at the hospital. I assume Lieutenant Tyson meant by a woman.'

'Thank you. Did you have the impression that Lieutenant Tyson meant to commandeer the hospital?'

'I don't know if he did or not. But by his statements about women and other comforts of the hospital, the men became quite aroused, and as the patrol moved towards the hospital, the expectations of the men became somewhat unrealistic.'

Pierce continued mining this vein, and Tyson thought it was rather smart of Pierce to show that the men had positive feelings before reaching the hospital and that these feelings were a result of their platoon leader promising them rape, pillage and plunder. Neither Pierce nor Brandt was going to be satisfied with proving only that he was a murderer. They wanted, also, to show that he was without integrity, venal, and debased. And there were two hundred people listening to this, including the press, people he knew, his wife, son, and mother. He wondered why he hadn't broken Brandt's neck.

The examination of Steven Brandt went on. Six or seven times Pierce drew the platoon to the hospital, then pulled them back with tangential or background questions posed to Brandt. Brandt seemed in no hurry either. He answered each of Pierce's questions fully and apparently objectively.

When Pierce finally took the court to the open square in front of the hospital, everyone was ready not only to hear but to believe what Dr Steven Brandt was going to say.

Pierce asked, 'How many shots rang out from the vicinity of the hospital?'

'About five or six in quick succession.'

'Could you tell approximately where they were coming from?'

'No. And neither could anyone around me.'

'So you can't say for sure if they actually came from the hospital?'

'No.'

'But in Picard's book and in previous testimony, it was stated that the hospital was the source of the sniper fire.'

'I never told Picard it was. I don't know where Picard heard that. I thought the hospital was the least likely place an enemy sniper would choose.'

'Did anyone around you at the time believe the firing was coming from the hospital?'

'Yes. Lieutenant Tyson did. He directed some fire back towards the hospital. I almost never got involved in tactical

618

questions, but this time I asked him to stop the firing at the hospital.'

'What did he reply?'

'He told me to mind my own business. Which I did. We had two wounded and one killed.'

'Could you name them?'

'Yes. Robert Moody was wounded in the leg. A light flesh wound. Arthur Peterson was hit here—' Brandt pointed to a spot on his right side, just below the armpit. 'The bullet passed through the – Can I use medical terms?'

Pierce smiled in sympathy. 'Best not.'

'Well, then, through the body and exited a bit lower on the other side. Both lungs were involved. Peterson was drowning in his own blood.'

'And the third man?'

'Yes – Larry Cane – he was shot in the heart and died instantly.'

'And you treated these men under fire?'

'No. The firing had stopped almost as soon as it had begun, and I was in no danger,' said Brandt modestly.

'What happened after the firing stopped?'

'The platoon directed a few more rounds of fire at the hospital. There were no glass windows. Only screens and louvre shutters, and I recall these being shot up. As I said, I still didn't think the five or six rounds that hit the three men came from there. Finally, Lieutenant Tyson gave a cease-fire.'

'Then what happened?'

'Then Lieutenant Tyson ordered four or five men to manoeuvre towards the hospital. They did and got right to the front door without anyone firing at them. I should point out that, as we approached the hospital, there were white sheets hanging from three or four of the windows, which I took to be a sign of peace or a signal that the hospital was neutral. Also, as I said, there was the Red Cross flag flying on a staff from the front of the building.'

'And there was no resistance from anyone in the hospital.'

'None at all.'

Tyson listened as Pierce backed up a bit, then took everyone to the threshold of the hospital again, then back again to the square in front of the hospital, then forward over the threshold into the front lobby. Pierce was pushing buttons on his tape recorder, forward, back, forward, and Brandt was responding like an audio tape. Corva objected now and then, but even Tyson could tell he didn't object to all he could have. He was giving Pierce a lot of leeway, and Pierce was growing a little cockier, letting Brandt make statements that Brandt would have a rough time explaining in cross-examination.

Finally Pierce got the platoon up the stairs of the hospital to the second floor where the main drama would unfold.

Pierce asked Brandt, 'How would you describe your reception inside the hospital?'

'Well, it was rather cool. We had just fired a few hundred rounds at the place, and if my guess is correct about the sniper not even being in or on the building, I can certainly see why they were less than enthusiastic to see us.'

'Was anyone openly hostile?'

'I wouldn't go so far as to say that. The men of the platoon were not very friendly visitors, either. I don't entirely blame them, though. It was this solitary sniper who caused what one might characterize as a misunderstanding, a feeling of distrust and hostility. It was not the happy arrival that the platoon had been expecting.'

Pierce looked pointedly at his watch.

Colonel Sproule did likewise, and Tyson thought they looked like they were doing a pre-attack watch synchronization. Colonel Sproule said, 'Colonel Pierce, if you have no objections, I'd like to adjourn this court until eighteen hundred hours.'

'I have no objection to a night session, your honour.'

Sproule looked at Corva. 'Does the defence have any objections to a night session?'

'No, your honour.'

'Then the court is adjourned until eighteen hundred hours.'

Tyson and Corva again went to the BOQ. Some of Brandt's morning testimony had been transcribed and was waiting for Corva, who took it from an MP at the door.

Corva and Tyson entered the apartment, and Corva took a bottle of premixed martinis from the bar refrigerator. He sat at the dining room table and began looking through the transcripts.

Tyson had a martini and a cigarette. He said, 'Where's dinner?'

'I'm not hungry,' said Corva.

'What if I am?'

'Eat your olive.'

'There is no olive.'

Corva shrugged as he read and drank.

Tyson said, 'How is the prosecution doing?'

'Not bad.'

'How is the defence doing?'

'Too early to say.'

Tyson paced around the living room. 'You're not objecting to some of Pierce's leading questions.'

'Why should I object to them? They're interesting. Look, Brandt is Pierce's witness. A prosecutor leading his own witness is just a shortcut to getting to what Brandt is going to say anyway. Let them dance.'

Tyson shrugged.

Corva said, 'I'm going to ask you about some of these statements that Brandt made, and you'll give me short and succinct answers that I can use on the cross-examination, which will probably be tomorrow.'

'Okay.'

Corva said, 'I hope *our* witnesses are as articulate and orderly in their answers.'

'I hope you are as articulate and orderly in your questions.'

Corva looked at Tyson. 'I wish all our witnesses weren't going to tell about a room-to-room battle in the same location and at the same time as Brandt and Farley told about a wanton massacre. It might confuse the jury.'

The court reconvened at 6 P.M., and Pierce pronounced, 'All the parties to the trial who were present when the court adjourned are again present in the court.'

Which, Tyson thought, was true. And if anyone took attendance in the pews, he could probably announce the same thing. The Army had an obsession with 'all present and accounted for.'

Pierce reminded Brandt that he was still under oath, but Tyson didn't think that was going to do any more good this time than it did last time.

Pierce began with warm-up questions, then questions of recapitulation, then moved again to the front doors of Miséricorde Hospital. Pierce and Brandt by this time had developed that sense of timing and mutual understanding of speech patterns that characterized long question-and-answer periods. But Brandt did not once anticipate a question, and though the examination was smooth, it did not appear rehearsed.

Pierce had finally reached the second floor of the hospital, and there was a palpable sense of expectation in the court, as Pierce asked, 'What did you see when you entered this room?'

'I saw immediately that it was an operating room. From what I could see, I didn't think the hospital was ever meant to fulfil the function of a general hospital. It seemed more a sanatorium than a hospital. My guess was that it was built by the French as a country rest home or a convalescent hospital.'

Pierce seemed infinitely patient as Steven Brandt gave his professional opinion of the architecture, layout, and setting of the place. Tyson thought that if Steven Brandt had been a crippled, unemployed veteran instead of a medical doctor, neither Pierce nor anyone else would have had much patience for this. Brandt got down to specifics. 'The operating room consisted of seven operating tables in an open space about thirty by forty feet. The walls were whitewashed stucco, as was the beamed ceiling. The windows were screened but not glazed as I said, and the floor was red terra-cotta tile. It was stark. There was electricity in the hospital, probably provided by a generator, and the operating room was lit by hanging incandescent fixtures. It was under these fixtures that the operating tables had been placed. Ceiling fans moved the air around, but the room stank of putrefying flesh and open body cavities. There were flies everywhere. I saw in an adjoining room a sink and toilet, and I assumed the water source was a collecting cistern on the roof. Hot water was boiled on a charcoal stove, also located in this adjoining room. The conditions were primitive, to say the least, and not very sanitary. My feeling for the men and women who were going about their jobs there was one of admiration.'

Pierce nodded in complete accord, though Tyson suspected he hadn't listened to a word of it.

Pierce asked, 'Who entered the operating room with you?'

'I can't recall everyone who was there, but I know I entered with Lieutenant Tyson, his radio operator, Kelly, Richard Farley, and I believe two more men. Farley was assisting Moody, who'd been hit in the leg. The other two men were carrying Peterson, who was semiconscious and crying out.'

'How many other people were in the room, and who were they?'

'There were about twenty hospital staff there. It was quite a mixture. All the doctors seemed to be Caucasian males. There were Oriental orderlies of both sexes. There were female nurses of both races – that is, Caucasian and Oriental. Most of the nurses wore white cotton dresses that I thought resembled nuns' habits. They wore crosses around their

623

necks. There were religious adornments throughout the hospital, and I made the assumption that it was a Catholic facility.'

Corva leaned toward Tyson, 'I've seen courts-martial run until midnight.'

Tyson said, 'Brandt seems fresh. He's enjoying himself.'

Corva observed, 'Pierce is in fine form, too. I think he'd like to finish up with Brandt tonight, while they're both on a roll. Sometimes you get a witness back the next day and the magic is gone.'

Pierce asked Brandt, 'Did any of the staff in the operating room formally greet you?'

'No. But Lieutenant Tyson said something to the doctor who was closest to the door. The doctor was working on a patient with a badly mangled leg. Lieutenant Tyson walked over to the operating table – it was the closest one – and began talking to this doctor.'

'In what language?'

'English at first. But the doctor was intent on his patient. He said a few words to the nurse in what sounded like French, then Lieutenant Tyson switched to French.'

'Do you speak French, Doctor?'

'No. But I'd heard enough of it over there by this time to recognize it.'

'Were Lieutenant Tyson and the doctor speaking amicably?'

'Not at all. I could tell from the beginning they were having strong words.'

'About what?'

'I suppose about Lieutenant Tyson's insistence that someone do something for Peterson. Actually, Lieutenant Tyson did make several asides to me and Kelly in English, so I knew what was going on.

Pierce continued his questions, and the responses provided more detail than Picard had done in his book and Farley had given in his testimony. After fifteen minutes of examination

624

concerning a segment of the incident that probably lasted one minute, Pierce asked, 'What was your opinion – your opinion at the time – not in retrospect, but at the time – of Peterson's condition?'

'I told Lieutenant Tyson my opinion several times. Peterson's wound was mortal. Only a thoracic surgeon in a well-equipped hospital room could have saved him. I saw a similar wound at a place called Phu Lai. I told Lieutenant Tyson that if Peterson had any chance at all, it was to get him on a medevac chopper. But he hadn't called one.'

'Did he give you any reason why he hadn't called one?'

'No, except that he was obsessed with the idea that if he were in a hospital, he should be able to get aid for his man. I explained that the hospital didn't look like it was equipped for what would have been open chest surgery. I think that was what this doctor was trying to tell him, too.' Brandt paused and said, 'Actually, I told him to forget Peterson. The man's blood pressure was dropping, and his breathing was very shallow. It was a difficult thing to say, but the man was as good as dead.'

'How did Lieutenant Tyson react to what you were telling him?'

'Not very well. He was very agitated, and I had the impression he was more interested in imposing his will on that doctor and the staff of that hospital than he was in helping Arthur Peterson.'

Tyson stood suddenly, sensing his chair falling backward. All noise including the court reporter's stenotype stopped. No one said anything for a second or two as Tyson stared at Brandt, his hands visibly shaking.

Corva looked at him but made no movement to get him in his seat.

Colonel Sproule said to Tyson, 'Will the accused please be seated?' Before Tyson could comply or not comply Sproule said hastily, 'The court will recess for fifteen minutes.'

625

Tyson and Corva walked in silence to Rabbi Weitz's office. Corva closed the office door and said, 'You scared the shit out of old Sproule.'

Tyson didn't reply.

Corva added, 'Brandt went a little white, too.' Corva went on, 'And the board will have no trouble believing you belted the French doctor.'

Tyson walked to the window and lit a cigarette.

Corva added, 'Of course, there was a positive side to that little scene. Colonel Amos Moore smiled for the first time in two days. I saw it. A tight little smile of approval.'

Tyson shrugged.

Corva said, 'They don't like the little shit, Ben.'

Tyson nodded slowly. 'But they believe him.' Tyson drew on a cigarette. 'Do you think Pierce himself believes that I ordered enemy soldiers to be shot?'

'Oh, yes. And it gives him the moral resolve he needs to prosecute this case. The fact of you not reporting the massacre may be legal or technical murder, but neither he nor the government would have had much heart for this case if that's all they had against you. No, they *have* to believe that your illegal order to commit selective murder led to the mass murder of everyone else in that hospital.'

There was a knock on the door, and an MP called out, 'Time.'

Colonel Pierce looked at his witness for some time, then asked, 'What was the result of this altercation between Lieutenant Tyson and the French-speaking doctor?'

'Lieutenant Tyson slapped the man across the face.'

Pierce nodded thoughtfully as if he'd heard this someplace before. Recalling that both Picard and Farley had described what followed as confusion, he said to Brandt, 'Would you tell us now, in your own words, what happened after Lieutenant Tyson struck this doctor. Take your time,

626

Doctor, and relate the incident as you recall it from your perspective.'

Brandt crossed his legs and leaned back in his chair. He put the tips of his fingers together and cocked his head slightly to the side so that he was looking obliquely at Pierce. Tyson thought Brandt was about to tell Pierce that he was a very sick man. Instead, Brandt said, 'The very next thing that happened was that Richard Farley swung his rifle and delivered a butt stroke to the doctor's groin. The doctor doubled over in pain. Then Lieutenant Tyson turned to one of his men, Hernando Beltran, and told him to pull the doctor's patient off the operating table. Beltran did this, literally throwing the man with the mangled leg on the floor. Two men lifted Peterson to the table. A white Caucasian female then placed a suction tube in Peterson's throat and with a foot pedal device began aspirating Peterson's blood. But Peterson would have needed transfusions of whole blood in order to stabilize his pressure, and he would have needed immediate exploratory surgery to see if blood was collecting in the abdomen. I think the hospital staff or some of them were ready to make a show of saving his life in order to avoid an ugly scene.'

Brandt looked at his surroundings, and his eyes went to the stained-glass windows where the light had long since faded. He seemed suddenly aware of the fact that he'd been testifying since morning, and he slumped a little in his chair. He cleared his throat and went on. 'Now that Peterson was on the table, Lieutenant Tyson began giving orders regarding other matters. His first concern, and properly so, was that the hospital should be searched thoroughly for hidden enemy soldiers. He ordered a room-to-room search.'

Pierce interrupted. 'Excuse me. Who did he give this order to? Who was present in the operating room? Could you describe the general command structure and deployment of this platoon?'

Brandt replied, 'There were a total of nineteen men who approached the hospital. As I said, it was a much reduced platoon. It was difficult to keep track of the comings and goings of everyone. Men were coming in and out, making hasty reports to Lieutenant Tyson. There were no sergeants in the platoon to give orders or supervise the men except Paul Sadowski, who had just been promoted to sergeant but who was not very experienced. There was virtually no command structure or organized deployment of the platoon. But eventually, about twelve men wound up in the operating room. It was then that Lieutenant Tyson began to attempt some organization. But the men were not at home, so to speak, in this sort of situation. They were running about, gawking at patients and staff. Some of them had not been in contact with ... other people for close to a year. That's the general impression I had. One of undisciplined behaviour. Inappropriate behaviour for the surroundings.'

Pierce seemed to find this interesting. 'Did this cause friction between the men of the platoon and the hospital personnel?'

'Oh, yes. There were several incidents.'

'Did Lieutenant Tyson correct the behaviour of his men?'

'Not that I saw or heard. He'd promised them a little treat, and he let them run loose. But as I said, most of them had gravitated toward the operating room where he was. Someone reported to him that the adjoining ward held six or seven wounded North Vietnamese soldiers. Their bloody khakis had been found lying around, and somehow the men matched the khakis to the soldiers, or perhaps there were other signs to indicate who was an enemy soldier.'

'And there were about twelve men in the operating room now?'

'Yes. And one of them was now having a verbal altercation with an English-speaking doctor. Then Beltran called out that Peterson had died. Then Lieutenant Tyson gave an order

to shoot any enemy soldiers who were found in the hospital.'
Brandt knew to stop there.

Pierce said, 'You heard him give this order?'

'Yes. He was five feet from me.'

'Can you recall in what form the order was given?'

'Not precisely. It was more of a response to these reports he was getting from a few men concerning the discovery of enemy soldiers in the beds. Lieutenant Tyson simply said something like, "Shoot them."'

'Meaning the enemy soldiers?'

'That was the subject at hand, yes.'

'Did anyone appear to follow this order?'

'Yes. A few men hurried off, and we heard five or six shots. Almost immediately afterward, I heard a long burst of gunfire right in the room. I turned, and this English-speaking doctor lay on the floor bleeding. I couldn't tell who shot him or why. I dropped to one knee, behind the operating table. There were more bursts of automatic fire. I saw the French-speaking doctor drop to the floor. Then I heard two loud single shots, and I discovered later that someone had executed the two North Vietnamese patients in the operating room. I saw them sometime later with bullet wounds in their heads. I should point out that I couldn't see much from where I was on the floor. I had no idea at first where the gunfire was coming from except that it was close. I even thought it might be enemy fire. But within a minute I realized it wasn't, because no one was reacting as though it was. Then someone began ordering the hospital staff into the adjoining room, making them leave their patients on the tables.'

'What was Lieutenant Tyson doing during this time?'

'He seemed to be doing nothing. He had his rifle cradled in his arm, he was smoking a cigarette and speaking to his radio operator, Kelly. I should say that a state of chaos existed now. There was random shooting throughout the hospital. I could hear voices screaming in Vietnamese. Most of the platoon had gone off into the rest of the hospital. There was a time when only Lieutenant Tyson, Kelly and I were in the operating room. Tyson seemed unable or unwilling to move from the spot and see what was happening.'

'Did you speak to him during this time?'

'Yes. I said to him, "They're shooting everyone."'

'And what did he reply?'

'He said he'd go and see about it. He seemed almost unconcerned ... detached. He and Kelly left, and I never saw them again until we'd all assembled outside the hospital.'

Pierce said, 'Let's go back to the time when the men were reporting to him about finding suspected wounded enemy soldiers. How many men reported this to him?'

'Two or three.'

'Did any of them make a suggestion as to what should be done with them? Or did they ask for instructions?'

'One of them, actually it was Sergeant Sadowski, told Lieutenant Tyson that the enemy soldiers were under guard. He asked what to do with them. That's when Lieutenant Tyson said, "Shoot them."'

'Those were his exact words?'

'Yes, "Shoot them."'

Pierce began a series of questions meant to replay the entire episode of the operating room. He tried to establish elapsed time, sequences, distances, positions of men, and names. But Brandt wouldn't commit himself to details or specifics, which, Tyson thought, was the right way to handle an incident that was chaotic when it happened eighteen years before. He noted, too, that Brandt's testimony did not perfectly coincide with Farley's, nor should it. It would have been suspicious if it had. He thought about his own five witnesses and their stories, and the sudden realization came to him that these men could not testify. Brandt and Farley diverted from the truth only on occasions when they sought to incriminate Tyson. But Beltran, Sadowski, Kalane, Walker and Scorello would have to relate an entire battle episode that never happened. As Brandt went through his account again, Tyson leaned to Corva and said, 'We have no defence witnesses.'

Corva replied, 'We never did. I'll talk to you about that tonight.'

Pierce took Brandt finally out of the hospital, into the rain-splashed courtyard, and it was as though everyone in the chapel breathed easier as they moved from the blazing fire, screams and gunfire into the quiet rain.

Pierce said, 'So now you were all together again.'

'Yes. Then Kelly, Lieutenant Tyson's radio operator, saw someone leap from a window of the hospital. He fired at the figure, a female, and she fell over before she could run. Then Lieutenant Tyson ordered one squad of men to deploy on each of the other sides of the hospital.'

'Why?'

'He said to shoot anyone who tried to escape. I stayed with him and Kelly and a machine-gun team on the courtyard side of the hospital.'

Tyson looked at his watch. It was 8.15 P.M. Corva must be hungry, he thought. The pews were still full, though there was some coming and going as MPs let people outside come in whenever others left. There seemed to be an inexhaustible supply of spectators, and Tyson found that interesting.

Pierce said to Brandt, 'Do you want a recess?'

'No, I'm fine.'

Pierce said to Sproule, 'If the court has no objections, we'd like to continue.'

Sproule replied, 'You may continue until twenty-two hundred hours, then we ought to adjourn.'

Pierce turned to Brandt again and picked up the questioning. 'You said Lieutenant Tyson was making false radio reports to his company commander, Captain Browder.'

'Yes. He was reporting enemy contact and giving progress reports regarding the approach to the structure which he described to Captain Browder as a large government

631

building. He was, in effect, going back in time and creating incidents that did not happen. Meanwhile, we were putting distance between ourselves and the burning hospital.'

Pierce, to everyone's surprise, moved quickly ahead to the French bunker. He asked Brandt, 'What was the mood in the bunker?'

'Somewhat subdued. We had the two bodies with us – Peterson and Cane. Some of the men smoked marijuana. Lieutenant Tyson passed around a bottle of scotch. A few men played cards. Lieutenant Tyson seemed intent on making them understand that they had to agree to a cover story for the incident. He coached everyone on what he should say if questioned. He congratulated them on a fine job. Then he even congratulated a man – Scorello – on using a phosphorus grenade to burn the hospital. He said something to the effect that there was no evidence to incriminate any of them. He even made up a body count.'

'Did Lieutenant Tyson indicate why he was going through this trouble of fabricating a story – why he didn't simply report to Captain Browder on the sniper and leave it at that?'

'Yes. He indicated that too much time had elapsed. He had to account for several missed radio reports. Also, we were supposed to join up with Captain Browder and the main body of the company before dark. But Lieutenant Tyson did not want his men mingling with the rest of the company in the state they were in. So he reported that we were still in the village of An Ninh Ha and would spend the night there. He also stated to Kelly, and I overheard this, that he wasn't going to have two dead and one wounded without being able to show an enemy body count. He was a man who did not like to look bad in front of his superiors. So, he fabricated a battle that would bring credit on him. His radio operator, Kelly, wrote up a proposal for a Silver Star for Lieutenant Tyson.'

Colonel Pierce concentrated on Brandt's recollections of the night in the bunker. Brandt, whose testimony had been almost dry, now described the atmosphere in the bunker in lyrical terms. He spoke about the flickering candlelight, the men speaking long into the night, the sound of nearby artillery fire, and the burning city of Hue, whose west wall was less than a kilometre away. Brandt described Tyson spinning his tale of a battle, and Brandt's story became a tale within a tale. Brandt described Moody crying out from the pain, administering morphine to him, and offering tranquillizers to the men, who declined, preferring marijuana and the lieutenant's scotch instead.

Brandt ended his story by describing the dawn breaking and the men climbing atop the concrete bunker watching the smoke rise from Hue, silhouetted against the rising sun.

Pierce let an appropriate amount of time pass, then asked, 'Did anyone in the bunker show any remorse?'

'A few men were quite shaken. But by and large, there was a feeling that the people in the hospital got what was coming to them. This was stated several times and in several ways by different people.'

Pierce, through Brandt, examined the psyches of the men of the first platoon. At five minutes to ten, Pierce said to Brandt, 'Did you ever consider reporting the incident as it actually occurred?'

'Yes. Nearly every day. At first, it wasn't physically possible for me to make contact with anyone who I could report to. But then we were given a brief two-day rest in a rear area. But on the way to camp, a delegation of six or seven men from the platoon took me aside and told me that if the story got out, they would assume it was me who let it out. They further stated that it would do no good to report the incident anyway, since no one would believe me if everyone else swore that there had been no massacre. They were right about that, of course. Considering the time, place and general conditions that prevailed, I saw no benefit in reporting what I'd seen. Of course, I should have, and that has been haunting me for nearly twenty years now. So when the opportunity arose to assist the author, Picard, by supplying the details of this incident, I immediately took it. I thought that a book would be an excellent format to tell the story of Miséricorde Hospital. I thought that if the Army and the government wished to pursue it, they would, and I would make myself available for any investigatory or legal proceedings that came out of the book's revelations. And I did, and that is why I am here.'

Pierce said, 'Thank you, Doctor.' Pierce looked at Colonel Sproule.

Sproule looked at his watch and nodded in satisfaction. Sproule announced, 'The court will adjourn until ten hundred hours tomorrow.'

Twelve hours after he'd taken the stand, Steven Brandt rose and walked off towards the side door.

47

At 10 A.M. on Wednesday, Colonel Sproule surveyed the chapel and announced, 'The court will come to order.'

Colonel Pierce said, 'All parties to the trial who were present when the court adjourned are again present in the court.'

Everyone sat except Pierce, who turned to Corva and asked, 'Does the defence wish to cross-examine the last witness?'

Corva replied from his seat, 'It does.'

Pierce instructed the sergeant at arms, and within two minutes, Steven Brandt appeared.

Brandt took the witness chair, and Pierce said to him, 'You are reminded that you are still under oath.'

Brandt gave a slight wave of the hand in acknowledgement which seemed an inappropriate gesture.

Tyson lit a cigarette and leaned across the table. He studied

Brandt's face, but there was no sign of any apprehension at having to face a cross-examination.

The spectator section was again full, and Tyson noticed that some people seemed to be in the same seats as the day before, though perhaps he was imagining it. The press corps all seemed to have made friends with one another and with some of the MPs.

Corva was reviewing the previous day's testimony and made no move to rise and walk towards Steven Brandt, who seemed somewhat confused. Several minutes went by, then Pierce stood and addressed Colonel Sproule, 'Your honour, did the defence answer in the affirmative?'

Sproule said to Pierce, 'I believe so.' Sproule turned to Corva. 'Does the defence wish to cross-examine this witness or not?'

Corva stood, 'Yes, your honour.' He came around the table, strode directly to Brandt, and stopped a few feet from him. Corva said to Brandt, 'Shoot them.'

Brandt seemed to move further back in his chair.

'Shoot them,' repeated Corva. 'Is that what he said?'

'Yes.'

'To whom did he say it?'

'To ... Sadowski.'

'And Sadowski replied what?'

'"Yes, sir."'

'And what did Sadowski say to elicit the order of "Shoot them"?'

'He said, "We found wounded and sick NVA."'

'And Lieutenant Tyson replied what?'

Pierce was on his feet. 'Objection. Your honour, counsel is badgering the witness.'

'Objection sustained.'

Corva said to Brandt, 'And Sergeant Sadowski left and shot them?'

'Yes.'

'Did you see him shoot them?'

'No.'

'How did you know he shot them?'

'I heard the shots.'

'That is how you know that Sergeant Sadowski shot them.'

'No ... I heard that he shot them.'

'Who told you this?'

'I don't recall.'

'Not Kalane?'

'Maybe it was ...'

'Not Walker?'

'No, it was ... '

'Objection.' Pierce was on his feet again. 'Counsel is badgering the witness.'

'Sustained. Mr Corva, if you don't mind.'

'Yes, your honour.' He looked directly at Brandt again. 'What did you say to Lieutenant Tyson when Lieutenant Tyson said to Sadowski, "Shoot them"?'

'Nothing.'

'Did you think Lieutenant Tyson's order was an illegal order?'

'Yes.'

'Yet you said nothing.'

'I was only the medic.'

'Only the medic.'

'Yes.'

'Did you tell Lieutenant Tyson that Peterson's wound was mortal?'

'Yes.'

'Then why did he not listen to you?'

'I don't know.'

'Did you tell him that only a medevac helicopter could save Peterson's life?'

'Yes.'

'Then why didn't you use one of the two platoon radios to call one?'

'It ... it really wasn't my job to use the radio.'

'Did you know how to use it?'

'No.'

'You didn't learn how to use a radio at Fort Sam Houston?'

'No.'

'Wasn't radio use a three-hour class at Fort Sam Houston?'

'No. Yes.'

'Why didn't you call for a medevac?'

'It wasn't ... I didn't have the frequency?'

'The platoon medic didn't have the medevac's frequency?'

'No.'

'Would anyone have given it to you if you'd asked?'

'I don't know.'

'Did you ask either of the radio operators to call medevac?'

'Yes. Yes, I did.'

'Who shot the Australian doctor?'

Brandt seemed momentarily thrown off by the switch in subject. 'I don't know.'

'Was it an American?'

'Yes.'

'You said you didn't know.'

'I didn't see who shot him.'

'Who shot the French doctor?'

'I don't know.'

'The burial mound was in the centre of a rice paddy.'

Brandt changed positions as though the change in subject necessitated it. 'Yes.'

'Where could a search be done to ensure privacy?'

'I don't know.'

'Were there trees or bushes around the burial mound?'

'I think so.'

'There are no trees or any vegetation on Vietnamese burial mounds. How would *you* have conducted the search?'

'I don't know. I wouldn't have.'

'Why?'

'It wasn't necessary.'

'You were two hundred metres away.'

'Yes.'

'Did Larry Cane die instantly?'

Brandt licked his lips. 'Yes. Bullet through the heart.'

'You said he was in the operating room.'

'Yes.'

'Dead.'

'Yes.'

'Did you have him carried there?'

'Someone carried him there.'

'Why?'

'I ... I don't know.'

'Why did someone carry a dead body up a flight of stairs?'

'I don't know.'

'Who killed Larry Cane?'

'A sniper.'

'He didn't die in the hospital?'

'No. Outside.'

'What was he doing upstairs?'

'I don't know.'

'Was he shot upstairs?'

'No.'

'Did Lieutenant Tyson ever strike you?'

'No.'

'On an occasion previous to this, did he not strike you in front of the entire platoon?'

'No ... we had words ... some pushing ... '

'Did you like Lieutenant Tyson?'

'Yes.'

'Did he like you?'

Brandt took a breath. 'No.'

'Why not?'

'I don't know.'

'Why did you like him?'

'He was a good leader.'

'Was he a good leader on 15 February 1968?'

'No.'

'The day before?'

Pierce stood again. 'Your honour, this is really too much. These questions are designed to intimidate and confuse the witness.'

Sproule said simply, 'Objection overruled. Continue.'

Corva continued, jumping from one incident to another. Brandt did not seem to enjoy the format. He began contradicting earlier answers, then he withdrew more and more into 'I don't know' and 'I don't recall' answers. Finally Corva said, 'Shoot them.'

Brandt ran his tongue inside his cheek.

'That was a direct order to Sergeant Paul Sadowski.'

'Yes.'

'You knew it was an illegal order?'

'Yes.'

'You watched Sergeant Sadowski leave to carry it out?'

'Yes.'

'Did Sergeant Sadowski leave by himself?'

'No.'

'Who was with him?'

'I don't remember their names.'

'How many?'

'Two or three.'

'You heard six or seven shots?'

'Yes.'

'Did Sergeant Sadowski or anyone report back that the order had been carried out?'

'No. Well, yes ... someone yelled into the operating room, "They're wasted."'

'Who was the someone referring to as wasted?'

'The six or seven wounded enemy soldiers.'

'You're quite sure?'

'Yes.'

'Who opened fire in the operating room?'

'I don't know.'

'How long were you with the platoon after 15 February?'

'Another month or so.'

'And you never found out who fired bursts of rounds into a crowded operating room full of patients, staff, and Americans?'

'No.'

'Previous testimony indicated it was Simcox.'

'It may have been. He was there.'

'And Lieutenant Tyson did not reprimand him?'

'No.'

'Do you expect anyone to believe any of this?'

'Objection!' Pierce was quite flushed by now. 'Your honour—'

'Objection sustained. Mr Corva, this is the last warning you are getting.'

'Yes, your honour. Mr Brandt, you stated that Lieutenant Tyson concocted a cover-up story for this alleged massacre.'

'Yes.'

'You stated that you went along with it.'

'No. I did not go along with it.'

'Then you reported a massacre.'

'No.'

'Why not?'

'They would have killed me.'

'Who?'

'The men in the platoon.'

'Do you think your superiors would have returned you to the platoon after you charged all the men in your platoon with mass murder?'

'I ... didn't know if they would—'

'Really? You thought you might have been ordered back to the platoon after you alleged that they were all mass murderers?'

'I thought the higher-ups wouldn't believe me. Or they'd try to cover it up.'

'Really?' Corva glanced towards the board, then back at Brandt. 'After you rotated back to the States in May of 1968, did you report the incident?'

'No.'

'Why not?'

'I ... wanted to forget it.'

'You said it haunted you.'

'It did. It does.'

'Based on what you observed, who did you actually see commit murder in that hospital?'

'I'm not sure.'

'Can you name any names?'

'No. Except perhaps Beltran. I saw him shoot the wounded man he pulled off the operating table.'

'Did Lieutenant Tyson see this?'

'Yes.'

'Did he take any action against Beltran?'

'No.'

'Mr Brandt, I listened to your testimony for a number of hours yesterday, and if there is *any* similarity to previous testimony, it has mostly to do with Lieutenant Tyson. The other participants in this incident have variously been described as doing a variety of things that they could not have done unless they were in two places at the same time. I realize that many years have elapsed since the event, and I wouldn't expect you or anyone to recall exactly the movements, or even the names, of nineteen men. Yet your testimony and previous testimony place Lieutenant Tyson in the same spot. Near the first operating table. And it pretty much leaves him there the whole time. Is that a correct assessment of Lieutenant Tyson's activities?'

'Yes, he was in the operating room.'

'And he never said much.'

'No. Except for a few orders.'

'Such as?'

'Such as, "Shoot them."'

'He didn't attempt to stop this alleged massacre?'

'No.'

'Did he aid or abet it?'

'Yes. By remaining silent.'

'Did he ever fire his rifle?'

'Not that I saw.'

'He mostly stood there, according to your testimony and previous testimony.'

'Yes. He never tried to stop it.'

'He stood there with his radio operator, Daniel Kelly, and had a cigarette.'

'Yes.'

'And you stood there in the same room with him.'

'Yes.'

'Were you afraid for your life?'

Brandt hesitated.

'Is that why you did nothing?'

'Yes.'

'Did Lieutenant Tyson appear to be afraid for his life?'

'I don't know.'

'Would you say that his troops went beyond the alleged order to shoot the enemy wounded?'

'Yes. They shot everyone.'

'Did Lieutenant Tyson order them to shoot everyone?'

'I never heard him give that order. Only the first order.'

'Were you surprised at that first order?'

'No.'

'Why not?'

'He was angry.'

'At what?'

'At the hospital staff.'

'So he gave the order to shoot enemy wounded?'

'Yes.'

'But no one else?'

'Not that I heard.'

'Did anyone threaten Lieutenant Tyson?'

'No.'

'Did anyone point a gun at him?'

'No.'

'Did anyone strike him?'

'No.'

'What happened to the hospital personnel who were ordered into the scrub room?'

'I already stated that someone threw a hand grenade in there.'

'Beltran.'

'Yes.'

'In earlier testimony you said you didn't remember.'

'Did I? I remember now.'

'Do you?'

'Yes. Beltran.'

'Beltran was a machine gunner. He fired his machine gun from the window.'

'Yes.'

'Did machine gunners carry hand grenades?'

'How should I know?'

'Did Lieutenant Tyson leave the operating room during the alleged massacre?'

'Yes. Towards the end. I didn't see him again until we were outside.'

'Where were you?'

'In the operating room. The whole time.'

'Why?'

'I didn't know where to go.'

'Why not go outside?'

'I suppose I should have.'

'Lieutenant Tyson tried to impose his will on the staff of the hospital.'

Brandt hesitated a moment, then replied, 'I don't know.'

'Did he care about Arthur Peterson?'

'I don't know.'

'Did you?'

'Of course. I was the medic.'

'Did you do everything you could for Peterson?'

'There was nothing to be done.'

'Except call medevac.'

Pierce stood again, 'Your honour, Steven Brandt is not on trial.'

Corva looked at Pierce, then at the board, then at Colonel Sproule.

Sproule said, 'Objection sustained. Mr Corva ... your line of questioning is becoming abusive.'

'Your honour, the line of questioning concerning Arthur Peterson stems from a totally uncalled-for remark made by the witness in earlier testimony.'

'That may be. But I think you made your point.'

'I think so, too, your honour.'

'Objection sustained. Proceed, Mr Corva.'

Tyson listened as Corva continued the questioning. Brandt, Tyson thought, was not at ease with Corva's style of questioning. Corva returned to the same points several times, but each time rephrased the question and received a slightly different response. Corva would then recapitulate the various answers to the same question. Brandt was in trouble, thrown off balance, and unable to recover his composure. His face and mannerisms betrayed that he was a man on the run.

After nearly two hours of questioning, Corva asked Brandt, 'Did you shoot anyone?'

'No.'

'Did you see Richard Farley shoot anyone?'

'No.'

'Did you see Larry Cane shoot anyone?'

'No.'

'Larry Cane was dead, Mr Brandt.'

Pierce got to his feet as Corva said, 'I have no further questions, your honour.'

Colonel Sproule almost breathed a sigh of relief and announced, 'The court will recess until thirteen hundred hours.'

Ben Tyson stared out the third-floor window of the BOQ. He said to Corva, 'What do you think?'

Corva lay sprawled on the couch and yawned. 'I think the board has reasonable doubt that you gave an order to shoot enemy soldiers.'

Tyson was able to see the Officers' Club a few hundred yards away. He saw a group of uniformed people who he took to be the board. Then he saw Brandt, then Pierce, Weinroth, and Longo. He envied them their freedom of movement. There were people dressed in civilian clothing outside on the cobblestones who he realized were media people. There were TV vans parked near the museum, and he saw two men holding cameras. 'What is the fascination with this?'

'What?'

'Media coverage. People outside the gates. I can see the main gate from here. Newspaper headlines. *Headlines*. There are important things happening in the nation beyond those gates.'

Corva yawned again. 'Don't be modest.'

Tyson turned from the window. 'How about the second assertion that I aided and abetted the massacre by doing nothing to stop it?'

'Also reasonable doubt. I think the board understands the troops mutinied and that you were no longer in command.' Corva sat up on the couch. 'But I couldn't get Brandt to help me out on that. If I were on the jury, I'd have lots of questions. Which is what will happen after lunch.'

'Right. So we're down to the cover-up.'

'Yes. That's about it. I wish I could think of a way to address that.'

'We could say that it haunted me, like Brandt said it haunted him; I kept meaning to report it, but with one thing and another I kept putting it off.'

Corva stood. 'We could say that. Hey, open the refrigerator.'

Tyson opened the bar refrigerator and took out a brown bag and two cans of beer. 'What is it today?'

'Chinese food.' Corva took the bag and began laying out containers on the dinette table.

'It's cold, Vince.'

'So what?' Corva found plastic forks in the bottom of the bag. 'Do you save these tea bags?'

Tyson said, 'Do you think the board would return a verdict of guilty based only on the cover-up?'

Corva nodded. 'Afraid so.' He heaped food from the containers onto a paper plate. 'Help yourself.'

Tyson helped himself to a beer. He said, 'Chinese food is what I had the night I saw Picard's book.'

'Really?'

'That was a long time ago.'

'It's almost over, Ben.' Corva cut into a piece of egg foo yung.

'For years after I returned from Vietnam, I wouldn't eat rice.'

'Me neither.'

Tyson remained standing near the window as Corva ate. Tyson said, 'You did fine with Brandt.'

'Thanks. That's how you handle articulate witnesses. You don't let them articulate. Everyone was tired of his windy bullshit anyway. The court reporter last night wanted to shoot him.'

Tyson smiled. 'I didn't expect him to start coming apart like that.'

Corva sipped on his beer. 'I couldn't have or wouldn't have done that with a pfc or with Farley. But Sproule gave me a lot of latitude with Dr Wonderful.'

'I think you planted some questions in the board's mind.'

'I think so. We'll see when they get a crack at him later.'

'You don't want to delve too deeply into the matter of Larry Cane.'

'No. He would have denied it.' Corva lifted a forkful of rice.

'You want to try any of this?'

'It's cold.'

'Right. So, what do you think? About our five witnesses?'

Tyson sat opposite Corva. 'They can't get up there and tell the story of the firefight, can they?'

'I really don't think so.'

'That was an okay story eighteen years ago when we were bullshitting Browder and the battalion commander. I don't think it's going to fly anymore.'

'No,' agreed Corva, 'and we shouldn't even let it on the runway.' He looked at Tyson. 'We have a problem, you know.'

'Yes, I know.' Tyson lit another cigarette. 'Will Sadowski, Scorello, Walker, Kalane, or Beltran take the stand and tell the *truth* about the massacre? And testify that I did not order anyone killed? That I shot Cane in an attempt to stop it? That my life was in danger? That the troops mutinied? And that the cover-up was not my idea?'

Corva wiped his mouth with a paper napkin and swallowed. 'That's what I'm trying to find out now. I've spoken to each of their attorneys, and they're not being very cooperative. Now that the trial has begun, everyone is having second thoughts about "all for one, and one for all."'

'Are they?'

'I told you, Ben, that before this is over, everyone will betray you in one way or another.'

Tyson drank his beer silently for a while. 'You're saying they won't testify on my behalf?'

'We're still talking about it. You see, there are questions of immunity, of perjury, and Fifth Amendment rights. But the bottom line, Ben, is that those men do not want to get up on the stand and have Pierce ask them if they killed babies and pregnant women. Or did they shoot doctors and nursing nuns? Who killed the babies, by the way?'

'Scorello. With a phosphorus hand grenade.'

Corva shook his head.

Tyson tapped his fingers on the table.

Corva said, 'What did Brandt actually do?'

'Pretty much what he said. Nothing. He was petrified. He thought they were going to kill him, too.'

Corva picked at some fried rice. 'Medics are always suspect, aren't they? They are never fully initiated into the psychotic circle. Medics, Army scout dog handlers, chaplains and chaplain's assistants, artillery forward observers ... all those people who joined up with us from time to time ... they looked at us funny, didn't they? Like they were visiting a travelling psycho ward where all the patients were armed to the teeth. They couldn't wait to get the hell back to camp. And when they left, we'd all laugh at them. But you know what? We *were* crazy.'

Tyson finished his beer. 'The platoon's instincts were correct about Brandt, as it turns out. They should have made a clean sweep of it.'

Corva said, 'They made a clean sweep of the hospital. They knew that they couldn't shoot a few people there like they did in the villages and get away with it.'

'No. That was civilization. So they destroyed it.'

Neither Corva nor Tyson spoke for some time. The phone rang, and Corva got up to answer it. He listened for a minute, then said, 'All right. Keep me informed.' He hung up and turned to Tyson. 'That was my office. They're still negotiating with our reluctant witnesses' attorneys.'

'And?'

'I don't know. They have very valid reasons for not exposing their clients to sworn testimony and cross-examination. If you were in their position and I was your attorney, I would not let you testify.'

'How about comrades in arms and blood oaths by the light of a flickering candle and all that?'

'I'd say my client doesn't recall any of that. I'd say that in the latter part of the twentieth century in a country run by lawyers, you can forget all of that. I'd also say, to save face, that my client's oaths, if any were in fact made, had to do with relating the story of a fierce firefight. Not a massacre.' Corva added, 'But we're still negotiating with them.'

Tyson said nothing.

Corva drew a deep breath. 'Sometimes, Ben, I think the less said, the better. Sometimes it is the defence and not the prosecution who winds up removing the reasonable doubt from the minds of the jury who had reasonable doubt until the defence witnesses started getting cross-examined. *Capice?*'

'I guess. But we're not offering much of a defence.'

'The prosecution didn't offer much of a case either. I'd like to throw it to the jury as soon as possible.'

'Do you want me to take the stand?'

'I'll let you know. And if you think of a good reason why you chose to ignore a mass murder, let me know.'

The phone rang again, and Corva picked it up. He listened. 'Okay, Sergeant. Tell them to start without us.' He hung up and said to Tyson, 'They're not going to start without us.'

'The court will come to order,' said Colonel Sproule.

Pierce made his announcement regarding all the parties being present.

Colonel Sproule addressed Colonel Moore. 'You informed me during the recess that the board has questions for the witness, Steven Brandt.'

Moore replied, 'Yes, your honour.'

Sproule said to Colonel Pierce, 'Recall the witness.'

Pierce motioned to the sergeant at arms. Brandt did not immediately appear, and after some minutes two MPs were sent to look for the sergeant at arms and for Brandt. Finally, after five full minutes, Brandt appeared and walked across the floor to the witness stand. Colonel Pierce said to him, 'The witness is reminded that he is still under oath.'

Brandt sat.

Colonel Sproule addressed the court. 'I have had an opportunity to see and hear the questions the board intends

to pose to the witness and have ruled on their admissibility.'
Sproule looked at Pierce, then at Corva, then back to Colonel
Moore. 'You may begin.'

Lieutenant Davis, the junior member of the board, began.
'Dr Brandt, did you discuss the hospital incident with your
own commanding officer? That is, the commander of the
Fifteenth Medical Battalion?'

'No.'

'Could you tell us why not?'

Brandt shifted in his chair and crossed his legs. 'As I stated,
I was frightened.'

'Would your commanding officer, a medical doctor, have
been unsympathetic to your story?'

Brandt replied, 'I don't know.'

Corva leaned towards Tyson, 'Dr Steve is going to like this
format even less.'

The questioning from the six-member board went on for
nearly an hour. Tyson could tell by the questioning that the
board did not find Steven Brandt to their liking. Their
questions focused on Brandt's reasons for not reporting the
crime and his reasons for coming forward after all these
years. They questioned him on his relationship with Tyson
and with the other men of the platoon. Tyson didn't doubt
that they believed Brandt's story of a massacre in broad
outline. But, just as with Farley, they couldn't seem to focus
on the details. Finally, Colonel Moore asked the last
questions. 'You stated earlier that you and Lieutenant Tyson
had an altercation sometime previous to this incident.'

'Yes.'

'You mentioned pushing.'

'Yes.'

'Who pushed whom?'

'Lieutenant Tyson pushed me.'

'Did you fall to the ground?'

'Yes.'

'Did you make a formal complaint against him?'

'No.'

'Could you tell us what the altercation was about?'

'I don't recall.'

'Did you bear him any ill will?'

'None.'

'Did you discuss the hospital incident with Lieutenant Tyson afterwards?'

'No.'

'Why not?'

'He was part of the cover-up.'

'Did you discuss this incident with *anyone?* Anyone in the military or in civilian life?'

'No. Not until I discussed it with Andrew Picard.'

'Did you, after you discussed it with Andrew Picard, attempt any communication with any government agency regarding this matter?'

'No.'

'Did the Army, then, contact you regarding this matter?'

'Yes.'

Colonel Moore looked to either side, and each member of the board shook his head to indicate that there were no further questions. But from where Tyson was sitting, the five heads turned towards the centre, all shaking in unison, gave the appearance of five disgusted people.

Colonel Sproule said to Steven Brandt, 'Thank you for testifying. You are excused subject to recall.' Sproule repeated the warning against discussing his testimony.

Tyson looked at Pierce, Weinroth, and Longo. They didn't look quite as smug as they had after Pierce's direct examination of Brandt. But neither did they look worried. In fact, they looked to Tyson like people who realize that the worst is over. That the end is near and that they are ahead and running downhill, while the opposition is only beginning the uphill portion.

Colonel Sproule finished with Brandt and said, 'The witness is excused, subject to recall.'

Brandt stood and walked, not too fast, towards the side door.

Colonel Sproule addressed Colonel Pierce. 'Does the prosecution wish to call a witness?'

Pierce replied, 'No, it does not, your honour.'

'Does the prosecution have anything further to offer at this time?'

'No, it does not, your honour.'

Colonel Sproule pronounced, 'The court is adjourned until ten hundred hours tomorrow.'

Tyson and Corva walked on the path leading to the BOQ. Tyson said, 'When will we know if we have any defence witnesses?'

'Tonight, I hope. I may have to ask for a continuance.'

'That's legal mumbo jumbo for a postponement.'

'Right.'

'I don't want a postponement.'

'Well, Ben, neither do I. But we need some time.'

'No. I want to be in court tomorrow.'

'We'll discuss it later.'

They came to a cross path on the lawn. The sun was behind the red-brick housing structures, and long shadows lay over the lawns. Corva said, 'It gets cold here at night.' He looked at Tyson. 'Going home?'

'Yes. To see David awhile. Marcy is still trying to accomplish some work, and she has dinner with a client tonight. You know how it is. Trying to juggle being a homemaker, mother, career lady, and still put in six to twelve hours in court.'

'Now, now.' Corva glanced at his watch. 'I'll be in the BOQ very late. Come over around ten, and we'll have a drink.'

Tyson asked, 'Where have all the soldiers gone, Vince?'

Corva replied, 'They all have lawyers now.'

48

Ben Tyson and Vincent Corva sat at the defence table. Tyson looked at his watch and noted that it was ten minutes to ten. The spectators were in place. The board began filing in.

Corva said to Tyson, 'I know how you must feel.'

Tyson lit a cigarette and replied, 'I don't feel betrayed. I don't feel bad. I don't know what those five men would have said that would make a difference.'

'They did all offer to make unsworn statements in extenuation and mitigation if a guilty verdict is returned. I think the presentencing presentation of extenuating circumstances is ultimately more important than the verdict in a case like this.'

'From the standpoint of how long I would have to spend in gaol, I agree.'

Corva nodded. He added, 'It's possible that they will return a verdict of not guilty.'

Tyson said nothing.

Corva said, 'Seeing as we don't seem to have any defence witnesses in the witness room at the moment, would you like a postponement?'

Tyson replied, 'No. You have a defence witness sitting next to you.'

Corva stayed silent a few seconds. He looked at the board, who were sitting at their table, talking quietly to one another. Corva said, 'It is very rare for the accused in a case like this to take the stand in his own defence.'

'You said last night I could make a statement.'

'Did I say that?'

'Yes.'

Corva put his hand on Tyson's arm. 'Listen, Ben. If you go

on that stand and make even a two-minute statement, you open a deep can of worms.'

Tyson didn't reply.'

Corva went on. 'I thought about it. Last night, after you left. I stayed awake and thought about it. You have to understand that if you are sworn in, and make a statement, Pierce will cross-examine you on that for a week. I mean that literally, Ben. And when he's through with you, Sproule has the right to question you. And when Sproule is through, the six members of the board will have a go at it. You are the celebrity. And if you decide to step out in public, they will own you for as long as they can get away with it. I'll try to limit the questions as superfluous and such, but it would be several days before I could make a case for that. Understand?'

Tyson nodded.

'The choice is yours. You may remain silent. That is your right, and if you do so no inference will be drawn from it, and it will not count against you in any way. Nor can it be commented on in any way.'

Tyson said nothing for several minutes. The sergeant at arms strode towards the middle of the floor. Tyson said to Corva, 'But I *will* make a statement, later, in extenuation and mitigation.'

'Yes. If you are found guilty, you will have that opportunity. I hope you don't have to take advantage of that opportunity. I know this goes against your grain. But trust me.'

'Sure.'

'All rise!'

Colonel Sproule walked to the pulpit and stood behind it. 'The court will come to order.'

Pierce confirmed that all the parties were present.

Colonel Sproule addressed Colonel Pierce. 'Does the prosecution have any further evidence to present?'

Pierce, still standing, said. 'The prosecution rests.'

Sproule turned to Corva. 'Has the defence any evidence to present?'

Corva stood. 'The defence has no evidence present.'

There was a stir in the court, and Sproule did not wait patiently for it to die down. He looked towards the pews, and the spectators fell silent. Sproule turned back to Corva. 'Does the defence, then, rest?'

'The defence rests.'

Colonel Sproule nodded perfunctorily and turned to Colonel Pierce. 'Does the prosecution have anything further to offer?'

Pierce answered, 'It does not.' Pierce said to Sproule, 'Does the court wish to have any witnesses called or recalled?'

'It does not,' replied Colonel Sproule. He, in turn, readdressed Pierce. 'Does the prosecution wish to present a final argument?'

'It does,' answered Pierce.

Colonel Sproule responded, 'Colonel Pierce' – he turned to Corva – 'and Mr Corva. I wish to remind both of you that in trial by court-martial final arguments are not required. If they are made they can be written or oral. In either case, they are customarily short. They are made generally in order to call to the attention of the court reasonably pertinent facts of the case and how they relate to the law. They may include elements of a summation, but they are not to be lengthy recapitulations of the trial.' He looked at Pierce. 'You may begin.'

Colonel Pierce came from behind the table and stood in the centre of the floor as he had done when he made his opening statement.

Tyson watched him, then focused on the board. The six members sat ramrod straight, very military, Tyson thought. Pierce carried himself reasonably well for a JAG lawyer. Tyson looked at the spectators. On this Thursday morning, in the fourth day of the trial, the pews were again full. Marcy had come in late. David was excused from school again.

Tyson's mother, staying with friends in Garden City and taking a limousine in every morning, looked weary. As Tyson scanned the sea of mostly white faces, he saw a big moon-shaped black face smiling, trying to catch his eye. Mason nodded at him from the fifth or sixth row. Tyson smiled and nodded back.

Colonel Pierce began with the traditional 'May it please the military judge, members of the court. You have heard the case of the United States against Lieutenant Benjamin Tyson. You have heard the testimony of two witnesses, Richard Farley and Steven Brandt, who related to the court the story of a cold-blooded massacre of civilians and enemy soldiers, of patients and staff, of infants and children. No, their testimony did not always agree in detail, their testimony was often contradictory, and their recall of names, events, and other specifics, which we have come to expect in trial testimony, was at times vague. But we did hear, did we not, the story of a massacre. And if the details were vague after some eighteen years, the broad outlines were still clear.'

Pierce rubbed his upper lip and hung his head a moment, then continued. 'Steven Brandt and Richard Farley were eyewitnesses to the events they described. These are events which are indelibly burned into their memories for all time – and not solely on account of their being eyewitnesses to the events, but on account of having been participants in those events. But their participation is not the issue here. What is the issue is the involvement of the accused in those events. If you remove from your mind the extraneous details of the testimony and the cross-examination and consider only the facts which relate to the accused and to the charges brought against him, then what remains is this: The first platoon of Alpha Company entered a building which two eyewitnesses describe as a hospital. By their testimony, we learned that there were upwards of one hundred – possibly two hundred – living human beings in that hospital. Their platoon leader, Lieutenant Benjamin Tyson, gave a verbal order to shoot sick and wounded enemy soldiers. Members of the board, if we stop right there, and if we are to believe the sworn testimony of two independent and unbiased witnesses, then the government can rest its case. But if we are to right a terrible wrong, if we are to redeem the honour and integrity of the American Army, then we cannot rest there. No, we must consider the remainder of the corpses that the witnesses saw with their own eyes, piled in the wards, strewn in the hallways, lying in the operating room, and sprawled about the grounds of the hospital. We must consider that these unarmed and defenceless people were shot and killed by troops under the command of the accused. We must consider that the testimony of two eyewitnesses agrees that the accused did not do or say anything to halt the actions of his rampaging troops. That, in fact, the accused, by his inaction, aided and abetted the massacre you have heard described. That, indeed, the accused, by his inflammatory order to shoot unarmed and convalescent soldiers, precipitated the general massacre which followed.'

Pierce turned and looked at Tyson, then looked out over the spectator pews for the first time, then again addressed the board. 'You could, I could, anyone with an ounce of human compassion and understanding could make or find reasons and excuses for everything the accused did or failed to do in that twenty or forty minutes. But who can excuse what happened afterwards? Who can excuse or understand an officer of the United States Army wilfully entering into a conspiracy with men under his command to obstruct justice, to fabricate a series of events that were intended not only to obscure the facts of a heinous crime but to turn that crime into an honourable engagement with enemy forces? Who can excuse or understand *that*? Who can excuse an ongoing cover-up of a capital and infamous crime that has continued up until this moment? Who can excuse an officer who, by his dereliction of duty, has perhaps and most probably ensured that no one else will be brought to justice for this mass crime?

Who can excuse a commissioned officer of the United States Army, in whom was placed special trust and confidence, from the obligations that he freely undertook when he took his oath of office?'

Pierce walked a few steps back towards the defence table, turned and concluded, 'The government has presented the facts which prove, beyond a reasonable doubt, that a violation of the Uniform Code of Military Justice occurred and that the violation was murder and that the specifications, as written, accurately reflect the nature of the violation; that the accused engaged in acts which were inherently dangerous to others and which evinced a wanton disregard of human life.'

Colonel Pierce took his chair.

Colonel Sproule turned to Corva. 'Does the defence wish to make a final argument?'

Corva stood. 'It does, your honour.'

'Proceed.'

Corva came out to the centre of the court and began, 'May it please the military judge, members of the board. You have heard the case of the United States against Benjamin Tyson. You have heard two witnesses, Richard Farley and Steven Brandt, who constituted the whole of the prosecution's case against the accused – whose testimony constituted the whole of the evidence which is necessary to prove the serious charge of murder. If we are to believe that the witnesses are unbiased and unprejudiced towards the accused, then we have failed to understand the true nature and underlying meaning of the testimony. Even if we are to believe that Messrs Brandt and Farley witnessed a massacre – and the defence does not contend anything to the contrary – then we must focus on two words: "Shoot them," the words Brandt contends were used by the accused in giving an unlawful order. Farley's testimony as to that direct order was somewhat different. So, we are to ignore the fact that two prosecution witnesses cannot recall, after eighteen years, names, places, or words of

658

their comrades. But we are to believe Steven Brandt when he says he can recall Lieutenant Tyson saying, "Shoot them." And we are to believe Steven Brandt when he states that Lieutenant Tyson did nothing to stop the troops under his command from committing murder. Yet Steven Brandt cannot even remember who committed the acts of murder which he says he saw or which he says he thinks he saw. Steven Brandt has a very selective memory.'

Corva paused and glanced at the empty witness chair, then at Pierce. He turned again to the board and continued, 'The prosecution has called to your attention the fact that the testimonies of the two prosecution witnesses do not agree in all respects. But when the witnesses made reference to Lieutenant Tyson, there seemed to be little inconsistency in their statements. If we are to believe that the variations in the testimony were due to the fact of the witnesses perceiving the event from different perspectives or that their different perceptions were a result of different personalities or sensibilities, then why are they in such agreement on the facts which tend to incriminate the accused?'

Corva paused, pulled at his lip awhile, then said, 'Brandt. Brandt has told you that he feared for his life. That he was approached by members of the platoon after the incident and threatened. If we believe that, why not believe that Lieutenant Tyson, too, feared for his life? The prosecution has stated that the accused engaged in a conspiracy to cover the facts of this alleged crime. If we believe Brandt that a conspiracy was hatched in that bunker and that Brandt went along with it only to save his own life, then why not believe that of the accused? For surely, if there were two outsiders among the men of the platoon, they were Benjamin Tyson and Steven Brandt. The testimony of the witnesses has in fact painted a picture of not only a massacre but a mutiny. And though the defence has stipulated to certain facts, the defence does not accept as fact that Lieutenant Tyson made no oral or written report regarding the incident in question. The prosecution asks you to infer from the lack of physical evidence that no report was made. But no such inference can or should be drawn. In deciding on whether or not Lieutenant Tyson properly reported to his superiors the events in question, the board should consider that no reasonable man would attempt to make such a report while his life was in imminent danger. If Lieutenant Tyson radioed false reports to his company commander while in the physical presence of at least a dozen men who had just committed mass murder, I think you can conclude that he acted reasonably. And in the days that followed, while still in the field, at a time of intense enemy activity, you can conclude why he made no report to his superiors. But sometime between 15 February and 29 February, the day Lieutenant Tyson was wounded and evacuated, can the prosecution, can the two witnesses, can anyone say that no oral or written report was made? Would it be beyond the realm of possibility for you to believe that an oral report was made to Alpha Company's commander, Captain Browder, and that Captain Browder had no time to alert his superiors before he was killed on 21 February? Would any amount of searching in the Army archives come up with a scrap of documentary evidence to show that the accused fulfilled his obligation to report a violation of law?

'Probably not. But that does *not* constitute proof that the accused made no such written report. And if the accused made such a report, oral, written, or both, and he observed that no action was taken on that report, what is he to do? Make a second report? Yes. And what if he did? And what if still no word comes to him acknowledging his report? What is he to conclude? That it was lost? That it was purposely lost? Would that be the first time such a thing happened? And when Lieutenant Tyson was wounded and medically evacuated and eventually left the Southeast Asian theatre of operations, what was his responsibility regarding this incident? Should he have pursued it? Undoubtedly. Did he? Perhaps. Did the prosecution prove anything to the contrary?

660

It did not. Is it the responsibility of the prosecuti~~on~~ the charges it has alleged, or is it the responsibi~~lity of the~~ defence to disprove the charges?'

Corva came closer to the board table so that he wa~~s within~~ a foot of it and looked up and down the table at the six members. 'The prosecution has proved to me beyond a reasonable doubt that a massacre of innocent and defenceless people occurred at the time and place stated in the charge sheet. I am convinced. But the enormity of this crime ought not to cloud anyone's judgement regarding the culpability of the accused in those events. The fact of a crime does not constitute the presumption of guilt of everyone at the scene of that crime. If it did, then the defence table ought to have at least two more people sitting at it: Brandt and Farley.'

Corva nodded, turned and walked back to the table.

Colonel Sproule stood behind the pulpit nearly motionless for close to a full minute.

Corva began straightening and stacking the papers on his desk.

Colonel Sproule said finally to Colonel Pierce, 'Does the prosecution have a rebuttal argument?'

'Yes, your honour.' Pierce stood and snapped at Corva, 'The suggestion that the government witnesses are indictable is obscene. If the accused had done his duty as an officer none of us would now be sitting here.'

Corva got to his feet and glared at Pierce. 'If the witnesses engaged in lies and cover-ups eighteen years ago, there is no reason to believe they are telling the whole truth now.'

Colonel Sproule said tersely, 'That will be all, gentlemen.' He asked Pierce, 'Does the prosecution have anything further to offer?'

'It has not.'

Sproule addressed Corva. 'Does the defence have anything further to offer?'

Corva stood. 'It does not.'

Sproule said to the board, 'The prosecution and the

.ence have rested. It only remains for you members to consider the evidence. This court will adjourn for the purpose of completing administrative matters and securing transcribed testimony that you may require in your deliberations. You are advised not to deliberate this case or discuss it in any way among yourselves until I have instructed you in your duties. The court will adjourn until 10.00 hours tomorrow.'

Tyson stood.

Corva put his papers into his briefcase.

Tyson lit a cigarette.

Corva snapped his briefcase shut.

Tyson watched the pews emptying and saw Marcy and David walking down the aisle, their way being cleared by MPs.

Corva said, 'Well.'

Tyson said, 'The defence rests.'

'Yes.'

'But the defence never played the game.'

'Nevertheless, the defence rests.'

Tyson shrugged. He looked at his watch. 'Lunch?'

'Why not?'

Tyson followed Corva towards the side door.

The last MP in the place, Sergeant Larson, stood at parade rest near the door. He said, 'Very nice, Mr Corva.'

'Thank you.'

'See you both tomorrow.'

Tyson nodded as he entered the corridor. It occurred to him that tomorrow there would be armed MPs as was customary on the day of the verdict. And that Sergeant Larson would be in charge of the escort that took him away in cuffs.

He suddenly remembered his dream and the man in the dream telling him he had five more years to serve. And the dream seemed now to be a presentiment of his sentence.

49

At 10 A.M. Colonel Walter Sproule called the court to order.

Sproule looked tired, Tyson thought, and he was sitting more on the high stool than he was standing. His face seemed whiter, and his eyes had a sunken appearance. Sproule waited until the court was assembled and the spectators had settled down. Then, as if someone had pumped air into him from behind the pulpit, he straightened up, rested his hands on the side of the pulpit, leaning slightly forward like a preacher about to deliver a message of hellfire and brimstone. Sproule's voice even sounded stronger as he spoke into the microphone. 'President and members of the board, you have heard the testimony in the case of the United States against Lieutenant Benjamin J. Tyson.'

Sproule began his charge to the jury, reading from typed sheets, behind the pulpit wall. He spoke in a steady voice with no inflections that would give colour or weight to any point he was making.

Within ten minutes of Sproule's opening sentence, Tyson knew that Sproule, who had been almost taciturn up to now, was going to give a detailed and lengthy charge to the six members who had, Tyson suspected, already made up their minds.

Sproule went on. He made the point that Pierce had made in his preliminary remarks, the point about technical murder.

'In assessing the witnesses,' Colonel Sproule said, 'you may consider the witnesses' relationship to the accused, their apparent intelligence, and general appearance of candour. In considering the extent of culpability of the officer charged, you may consider his rank, background, education, Army schooling, and his experience in the field during prior operations involving contact with hostile and with friendly Vietnamese. You may consider his age at the time of the alleged incident and any other evidence which might help you in determining if the accused wilfully aided, abetted, ordered, or concealed a mass murder. But first you must be certain beyond a reasonable doubt that the testimony of mass murder which you have heard was truthful.'

Sproule went on in a somewhat convoluted manner, explaining the merits of the government's case, then the merits of the defence. He pointed out weaknesses in both cases and said, 'You must be satisfied from the evidence, which consists solely of testimony, that the accused acted unlawfully, and further that any unlawful acts that the accused may have committed constitute murder. You must have an abiding belief, amounting to a moral certainty, that Lieutenant Benjamin Tyson is guilty as charged. I must remind you that because of the statute of limitations, there is no lesser included offence of which you may find him guilty. You may not return a verdict of manslaughter. You may not return a verdict of dereliction of duty, conspiracy, or any other lesser offence. You may only return a verdict of guilty or not guilty to the charge and to one or both of the specifications.'

Colonel Sproule explained the procedures under which the board had to operate, and it was apparent that he was explaining it not only to the board, who most probably knew the procedures, but to the civilian spectators and the press. He said, 'There is no possibility in a trial by court-martial of a hung jury. The first vote on the charge will be decisive. To convict, four or more of you must have voted guilty. To acquit, three of you or more must have voted not guilty. So I urge you to deliberate for as long as you feel necessary before you cast your first and only ballot. If you vote to convict on the charge of murder, then you must vote on the specifications. You may vote to approve one or both of the specifications. If you cannot in good conscience vote for either specification as written, but you have voted to convict on the overall charge, then it is within your power and your duty to change the wording of one or both specifications so that it comports with your reasoning behind your guilty verdict. I warn you, however, that a rewording of the specifications may change their meaning to the extent that they define manslaughter. In such a case, the accused would be not guilty of any chargeable offence under the Code.'

Colonel Sproule said, 'If you have reached a verdict by sixteen-thirty hours, you will return to this court to announce that verdict. If you have not reached a verdict by that time, you will be housed in the post bachelor officers' quarters and will not deliberate there. If you wish to deliberate this evening, you must arrange to be taken back to the deliberation room that has been set aside for you in the adjoining office wing.'

Colonel Sproule continued, 'I must remind you that you have sworn not to disclose or discover the vote or opinion of any particular member of the board. That is to say your vote and your reasoning for it are to remain secret after this court is adjourned and for all time.'

Colonel Sproule leaned farther to the side of the pulpit toward the board and concluded, 'The final determination as to the weight of the evidence and the credibility of the witnesses in this case rests solely upon you members of the court. You must disregard any comment or statement made by me during the course of the trial which may seem to indicate an opinion as to the guilt or innocence of the accused, for you alone have the independent responsibility of deciding this issue. Each of you must impartially resolve the ultimate issue as to the guilt or innocence of the accused in accordance with the law, the evidence admitted in court, and your own conscience.' Colonel Sproule straightened up and announced, 'The court will be closed.'

Tyson looked at his watch. The charge to the jury had taken a full forty-five minutes, and now all the words that could possibly influence them had been spoken.

Benjamin Tyson stared silently out of the window of Rabbi Weitz's office. It appeared that all the spectators had left the chapel and were now milling about over the lawns in the cool autumn sunshine. There were, in addition, several hundred people across the road behind MP barricades.

Corva poured himself a cup of coffee. 'Do you want to go outside?'

'No.'

'Don't you want to see your family?'

Tyson continued to stare out of the window. 'No.'

Corva came up behind him and glanced out the window. 'They look properly subdued. Respectful. It wasn't such a circus.'

'Yes.' The scene actually reminded him of a cigarette break outside a funeral home; people are introduced, there is the occasional brief smile. Everyone has their back to the place, not wanting to be reminded of why they are there. The final sermon is about to begin, so no one strays too far.

Corva turned from the window and stood beside the desk. He put cream in his coffee. 'Are you satisfied with how the trial went?'

Tyson said with a touch of sarcasm, 'I suppose if one has to be tried for murder, that was as good a trial as one can expect.'

'I mean,' said Corva, a bit impatiently, 'are you satisfied with how I represented you?'

'I'll let you know after the verdict.' Tyson noted that Corva's manner was somewhat cool. He supposed that was a defensive response. He felt badly for Corva having to wait here with him. Tyson said, 'Why don't you take a walk?'

'You mean I'm fired?'

'No. A *walk*. In the fresh air.'

'I wouldn't get fifteen steps before the media surrounded and annihilated me. I'll stay here until we're called. Or until

666

four-thirty.' Corva added, 'But if you're going to smoke, open the window.'

Tyson opened the window and felt the rush of cool, crisp autumn air. 'How long do you think this will take?' He turned from the window.

Corva shrugged. 'The trial was relatively short. There isn't much to consider except testimony. They may ask for transcripts of that.'

Tyson waited, then asked again, 'How long? Days? Hours? Minutes? Do I have time to finish a cigarette?'

'Court-martial deliberations are usually short. There is only one vote, and it is binding.' He paused. 'I suspect that everyone's mind was made up as they rose from their seats.'

Tyson nodded distractedly.

Corva said, 'There is no reason for them to pretend they agonized for days. In fact, there is subtle pressure on them to make up their minds. They are officers. They have heard the case. They have duties awaiting them. They would rather be back with their units than here. So, to give you a precise answer, I expect a verdict before four-thirty.'

Tyson looked at the wall clock. 'Six hours.'

'Yes. More than ample time.'

Tyson contrived a smile. 'Nervous?'

'Anxious.'

'You going to break your streak?'

Corva smiled wanly but didn't reply.

Tyson and Corva conversed on various irrelevant topics. No subject seemed appropriate, and each short foray into idle chatter inevitably led to something they didn't care to pursue. After an hour and a half, Corva opened the door and asked the MP to bring them newspapers and magazines. He said to Tyson, 'I'll ask you one more time – you're authorized to go back to your quarters – do you want to go?'

'No.'

'Do you want to go to the club for lunch?'

'No. I'm not particularly hungry. You can have something

667

brought in.'

'Are you feeling sorry for yourself?'

'No. I'm feeling sorry for you. And for my family.'

'Can I send an MP to bring your wife here?'

'No.'

'Your son?'

'*No*. And not my mother or my sisters or my minister or anyone.' Tyson's voice rose. 'Why can't you understand that I cannot face anyone now? Why can't you understand that if I see anyone ... I don't want anyone to see me in my present condition ... Can't a man suffer alone, in dignity, anymore?' He pointed to Corva. 'Would *you* want your family around you?'

Corva replied in a soothing tone, 'I might, Ben. I might want their support —'

'Oh, fuck support. That's an idiotic word.'

Corva drew a deep, patient breath. 'I just wanted to make sure you understand that this may be the last time ... for some time ... that you can speak to them without ... guards present ...'

Tyson paced across the small office. At length he said in a calmer tone, 'I don't mean to take this out on you. You just happen to be here. So leave.'

'No, sir. My personal policy is to stay with the accused.'

Tyson stopped pacing and turned to Corva. 'Well? Take a guess. As long as you're here, entertain me. Take a guess.'

Corva said evenly, 'Within the narrow confines of the charges and from a legal point of view, the government proved its case.'

Tyson said, 'So what is taking them so long? They're officers. Why can't they make up their minds?'

'Because the defence proved other things. Things that went beyond what they'd expected to hear.' He looked at Tyson. 'I'm not upset with you for holding some of this back. I asked you to. I wanted it revealed spontaneously, in its own time. And the board listened, and their impassive faces betrayed their emotions. They are human; therefore, they are now questioning *themselves*.'

Tyson didn't respond.

Corva said, 'Right now, one or two of them are making arguments to try to influence a second or third member to say, "The hell with the law." That can be the only reason for any delay.'

'Will it happen? Will three of them say, "To hell with law"?'

Corva glanced at Tyson, then looked off at the rabbi's bulletin board. He said, 'If they say the hell with the law, then they are saying the hell with the Army. They are part of the system, the embodiment of the Code. They are sworn officers. They have more of a vested interest in this system than any civilian juror has in the civilian judicial system. What would you do in their place? How do you vote?'

Tyson thought a moment, then replied, 'I vote guilty.'

'Me too.'

'So what is taking so long?'

'I honestly don't know. I told you ... They are having some problems getting to the vote. Colonel Moore is not calling for the vote because one or two of them is sticking his or her neck out and making a pitch for you. Maybe Moore is making a pitch himself. Maybe Davis is on your side, too. Maybe Sindel is the one pushing for a quick guilty vote. Maybe Laski would have been the third person we needed on your side. I don't know. Nobody knows ... juries never fail to surprise me.'

'Even military juries?'

'Even them sometimes.'

'You'd be damned surprised if you won this case.'

Corva began to smile, but the sound of footsteps in the corridor brought him to his feet. There was a knock on the door, and an MP opened it, carrying a stack of newspapers and magazines. He said, 'Got next month's *Playboy*, too. Get you anything else, Mr Corva?'

'No, thanks.'

The MP left. Tyson and Corva read desultorily. At half past noon, there were again footsteps outside the door. They stopped. There was a knock, and the door opened. Sergeant Larson said, 'Can I take your lunch order? Or are you going out?'

Corva replied, 'Have sandwiches and coffee sent, Sergeant. Surprise us. But no white bread and no mayo.'

They waited a half hour, and Tyson commented, 'It usually takes fifteen minutes to get sandwiches from the mess hall. Maybe they've reached a verdict.'

'We'd still get the lunch before we were called. Try to relax.'

'I'm relaxed. I'm bored.'

Again there were footsteps, a knock, and the door opened. Sergeant Larson entered with a cardboard box which he set down on the desk. Tyson saw it was crammed with sandwiches, salads, and desserts. Larson said, 'My wife. She's been insisting,' he added with some embarrassment. 'Hope it's okay.'

Corva said, 'Tell her we appreciate it.'

Tyson took a wrapped sandwich, though he didn't want one. 'That was thoughtful of her, Sergeant.'

Larson smiled and left.

Corva found a chicken cutlet sandwich on rye bread and bit into it. He said, 'As I told you once, and as you see and hear every day, you are not guilty in the public mind.'

'I never thought much of American public opinion and judgement before. I'm a snob and an elitist. I don't deserve to take comfort in what they think now.'

Corva found a can of cola and popped it open. 'You have a good grasp of who you are and the world you live in. Unfortunately, who you are and the world you live in don't get along.'

Tyson discovered two beers in the cardboard box and drank both of them without offering one to Corva.

Corva ate with no apparent loss of appetite.

Tyson went to the men's room under escort. Corva went on his own. The afternoon played itself out in boredom and anxiety. The sunlight was beginning to fail, and a wind came up off the water, scattering the red and gold leaves over the lawns and sidewalks, and rustling them against the side of the building. Tyson went to the window and noticed that the crowd had thinned and those who had not gone back in the chapel were huddled against the chill wind. Tyson said, more to himself than Corva, 'Last autumn I raked the leaves and threw around the football with my son. I split logs and built fires in my fireplace. We went to a farm out east and bought pumpkins and gourds and apple cider. We came home, and I made hot rum toddies. I like the smell of autumn.'

Corva replied in an equally distant voice, 'Me too. I missed it in Cu Chi. I had my brother send me a shoebox full of leaves.' He smiled to himself. 'I gave them to people who said they missed the fall.'

Tyson said, 'Sounds like you were fishing for a psychiatric discharge.'

Corva picked up the *Daily News*. The headlines read simply: *VERDICT TODAY?*

Tyson looked at it. 'Good question.' He looked at the wall clock. It was four-sixteen.

At four-twenty, Corva stood and went to the window. 'No one seems to be leaving. The press vans are still there.'

At four twenty-five, Tyson stood. 'I didn't want to have to sleep on this. Have me put up in the BOQ. I'm not going home tonight.'

Corva replied, 'All right, I won't argue with you.' He added, 'It may be nerve-wracking to have to wait, but it is not a bad sign. Something happened in that deliberation room.'

'But what?'

At four-thirty, Corva snapped his briefcase shut and took his trench coat from the coat tree.

Neither Tyson nor Corva heard the footsteps this time, but they heard the gentle knock on the door, as gentle, Tyson

671

thought, as the footsteps must have been, and he knew they hadn't come to excuse him for the day.

The door opened, and Sergeant Larson stood a moment without speaking; a moment too long for Corva, who snapped, 'Well? Are we excused?'

'No, sir. The Board has reached a verdict.'

Corva nodded stiffly. 'Thank you.' He rehung his coat and said to Tyson in a strained voice, 'Let's hear what they have to say.'

Tyson walked towards the door being held open by Sergeant Larson. Larson said to Tyson, 'Sir, you should take your cover.'

'What …?' Tyson stood motionless for a moment, then said, 'Yes, of course. I won't be coming back here either way, will I?'

'No, sir.'

'Thank the rabbi for us, if you should see him.'

'Yes, sir.'

Corva led the way into the corridor. Again, Larson caught up and walked ahead. He seemed to sense that his charges were in no hurry, and his pace was not fast. They entered the courtroom, and Tyson heard a hush fall over the crowd in the pews. He looked and saw that the chapel was completely full, like Easter Sunday, with people in the aisles and in the vestibule.

He strode purposefully past the table where the board was already assembled, past the prosecution table without looking at Pierce, Weinroth, or Longo, and took his place beside Corva at the defence table. Corva had remained standing, so Tyson did the same. He noticed, too, that the prosecution was now standing, though this was not required.

Tyson brought himself to look at the right front pew. Marcy was dressed conservatively in a tweed business suit. She crossed her legs, smiling at him encouragingly. David, seated next to her, looked sad, he thought, though perhaps scared was a better word. He wondered what was going on inside the mind of a sixteen-year-old. Tyson's sisters, all pretty, lively women, were maintaining a show of optimism. His mother, who rarely showed any emotion other than haughtiness, impatience, or annoyance, now looked bewildered and old. Tyson contrived a look of unconcern and faced the board. He tried to read their expressions, but there was less there to read than there had ever been. The only flicker of emotion came from Major Virginia Sindel, who inadvertently made eye contact with him, then dropped her eyes.

Tyson realized Corva was speaking to him. Corva whispered, 'There is a quirk in the wording of the Manual for Courts-Martial. Verdicts of not guilty are announced with the words, "It is my duty to advise you ... " Guilty verdicts with the words "inform you". I wanted to know that so you could prepare yourself before you hear the actual verdict.'

Tyson kept his head and eyes straight ahead and said, 'Thank you.'

Not more than a moment later, Colonel Sproule turned on his microphone and announced, 'The court will come to order.' Sproule looked out at the pews, then regarded the press section a moment, then looked at the prosecution and finally at the board. He said, 'All parties to the trial who were present when the court closed are now present.'

Colonel Sproule addressed Colonel Moore, asking, 'Has the court reached the findings in this case?'

Moore stood and replied, 'It has.'

Sproule then asked, 'Are the findings reflected on the finding worksheets you were given?'

'They are,' replied Moore.

Sproule looked at the prosecution table. 'Will the trial counsel, without examining it, bring me the findings?'

Major Judith Weinroth stood and went directly to Colonel Moore, who handed her the findings. She made a show of not looking at the long sheets of paper and walked the five paces to the pulpit, handing the two pages up to Colonel Sproule.

She waited in front of the pulpit facing it.

Colonel Sproule adjusted the pulpit light and examined the sheets of paper closely, turning them both over several times. Tyson, Corva, and everyone in the chapel, including the court reporter, had their eyes on Sproule's face to see any trace of emotion. But Colonel Sproule's face revealed nothing but concentration on the forms before him, and Tyson thought he had the look of a man grading a school essay on a dull subject.

Colonel Sproule looked up abruptly and said to Moore, 'I find no defects of form.' He handed the two pages down to Major Weinroth and said, 'Will you return this to the president of the court?'

She took the papers, but they somehow got loose from her grasp, and they fell to the red-carpeted floor. She knelt hastily to retrieve them and lingered perhaps a half second too long in gathering them before she rose. Her face was flushed as she strode across the floor and handed the papers back to Colonel Moore, who gave her a sympathetic look. Major Weinroth turned and walked back to the prosecution table, carrying herself the way someone does who knows there is a room full of people looking at them. As she approached the table, her face still towards the spectators, she made eye contact with Pierce, and her head bobbed slightly, but no one could say for sure if it was in apology for the dropped forms or in triumph.

Colonel Sproule turned and looked at Tyson. He said, 'Lieutenant Benjamin Tyson, please report to the president of the court.'

Tyson replied in a strong voice, 'Yes, sir.'

Corva reached out and, in full view of the court and spectators, squeezed Tyson's hand.

Tyson came around the table and walked across the red carpet, centring himself directly in front of Colonel Moore. Tyson saluted but maintained the protocol that this was one of the few occasions when no verbal report was made.

Colonel Moore and Benjamin Tyson faced one another. The remainder of the board stayed seated. Corva had remained standing, though it wasn't required that he do so. The prosecution was standing also, and they blocked the view of some of the spectators sitting on the left of the nave. The media stood, perhaps to get a better view, and the people behind them began standing, perhaps because the press was blocking them. Then others began standing, even those whose view was not obstructed, and within a few seconds the entire chapel full of people was on its feet, standing and waiting.

Colonel Sproule began to say something into his microphone, then hesitated and turned to Colonel Moore. 'Proceed with the verdict.'

Out of the corners of his eyes, Tyson saw that the board was staring straight ahead, resisting their natural desire to look at him. Moore, without referring to the findings sheet and looking Tyson directly in the eye, spoke to him as though they were the only two people in the room. 'Lieutenant Benjamin Tyson, it is my duty as president of this court to inform you—'

There were audible reactions from a few of the people in the pews who understood what the wording signified.

'—that the court, in closed session and upon secret ballot, two-thirds of the members present at the time the vote was taken concurring in each finding, finds you, of the charge of murder, guilty.'

Tyson stood perfectly still, showing Colonel Moore and the board no more emotion than they'd shown him all week.

Someone in the pews shouted something, and a woman sobbed, though he didn't think it was Marcy or his mother, neither of whom was prone to sobbing.

Colonel Moore continued, 'Of Specification One, guilty, and of Specification Two, guilty; excepting that in both specifications the words, "shooting them", and the words "ordering them to be shot," will be deleted, leaving the words "causing them to be shot."' Colonel Moore looked at Tyson and gave a brief nod to indicate he was finished.

Tyson saluted, turned, and walked to the defence table, not meeting Corva's or anyone's eyes, not once looking at his wife and son.

Colonel Sproule surveyed the chapel and the altar area where no one was sitting but the five members of the board. He had the quizzical appearance of a man who had never seen such a thing. He announced into the pulpit microphone, 'This court will reconvene Monday at ten hundred hours for the purpose of arriving at an appropriate sentence. This court is adjourned.'

But no one moved towards the doors. Instead, everyone stood silently as Sergeant Larson, now armed and wearing a helmet, approached Tyson with another armed MP. The MPs stood self-consciously before the defence table. No one said anything until finally Larson asked politely, 'Sir, will you come with me?'

Tyson shook hands with Corva, took his hat from the table, and came around to join the MPs, still not trusting himself to look at his family. The MPs moved to either side, flanking him, and walked across the altar floor through the side door and down the long white corridor. Tyson noticed that the corridor was deserted and quiet except for their footsteps.

They came to a door that exited to the back of the chapel grounds, and an MP standing there opened it.

Tyson put on his hat and walked out into the cool twilight. He noticed first the western sky to his front, a deep blue, then towards the horizon a nice orange and yellow beyond the lights of the bridge.

Burly MPs formed a wedge around him and escorted him towards a dark-coloured staff car. The chapel and corridor had been deathly still, but now a raucous noise assailed him: the shouts of dozens of people, then dozens more as people converged on the rear of the chapel. He saw a television camera. Then there were flashbulbs lighting up the pleasant, comforting dusk. Microphones were pushed towards him, but the MPs pushed back hard. Above the general bedlam he heard a man shouting, 'Let him go! Let him go!' A woman had somehow slipped past the phalanx of MPs and reached out to him sobbing, 'God bless you, God bless you.' As she reached him an MP caught her arm and pulled her away.

Tyson found himself at the car, then in it. Sergeant Larson slid in the rear beside him, then the other door opened and another MP slid in to Tyson's left, jamming him in between them. Both doors slammed shut, and Sergeant Larson said, 'Please put your hands on the back of the seat in front of you.'

Tyson did as he was told, and Sergeant Larson snapped a pair of handcuffs over his wrists. Tyson was surprised at how heavy they were.

The car began moving slowly over the back lawn, through the milling crowd, the headlights flashing from low beam to high, and the horn honking in a rhythmic cadence. The driver swore.

The MP to Tyson's left said, 'I don't have to worry about your all-night runs anymore. Do I?'

Tyson turned his head and found himself looking straight into the beady eyes of Captain Gallagher. Tyson began to say something unpleasant, then realized he was no longer free to say to Captain Gallagher the things that needed saying.

Gallagher seemed to sense this, and realizing, too, that the sport was gone, his face softened. He said, 'We were parked there for an hour waiting, but to tell you the truth, Tyson, I didn't want to see you in this car.'

'Yes, sir.'

The dark staff car was clear of the crowd and had picked up a two-jeep escort: They were rolling fast now up Lee Avenue.

Tyson noticed for the first time that the man in the front passenger seat was a civilian. The man turned in his seat and said, 'We have some talking to do before they sentence you, ace.'

Tyson looked at Chet Brown. Tyson replied, 'I don't think so.'

Brown shrugged and turned back towards the front. He said, 'We'll see.'

Gallagher produced a hip flask and unscrewed the cap. 'Let me buy you one.'

Tyson said, 'Don't need one.'

Gallagher, too, shrugged and put the cap back on. He hesitated, then shoved the flask in the side flap pocket of Tyson's tunic. 'Keep it.'

Tyson realized they were not heading off-post and knew they were not going to Fort Dix.

Gallagher watched him a moment and said, 'Just the post lockup. Over the weekend. Until sentencing Monday. Then ... then ...'

'Then,' said Brown from the front seat, 'it depends on the stubborn son of a bitch where he goes next.'

Tyson ventured a soft 'Fuck you,' and no one seemed to mind.

The car stopped at the provost marshal's office, and Tyson found himself in a small cell whose walls were made of glazed beige block. Sergeant Larson removed the handcuffs and left, slamming the barred cell door. Brown stood on the other side of the bars as the MPs went into the office to do the paperwork on the prisoner. Brown said, 'All we want is an assurance from you ... in writing ... that you will never speak of any of this ever again for the rest of your natural life.'

'Go fuck yourself.'

'Except, of course, for a few well-chosen words now and then regarding the positive side of your experience with the government and with military justice.'

'Take a walk.'

'In effect, you've lived up to your end of the deal so far without even agreeing to it. You haven't said one word to the media about anything. We appreciate that. And your lawyer has been decent, too.' Brown pulled a folded sheaf of papers from his breast pocket. 'You read this and you sign it.'

'Shove it, Chet.'

'One of the things this says is that you won't bring up questions about your recall to duty or about the fact that the actual perpetrators of the crime are beyond the reach of the law. The government is very sensitive about that.'

'I'm a little sensitive too.'

Brown leaned closer, his hands on the bars, and his face between them. He kept a close eye on Tyson standing about eight feet away, as though acknowledging that Tyson, though caged, was dangerous. Brown said musingly, 'Did you know, Ben, that of the twenty-five men originally implicated in My Lai, about eighteen never had charges brought against them because they had been discharged by that time? Well, the government has had ample time to plug that loophole but hasn't. And of the men implicated who were still in the service, most were never charged because the local commander didn't bring charges, such as General Peters brought in your case. Of course, Peters needed a little prodding. But the Army likes their system. And of the other men who were charged for My Lai, all were acquitted except Calley. That's what we call the My Lai mess now. And after all these years, the system hasn't changed. The government, the Justice Department, would like to change that system so that the United States is never again embarrassed by an inability to prosecute its servicemen for war crimes. That's a noble goal.'

'It's so noble that no one has thought about it for twenty years.'

'Well, it takes something like this, doesn't it? The point is the Army doesn't want its system changed. So there's a fight on now. What we don't need is you confusing the issues.'

'Who are *we*? If I knew who you worked for, I might listen to you. You may be an Army man for all I know. You may be a JAG man.'

'I may be. I may be a civilian. Doesn't matter.'

'Sure does.'

Brown ruffled the papers in his hand. 'If you sign this, then no matter what sentence you are given, the President will give you a full pardon within thirty days. While you're still at the Dix stockade. You'll never see Kansas.'

'Where were you before the verdict, bozo? When I needed you?'

Brown smiled. 'Oh, I couldn't do anything about the verdict or even the sentence they hand you. I can't get to a military jury. But I can get to the chain of command and see that you are released by ... let's say Thanksgiving. Turkey in your dining room in Garden City. Tastes better than the turkey in Leavenworth.'

'You searched my house.'

'K and G Cleaning Service cleaned your house.'

'You're a shit.'

Brown threw the folded papers through the cell bars, and they landed in the centre of the concrete floor. 'Among other things, you agree not to talk to the press, you agree the government has treated you fairly, you agree not to write, lecture or utter any public statements, and so on. And I agree to make you whole again. Including your overpaid job.'

Tyson looked at the papers on the floor. 'Okay, Chet. I'll read it if you'll beat it.'

'Right. *Adiós, amigo.* Get a good night's rest. And hey, you handled yourself well. I would have been shaking in my boots. And Monday, if you play ball, and they hand you ten to twenty, you can smile at them.'

'Right.'

'You'll have no visitors tonight, so don't think about giving that to your lawyer to smuggle out of here. I want it back at 6 A.M. tomorrow. Signed or unsigned.'

'How about my copy?'

Brown laughed as he turned and left.

Tyson looked around the cell, then sat on his bunk. He glanced again at the papers lying on the floor, then took off his hat and shoes and lay back on the narrow Army cot. 'The quarters keep getting smaller.'

Sergeant Larson came to the cell door. He said, 'You want dinner?'

'No thanks.'

'Okay. Your lawyer called. He said he'll see you at seven A.M.'

'Okay.'

'He said to think about a statement you'd like to make in extenuation and mitigation before the sentencing.'

'I'll think about it.'

'Anything I can get you?'

'The keys.'

Larson smiled. 'The evening papers will be full of this. You want the papers?'

'You read about one court-martial, you read about them all, Larson.'

'Right. Was everything okay?'

'What ...?'

'The lunch. I have to tell my wife.'

'Oh. Yes. Great veal cutlets.'

'It was chicken.'

'That's right.'

'Hey, what was it like over there?'

'Where?'

'Nam. What was it like in combat?'

Tyson thought a moment, then replied, 'I couldn't tell you.'

'Weren't you in combat?'

'I guess. But I'm home now. The war is over.'

50

At five-thirty on Saturday morning Tyson was awakened by
an MP and taken, in his underwear, to the latrine and shower
room. The MP provided him with a standard-issue box of
toiletries. The MP also gave him the rules and added, 'You
have twenty minutes.'

Tyson shared the small facility with two other prisoners,
who didn't have much to say, though one of them offered,
'You got the biggest royal fuck I ever heard of.'

The other one only commented that he'd never shared a
latrine with an officer. Tyson didn't know if the man meant it
was an honour or an inconvenience and thought it best not to
ask.

Tyson shaved and showered and folded his towel into a
square as he'd been told, placing it on the sink. He helped the
other two prisoners clean the latrine and was wiping the
shower dry when the MP returned. 'Back to the cells, men.'

Tyson was escorted back to his cell in his underwear. He
dressed in his uniform but left the tunic in the metal wall
locker. He combed his hair in a small polished metal mirror,
an Army field mirror, that was hung too low on the wall and
didn't reflect his image well, which might be more of a
blessing than a nuisance, he thought.

At 6 A.M. sharp, Chet Brown arrived with a container of
coffee.

Brown looked at the papers still on the floor where he'd
thrown them. He said, 'This offer is not good after the
sentencing. So don't try to play it that way.' He offered the
container through the bars.

'Keep it.'

Brown shrugged, peeled off the lid, and drank the coffee himself.

Tyson sat on the edge of his cot and lit a cigarette.

Brown continued, 'Don't think if you get off with a year or two you can do that standing on your head, Ben. Gaol sucks. And people like you don't do well in gaol.'

'Who are people like me?'

'They could hand you ten to twenty. And I won't be back with this offer. Because if they give you ten to twenty, then nobody has to worry about you becoming a public nuisance.'

Tyson flipped his ash into a tin can filled with water.

Brown added, 'They could order you hanged, you know.'

Tyson yawned.

Brown said, 'What's the big deal about agreeing to something that you're already doing?'

Tyson looked at his cigarette as he replied, 'Because, shithead, if I want to do something, then that's all right. If I don't, then that's all right, too. But if you try to put a gun to my head to make me do something, then all I can do is say fuck you. *Capice?*'

Chet Brown looked annoyed. He said in a sarcastic tone, 'You didn't have all these scruples when you watched your men mow down nuns and babies.'

Tyson drew a deep breath. 'No. No, I didn't. That's why I'm here. But that doesn't mean I have to deal with you. Leave.'

Brown began to say something, then changed his mind. He looked at the papers on the floor. 'I'll take those.'

Tyson stood and kicked the folded papers near the bars.

Brown said, 'Step back, killer.'

Tyson stepped back.

Brown squatted quickly and snatched the papers, spilling coffee on his trousers. 'Damn it!'

'You're a little jumpy this morning, Chet.'

Brown blotted the coffee with a handkerchief. He said to Tyson, 'Look, if everything goes all right for you, maybe we

683

can talk about government job opportunities. Look me up.'

'How do I look you up, Chet?'

'Just make a public statement I don't like. You'll hear from me.'

'Don't threaten, Chet. It makes me mad.'

'Just trying to be helpful. I like you.'

Tyson said, 'You wouldn't know anything about the whereabouts of Dan Kelly and Sister Teresa, would you?'

'I might.'

Tyson and Brown looked at each other, then Brown said, 'You may hear from them shortly. Then again, you may not.' He turned and walked through the door into the provost marshal's office.

A quarter of an hour later, an MP appeared with a breakfast tray from the mess hall and a newspaper. The MP opened the cell door and set the tray on the cot and handed the newspaper to Tyson. 'Last night's final.'

Tyson looked at the copy of the *New York Post*. The headline in red shouted, *GUILTY!* Tyson said, 'Get it out of here.'

The MP shrugged and left with the newspaper.

Tyson found he was hungry and finished the breakfast of scrambled eggs, bacon and coffee. There were also grits, which the Army apparently still blithely served to soldiers, who stuck their cigarettes in them. 'Typical.' He wanted another cup of coffee but didn't ask. A radio in the provost marshal's office was playing a sort of music, a hard screaming rock that he thought shouldn't be allowed over the public airwaves until after 6 P.M. He decided he didn't like prison life.

The cell was cold, and Tyson put on his tunic and tightened his tie. There was no window, and he didn't know what the weather was like outside, but since he wasn't going outside, it didn't matter.

At 7 A.M., the door of the provost marshal's office opened again, and Corva came into the small passageway between

684

the three cells. The MP opened the cell door, Corva entered, and the MP closed and locked the door.

Corva took the plastic moulded chair and pulled it up facing Tyson, who was sitting on the cot. He opened his attaché case and laid it on his lap. Tyson noted the attaché case made a better prison lap desk than the briefcase Corva usually carried. Tyson observed, 'You seem at home here. I guess you've visited a lot of your clients in gaol. Like all of them.'

Corva ignored this and said without preamble, 'Our goal now is to keep you out of gaol.'

'I'm *in* gaol, Vince.'

Corva produced a pint of Dewar's from his briefcase and threw it on the cot. 'Put that out of sight. They don't mind if you drink, but they don't want to see it.'

Tyson put the bottle under his pillow from which he took Captain Gallagher's hip flask, which was empty. 'Give this back to Gallagher.' He threw it to Corva, who put it in his attaché case. Corva said, 'Is there anything else you need? Stamps—'

Tyson laughed derisively. 'Writing paper, candy? Christ, Vince, I used to say that to the guys in my company who got locked up.'

Corva said coolly, 'Well, you won't be here long.'

'Will you come to Kansas to see me? We can have a reunion. Corva's clients.'

Corva smiled unexpectedly, then laughed. 'Corva's clients. I like that. Corva's cases. No, clients.'

Tyson regarded him icily for a moment, then leaned forward on his cot and said slowly and distinctly, 'Get me the hell out of here.'

'Working on it.' He looked at Tyson and said pointedly, 'Just for the record – you wanted a trial.'

Tyson didn't speak for some time and then said, 'No one *wants* to be tried. I may have thought I needed it. I'm not sure *how* I felt before Sproule said, "The court will come to order."' Tyson added, 'Also, for the record, someone with brains would have convinced his client that a court-martial was not a good idea. Someone with brains would have got this thing dismissed before it got this far.'

Corva seemed to be counting to ten, then said, 'There was a time, not so many years ago, when these charges might have been dismissed. But I don't think that was so good a thing either. Point is, this is the new Army.'

'I'm old Army.'

'Good point, I'll bring it up. Anyway...' His eyes fell on the place above Tyson's top left pocket where the service ribbons were worn. 'I see you've undecorated yourself.'

Tyson nodded. 'I couldn't very well wear the Silver Star or the Vietnamese Cross of Gallantry for heroism on 15 February 1968. Could I?'

'I suppose not.' Corva said, 'Let's do some work. Okay, if you were paying attention during the verdict reading, you might have heard Colonel Moore say, "Two-thirds concurring." The actual number tally of votes guilty or not guilty is secret, but they will announce an approximate fraction. With a six-member board, if the vote was five to one for conviction, Moore would have said, "Three-fourths concurring." But now we know what I suspected. Two people on that board voted for acquittal, which means there are two people on that board who will argue very strenuously for a light sentence. Follow?'

Tyson nodded.

Corva continued, 'So, Pierce is pissed and a little worried. So he's prepared to go into the sentencing session with a strong argument when they ask him for his recommendation for an appropriate sentence. But now that we've got him on the run a little, he's come to me with a proposition. To wit: If we don't sit there for a week – offering extensive extenuation and mitigation – like everything from bringing in Levin and your wife to testify to your character and the reading of award citations and on and on – then he will recommend an appropriate sentence of five years. Now, understand, this session is very important in a court-martial. I've seen serious crimes extenuated and mitigated to the point where a board will hand out less than a year gaol time. The Army is different from civilian life, as you may have noticed. A soldier can be reduced in rank, forfeit pay, confined to barracks, and all of that. So actual gaol time tends to be less than you'd expect for some crimes. And the board will base the sentence not so much on what you did, but who you are, the sum total of everything you've accomplished as a man and an officer. And even how you've behaved at the court-martial.'

'How about how you've behaved?'

Corva nodded. 'Yes, that too. And that's no joke, Ben. I couldn't get away with my civilian theatrics with that bunch. There is a very famous case of a captain who hired a civilian lawyer who was not only obnoxious but insulting to the board, threatening them with civil suit over something or other. The captain got the max in Kansas. So if I didn't seem like the lawyers you see on TV, that's why. Okay?'

'Okay.'

'So what should I tell Pierce?'

'How about, "Pierce, go fuck yourself?"'

Corva smiled. 'Okay. But I'll put it a little differently. Next point. The board, as you noticed, changed the wording of the specifications. In other words, they didn't believe Brandt or Farley that you, yourself, ordered your men to waste everyone or that you, yourself, engaged in any acts which were inherently dangerous to others or evinced any wanton disregard of human life. That was a slap in the face to Pierce, not to mention the fact that they called Brandt half a liar, and Farley, too. One of the commentators on a late night news show last night said Brandt stands convicted as a liar. So you've got your Pyrrhic victory, and Brandt has a public relations problem. But you're the one in the slammer. Worth it?'

Tyson shrugged. 'We'll see when the sentence is announced.

And I'm not through with Dr Brandt yet. When I take the stand in extenuation and mitigation, I have a few things to say—'

'Like hell you will. When you get up there, you'll talk about *you*, not Brandt. We had our chance to impeach Brandt's testimony.' Corva studied Tyson's face. 'When you take the stand, Ben, you tell the truth. You'll tell the court who murdered the people and who did not. You'll tell them you killed Larry Cane. You'll tell them your troops mutinied, went on a rampage, and you were almost shot trying to stop it – who pointed the rifle at you by the way?'

'Farley, Simcox, and Beltran.'

Corva shook his head. 'Anyway, you'll tell the court you were scared shitless and that's why you failed to make a report and swear to criminal charges. And you'll tell them you felt some loyalty towards your troops, misguided though it was. You will not tell them about Brandt fucking the little girl. *Capice?*'

Tyson nodded. 'Do I – I mean about Cane – is that necessary?'

'Absolutely.' Corva looked at him closely. 'The board understands that what they heard from Brandt and Farley was the story of a mutiny. They don't like to hear about troops mutinying. It scares officers. But they like it even less when they hear that the officer in charge stood there with his finger up his ass, whistling "The Stars and Stripes Forever."'

Tyson nodded. 'I understand.'

Corva went on, 'The annals of military history are filled with stories of officers quelling mutinies though they were outnumbered by their troops a zillion to one and full of stories of officers dying in an attempt to prevent mutinies, massacres, rapes, pillaging, and what have you. A good part of the officer's code is based on this mental image of chivalry and is a direct product of the knight's code. They teach you that?'

'I missed that class.'

'Anyway, you will get up there and tell them that indeed you did put your life on the line, shot an American soldier as was your duty, and were assaulted and knocked unconscious and so forth. You will tell them you did your duty. Right up to the point when you reached the safety of a base camp and did not initiate charges of mutiny, mass murder, arson, striking an officer, and so on. *That* is where you fucked up. That is what you will tell them.'

'Will they believe any of it?'

Corva leaned across his attaché case. 'If you tell it to them, Ben, they will believe it. It is the story that fills in the missing pieces for them. It also happens to be the truth. And just as the board knew Brandt and Farley were lying, so they will know you are not.'

Tyson sat quietly for a long time, then said, 'I feel bad for the rest of them. The ones who signed sworn statements and for the dead, whose families thought they were heroes. For Larry Cane's family, who thought he died in action...' Tyson looked at Corva. 'But it is time to set the record straight, isn't it?'

'Yes, it's time. Especially if there are men who didn't shoot anyone. Are there?'

Tyson nodded. 'Some of them are dead now. Only Kelly, me, and Brandt never pulled a trigger.'

'How do you know that Kelly and Brandt didn't? You weren't there the whole time.'

'It came out afterwards. But I assumed from the beginning they didn't. Brandt was a lot of things, but he wasn't a ...'

'A what? A killer?'

'Right.' Tyson said, 'If we're setting the record straight, why can't we set it straight regarding Brandt?'

'That is one story I don't think they'll believe, if *you* tell it.' Corva added, 'That's why I'm going to have Kelly tell it.'

Tyson stood.

Corva remained seated.

He explained. 'I heard from Colonel Farnley Gilmer, who

was good enough to keep the Article 32 investigation open as is sometimes done even during trial. He informed me that Daniel Kelly has shown some signs of life. Specifically, a law firm claiming to represent Kelly has contacted Gilmer. The firm, incidentally, is Conners, Newhouse, and Irving, who coincidentally are secretly famous for representing CIA people. So, apparently somebody somewhere decided it was okay to surface Kelly for a one-shot public appearance.'

'Kelly decided. He would have insisted.'

Corva observed, 'But not to testify at the early part of the trial. That would have put him in a position of having to lie if he were our witness or having to tell the truth as a prosecution witness. If indeed Pierce called him at all. Now that the smoke has settled, he's coming in as your witness in extenuation and mitigation only. He can be cross-examined on anything he says, but I think Pierce will have the sense not to do that.'

Tyson said, as if to himself, 'Daniel Kelly ... God, he could have blown this case wide open. His story would not have agreed with ours or the prosecution's. He would have told the truth.'

Corva nodded. 'The old infantry vets on that board will understand that Kelly, as your radio operator, was rarely more than an arm's length from you every minute you were in the field. He was your shadow, your aide, your *consigliere*.'

Tyson said, 'I don't know about that last thing. But I do know that he even followed me when I went off in the bush to take a crap. The only two times I can recall when we were separated for any length of time was when he knocked me out in the hospital and then later at the Strawberry Patch we got separated by refugees.'

Corva said, 'I could reopen the whole case because of his appearance. But I don't think it would lead to an acquittal. The point remains that your cover-up amounted to condoning mass murder, and the words "caused to be shot" and "inherently dangerous acts" and so forth would be interpreted as your striking of Dr Monteau which ignited the

690

massacre.' He looked at Tyson. 'It did, you know.'

'I know.'

'But anyway, if we reopen the case, Pierce may just switch around some wording on the charge sheet now that he has more of the facts.'

'I don't want a retrial, Vince. Everyone's had enough. I just want to keep out of gaol. I can live with the guilty verdict.'

'I understand. And you can live quite well with Kelly testifying that he saw Brandt raping a young girl.'

Tyson drew a long breath. 'Yes.'

'What, by the way, happened at the Strawberry Patch? Harper thinks Brandt failed to go out after you under fire. Failed to treat you.'

Tyson shook his head. 'He treated me. He treated me to an overdose of morphine.'

Corva's eyes widened. 'Jesus Christ – '

Tyson said, 'But, obviously, neither Kelly nor anyone was witness to that. I'm not one hundred per cent sure of it myself. The nearly perfect crime.'

Corva nodded. 'And you can't tell that in court, Ben. He'll sue the pants off you. The board may believe it, but ... without corroboration ... and coming only from you ... forget it. That's done with. You'll never settle that score.' He glanced at Tyson and said, 'That was a hell of a crew you had there, Lieutenant ... rape, murder, conspiracy, revenge, mutiny ... what else? Steal chickens, too?'

Tyson snapped, 'As a matter of fact, they were not bad. Not in the beginning. But you can only log so many miles on a man and imprint so many obscenities on his brain before he begins to malfunction. You know that. Don't *you* judge them!'

'Sorry.'

'*I* don't judge them too harshly. I don't even judge Brandt harshly. I mean about trying to kill me.'

'Because you'd thought about killing *him*.'

'Yes, that's why.' Tyson smiled. 'I related to that. I could see his point. The Nam solution – someone bothering you? Annoyed? Upset? Administer five to ten rounds of 5.56-millimetre M-16 ammunition. Or, if you're a medic, a good-bye dose of pure morphine.'

Corva snapped his attaché case closed and stood. 'I'll be back tomorrow. I'm going to mass at the chapel at ten A.M. Then I'll be here. And we'll go over the E and M.'

'Do you want to do it this afternoon? I'm free.'

Corva smiled. 'Today I'm going to spend the day with Daniel Kelly at his lawyers' midtown office.'

'Good. You'll like him.'

'I might have, eighteen years ago. Men change.'

'Do they? I don't think so.'

Corva walked towards the cell door. He hesitated, then said, 'One more thing ... This is not certain, but Colonel Gilmer tells me he has heard from Interpol ... '

Tyson moved toward Corva. 'They've found her.'

'Maybe. And not in France where everyone was looking. But in Italy. They think it's the same woman. I'll know today.'

'I don't think I want her called.'

'Well ... we may not be able to.'

'What do you mean?'

'I'll talk to you about it after I speak to Gilmer.'

'There's no reason to call her. The case is done. We have Kelly for E and M. And I'll testify on my own behalf.'

Corva rubbed his nose and said, 'She can tell the court that you saved her life at the hospital.'

Tyson didn't respond.

Corva added, 'Ben, if this woman in Italy is *the* Sister Teresa, I'd like to talk to her. And I think if she is your friend, she'd want the opportunity to help you. You helped her.' Corva looked at Tyson awhile, then said, 'If it was more than a friendship ... and it went bad ... then maybe it would be best to leave her be ... '

Tyson looked at the floor awhile, then stated, 'The woman was a nun, Vince.'

'Of course.'

Tyson rubbed his lip for some time. 'None of your surprise reunions. Okay?'

'Okay.' He drew an envelope from his side pocket. 'A letter from your wife.'

Tyson took it.

Corva said, 'She loves you deeply, madly, passionately.'

'Are you reading my mail?'

'No, no. My wife told me. My wife is staying with your wife this weekend.'

'Who are you staying with this weekend?'

'Kelly and his rather unorthodox lawyers. And this Sister Teresa is a hard call. I have an interpreter lined up just in case.'

'Really? You're not as incompetent as you look. What language? Greek?'

'No, French.'

'Why not Vietnamese?'

'For one thing, they're harder to find. For another, the last thing I want in that courtroom is a Vietnamese. You know?'

Tyson nodded. '*Compris.*'

'Anyway, if I can't get the whole show on the road by ten hundred hours Monday, I'll ask for another day or two.' Corva glanced at his watch. 'I need my breakfast. You screwed up my whole weekend.'

'Mine is a little screwed up too. I have theatre tickets for tonight. I want out of here, Vince. Monday night I want to be watching football at home. In Garden City.'

'I'll do everything I can. You know there's no bail in the Army. But I may be able to secure what they call deferment. That's like back to house arrest until the case is finally settled with reviews and appeals and all that.'

'Do it.'

Tyson thought of Chet Brown. He said, 'Is there any way we can negotiate the sentence? I mean is that legal?'

Corva looked at him. 'In military law, there is virtually no plea-bargaining or sentence negotiations. And by law, it must originate with the accused and his lawyer. Why do you ask? Has someone been talking to you?'

'No, I just wondered.'

'By the way,' said Corva, 'you can have visitors in addition to your attorney.'

'I don't want visitors.'

'Okay, I had to ask.' Corva turned and pushed a call button on the wall near the cell door.

Tyson commented, 'You know your way round these places.'

'I've been in gaol before. A piece of advice about that: Follow all their idiotic rules. Military prisons are no place to try to exercise your rights.'

An MP came with the keys and opened the cell door.

Tyson said to Corva, 'I want you to tell me how you got the Bronze Star in the tunnel.'

Corva smiled. 'One of these days.' He walked from the cell, and the MP shut the door. Corva said through the bars, 'The first platoon of Alpha Company has nearly completed its exorcism.' Corva left with the MP.

Tyson stood in the centre of the small cell for a full minute, then stared down at the envelope in his hand. He opened it and read the note inside:

Dear Ben,

I understand why you didn't want to see me while you were awaiting the verdict, and I'll understand if you don't want me to visit you now. But I will not understand if you don't send me a letter today to tell me you still love me.

David sends you his love, as I do.

Marcy

P.S. You looked quite brave up there. Your mother says you should punch Colonel Pierce in the eye.

Tyson read the short note again, then rang the bell. When the MP came, Tyson asked him for writing paper and pen.

51

The cell door opened at nine-thirty on Monday morning, and Tyson and Corva walked into the provost marshal's office. Corva said to Captain Gallagher, 'No cuffs. Right?'

Gallagher nodded. 'But if he gets away, you will be held accountable.'

Corva said, 'Don't be an ass, Captain.'

'Yes, sir. I try not to be.'

Corva and Tyson left the office and got into the back seat of an olive-drab staff car. Two MPs whom Tyson had never seen sat in the front. The car headed toward the post chapel.

Tyson said, 'That was not one of my better weekends.'

The car delivered them to the rear door of the chapel's office wing. They were met by two more armed MPs and taken directly to the courtroom.

It was a brilliantly clear day, and the four south-facing windows were alight with the morning sun. Tyson took his place at the defence table and remarked to Corva, 'I feel at home here.'

Corva nodded as if he'd heard this before.

No one else had arrived yet except the spectators, and Tyson looked out at the pews. The press was in full attendance, but the pews were only about three-fourths full, and most of the spectators were military. His sisters had gone home to husbands and jobs, and only Marcy, David, and his mother remained in the first pew, the remainder of the seats being left vacant. Marcy wasn't looking at him, but David waved and Tyson waved back.

He didn't see anyone else he knew except Colonel Levin,

who, he'd been told, had taken leave time to attend each session.

Tyson began to turn his attention back to the court, but some movement caught his eye, and he saw walking down the middle aisle, Steven Brandt. Brandt took an empty place in the pew almost directly behind Marcy. Tyson nudged Corva. 'Look.'

Corva looked, and his eyes widened.

'What,' asked Tyson, 'is *he* doing here?'

Corva replied, 'A witness may be present after the verdict. I guess he's here to see you sentenced.'

Tyson stared at Brandt until finally Brandt looked up. Brandt leaned back and folded his arms. He smiled at Tyson.

Tyson, still staring at Brandt, said to Corva, 'I'm going to kill the son of a bitch.'

'Cool down, people are watching you.'

Tyson saw that was true. People were looking from Brandt to Tyson and back again. Tyson sat back in his chair. He lit a cigarette. 'Bastard.'

After a few minutes he became aware again of his surroundings. He sensed a somewhat less tense atmosphere in the court, though he didn't know why there should be. He didn't consider his sentencing an anticlimax; it was the most important thing in the world for him at the moment. And today or tomorrow, he knew, depending on testimony, he'd take the stand himself. He looked at Marcy again, but she was still not looking at him. She was staring straight ahead. His note to her had been simple: '*I love you. But if I am sent to prison, I don't want or expect you to wait.*'

He thought that was all right, but apparently, according to Linda Corva, it was not. *Women*, he thought. When he was younger, he'd never liked female intermediaries involved in his *affaires d'amour*. But they could be useful as a source of information, if not comprehension. He'd have to write another note.

The prosecution walked in, and Tyson thought they looked

like three pigs heading back to the slop buckets for seconds.

The board entered very solemnly, together and in order of rank as usual. Tyson suspected that Colonel Moore ran his whole life by the manual for drill and ceremonies. Tyson said to Corva, 'In a three-seat crapper, would he take the middle seat or the far right?'

Corva looked up from his papers and followed Tyson's gaze. 'Oh ... the place of honour is usually the far right. But at a dais or court-martial, he takes the middle. I'd say it was the same for a three-seat crapper. I'll check, though.'

The sergeant at arms strode to the centre of the floor and the spectators began to rise before he announced, 'All rise!'

Colonel Sproule entered, and Tyson noticed for the first time that Sproule's pants were too long.

Sproule stepped up behind the pulpit, turned on the light, adjusted the microphone, and surveyed the court with his myopic eyes, as though, Tyson thought, he wanted to be sure he was in the right place. Sproule said, 'The court will come to order.'

Pierce stood and said, 'All parties to the trial who were present when the court closed are now present.'

Colonel Sproule glanced at something on the pulpit and said, 'The purpose of this session is to hear testimony and to present to the board other evidence and documented facts which may be considered by them as extenuating or mitigating facts or circumstances which may be considered by the board in determining an appropriate sentence. The court will now hear the personal data concerning the accused shown on the charge sheet and any other information from his personal records relevant to sentencing. The court will also receive evidence of previous convictions, if any.'

It was Captain Longo who stood and said, 'The first page of the charge sheet shows the following data concerning the accused.' Longo began reading the personal data sheet.

Tyson leaned toward Corva. 'We're playing the B team today.'

Corva said, 'They are all the B team every day.'

Longo continued to read the standard data from the charge sheet, but when he came to 'term of current service' he paused and said in a snide tone, 'Indefinite.'

Corva was on his feet. 'Objection, your honour.'

Sproule didn't bother to ask what the objection was. He said to Captain Longo sharply, 'Captain, this is not an audition. Just *read*.'

Longo seemed crushed and bowed his head. 'Yes, sir.'

Tyson noticed that Pierce and Weinroth exchanged looks as if to say, 'I knew we shouldn't have let that schmuck open his mouth.'

Longo completed the reading in a monotone, then sank low into his chair, as Major Weinroth stood. She began reading data from Tyson's old personnel file, though little of it seemed relevant any longer. Tyson realized he'd never heard her speak more than a word or two before, and he was surprised to find she had a deep, husky voice which he found sexy. Then he discovered that he was thinking about sex, then his mind drew him to Kansas and a place where there was no sex of the type he favoured. He had a sudden urge to bolt, to dash into the pews, into the arms of his supporters, who would carry him to safety. He whispered to Corva, 'I'm making a break for it.'

'Pay your bill first. Calm down.'

'I'm getting restless.'

'I see that. You want a recess?'

'No. I'll be all right.'

Corva poured them both some water. Tyson lit a cigarette and blew the smoke toward Weinroth, who glanced up at him as she read. She finished reading the data and said to Corva, 'Does the accused have any objection to the data as read?'

Corva replied, 'Not the way you read it.'

A few people laughed, and Corva said, 'Give me a moment.' He leaned toward Tyson. 'All right?'

Tyson shrugged. 'I wasn't paying attention.'

Corva whispered, 'The medals and citations and letters of commendation from your first term of service sound good to the board. And Levin's letter was a bit of a surprise. The board knows you did your job the first time around, and they know you've been a good soldier under Levin's command, too.' He added half jokingly, 'That's an automatic ten years off the sentence.'

'That brings us down to sixty years. What if I can recite the Infantryman's Prayer by heart?'

Colonel Sproule cleared his throat pointedly.

Corva remained in his seat and said, 'The accused has no objection to the data as read.'

Tyson said to Corva, 'Why am I still the accused?'

'I don't know. Never thought about that.'

Colonel Sproule announced, 'These documents will be marked as exhibits and made a part of the court record. Copies of all documents and records that are relevant to the imposition of an appropriate sentence will be presented to the members of the board preceding deliberations on sentence.'

As the exhibits were marked, Tyson studied the board closely. Two people there had voted for acquittal, but for the life of him he couldn't guess which two.

Corva saw where he was looking and said, 'Major Sindel. That was who my wife said.'

'Possible. Who else?'

'Beats me. The rest of them look like they spent the weekend building a scaffold.'

Tyson said, 'Maybe McGregor ... no, Morelli ... he liked your style ... you remind him of his Uncle Vito's mouthpiece.'

'Are you all right today?'

'I didn't sleep well.'

'I'm not surprised.' Corva looked at his client with some concern.

Colonel Sproule addressed Colonel Pierce. 'Does the prosecution have evidence in aggravation?'

Pierce replied, 'It does not.'

Sproule turned to Corva. 'Does the defence have evidence in extenuation and mitigation?'

'It does, your honour.'

'Does the defence have evidence to be submitted and marked as exhibits?'

'It does not, your honour.'

'Does the defence, then, intend to call witnesses in extenuation or mitigation?'

'It does, your honour.'

'Then call your first witness, Mr Corva.'

Corva turned to the sergeant at arms and said, 'The defence calls as a witness Mr Daniel Kelly.'

The door opened, and Daniel Kelly strode into the court. Tyson saw at once that the slight twenty-one-year-old he remembered was now a powerfully built forty-year-old man who walked with the movements of an athlete. Kelly's fair skin was bronze, and his long straw-coloured hair fell across his forehead. Tyson noticed that his eyes darted everywhere at once, taking in the whole scene, noticing possible ambush sites, registering places of cover and concealment, heeding signs of booby traps, and discerning good fields of fire. Kelly wore black flannel slacks, a white turtlenecked sweater, and a beige-coloured suede sports jacket. Kelly stopped at the witness chair, looked at Tyson, and gave a thumbs-up. Tyson returned the greeting.

Corva said to Sproule, 'Your honour, we intend that this be sworn testimony.'

Sproule nodded to Pierce, who approached the witness chair with the impatient movements of a man who thinks he should be somewhere else by now. 'Raise your right hand.'

Kelly, still standing, raised his hand.

Pierce recited quickly, the words running together, 'Do you swear that the evidence you shall give on the case now in hearing shall be the truth, the whole truth, and nothing but the truth, so help you God?'

'I do.' Kelly sat without Pierce inviting him to do so.

700

Pierce said, 'Please state your name, residence and occupation.'

'Daniel Kelly, Edgerton, Ohio, importing and exporting.'

Pierce, who had been given some general information by Corva regarding expected testimony, had apparently learned a few other things about Daniel Kelly and didn't intend to let his first statement go unquestioned. 'You are a *current* resident of Edgerton, Ohio?'

'Yes.'

Pierce seemed sceptical. 'Could you be more specific concerning your occupation?'

'Yes. I import and export things.'

Someone laughed.

'From Edgerton, Ohio?' asked Pierce dubiously.

'Yes.'

Corva said, 'Your honour—'

Sproule put out his hand toward Corva and said to Pierce, 'Perhaps you'd like to hold the cross-examination until after the defence has examined its witness, Colonel Pierce.'

Again, a few people snickered.

Colonel Sproule said, 'Mr Corva, you may begin.'

Pierce returned to the prosecution table, as Corva stood under the pulpit facing Kelly. Corva began, 'Mr Kelly, could you state your former grade, organization, and duties while serving in the Republic of Vietnam?'

Kelly replied in a well-modulated voice, 'I was a Specialist Four, serving with the first platoon of Alpha Company, Fifth Battalion of the Seventh Cavalry, First Air Cavalry Division. I was the platoon leader's radiotelephone operator, known as an RTO.'

Tyson noticed, too, that Kelly's diction and choice of words had improved since Vietnam.

Corva said, 'You were Lieutenant Tyson's personal radio operator, were you not?'

'For most of the time I was there, yes.'

'And as an RTO, you had close and frequent contact with

701

your platoon leader.'

'Every day. We slept in the same foxhole. I had to provide him with radio contact at a second's notice, so we stayed fairly close.'

Corva asked a series of questions to establish Kelly's past and present relationship to Tyson, then asked, 'Are you generally aware of the circumstances of this trial?'

'Yes, I am.'

'You're aware Lieutenant Tyson has been convicted of murder.'

'Yes, I am.'

'And you have offered to appear in his behalf to offer testimony that may establish extenuating circumstances for the crime of which he stands convicted.'

'Yes, I have.'

'Mr Kelly, could you tell the court what happened on the morning of 15 February 1968? The incident of the burial mounds. Begin, please, at first light.'

Kelly replied, 'At first light, nineteen of us moved out of our night defensive positions.' Kelly continued his narrative in the short concise sentences favoured by the military, using military terminology of the period and using it accurately. Tyson had the impression that Kelly was relating last week's events, and he thought others shared that impression.

Tyson watched the board. He could see that Moore, McGregor, and Bauer were favourably impressed with Daniel Kelly. But he didn't know if that was going to do Benjamin Tyson any good. He glanced at Brandt, who seemed to be getting a little uneasy.

Kelly concluded, 'We resumed the patrol, in a southeast direction, toward Hue.'

Corva asked, 'So, the only men who were with you on that burial mound were Lieutenant Tyson, Richard Farley and Harold Simcox.'

'Yes.'

Colonel Pierce stood. 'Your honour, if it please the court, I have been exceedingly patient, listening intently for anything that sounds like it might be extenuation or mitigation for the offence of which Lieutenant Tyson has been convicted.'

Sproule looked down at Corva. 'Mr Corva?'

Corva replied, 'Your honour, the nature of testimony offered in extenuation or mitigation is often such that it does no more than to establish the accused's state of mind or his intentions or the general conditions that prevailed at the time. I intend, your honour, for Mr Kelly to be up here for some time. Now, the prosecution can object to this and that, but I assure the court that I will get this story told one way or the other, even if it means Mr Kelly sitting here for the next week while I reply to objections. Your honour, do not take offence. Lieutenant Tyson stands here convicted of murder. And I am standing here to do everything in my power to see that the board has every pertinent detail that surrounds this incident, so that they may arrive at an appropriate sentence. I want the members of the board to discover as much as I know and Mr Kelly knows about Lieutenant Tyson and about Miséricorde Hospital before they vote on a sentence. Though it may not all appear to be pertinent as it unfolds, I assure the court that this evidence is pertinent and that the court will recognize it as such by the time the witness steps down. That is my intention, your honour.'

Sproule thought about that for a moment, then said, 'Colonel Pierce, Mr Corva, would you approach the bench?'

Pierce and Corva stepped up to the higher level of the pulpit on the side away from the witness chair. Colonel Sproule faced them and addressed Pierce in a low voice. 'Colonel, if I am to believe Mr Corva, he is attempting to establish what he believes are extenuating and mitigating circumstances for the crime which you have proven. I suggest you let him do that. Unless you have good and substantive objections to the testimony, I will overrule you. If this testimony takes you somewhat by surprise because of the sudden appearance of this witness, I will give you ample time to prepare a cross-examination during which you may address these objections within that format. I remind you that the defence has the benefit of the doubt in these matters. The charges having been proven, I intend to give the defence even more leeway in presenting facts which might lessen the sentence. I believe the board is looking for those facts.'

Pierce stayed silent for a moment, then responded, 'Yes, your honour.'

Sproule turned to Corva. 'I'll let the man talk, Mr Corva, but I strongly suggest you do not attempt to retry this case in this session.' Sproule looked from one to the other and said tersely, 'Understood?'

They both answered in the affirmative.

Sproule faced forward on the pulpit and said, 'Proceed with the examination.'

Pierce went back to the prosecution table, and Corva to the witness chair. Corva addressed Kelly. 'During the burial mound incident, did you hear Lieutenant Tyson give an order to shoot the peasants who were burying the dead?'

'Yes.'

'Now ... I'm going to ask for an opinion, Mr Kelly ...' He glanced sharply at Pierce. '... And the court knows it is only your opinion. But as a man who had served with Lieutenant Tyson in the field for approximately eight months before that incident, what was your opinion of that order?'

Kelly replied, 'On the face of it, it was an illegal order. But it is my opinion that it was not given in earnest. It was meant to shame.'

'To shame whom?'

'Me, for one. Farley, Simcox and I were making threatening gestures toward the peasants, generally being abusive. The strip search, for instance, could have been handled with more tact. I could see that Lieutenant Tyson was becoming annoyed with us. So, in a manner of speaking, he called our bluff. And we *were* bluffing. We had no intention – at least I didn't – of shooting those people. It was a bluff that we used too freely with the Vietnamese. After Lieutenant Tyson gave the order, no one moved for some time. He did not repeat the order or attempt to enforce it in any way. He then said, "Okay, heroes, let's get moving." Or words to that effect. He said it with sarcasm.'

Corva asked, 'Did you discuss this with him afterward?'

'No. There was nothing to discuss. If I had thought he was serious about the order, I would certainly have discussed it with him. But the order was too out of character to take it as anything but what I said it was.'

'Did you discuss it with Farley?'

'No.'

'Do you think Farley understood that the order was a bluff? Meant to shame?'

Pierce got to his feet, thought better of it, and sat.

Tyson could see that the board and Sproule were intent on hearing the story. And Pierce, as Corva had suggested sometime ago, knew when to withdraw. Pierce had to weigh the effects of letting Kelly tell the story against the effects of not letting him tell it.

Corva repeated the question to Kelly.

Kelly replied, 'Farley was not a man who understood subtleties. Yet, on this occasion, I believe he understood that Lieutenant Tyson did not mean for us to shoot those people. Simcox understood it. He commented to me as we left the burial mound that Lieutenant Tyson was too soft on the gooks. I don't think he would have said that if he believed that Lieutenant Tyson's order to shot them was meant in earnest. Farley was in earshot and responded, "Yeah."'

Corva nodded, then said, 'Thank you. We can move on or rather, move back, to an incident of some months previous to this incident which occurred in either late November or early December. I'm referring to an operation that was known as a cordon. Alpha Company was working with the Vietnamese National Police at a village south of Quang Tri. Do you recall this operation?'

'Yes. We'd done four or five of them before. Regarding this particular one, everything went as planned. The village was surrounded two hours before dawn. At dawn, we sent a few squads in to be sure the village was not infested with armed enemy soldiers. Then the squads withdrew. Sometime later, within the hour, a large Chinook helicopter landed, and about forty or fifty National Policemen got out. Their officers exchanged some words with our officers, who assured them the village did not harbour any large enemy force. The National Police then entered the village with the objective of finding VC who might be hiding in holes or tunnels, VC sympathizers, VC political cadres, arms caches, documents, and that sort of thing.'

'What was your personal opinion of this sort of operation? I ask that, because I was an infantry officer and know my opinion of it.'

Kelly replied, 'These operations were distasteful to me personally and to many other men in the company. The National Police usually – no, always – behaved very badly toward the local population. After we'd swept through the village, we were normally not allowed to go back to see what they were doing, but you could hear the screams.'

'Screams?'

'Yes. They would vigorously interrogate the villagers.'

'How vigorously?'

'Usually with the aid of electric shock treatments to the genitals. They brought their own hand-cranked generators. They would also suspend people by rope or wire upside down into the wells until they nearly drowned. They used other means of interrogation which were peculiar to the Orient and which probably should not be discussed here.'

'Of course. Now, you said Americans were not allowed in the village during this period of interrogation.'

'Correct. However, the officers in the American unit involved sometimes entered the village for purposes of discussing tactical matters with the National Police commanders. As Lieutenant Tyson's RTO, I, of course, would go with him. On those occasions, I personally observed what I stated earlier.'

'How did Lieutenant Tyson feel about these operations?'

'He had negative feelings toward using American troops as accomplices to this sort of thing. He wrote a memo once to the battalion commander protesting against what he said amounted to condoning these brutalities. He made the point that it was demoralizing for his troops to see the results of it, as we always went through the village after the police had gone. After his letter to the battalion commander, Alpha Company never again participated in these joint operations with the National Police.'

Corva asked, 'What happened on that particular operation? The one that led to the altercation.'

'Lieutenant Tyson's platoon was stretched out along a dike, forming a side of the cordon. From here we could see into a part of the village. The National Police had a dozen people, all naked, of all ages and sexes, lined up at a well. We could see them lower the first person down the well.'

'What was the purpose of this sort of thing?'

'It was supposed to encourage the villagers to point out the VC spider holes, tunnels, arms caches, and turn in any VC among them. But, to my mind it was – or became – nothing more than a thinly disguised sado-sexual orgy. They often got a VC or two and a weapon or two, but the price was too high.'

Tyson looked at the board, then at Colonel Sproule, then at Pierce. And finally at the spectators. Kelly's narrative had created an atmosphere of intense interest, except at the prosecution table where the atmosphere was more one of uneasiness.

Corva said to Kelly, 'Go on, please.'

'Yes. Lieutenant Tyson suggested we go into the village to talk to the local Viet commander. He always did that.'

'Why?'

'To try to get them to take it a little easy. The presence of

707

Americans usually accomplished that, until you turned your back. Lieutenant Tyson's objections to this sort of operation were partly humanitarian but partly practical. He doubted if any hearts or minds could be won by subjecting an entire village to mass torture and humiliation. He observed that after the National Police went back to their barracks, we would still have to deal with the locals in our area of operations.'

'So you went into the village.'

'Yes. We went into the village. And while walking, we spotted Steven Brandt.'

Pierce was on his feet. 'Objection. Your honour, this has gone on long enough. This is totally irrelevant.'

Sproule looked down at Corva, then at Pierce, then back to Corva. He said to Corva, 'Explain to the court, Mr Corva, how the line of questioning you are pursuing will extenuate or mitigate the circumstances surrounding the incident for which Lieutenant Tyson stands convicted.'

Corva replied, 'Your honour, it is my intention to demonstrate to the court that there was bad blood between Lieutenant Tyson and the prosecution's witness, Steven Brandt, and that the hostility that existed between Lieutenant Tyson and his former medic was of such intensity that it has prevailed up until the time that Mr Brandt took the stand in this court. I intend to show that Mr Brandt's statement, that there was no such hostility and animosity, was a lie.'

Sproule said, 'It's a little too late for that, isn't it, Mr Corva?'

'Your honour, if I can demonstrate through this witness's story that Mr Brandt's feelings for the accused were biased and hostile, then I can demonstrate that Mr Brandt's testimony was likewise biased and hostile, which in turn will let the board put the proper coloration on Mr Brandt's testimony and may influence their deliberations on an appropriate sentence, which is the purpose of this session.'

Sproule's eyebrows arched slightly. 'That is stretching it a bit, Mr Corva. I don't know what your true purpose is in pursuing this story. However, you may continue, with caution. Objection overruled.'

Pierce sat and slapped his hand against the table in a rare show of ill temper. Corva said to Kelly, 'You saw Mr Brandt in the village. Did he belong there?'

'To some extent. Medics, as well as officers, could and did enter these villages while the police were conducting their searches and interrogations. The medics were often needed.'

'What happened next?'

'Lieutenant Tyson said to me, "Keep back, I want to follow him," meaning Brandt.'

'Why? What did he mean by that?'

'It was Lieutenant Tyson's observation that Brandt was acting improperly.'

'How so, Mr Kelly?'

'Brandt was taking pictures. This was strictly forbidden by the National Police. They did not want pictures.'

'What was Mr Brandt taking pictures of?'

'Mostly of naked women being tortured and humiliated.'

Corva waited for Pierce. Pierce did not object. Corva said, 'Go on.'

'Lieutenant Tyson noticed that the National Police were not stopping Brandt from taking pictures. In fact, they seemed quite friendly toward Brandt.'

'Did you notice this also?'

'Yes. And I once saw Brandt on a previous cordon operation give a National Police captain what looked like medical supplies from his bag.'

'Continue.'

'After Brandt finished with his pictures, he entered a hootch – a Vietnamese house – with two National Policemen. Lieutenant Tyson and I discussed this for some time, then went into the house. A policeman put his hand on Lieutenant Tyson's arm to detain him. Lieutenant Tyson pushed the man away, and we entered the house in which Brandt had gone.'

'And what did you – *you* see, Mr Kelly?'

Tyson turned from Kelly and stared at Steven Brandt, whose expression was fixed and rigid. Tyson kept his eyes on Brandt as Kelly replied, 'I saw three naked females. One of them was curled up in a corner weeping, and a policeman was pulling her by the arm. Another female was performing fellatio on a second policeman, and the third female was being raped by Mr Brandt.'

Pierce jumped to his feet and shouted something that was drowned out by other sounds in the chapel, which ranged from gasps to a few shouts. Tyson caught Brandt's eye for a moment before Brandt turned away.

Colonel Sproule signalled to the sergeant at arms, who went to the Communion rail and held up his hand for silence. The well-disciplined crowd fell silent.

Colonel Sproule announced, 'If there are any more outbursts, I will clear the court.' He looked at Pierce, who was about to state his objection again, and Sproule said, 'Objection overruled.' He said to Corva, 'I wish to put some questions to the witness.'

'Yes, your honour.'

Sproule looked down the side of the pulpit. 'Mr Kelly, the court would like to know how you determined that what you saw was rape and not ... not the normal activities of men and women.'

Kelly glanced up at Sproule, then turned back to his front and replied, 'I don't see anything normal in group sex, your honour, but that might be my personal prejudice. To answer your honour's question, I assumed from the circumstances that the men did not know the females very long. About five minutes, I think. Also, the females were weeping. All of them. Also, they were very young, your honour. The one who was with Mr Brandt was not more than twelve or thirteen. Even making allowances for cultural differences and the earlier onset of puberty in tropical climates and such, this was quite young. Also, when Mr Brandt stood, I could see blood on his genitals and thighs, and I remember making the assumption that the girl had been a virgin, though, of course, she may have been having her period. Also, your honour, the girl looked to me as though she had been struck in the face. It was for these reasons, your honour, that I concluded that what I was witnessing was a mass rape and not a party.'

Sproule nodded and swallowed. 'I see.'

'And also, your honour, Mr Brandt had a look of fear on his face when he saw Lieutenant Tyson and me. He jumped immediately to his feet – he was on a sleeping mat on the floor – and exclaimed, "Don't!"'

Sproule asked, 'Don't what?'

'Lieutenant Tyson and I had both levelled our rifles at our hips. This was a precaution against any attempt by the two policemen to go for their guns. They could sometimes be hostile. But Brandt thought Lieutenant Tyson or I was aiming at him. So he shouted, "Don't!" Then he shouted, "Please!" as he grabbed his fatigue pants. He was still wearing his bush jacket and boots. Then he bolted through a window leaving behind his medical bag and rifle.'

Colonel Sproule asked, 'Did you follow him?'

'Yes, your honour. But first we gathered up Brandt's equipment and escorted the two policemen out of the hootch. Several policemen were converging on the hootch now, and an ugly scene seemed about to take place. There was some shouting back and forth between Lieutenant Tyson and myself on one side and about a dozen police on the other.'

'Did you feel you were in danger?'

'There was an element of danger. But in the end, we simply turned and walked away. We got back to the dike, and Brandt was there, fully clothed by now. Lieutenant Tyson approached him. I should have pointed out before, your honour, that Lieutenant Tyson had mentioned to me on a few previous occasions that he thought Brandt was taking advantage of his status as a medic to further his private interests in the local women. Lieutenant Tyson was

711

concerned about this.'

Sproule said, 'So this was the incident that caused the alleged animosity between Lieutenant Tyson and Mr Brandt?'

'Yes, your honour, but the animosity deepened after Lieutenant Tyson confronted Mr Brandt on the dike.'

'What did Lieutenant Tyson say to Mr Brandt when he confronted him on the dike?'

'Not too much, your honour. Lieutenant Tyson kicked Mr Brandt in the groin. Then he slapped him around but only hit him once or twice with a closed fist. Then Lieutenant Tyson threw Mr Brandt into the flooded rice paddy, drew his forty-five, and instructed Mr Brandt to sit in the water or have his brains blown out. Mr Brandt sat in the water. Then Mr Brandt began to complain that the leeches were finding him. He became quite agitated and began to weep, then he became hysterical.'

Colonel Sproule said nothing for some time. He touched his fingers to his lips in thought, then asked, 'Were there any other witnesses to this incident on the dike?'

'Yes, your honour, the entire platoon could see from their positions on this long straight dike. But no one thought it wise to interfere with what appeared to be a personal matter. In fact, I passed the word down the line for the men to remain in position and continue with their mission of watching the village for anyone trying to escape.'

'But no one else knew the cause of this incident on the dike?'

'No, your honour. And never did know. But I think there were some good guesses.'

'Do you know if Lieutenant Tyson took any legal action against Mr Brandt or if Mr Brandt took any such action against Lieutenant Tyson?'

'There was no such action taken by either party, your honour. Not that I know of.'

Sproule asked Kelly, 'How did the incident end?'

712

'After about thirty minutes, Lieutenant Tyson had calmed down somewhat and told Mr Brandt he could come out of the water. Mr Brandt did so. Mr Brandt then undressed on the dike, and I observed perhaps thirty leeches on his body. He was very agitated. He was weeping actually, pleading with someone to help him take the leeches off. Several men went to his assistance with insecticides and lit cigarettes. Mr Brandt had lost some blood to the leeches, and as a result of his physical and mental state, we called in a helicopter to take him away.'

Sproule asked, 'Would a man have rejoined his unit after such an incident?'

'Not normally, your honour, but Lieutenant Tyson and I went back to the rear area that night on a resupply helicopter and paid a sick call on Mr Brandt, who was in the battalion aide station. Lieutenant Tyson informed Mr Brandt that he expected him back in the field within twenty-four hours, or he would have him court-martialled on a variety of charges. Mr Brandt indicated that he didn't want a public record of this incident as he planned to go to medical school. Lieutenant Tyson felt that he had solved Mr Brandt's problem and thought that Mr Brandt's continued presence in a combat infantry company would be useful to Mr Brandt and to the company. Mr Brandt was a good medic. So the matter rested there, which answers your honour's question of Mr Brandt's return to his unit.'

Colonel Sproule nodded. 'And that was the end of the incident?'

'No, your honour, this is the end of the incident.'

'Quite so, Mr Kelly.' Colonel Sproule looked at Corva for some time, then nodded to indicate he should proceed.

Corva said to Kelly, 'And from that time on, how would you characterize the relationship between Lieutenant Tyson and Mr Brandt?'

Kelly replied, 'I don't think Mr Brandt liked being humiliated in front of the entire platoon, nor did he like the

713

leeches. I think I would characterize the relationship between the two men as cool.'

'Do you think Mr Brandt held a grudge against Lieutenant Tyson?'

'I believe so. Neither of them was what you would call the forgiving type.'

'Do you think Mr Brandt held this grudge up until the time of the hospital incident, some two or three months later?'

'Yes. In fact, that morning of the burial mound incident, he and Lieutenant Tyson had words.'

'About what?'

'About Mr Brandt feigning illness to get out of the field.'

Corva asked a few further questions, then said to Colonel Sproule, 'I have no further questions regarding this incident, your honour. I would like to go on to the hospital incident if you have no further questions.'

'I have none. And if the board has any, we will ask them at the end of your examination of Mr Kelly. We will take a recess at this time and reconvene at fourteen hundred hours. I would like to see Colonel Pierce and Mr Corva in my chambers. The court is closed.'

Tyson looked out to the pews and saw Brandt hurrying, head down, towards the doors.

Corva said to Tyson. 'Feel better now?'

'No.'

'Good. You should not. But I can.'

52

The court reconvened and Daniel Kelly retook the stand.

Colonel Pierce stood and said, 'Mr Kelly, you are reminded that you are still under oath.'

Corva stood under the pulpit and faced Kelly. After a few

preliminary questions, he said to Kelly. 'Could you relate to the court the events that led up to the hospital incident?'

Kelly replied, 'Yes, I can,' and began a clear, detailed account of the approach to Miséricorde Hospital. The account, Tyson noticed, was much more lucid than Brandt's or Farley's, but did not differ from those accounts in any major details, nor did it differ from the account in Picard's book, which Tyson knew everyone in the court had read.

Tyson glanced into the choir loft and saw a few silhouettes. The pews, which had been a fourth empty at the morning session, were now full again, no doubt as a result of word getting out about the testimony. He did not see Brandt, and suspected the good doctor was on his way back to Boston.

Tyson looked at the press section and saw that those pews were full as well. There had been no sketch artists at the morning session, but there were five at the Communion rail just now, kneeling, their sketch pads on the rail, their eyes on Kelly.

Tyson looked into the right front pew and saw that David was not there, though Marcy was, and the expression on her face was taut.

Tyson had picked at his lunch in his cell, waiting for Corva to join him, but Corva never came. And they had barely five minutes together before Sproule called the court to order. During that five minutes Corva had told him that the session in Sproule's chambers – the head chaplain's office – had been heated. And Tyson did not know how much more Corva could get away with. He saw, though, that Corva was being a bit more cautious in the wording of his questions, and so far Pierce had no reason to object. Corva's questions emphasized the physical and mental condition of the platoon since he was no longer trying to prove that nothing illegal had occurred, but was now showing why it had occurred. Tyson felt more at ease with this approach.

Corva said to Kelly, 'So you entered the hospital after you were certain the enemy sniper had fled. You had two wounded: Robert Moody, who was lightly wounded in the leg, and Arthur Peterson, whose wound was serious. You have stated that you knew it was a hospital before you ever reached it and that no firefight of any significance occurred as you approached the hospital. There was a single sniper. Correct?'

'Correct.'

'Now, Mr Kelly, you are in the hospital, and here is where previous testimony diverged even further. What happened in the hospital to cause the incident for which Lieutenant Tyson has been convicted?'

Kelly paused for the first time in his testimony, then spoke. 'We carried Moody and Peterson inside. The staff was preoccupied with their duties and I remember thinking that they showed no signs of having been affected by the recent shooting. Lieutenant Tyson detained a nurse who informed us that all the doctors were upstairs. We carried Moody and Peterson upstairs.'

Colonel Sproule interrupted. 'Mr Kelly, I think the court is wondering about a missing detail. There seem to be two versions of the death of Cane. One is that he was killed outright by the sniper outside the hospital. The other version is that he died in room-to-room fighting. Since it appears there was no room-to-room fighting, I assume he died outside the hospital. Yet, you don't mention his death in your account.'

'That is because Larry Cane was still alive when we entered the hospital, your honour.'

Sproule thought a moment, then said to Corva, 'Proceed.'

Corva addressed Kelly. 'What did you find upstairs?'

'There were three wards. One was a sort of general ward filled to overflowing with wounded. Mostly civilian refugees from Hue, I believe. The second ward was marked in French "*contagion*". We only glanced into that ward, a small room with ten beds, all filled. The third ward was paediatric and obstetrics. This had perhaps thirty beds and was full, also. In

716

addition, there were wounded and sick all over the corridors. There were people who appeared to be neither wounded nor sick, but just refugees. There were perhaps a hundred people in the hospital, but there could have been two hundred, for all I know. We discovered also an operating room. It was there that we carried Arthur Peterson. I should point out that we were not completely certain the hospital was secure and that the platoon was making room-to-room searches. We found a pile of bloody khakis which we took to be enemy uniforms and in fact found about a half dozen young men in the beds whom we took to be enemy sick and wounded.'

'What was the platoon's reaction to this?'

'Pretty much the same reaction they had to the peasants burying the enemy dead. It was not rational, but then neither were we. It is only in retrospect that it seems we overreacted to the fact that the hospital held enemy sick and wounded.'

'Did anyone threaten these sick and wounded enemy soldiers?'

'Not that I could see. But Sergeant Sadowski put a few men in the ward to keep an eye on them.'

'What happened in the operating room?'

'I was in the operating room with Lieutenant Tyson and several other men. It was a large room that actually held six or seven operating tables. It was very primitive, as I recall. There were people on each of the tables, and there were nurses and doctors in attendance. Lieutenant Tyson spoke to a man who identified himself as the chief of staff.'

'In what language did they speak?'

'Mostly French, but some English. The gist of the coversation, most of which I learned of afterwards, was that Lieutenant Tyson, of course, was asking – actually insisting – that Peterson and Moody be treated. Peterson was at this point lying on the floor of the operating room. Moody was sitting against a wall. This doctor knelt down and examined Peterson perfunctorily and announced that the man was beyond saving. Lieutenant Tyson told him to try. The doctor explained – and again this is what Lieutenant Tyson told me afterwards – that the hospital was on the triage system. That is, anyone whose wounds were very severe would not be helped because that would tie up too much of the hospital's resources for little or no gain. The lightly wounded, such as Moody, would not be helped because they could live with their wounds. It was those people in the middle group who would be tended to. Apparently neither Peterson nor Moody qualified for this group. Moody was actually being tended to by Brandt right there on the floor of the operating room anyway.'

'But Peterson was dying?'

'Yes. He'd been shot in the side, and the bullet exited on the other side. He was gagging and spitting up frothy white blood. Apparently he was drowning. He was semiconscious, and kept calling out for help. In fact, while he was lying on the floor, he pulled at Lieutenant Tyson's trouser leg. Lieutenant Tyson knelt a few times while he was arguing with this doctor. I was kneeling on the floor, holding Peterson's hand.'

'Do you recall who else was in the room?'

'People kept coming in and out. But Farley and Cane were there almost the entire time. There were several Oriental staff in the room, again coming and going. There were also perhaps five or six Caucasians, which was one of the reasons the men of the platoon kept coming in and out.'

'Why?'

'To see the Caucasians. Other than GIs, none of us had seen Caucasians in some time. It was a novelty. There was one Caucasian woman, too, a rather good-looking woman, and that caused a little stir. As I suggested, it wasn't an operating room of the type we picture, but only a large whitewashed room with a red tile floor and six or seven tables.'

'How long did this altercation between the doctor and Lieutenant Tyson last?'

'Hard to say. Maybe five minutes before Lieutenant Tyson finally levelled his rifle at the man and ordered him to do something for Peterson.'

'And what did the doctor say?'

'I'm not sure, but I could tell by his motions and his tone of voice that he wasn't intimidated. He seemed to want to return to his patient, who was an Oriental male lying naked on the closest table. The man's leg had been shredded badly by some sort of explosive device. The man's clothing, a khaki North Vietnamese Army uniform, was on the floor. So, the doctor turned away. Lieutenant Tyson spun him around and slapped him across the face.' Kelly paused.

Corva let the silence continue for some seconds, then said, 'What happened next?'

'Several things were happening concurrently now. First, Farley delivered a horizontal butt stroke to the doctor's abdomen, which caused him to double over. Hernando Beltran had entered the room and gone to the operating table where the wounded enemy soldier was. Beltran pulled the man off the operating table and onto the floor. The man was screaming. Peterson was crying. The doctor was moaning in pain. The nurses were becoming frightened. Then from the rear of the operating room comes this tall Caucasian, running at us. He was shouting in English and had an accent that I believe was Australian. We'd worked with Australian troops for a week once, and that was how I could identify the accent.'

'What was the man shouting, Mr Kelly?'

'He was being very abusive. Everyone was stunned to hear this English-speaking man. He hadn't said anything up until that point.'

'What was he saying now?'

'He began by telling Lieutenant Tyson to get out and take his men with him. Then he began to swear, calling us all fucking murderers. Then he moved on to larger issues, such as the fact that all we knew how to do was kill and hurt people. That we had no right to be there – in Vietnam. That the war was this and that. The sort of stuff you saw in the stateside newspapers.'

'Did Lieutenant Tyson respond?'

'No. The man was obviously overwrought. But while this was going on, Beltran and someone else had laid Peterson on the now vacant operating table. Another doctor approached, but he spoke no English or French. I believe he was German or Dutch. He was indicating by his motions that he would operate on Peterson. In fact, someone had put a tube down Peterson's throat, I suppose to suck the blood out. But no one was paying much attention to this doctor by now. The French doctor was somewhat recovered from the butt stroke, and extremely angry, but I had the distinct impression that the medical staff there had properly evaluated the situation and were about to cooperate. But there was still this Australian doctor who wouldn't calm down. And then there was Beltran, who had found another NVA soldier and had thrown him off the operating table, too. Lieutenant Tyson shouted to Beltran to get out. I'm telling you what I remember, but it was somewhat confusing, because everyone was very hyper. I would imagine that these people had had about as little rest as we had and tempers were very short. But as I said, the Australian was exhibiting the most provocative behaviour.'

'What do you mean by provocative?'

'He began pointing.'

'Pointing?'

'Yes. At each of us. He would point and shout such things as, "You! Get out!" or, "You are a bloody fucking murderer. You. You. How dare you." That sort of thing.'

'How did the men react to this?'

'Not too well. As I said, we were wet, tired, frightened. We knew we were headed toward Hue. I don't think anyone expected to come back from there. And then here was this doctor, one of our own so to speak, calling us names. Someone shouted to him that he wouldn't speak to the VC or NVA that way, which was probably true. Also, I think the general feeling was that the enemy had caused all this misery, not us. As I said, the rest of the staff were willing to cooperate

720

regarding Peterson, but I had the impression they were not pro-American types. They didn't greet us very warmly. That, I think, set up the psychological atmosphere for what eventually happened to them.'

'And the Australian doctor was still being abusive?'

'Yes. He couldn't get himself under control. Something inside him had obviously snapped. Two Caucasian males tried to pull him away, but he pushed them aside. Most of us were ignoring him, but somehow Larry Cane got into a screaming match with him. They traded insults for some seconds. Then the Australian poked Cane with his finger and said, "You're a stupid son of a bitch." Cane pulled the trigger on his rifle and fired a burst into the Australian's abdomen.'

Corva said, 'This was the first shot that was fired?'

'Yes. But that's all it took. Beltran went over to the two North Viets on the floor, pulled his pistol, and shot them both in the head. Then Cane, for a reason I'll never comprehend, fired his M-16 into the far wall, splattering stucco all over. People were screaming, dropping to the floor. The Australian doctor was lying against a wall where he'd been thrown by the impact of the bullets, bleeding badly from the abdomen. Then Brandt, apropos of nothing really, yelled out, "Peterson's dead." Cane then turned and shot this French doctor in the back.'

'What was Lieutenant Tyson doing during this time?'

'Same thing as I was doing. Diving for the floor. Cane had obviously gone around the bend. It happened really very quickly. At least I think it did. Then Lieutenant Tyson got to one knee and drew his pistol. He aimed it at Cane and ordered him to drop his rifle. Cane was reloading another magazine. Lieutenant Tyson again told him to drop the rifle. It was all very tense.'

'And did Cane drop the rifle?'

'He did after Lieutenant Tyson shot him dead in the chest.'

Ben Tyson sat with his elbows on the table, his chin resting on his hands, staring intently at Daniel Kelly, as was everyone. Tyson listened hard for a sound, but there wasn't any. Corva seemed to have nothing to say and neither did Kelly.

Finally, Colonel Sproule asked Kelly, 'Are you saying that Lieutenant Tyson shot Cane?'

'Yes, your honour. Shot and killed him.'

Sproule nodded, almost wearily, thought Tyson. Tyson looked at the board and saw Colonel Moore staring at him, as though seeing him for the first time. Tyson also saw Major Bauer's head nodding slowly and rhythmically.

Corva came over to the defence table and poured himself some water and drank it. He never looked at Tyson but turned and went back to Kelly.

Tyson sat back in his chair and turned his head toward the prosecution table. Pierce seemed not upset and not uncomfortable. He seemed, if anything, relaxed, as if it were all beyond his control now. Tyson looked at Colonel Sproule, who seemed thoughtful. Probably, thought Tyson, this case, whose facts had eluded him, was now becoming clear and tidy in his mind.

Corva said to Kelly, 'What happened next?'

'The operating room was in pandemonium, as I recall. Beltran was at the door and wouldn't let anyone leave. Richard Farley ran over to Cane and knelt beside him. Cane and Farley were from the same town somewhere in South Jersey and had enlisted together under the buddy system which guaranteed that the men would stay together during their enlistment. Farley was very distraught and was screaming at Tyson that he had killed his friend to save a bunch of gooks. Of course, Cane had in fact killed two Caucasians, but as I said, Farley was distraught. No one and nothing was making much sense. Even now I can't make much sense of it.'

'Did Lieutenant Tyson at any time give an order to kill wounded enemy soldiers? Or to kill anyone?'

'No, he did not.'

'You were with him for the entire time?'

'Yes. Except for a period later, after the shooting began.'

'How much time had elapsed since you entered the hospital?'

'About fifteen or twenty minutes.'

722

'You described the operating room scene as pandemonium. Could you give any details?'

'I recall that Beltran was giving orders. Nearly the entire platoon was in the operating room by now and Beltran ordered them to find all the gooks and kill them.'

'Was Beltran in a leadership position?'

'No. He was a pfc. He was a machine gunner. But he was prone to giving orders. Lieutenant Tyson told him to shut up. But Farley was now standing to Lieutenant Tyson's side, aiming his rifle at him. Lieutenant Tyson was still on one knee with his pistol in his hand and his M-16 on the floor. Farley told him to drop his pistol.'

'Did he?'

'No, Lieutenant Tyson stood and told Farley to drop his rifle. But now Beltran had his machine gun trained on Lieutenant Tyson. A few of the men meanwhile had gone back to the ward where the enemy soldiers were lying in bed. We heard six or seven shots, and I assumed they'd killed the wounded NVA.'

'What were you doing during this time?'

'Not too much. It was a very chaotic situation. I tried to calm people down, but it was beyond that at this point. Another man, Harold Simcox, was pointing his rifle at Lieutenant Tyson now. Lieutenant Tyson told them – Beltran, Farley, and Simcox – to drop their weapons, but they didn't. Simcox was one of those men who had a bad attitude towards any authority. There was no bad blood between Lieutenant Tyson and Simcox, but Simcox was a rabble-rouser, and as soon as he smelled a mutiny, he joined the mutineers. There are always a few like that.'

'So now three men were pointing their weapons at Lieutenant Tyson. What was his response?'

'His response was to tell the three men they were under arrest. He told me to call battalion headquarters and make a report.'

'Did you?'

'No. Lieutenant Tyson's estimation of the situation was faulty. Had I attempted to make the radio call, I'd have been shot. And so would Lieutenant Tyson. He was letting his ego get in the way of his judgement.'

'What was the response of Beltran, Farley, and Simcox to being told that they were under arrest?'

'They had a negative response to that. Farley again told Lieutenant Tyson to drop his pistol, and this time he threatened to shoot him if he didn't. At this point, it seemed to be a standoff. Then we were momentarily diverted when one of the staff, a young Caucasian male, jumped from the window. It was two storeys, but there was shrubbery outside. Beltran ran to the window, rested his machine gun on the ledge, and fired.'

'Did he hit the man?'

'He said he did. Then Beltran turned from the window and ordered all the remainder of the staff into a side room that looked like a scrub-up room. It had sinks and a toilet. Then he sent a few men out to round up any other staff members, Caucasian and Orientals.'

'Would you say that Beltran, then, was *the* leader or *a* leader of this mutiny?'

'Sort of. He was giving orders, and people were taking them. He was on a power trip. He was also shouting that this was a communist hospital. It was actually Catholic, and there were crosses and such all over the place, but he didn't seem to perceive this.'

'And Farley and Simcox still had their weapons trained on Lieutenant Tyson?'

'Yes. And the Australian doctor was taking his time about dying. He was still on the floor crying out in pain. But Farley wouldn't let the hospital people go near him. His reasoning as best as I could determine was that if they couldn't find the time or space for Peterson, then they shouldn't worry about the Australian. There was a certain degree of symmetry and logic to that. During these few minutes, other people in the hospital were trying to run away, but they were shot by the men of the platoon whose natural reaction was to shoot anyone running away. At this point there was no full-scale massacre in progress, but the deaths were mounting up, and I believe that some of the men were thinking along the lines of eliminating evidence and witnesses.'

'Including eliminating Lieutenant Tyson?'

'Yes. I think so. Farley and Simcox looked as if they were trying to get up the nerve to shoot him. Beltran was inciting everyone who would listen to him. Lieutenant Tyson was ordering me to give him the radiophone. At this point, I decided that Lieutenant Tyson was part of the problem and not part of the solution. So I struck him and knocked him to the floor.'

'What was your intention in doing that?'

'Partly to get him out of there since he wasn't going to leave on his own. Partly to save his life. After he was on the floor, Farley and Simcox, I believed, wouldn't think it necessary to shoot him. Apparently this was an accurate assessment, because they turned away from him and joined Beltran and a few others who were shoving people into this washroom. I asked a man named Walker to give me a hand, and together we carried Lieutenant Tyson out of the operating room, down a short corridor, to the first door we came to which turned out to be a small room that appeared to be a laboratory. We put him on the floor, and I told Walker to stay there with me. We sat there awhile, listening to the shooting and the screaming. I never actually saw the indiscriminate shooting. Up until that point, the deaths had been caused by some specific factor, no matter how unjustified or illogical.'

'How long did you stay there?'

'Walker and I stayed there about ten minutes. Then the shooting stopped, and we left to see what was going on. In retrospect, I should have stayed with Lieutenant Tyson, but I didn't think he was in any real danger any longer. I saw all I wanted to see in the hospital and came back to the laboratory about ten minutes later, but Lieutenant Tyson was gone. I guessed that he'd left the hospital, because I hadn't seen him while I was looking around the hospital, so I went outside and looked around.'

'Did you see him there?'

'No. And I didn't want to go back inside that hospital. I had some fear for my own safety. I was also angry at Lieutenant Tyson for leaving the laboratory.'

'Would you describe what you saw in the hospital after you left the laboratory?'

'I'd rather not.'

'All right – what did you do outside the hospital?'

'I was trying to sort all of this out in my mind. I sat on a stone bench in the courtyard and had a cigarette. I saw the hospital begin to burn. The platoon began to assemble outside. One of the last people out was Lieutenant Tyson. The platoon surrounded the hospital and watched it burn. Several people who had not been shot tried to escape through the windows and doors, but they were shot. We stood around in the rain and waited until the hospital roof collapsed. Then we formed up and began moving toward Hue.'

'Did anyone threaten Lieutenant Tyson at that point?'

'During the rest breaks in the patrol there was some discussion about killing him, but no one did anything about it. Lieutenant Tyson was sort of a prisoner, and he never said a word to me or anyone as we walked. We carried Moody in a stretcher and Peterson's body in a poncho. Farley carried Cane's body for a while, then we took turns in carrying it. We walked in single file, and no one could see anyone else's face. It was very surreal. The more we walked, the more the adrenaline boiled out. The rain was coming down hard, and the villages seemed dead. To our front we could see Hue burning in the rain. We could actually see the flames now and hear the small-arms fire. It was early, but we decided it was time to pull in for the day. Everyone was very tired. We found an old French pillbox – a round concrete bunker – and set up there. Lieutenant Tyson kept making radio reports to Captain Browder of this sniper fire, and as long as he did that, he was safe. But everyone was wondering what he'd say when he got a chance to go back to base camp.'

Corva asked, 'What happened in the bunker?'

'We sat around. A few candles were lit. Everyone was soaked. We changed into dry socks and we heated C rations. We had to keep the two bodies in the bunker so the animals wouldn't get them. Normally, we would have called for a chopper to get rid of the dead and wounded, but we were supposed to still be in An Ninh Ha exchanging fire with snipers, so we couldn't give our grid coordinates. Browder kept calling asking if we needed artillery support and all that. Lieutenant Tyson said no, there were civilians in the area. Finally Browder said to do something about the snipers. So Lieutenant Tyson reported that we were going to move on this building where the sniper fire was coming from. Actually, it had been two hours since we left the village of An Ninh Ha. Finally, Lieutenant Tyson reported that we were now in heavy contact with an NVA force in a large building. Then he reported an assault on the building, then reported a room-to-room fight, then victory. It was bizarre. Browder said fine job. Browder reported that he was near Hue already. So were we, but he didn't know that. He gave us his grid coordinates. He wasn't more than a kilometre from us. But we said we couldn't reach him before nightfall and we'd stay in An Ninh Ha and link up in the morning. We were making all this up, of course, and feeding it to Lieutenant Tyson as he was talking with Browder on the radio. After Lieutenant Tyson reported that we were going to stay in An Ninh Ha, we started to talk about the battle as though it had really happened. I think the men reasoned that everything about the war was so unreal anyway that this battle and the body count we came up with was as real as the stuff MAC-V put out. So we smoked some grass, and Lieutenant Tyson passed around a bottle of scotch. We played some cards. We slept. We woke up in the middle of the night. A few guys threw up outside. Brandt gave Moody another shot of morphine. The radio crackled all night, and every hour or so I made scheduled night reports. By dawn, we had our story down pretty well. In fact, by dawn, it was not a story, it was the truth. What really happened became that night's collective nightmare. We had done a neat switch with reality. I even wrote up a Silver Star for Lieutenant Tyson that night. The next morning we linked up with the rest of the company, got Moody medevaced, and got rid of the corpses. We swapped war stories with the other two platoons. Captain Browder said he was very proud of us. We reported, I think, twelve enemy KIA. We didn't want to overdo it. Actually Browder didn't believe a word of it. The time sequence and all the little details were wrong. We'd never asked for artillery to support us, for instance. Browder was a pro, and Lieutenant Tyson wasn't exactly convincing on the radio or in person. But we had two killed and one wounded, though we had no captured weapons. One of the other platoon sergeants asked us sarcastically if the twelve NVA we killed were unarmed. But the after-action reports were written, and no one higher up asked any questions or even did an after-action survey of the battle scene to the best of my knowledge. But it was a very tumultuous time. We moved on to other problems. Within a week, nobody cared what happened in An Ninh Ha in the hospital that now has a name. But I told you what happened, though I swore in the bunker I never would. So even though I swore to you here that I would tell you the truth, you understand that my story could be as phony as the rest of them.'

After a full minute, Corva said, 'The defence has nothing further.'

Sproule asked, 'Does the prosecution wish to cross-examine?'

Pierce replied in an almost weary tone, 'The prosecution does not.'

Colonel Sproule looked at Colonel Moore. 'Are there any questions by the court?'

Colonel Moore replied, 'The court has no questions.'

Colonel Sproule said to Kelly, 'The witness is excused.'

Kelly stood, but instead of turning to his left and leaving, he turned right and walked towards Tyson with the self-assurance of a man who knows no one is going to challenge his movements.

Tyson stood, and they grasped each other's hand. Tyson said in a quiet voice, 'Hello, Kelly.'

'Hello, Lieutenant.'

'Thanks for coming.'

'No problem. You should have come to Angola with me. You wouldn't be here now.'

'No, I'd be dead now.'

Colonel Sproule looked at Kelly and Tyson, then looked at his watch and said, 'The court is adjourned until ten hundred hours tomorrow.'

The board, the prosecution, and the spectators stood and began drifting off.

Tyson saw the MPs approaching and said to Kelly, 'See you later maybe.'

'Don't think so,' said Kelly. 'Flying out in about two hours.'

'Where to?'

'Here and there. Doing a gig in Central America now.'

'Your number is going to come up one of these days, Kelly.'

'Maybe. But it's been fun playing.'

'You missed a good reunion. Sadowski, Scorello, Kalane, Beltran, and Walker. Only DeTonq is not present or accounted for.'

'DeTonq's still there, Lieutenant.'

'Maybe. Maybe he made it back.'

'No, he's there. In place.'

'In what place?'

'Hue. Agent in place. Posing as a Frenchman. We need intelligence there.'

'You're making that up.'

'Maybe. But we'll be back there someday.'

'Without me.'

'With or without you.'

Tyson said, 'Thanks again.'

'Anytime, *amigo*. I'll look you up next time around.'

'Try Leavenworth.'

'I'll try Garden City first.' Kelly winked, turned, and walked away as the MPs flanked Tyson.

53

The MP car pulled up to Tyson's housing unit at 7.30 A.M. and Sergeant Larson unlocked Tyson's handcuffs. He said to Tyson, 'One half hour, sir. We'll honk at eight hundred hours.'

'Right.'

Larson added, 'There will be an MP stationed at the rear of your unit, sir.'

'Swell.' Tyson opened the car door and walked quickly up the path of his attached unit. David opened the door before he reached it and stood smiling in the doorway.

'Hello, Dad.'

'Hello, kid.' They shook hands, then embraced. Tyson went into the house, and David closed the door. Marcy came quickly down the stairs, dressed in a grey suit and high heels, suitable for trials or business meetings.

Tyson embraced her, and they kissed, but they both sensed an estrangement between them. She said to him, 'Would you like breakfast?'

'No thanks. They serve breakfast early there. I had eggs and grits.'

Marcy, David, and Ben Tyson went into the dining area and sat around the table, half of which was piled with Marcy's paperwork. They talked about David's school for most of the next twenty minutes. Tyson had coffee, David had two bowls of cereal, and Marcy sipped on a weak herb tea. 'My stomach,' she explained. 'Tension. Not really sleeping well.'

Tyson looked at his watch. 'I'd better start saying good-bye

730

now.' He stood and said to his wife, 'I'll see you in court, as they say.'

'Do you want David there?'

Tyson looked at his son eating his cereal. Tyson said to him, 'Do you want to go to a court-martial, or do you want to go to school?'

David smiled weakly. 'Court-martial.'

'Good. Maybe you'll be a JAG lawyer when you grow up.'

Marcy said to Tyson, 'Say hello to Vince for me.'

'Okay.' He found his hat on the couch.

She added, 'What is happening today, Ben?'

He replied, 'I'm not certain. Except that we're still presenting extenuation and mitigation. Corva may ask Levin to testify today.'

She asked, 'What time do you think it will end?'

'I'm not sure. Depends on how many people Corva has lined up.' He paused and asked, 'Do you want to testify?'

'Me?'

'Yes. The wife often testifies to her husband's character during E and M.'

'Really? How bizarre.'

Tyson shrugged. 'The Army is all one big family.'

She thought a moment, then smiled. 'Do I have to tell the truth?'

'No, no. They expect wives to lie.'

'Well, I will, of course. But I don't think you really want me to testify.'

'No, I don't. It's not my style. But Corva thinks it's a good idea. You know how these Italians are with family. In Italian courts they herd in the whole family – old grandmas and little bambinos, all screeching and crying.'

Marcy frowned. 'I hate it when you make ethnic generalizations.'

'Corva seems to enjoy it. He does it to me. Why should it bother you?'

She started to say something, then just shrugged.

731

Tyson nodded towards the paperwork and her attaché case on a chair. 'Do you have an appointment this afternoon?'

She nodded. 'But I've arranged it for five, in midtown. If the court adjourns at four-thirty, I can make it easily.'

'I'll pass a note to Judge Sproule.'

Marcy drew a deep breath and said nothing.

As Tyson checked his watch, the car horn blew twice. He said, 'There's my limo.'

David stood again and they embraced. Marcy took his arm and walked with him to the front door. She said softly, 'I never know when I'm going to see you again.'

'Well, if you come to court at ten, you'll see me.'

'You know what I mean.'

'Tomorrow,' said Tyson. 'I'll work out something for tomorrow.'

She squeezed his arm. 'Can you get forty-five minutes?' She winked suggestively.

He smiled. 'I'll try.'

'I know you would like to be a little nicer to me, but you're trying to make this easier on me by being – cool. It's not making it easier.' She said, 'Ben – Kelly's testimony –'

'Yes?'

She took his hand. 'I had no idea –'

'I'm no hero. But it's nice to know you think so.'

The horn blew again.

They kissed, and Tyson left quickly.

He got back into the MP car and sat beside Sergeant Larson, who didn't produce the handcuffs this time. Larson said, 'BOQ. Correct?'

'Correct.'

Tyson looked out the window as the car moved slowly to the BOQ, a short distance away. He remembered the route he used to take between his house and the BOQ. He had not been allowed to vary his route or make any stops or detours. Straight and narrow. He'd hated that, but now it looked like boundless freedom in comparison.

Filmy black clouds raced across the morning sky, blowing from east to west, and there was the smell of rain in the cool air. The few trees on the route looked more bare than they had the day before, and the limbs seemed blacker, giving them a forlorn appearance against the stark institutional buildings.

The car stopped in front of the BOQ, and Sergeant Larson said, 'Nineteen-fifteen hours, sir.'

'Right.' Tyson got out, entered the far right door of the building, and went up three flights of stairs. He knocked on Corva's door. The door opened, and Corva showed him in.

They sat at the dining room table, and Tyson poured a cup of coffee from a mess hall thermos jug.

Corva said, 'How is Marcy?'

'Fine. Sends you her regards.'

Corva nodded as he rifled through a folder of yellow paper. 'David?'

'Fine. All the Tysons are fine. How are the Corvas?'

'Fine. How's gaol?'

'Gaol sucks. I'm in charge of the latrine detail now – my first command since I was CO of Alpha Company.'

Corva chewed absently on a Danish as he jotted notes on his pad. He said, 'Today should be the last day.'

Tyson nodded.

Corva continued, 'Colonel Levin is prepared to testify on your behalf today.'

'No.'

'Why not?'

'Give the man a break, Vince. He's got enough problems being a middle-aged Jewish lieutenant colonel. He wants his full bird before he gets out.'

Corva said impatiently, 'How about Marcy, then?'

'No.'

'Why not?'

'Because I'd like to keep it dignified, if you don't mind.'

Corva thought about that a moment, then asked, 'How

about your minister, Reverend Symes? He is most anxious to speak for you.'

'Symes is most anxious to speak, period. He'll begin at my baptism.'

'Well, how about—'

'No one. Not my ex-scout leader either. Let Kelly's statement stand by itself.'

Corva leaned across the table. 'Look, Ben, now that you've established that gaol sucks beyond a reasonable doubt, let's try to make sure you don't go back this afternoon.'

Tyson nodded.

Corva continued, 'Testimony regarding your character is the last thing that board will hear before they go off to vote on a sentence.'

'My character is irrelevant. The board has the facts.' Tyson stood and went to the window. The sky was darkening, and a few drops of rain splattered against the glass.

Corva said, 'You're not in the best humour this morning.'

Tyson shook his head. 'I woke up in gaol this morning.'

Corva stood and took a step towards Tyson. 'Talk it out.'

Without turning, Tyson said, 'It's all hitting me now. Farley, looking so pathetic. Brandt, being destroyed by Kelly. Sadowski, Scorello, Beltran, Walker, Kalane – now they've got to live not only with what they've done and with everyone knowing about it, but also with the fact that they didn't take the stand like men – because some wimpy lawyers got to them.'

Corva laid his hand tentatively on Tyson's shoulder.

Tyson went on, 'And if I go to gaol – what does a man say to his wife when he comes home after some years in gaol? Do women wait? What is your experience?'

'Ben, that's enough.'

Tyson said, 'And David's life would be ruined—'

'Enough!' Corva grabbed Tyson's shoulder and with a surprising strength spun him around and shoved him towards the wall. 'Enough!'

Tyson clenched his fist and glared down at the smaller man.

734

Corva glared back. Finally Tyson said, 'Okay. Had a bad night.'

Corva went to the table and poured more coffee. He said, 'Do you still want to take the stand?'

'Yes.'

'Do you know what you want to say?'

Tyson nodded.

Still standing, Corva shuffled through some papers on the table. He said, 'The last piece in this Oriental mosaic fell into place last night.'

Tyson looked at his lawyer.

Corva picked up a telex message and glanced at it. He said, 'At first I thought it was the government who was somehow keeping her under wraps, the way they kept Kelly under wraps. But I should have known – '

'She's dead?'

'No, no. She's very much alive and well. It was the church who removed her from the world.' Corva added, 'I told you Interpol thought she was in Italy, and she is. In a place called Casa Pastor Angelicus. It is a sort of cloister for nuns built on a hill outside Rome. She is effectively cut off from the outside world.' Corva added with a half smile, 'I don't think a subpoena would ever reach her.'

Tyson stayed silent a few seconds before asking, 'How – how is it that she is there?'

'Well, apparently when the first public stories of this appeared in May or June, someone, perhaps in the Vatican, got wind of it and had her sequestered. I would doubt that she knows anything about your difficulties.'

Tyson nodded. 'Well, I suppose it's just as well, isn't it? It's good that there are places left in this world where people can live in absolute peace. So,' he said, 'that is a closed chapter.' He rubbed his brow. 'Thank God somebody was spared from all this.'

'But perhaps someday, when this is over and she returns to her hospital work, you might visit her.'

Tyson shook his head. 'No, I think, as Kelly said, this is the end of the incident. Whoever walked away from that hospital should keep walking, in different directions, and never look back and never reach out to one another. Not ever again.'

Corva replied, 'Maybe you're right. No more reunions. Though,' he said musingly, 'I would have liked her to tell the court and everyone that you saved her life. That is a story that should be known.'

'Is it? It doesn't fit, Vince. Vietnam means loss. Lost war, lost honour, lost innocence, lost souls. Don't confuse everyone with a story of two people who found something in each other.'

'You're too cynical this morning.'

'Well, then, let's say it is a private story and it's just as well that it won't be used for any public purpose. I would never have let you call her to the stand anyway.'

'I know that. I just wanted to find her for you.'

'Thank you.'

'Time to go.'

54

Ben Tyson sat at the defence table. Pierce, Weinroth, and Longo were already at their table. Tyson said, 'Why do they always beat us here?'

'I once stole Pierce's water pitcher, and he's not going to let it happen again.'

At 10 A.M. sharp, the sergeant at arms called out, 'All rise!'

Colonel Sproule entered the court and took his place behind the pulpit. 'The court will come to order.'

Everyone sat. Tyson saw that the chapel was still filling with people and the MPs didn't seem to be stopping anyone from cramming in. This was going to be a short session.

He looked up into the dark choir and saw, standing at the railing, Chet Brown. Brown waved a cheery greeting, but Tyson did not acknowledge it.

He looked into the front row and saw Marcy, who blew him a kiss. David was there, as was his mother, as Corva had insisted. Also in the front pew now was Karen Harper, minus her friend. She was sitting a few feet from Marcy, and they occasionally exchanged a word or two.

The chapel smelled of damp clothing and chilly rain. The persistent drizzle ran down the stained-glass windows giving them a flat lifeless appearance, making the depictions on them look like cartoons.

Tyson looked again at the prosecution table. Pierce, Weinroth, and Longo sat talking in low whispers, and for the first time since Tyson had seen them at the hearing, they looked quite human. In fact, he even credited them with human attributes, such as love, money problems, and family cares. He noticed, too, that Major Judith Weinroth was very much taken with Colonel Graham Pierce, and he fantasized for them an affair.

Tyson looked at Colonel Sproule, shuffling papers behind the pulpit. The man was a product of another era. He had sat there, day after day, literally and figuratively looking down on the court. And clearly he had been shocked in an old-fashioned sense of the word by what he'd heard.

Tyson looked now across the open space at the board table which was empty. Beyond the table, in the wing of the altar area, stood two armed MPs at parade rest. Tyson spoke to Corva while still looking at the two MPs. 'The armed and the unarmed.'

Corva nodded.

'That's another way to divide the world.'

Again Corva nodded. 'That's the way it's always been.'

'I have a small sense of how the Viet peasants felt when they had to deal with us. How do you deal with a man carrying an

M-16 rifle if you're carrying a basket of vegetables?'

'Very carefully.'

'Right. The Aussie doctor didn't understand that.'

'Apparently not,' replied Corva as he looked through some papers on the table. 'Are you ready for your courtroom debut?'

'I ought to be.'

'True.'

Corva noted, 'A jury often knows how they're going to vote on a verdict. There are only two choices. But sentencing is much more complex. What you say may make a difference.'

'In other words, don't blow it.'

Corva didn't respond.

Colonel Sproule caught Colonel Pierce's eye and indicated he was ready.

Colonel Pierce stood and said, 'All the parties to the trial who were present when the court closed are now present except the members of the board.' Pierce sat.

Colonel Sproule turned to the defence table. 'Will the accused please rise?'

Tyson stood.

Sproule said, 'Lieutenant Benjamin Tyson, you are advised that you may now present testimony in extenuation or mitigation of the offence of which you stand convicted. You may, if you wish, testify under oath as to these matters, or you may remain silent, in which case the court will not draw any inferences from your silence. In addition, you may, if you wish, make an unsworn statement in mitigation or extenuation of the offence of which you stand convicted. This unsworn statement is not evidence, and you cannot be cross-examined upon it, but the prosecution may offer evidence to rebut anything contained in the statement. The statement may be oral or in writing or both. You may make it yourself, or it may be made by your counsel or by both of you. Consult with your counsel if you need to, and advise this court what you wish to do.'

Tyson replied, 'I wish to make a sworn statement, your honour.'

Sproule nodded as though in approval. He turned towards the sergeant at arms and said, 'Sergeant, call the board to court.'

Tyson felt his heart beating heavily for the first time since this began. He wanted a drink of water but didn't take the cup in front of him.

Corva leaned towards him. 'I am not going to ask you questions or elicit anything from you. You are on your own, Lieutenant.'

'That's fine. I've heard enough out of you to last me a lifetime.'

Corva grunted.

The members of the court-martial board arrived in their usual single file and went to their chairs in order of rank, but this time, the court already having been called to order, they sat immediately.

Colonel Sproule wasted no time either. 'Lieutenant Tyson, will you take the stand please?'

Tyson walked unhesitantly towards the witness chair and reached it at the same time Pierce did. The two men stood less than three feet apart, and at this distance Tyson was able to see freckles on Pierce's remarkable scarlet skin.

Pierce said, 'Raise your right hand.'

Tyson raised his hand.

Pierce and Tyson looked directly at each other as Pierce recited, 'Do you swear that the evidence you shall give shall be the truth, the whole truth, and nothing but the truth, so help you God?'

'I do.'

'Please be seated.'

Tyson sat.

Corva, still at the defence table but standing now, said, 'Your honour, members of the board; Lieutenant Tyson will make a statement.' Corva sat.

Tyson found himself looking at his surroundings from a different perspective. He could no longer see Sproule, whose fidgeting with his hearing aid was distracting. But he could see Pierce, sitting at the table ten feet away directly in front of him. Pierce was leaning forward over his crossed arms as though very eager to hear him. Tyson suspected this was meant to unnerve him, but realizing that, he found it somewhat ludicrous. Weinroth and Longo were sitting straight which looked more appropriate to the military surroundings. The board was to his left, and he could see them by turning his head slightly in that direction.

Beyond the prosecution table but partly blocked by it was pew after pew of heads and shoulders, all eyes on him. Tyson said in a normal conversational tone of voice, 'I realize that any statement I make here in extenuation and mitigation could only be construed as a self-serving one. But the military system of justice is unique in that it allows a convicted man to present certain facts which may diminish his sentence. But I'm not certain that it would be appropriate for me to go into personal details of my life, as you know them as well as anyone, due to the public attention that has surrounded not only this trial, but my personal life. And I'm not certain it's necessary to attempt to convey to you any more of the horrors of war than you've already had conveyed to you. I understand that the Code specifically recognizes combat fatigue and all that this term implies as an extenuating factor in cases such as these. But I know, and you know, that the crime for which I stand convicted was not the crime that occurred in that hospital, but the crime that occurred some days later in base camp, when I walked past battalion headquarters and failed to enter there and do my duty. That crime did not occur under conditions of battle fatigue. I cannot sit here in good conscience and tell you that if I had it to do over again, I would do my duty as I clearly understood it. On the contrary, if I had it to do over again, I would do the same thing. And though my life and freedom depend on it, I cannot tell you why I would again wilfully commit the same crime. I know that I briefly considered reporting this crime of mass murder. But only briefly; and that was a result of my officer training such as it may have been. I did not wrestle long with my conscience before deciding that I would not do my duty. And after I had made the decision not to speak of this crime ever again, I felt that I had made the right decision. If I said otherwise to you, you would wonder, and properly so, why I did not rectify my original decision which I know full well was both an immoral and illegal one. So I stand here convicted of a crime I did commit, and we should let the matter rest there.'

Tyson surveyed the silent court, then continued, 'As for my men, you may have the charitable thought that I was protecting them out of a sense of loyalty, comradeship, and that special paternalism that exists between officers and men. There would be some truth in that thought, but you know and I know that loyalty, comradeship, and paternalism should not extend that far. I do feel some natural regret for the lives that have been perhaps ruined or altered by the public testimony we have all heard here. But balanced against the lives that were ended at that hospital, there cannot and should not be too many tears shed for any of the men of the first platoon of Alpha Company. I do feel some sympathy for the families who have discovered things about their sons and husbands that were best left undiscovered. A day or so after I killed Larry Cane, I wrote his family a letter of condolence in which I said he died bravely. He was a brave man in many ways, but he did not die bravely, and I again offer my condolences to his family.'

Tyson looked at the board and addressed them directly. 'When my attorney, Mr Corva, asked me if I would like to make a sworn statement in extenuation or mitigation on my own behalf, I told him I could think of no extenuating or mitigating circumstances that I could swear to.' He paused and looked directly at the board, meeting each member's eyes. 'Sitting here now, I still can't.'

Colonel Sproule waited some time, expecting more. Finally realizing that Tyson had no intention of offering anything further, he addressed Colonel Pierce. 'Does the prosecution wish to offer anything in rebuttal to the statement of the accused?'

Pierce stood and began to reply, but Corva had come across the floor and was in front of the pulpit. Corva said, 'The accused has not finished, your honour.'

Sproule's eyebrows rose. 'It appeared he had, Mr Corva.'

'No, your honour.' Corva turned to Tyson, who gave him a sharp look. Corva said to Tyson, 'Would you characterize your state of mind after the incident as remorseful?'

Tyson sat back in the chair and crossed his legs. He stared at Corva awhile, then replied, 'Yes.'

'And do you feel remorse now?'

Tyson replied tersely, 'I suppose.'

'And would you describe yourself as haunted by this incident?'

Tyson looked at his lawyer. Clearly Corva did not intend to let his statement stand as it was. He studied the man's face and saw he was very distraught.

'Are you *haunted* by what happened at that hospital?'

Tyson snapped, 'Wouldn't you be?'

'Did you seek psychiatric help after you returned from Vietnam?'

Tyson could see the board out of the corner of his eye, and he noticed that some of them looked uncomfortable. He kept silent.

'You *did* seek psychiatric help, didn't you?' he went on without waiting for an answer. 'By shooting Larry Cane did you believe you did everything humanly possible to stop the mutiny and massacre?'

'Hard to say.'

Corva's voice rose. 'Can't you give me more complete answers?'

There was a stirring in the spectator pews. Tyson looked past Corva at Pierce, who was no longer staring at him, but at Corva. Weinroth and Longo were glancing at each other.

'Don't you think,' asked Corva, his voice becoming louder,

'that combat fatigue mitigates what happened at that hospital? That if the UCMJ recognizes that, then maybe you should too?'

Tyson uncrossed his legs and leaned forward. His voice was taut. 'I don't think I want to retry this case now.'

'Were you or were you not suffering from combat fatigue? Answer the question.'

Tyson stood. 'I told the court what I had to say! There is no extenuation or mitigation.'

Corva began to speak, but Sproule cleared his throat. 'Mr Corva, does your client wish to conclude his statement?'

'No.'

'Yes,' said Tyson and stepped away from the chair. Corva blocked him. There was open talking in the court now. Sproule called for quiet and said to Corva, 'This is most unusual.'

Tyson looked into Corva's eyes. It suddenly occurred to him that Corva had been under tremendous strain, had hidden it well, and was now about to snap. Tyson took his seat and said in a calm voice, 'I suppose battle fatigue could explain almost all of what happened.'

Corva seemed to be getting himself under control and nodded quickly.

Sproule spoke. 'Mr Corva, do you want a recess?'

Corva rubbed his cheek. 'No, your honour.'

Tyson said, 'Your honour, I've concluded my statement.'

Corva stood silently, as though in a daze.

'Very well,' said Sproule with a note of relief in his voice. Sproule looked at Pierce and asked for the second time, 'Does the prosecution wish to offer anything in rebuttal to the statement of the accused?'

Pierce stood and made an exaggerated shrug. 'It appears that defence counsel has already done that.'

There were a few tentative laughs which quickly died away.

Sproule looked at Colonel Moore. 'Does the board have any questions for the witness?'

Colonel Moore, apparently without consulting the board, replied tonelessly, 'We have no questions, your honour.'

743

Sproule said to Tyson, 'You are excused, Lieutenant.'

'Yes, sir.' Tyson rose and nudged Corva back toward the defence table. They both sat.

Colonel Sproule said, 'We will take a five-minute break in place.' Sproule made a show of concentrating on some paperwork as did the prosecution team and the board.

Tyson leaned toward Corva. 'Are you all right?'

Corva sipped some water. 'Better.'

'Are you well enough for me to beat the shit out of you?'

Corva smiled wanly. 'I just slipped a little.'

'Don't get personally involved with your clients,' advised Tyson.

Corva didn't reply. The minutes ticked by in silence. Sproule looked up from his papers and cleared his throat. He addressed Pierce. 'Does the prosecution wish to present an argument for an appropriate sentence?'

Pierce let a few seconds pass, then replied, 'The board has the facts and will reach a decision on an appropriate sentence.'

Sproule turned to Corva. Sproule asked, 'Does the defence wish to present an argument for an appropriate sentence?'

Corva, without standing, replied, 'The defence, too, believes the board has the facts it needs to reach an appropriate sentence.'

'So,' said Sproule with uncharacteristic informality, 'that's it.' Sproule turned to the board and said, 'It is my duty now to instruct the board on matters of punishment.' He cleared his throat and began. 'It is your sole responsibility to select an appropriate sentence, and you may consider all matters in extenuation and mitigation in arriving at that sentence. You may take into account the background and character of the accused, his reputation and service record, including awards, medals, conduct, efficiency, fidelity, courage, bravery, and other traits of good character.

'You must also consider that the desired effect of a sentence is not primarily punishment, deterrence, rehabilitation, or the protection of society. The end product of a conviction in a trial by military court-martial and the sentence arrived at is to reflect

744

military goals, which include the maintenance of good order and discipline, the continued ability of the service to carry out its mission, and the preservation of the service concepts of duty and honour. In the case where the accused is a commissioned officer, he should, by custom and often by law, be held accountable to a higher degree for the preservation of these goals, concepts and ideals than an enlisted man would be. However, he should not be held accountable to such a degree as would impose unrealistic or unattainable standards on the officer corps.'

Sproule went on, 'In considering your verdict, you should also take into consideration the prevailing conditions at the time of the offence. You should not take into consideration any outside influences, real or perceived, and you should not be subject in any way to command influence.'

Sproule glanced around the room, then concluded, 'Though there is not and should not be a statute of limitations for the crime of murder, you may consider in arriving at an appropriate sentence that the offence for which the accused stands convicted occurred over eighteen years ago. Also, due to the special circumstances of the accused having been a civilian for nearly eighteen years, you may take into account his civilian accomplishments, his community standing, his marital status, and his age in arriving at your sentence.' Colonel Sproule looked at Colonel Moore. 'Do you have any questions?'

Moore looked toward either side of the table, then said, 'We have no questions.'

Colonel Sproule instructed the board, 'You may deliberate the sentence in the room set aside for that purpose. If you have not reached a sentence by fourteen-thirty hours, you may continue deliberating in the deliberation room until you do reach a sentence. Please keep the court informed of your progress. The court will be closed.'

Tyson and Corva found themselves back in Rabbi Weitz's office. The rabbi, too, was present. He said to Tyson, 'I came. I was there today for the first time. Whose side were you on?'

745

Corva said, 'That's what I'd like to know. That was the absolute worst statement I ever heard from an accused.'

Tyson saw that Corva was nearly himself again, though he seemed somewhat sulky.

Corva added, 'It would serve you right if they took you at your word.'

Rabbi Weitz joined in. 'If that was supposed to be reverse psychology, my friend, I hope the board responds.'

Tyson said irritably, 'I said what I had to say.'

Corva responded, 'Your ego will be your downfall one of these days ... maybe today.'

'You said I could say what I wanted.'

'You were supposed to say that the murderers were walking free. That before they imposed a prison sentence on you, they should consider that. I thought you understood what we have been driving at ... oh, the hell with it.'

Rabbi Weitz took his attaché case, headed for the door, and opened it. 'While they are considering an appropriate sentence, maybe they will consider an appropriate place to hold courts-martial next time. God bless both of you.' He left.

Corva sat at the rabbi's desk, drinking ice water.

Tyson stood at the window and looked out into the rain. On the lawn, not ten feet away, stood two MPs in rain gear, M-16 rifles slung on their shoulders. 'There's no place to run.'

'What's that?'

'They have MPs with rifles out there.'

'What did you expect?'

Tyson shrugged. He turned from the window. 'Why did you do that?'

'Do what?'

'You know damned well what.'

Corva stayed silent. At length he responded, 'I did it because I couldn't sit there and watch you walk jauntily to a firing squad with your fucking stiff upper lip.'

'Well, I did it my way, and you did it your way. And the result was a dog and pony show.' He glanced at his watch and asked,

'How long will this take, and how long will I get?'

Corva said, 'They have a lot to consider. Sometimes this takes longer than the verdict. It could go on for days.'

Tyson nodded, 'Take a guess then. What's your experience with sentences, or shouldn't I ask?'

Corva smiled thinly, then said, 'I could have fifty years' experience with sentences, and I couldn't call this one. It could be anywhere from no gaol time to ten ... fifteen years.'

Tyson sat in a visitor's chair and looked at the clock. 'Eleven-fifteen hours.'

'What's the real time?'

'Quarter after eleven.'

'Well, be prepared for a wait.'

'Is it your policy to stay with the accused while the sentence is deliberated?'

'I guess. We're authorized to go back to the lockup if somehow you'd feel more comfortable there.'

'I think we'll stay here.'

'Right.'

They sat in silence for some time, then Corva began speaking. 'You remember what we used to say in Nam – you can't tell the good guys from the bad guys. So kill them all and let Saint Peter sort them out. Well, the first time I heard that, I thought it was funny. Then when I saw it happen – the killing of civilians – it wasn't so funny. But by the time I was ready to go home, it started to make sense, and that scared the hell out of me. I think – I know – that when you're there, you lose touch with external reality and create your own inner reality. That was the missing piece in your little speech. The gap between knowing what your duty was, deciding not to do it, then feeling fine about deciding not to do it even though it went against what you believed in.'

Tyson lit a cigarette. 'I keep going back there in my mind. Trying to experience it again, trying to feel what I felt, think what I thought. But the more I try to do that, the more elusive the whole thing becomes. It's funny that my most vivid and I think accurate memories are of the first days and weeks in Nam.

While I was still open to outside reality. But as the weeks went by, with each passing month I began to block, to distort, and especially to deny. We, all of us, got heavily into denial. You could have five men killed in the morning, and by lunch they didn't exist. You could kill a peasant through carelessness, and before you even reloaded, he was a hard-core VC armed to the teeth. So maybe what happened at the hospital was not what Brandt said or Farley said or what I told you or what Kelly told all of us. Maybe it was something else. Maybe if I'd gone into battalion headquarters and seen the colonel and told him what had happened, he'd have told me I was crazy. He'd wave an after-action report in my face, and show me my proposal for a Silver Star and tell me to get a grip on myself.'

Corva said, 'Oh, Christ, Ben, what a place that was. Are we sane now?'

'You bet.'

'Right.' Corva said, 'By the way, I have a verbal message for you from a Major Harper. Want to hear it?'

'No.'

'Okay.'

Tyson drew on his cigarette. 'What's she want?'

Corva said, 'She wants you to know that she's being released from active duty at midnight tonight. She says she would like to buy you a drink tomorrow at a midtown bar of your choice.'

Tyson thought about that awhile, then said, 'There was a woman I could have gone for.'

'You did. But, hey, that's another story. Make her take you to a hotel bar – then if it's going right, you just have to point up.'

Tyson smiled. 'You're disgusting. If I meet her, I want you along to chaperone.'

'I'll be there. And so will you.'

Tyson looked at him but said nothing. After a few minutes he said, 'That Sindel woman isn't bad-looking either. Must be the uniform. Why am I so attracted to uniforms?'

'Don't know. Ask your shrink.'

'My shrink once said that when a soldier goes to war, all is pre-forgiven.'

748

'Did he? I wish I had him on the board.'

'He's dead.'

'Right.'

They both glanced at their watches. Corva said, 'Hungry?'

'No.' Tyson lit another cigarette. 'Why do you think I will be able to meet Karen Harper in a bar tomorrow?'

Corva replied, 'I'm optimistic. So, apparently, is Harper. But I think some of them want to hand you a gaol sentence – to show that the military doesn't give a damn *why* you failed to act like an officer. That's the traditional approach. They court-martialled that Captain Bucher who surrendered the *Pueblo*. They would have court-martialled Custer if he had survived the massacre. The military gets off on showing toughness when compassion is called for and compassion when toughness is called for. What they say, in effect, is, "We don't live by civilian concepts of right and wrong. We have our own code and our own requirements." Where else can a man get five years in gaol for dozing off at the wrong time and wrong place?'

Tyson nodded. 'I thought about that. Sproule was telling them to go easy. But he's a judge. He's not really part of the corps. Those infantry officers are coming from someplace else. Aren't they?'

'We'll see.'

'Tell me a war story, Corva. I'm bored. Tell me about the tunnel and the Bronze Star they gave you.'

'Okay,' Corva began with enthusiasm. 'I crawled into this tunnel, and it narrowed and narrowed until I had less than a foot of free space around me.'

'I know that.'

'Right. So I flip on the miner's lamp, and there's this Oriental gentleman there who I assumed was a member of the People's Liberation Army, though I saw no shoulder or collar insignia on his black pyjamas. So I reach back into my pocket – it was a tight space, remember – and pull out my little plastic card and quickly peruse the Rules of Engagement—'

Tyson laughed.

'Don't laugh at me. This is serious. So I'm up to rule six or seven now, and I think I find what I'm looking for – "Meeting a gook face-to-face in a dark tunnel." And it says, "Shoot first and issue a challenge afterwards." So—'

There was a knock on the door, and Tyson looked at the wall clock. Five after noon. *Lunch*. The door opened, and Sergeant Larson stepped into the office and, remembering last time, said immediately, 'The board has reached a sentence. Will you come with me, sir?'

Tyson stood quickly, snatched his hat off the desk, and was out of the door, followed by Corva and Larson. They strode quickly down the corridor, turned, and entered the chapel. Tyson walked directly to the defence desk and stood behind it. Corva caught up and took his place beside Tyson.

Tyson glanced out over the pews and saw they were half empty. Obviously no one expected this so soon. But Marcy, David, and his mother were being escorted up the aisle by an MP. Other people were hurrying in.

Pierce, Weinroth, and Longo sat at their table, but for the first time the table was clear of papers.

The board sat stoically in their seats, not speaking to one another as they'd sometimes done before Sproule arrived.

The sergeant at arms marched to the middle of the floor and called out, 'All rise.'

Colonel Sproule strode in and went to the pulpit. He squinted out over the pews, hesitated, then said, 'The court will come to order.'

Pierce stood. 'All parties to the trial who were present when the court closed are now present.'

Sproule turned to Colonel Moore. 'I have a communication that you have reached a sentence. Is that correct?'

Moore replied from his seat, 'That is correct.'

Sproule turned to Tyson. 'Lieutenant Benjamin Tyson, will you report to the president of the court?'

Tyson stood, and Corva with him.

There were still people coming into the chapel, but there was no noise beyond the sound of soft footsteps and from the open doors, the occasional splash of a car going through the wet street.

Tyson walked across the red-carpeted floor and stood again directly in front of Colonel Moore, who rose. Tyson saluted and stood at attention.

Colonel Moore looked him squarely in the eye, as he said, 'Lieutenant Benjamin Tyson, it is my duty as president of this court to inform you that the court, in closed session, in full and open discussion, and upon secret written ballot, all of the members concurring, sentence you to dismissal from the Army of the United States and to forfeit all pay and allowances that may be due you or have accrued as a result of your past and present service as a commissioned officer in the Army of the United States.'

There was no sound in the chapel, as if, Tyson thought, someone had turned off the audio portion. He waited for a sound, but there was none, and Colonel Moore seemed to have finished, but he couldn't have, and Tyson stood there until finally Colonel Moore sat down.

Someone in the pews was weeping, everyone was standing. Tyson found Corva beside him. Corva said, 'Well, are you going to stand there, or do you want to go home?'

'Home. I want to go home.'

Colonel Sproule looked at Colonel Pierce and asked the required question, 'Has the prosecution any other case to try at this time?'

Pierce already had his briefcase in his hand and in a breach of military etiquette spoke as he was on his way to the side door, 'No, your honour, I have nothing further.'

Colonel Sproule announced, 'The court will adjourn to meet on future call.'

Tyson turned towards the side door, and Corva gently turned

him towards the communion rail. 'We're leaving through the front door this time. Lots of people out there want to say hello.'

Two lines of MPs had formed up in the wide centre aisle, and Tyson and Corva walked between them, joined by Marcy, then David, and his mother, who kissed him. No one spoke as they headed out into the October rain. Marcy took his hand and squeezed it as they entered the vestibule.

Out on the rain-splashed steps, Tyson was greeted by the sight of umbrellas, hundreds of umbrellas, and as he walked down the steps with his family, the umbrellas tilted to cover them from the rain. Tyson kept his hand in Marcy's and put his arm around his son.

Marcy said, 'We're all packed and ready to go home.'

'Then, let's go home.'

'I'm pregnant.'

'I forgot my hat.'

'What?'

'My hat. Inside.'

'Leave it.'

'What did you say?'

'Leave it.'

'No, I mean before?'

'Pregnant.'

'Who?'

'*Me!*'

'Oh!'

'Happy?'

'Yes, very,' he said.

'Love me?' she asked.

'Always.'

PLUM ISLAND

Nelson DeMille

Wounded in the line of duty, NYPD detective John Corey
is convalescing on Long Island when Tom and Judy
Gordon are found murdered on their patio. Corey knew
the young, attractive couple, and Sylvester Maxwell, the
local police chief, wants his big-city expertise. Maxwell,
however, gets more than he bargained for.

The early signs point to a burglary gone wrong, but
because the Gordons were biologists at Plum Island, the
off-shore animal disease research site rumoured to be
involved in germ warfare, it isn't long before the media
is suggesting that the dead couple stole something
very deadly.

John Corey's investigations lead him into the lore,
legends and ancient secrets of northern Long Island. But
they are secrets more dangerous than he could ever have
imagined – and he becomes trapped in a crime with
global implications . . .

'An ingenious . . . thriller. You'll be rewarded with a
climax as funny as it is tense'
Time Out

'Chilling . . . that rare breed of suspense novel that keeps
you sitting on the edge of your beach chair even while
you're laughing out loud'
Newsday

THE CHARM SCHOOL

Nelson DeMille

Deep in the heart of Russia, a group of casually dressed young men are learning a different kind of lesson. The undergraduates sprawled around a game board aren't chilling out on campus: the young KGB agents attending the Charm School are brushing up on their American.

When a young tourist goes to the aid of a stranger on a dark Russian road, he is astonished to find a fellow American on the run. The man has been missing for over a decade, plucked from the jungles of Vietnam to become an unwillling tutor at the institution. Now his former students are poised to strike at the heart of America.

'Definitely the Russian spy story to top them all'
Sunday Times

'Takes us inside the Russian psyche – a strange and fascinating world of paranoia, fear, illusion and deep humanity. The best thing to come out of Russia since Gorky Park'
Mark Joseph

Time Warner Paperback titles available by post:

☐ Cathedral	Nelson DeMille	£6.99
☐ The Talbot Odyssey	Nelson DeMille	£6.99
☐ The Charm School	Nelson DeMille	£6.99
☐ Plum Island	Nelson DeMille	£6.99
☐ The Lion's Game	Nelson DeMille	£6.99

The prices shown above are correct at time of going to press. However, the publishers reserve the right to increase prices on covers from those previously advertised without prior notice.

timewarner
paperbacks

TIME WARNER PAPERBACKS
P.O. Box 121, Kettering, Northants NN14 4ZQ
Tel: 01832 737525, Fax: 01832 733076
Email: aspenhouse@FSBDial.co.uk

POST AND PACKING:
Payments can be made as follows: cheque, postal order (payable to Time Warner Books) or by credit cards. Do not send cash or currency.

All U.K. Orders	**FREE OF CHARGE**
E.E.C. & Overseas	25% of order value

Name (Block Letters) _____

Address_____

_____

Post/zip code:_____

☐ Please keep me in touch with future Time Warner publications

☐ I enclose my remittance £_____

☐ I wish to pay by Visa/Access/Mastercard/Eurocard

Card Expiry Date

_____